CW00515033

The Cleaving of Paycocke's

by

Orlando Wysocki

four o'clock press

Copyright © Orlando Wysocki 2008
Cover Design by Jag Lall @ Discovered Authors

This first edition published in Great Britain in 2008 by
Four O'Clock Press - a Discovered Authors' imprint

ISBN 978-1-906146-60-3

The right of Orlando Wysocki to be identified as the Author of the
Work has been asserted by him in accordance with the
Copyright, Designs and Patent Act 1988

All rights reserved.
No part of this publication may be reproduced, stored in a
retrieval system, or transmitted, in any form or by any means
without the prior written permission of the Author

Available from Discovered Authors Online –
All major online retailers and available to order through all UK
bookshops

Or contact:

Books
Discovered Authors
Roslin Road, London
W3 8DH

0844 800 5214
books@discoveredauthors.co.uk
www.discoveredauthors.co.uk

Printed in the UK by BookForce Distribution
BookForce Distribution policy is to use papers that are natural,
renewable and recyclable products and made from wood grown
in sustainable forests wherever possible

BookForce Distribution Ltd.
Roslin Road, London
W3 8DH
www.bookforce.co.uk

Acknowledgements

Although the words are mine, they would not have reached the page without the generous help of the following:

Elizabeth West, whose kind suggestions lit the kindling in the book's early phases. Martin Atkinson, Glen Moon, Anna Forrest and Christopher Calnan of the National Trust, whose devotion to historic buildings has no limits. Leigh Alston, a nonpareil in the field of timber-framed architecture, who shared his well of knowledge with me. Michael Horne was a source of interesting nuggets concerning Coggeshall's history, while my good friends Jolie, Ed and Pip of the Suffolk Howlers furnished many snippets of daily Tudor life. I thank my daughter Izzy for believing in me and for wading through my initial manuscript. I also owe a debt of gratitude to Professor Christine Temple of Essex University for proofreading and for insights which improved the telling of my story. I have massaged history to some extent to produce this novel, but any factual errors are mine and mine alone. You may visit Paycocke's House, which exists today and looks much as it did in 1509. It has been the background to many a strange incident and fascinating character, but the tale within these pages is imagined.

Also, of course, my thanks go to all at Four O'Clock Press, particularly my author manager Michaela Unterbarnscheidt, my editor James Randall and designer Jag Lall. I would like to mention especially the artist and photographer Linda Wood, who together with Stuart Peacock spent a cold January night creating the photographs for the cover.

Finally, my thanks go to Sally Stow for her unflagging support during the dark hours of self-doubt which strike all writers.

In addition, I would like to acknowledge the following reference sources:

A Social History of England by Asa Briggs (Weidenfeld & Nicolson).
English Social History by G.M. Trevelyan (Longman).
The Earlier Tudors by J.D. Mackie (Oxford).
Henry VII by S.B. Chrimes (Methuen).
The Tudor Age by James A. Williamson (Longman).
The Tudors by Richard Rex (Tempus).
Great Men of Essex by C. Henry Warren (Desert Island Books).
The Paycockes of Coggeshall by Eileen Power (Methuen).
Medieval People by Eileen Power (Pelican).
Lost Voices of the Edwardians by Max Arthur (HarperPress).
Conrad Noel: Autobiography ed. Sidney Dark (Dent).
Conrad Noel, Prophet & Priest by Jack Putterill (Plumridge).
Gustav Holst and Thaxted by Imogen Holst (Mark Arman).
Gustav Holst by Imogen Holst & R. Vaughan Williams (Oxford).
Paycocke's House by H. Avray Tipping, in Country Life Magazine, June 30th 1923.
A History of Coggeshall by G.F. Beaumont (John Lewis)
The Elements of Style ed. Stephen Galloway (Mitchell Beazley).

Prologue
May 1487

John Paycocke saw blood where there was none, only where it had been, a shadow of past lives. He was a butcher accustomed to carnage and to life spilling easily from carcass to clay, yet now John's palms flushed crimson with guilt and shame.

But which man would not have done the same for his three sons? A tarnished coin has as much value as one shiny with dew. With such wealth he might be a butcher no more, but a clothier, prosperous and fat on good venison and boar, his sons growing strong by his side. He might move to Coxhall, build a house and in times to come his own sons would build houses there too and the future of the Paycocke family would be assured.

It had been a dream turned sour by knowledge and curdled further by the realisation that there might be no way back, the riches tainted. Once something is known, it might not be unknown. A royal coin taken can never be returned. This John knew he must live with, he and only he. He was proud to serve the house of Tudor, but at what cost would it be?

As the wain left Suffolk for Essex he turned one last time in the direction of Walsingham to the north, where lately King Henry had been on Easter pilgrimage, praying to Our Lady for a miracle. John uttered his own prayer, for such a miracle would serve him well.

Paycocke would pray for Henry too, a good man, despite all, that he might vanquish the pretender Simnel and that he might return England to a peace and stability squandered by the reckless third Richard. He would pray for his sons: John, Robert and young Thomas. He would protect them. Aye, he knew as yet not how, but he would find a way.

*   *   *

20th February 1923

Holst adjusted his spectacles and peered at first violin. Smythe nodded only with his eyelids, flicking his bow an inch in the air to firm his assent. How strange they all looked in their rehearsal garb, these musicians so recently in a different uniform, their lives spared for reasons Gustav could not fathom. He raised his baton, holding his breath to accentuate the complete silence.

Cello came in a hair early and Gustav blamed himself: he had twitched; his signals had not been clear; his hand was shaking; nerves. As it ever was. As it had come to be. A dizziness washed over him and he closed his eyes. *The Planets* had proved to be a millstone in its triumph by dint of its ravenous expectation, emphasising his mortality. He stepped from the rostrum and looked around. Reading. Yes, he was at Reading. It was good to know where one stood.

"Gentlemen," he said. Rows of faces inclined to him. "Gentlemen..." He had forgotten what he intended to say, as if the altitude drop from rostrum to stage had compromised his memory. Did these musicians see failure spark from his eyes, he who had promised so much? From *The Planets* down to earth. Gustav had thought his new opera *The Perfect Fool* worthy, its scoring more elegant than even *Saturn*, and yet who knew the minds of the critics? Doubt. They might distill doubt from talent, reduce his piece to farce. Now he himself was unsure as to the merit of the libretto, was vexed by fears that his works exhibited a single dimension. His head throbbed and he gripped the bridge of his nose between his thumb and ring finger, aggravating the ache in an effort to make it pass. How could he rehearse? He ought to dismiss the orchestra, but that would be yet more failure. Holst turned to face the musicians once more and an excruciating pain torched his arm. The neuralgia again. The players seemed to loom en masse, filling his vision with their monochrome and their whispering voices. He stepped back, finding air. The baton escaped his hand and he clutched for it, before falling from the stage and smacking his head on something unyielding.

Gustav lay still, imagining forcing his eyes open, picturing himself raising his body and saying, 'It is all right. I am quite well.' But all was not well, he knew that. All had never truly been well, nor might it ever be well. There was Isobel and there was Imogen. If only Imogen were here. If only he could see the world through his daughter's eyes, fresh and untainted, then he might rest.

The perfect fool. He lost consciousness.

Chapter 1
Ends

It should be a crime to want days over, even those that are fogged with pain and regrets. Simon Chance watched his wife turn her back on him and he wished for tomorrow, for the day after, for next month, next year, some indefinable time when the hurt would leave him, any time that was not now.

Robin's charcoal-suited figure grew smaller as she walked away, until she disappeared into the distance. Simon leant against the front door, oblivious to the limewash rubbing off onto his jacket, stippling him with its white fingers. She had waited until this moment to tell him, now that Paycocke's House was closed to the public for the winter, its season over and hibernation begun. A clean break? For her, maybe; just a greenstick fracture. But for him, would it ever mend? Could he ever wish her back?

Simon looked up at Paycocke's, its chimney's smoke attaching it to the sky like an umbilical cord. He would later see this day with a clearer vision, just another Monday, but a day of secrets and lies beginning to unfold, the day Robin left him. And Paycocke's? The house would never leave him.

When Robin had agreed to marry him, their student debt crises had meant stale muffins and tea long past its sell-by. Several thousand breakfasts later the 'I do' became 'I don't' and there were croissants and lapsang souchong, but the complete absence of laughter and mutual love.

"We have to talk," Robin had said. She took a breath so deep it slashed the air between them. There had been no warning; yesterday had been like any other, or had *that* been the warning? There were platitudes, pregnant words. She put her hand on his and her fingers held a warmth that only felt skin deep. Simon fixed his gaze to the kitchen table, picking out first the spot where Skimble had clawed the soft pine and then the scars of their

9

daughters' drawings, faded impressions of stick men from another decade, a different life.

"Dammit, I'm sorry, Simon, I owe you more than that." Robin's American accent, tempered after twenty years in England, took over again in times of stress, times when she couldn't meet his eyes.

Simon looked up at his wife, his forehead creasing into a stave of lines. His thoughts hovered over the main issue, alighting only on trivia: a trace of powder on her silk blouse; the tiny crescent moon studs that she wore in her ears; the single white hair he had never noticed; the way she said, 'Sorry.' There was already a distance between them, he and his ex-wife elect now. He held his chin in one palm, his fingers against his lips as though they could stop the words coming out. He could do no more than shrug the question. "Why? Why, Robin?"

She looked away. "It's been coming a long time, Simon... Don't you see? We've grown apart. It would have taken more than the house to save us, a whole lot more. I thought it could... I thought... but..." She bit her bottom lip.

He wondered when was the last time they had made love. The day they had moved into Paycocke's, months before, high with the excitement of the house, with its five hundred years of passions buried in the timbers. The memory made him smile, even though the cutting edge of their own passion had been so quickly blunted by the mundane. But that wasn't it. There was something else in Robin's dark green eyes, a fence over which he couldn't see.

Robin seemed to sense pleading in his look. "Jeepers, why can't you be angry, Simon? Why can't you be goddamn angry? You... you always have to take the moral high ground." She pushed back her hair from her eyes with perfect coral nails and was brutal on the threatening tears, blinking them away. "Oh, Simon, speak to me."

Simon shook his head, lost. "I don't know. I just don't know." Then the questions poured out. "But what are you going to do? What about the girls? Do they know? How long have you felt like this?" He massaged his brow with his fingertips. His whole face felt old, used, second-hand.

Robin looked away. "It's not just you, Simon. It's me. It's this house. It's everything."

"The house? What do you mean, the house?"

"Since we moved in, everything's gone wrong. I don't know... this place gives me the creeps. We should never have come here. It was a mistake, another damn Band Aid. It's weird, Simon. And it's not just me, Cassie feels it too... and Alex. But anyhow, that's beside the point. It's not the house, it's us. We've changed. You've changed. I've changed." Robin sighed, punctuating her staccato list. "No, that's wrong. I haven't changed. That's the problem. Look, Simon, there's someone else."

"What?" Simon's heart seemed to ricochet around his chest and he could hear its beat pulsing in his temples. He stood up and cracked his head on a low beam. "Ow."

Robin laughed as she did every time he bumped his head, still several times a day. Simon felt dizzy and Robin held him, tightly but not close.

"You see what I mean about the house?" She grinned to try and lift the moment, but for him it remained anchored in despair. "Maybe you'd better sit down, honey."

So he was still her honey. That was something. Something or nothing. "Who is it?" he said, wondering if he really wanted to know, whether he could handle knowing. He stared out of the window into the courtyard. The clematis was dying back for the winter, its purple blooms withering, drying out.

Robin inhaled. It was like the breath she took when she had to give one of her clients bad news. 'We can't take out that wall' or, 'Your colour scheme is too dark' or, 'Boy, whoever did this had lousy taste.' So this time it had turned out to be her with the lousy taste. Her voice shrank, becoming as small as he had ever heard it. Confidence seemed to desert her and Simon welcomed the tiniest of pyrrhic victories. "Abby Williams."

"Abby? Abby Williams? But Abby's..."

"A woman." Robin held his hands between hers.

"But..." Simon closed his eyes and shook his head, as though the bump he had taken were making this happen.

"Yeah." She sighed, trying to persuade him that this was hurting her as much as him.

"You can't be…"

"Simon. I'm sorry it had to be this way. Gee, this sounds like such a cliché, Simon, but I truly am so sorry. I tried so hard…"

"But…"

But there was no more. Robin took a holdall and walked through the falling leaves down West Street into the centre of Coggeshall. He watched her figure dwindle, enveloped by the perspective, and he was unable to feel anger, only loss. Gripping the frame of the huge front door, he made his wish for time to pass and then slammed the three inches of solid wood shut. Simon leant back against the wall and slumped to the floor, even the 'Why?' eluding him.

Six months ago, when the opportunity arose to run Paycocke's House for the National Trust, Robin had been all for it. She had been sick of the Northern Line, couldn't wait to leave Hampstead for East Anglia's open skies. Paycocke's had been 'totally awesome' and 'a dream'. He could just as easily run his book business from here and her clients were spread out all over the south east, anyway. Cassie was mixing with a bad crowd; Alex needed better air for her asthma. Simon was crowbarred away from his bookshop in Flask Walk, persuaded of this new start. In return for living at Paycocke's Simon and Robin would open the house to the public. It would be fun. It would bring them all closer together. It was a New Deal.

He sat down at the huge trestle table and ran a finger over its polished surface. There were small craters where pests had burrowed over the centuries. Dust would settle on the furniture this winter, the room unused, too cold to entertain. Paycocke's creepy? What could she mean? Simon loved the house, had so the minute he first saw its silvery limewashed timbers lording it over West Street. And now what? He put his head in his hands. Paycocke's creepy? No. Never.

*   *   *

"Dad? Where's Mom?" Simon and Robin had often joked that their daughters had been brought up bilingual: English and American. Cassie stood at the landing half-way up the stairs. The low autumn sun cascaded through the leaded glass behind her and Simon had to shield his eyes.

"Gone... out. Gone." He shook his head at his daughter, her thin silhouette framed by the window, frail, almost transparent. "Gone."

"She told you?"

Simon lifted his head. Great, so Cassie knew already. She came down a step towards him. He noticed that the stairs didn't creak in complaint the way they did when he trudged up and down.

"You OK, Dad?"

Simon brushed his hand through his hair and looked at the floor. Cassie dissected his expression of disgust. "It's not the end of the world, Dad."

"Isn't it?"

"She's staying in Coggeshall."

"Oh."

"Sorry, Dad, but it is the right thing to do. You'll see. Eventually."

"How long have you known?"

"I don't know, Dad. A while." Cassie was vague; it seemed to suit her shadowy figure, first eclipsing then dancing in the sunlight. "She couldn't talk to you. How could she? It was burning her for so long, and you... you weren't there for her." Then she was beside him, touching him, her long fingers on his shoulders, massaging the pain he didn't know he had. In that moment he lived again. "It *is* for the best."

He raised his chin; it felt so heavy. "Am I really the last to know?"

"Dad, don't be too hard on her."

"On her?" Simon spat out the words, thumping the oak table.

"She needs to find herself; give her that much."

"Find herself?" His voice rose with incredulity. "Find herself?"

Then plummeted with despair. "Find herself." *And lose me.*

"It'll be OK, Dad."

"No."

She nuzzled his hair and he smelt Robin's perfume.

"Oh Cassie, what am I going to do?"

She touched his neck with her cool hands. "Chill, Dad. You have the book business and Paycocke's, and Alex will still be here for a couple of years. Things will turn around."

"And you?"

"Me?"

"You said Alex? What about you?"

"Yeah, me too, I guess. I don't know. Alex has school to finish. I…" Cassie shrugged.

"Have your gap year?"

"Yeah, whatever."

"Gap life, more like," he said, resurrecting a running family joke. "So you guys are staying with me?"

"Does it matter?"

"I suppose not." Simon could resign himself to anything. He curled his legs up to his chest and rocked on the chair. He could no longer hear his heart, unsure whether that was good or bad.

Cassie broke the silence that had swamped them. "Tea?"

"Tea," he agreed.

She made Earl Grey, Robin's favourite. Ginger nuts, too. He found himself zooming in on the details; everything else was too much. The Wilde quotation on the biscuit tin; Robin had loved Oscar. *Had* loved. Life reduced to the pluperfect in seconds. Simon looked at his reflection in the grandfather clock, a waste ground of emotion. He must have a picture of himself in the attic, a painting that stayed young and handsome, more harshly youthful with every passing minute, while he deteriorated. He sipped the tea.

"What's that stuff about the house?" he said.

"Huh?"

"Mom said she hated the house. She said it gave her the creeps. You know what she meant?"

"I don't know. Maybe something about the panelling being

hosed. Abby said…" She cut off her words with a brisk change of subject. "Or maybe it was that time Alex saw the ghost."

"That was not a ghost." Simon almost laughed, almost forgot himself. What he would give for the resilience of being nineteen again. "That was just a car headlight reflected in the mirror."

"Alex said…"

"She was half asleep. There's no such thing as ghosts." He gave a glimmer of a grin and she leant across the table and touched his cheek.

"What about the Imogen Holst thing? When the Holsts were here she saw some freaky stuff." Cassie's long blonde hair flopped in front of her eyes like a veil and she tucked it behind her ears in an automatic gesture. "You really think there's no such thing?"

"OK, then. Probably no such thing." Simon hedged his bets.

"That's more like it, Dad, sitting on the fence." Cassie's laugh made her face grow.

"I fell off the fence a long time ago, darling." He wanted to make the moment linger a while, this by-product of Robin's departure, a sudden unexpected closeness with Cassie. It cut through the confrontations about university, boyfriends and the state of the bathroom. He was glad she was here, breathing her freshness, looking into those muddy blue eyes, proud of his part in creating her. He smiled and took a biscuit from the tin, dunking it in his tea for a second too long. It wilted en route to his mouth.

"And…" He bit his bottom lip, relished the physical pain. "And… Abby?" At least he could say her name.

"It's cool." Cassie gave the smallest of shrugs.

"It was… I don't know… a shock. Shock's too small a word." He put his arms out, palms facing up. "How did I not know, Cassie? How did I not see it coming? How?"

"Look, Dad, don't beat yourself up. It's not a lifestyle choice. It's Mom. It's who she is, who she needs to be, who she's… always been. But she's still Mom. And she's still Robin." Cassie put her hand on his arm. He couldn't remember when he had been so aware of her touch. "We'll be all right."

Simon stared into his tea, its surface scumming over. *Who she's always been.* "Yeah. You're right." He forced brightness. "What are you up to today?"

"Nothing much. I want to go up to London, go over some scripts with Joanne. I have an audition Friday. You?"

"I don't know. End of season accounts for the house. And I need to send a few invoices out. Like you say, nothing much." Just another day: a few invoices; do the accounts; my wife leaves me. Not much.

"Dad?" The word was drawn out, almost to breaking point. The begging bowl signal.

"Uh-huh?"

"Could you sub me for the train fare?"

He snorted, tried to smile. Normality resumed. He went to his study and pulled out his wallet from where it had fallen behind the printer. One lone purple twenty peeked at him. He frowned – he could have sworn he had more cash than that. He held up the note and she plucked it from his grasp in case he changed his mind.

Cassie kissed him on the cheek. "Thanks, Dad, you're a sweetie."

"Yeah, a soft centre. Strawberry cream, that's me." *The one everybody leaves until last.*

"Aw. Poor Daddy." She mussed his hair.

"Need a lift to the station?"

"No, thanks, Dad, I'll walk."

Cassie looked into his eyes, and he felt the brevity of life slap him across the face. He would have her for such a short time.

"And Dad?"

"Yes?"

"Don't do anything silly, will you?"

He looked away, wondering how silly things could get.

"You promise?"

"I promise."

Simon flinched as she slammed the heavy front door behind her. *Imogen Holst, Of course there was no such thing as ghosts.* She'd been sixteen, impressionable, imaginative. But the Holsts had stayed at Paycocke's for such a short time; in fact, no one stayed at the house long. What had brought the family there? What had made them leave? What made everyone leave Paycocke's House?

*   *   *

Halfway down the street Cassie looked back at Paycocke's, its façade merging into the grey afternoon, forbidding and brooding but at the same time powerless and looking sorry for itself. Much like Dad. The wind blew her hair into her face, obscuring her eyes. For a brief instant she felt a pang for her father, but then she took one last look at the house, squeezed out a smile, and walked in the opposite direction to the railway station.

He had brought it on himself, really, hadn't he?

Chapter 2
Falling Leaves

The house felt empty now, barren and cold as though the life had been sucked out of it with the departure of his wife and daughters. It held Simon in its cold embrace and he had a flashing thought that this was how it would always be from now on.

He gazed out of the oriel window onto West Street. A strong breeze whipped up a mixture of willow and horse chestnut leaves, not yet brown, not yet at that crisp underfoot stage. It had always been a favourite family pastime in autumn, crunching through the leaves on Hampstead Heath, hand-in-hand, a daisy chain of Chances, their little girls so trusting and vulnerable, a parent at each end. Now the chain was broken, its links no longer needed, and the leaves chased each other down the street in Robin's wake.

Although the sun still streamed in through the window, spotlighting the swirling dust, Simon felt a chill in the hall and lit the wood burner. Sitting at the table he took out the accounts folders, but the numbers merged into one another. *What did it matter?* He slumped in the yew carver, its high comb back supporting his head as he looked up at the ceiling. Amongst the elaborate carving on the beams above him he picked out the initials 'TP' and 'MP', Thomas and Margaret Paycocke, so sure of their love for each other that they had stamped it on their house. He wondered if Margaret could have walked out on Thomas, leaving behind those carvings.

"Oh, Thomas, Margaret, what did I do?" He rubbed his hands together; they were freezing even though the fire was throwing out waves of heat. He wandered up the narrow back staircase in the east wing, where every creak announced his arrival. He looked into Cassie's room, long and low, facing out over the back of Paycocke's into the Edwardian garden, where the lavender now held only a hint of its summer lustre.

Ghosts? Letters written by Gustav Holst's daughter Imogen told of Thomas Paycocke's ghost being seen in the entrance hall, and that Cassie's room was haunted by the looms that had shuttled there in the eighteenth century. That had made both Cassie and Alex want it, so they had had to toss a coin. He remembered Alex's pleading in a squabble that mirrored their earlier years. Weeks' worth of Cassie's clothes now sprawled across the floor and relaxed on the sofa. No weaver would want to haunt this mess.

Alex's room was up on the top floor, its vaulted ceiling following the contours of the roof, baking her in the summer. Slung from two rafters was a hammock full of cuddly toys, a menagerie awaiting inevitable exile from the teenager's life. He plucked a faded Penguin from the bookcase that had had the removal men cursing as they inched it up the narrow stairs: *A Vindication on the Rights of Woman* - Mary Wollstonecraft. Simon was impressed; for all his interest in books these days, at fifteen it had been Dennis Wheatley and Alistair MacLean that had stoked his fire. He opened the cover. There was an inscription in neat black ink: 'To my own Vindication, love J.' The tail of the last letter curled around and the author had put a smiley face inside the resulting circle. He put the book back where it belonged, between Wolff and Woolf, smiling at Alex's powers of organisation.

Simon shivered and pulled his zippered fleece up around his neck. It felt as though the heat had been drained from the house, that all its warmth had left with Robin. Although the window was closed, the curtains billowed out like limp spinnakers. His little finger could fit into the gap between the frame and sill. On moving in, they had thought the draughts would keep them healthy; right now Simon could worship at the altar of central heating. Blowing into his fist he heard the noise, like a pager going off, persistent and repetitive, calling him. He thought it came from one of the public rooms.

The beeping grew louder as he approached, and when he stood at the entrance of the master bedroom he saw that it was coming from an oak chest beside the four-poster. Sitting there was a Staffordshire dog, a basket of flowers in its mouth. The spaniel berated him with the irritating sound, oblivious on a squat plinth containing a tiny spring-loaded alarm, designed to go off in case a member of the public lifted the piece.

"Hello. What's set you off, then?" He lifted the figure off the base and the volume of the beeping increased. Putting the dog back on its pedestal the alarm stopped. "Must be a loose connection." Picking it up again, he set off the alarm. Putting it back, the beeping ceased once more. He laughed at the dog with its ridiculous cargo of flowers. "I don't know what it was. You explain it." He went to the window and looked out onto the main road. The wind had taken a firmer hold of the day and more leaves rolled down the street towards the crossroads. He leant forward with his head against the icy glass. As he did this, the alarm went off behind him again. He turned; no, not the alarm but the telephone this time, shrill with the ring tone that Alex had programmed into it. Vivaldi; she planned to change it with every season. He ran downstairs and picked it up a second before the answer phone cut in.

"Simon Chance."

"May I speak to Robin, please?" A woman's voice.

"She's not here." His normally affable telephone manner cracked as he fought to control the vitriol. "Is that Abby? Abby Williams? You've got a nerve."

"No, oh, no. It's Eleanor, Eleanor Simmons." He picked up a trace of Yorkshire in her, a hint of the Dales.

Simon's anger ebbed. "I'm sorry. I… I thought you were someone else." He forced himself to be friendly. "Can I help?"

"You'll be Simon, Robin's husband?"

How was he supposed to answer that? '*Not anymore?*' He took a deep breath and managed not to commit himself. "Uh-huh."

A bounce entered her voice, like a telephone salesman, someone who wants something. "Maybe Robin's mentioned me?" she said. *No.* Another thing Robin hadn't touched on.

"I teach at the primary?" Everything she said was a question.

"No, no, she hasn't told me anything. She's… away… for a while." He parked his bottom against the kitchen table.

Eleanor seemed to detect his languor and became more

hesitant, her accent moving further north, or maybe that was just his imagination. "Well, perhaps I should call back when she's there."

When would that be? Simon shook his head and sighed. "No, that's all right. What's it all about?"

The bounce returned. "Well, Year 6 is doing a project on local history, and Robin kindly said that once the season was over she'd open Paycocke's for the class to have a look around."

He tried hard to volley back the enthusiasm he didn't feel. "Great, what a lovely idea. Just like Robin." Just like Robin, to land him with this, ten-year-olds tearing around between the Nankin porcelain and the cranberry glass, wiping sticky fingers on the Durham quilt. He shuddered.

"Yes, it would be fun. Why don't you come over next week sometime, have a cup of coffee and we can thrash out the details." He began to feel on more solid ground, and felt a smile intrude into his words.

You could tell she was a teacher, standing for none of this up-in-the-air malarkey. "Well, I want to get the groundwork done before half-term, so I'd like to get the ball rolling as soon as I can. How about this evening?"

Simon felt cornered. He stood up and looked out of the kitchen window. Leaves collected in the courtyard, bundling up as though for warmth against the whitewashed wattle and daub.

"Simon, are you there?"

"Yes, yes, sorry… Eleanor. Just checking my diary. Tonight's out, I'm afraid. I have… a meeting." A meeting. Simon rolled his eyes at his own stupidity. Of all the excuses: I'm washing my hair; I missed the bus; the dog ate it. Eleanor was a teacher; she had excuse radar. He tried to pick up the pieces. "How about… Wednesday?"

"It'll have to be lunchtime?"

"That's fine."

"About one?"

"Great. You know where to find us?"

Eleanor laughed. "You can hardly miss fifty feet of mud and stud."

Simon laughed too, in spite of himself. "The bell's a bit stiff and it looks like it'll self-destruct, but it does work."

"Grand. I'll see you Wednesday, then." The telephone went silent. Simon's footsteps clattered on the loose parquet as he went through to his study and put the handset back on the base.

Wednesday, forty-eight hours. The distance between yesterday and today seemed like a chasm. How far away was Wednesday, with empty nights spanning the abyss? He had to speak to Robin, maybe when Alex got back from school. There had to be some way forward.

He fired up his laptop. Maybe he should get on with some work, pick up any emails, check the website for new orders, catalogue the latest batch of books, anything. Paycocke's was beautiful to look at, but it paid no bills. At the top of his inbox he saw Martin Sparrow's name.

"Sparrow? Martin Sparrow? What on earth...? Sparrow?" *Martin Sparrow, crawling out from under his stone. And why, after all this time?* Simon shook his head at the memory of the man, arrogant, selfish and so damned charming he still made him smile. And how in the hell did he get Simon's email address? How long had it been - had email even existed then? He hovered the cursor over 'delete'. *Damn, what did the man want?* The subject line was irritating, just like Sparrow himself, 'Open me, you know you want to!' Simon resolved not to, although it nagged at him like a desire to pick at a scab. Instead he gazed at the beams in his study, and fingered a long gash in one stud where the green oak had split as it seasoned, holding that scar throughout the centuries. He tried to remember what Cassie had said about the panelling. It was wrong; what did she mean, wrong? It was early sixteenth century, contemporary with the house. What was wrong with that?

The screensaver activated, and Simon watched the scrolling books fill the display, hypnotising him. He walked through the entrance hall into the dining room and stared at the walls. What could be wrong? The oak linen fold panels had lined the walls of Paycocke's House for five hundred years. It was intricate and elaborate, gracefully mimicking the soft folds of draped material, appropriate for the clothier Thomas. But hadn't he read somewhere that linen fold was a Gothic pattern, maybe that was it; maybe you would expect something with more of a Renaissance feel to it, something more ornate in a Tudor house.

Or maybe a panel swung open at midnight and unleashed a stream of the undead. He laughed at the thought and then crossed his fingers against it, like the belt-and-braces conversion of a death-bed atheist.

He caressed each wooden panel, working his way up and down the smooth wood, looking for notches or knots which might represent some sort of lever. Secret passages? Now he thought he was losing his mind. He knocked the wood, but it all sounded the same. Hollow. The east wall echoed to the sound of his tapping and he wasn't even certain what he was looking for. Something, anything out of the ordinary, but today he couldn't say what was ordinary and what was bizarre. The panelling stretched several feet above his head to the dark oak beams of the ceiling. He fetched a step-ladder and probed the panelling from his precarious perch. His hair dusted the cobwebs on the ornate stop-chamfers decorating the end of each beam. Although the carvings were not as elaborate as those in the main entrance hall, Simon marvelled at the craftsmanship that had gone into the work, perfect foliates even at this close range.

Then he saw the ledge. So obvious it was from his elevated position, he wondered why he had never noticed it before. Across the room from where he stood, where the linen fold above the fireplace reached up to the ceiling, he saw that the panelling stopped short of the beams by a few inches, leaving a narrow but dark ledge.

In his rush to get down, Simon missed a step on the ladder and lost his balance, falling onto his ankle. He sat on the floor, cradling his foot until the pain subsided enough for the battery of his cathartic expletives to run down. "Bastardly. Bastardly and Muttley," he said, rocking back and forth. He stared at the spot on the wall which had proved his downfall. But the ledge. Why would there be a ledge?

Putting his hand on the polished Jacobean table, he pulled himself to his feet and tested the weight on his injured ankle, finding it wanting. He walked the aluminium ladder like a Zimmer frame towards the fireplace wall. Using his good foot and his other knee to haul himself up the ladder, he rested on the platform, sweat beetling down his brow. His ankle shrieked.

It looked like it hadn't been dusted in centuries. Spiders had grown up, lived and died there, their mummified corpses curled up towards him like arthritic hands. As his eyes became accustomed to the gloom, in the midst of the spider graveyard he saw a small dark shape, silhouetted against cushions of dust. He reached over and felt it, velvety with the dust of decades but hard in his fingers, then he held it up to the remains of the day's light. A key.

"Hey, Dad."

Simon turned, caught red-handed, and almost lost his balance again. He stretched out a hand and steadied himself against the wall. "Alex, hi. Hi. What are you doing home so early?"

"It's four o'clock, Dad. I'm always home this time." Alex affected that default teenage tone of accusation.

Simon was flustered. "How was school?"

"Fine."

"Good day?"

"What are you doing up the step-ladder?"

"I'm looking at the panelling."

"Oh yeah. Abby said it was funny."

Simon almost parted company with the ladder as his balance deserted him again. "What do you know about Abby?" He could not manage more than a monotone.

His daughter shrugged, her light brown ponytail bouncing against her shoulders for a split-second. "You know. She has that shop in the village. And, you know."

"Oh hell, Alex, did everybody know except me?"

"Dad, these things happen. You should be happy she's found the courage to come out."

I should be happy? I *should?*

"Are there any biscuits?"

Simon was speechless at Alex's priorities. "In the kitchen."

"What kind?"

"Does it matter? I don't understand, Alex. Your mother left me this morning, left us. She walked out." He had to spell it out. "For another woman. And you want to know what biscuits we have?"

Alex smiled. "It'll be cool, Dad."

Simon shook his head, unleashing a cloud of dust from his hair.

"You could use some Head and Shoulders." Alex broke the moment, and Simon lost his first tear. His daughter put her sports bag down and held out her arms.

"Simon Chance – come on down."

"I can't. I've done my ankle."

"Take it easy, Dad. One step at a time, like running a marathon." He inched his way back down to ground level, his foot screaming. Turning around, the ceiling looked far distant and his head swam. "Take my hand."

"Thanks, Ally."

"What you got there?"

He opened grubby fingers to reveal the old flat key lying in his palm. It was less than an inch long with a heart-shaped cut-out. Simon rubbed it between his fingers. There was no rust, only a dull sheen. Simon smiled at Alex, felt his love for her underpinning his existence. He ran his fingers through the red streaks in her hair, a gesture that she usually hated. But this time she touched his chin, where dust had settled on his Velcro-like stubble. To have come this far and have Cassie and Alex to show for it, that wasn't too bad, was it?

"A key," he said, shrugging. "It's a key."

Chapter 3
Making the Bed

Two days was all it took to realise that the bed didn't make itself, Monday and Tuesday nights spent churning up the sheets when the ibuprofen wore off.

Simon would have been listless had it not been for the sharp pain of his injured ankle punctuating his day. Thanks to Alex it was on the mend.

"RICE, Dad," she had said, masquerading practicality as gentleness, probing his swollen foot with her long pale fingers, asking whether this or that hurt, and ignoring his answers.

"Ow." He sucked his teeth. "Rice? Ah, that's worse. That's definitely worse. Ooh. Not so bad there. What do you mean, rice?"

"Rest, Ice, Compression, Elevation. Good job I was here." Alex shuffled her father into the sitting-room and arranged him on the sofa with a bag of frozen peas and a piano stool. "It's just a slight sprain. Julia did the same on the astro the other week and she's right as rain. Of course she's not as old as you." When Alex laughed, her face grew full, inhaled life and spread it around like a contagious disease. Simon had to laugh too.

Two days laid up gave him plenty of time to think, plenty of time to prevaricate and to let his anger diminish to a sturdy simmer. Alex helped him down the stairs in the morning, gave him a fresh ice-pack, and settled him down with a stack of book catalogues, his laptop and instructions not to move. Simon ignored his work and his overflowing inbox, especially the nagging email from Martin Sparrow.

When Sparrow had arrived at Groves and Palmer fresh from Balliol, he had impressed the publishers with his hummingbird ability to dart from topic to topic, extracting the nectar of importance and then move on. With a confidence honed in Marlborough College, he made Simon, though several years older, feel ponderous by comparison. The ebullient Sparrow skipped several rungs on the promotional ladder while Simon fidgeted with the small print, and in the end it was a relief to quit the Cambridge firm when Robin decided to set up her design business in NW3. Simon knew he wasn't cut out for the sabre-toothed side of business life.

To Simon's surprise, Martin Sparrow followed him out of the Fens a year later and contacted his old colleague with a proposition.

"We set up on our own. Take on the big boys. They're all so swamped by tradition, they're haemorrhaging money. We go international, the States. There's money in them thar hills, Simon my boy. I rustle up the clients – there are oodles of collectors that side of the pond, just itching to be bled. You locate the books and, bingo, Robert is your uncle. Richer than your wildest custard creams. Sparrow and Chance. How does that sound?"

"Oodles? Oodles?" Simon laughed. "You're not just behind the times, Martin, you're behind behind the times."

"That's for the Yanks. They love all that stuff. I've been boning up on my Wooster-speak for them, too. BBC accent and a well-cut suit, they can't resist it."

It was true that Martin Sparrow had the finest suits that Simon had seen in a leather elbow patch world. Although Simon didn't know Alexander McQueen from Steve McQueen, Robin had reverentially pointed out Sparrow's immaculate Anderson and Shepherd three-piece. Martin was clearly right about American gullibility.

"But your wife's a Yank, isn't she? Sorry about that." Sparrow laughed at the ambiguity. On sober days he knew it was ludicrous, but in some ways Simon couldn't help liking his ex-colleague, so full of disrespect for the system and yet never feeling the need to point out that his overcoat cost more than Simon's car.

Sparrow's idea was tempting, although impossible. Robin had spent years sloughing off her American past; she would never agree. "Robin's just got the business into the black, Martin. She's established a good client profile…"

Martin impersonated a police siren. "Bee-bow-bee-bow. Office-speak detected, Simon, don't give me that, pleeease."

"Sorry, Martin. But anyway, the girls, they're still too young…"

"Tell you what, old chum, I'll pop around tonight, see the wife and two veg, give them the old Sparrow Arrow…"

"And Robert is your uncle?"

"Indeedy-do." He launched into a WC Fields impersonation. "Whaddya say, huh? Whaddya say?"

"Thanks for the offer, Martin, but I'm not ready for the States."

Martin smiled, dropping the ham. His voice shrank. "Yeah, well, I *am* ready, Simon." He clicked his pen open and closed in annoyance; this clearly hadn't gone the way he had expected. This moment was like an optical illusion, because he recovered his larger than life persona in a second. "I don't know if they are ready for me, but the Sparrow mind," he brandished the ballpoint at Simon, "is made up. New York here I come. New York, New York. Look, Simon, how about 'Chance and Sparrow'? My final offer. You'll never look back."

Martin Sparrow was not made for looking back. Simon, with his throbbing ankle as constant company, could only look back. He had no regrets about ditching his mired PhD back in Cambridge, had done it happily to look after Cassie. Robin had joked he was a low-flyer; that was what passed for a joke with Robin. Of course she had been right. He had always been lacking in ambition and drive, and as he brooded on the sofa his thoughts queued up to compete for the gold medal in failure: career; money; relationships. He had screwed them all up.

He returned to the mysterious key, an itch he couldn't scratch. It fitted none of the locks in the house. What was it for? He took some photographs and posted them on the bulletin board of an antiques website, then had to stop himself pulling up the bookmark every half hour to see if there was any information. It was something to think about that wasn't Robin.

"It's only a key, Dad." Alex teased him.

Cassie scorned the fuss. "The electrician probably dropped it when he was re-wiring."

"Dropped it on a ten-foot high ledge? Right."

"Who cares, anyway?"

"No, no. It's important. I can feel it." He did. The key felt alive to his touch, cool but at the same time vibrant. It had drawn him. It had wanted to be found.

Simon lay back on the sofa, his leg stretched out on a footstool, RICE, and turned the key over in his hand, willing it to give up its secret, but it caught the light of the fire and mocked him with its resistance. Abby. Abby Williams. The thought of her stabbed at him.

The doorbell rang, echoing through the house. The grandfather clock in the hall had just squeaked out a single anaemic chime – one o'clock. Alex wasn't back from school yet and as for Cassie, heaven knew where she was. She had disappeared with another twenty pound note and promises of being back for dinner. Simon reached for his walking stick and hobbled out to the front door. On the way the bell rang twice more.

"All right, all right, I'm coming."

He swung the huge door ajar. A slender woman stood framed there, her left hand tugging on the bell-pull. Her deep brown hair was held back into a loose ponytail and she carried a folder. Canvasser. Jehovah's Witness. His heart sank at his own stupidity. Why had he not ignored the bell?

"Hello?"

"Does your bell not work?" The woman smiled, but her eyes looked past him into the cavernous hall.

So this is Paycocke's. This is what the fuss is all about. It's the right place, but he knew that already, didn't he? 'Softly, softly.' Him and his daft clichés. Why not just come straight in and say what you want? 'Because there's a plan, Eleanor. You've got a have a Plan. And first up, you are going to get to know Simon Chance.' Well, he pays the piper. He's not bad-looking, this Simon, is he? Shame for him. Still and all, reap what you sow.

"Yes... yes, I think it does."

"You can't hear anything. Look." The woman demonstrated

and Simon winced as she tugged at the rusty chain. The bell rang inside the house. A shadow of red lit up the woman's cheeks. "Oh."

"Told you it worked."

"Well, not out here it doesn't." She wouldn't let it rest.

"Well, there's several inches of oak between outside and in."

"Aah." She tacked. "Simon?"

He jibed. "I've got enough brushes, I'm an atheist, I have a poppy already and Labour's too right-wing for me. Does that cover it?" His ankle complained and he had had enough.

The woman's face creased with incomprehension, then relaxed into a real smile. "No, I'm not selling anything and I promise I won't try to convert you. Eleanor Simmons." She offered a hand. Simon dropped his stick.

The man's frozzed. Hell fire, the whole place is like a fridge. What the heck's so special about it? That's what I'd like to know.

"Oh, hell, I completely forgot. Eleanor, yes, of course. I'm really sorry. Oh, hell." He reached for his stick and lost his balance. Eleanor steadied him with a hand that had practised on years of children.

"That's a lot of hell for an atheist." She laughed.

"I'm so sorry. I completely forgot. I wish I could say I hadn't, but it totally slipped my mind. Totally." His embarrassment was reducing his vocabulary. "Come in, come in." He limped out of the way of the entrance.

"Look, let me get the door." She picked up his walking-stick. "You take this."

Simon took the offered lifeline. "Thanks. I'm so sorry…"

"That'll do. Is it a bad time?"

"No, no, not at all. Just…" Simon gestured at his ankle.

"What did you do?"

"Fell off a ladder." He almost did it, almost added 'Miss' on the end in deference to her natural authority, even though she was at least ten years younger than he was. Her eyes searched him out, no matter how hard he tried to hide. He was swamped by a feeling of guilt over something he hadn't done.

She grinned again. "I bet. Do you want me to have a look

at it? I've an HSE." Simon stared. "Health and Safety Exec. First Aid."

"Yes. Right. Lovely. Yes. Shall we have some tea?"

Eleanor parked him back on the sofa and Simon gave her directions to the kettle.

"RICE," he said, as she turned his ankle over in her firm hands. "Rest, Ice, Compression and…" He clicked his fingers.

"Elevation."

"That's it. My daughter, Alex; she fished out the frozen peas."

"Good for her. Bright lass. Probably saved you a lot of pain." Eleanor smoothed down her moleskin skirt and sat on the sofa beside Simon. "There's no real damage – you'll be walking in a day or two. Milk?"

"Yes, please, just a drop."

Eleanor leant down for the milk jug, and as she did the clasp came loose on her ponytail and a curtain of wavy hair flicked across her face. There were traces of gold highlights picked up by the shaft of sun playing across the sofa, or maybe it was his imagination. Simon picked up the hair-grip from where it fell and handed it to her. With her hair free, the authority he had glimpsed seemed to dissipate. Exposed, she picked up her teacup.

Stop looking at me like that, will you? Do you know something? You can't, can you? Come on, get a hold of yourself, Eleanor, stop faffing. Of course he knows nothing. Those sad eyes of his, they can't see any further than the end of his nose.

"Thanks. Spring must be loose," she said, putting it in her handbag. "Anyway, to business."

"Yes. Now, Robin…" Simon took a deep breath, "my wife, has…"

She put two fingers on the back of his hand, a brief butterfly-like touch. "I know. It must be hard for you."

Simon almost dropped his tea. "What? *You* know as well?" He put his cup on the floor and rubbed his eyes with a thumb and index finger, picking at tiny nuggets of sleep.

Eleanor gave him the sort of look she probably saved for a grazed knee. "Simon, everybody knows. You can't keep a secret in a small town like this. Especially not when you're running a place like Paycocke's."

He slumped back into the cushions and crossed his arms. "It's not so much that I mind her leaving me... well, it is, but... But for another woman? She's been hiding this from me all these years. Why didn't I know? Why did I not see it?"

Eleanor's voice dropped. "Sometimes, if you want to see, you have to look, Simon."

Of course he knows nothing. How could he? It's going just like the Plan said it would. And we're not taking him for much of a ride, are we? Not compared to his Robin? He won't even notice we're here. But those sad brown eyes — that's what it's like when trust has been snapped in two. You've just joined a club, lad, the Mile Low Club. But don't worry, it doesn't get any worse. Although I'm making no promises.

Simon stared into the palms of his hands. This was hurting too much. He pushed the conversation out toward the periphery of his emotions. "What's this about the school trip, Eleanor?"

Simon had his reservations about thirty ten-year-olds in Paycocke's — the memory of Cassie and Alex ripping up their pillows to tar and feather each other was still strong. However, he accepted Eleanor's suggestion and agreed on a date in November when the class could come over. Cassie could do her talk; she was great with kids, exaggerating the ghosts and gossip that they liked and turning the history of the Paycockes into soap opera.

They stood for the awkward goodbye of new acquaintances and he had to open the sore.

"So, do you know Abby?"

"Yes, of course, everyone does." Everyone except him, it seemed.

"Oh?"

"The only snake in Coggeshall," she said, by way of explanation.

"What?"

"Yes, it's a huge python, thick as your arm. If you ever go round her house it's like a tropical rainforest."

"Oh." Simon twisted his lip, trying to feign disinterest in

Abby's snake. He supposed it at least had more cachet than being dumped for a guy with a Ferrari.

"She runs the Zebra boutique up Stoneham Street."

"Oh." The name meant nothing.

"She's nice, Abby is."

'Nice'. Robin had left him for someone who was 'nice'. His insides boiled. He would find out exactly how 'nice' she was. Right now.

"Did you drive up from the school?"

"Yes, it's my lunch break, but…"

"Could you give me a lift? Just to the crossroads." *It's my turn to get what I want.*

Eleanor gave way and gestured towards the front door. "The car's right outside."

"On the double yellows?"

"He doesn't come up this far."

She let Simon and his walking stick out by the side of the road and he disguised his intentions by shuffling towards the newsagent's. He waved at Eleanor's Focus as it disappeared up the hill, then realised he had forgotten to set the burglar alarm. "Damn." Going back to set it would be an excuse, evasion, displacement. There had been enough of that already. His resolve strengthened.

'Zebra'. 'Up Stoneham Street'. He had never noticed the shop before, but there it was, all plate glass and Sixties' graphics nestled between the sweetshop and the baker's. The door opened and a woman came out, well-dressed, hair tamed by the light breeze. Was that Abby Williams? His heart skipped and he turned back to scrutinise the cards in the newsagent's window, strengthening his alibi by muttering to himself. "Sixty pounds for a Chesterfield – mmm, not bad…" He saw in the window's reflection that the woman had gone and he hobbled across the road.

The door to Zebra was flanked by two bay trees in pots, each four feet tall with a perfect orb of leaves. Had it been anywhere else they would have been nicked by now. Maybe that was why he had liked this place so much, the perfect antidote to the Finchley Road. It was where they could grow tomatoes, grow closer, grow old. He passed by the sentinels into the shop, bright and airy. A bell rang as he entered, a warning bell. No one came out to serve him; silent ranks of russet and ochre pullovers echoed the falling leaves outside. He put a hand on a rack of raw silk jackets to take the weight off his throbbing foot. Expensive: beige; fawn; oatmeal; taupe. Colours which would mean something to Robin – she could smell 'expensive' – but which merged together on his own mental palette. Robin would have shopped here. Was this where they had had their first kiss? He fought the urge to consider himself bereaved. Had it been another man he would have had someone to battle against, a known enemy. But this – Robin had changed the rules of engagement in an instant and he no longer knew what they were. Yes, darn it, he felt bereaved.

The bell rang. Second warning. He turned and saw the woman come in.

"Hello." It was a bright 'hello', U-shaped with friendliness as if she had known him all her life, the 'hello' of someone trying to sell him something. A man, an easy target for a quick sale: a scarf; a pair of gloves; always the accessories. "Lovely afternoon," she said, filling his silence.

His stomach seemed to rise up and grab his vocal chords, plaiting them so that all he could manage was a garbled, "Hi."

The woman picked up on his reticence. "I'll just leave you to have a good nose, shall I?"

Simon found the words he had lost. "Abby? Abby Williams?"

She gave him a crimson beam. "Yes. Have we met?"

"No. Simon. Simon Chance."

The beam diminished to a smile, but what it lacked in size it now made up for by sincerity. "Simon." She held out a hand, which he stared at, then he looked at her, shaking his head. "We should talk," she added. The smile never left her lips, but her eyes held pity; that he did not need. "But not now. Not here."

She was so young. He wanted to pull both ends of her chiffon scarf tight around her thin turkey neck, until the fabric tore. He stared at her. She couldn't have been more than twenty-five, her skin pale and perfect, with little make-up; only a small mole on her upper lip drew his eye. His wife had left him for a younger woman – wasn't that supposed to be his territory?

"Please, Simon. I understand how you feel. I know how hard this is."

Her reasonableness was the back-breaking straw. "No. No," he screamed. "How could you know? How could you understand?" Simon took hold of the rack of jackets and threw it to the floor.

Abby screamed. "No." *She's afraid. Good.* "No, please, Simon. Please. This won't solve anything." Her voice faded into the distance as his mind fogged. He felt her hands try to pull him off, but he shrugged her aside, yanking several storeys of precision-folded sweaters from a shelf and tossing them up in the air. "No, stop it, please. Simon." Whirling his walking-stick around his head, he arced it like a javelin into a mirror, crazing it into a hundred pieces.

"You... you... both of you... lying... what have you done?" He turned around to face her, but his feet slipped on a lavender pashmina. Without his stick to steady himself, he put his weight on his twisted ankle, lost his balance and crashed to the floor.

The humiliation broke him and he started to weep into the sleeve of a crumpled Max Mara. Abby pulled the blinds on the gaping window, turned the shop sign to 'Closed' and took Simon up in her arms.

"Hey, it's OK, Simon. Let it out. It's OK. I've got you now."

He told himself he should hate her, but he clutched at her compassion. Her eyes locked with his and through the mist of his tears he saw that the pity was gone.

Abby pulled out a bottle of Laphroaig from behind the counter, and sloshed two fingers into a china mug. She held it to Simon's lips. "Better than sweet tea."

Simon spluttered, but sipped the whisky. It warmed him and drained the pain from his foot. His anger retreated. Her face, six inches from his own, was one he might have called beautiful in another life.

"Take your time."

He looked around the mayhem of the boutique. "I'm sorry."

"More?"

He shook his head. "This is good."

"Daddy's panacea."

So she had a 'Daddy'; Robin had always been a sucker for the English class system he detested. He felt snide remarks well up inside him, observations he was ashamed to be making, and he fought to suppress the vitriol. "I don't know what came over me."

"It was a normal reaction, Simon. And it's my fault. I should have been more open with you. We both should."

Simon clamped his eyes shut as he revisited the reality of his life now. His words were slow, deliberate. "Even so, I shouldn't have... Let me help you get things straight."

"It's fine. Really it's fine. A few things knocked over, that's all. I'll close up early and get the dustpan and brush out."

"I'll pay for the damage."

"It's not a problem, Simon."

Simon stared at the woman who had stolen his wife. He closed his eyes to guard the tears he could not control. "I want her back," he said.

Abby knelt down beside him, her eyes filming over. "It's not that easy," she said. "You just come to, get your breath back, and I'll run you back to Paycocke's. All right?"

He nodded.

Back to Paycocke's, to emphasise his pain. What was it Robin had said? Or was it Cassie? 'Abby said the house was all wrong.' Abby's face was still close to his, her breath smelling of spearmint, clean and unimpeachable. "Can I ask you something?"

She hesitated, as though he might tip over the edge again. "Yes?"

"Robin said you thought Paycocke's was weird. Why, exactly?"

Abby scrunched her brow into unaccustomed wrinkles. "Weird? I don't understand. What did she tell you?"

"I can't remember. I've spent the last couple of days trying to blot out that morning, but it was something... something about the panelling."

"Oh yes, the panelling. Have you noticed? I think it's upside-down."

Chapter 4
Washing

Simon looked at the panelling. Abby was right – it was exactly as she had described.

"You remember the Hampton Court fire back in the Eighties?" she said. "My father was involved with some of the restoration work on the panelling in the King's Apartments. He used to bore me witless with his stories. But anyway, this one stuck."

"Go on."

She shaped a rectangle in the air with her two forefingers. "A panel looks like this. Now, mediaeval carpenters were very pragmatic, always with an eye to saving time and effort. So the bottom edge of the panel," she drew a finger from left to right, "was always flat, so that when it came to dust, it could just be wiped clean. The top edge would have more complex carving, fluting and so on, because that way, it would collect less dust. On *your* panelling at Paycocke's, the bit above the fireplace, it's the other way round."

How come he hadn't noticed before? He stood in front of the inglenook and laughed. How had he missed it? On the other walls, he saw that the panelling was correctly oriented, with the flat edge at the bottom. But this one... He ran his fingers along the smooth surface. Why was it upside-down? Why had it spooked Robin so much? He shivered, although the afternoon was Indian summer warm.

"Hi, Dad, what's up?" Cassie passed in front of the dining room door, her long brown leather jacket on.

"Cassie, hi. Not a lot. Well, yes a lot, I suppose. I went to see Abby." Simon was still staring at the panelling as if an answer were imminent.

"And?"

He took a deep breath. "She's..."

"She's nice, isn't she?"

'Nice.' There it goes again. "I wasn't going to say that."

Cassie hooked her arm through his. "Give it time, Dad."

"Cassie? You know that Paycocke's talk you do for the public?"

"Uh-huh?"

"That bit when you come in here and start talking about the restoration? Something like, 'Charming though the bressumer above the fireplace is, with its delicately carved animals...' dum-di-dum, et cetera..."

"Dad, can we do this later? I have to go into Colchester." She tapped her wrist.

"So what do you know about the fireplace?"

"This and that. Listen, Dad, I have to shoot. I need to get to the shops."

Simon sucked his teeth in frustration.

"It's just I need to pick up a new print cartridge. Mine's low. I've had to print off a lot of CV's and stuff for my portfolio. They chew up the ink, you know. And those recycled cartridges last hardly any time at all."

"All right, I get the point. Will you be back for dinner?"

"Yeah... no... I don't know, Dad. I'll pick up something when I'm out. Er... Dad?" Cassie hesitated. From the age of four, she had always blown her pocket money by eleven o'clock on a Saturday morning. Alex, on the other hand, had built up a healthy stash of premium bonds and Post Office savings by the time she left primary school. Graduating from Smash Hits to Cosmopolitan, Cassie could be guaranteed to spend all her money in one go. What hadn't disappeared at the paper shop went on Walnut Whips. "Could you sub me twenty, Dad? I'll pay you back."

Simon opened his wallet and passed the note across. It disappeared from his grasp like a rabbit into a hat. Now you see it, now you don't. Whatever had happened to the Walnut Whips?

"Love you, Dad. See you later."

He stared back at the panelling and chuckled to himself. Upside-down?

"Hi, Dad, I'm back." Alex swung her bag inches from a Spode

bowl as Simon flinched. He prompted the usual monosyllables with his interest in her school day.

"Did you see Cassie?"

"She was at the bus-stop."

"Did she say anything?"

"Does she ever?" Alex shrugged. "Have you got my PE kit for tomorrow?" Just like Alex, organising tomorrow while today was still warm.

Simon thumped his head in a faux-melodrama. "I washed it, but..."

"It's still in the machine."

"I've had a lot on."

"It's all right, Dad, I know. I'll go and hang it out now."

Simon watched his daughter go out into the garden with an armful of whites. The temperature had dropped, but the wind was still strong and her Fred Perry clung with desperation to the washing line. The sky was turning slate in the distance and with rain forecast, this might be the last drying day. Alex reached up to the washing line, so healthy that sparks seemed to come off her, so full of potential that he could cry.

How dreadful it was to love one child more than another. Guilt pounded at him.

She came in with the empty clothes basket and Simon turned away so that she wouldn't see his ashen face.

"I need to get some work done, Al," he said. "I've been out of the loop for a few days."

"No sweat, Dad. I have some French to do." She clomped up the stairs.

Simon turned his computer on, pouring a tumbler of Glenfiddich while the machine was booting up.

Three new emails, plus the lurking one from Sparrow. He would have to look at that later; he still wasn't ready to face it. Two of the others were from eBay and he realised that even though the last few days had passed like mud, he hadn't found time to check his listings. He linked to the auction site and saw that he had won an early McEwan first edition for, well, all right, then, several songs. All the same, there was room for profit there.

One of his sales was also going well: a Thomas More's *History* volume that he had picked up at a car boot for a pound was generating a fair amount of interest. Only half an hour left and it was already up to £32.01. He laughed at the penny, one bidder's misguided attempt at cunning. He would come back to check the denouement later.

"Just a quick look at Antiques World," he said, clicking on his favourites. Expecting the usual nothing, this time he was surprised to see 'one reply' next to his 'Mystery Key' thread.

'KeyMaster' stood next to his query in bold. He always tried to imagine the person behind the web name, the character relishing the obscurity. His own, 'OldManBooker', had never felt more appropriate than now, wretchedly under the thumb of his years. With more and more of his business being done online, he wondered whether OldManBooker's burgeoning reputation would soon outstrip his own.

KeyMaster evoked an Arthurian holder of the keys to Knowledge and Myth, a bark-faced servant of Good, whose life was subjugated to the care of keys. That or an off-duty civil servant in Milton Keynes.

Simon clicked open the thread. 'Real distinctive key, has a European feel to it. IMO size and shape indicate it is probably a padlock key, quite early, an Eagle or a Dalab, maybe. Specific markings? Could you post more photos, or better still, email me offline at *keymaster@aol.com*? Let me know if you're interested in selling.'

So, not Milton Keynes, then, unless KeyMaster had strayed from New England to Old: 'Real distinctive'. Simon decided to hold fire; he didn't like 'taking things offline' – there were too many Web-weirdoes about, hiding behind fake identities. He tossed the key into his in-tray where it sank behind a mounting pile of papers. He would do some research of his own. Posting a 'Thanks, I'll get back to you,' he switched to eBay.

The More had climbed up to an incredible £94; it couldn't go any higher, surely. Checking the bid history he saw that two bidders were trying to outmanoeuvre one another: 'fitzall' and 'thebookie' had kangaroo-hopped above each other in healthy increments, sending the price way beyond his expectations. They must be collectors, with that 'must-have' gene that transcended common sense. No book dealer would pay so much; there wasn't enough profit in it.

Fifteen minutes to go. Simon switched to his email. 'Open me, you know you want to!' "OK, Sparrow, what do you want?"

'Hey, Simon, long time no sea, and have I got a deal for you. *Medicina* – remember? Give me a buzz on 07793 219876. Love to Robin, M.'

'Long time no sea.' In two years Sparrow had graduated from tea-boy to a forty-foot Swan he kept on the Solent. He had taken Simon and Robin around the Needles, sailing close to the wind in every respect, touching Robin's hair as it danced in the breeze and mooring his tanned cheek next to hers as he pointed out something on the horizon. Something where there had been nothing, well, nothing that Simon could see, anyway, nothing except for Sparrow's transparent intentions. 'Love to Robin'? What would Sparrow say now? He wanted to laugh, but couldn't. In Sparrow's presence, Robin's Missouri accent (she pronounced it 'Misery', she meant it, too) had deepened slightly, her hair seemed blonder and her tales of bagging an Ozark eight-pointer shaggier.

'*Medicina*' – they had buried that one years ago. Another Sparrow goose chase.

"What's the French for werewolf?"

Simon surfaced from the past with his chin resting on a palm, staring at the crumbling brickwork of his study wall. "Huh?"

"Hallo, Earth to Dad." Alex waved her hand in front of his eyes, a handful of silver rings blurring his vision.

Simon forced a small laugh and pushed his hair back. "Sorry, sweetheart, I was somewhere else."

"Anywhere good?"

He shook his head.

"Werewolf?"

"No idea. Something-loup? Loup-something, I don't know? Why are you asking me?"

She put her hands on his shoulders and tickled the nape of his neck. "Because you are one? Oooooooowwww," she howled.

"Hey, watch it." He tilted his head from left to right and heard his neck creak. "You could always look it up, you know."

"Yeah, I suppose." Peering over his shoulder Alex saw the eBay logo on a background window, chirpy primary colours in a bouncing sans serif. "Sold anything?"

"Oh, yes, that reminds me." Simon switched to eBay and refreshed the More sale. "Hey, Alex, look at this." There were less than two minutes left. "Jeez, Al, a hundred and thirty."

Simon refreshed once more.

"Hundred and forty, Dad. It's with fitzall now."

"I don't believe it. Cost me a pound."

"Refresh it, Dad, refresh it again." Alex urged him on, infecting him with her excitement.

"Wow, one sixty - thebookie really wants it."

Alex yelped with delight. "Click, Dad."

"Come on, fitzall, you need this book, come on, my son." He willed the unknown bidder onwards. "Yes. Yes, a hundred and eighty squid. This is crazy, Alex."

His daughter bounced up and down at his shoulders, the way she used to on his knees when she was five, symmetrical pigtails flying, a rollercoaster scream pounding his ears. Her hair was a sun-bleached blonde then, as fine as silk thread. It slipped through his fingers like water, like moments he could never have again.

"Two hundred – thebookie." Alex clapped her hands.

"Ten seconds. I just don't believe it." Simon did another refresh; the screen seemed to stall, not wanting to give up its secret, but then loaded the page in a last-ditch flash. 'Seller status: your item sold for £275!' Fitzall.

They both stared at the screen, mouths hinged open. Simon broke the silence with his mantra, "I don't believe it, Alex." He shook his head. "I don't believe it." He felt exhausted and leant back in his leather swivel chair. "Two hundred and seventy-five sovereigns, Alex. Two hundred and seventy-five smackers. Be-bop-a-moolah. I just don't…"

"Believe it, Dad. Believe it." Alex laughed.

"Who is this fitzall, then? Obviously knows nothing about books. I would've been pleased to get fifty."

"You've probably got thebookie to thank."

"Cheers, the bookie, whoever he is. Doesn't know much more than the other guy." "This calls for a celebration. Fancy popping down to the White Hart for dinner?"

Alex smiled and Simon felt her tender touch on his shoulders. "Let's."

"This is the best thing that's happened since... since..." Simon's mood went into freefall.

"Don't, Dad." Alex hugged him, her embrace making him feel small and wanted, taking tiny steps again.

"You're right. Let's go. I'll just send an invoice to this fitzall guy."

"OK, I'll run up and change. Two minutes." Alex kissed his head and peppered up the stairs.

Simon rubbed his hands together. He clicked on 'Send Invoice' and saw that hiding behind 'fitzall' was Mark Fitzwarwick from Clacton. "Local boy, eh? Well, Marky, I hope you still like to be beside the seaside, because now you're £275 lighter." He fingered the More book, wondering why both fitzall and thebookie had wanted it so much. Either way, at that price he'd better not leave it on his desk waiting for a spilt cup of coffee. He wrapped the book in some acid-free paper and enveloped it in bubble-wrap. It could go Special Delivery in the morning. He hit 'Print' to get a copy of the invoice and put his jacket on. "Oh, what?" The monitor shot back the message 'Unable to locate printer driver' and the printer stood there, mute and inanimate. He yanked the USB cable from the back, plugged it in and tried again. It was defiant and Simon had reached the end of his technical knowledge. "Damn."

Alex poked her head around his study door. "Ready?"

"Bloody printer's on the blink."

"Have you tried re-booting?"

"It takes so long. Can I send you the link and you can print it off on yours?"

"You can't, I'm running a defrag."

"A what?"

"Never mind. Look, log in on Cassie's; it's always on standby."

"Does she know how much that costs?"

Alex smiled and rubbed her chin in a parody of her father. "I think you have mentioned it before. Just once or twice."

Simon let out a sigh and stomped up to Cassie's room. Her Dell was indeed on standby with no password lock on it; just like Cassie. He was willing to bet that no hacker could circumvent Alex's system, but Cassie's was a joke. A minute later he was clutching the invoice, which he parcelled up with the book, ready to post.

The sky was stained with dusk as they ambled down to the pub. Alex put her arm in his, an ostensible nod to his unsteadiness, and he was beginning to feel touched by a consolation prize in all this. Alex and Cassie – he felt closer to them than he had in years. He had let things slip. That would change.

The wind had dropped, but they could feel the hints of the first autumn chills and were glad to get inside. Simon toasted Mark Fitzwarwick with a Chablis and ordered a squid-ink pasta. Alex went for the vegetable lasagne and Simon hoped she wasn't resurrecting her old vegetarian habits. They had been able to shoot that one down with a well-aimed bacon sandwich, but Simon didn't think he could get away with that again. 'He' instead of 'they'; he was already thinking along those lines.

"Don't look, Dad." Alex's fingers found his.

He looked and his stomach yelped. Robin and Abby were coming through the door. He raised his wine glass to hide his face and stared through the golden filter at the women. His wife looked great. Her hair sprang with life and she wore a suit he hadn't seen before. At least he thought he hadn't seen it before. Her steps were light, and her expression, too, was unburdened. The way she touched Abby's arm, the way she inclined her head, these were new to him. Had he ever known her? She was laughing and he struggled to remember the last time he had seen her laugh, and how much longer since he had been the one to make her laugh. The two women took a table around the corner of the L-shaped room, then all he could see was Abby's back. He put his glass down.

Alex took his hand across the white linen. "One day at a time, Dad."

Simon sighed. "Yeah." He moved his chair so that Abby was out of line of sight, out of his line of fire, and picked up his glass again, taking a large gulp that insulted the wine.

"We'll get there. You'll see."

Simon just nodded and the food arrived.

"They have a great chef here," Simon said, curling the noodles around his fork. It hung in mid-air on its way to his mouth, suspended above the deep black glow of the pasta on his plate, its inky sauce glinting in the candlelight.

He had been able to print out the invoice on her PC, yet Cassie had said her black ink cartridge was empty.

Alex caught his eye. "What is it?" she said.

"The washing," he said. "It's still on the line."

Chapter 5
Going Dutch

Dad didn't have a clue. Loser. He always ran his own course and always blinkered. The way his hair flopped over his eyes was just a microcosm of his own life, letting it go past the point where he could control it. And Mom? He hadn't seen it coming and he never would. Cassie would pick up a print cartridge in the morning. Always make a lie as close to the truth as possible. Poor old Dad. But, yeah, he asked for it. And that stuff about the fireplace? What was he on about? Mom's just left him and he's wittering on about the fireplace.

Cassie got off the bus in the buffeting wind and hurried over to Roach's house, one of the pastel cottages snuggled in the depths of Colchester's Dutch Quarter. She pulled her jacket collar up around her neck, the wind failing to make a dent in her pallor. She put her head down and weaved between the rush hour traffic. She hoped Roach had the gear.

Roach's place was in an alley off an alley, a place where the sun didn't shine, where the buzzer didn't work and the paint peeled off the door frame in blisters. The knocker was loose, but she rapped the dull brass anyway. The wind had chased her down this narrow gutter of town, and it pelted her ankles with burger cartons and cigarette packets. She tucked herself into the narrow doorway and knocked again. Where the hell was he?

She heard a shuffling from within, and the door opened.

Roach stood barefoot in the opening, either half awake or half asleep, she couldn't decide. He scratched his black stubble and squinted at her as if he couldn't bear the brightness, although the alley was swaddled in gloom. He reached up and smoothed a dense caterpillar eyebrow, yawning. "Cass, babe, what's up?"

"I called you yesterday, Roach?" She hadn't meant it to be a question, had wanted it to sound more forceful.

"You did? You did." Roach nodded in agreement.

"You didn't get back to me?"

"I've, like, been busy, yeah?"

"Have you got the Tryph?"

He smiled and although his eyes were trampled by an army of crows' feet and his hair looked like it had been washed in cooking oil she saw why she'd been attracted to him in the first place. Even this haggard he was better looking than any man she had ever known and he knew it, too, trading on his father's Italian genes. Great looking, great in bed, what more could you ask for? Roach held his arms out like the Messiah. "Would I let you down?"

"Yes." Cassie grinned.

Roach laughed. "Come in, babes. Relax, I got your Tryph."

The house smelt like an ashtray. Clothes lay in random mounds; a half-eaten pizza might have been there a day or a week. A pyramid of empty cans stood incomplete beside the fireplace. The rank odour of stale beer competed with the cigarettes.

"Excuse the mess. We had a bit of a party last night. I only just had breakfast."

"Off a mirror?"

Roach shrugged and pulled at an ear, seeming to fish for an answer. "Yeah, right. Nice one, Cass." Roach gestured at the sofa. "Hey, sit down, babes. Make yourself at home."

She moved a pile of newspapers and sat down on a red cushion, its pattern blurred by years. A stack of CDs wobbled next to the hi-fi, almost all the discs divorced from their cases. If Alex was here, she'd have a fit. Either that or an orgasm putting them all into alphabetical order.

Roach gave one of the early morning coughs that battered his lungs. "I was just about to skin up, yeah?"

"Roach by name..."

"On form today, Cass."

"You know I don't do drugs, Roach."

"Whoo-hoo. Of course you don't. Tryph's Smarties, right?"

"That's different."

"Sure." Roach slumped back on the sofa next to Cassie. "That's why they banned it. That's why you come to me instead of going to Boots."

Cassie ignored him, gesturing at the room. "Why do you do all this, Roach?"

"All this? All this?" Roach laughed through his nose. "One day, all this will be yours, babe." He twiddled his fingers in front of his eyes.

"This is all an act, isn't it?"

"If you say so." He took her hand and traced circles on her wrist with the tip of his finger. It made her shiver. She wanted him. Roach yawned again. "I could use some fresh air. Want to go for a walk?" He bent forward for a pair of boots lying under the table, tugging them on without socks.

Cassie reached out and grabbed his arm. "Look, have you got the Tryph?"

Roach rolled his eyes and laughed. "Oooh. Poor little rich girl. Take it easy, babes."

Cassie couldn't let that go. "Rich? You think because we live at Paycocke's we're rich? Dad limps from week to week on whatever dusty old books he happens to flog, not even noticing that Mom is having it off with Abby. I pay off my credit card bill with another credit card. As a family we are beanless. Alex is the only one with any cash and she's probably got it tied up in a ten-year gilt-edged index-linked asbestos-lined fucking piggy-bank. Now where are the pills, Roach?"

Roach laughed, filling the room. "You crack me up, you really do." His laugh mutated into a cough. He stood up, laces trailing behind his boots like streamers. "Back in a sec." She heard him climb the stairs in his scuffed Timberlands, still chuckling. Damn, just because they lived at Paycocke's, everyone assumed they were rolling in it. There was never any money, nothing ever happened in the village, and there was the dreary public to deal with three times a week. Thank God that was over. It was a good job she was a decent actor. And why was Dad so interested in the sodding fireplace? Maybe it was that old vicar geezer – hadn't he said in his book that there was supposed to be buried treasure at Paycocke's? She wouldn't mind a slice of that. And then there was Mom. Blimey. Who'd have thought it? Her mind wandered as she stood up and went over to the window. The curtains were steeped in a smoky marinade that would never come out, and the window panes were so grimy she couldn't tell whether the dirt was inside or out. She felt dizzy, suddenly too warm and she pressed her forehead onto the glass.

"Here you go." Roach stood at the door, waving a small box. "Catch." He tossed the Trypholine over to Cassie. She fumbled it and it fell to the floor. "Butterfingers." As she bent down to pick it up, the dizziness mugged her again and she put out her hand to the floor. It was somehow distant and seemed to have developed a camber, the box sliding away from her. Roach's voice receded. "Cass, you OK, babes?" Then the floor felt solid again and she had the box in her grasp. A tear of sweat snaked past her eye. She gripped the box in case it harboured any ideas of escaping.

"It's OK. I stood up too fast." She shook the box. "Glass of water?"

"Yeah. You sure you're OK?"

"Yes." Her impatience came out in a hiss.

Cassie struggled with the childproof lid. It came off with a snap and evaded her, rolling off into a corner. She took out one of the small tiger-striped capsules and rolled it in her palm. Just a helping hand, really, a confidence booster. A placebo. That's all it was.

Roach passed her a mug of water. Cassie placed the pill on her tongue, swallowed it with a gulp and started to feel better. Stupid. She smiled at Roach. "Cheers."

Roach chased after the errant lid and twisted it back on the bottle. "You know you don't need these, Cass? You don't need to lose any weight. You look great as you are."

Cassie tossed her fringe, loosening strands of damp hair from her forehead. "Well, I need to stay looking great. What do I owe you?"

Roach helped Cassie to her feet. "Three of the big purple ones."

Three. Cassie knew without looking that she was short. She would have to tap Dad up again. "Can I owe you?" Bloody hell, she could do with some buried treasure. She'd have to keep an eye on Dad, especially if there was cash involved.

Roach spread his arms in apology. "I need to pay the rent, Cass."

"End of the week." She put her hands around his waist. He was slim and wiry; the black leather belt he wore was just an accessory. She felt his pelvis hard and unyielding beneath her fingertips. Roach smiled at her, but the fading day cast a shadow across his eyes and she couldn't see what lingered behind his expression.

"I could still use some fresh air," he said.

"Open the windows."

"They're stuck."

"Unstick them."

"With what shall I unstick them, dear Cassie, dear Cassie?" Roach erupted into song and danced around her while she laughed.

"This place is a tip, Roach. It stinks, it festers, and the washing-up hasn't been done for a week..."

"Two."

"...it has never, ever been Hoovered..."

"Dysoned."

"...your clothes are rotting in their own sweat and you have enough beer cans to start an off licence."

"Except they're empty."

She waved her arms at him in mock despair. "You need a housekeeper, Roach."

"Are you applying?"

He always had an answer. Even hung over, tasting cold turkey leftovers, Roach always had an answer.

"And the dope? The dope..."

"I love it when you talk sense to me," he said, wagging a finger at her.

"Sense?" She seemed to be getting through to him.

"Sense. Sense and sensimilia. Yeah." He buried his face in her neck.

Cassie laughed. "You are the pits, Roach."

He lifted a tender hand to her face and brushed her hair from where it was clouding her vision. "Stay."

"Stay?" Cassie lost her resolve in his dark eyes.

Roach wasn't smiling, but the corners of his mouth twitched in that way she loved, his eyes black and unfathomable. He enveloped her hand with his and drew her to him. "Stay."

She hinted at a smile. "Roach?"

"Yeah?"

"Can you brush your teeth?"

Chapter 6
Blackberrying

Cassie's lie niggled at Simon like a loose tooth. And she didn't come home last night. She didn't come home. 'Cassie, come home.' He hadn't thought of that since the girls were small.

Not far from their home in London, the bathing ponds on Hampstead Heath were child magnets. It had never seemed to matter what time of year it was, because Cassie and Alex had no thermostats. They took a long run-up, cried 'Geronimo', and landed with the maximum possible splash, giving Simon goose-pimples by proxy.

On a warm day he and Robin sat on the grass with the Sunday papers, reading out snippets of news or teasing each other with cryptic crossword clues.

"'Past tense for smoky armadillo,'" said Robin, as the girls screamed below.

He tickled her feet. "Give us a clue?"

"Stop it. Seven letters. Ends in 'M'."

"Give up." He kissed her big toe. It wiggled in protest.

"You can't give up. Come on, Simon, use what passes for a brain in there." She hit him with the Review section.

"Ow, I definitely give up."

"If at first you don't succeed… give up – I guess that's the Chance philosophy, huh?"

"OK, you win." He sat cross-legged in silence for a full minute, staring into the distance where the trees could make you forget the smouldering city. He opened and closed his mouth in approximations of words and counted letters on his fingers. Then he stopped and smiled at his wife. "Right."

She stroked his knee. "Way to go, Simon. See, everything comes to he who waits."

Simon raised his eyebrows.

"So?" Robin prodded him.

"No idea. Can I give up now?"

She grabbed him and they rolled off the tartan rug, gathering grass clippings in their hair and green stains on unforgiving linen. They kissed and it had felt to Simon as though it would always be like this.

When it was time to go, there were ice-cream bribes and no-story-tonight threats to extricate the shivering girls from the pond.

"Just one more go," said Cassie.

"Me too."

"Me three."

And then one more go after that. And one more. Until it was, "Cassie Jo, Alex Edie, get your butts over here, right now." And Alex trotted over to be wrapped in a towel, her hair plastered dark across her tiny nose and water collecting in the dimples he loved.

Cassie pushed her luck until the rallying cry came, "Cassie, Cassie come home."

They set off towards the East Heath Road, dwindling figures every so often turning around to mark her progress. Cassie chased them across the grass, showering passers-by as she ran. "Don't leave me." She jumped into Simon's arms, clasping thin fingers around his back and soaking his polo shirt.

It was odd that he should have recalled the phrase now, risen back up above the horizon of memory. Cassie come home.

Her bed had not been slept in, but since she never made it, it was hard to tell. Clothes dripped off her exercise bike, but from when? Drawers gaped at him, pleading their innocence, and Simon gave up. He would speak to her later.

"Did you hear Cassie come in last night?" he said over breakfast.

Alex was reading the back of the muesli packet. "Nope."

"Did she say anything to you about what she's up to today?"

"Nope."

And then Alex was gone too.

He booted up his laptop, the printer surging into life as Alex had predicted. He probably should check for viruses. But not now. When Alex got home – it would give her a chance to earn her allowance for a change. She could run her defrag, whatever that was.

There was an email from fitzall:

'Hi Simon,

I'm the one who won the Thomas More last night. Just to say that I'll be working over in Braintree for the next week or so, so if it's OK by you, I'll pop in and pick the book up. Save on the postage. Can you give me a buzz on 07781 564543 and we'll fix a time.

Sweet,

Fitz.'

He sounded like an old friend already. Simon turned the parcel over in his hands; shame he had already wrapped it. Still, at £275 he couldn't blame the man for wanting to save on stamps.

Sparrow's email still taunted him. He drummed his feet on the parquet, trying to decide what to do. Finally, he picked up the telephone and dialled Sparrow's mobile. Answer phone. The voice hadn't changed, cocky and confident, a tanned and moneyed accent used to having its own way. "Heyyy, Martin Sparrow. Sorry I'm not around right now, but leave me a message and I'll get back to you. As soon as I can."

The beep sounded before Simon was ready. "Ah, Martin, hi. Martin, it's… it's Simon Chance. You sent me…"

The phone clicked and Sparrow came on the line. Simon wasn't sure if anyone had ever sounded so pleased to speak to him. "Simon." The word lasted three full seconds, tailing off into a, "How the devil are you? It must be years?" He didn't really want to know how the devil Simon was, launching into the next part of his spiel without waiting for a reply. "Just got back from the States and thought I'd give my old mate a ring. *De Medicina*? *Artes*? Yes?" The line went silent as Sparrow allowed Simon to absorb his words. It was not a privilege for which his ex-colleague was renowned.

'*Old mate*', *the canny revisionist.* But the bait was too much and he couldn't help smiling. They had drunk a lot of pints together speculating on *De Medicina* in those Groves and Palmer days. They could have wallpapered Buck House with what-ifs. The book that could change the world, if it even existed. "*De Medicina,*" Simon repeated, laughing through his nose. "That's going back a bit, Martin."

"Yessiree. I've got something, Simon. And I thought..." he paused, his deliberate absence of dots and dashes the Sparrow Morse code for 'dramatic effect', "...of you."

"How sweet."

"This could be the biggie. I have a real lead."

"Go on."

"We should meet up." Sparrow's tone flattened; this meant serious. Sparrow without body language was still only too easy to read.

Mostly, Simon wanted to put the receiver down and dismiss Martin Sparrow from his life. But a small part of him wanted to see the man ravaged by the years, a Sparrow brought low by high living. "Yes, we should. I'm up in town at the end of the month. Meeting with the accountant."

Martin ignored him. "I've got a yen to see some good old English fields again. Why don't I come out to see you? I hear you've got a fancy new gaff? Paycocke's, isn't it?"

How did he know that? "Yes, that's right."

"How about this weekend? Saturday all right with you?"

"Saturday?" Simon knew that no attempts to filibuster would derail the Sparrow express. "Yes, OK, why not? Saturday." He had forgotten any plans made when Robin and he were still together, plans that didn't know they would never see daylight.

"Three-ish sound good?"

"Three? Fine."

"You can give me the guided tour. Surprise me."

"Sure." The telephone call seemed to have reached its natural conclusion, but Simon sensed there was more.

Sparrow became even more affable. "How's Robin?"

"Robin?" Simon was becoming aware that his every response

was a question, that he was playing for time, taking the ball out near the corner flag in the dying minutes.

"Your wife, remember? The good-looking one. I'm looking forward to seeing her again. Now that I can speak her language, y'all." He said the last sentence in a grotesque interpretation of a Southern drawl.

"She's... not around," Simon hesitated.

Sparrow left the slightest of pauses in the conversation, inviting Simon to divulge more information. He remembered it as a Sparrow tactic from the old days. The old days, old habits, old dogs, old tricks. Simon resisted the temptation to explain.

"Oh, too bad. Well, I'll see you Saturday, then."

"Yeah. Great." He tried to pitch some more enthusiasm at the idea.

"Good to speak to you again, Simon. Be like old times." Martin Sparrow laughed. "Just like old times."

Simon hoped not.

The sun leaked in through the study window, bouncing off the laptop screen and turning it into a dark mirror showing his face, too pale from a summer spent indoors. He tried to imagine that he appeared careworn and wise in the reflection. Probably not - he just looked knackered. There were strands of grey that Sparrow would never have seen and he was putting on weight. Finishing up the girls' leftovers didn't help. When they bothered to show up for dinner, that was. Damn. Perhaps he could fit in a haircut before Saturday. Sparrow would just love to see him going downhill.

He shivered; he needed to crank the storage heaters up. There was a chill in the entrance hall, its high ceiling ('much higher than you would expect in a domestic house of this period, a real testament to the Paycockes' wealth,' as Cassie said in her talk) losing what little heat there was. He lit the wood burner, but was still cold despite the blaze. The room faced north and the October morning saw it gripped by gloom. He had to get out of the house. Maybe he could pick some blackberries.

As he opened the huge front door, he was overtaken by a swooping daylight highlighting the carpenter's mark on the door frame. The mark which joined the two beams was exactly like a bird's footprint, a scratched trident in the oak, as though a crow had once stood there; a crow, or maybe a large sparrow. A Sparrow, the bastard.

It was warmer outside than in, autumn held in check for one last day. He crossed the bridge over the River Blackwater and went up the hill, ankle throbbing, then cut down a footpath where no one knew him.

There were not enough blackberries left for a pie. The birds had been there before him.

*   *   *

Cassie was home when he got back with his unneeded trug. It had to be her, anyway. Alex would still be at school and the burglar alarm was off. "Cassie," he called. There was no answer, but that meant nothing. The wood absorbed the sound like a sponge. It came in handy when Alex had friends around, the sound of the Chemical Brothers thudding away at the innocent timbers. He put his tiny collection of berries on the hall table and knelt down to stoke up the fire. The room didn't seem any warmer.

Some tapping came from outside, a sharp insistent noise like a coin on glass. Someone who didn't know they had closed for the winter. Of course, most people thought the doorbell was going to fall apart, so didn't dare use it, but there was a knocker about as big as a horseshoe, difficult to miss. He opened the door; there was no one there. He must have imagined it.

As Simon clicked the latch shut the tapping started again. It was a sound that didn't want to be heard, almost guilty in its perseverance. If Simon turned his head away he couldn't hear it. He approached the window and the sound seemed to grow less distinct, as though it knew he was coming. As he opened the door again, the tapping stopped. There was no one outside. He stepped into the street, went over to the oriel window and peered into his house. The room looked warm and cosy; the burner's glow cast a homely light over all the dark wood. Stepping back from the window he saw two sets of fingerprints on the glass, small crescents tattooed on the panes. Kids.

As he drew back, he saw in his peripheral vision a white shape blot out the glow of the fire. When he put his face back to the window it was gone, a pale blur so brief that it must have been a shadow. Then the front door opened and Cassie stood there.

"Dad? What are you doing?"

She wore an old white shirt, paint-spattered and frayed, once his and too large for her, much too large. It swept down over her jeans and made her look smaller than she really was.

"Oh, nothing, just checking the windows." Simon smiled, feeling as though he had been caught in the act. He countered. "Out late?"

"Yeah, I was with a friend."

"No problem."

"I know."

He parried. "Did you pick up your print cartridge?"

"Oh, yeah. Yeah, I did, thanks."

Thrust. "Only I needed to print something out and mine was playing up, so I borrowed yours." He waited.

She looked at him, the blueness of her eyes greyed and opaque in the dim room. He could detect no shred of concern in those stagnant pools. "And?" A hard-edged word, an accusation, a gesture of defiance. Just like Cassie.

"Only that it seemed to be working fine to me."

Her reply was too swift, too smug. "If you shake the cartridge and hold it in your hands for a minute to warm it up, you can squeeze a bit more life out of it." She smiled, holding his gaze. Then she melted the ice of the moment with a Cockney riposte. "Don't you know nuffink?"

Simon laughed. "No, I guess not."

"I'm making coffee – want some?"

The cartridge. He remembered the invoice. Bugger, he hadn't called fitzall.

"Dad?"

"Uh?"

"Coffee?"

"Oh, yes, please. Thanks. I just need to make a phone call."

In his study Simon fingered the More book while the dial

tone shrilled away. He leant back in the swivel chair and shielded his eyes from the watery sun that was occasionally penetrating the low clouds.

"Fitz."

"Hallo, Mark Fitzwarwick?"

"Right you are, what can I do for you?" The man's voice was brisk, London battling with Essex.

"My name's Simon Chance, you won a book on eBay…"

"Monster. Been looking for that for ages."

Simon found his tone strange. He didn't think it was that hard to find but didn't want to disabuse Fitz. He hadn't paid for it yet. "Glad you won."

"Yeah, it was touch and go for a while back there."

"So, you want to come over?"

"Yeah, like I said, I'm in your neck of the woods at the moment, so I can drop in any time to pick it up."

"Great. I work from home, so I'm in all the time."

"Tomorrow suit you? After my dinner?"

Simon hesitated.

Fitz rescued him. "About one?"

"Great."

"Cash OK?"

"More than OK, yes."

"See you tomorrow, then."

"Right you are."

Simon put his hands behind his head and massaged his neck. If only all sales went that well. He looked up at the ceiling. £274 profit, well, minus the eBay fees a bit less, but still handsome. Simon felt almost guilty about taking Fitz for a ride on a book which shouldn't have fetched more than fifty. Almost guilty, but not quite.

He stared at the ceiling. There was a trapdoor set in one corner, about two foot square. His brow buckled. Directly above his study was the bathroom, wooden floored, planks scarred with age, but just a series of floorboards. So where did the trapdoor lead?

Chapter 7
1923: The Garden

The summer of 1923 carved my life in two – before and after Paycocke's. As we closed the door on the house for the last time I trembled like a falling leaf, trembled for the path not taken. I could not do more. The house had broken my will. Or perhaps its will had simply been stronger than my own. I had made use of Edward in a most despicable way, but he had been so like a tram-car and not to be deviated from his rails. I could not return his boundless love and I could not do other than I did.

As earth becomes wet, it takes on a darker hue. As one digs deeper into the soil, it becomes blacker; it clings to itself in great clumps where only the most intrepid weeds venture. All life aspires to the light and I am no exception. I shall not readily forget our time at Paycocke's, but there was too much that was dark there, too much that I had not foreseen.

*   *   *

Yet when I first saw Paycocke's it looked so exquisite, beaming in the warm sun, too delightful for words. It was such an extraordinarily beautiful house, more like a dream or a fantasy. It was so romantic that we should live in a fantasy.

Gussie's fall at Reading had impacted greatly upon his nerves. Needing complete peace and quiet, we decided to retire to Coggeshall so that he could recuperate. It was a far cry from our lives in previous years, riding on the wake of my father's fame, he the toast of London. I don't think he was altogether prepared for the success that *The Planets* brought him. To me he was still my dear, dear father, a jolly dreamer and never the slave to celebrity.

Of course we had spent a good deal of time in nearby Thaxted in the cottage on Monk Street, so we knew the area very well. In fact, it was the rather dashing Reverend Conrad Noel of Thaxted who pointed us towards Paycocke's House. He had lived there himself some years before, making great sport of its restoration and he was as delighted as we were that we should take it for the summer. (I am led to believe that he is called 'The Red Vicar' by those unsympathetic to his socialist leanings. If so, it is a name he should bear with pride, for never have I met a man more predisposed to equality among all.)

Driving down the hill into Coggeshall on the main road, we spied Paycocke's House on the right hand side, every part as magnificent as Conrad had described. To the left of the building there was a gigantic oak gateway carved in a linen fold fashion, with two wooden figures, a mummer and a fool, standing guard over it. The front of the house was a full twenty yards long, with a most stunningly carved beam running its length. Playful deer and fearsome dragons scampered along the woodwork, together with all manner of flora and fauna of such delicate beauty that I wanted to stay there the whole afternoon and examine it.

Gussie dragged us into the house, saying there was much more to explore. He whooped with delight, and his long legs took the stairs two at a time. He reminded me of nothing more than Just William, off on one of his ill-conceived adventures. It was good to see him frivolous once more, as he had been in such low spirits that Iso and I had despaired for him. I myself stood in the grand hall, stared at the incredible ceiling and whirled around like a top, dizzy with delight that we should be living in this marvellous palace. It was as if I were ten years old again.

Paycocke's brought out the child in my father too as he raced up and down the many staircases in a maddening game of Hide and Seek. It seemed that I should never find my way about this labyrinth of a house, with more discoveries to be made around every corner.

That first week there was so much to be done, for the house had been empty some little while. We engaged a cook, housekeeper and parlour maid and determined to invite our revolutionary vicar to tea in thanks for his part in providing us with this wonderful home. In truth, Conrad had learnt of the house through his cousin Noel Buxton, the politician, who had himself owned Paycocke's for some time. It had become rather dilapidated in the latter years of the last century, and was indeed on one occasion on the point of demolition. It had been turned into a row of cottages and the beauty of its front elevation utterly hidden by boring Georgian plasterwork. Buxton beseeched his cousin to take the tenancy of Paycocke's and supervise a major restoration of the house. Conrad thought the exercise to be great fun and agreed. So hurrah.

The night before Conrad came for tea was hot and still. I had a small bedroom at the top of the house, miles from Iso and Gussie. Conrad had told us, tongue in cheek, tales of how the ghosts of Paycocke's lurked in the long, low-ceilinged Weaving Room, operating the hand loom. He also told of a visit he had once had from a merchant by the delicious name of Tudor Pole, who had seen a ghostly apprentice at Paycocke's, begging his master for the hand of his daughter in marriage. In conspiracy, he had also related to Conrad the tale of a great treasure, supposedly buried at the house. Treasure and ghosts, how utterly ripping. And far from scaring us, we were all excited at the prospect of meeting a visitor from the spirit world, Iso most so, insisting that she should occupy the said Weaving Room.

Disappointed, I settled for my own tiny chamber, whose huge grey beams stretched up to the roof where spiders scurried away at their endless chores. The vaulted roof held the heat prisoner, making the room fearfully hot. I tossed and turned under my blanket, unable to sleep. I so wanted to be wide awake and charming for Conrad Noel, yet the harder I tried to go to sleep, the less tired I felt.

I was dropping off when I heard the noise. At first I thought it had been in my dreams, the night seemed so still. Then it came again, a scuffling sound outside my window.

"Hello," I said, to whom I did not know. I pulled the covers aside and sat on the edge of the bed, my heart pumping like an engine. I opened the window a fraction and the inky night seeped into my room. There was silence for one brief, safe moment and then the shrieks began, a series of dreadful and unearthly cries, each tailing off into a banshee wail. I pressed my body close to the wall, unable to move. I felt as though it would never end, each wail burning my heart with its beseeching and plaintive cry. It was such a horrible yet compelling siren that it was all I could do not to be drawn down the stairs toward it. I held my ground until it was over, and then there was a gaping hole in the night where the sound had been. I stared through the window at the moonless sky, but whatever it was had gone, and had left in its place an awful muteness.

I lay awake for hours. What could it have been? I sat in bed cocooned in blankets, although the night was stifling. Each whisper of the breeze mocked my fear and eventually I slept, wondering whether I had imagined it all.

As is the wont of bright mornings, the terrible night had a distant and alien timbre. The aroma of kedgeree wafting up the stairs bestowed such a mundane feel upon the day that I went downstairs much recovered. Gussie was sitting at the breakfast table with the newspaper open, devouring stories of the Soviet Republic while his poached eggs grew cold. Iso was nowhere to be seen.

"Good morning," I said. My father folded the paper and put it on the table, his Bolshevik-induced frown erased and replaced by a welcoming smile. I shuddered at the thought that he might become the sort of person who writes letters to The Times. He looked at me over the top of his spectacles. "My dear Imogen. Have you slept well?"

"Somewhat restlessly, I am afraid."

"The heat, no doubt. You do look a little pale this morning. I had thought I might take a walk over to Markshall this morning, if you would care to join me?"

I pleaded fatigue. Gussie's long and loping stride leaves me struggling for breath, and I wondered that he should have the energy for such an exploit, for he had not been himself for some months now. Persistent headaches and nervous attacks had left him frail and anaemic, a thinner version of himself in every way. Even the thunderous applause that greeted *Planets'* last outing in London failed to rouse him. His smile could not hide the tiredness that creased his kind eyes and I asked after his own night, although my motive was not wholly altruistic.

"Passable. The fresh air will do me good, I am certain." I waited for an allusion to the cacophony of the night, but none came.

"The Reverend is coming to tea."

"Ah yes, indeed, dear Conrad, of course. I shall return with time to spare." He tapped his newspaper. "We have a great deal to discuss." Pleased to see my father so animated, I hoped that he would not monopolise the dashing vicar with dull talk of politics when there was so much else of interest to pursue. With that he was gone, eggs untouched.

My mother's soprano drifted through the open window and I chased her down the garden. Oh, and what a garden Paycocke's had, laid out in the latest style by Conrad's wife Miriam. So talented was she that I thought her Gertrude Jekyll's equal at the very least. Iso stood by the wisteria vines, the morning sun behind her bouncing on her blonde hair. She was carrying a wicker basket and looked impossibly elegant in a quite simple ivory sponge cloth dress.

"Why, good morning, Imogen," she said.

I determined to say nothing of ghosts and counted myself fortunate to have such a practical mother. Should she meet a supernatural being in the middle of the night she would doubtless invite him in for tea and scones with raspberry jam. Before morning she would have his life history. And death history, come to that.

I was surprised when she herself referred to the night's mayhem. "Did you hear the howls last night?"

"Oh, yes…" I was struck with an immediate urge to spill out my story of the night's events.

"There must be a nest nearby. A tawny, I expect, although I should very much like to see a little owl."

'Owls', not 'howls'. I was disillusioned. Perhaps it *had* all been a dream. "I did hear something." Nothing like the gentle 'hoo-hoo-oooo' of the tawny owl, nor the creaking gate cry of its young, but I did hear something, I was sure of it. It could not have been a dream.

Iso felt the pang of my disappointment and her eyes grew

bluer and more alive. She put her arm through mine and we walked back toward the house so white and welcoming in the bright day. "What shall we give the Reverend this afternoon?"

"Scones."

"And caraway cake."

"And tea bread, of course." I counted off the treats on my fingers.

"Shortbread…"

"And strawberries."

"What else for a Red Vicar?"

And we laughed in each other's arms and I thought everything should all be fine, except that when we approached the house I saw that the flower bed under my window had been disturbed. The scarlet peonies had been roughly pushed aside and there were scratch marks on the bare earth, as though someone had been trying to dig up something. Or bury it. I picked up some of the fallen petals; they had lost their lustre and their velvet softness.

*   *   *

Conrad would know. If there was anything to know about Paycocke's then he would have the answer, since he had built the house, or rebuilt it, rather. He more than anyone would know of its ghostly aspects.

I had to weave through all the political conversations and interminable chatter about the music at Thaxted, for my father had been involved with the choir there for many years, but at last I seized my opportunity. I rather fancied myself as a beautiful sparrow hawk diving in for the kill. We were sitting in the garden in the shade of the hornbeam tree and Conrad was asking my father about his latest work.

"So, how goes the Keats' symphony?"

Gussie shook his head. I knew he feared his gift in decline. "Slowly."

"Adagio?" Conrad Noel was ever the wit. He raised a small smile from my father and reached forward to clap him on the shoulder. "Come, Gustav, I have great faith in you."

"You are paid to have faith."

"But not in you. You are a great composer, my friend. Such a gift does not wither upon the vine."

"You have greater belief than I."

"Then we shall revive your gift." Conrad thumped the table and the teacups rattled in complaint. His dark, curly hair quivered like springs and he turned to my mother and bowed. "My lady Isobel, would you sing with me?"

My mother smiled; she was always undone by the irrepressible vicar. "But of course." Conrad Noel's charisma shimmered in the air, drawing the best from everyone.

"Never a more perfect setting for *The General Dance*, I think." He sang the first few words in his succulent baritone, "This I have done…" Then he looked at me and winked, speaking the remaining words of the line, "…For my true love."

My father roared with delight as Conrad and Iso gave a spirited rendition of the beautiful song, which Gussie himself had set to music. If I remember correctly, he had dedicated the piece to Conrad. I myself joined in for the refrain. It had a wonderfully lyrical melody, and I have always counted it among my father's finest compositions. To see him happy for a short while again was bliss.

They finished to loud applause.

"It is true," I said. "There never was a finer setting than Paycocke's. You have performed wonders with this house." The house gleamed in the afternoon sun, its bleached walls pure and alive, vibrant with the day. We all could feel it.

Conrad held up his hand in modesty. "I did little but bring Paycocke's House back to its rightful status."

"Nonsense. You have given it life where there was none," Gussie argued. "I have seen the photographs. Before the restoration it was calamitous. Only you had the audacity and belief to strip the veneer from the front. But for you it would still be… just another Georgian terrace."

Conrad was trying hard to field the compliments with his accustomed self-effacement, but I could tell he was touched by our flattery. The words of true friends are frequently the most telling.

"How did it look when you first saw it?" I asked.

"Rather sorry," he said, shaking his head. A light seemed to go out in his deep brown eyes as he remembered the occasion. "It had been greatly neglected. There was a fiendish atrophy at work and the house was suffocating under the weight of centuries. The studwork had been covered up, carvings painted over. The very heart of Paycocke's was concealed." He seemed to grow uneasy with the recollection. "Far be it for me to wander down an anthropomorphic path, but..."

"You mean its soul? You think the house is haunted?" I interrupted in excitement, and then clapped a hand to my mouth for my rudeness. "Oh, I do apologise..."

"No need, Imogen, my dear." Conrad smiled and looked at me, through me, with those penetrating dark eyes. His gaze had the air of a challenge. "Ghosts? Certainly there are strange things in this world and beyond." Infuriating as usual, he refused to confirm or deny, just tipped his head to the side in that enigmatic way of his. He clasped his hands together. "What I do know is that when the restoration was complete, Paycocke's House seemed to me to sigh."

The company became silent. Whether with reflection or embarrassment, I am uncertain, but Gussie cracked the ice. "'No restoration without revolution'," he said, quoting one of Conrad's most famous sayings. We all laughed a little too readily.

Conrad asked my father about his walk to Markshall. Gussie was telling him about an oak tree there which was hundreds of years old. My attention wandered to the fence, where I could see a figure in the garden next door. It was a boy, perhaps fifteen or sixteen years of age, not much younger than I. He held onto the bars of the fence as though they were his gaol, and a toe of his scruffy boots was wedged between two of the slats.

He acknowledged me with a wave so small it only needed one finger. I grinned back and mouthed, 'Hello.'

Instead, I should have made him go. Oh, how I wish that I had made him go.

Chapter 8
Sloes

Simon couldn't reach the trapdoor, short by two feet even standing on his swivel chair, rocking on its castors. He took the broom from behind the door and stretched up toward the wooden recess. A cloud of dust drizzled on his face as he harvested the Addams Family cobwebs that had gathered over the opening. He spluttered.

"Coffee, Dad." Cassie came into his study with two steaming mugs, mugs from the Denby birds collection.

He hesitated, knowing she would pass him the robin. "Thanks." Just thoughtless.

"What are you doing?" Cassie gestured at the ceiling, her milky coffee sloshing in her wren mug and spilling onto the parquet. By coincidence Robin and he had given each other the mugs in their Christmas stockings one year. Simon couldn't even remember which year; one when their minds thought alike. Great minds they were then. A Hampstead Christmas, that was all he knew, snuggled up to an illicit log fire, mulled wine besmirching the air with cinnamon. 'Robin' had been an obvious choice, but she had given him the wren.

"Dad? Are you here?"

"Oh, yeah. Thanks."

"What is it?"

He had a sudden urge to keep it to himself, guard the secret like a walnut in its shell, safe and for him only. But what secret? There was nothing to tell. "I don't know. Probably nothing. I was just on the phone, staring at the ceiling, and I noticed the trapdoor." He waved the robin mug upwards.

"So?"

"Well, it's the bathroom above us, right?"

"Yes?" It was a long, drawn out where-are-you-going-with-this 'yes'.

"So, there's no matching trapdoor up there, is there?"

"I've never noticed."

"Well, take it from me, there isn't."

"So?"

"So why?"

"Why not?"

"It has to go somewhere. Look, humour me, will you." Simon put his mug down on the desk, making a ring on the MDF. He stepped out into the courtyard. It had turned into a wind trap in the late afternoon and he shivered.

"Oh, Dad." Cassie trudged after him, cupping her wren in both hands.

He pointed at the wall. A climbing rose was losing the last of its blooms, petals clinging to dead heads like hanged men. "Say my study ceiling is about ten feet from the ground?"

"OK?"

"Now look at the bathroom window. It's, what, about four feet higher than that?"

Cassie shivered and stamped her feet, distracted. "Go on."

"Well, when you're in the bathroom that window is only about a foot above the floor, meaning that even allowing for the joists and floorboards there's a space between the two rooms, maybe eighteen inches to two feet high."

"And?"

"Why?"

Cassie continued to be exasperating. "Can we go inside now?"

His coffee was lukewarm. Simon pushed it to one side and climbed up onto the work surface.

"Hey, Dad, be careful. Mind your ankle."

"Pass me the broom, will you." With his grimy fingers he brushed his hair back from his eyes and squinted through the darkening day. The trapdoor seemed to retreat into the shadows as though it did not want to be noticed.

Cassie sighed, but gave him the broom anyway. He tapped at the trapdoor, but it didn't budge. It sounded solid. He put some weight behind the handle, but still felt no give. He gave another shove on the broom and felt his balance start to go astray.

"Careful." Cassie held his leg as though it would somehow stall his crash-landing.

"There's something holding it, something stopping it from opening," he said. "I just can't see… Get me a torch, Cass."

"Oh, for heaven's sake, Dad…"

"Get me a bloody torch, will you?"

"All right, all right, no need to get stressy."

Simon's face twitched and he bit his lip. He took a deep breath and his voice dropped, a pretence of calm. "Please. Please can you get me a torch? In the kitchen. On the shelf."

She came back with the big black rubber torch, and as she passed it to Simon it rattled. He turned it on. Nothing happened. He shook it and heard the noise of batteries sliding up and down.

Cassie tried hard to hide a grin. "Oh yeah, Alex was looking for some batteries for her CD player yesterday. I told her there might be some spare ones… in the torch."

Simon flung it down on the wooden floor and the glass cracked. It rolled into a corner. "Bloody hell. Why is nothing ever there when I want it? I've had enough of this. And why leave two fucking batteries in there? Why?" He jumped off the work surface, wincing as he landed on his sore ankle. He picked up the torch and glared at it.

Cassie put her hand on his wrist. Her fingers were thin and cold; she had poor circulation, just like her mother. Robin had had icy feet in bed; he missed those icy feet.

"Don't you think you might be taking this a bit too far, Dad?"

"What?"

"First the panelling, now the trapdoor. Is the house spooking you too?"

The house had never spooked Simon. He was too prosaic for that. Maybe he *was* getting too involved. Maybe Cassie was right. One chance remark by his wife's lover and suddenly he was trying to take the house to pieces.

He put the torch down on the table; its sound was now a death-rattle. Simon sighed. It was all stupid.

*   *   *

Mark Fitzwarwick pounded out another mile on the seafront, the wind in his face feeding his determination and strength. He sprinted the last hundred metres to the concrete breakwater. Sweet as a nut. Sweet as a nut. Sweet... as... a... nut with every stride. He came to a halt and put his hands on his knees, breathing heavily and laughing in great gasps. That Simon Chance, he could not be serious. He slowed his breathing; everything under control. The wind started to chill the V-shaped sweat patch on his chest, and he stretched his arms, hearing his elbows crack. What he had was gold, more than gold. The game was begun. There was no going back. 'Wealth untold,' the letter had said, that was worth the risk, worth any risk. His stomach flipped with unease every time he thought of it. Yeah, he could be caught, but it wasn't the Old Bill who scared him, no way, it was the lines between the lines of the old geezer's letter. 'There are forces at work about which we know little, Mr Fitzwarwick.' How could you know your enemy when you couldn't see him? Patience. Patience and time, that's all it took. Fitz had plenty of both.

He rolled his head around, felt lean, felt supple. Needed to. Receding hair shorn, there were no dams to stop the sweat rolling down his cheeks. He tasted its salt then let it go on its way south.

Fitz started to jog in the direction of the pier; it rose and fell with his motion. The fartlek technique. Jogging, then sprinting, then slowing down again. Always moving, he was always moving towards the goal. He would be surprised if Chance suspected, had any clue of what was happening.

Two hundred and seventy-five quid. He shouldn't laugh; it would disrupt his rhythm. Look on it as an investment. Left, right, left, right, his muscles felt warm as though Ralgex ran through them. Left, right, left, right, his tracksuit trousers billowed in the wind. This was the slow part, teasing Chance out into the open, playing with him.

Tomorrow would be fast again. Just thinking about it made him pick up his pace, and he was racing as he reached the pier, its grey arm snaking into the thrashing sea. A few fishermen in orange cagoules were packing up their gear and their prizes: dab, whiting, maybe even a few bass. Fitz didn't need squid or lug for bait. Not when he had More. Not when the fish brought its own bait to the party.

He turned inland, slowing his pace again, came to the main road and stopped at the zebra, jogging on the spot, waiting for a gap in the traffic. The gap appeared and Fitz started to walk across.

The Subaru Impreza came out of nowhere, a streaking yellow blur, its fifty miles an hour seeming much faster, exacerbated by the growl from the exhaust. Its horn screamed with aggression, competing with the bass streaming from the open windows.

Fitz turned to face it, hands on hips. Even at twenty yards away he could see the eyes of the young driver fuelled by testosterone. Eyes that thought they held power, but which realised their mistake just in time. The kid stamped on the brakes, locking the wheels and the car slew left, leaving tread on the asphalt. It rocked to a halt on the wrong side of the road and stalled.

Fitz didn't flinch, just stood poised on the balls of his feet, watching the car skid. He walked over to the Subaru, the smell of burnt rubber flaring his nostrils. The kid was quaking and Fitz thought maybe he had learnt his lesson, suffered enough. He opened the car door and beckoned the boy out with one finger. The driver obeyed, his thin T-shirt rippling in the wind.

Fitz pointed to the bonnet of the car and walked around to the front. He turned to the kid and said one word: "Don't." He slammed a boxer's fist into the bonnet, leaving a deep dent in the metal. Then his face relaxed and he smiled. "Don't fuck with me." Pleasant, like a meeting a neighbour in the park. Then he was gone, fartlek, sprinting home. That was the enemy he knew.

Back in his Victorian terrace on Cambridge Road, Fitz drew the curtains against the blackening sky and woke his PC. It would be a shame to lose the momentum now. He grabbed a towel from the downstairs loo and mopped his face in front of the hall mirror. It felt good to be back in the ring again. He winked at his reflection, then hung the towel across his shoulders. While the computer came back to life he poured himself a tumbler of sloe gin. Last year's batch, the intense ruby colour had faded to a tawny, the Benylin sweetness dulled by the passing months. Maybe less sugar this year, he thought. Sloe gin, fast gin, sloe gin. Fartlek gin. It would soon be time to pick the sloes again. Harvest time.

Fitz sat down at the table and flexed his fingers. He logged on to eBay and closed down thebookie's account. Yeah, you could be anyone you wanted: fitzall; thebookie; or both. He laughed. End of round one.

Chapter 9
Horse Chestnut,
Beech and Ash

Simon was stacking a wheelbarrow load of logs beside the hearth when the doorbell rang.

"Hi there." The man at the door brushed a hand through what seemed to Simon to be invisible hair. He peered into the hall. "Whoa. Fantastic place you have here."

"Hallo?"

The man laughed at Simon's confusion. It was a relaxed and easy laugh. "Sorry, where was I? Mark Fitzwarwick. Fitz. I'm fitzall off of eBay." He stretched out a hand.

"Oh, hell, yes, of course – fitzall." He shook off his gardening glove, scattering a confetti of dry earth onto the rug, and took Fitz's hand. There was a shade of a second when each man gave the stronger grip, and then the touch was over. "Simon Chance. Come in, come in." He waved Fitz into the house and closed the door.

The guy reminded Simon of a six year old Alex at Disneyland for the first time, awed by treats all around her.

"Blimey, what a place." Fitz stared at the ceiling with its intricate carvings in the oak: swirling foliates, delicate flowers and the Paycockes' initials. "That is some ceiling, eh? It's what, Henry VII, Henry VIII?"

"Yeah. About five hundred years old," Simon said.

"Beats Artex, eh?"

Simon laughed.

Fitz's gaze moved from beam to beam. He pointed at a repeated carving, which looked like an elongated ace of clubs, or a clover leaf with a split stalk. "Merchant's mark, is it?"

Simon was surprised. It was unusual to meet someone who recognised the Paycocke logo. "That's right."

"I love old places, me, but this is incredible."

Simon smiled; he understood Fitz's love at first sight. He

had never had that creepy feeling about Paycocke's the way Robin had. He loved the place, perhaps even more so now that he had it more or less to himself. He was at home here; he couldn't imagine wanting to leave. Every day he saw something new, surprising, exciting or mysterious. The house embraced him, consoled him, valued him, and he enjoyed sharing it. "And Paycocke, Mark, he was just a self-made man. Made a fortune in cloth and built this place to show off."

"Fitz. Call me Fitz. Only my Mum calls me 'Mark'. Amazing. And look at these studs." Fitz turned his attention to where the vertical beams striped the walls. "Fuck my old boots. This place ain't going to fall down in a hurry. Bit wasteful on the old oak, weren't they?"

"All for show, Fitz."

"And why not? If you got it, flaunt it."

"Times don't change."

There was a moment's silence while Fitz traced a carpenter's mark with his large, sensitive fingers. He seemed to be running low on superlatives. "Blimey." Still looking at the wall, he backed away and bumped into Simon's wheelbarrow, knocking several logs onto the floor. "Sorry, Simon, my son, let me pick those up for you." He took a log in each hand and dropped them back in the barrow. "Ash. Lovely. I love ash, me. How does it go? 'Ash wood green and ash wood brown are fit for a queen with a golden crown.'"

Simon shook his head. "Huh?"

"You know that old poem about firewood? My gran used to recite it to me when I was little." Fitz laughed. The house often had that effect on people, unleashing an avalanche of emotion and chatter. He had seen more people smile in Paycocke's than on Hampstead Heath, that was for certain. He let Fitz ramble on. "There was a line about oak, too. How did that go? 'Oak logs when dry and old keep away the winter cold.' I can't remember how it goes on, but it's about all the kinds of wood and how they burn." He held another log up to the light. "Beech. Lovely. 'Beech wood fires burn bright and clear, if the wood's kept for a year.'" Fitz registered Simon's inability to squeeze a word in, and smiled. "Rabbit, rabbit. Sorry about that, mate. I get carried away sometimes."

"No problem. Don't worry about it. Do you want to come through? I've got the book."

"The book? Great stuff." Fitz thrust a hand into the deep pocket of a frayed parka, and pulled out a thick manilla envelope.

They went through into Simon's study. The shelves of books that surrounded his desk could not mask the beauty of the small room, and he saw it with Fitz's eyes, as though for the first time. "Fantastic. You work here?"

"All day."

"You're in the book trade, right?"

"Yeah, right. Do quite a bit of buying and selling."

"I only ask, 'cause I've seen your moniker on eBay a lot. Power Seller. It's 'oldmanbooker', isn't it?"

Simon grinned. "Yeah. Daft, eh?"

"No, not a bit of it. Nice one. You're younger than I expected, mind."

Simon picked up the parcel and handed it to Fitz. "I'd already wrapped it."

"No sweat. I'll have a quick shufty, if that's OK?"

"Sure."

"And this one's for you." He gave Simon the envelope. "I'd count it if I was you. You don't know me. And even if you did, I'd still count it. Especially if you knew me." Fitz chuckled.

Twenty-seven ten-pound notes and one fiver, all new, freshly cashpointed.

"All right?"

"Right you are." Money for old rope. He watched Fitz unravel the old rope of the brown paper package. He seemed pleased enough, but Simon still couldn't credit how anyone could have paid so much money for a relatively common book. One born every minute, he thought, although something told him that Fitz had been born in the other 59 seconds.

"Monster," Fitz said. "Just what I've been looking for. Cheers, Simon."

Simon waved the bunch of banknotes. "Pleasure's all mine."

The two men smiled. The transaction over, there was an inch of uncomfortable silence between them. They both spoke at the same time, but Fitz filled the gap first. "Well, that's that. I'd best be off, let you get on."

"No problem. Nice to meet you, Fitz."

"You too." Fitz turned as they reached the front door. "It's a sort of period of mine, this More thing." He flourished the book. "If you come across anything else like this, give me a ring."

"You got it, Fitz." *You got it?* Just as Robin would have said. He never said, 'You got it.' Leave Americanisms to the Americans. He shook his head and snorted out a laugh. "Absolutely. Cheerio, Fitz."

Fitz looked back at the wheelbarrow full of wood. "Some nice horse chestnut you've got there, too. Lovely, burns a treat. Now how did that one go?"

That was more like it. Simon felt the new banknotes warming in his hand and laughed. He and Paycocke had a lot in common - they were both in the wool trade, Paycocke making cloth, and Simon doing the fleecing.

He turned his attention back to the barrow-load of wood and started stacking it by the burner. Horse chestnut, beech, ash, the logs all looked the same to Simon; how on earth could Fitz tell the difference? Anyway, it was all going the same way – up the chimney, up in smoke. The room was cold after the cosiness of his study. He would probably need to keep the fire lit throughout the winter.

Then came the tapping at the window again, sharp, insistent, like a coin on glass. It sounded closer this time, in the room with him. He waited, still as a stone, angling his head towards the wood burner, trying to see a reflection, but it showed only the opposite wall. The tapping grew louder, more urgent. He swivelled around, as though he might catch the perpetrator. Expecting nothing again, he saw Fitz rapping at the pane, shrugging and pointing to the road. Simon smiled, massaging his forehead with his fingertips. He opened the door.

"Sorry to hassle you, Simon. Bloody car won't start." He looked up the road at a red E-registration Ford Escort. "Third time this week. I've had a bellyful, I can tell you. Can I use your phone?"

"What's the problem?"

"No idea, mate."

Simon put his glove on the trestle table and went into his study. The handset was gone. "This is going to sound stupid, but I don't know where the phone is."

"Kids?"

"Two. Girls."

"There's your answer."

"Yeah." Simon fished out his mobile from his coat pocket and dialled their home number. They heard a faint ring from the top of the house.

"Bingo," said Fitz.

"Follow me. You can take a look at the rest of the house on the way."

"Brilliant."

"Mind the rug on the way up. It buckles up. One of these days I'm going to trip on it and go flying through the window."

"Gotcha."

As they went up the stairs Fitz ran his hands along the beams. "If these could talk, eh?"

"Been there a long time."

"But they're not original, these ones, are they? You can tell they've been re-used. See these old mortise pegs? And the beams aren't the same width as the others in the hall, are they? Came a good bit later, my guess."

Simon was surprised at Fitz's astute observation. He hadn't seen it himself until the Trust's Property Manager had pointed it out. "Sounds like you know a bit about old houses, Fitz."

"I should do, Simon, should do." He didn't elaborate, just stuffed his hands deeper into his pockets. Simon wondered at the size of the pockets that could hold such fists.

They went through the main public bedroom and Fitz pointed out the elegant rolled ceiling beams. He was beginning to impress Simon. He'd have to remember some of this stuff for when the house opened again. Next spring. It felt lifetimes away.

The noise of the ringing telephone came from Cassie's room.

That was right; she had spent most of the previous day barricaded in her room making calls.

"Sorry about the mess," Simon warned, even before they went into her bedroom. "Bit of an earthquake zone."

"Don't worry about it. Great room. When I was her age I had to share with my brother. We got on each other's nerves something rank."

Fitz called the breakdown company. "Three-quarters of an hour, minimum."

"Cup of tea while you wait?" Simon offered.

"Tell you what: fancy a bevy? What's the pub like?"

They strolled next door to the Fleece. Fitz went up to the bar and greeted the barman with a thumb and forefinger pistol gesture. He came back with two pints.

"Cheers." Simon raised his glass.

"Least I could do."

Fitz took a long pull of Abbot and Simon tried to jump-start the conversation. "So what's your line of business, Fitz?"

"Antiques. Buying, selling." It was the shortest answer Simon had had all afternoon. "You know. This and that."

"You're in the wrong place, then," Simon laughed. "There's a sign on the by-pass, that says 'Coggeshall, Centre for Antiques' and there's hardly a single antique shop left."

"Maybe they mean the people, mate."

Simon laughed. "Could be." The pint turned into two, and when the breakdown truck failed to materialise Simon felt obliged to knuckle down to a third. Anyway, who did he have to go home to? Home? Should he even call it that now?

Drinking in the middle of the day always made him feel sleepy and morose, whereas it had the opposite effect on Fitz, who grew more animated and talkative, turning heads in the cosy bar. The third pint became four and Simon vaguely worried if Fitz was bothered about being breathalysed.

Fitz explained his interest in Tudor history. "What it is, mate, is that I've been researching my family history. The Fitzwarwicks go back centuries. And they weren't all bruisers like me, you know." He rippled a sword tattoo on his forearm and laughed. "There was a lot of Fitzwarwick land and money at one time. Trusted by royalty, we were. Some of the most important people in English history were Fitzwarwicks." He listed his ancestors on his enormous fingers. "There was a Fitzwarwick at Trafalgar; Wellington's right-hand man, he was. A Fitzwarwick was one of Henry VIII's most trusted sidekicks. One of us was a spud basher with Raleigh's lot, and I wouldn't be surprised if we were mentioned in the Domesday Book. Anyway, at some point along the line we were done out of our land, probably during the Reformation, like, and since then we've always been paupers."

The beer started to erode Simon's attention and he lost track of Fitz's thread. He offered sporadic noises of encouragement and wished he hadn't succumbed to the last pint.

Fitz was just taking a diversion to colonial Virginia on his eclectic tour through British history when they were interrupted by one of the other customers. Simon put his hand up to his face and rubbed his eyebrows, hiding a beer-fuelled yawn as he did so. He expected that Fitz was about to be asked to keep his voice down.

"Mark Fitzwarwick? The King of Clacton?" The man looked at Fitz in expectation, a half-smile ready to erupt. He was in his forties, face road-mapped with the capillaries of serious drinking. He rocked on his feet, lager rippling over the edge of his pint glass.

Fitz looked down at his beer. "No. Some mistake, mate. I don't know what you're talking about." His gaze was welded to the table.

The man persisted. "It is you, isn't it? Let me buy you a drink, mate. Many's the night I watched you in the ring, my old son. 'King of the Ring, the Clacton King', that was you, weren't it?" He leant forward over their table to get a better look at Fitz. He smelt of stale smoke and yesterday's fish and chips. Simon drew back his head from the odour, a reflex that brought him to the man's attention.

He turned to Simon so quickly that his eyes were a fraction of a second behind his head. He pointed a quivering finger inches from Simon's nose. "You... can fuck off, sunshine." His eyes widened, lakes of bloodshot anger.

Simon felt sick. Fitz's hand whipped out like a frog's tongue and grasped the man's finger. He drew it towards him, squeezed it like a mangle as his knuckles started to blush. A semi-laugh dripped from his words. "I suggest you leave my friend alone, all right?" He bent the man's finger back, taking it to the point of last resistance, and then stopped to drain the last of his pint. He licked his lips in appreciation, then turned to face the man. His smile was empty. "All right?"

The man's face was turning grey and his other hand relaxed its grip on his beer glass. It tipped forward and lager started to spill onto the floor. Fitz took the glass from him and put it down, a small pool of beer forming at its base. Picking up a beer mat, Fitz shepherded the growing puddle away from his side of the table. "Now, please go," he said. "You're getting on my wick." He gave the man back his finger.

The man put the swollen digit up to his lips and looked sideways at Fitz. "You…"

Fitz raised a hand and the man was silenced. Fitz's middle finger twitched and the man slunk away muttering, without his drink.

"Cheers," said Simon, his forehead damp. "What was all that about? Did you know that bloke?"

"No. Ancient history, that's all. Surprised people remember that far back." Fitz peeled his parka from the back of the chair. "I think we should go now." He nodded towards the window to where the breakdown truck was arriving.

They shook hands. "Enjoy the book," said Simon.

"Yeah, cheers. Give me a buzz if you get anything else in that line." Fitz threw his parka onto the passenger seat where it joined his mobile and the More book in a haphazard pile. He saluted Simon and turned to the truck driver.

Simon felt in his pocket for the Yale.

"Hello, Simon." The voice had lost some of the confidence that came from being in her natural habitat. "How's your foot?"

"Abby." The lunchtime drinking slowed his thoughts. "Hi. Foot's OK now, yeah, not too bad, thanks."

She wore the same crimson lipstick as when he had seen her

in Zebra. Those lips had kissed Robin, mingled with her favourite coral, two perfumes becoming one. He suppressed the image, and tried hard not to stare at Abby's mole. "Wednesday. I was completely out of order. I'm sorry."

She shushed him. "No, Simon. It's all our fault." 'Our' – the word made Simon give an inward wince. "We've handled it really badly."

They stood in Paycocke's doorway and Simon had the impression that this was no chance meeting in the street. He held an arm up to the massive doorframe, subconsciously putting a barrier between them.

"May I come in for a moment?" she said.

Simon felt his eyelid tremble and rubbed it. "Yes, of course."

It was colder inside than out. The logs lay half-stacked by the burner and Simon started again on the barrow load, anything to keep his hands busy, anything to defer the embarrassment of eye contact.

"Horse chestnut," she said. "'Chestnut's only good, they say, if for years 'tis stored away.'"

He knelt on the coarse drugget and looked at her. "What do you want from me, Abby?"

"I'm a... a go-between."

"'The past is a different country.'" That was true, never more so.

"Sorry?"

"L.P. Hartley."

"Oh."

Simon turned back to the logs, unwilling to contribute to the filling of the difficult silence.

"Robin needs a few things. And..." Abby hesitated.

"And..."

"She wants to talk."

"Talk?" He stood up, the melange of beer and sudden altitude making his head spin. "I don't know what there is to talk about." Maybe they had run out of things to say to each other years ago. But no, that couldn't be right. For her to leave him for Abby, she must have been hiding her feelings for years, desperate to come to terms with her sexuality. She lied to him, she betrayed him, she cheated him. For years. For what? For everything. He slumped in the carver, head in his hands. Poor Robin, poor darling Robin.

Abby approached him and put her hands on his shoulders. "You owe me a Scotch," she said.

Chapter 10
The Carriageway

Had the Markshall oak been there a thousand years I could not have been induced to join the conversation. I excused myself from the company; Conrad smiled as I arose, his eyes sparks. I took a circuitous route over to the fence where the boy stood, looking like Christabel Pankhurst chained to her railings, but nothing like as doughty, his mean apparel underlining his somewhat wan expression.

He took a step back, as though I were about to castigate him for his boldness. He was older than I had at first thought, being thin and wiry. I put my hand through the bars of the fence.

"Good afternoon," I said. "Imogen Holst, at your service." He was shocked by my behaviour and turned an attractive shade of radish. Staring at my outstretched hand, he looked at the ground, where he seemed to find a sudden great interest in a clump of speedwell doing its best to invade our garden with its pretty blue flowers.

"You mustn't mind me." I smiled at him and it chipped away at his shyness. Much as I adored my family, it was good to find some people of my own age. Up to that moment I had been limited to letters to old school friends from St. Paul's; I was not going to let this young fellow escape.

"Edward. Edward Daynes." He was still loath to approach my hand, as if it were a tiger behind the bars, benign to observe, but lethal within arm's length.

"Then we shall do away with formalities." I dropped my hand. "Do you like Battenberg cake?"

He nodded, his pallor returning.

"Then come to the front of the house and I shall see you there in two minutes." I wrapped a piece of cake in a napkin and ducked through the carriageway doors into West Street. Relieved of the fence between us, I could see that Edward had the greenest eyes I had ever seen, twinkling emeralds garnishing huge black pupils. They were looking everywhere but at me. He unwrapped the Battenberg with a certain reluctance.

"Thank you, Miss Imogen," he said.

"Now, less of the 'Miss' – 'Imogen' will do." I was determined to dash his unnecessary politeness into the gutter. "I usually leave the pink squares until last," I said. "What do you do?"

"I don't know. Me mother don't make Battenberg. She don't make any cake no more." He looked directly at me for the first time. "Is there a proper way to eat it, then?"

I laughed and punched him lightly on the shoulder. "Of course not. You must eat it how you like." Edward was not used to being punched by girls and he assumed his crimson hue once more. I changed the subject. "Tell me about Coggeshall. We haven't been here long."

He pointed his slice of cake to a building on the other side of the road. "That's the school," he said. "The old Hitcham School. My pa went there when he was a lad." He struggled with his words, choosing them carefully. "He's Albert Daynes, the carpenter," he said, as though I should recognise the name.

"My father is Gustav Holst, the composer." It felt like we were playing a game of Happy Families, although clearly neither of us had heard of the other's parent. I was secretly disappointed that Gussie's fame had not penetrated this far into the wilds of Essex.

Edward offered to show me something of the village. In fact it is truly a town, having been given a market charter by Henry III, but Edward said that most of the local people call it a village, and I must admit that it somehow feels more cosy that way. We started at the splendid clock tower on Market Hill, and walked up Church Street to St. Peter-ad-Vincula's. With every stride of his gangly legs Edward seemed to feel on more solid ground, becoming quite the chatterbox.

"Paycocke money built a lot of this church," he said, lowering his voice. "Course they called it Coxhall in them days, not Coggeshall."

I wanted to find out whether Mister Paycocke's motives were

altruistic, or if he merely hoped to buy his way into heaven, but Edward could not enlighten me. In any case, to have built such a splendid house as ours, I assumed his celestial passage was already assured. It appeared that every second building in the village had a Paycocke connection: the White Hart; Constantynes; Huttley's; houses on East Street and Bridge Street. Astonishing that one man could be so wealthy.

Returning down Church Street, Edward pointed out a small and innocuous-looking house set back from the road, as though it were shy of its status. "Haunted, that one," he said. "No one ever lives there for long. Bad smells, lights go on and off for no reason, doors slam shut." He shivered. "Wouldn't go in there if you paid me."

"I would. I'd do it for nothing."

An idea seemed to ferment in Edward. "Well, I suppose if there were two of us…" He was finding a certain attraction in the idea of safety in numbers.

I smiled in what I hoped was an enigmatic fashion. "Are there many ghosts in Coggeshall?"

"Oh yes, not half. They say there's an old monk who stalks the abbey at night. And there's this woman who was hunted down as a witch hundreds of years ago. And have you heard about Robin?"

"Robin?"

"He was a woodsman about 400 years ago. He's supposed to have carved a beautiful statue called 'The Angel of Christmas' or something like that. Anyway, the statue got lost around the time Henry VIII was tearing up the monasteries. Folk say that he wanders the village at night trying to find his lost carving, and that you can hear his axe chopping in the distance.

"They named the stream after him – Robin's Brook." Edward was matter-of-fact, as though ghostly witches, monks and woodcutters were as normal as barrow boys.

"Don't you find it all exciting?" I said, and with the distance that daylight affords I told him about my own experience in the night.

"Sounds like a fox," he said, but he thrust his hands into his pockets and kicked out at a pebble. His boots were cracked and dry, and ancient mud flaked off the sole. His animation had deflated and although I wanted to press him further about my ghost, we walked to the end of the road in silence.

"My mammy used to work there." Edward pointed at the Chapel Commercial Hotel opposite us, a long building with a prosperous new sign, gleaming black in the dazzling afternoon sun.

"Used to?"

"She ain't… she's not well. These few months."

"I'm sorry to hear that."

"S'all right. You're not to know." The sullenness did not match his eyes, sharp and bright. He was drawing his lower teeth over his top lip, caught in the throes of a debate with himself. Then he turned to me. "Do you want to know a secret?"

I nodded.

"You got to swear not to tell."

I placed my hand on my heart. "I shall be utterly, utterly oyster," I said, with great gravity.

He paused to digest my promise.

"It's Paycocke's, your Paycocke's. There's something you should know, about the restoration. Only I know. My father and uncle Billy worked there for a bit, for Ernest Beckwith and that Buxton bloke."

Buxton. Noel. Conrad. I clapped my hand to my mouth. So diverted had I been with Edward that I had completely forgotten our guest at Paycocke's.

"I must go," I said.

"But…"

"I'm so sorry, Edward. There's no time. I simply have to go."

"Wait." He felt in a pocket of his trousers and pulled out a shiny key. The bright metal winked in the sun and before I could protest he had pressed it into my palm. "I will see you again… soon. This key says it."

I ran all the way back to Paycocke's, and when I arrived the key had impressed itself into my perspiring hand, leaving behind the harsh scent of metal on my skin.

* * *

Edward was lost. Imogen's voice had floated over the garden at Paycocke's, carried by a breath of a breeze. Her voice was the sweetest sound he had ever heard, dancing in the air like a sycamore pod. He caught scraps of words, conversational leftovers, and made them his own. When she laughed it was like she had become the sun and the world span around her. Even the imperious Reverend was held by her spell. When she sang that song, he thought that the nightingales would leave early for Africa, shamed by the comparison. He was in a trap from which not even Houdini could escape.

Edward knew the Reverend well; or by reputation knew him well, since his father often spoke of the Red Vicar in awed tones. Not only had he overseen the work at Paycocke's House in recent years, but news of his exploits at Thaxted had travelled far if not always to great acclaim. Edward's father had been honoured to be considered an equal by this unusual clergyman, his opinion highly valued, his skills as a carpenter prized.

Imogen turned towards the fence and saw him. The sun shone behind her, making her look as though she had a halo, golden and pure. He felt his ears catch fire. He stepped back from the fence, but his hands still held fast to the bars, the wood embossing itself on his fingers as he peeled them off, one by one. She spoke, a silent word that belonged only to Edward, "Hello."

Edward's heart thumped at his chest. He wanted to run and he wanted to stay, but in the end he had no choice. He had heard them speak of giant oaks; well, that was how he felt, as though he would not be able to move for a hundred years.

Imogen walked towards him, glided on the haze of summer, heat-white and blazing like the Angel Gabriel. Her smile paralysed him further. He watched her draw nearer and she became his fate, his dreams. She must be taking all the air around them, since he could no longer breathe. She put out her hand, delicate and pale, and spoke to him. "Good afternoon. Imogen Holst, at your service."

At his service. No, that was wrong, for he would die to serve her. Die like his uncle in the War, die for a greater cause than his own life, die for love. Still he could not speak, so shell-shocked was he that he could merely stare at her feet, where he longed to lie. He dredged up his courage, fighting for breath as though he were emerging from a cloud of mustard gas, and spoke words he had come close to forgetting in that blinding minute. "Edward. Edward Daynes." So this was love.

Imogen offered him cake and he nodded, anything to prolong the moment. She was carrying a straw hat and put it on, its rose-coloured ribbon draping down over her hair as she turned to go. It burst the halo that the sun had given her, allowing him to breathe once more and he watched her walk over the lawn without crushing the grass.

Racing around to the front of the house, Edward examined himself. His boots were boots, nothing to be done. His hands held honest grime from a morning's graft. He spat on them and wiped them dry on his stockings; she would never know. He rolled up his frayed cuffs and brought his disobedient hair to heel.

The cake, in an ivory napkin folded by her hands, was almost enough to bring him to a standstill again, and she tried to put him at his ease, saying something about the different squares of the Battenberg. It reminded him of his mother, whose cakes had once been considered the best in Coggeshall. She seldom left her bed now, or if she did just sat night after night in the parlour, no strength even to beat an egg, her lace tambour and hooks collecting dust on the dresser.

"She don't make any cakes no more," he said. Even too tired to bake, she was, always too tired. Edward was drawn back to his earlier sadness. His mother had become so thin these past few months, even though she sometimes had a hunger like five men on her.

She was stubborn with it too, refusing to see a doctor. 'It'll pass. No sense in wasting good money.' It hadn't passed yet, though.

Imogen said her father was a famous musician. He had a foreign-sounding name, and Edward remembered overhearing tittle-tattle in the Post Office about 'the new German bloke in the village.' There was still fierce resentment for fallen Tommies. But Imogen sounded English to Edward, as English as himself, maybe more so. He wished he had paid more attention to the gossipmongers, if only so he could say something intelligent about Imogen's family. However, she had not heard of his father either, so they were well matched. He revelled in that small similarity.

The cake was soft as feathers and prevented his mouth from descending into further embarrassments. They walked awhile in silence, each second like the tick of a clock in that he knew it was there, needing to be filled, reminding him of its presence by the absence of words. She wanted to see the village, so he took her on a short tour and pointed out the churches and the schools, and told her some of the legends of Coggeshall. Her eyes grew large at his tales of Coggeshall's ghostly past and her attention zigzagged like a hare from one building to the next as he conjured their strange histories. It was then that he decided he could trust her, that he could share with her the secret that had been gnawing at his insides over the past few years. She would not think him stupid. He laughed inwardly at his foolish infatuation of an hour earlier, hardly able to utter his own name in her presence. Now that he knew her, now that they were friends, now that he truly did love her.

"Do you want to know a secret?" he asked, dropping his voice in conspiracy, for they shared something.

She nodded.

He asked her to swear on it, knowing that she would not be shocked, but that she would realise its importance. She said something about oysters that confused him and he was about to reply that some folk thought Paycocke's had been built upon a bed of crushed oyster shells, and then he realised that she meant she would be like an oyster and guard his secret well.

"It's about Paycocke's House. There's something you got to know. It's about the restoration. There's only me knows. My uncle Billy was there all the time working for Buxton. It's…"

He got no further. Imogen put her hand to her mouth. "I must go," she said. Edward cursed himself; what had he done? He had scared her. Something he had said. He had been too forward. He bit his lip and fought back the emotion. He might have known it. Why would someone like Imogen Holst ever be interested in a nobody like him? Why did he ever imagine they could be friends? Anguish shredded the infant security he had allowed himself to feel while they walked together, and he stared down at his worn-out old boots.

She put her hand on his arm, a touch he vowed to remember forever, a touch that lifted his heart to the clouds. Their eyes locked, hers as blue as the open sky, and she winked at him. "I simply have to go," she said.

"Wait." He had to see her again, any excuse, no, any reason would do. He fished in his pocket for the key to his box, the box where he kept everything that had ever mattered to him: his best marble; a lock of his grandmother's hair; a Gatling gun shell; an adder's skull. He had to see her again, for he would have to get the key back. He felt it in his hand, felt his fingertips meet in the heart-shaped cut-out on the key's handle. The key represented everything he valued - he would have to get it back. "Take this," he said. "I will see you again... soon... the key says it."

And then she was gone, running up West Street away from him, disappearing without a glance. He fought the pain that welled within him that she could be so curt, could flit away with so little care. He looked down at his boots. They had sloughed off all the dried mud and dirt like an old skin. The leather looked softer, newer. The key *had* represented everything he valued, but things change.

Chapter 11
Shopping

"How was your audition?"

"Huh?"

Staggered breakfasts had become Robin's immediate bequest. Alex had already left, for an away match at Ipswich. Simon was pushing Sultana Bran around a bowl when Cassie came down in her dressing-gown, hair ratty and eyes still glued together with sleep.

"You had an audition yesterday."

"Oh, yeah, that. Listen, Dad, did you get anywhere with that panelling, the fireplacey stuff you were on about?"

Simon stared at her, unused to the interest in his life.

"Just wondering, yeah?" Cassie sat down at the end of the table and reached for the orange juice. She slopped some into a glass, but her aim was shoddy and she made a small puddle on the pine table. She stared at the spilt juice, as though she were willing it to evaporate. "I'll get it in a minute, Dad." She yawned.

"So, how did it go?"

"What is this, the Spanish Inquisition?" She yawned again and rubbed her eyes.

"I care, Cass."

"Yeah, well, you know."

"Yes?"

"Some you lose…"

"Some you win…"

"Some you get thrashed in."

"So no dice?"

"No, as you say, dice." She poured some Special K into a bowl. The last remnants of the packet cascaded out, the dust of the box that no one ever ate. "Any skimmed?"

"In the fridge."

She reached for the semi-skimmed and dribbled some onto

92

her cereal. Only her crunching pushed a wedge into the silence.

Simon flattened the packet for recycling. "I'd better go to Sainsbury's this morning," he said. "Need anything?"

Cassie shook her head, her mouth full.

"Want me to put you on some bacon?"

"No, you just get on, Dad. I can fend for myself."

"What was it, then?"

"What?"

"The audition?"

Cassie's mood snapped like an over-tightened guitar string. "Leave it out, will you, Dad? Nothing, it was nothing. An advert. Nothing. It doesn't matter."

Simon held his hands up in surrender. "All right, all right. Take it easy, Cass." He scraped his chair back and stood up. "I'll be off, then."

Cassie looked down at her congealed Special K and pushed the bowl away. "Yeah."

*   *   *

Sainsbury's was molten, parents with nothing better to do with their children than to subject them to an hour's hanging off the trolley and whining, 'Can I have this?'

The aisles were blocked with a mixture of unravelling tempers and garrulous hobby shoppers for whom a Saturday at the supermarket was a social opportunity. Simon gave up all hope of efficiency. As long as he was back by three for Sparrow. Martin had him wondering: *Artes*, the Roman encyclopaedia – Celsus, wasn't it? Only the medical volumes - *De Medicina* – had survived. The other texts, the science, the philosophy, the agriculture, they were dust in the wind, lost centuries ago, surely. What could Sparrow possibly have found out?

An overweight man in a baggy green Nirvana T-shirt pulled up by the bottled water. Simon saw him too late to put the brakes on and his trolley caught the man's foot.

"Oi, watch it, mate."

"Sorry," Simon said.

"Yeah." The man turned away and Simon humped six bottles of Evian into his trolley. *De Medicina* itself had become a standard medical text when it surfaced in fourteen-something, having been lost for centuries in the murk of the Dark Ages. But if that one had been found, why not the rest? Why not? The implications of finding the other volumes... well, he didn't know that it would change the world, but it would be a massive coup. He laughed to himself. Sparrow certainly knew how to dangle bait.

He checked his shopping list: Special K; muesli; those apricot bars that Alex liked. The heavy trolley was beginning to acquire more momentum as he slid it over to breakfast cereals, so he parked it at the gondola end and walked through the gridlocked traffic. He eased past a gaggle of chattering pensioners to the shelf. A boy stood in front of it, leaning against an empty trolley, pushing it forward and back to emphasise his boredom.

"Excuse me," Simon said, smiling. "Can I just squeeze through?" He pointed down to the Special K.

The lad couldn't have been more than eight or nine, with a number two haircut and a round face that looked like an advertisement for pies. He scowled down at the cereal.

"Excuse me," Simon repeated, gesturing at the trolley.

The boy looked straight through Simon with empty grey eyes and said, "Fuck off."

Simon was astonished. "What?"

"You heard."

Simon spluttered. "Have you any... What the... Where..."

The boy raised a hand and turned the palm outwards to face Simon. "Talk to the hand."

That was it. "You little runt. Get out of the way, you brat."

The boy's voice dropped, intelligence appearing in it for the first time. He sneered. "Don't you fucking touch me." He sniggered, then cried out, "Paedo. He was touching me. Mum, Dad. He's a paedo. Don't let him get me. Mum."

Shoppers turned to face Simon, shock and anger rendering their faces rigid. He held up his hands in a gesture of innocence. "No. I never touched him. I wasn't doing anything. No."

The boy put his face in his hands, his shoulders shaking.

The overweight man from the water aisle took a step towards Simon, his huge fist curled at the ready. "You disgusting pervert…"

"Stop." The voice looped from behind the fat man. "I saw it all." It was a strong voice, a woman's voice, a voice with a hint of the Dales. "Daniel Slater, you should be ashamed of yourself." She faced the growing audience. "One of my lads, trying it on."

The store manager was burrowing her way through the people with 'Excuse-me's. "Is there a problem?"

Eleanor Simmons took control. "No problem. This is Daniel Slater, Year 6, and he'll not see Year 7 if he carries on like this. This gentleman," she pointed to Simon, "was trying to reach the cereal and Daniel was being his usual helpful self, weren't you, lad?"

"Is that right?" The manager winked at Daniel. "Was it just a bit of a trick?"

Daniel was shaking for real now, found out. He lifted his face up, the defiance drained from his expression. He nodded.

"He's got previous," said Eleanor.

The manager turned to Simon. "I am sorry, sir."

Simon felt his heart running wild. "Let's say no more about it." He glared at the Slater boy, who turned away.

Eleanor smiled at him. It was a smile he hadn't seen before, one that seemed to start inside her. "You could use a coffee, I'll bet," she said.

There's a turn-up for the book. Fancy gormless Daniel Slater coming to the rescue. Little toe-rag. Come on, Mr Sad-Eyes, have a coffee with your New Best Friend.

Simon's stomach felt acid. He didn't want coffee. He wanted to be home, under the duvet. "Yes, that'd be good."

Five minutes later it was no more than a nasty might-have-been, and Simon felt embarrassed at having been so shaken.

Eleanor stirred her cappuccino, laughing. "He's a bit of a rabbit, really, that Daniel Slater."

"You could have fooled me. He's itching for some serious trouble."

"Oh, his brother was the same – all mouth and no trousers. He was in my class two years ago."

"And you teach twenty of these?" Simon shook his head in amazement. Eleanor was quite calm about the whole incident, almost amused. Her hair was in weekend mode, a natural wave flowing past her dark brown eyes, tickling her collar-bones as it fell onto her sleeveless cotton shirt. He found himself looking for the golden highlights he had seen at Paycocke's, but in the harsh neon of the cafeteria he could only see the deep chestnut brown.

"Oh, it's more like thirty. But they're not all like Daniel," she said.

"I don't know how you manage."

She looked at him over the top of her cup. "I've had plenty of practice – I've a twelve-year-old of my own. Jack."

He looked at her again, a double-take. "You can't be... I had no idea you were that old... sorry, I didn't mean it that way..."

Oh, you are a cack-handed old thing. I could like you in another life. But I need to know a bit more about Paycocke's. It's the Plan, you see.

"You're putting your foot in it today, aren't you?" And her foot touched his, her mule brushing his shoe. It was such a brief touch that it must have been an accident and she shifted her position in her seat. "How *is* your foot, by the way?"

Simon rolled his ankle to test it, only feeling a slight discomfort. "Fine. Well, better than it was. Thanks. For the other day, I mean."

"Nothing to thank."

"Well..."

"How's everything else?"

Simon smiled at the euphemism, the 'everything else'. "I lost it for a while back there." He closed his lips and let out his breath through his nose. "I'm lucky to have Cassie and Alex to help me through this."

"If I can help..."

"Well, thanks, but..."

"It's not an offer out of politeness, you know. When you get to know me, you'll find out that polite is the last thing I am."

Simon laughed, at last feeling at ease. There was a hole in the conversation and he didn't rush to fill it.

"If you need a shoulder to cry on, someone to talk to that's not family, give me a shout, eh, Simon? I know what you're going through."

His gaze met hers. How could she possibly know what he was going through?

*   *   *

They drove back to Coggeshall in an informal convoy, her silver Focus waiting at amber lights for him in moral support. He wondered if Robin would want the family Citroen, stippled with the acne of incipient rust, ancient sherbet lemons stuffed down the backs of the seats. He waved at Eleanor's car as it turned up Stoneham Street. She held up a hand in return, an ambiguous gesture that could just as easily have been two fingers, but wasn't. At least he was sure of that, and sure that she was as uncertain as he, as anybody.

"Alan and I came down south for his job. Insurance. He sold life insurance. Good at it, too. Not a smooth talker, Alan, but someone you immediately felt you could trust. And that was the problem – he fell for one of his clients. And nobody will sell you life insurance for your marriage – when that dies…" Eleanor spread her arms out. "You just have to get on with it. Do your grieving in private."

"And your son?"

Aye, I'll trade a few confidences with you, Simon. And you'll tell me what I want to know in good time. You have to.

"Jack took it badly. Adored his Dad, he did. Still does, even though he buggered off to Brighton two years ago with the Mark II. Oh, he sends money on Jack's birthday, took him up the London Eye last year, has him over in the holidays. He draws the dividends, does Alan." She laughed. "But he left me with the premiums to pay: the school run; the dentist's appointments; getting the stains out of his football socks." The words themselves were bitter, but her tone was resigned. Her shoulders dropped and the collar of her shirt slipped down. Simon could see the small hills of her clavicular notches, their faded bronze alluding to the summer past, and for the first time since Robin had left, he felt able to be the listening one, the one exuding the calmness and wisdom.

He pulled up behind a Nissan Micra on the yellow lines outside Paycocke's. The enormous oak door gaped open and an elderly couple stood in the entrance hall, admiring the carvings. At first he was confused; who on earth were they? Astonishment turned to concern and panic. Hell, he hadn't set the alarm. Where was Cassie?

Simon couldn't keep the gruffness out of his voice. "Yes? Who are you? How did you get in?"

The man dropped his walking-stick, its brass duck head clattering to the floor. "Oh, I'm sorry. Have we…"

"Don't apologise, Geoff, we've every right to be here." The woman was polite but forceful. "Your colleague let us in five minutes ago. We were just passing and the door was open…"

"How could it be? We're closed for the winter."

"I showed him our membership cards, and…"

"Who?"

"He was very nice."

"Who was?" Simon felt control drifting away from him.

"Your colleague. The young man."

"What are you talking about?" Simon fought to suppress a burgeoning panic. Cassie's boyfriend. It must have been Cassie's boyfriend. "Cassie," he yelled up the stairs. "Cassie, where are you?" He picked up the walking-stick and turned back to give it to the couple. "Please go, we're closed."

"But he said it would be fine."

Simon was going to throttle Cassie. "What young man?"

"The one with the box. He was doing stock-taking, he said. Isn't that right, Geoff?"

Her husband nodded, fiddling with his white moustache, avoiding eye contact. "End of season stock-taking." Geoff touched his wife's arm, sensitive to Simon's impatience. "I think we ought to go now, Mary."

Simon picked up a Paycocke's guide lying on the table and

thrust it at Geoff and Mary. "Take this, read about it, come back in the spring," he said, wringing out a smile. "Do come back. When we're open." He herded them out into the street and closed the door.

Box? The man had a box?

He rushed outside in time to see the couple judder off up West Street in the Micra. Stock-taking? What did that mean? The Trust always called to make sure someone was at home before they came. Something was wrong.

Cassie was not in the house. Her room was untouched, the only clue to its recent occupancy the vague scent of deodorant fighting a losing battle with the stale air. He flung the window open. "Bloody hell, Cassie."

Everything seemed to be all right; nothing appeared to be missing. He would have to run through the inventory later. Perhaps it had been a friend of Cassie's with a box of CDs or something. Something probably being the Chinese snuff bottles, which he could swap for an ounce of blow. How was it that Cass had managed to leave behind the dregs of Camden Town only to hook up with another species of low-life? But even so, why would she let strangers into the house?

Simon was annoyed with himself for not having probed Geoff and Mary properly. He would have to wait until Cassie came home. Whenever that was.

The alarm went off on the Staffordshire dog, shooting its penetrating bleeping down the stairs.

"Oh hell," said Simon. "What now?" He took the steps two at a time and reached the top just as the beeping stopped. He stared into the public room at a man wearing a smirk and with an out of place tan. The guy's blond hair was swept back over his forehead and he clutched a small box under his arm. "Well, well, well," he said.

"Martin bloody Sparrow," Simon said.

Martin swivelled his head at the carved ceiling and whistled. "Paycocke sure knew how to live, didn't he?"

Chapter 12
1515: A Hard Beginning Maketh A Good Ending

Thomas Paycocke knew how to live, and he knew how to die. Like Margaret, his dear wife, his honeysuckle, who died with dignity, though racked by the sweats and not the woman he had loved. She died with grace and in Grace. God be with her.

Her tomb felt warm to his touch. It was the sun, he thought, streaming through the high windows of the church and staining the flagstones with yellows and reds. But the sun was still cloaked by St. Peter's spire and the day was yet young. He would have to be away before the midday Angelus; he was not ready to test his faith with the words of prayer. "Miserere nostri Domine," he muttered. "Have mercy on me, Lord. Have mercy."

He picked up his hat and pulled its brim down to leave his face in shadow, but he was recognised time and again as he trudged home: Peter the smith; the fuller Taylor; a hind servant whom he knew by sight. They all stopped to pay their respects, to offer condolence, but there was none to be had.

Thomas arrived back at the Paycocke house uncertain how it was that he had managed to negotiate the way from the church. His head tipped forward as though it were lead; he thought only of the house they had loved together, a house now his alone, the mockery of the 'T' and 'M' carved for evermore in the ceiling beams of the hall. Though slow of tongue, the journeyman Kees had made most fine work of rendering their love in the green oak. 'T' and 'M' - Thomas and Margaret, the last place he would ever see them together; in very truth, while he remained alive. He shook his head. No, he was not ready to set eyes on those carvings. Mud spattered his hose as he took the horses' entrance which led to the back of the house.

Robert Goodday, the clerk, a man of twenty summers, but whom Thomas trusted as no other, was grooming a mare with fluid and confident strokes. He looked at Thomas and bowed his head the once. "God you save and see, master," he said.

"Good morrow, Robert." Thomas pursed his lips, nodding at the younger man. "How goes it with you this day?"

There was silence between the two men, a silence filled with knowledge. The clerk patted the chestnut's haunches and took a step towards Thomas. "Well, Master Thomas."

Paycocke held up his right hand. "It's to be 'Thomas'. Only 'Thomas'. You are as my right hand, Robert. You know me as no other. From this day forth it shall be only 'Thomas'."

Robert nodded his thanks, the smallest of smiles tinkering with his lips. "It is most well done. Thomas."

"Will it please you to take your ease, Robert?"

"Aye, indeed."

"Then take dinner with me, for I am passing hungry." Thomas could not eat alone, could no longer look at Margaret's empty seat. The room with its grand carvings and bright wall hangings could bring him no solace.

"That would be well, Thomas."

The two men ate some hodgepot together, for Paycocke had not become wealthy by wasting leftovers, and they washed the stew down with strong ale. Goodday was thin but powerful, long but not so that he had to stoop to enter the house. His clothes had been his father's before him and the older Robert had been a shorter man, so the sleeves of his son's shirt fell shy of the wrists. Thomas made up his mind to give the lad several ells of cloth for a new suit of clothes, if he would accompany him. London was a parlous journey, but now that Margaret had passed on, it was a journey he must make, and Robert the only man he might trust.

So it had come to this. He had always known it would, since the reading of his father's will those years ago, foreshadowing the destruction of the Paycocke family. What had he meant? If only Thomas had asked him while he was alive. What he would give to see his father's face once more, hold his hard hands, be touched by his soft heart. Thomas felt the lesser man, but what had his father done that he had feared damnation? And how many times had Thomas knelt before the altar praying for guidance, pleading for his father's soul, but with no knowledge of his crime? He had been the best man who ever lived.

'My last and most terrible legacy is for William Spooner, tenant, master builder, friend and trusted adviser, to whom I bequeath the sum of twenty pounds and the guardianship of my most shameful deed, one that would destroy the very name of Paycocke and all Paycockes to come and one which will haunt me throughout eternity. May it never be known. John Paycocke, 1505.'

William Spooner was a hulk of a man who had been almost part of the Paycocke clan, a man who had dandled Thomas on his knee and shared bread with the Paycockes in times both good and hard. Trusted with all manner of works on the properties of John's growing empire, he was a godly man like Thomas's father. Thomas had valued him highly too, entrusting him with the design of Paycocke's House itself. Spooner's very soul lived in his walls, his sweat and blood made real in brick and wood. But where was he now? And what had he done to deserve John's fearsome bequest?

The dreams were plague in the years that followed his father's death: John in Hell's furnace, his screams bringing Thomas to thankful consciousness in brooks of sweat, Margaret holding him in her arms like the babe she would never have, smoothing his brow with her kisses. "My dear Thomas." Never asking, never complaining, her feelings as dear to him as her capacity for business, his partner in every sense. And gone, her last frail grip on his hand slipped away, just days ago, yet it might have been years.

So what was there now to lose? With Margaret passed on without issue, there were no Paycockes to come, save for his brothers, and he must act according to his own conscience. As far as Thomas was concerned, there was the eternal soul of his father John to be saved. He had tried to buy absolution, had given a deal of money to the church, and this had tempered his dreams for a while, quelled the images of his damned father. But now the only hope of resolution lay with Spooner, gone these past years to London to serve the new King.

"Thomas? Master Thomas?" There was a rapping that hauled Thomas from his thoughts. Robert tapped the handle of his spoon upon the oak table. "Are you well, sir?"

Thomas looked across at Robert's carefree face, and scolded himself for wishing to inflict premature lines on the lad. He had hair like hay and deep nut-brown eyes that would be the tinderbox for many a girl's heart. "Fatigue, methinks. That is all." How could he take this innocent lad to London? He who had done naught? It must be a Paycocke struggle alone. It was John and Robert he should ask. But he knew his brothers only too well, and they had their own families to consider.

"You have not touched your food, you who are passing hungry."

Thomas looked down at his bowl, where the roots and meat had now cooled. He stirred it with his spoon, fishing out an apricock. He stared at it for a few seconds, then let it fall back into the wooden bowl. "Aye," he said. Robert's own dish stood empty and he scoured it with a piece of manchet, sopping up the last of the juice and popping the bread into his mouth. Of all the people who had spoken to him since Margaret's death, none had said as much as Robert. Robert had said very little. Their eyes locked across the table, and Thomas knew he trusted this man with his life and this man only.

"Might I be of aid?" Robert cleaned his knife on a last chunk of bread. His actions were methodical: he wasted nothing, neither time nor vittals. "Something troubles you, Thomas."

Paycocke sighed. He felt old beside Robert, his best years behind him. His beard was streaked with grey now and lines traced his face. He was right: it was fatigue, the fatigue of living. But he also knew that he was compelled to do what was right by his father, to find William Spooner and learn of John's horrible secret. Only then might the Paycockes rest in peace. He put his elbows on the table, and held his hands up before his face, joining the fingertips together as though they were a steeple. "You recall William Spooner, Robert?"

Robert pushed his bowl away and scratched the side of his head. "William? I do know a John and an Emma..."

"His brother and sister."

"Is that so? John lives close by us still. He did teach me my letters when I was small."

"Aye, good men and true, the Spooners."

"And this William?"

"He departed Coxhall some few years ago, to pursue his trade in London. There was much work to be done following the accession of the eighth Harry. Aye, and fortunes to be made, too. The King would build fine new palaces in London and a man of skill such as William Spooner would be in great demand. And in truth, William was ever an ambitious man, but my father loved him all the same."

"And…"

"There has been no word of him since." Paycocke took a deep breath and his chest filled his doublet as it had not done for many weeks, since Margaret first fell ill. He folded his big hands together. "I must find William, Robert. He holds the key to my father's death, and without that knowledge I cannot live."

The boy tipped his head to one side and smiled. "Then it is done, Thomas. We leave for London at your convenience. I am your vassal."

"You are my equal."

"And yet I am still your vassal."

"And I yours, my friend."

Robert smiled. "As you will."

"Then I shall visit my carders and kembers this day, leave instruction for the shearmen and fullers, and we shall depart on the morrow."

"'Tis well done."

"'Tis well done indeed, Robert. You are your father's son, a fine man and a good companion."

The sun was low in the sky when they met the following morning in West Street. Thomas hoped the way would be smoother than the street in front of his own house, for here it was pock-marked with holes and sad with neglect. He would renew this stretch upon his return, and pray his horse did not cast a shoe before that time.

The two men broke their fast with dark ravelled bread and herring while the mounts were readied. Robert's hunger remained unabated and he ate and talked with gusto, with the confidence and happy ignorance of the young. Thomas wished his own appetites were as hearty. "I have spoken with John Spooner this day. It is as you say, Thomas, that there has been no word of his brother William." He waved a crust in Thomas's direction. "None the less, it is said that he worked for a time at a place called Cheapside. Some journeymen who passed through Coxhall on their way to Melford but six months since reported having met him in an ale house near there. Taggy's, they did call it. But whether he is still at this place…"

"Cheapside. I know of it."

"To find one man in a town of seventy thousand will be no easy task, Thomas."

"I have been many times to London to trade at Bakewell. The town is something of a labyrinth, but I flatter myself that I know a little of its ways."

"Even so…"

"Mayhap William will come to us, Robert."

Thomas stopped by the door to his house as they left, the huge door with its perfect folded linen pattern, and he touched the carpenter's mark. It was like a bird's footprint, but a large bird. He put his trust in God to give him the wings to return and see the mark once more. Taking one last look around the entrance hall, he closed his eyes to blot out Kees's 'M' and 'P', still a dagger in his heart, and focused instead on the Paycocke's merchant mark, carved in profusion. What lay in store for the Paycocke family? Would he ever see the ermine tail again? He placed his hand on his heart and made the sign of the cross. He would have faith in God, for only He knew what was to come. Still, there was a seed of uncertainty within him; would he preside over the destruction of his family? The doubt nestled in him like a pearl held inside an oyster, growing harder and stronger, awaiting its moment of release.

Thomas knew how to live: with respect for all men, whether they knew their letters or not; with respect for the King; with respect for the Lord. He hoped he would be able to die like Margaret when it came to his turn.

"Away," he said. "To London."

They took the old Roman road out of Coxhall and without looking back they were gone.

Chapter 13
Wine and Wenches Empty Men's Purses

It was not clear whether the walls of London existed to keep men out or to keep men in.

"It is not that I pay heed to pishery-pashery, Robert, but this place has me wary."

"But you do know London well, Thomas?"

"Aye, true, but it is like the shifting sands, always changing, always moving, never the same. These are dangerous times, Robert."

Once in Cheapside, they found Taggy's down a murky street called Rose Alley, and no fresh and fragrant York or Lancastrian rose was it, but a stinking gutter of a lane that led nowhere, its cobbles greasy although there had been no rain.

Thomas fingered the clay charm at his neck, a gift from Margaret, for which very reason he trusted it to watch over him in times of threat. Yet he felt protective of the young Robert, as though he were the son he would now never have. The sun was setting over the squalid Thames and the air held the scent of violence. Only a meagre shaft of light penetrated the dark tunnel and that was fading to grey as they waited. Thomas pulled his second-best cloak around his dark red woollen coat – it would not look good to appear too gentrified.

Before they could enter, a man stumbled from the door. He put his hand out to balance himself and missed the doorframe, falling to his knees at Thomas's feet. He steadied himself on all fours, the edge of his ragged once-ochre sleeves dipping in the fetid puddles where uneven cobbles met. He examined the blunt toes of Thomas's shoes, well-made, well-fitting, then lifted his gaze.

Thomas's hand moved to his knife. The man on the floor was drunk, that much was clear, and although he appeared harmless, there was no accounting for what he might do. *When ale is in, wit is out.*

The man watched Thomas's hand creep beneath his cloak. "Beg pardon, sir, I cry you mercy," the man said, struggling to his feet. He wore no hat, and his hair was long and grey, months since it had seen a comb, knotted together like old rope.

"No harm done," said Thomas, holding out a hand so that the man might stand. He gestured to Robert to step aside so that the drunken man could pass, then held up one hand. "Good even, my friend. Tell me, is this the alehouse they call Taggy's?"

The man coughed out a laugh. "Alehouse? That's one word among many. Just as soon a nunnery, you might say." He moved to leave, but Thomas rested a light hand on his arm.

"I seek a man they do call William Spooner. Know you of him?"

The man's eyes were dull and cloudy; he showed no recognition of the name.

Thomas continued. "A hefty man, uncommonly long, hands like trenchers."

"I know him not." The reply seemed too fast, and before Thomas could react, the man had slipped his grasp and ducked out of sight down a near alley. There was a brief sensation of fresh air in the space he had occupied, quickly filled by the stench which by now was normal.

"Shall we follow?" Robert moved to chase the man, but Thomas held his hand up.

"'Tis of no import, Robert. If one man knows William, then I wager many will. And our visit to this quarter must be brief." He looked up at the pewter sky. "We tarry overlong and I do not wish to be here when night falls."

Robert opened the door to Taggy's. It was warm within, although there was a suffocating smell of sweat long given. Heads turned at their entrance and conversations were muffled. The company was poor, wretched even, and Thomas was aware of several pairs of eyes gauging the whereabouts of his purse.

A young girl of no more than fifteen sat slumped in a corner of the room, a tankard of warm ale before her. She wore a grubby kirtle of goose-turd green, and the hue of her face made a sickly match. She seemed too weak to move, not even noticing that the men had entered the room. "The green sickness," whispered Thomas.

"No need to talk among yourselves, gentlemen." A woman approached them from a side room. Her apron had once been sheep-coloured, but now was ingrained with the dirt of years. Thomas's professional eye marked it as no cheap fustian, but the finest of linen, although now in its darker days. She was as skinny as a maypole, but not so well decorated, her dark hair scraped back under a plain coif, exaggerating the sharpness of her cheekbones. She approximated a smile. "Will it please you to eat?"

Thomas smiled in return. "I have no great stomach. Some ale will suffice."

She nodded. "Aye, so be it. Ale it is."

Thomas and Robert sat down on a bench, which shook as it took their weight. The eyes that had followed them returned to their own affairs.

The woman returned with two tankards. She waited as Thomas felt within his purse for pennies. He held them out, pausing before he dropped them into her outstretched palm. "Taggy, is it?"

Her eyes narrowed. She tested the edge of the coins to be sure they had not been filed. "Who asks?" she said.

"Paycocke. Thomas Paycocke of Coxhall."

She lowered her face closer to Paycocke, so close he could smell decay on her breath. She smiled again, assuming an air of grandeur. "Well, Mister Thomas Paycocke of Coxhall, we are happily encountered, are we not? And how might else might we serve you this even? What," she winked at him, "other pleasures do you have?"

Thomas took a long draught of the weak and tepid ale. The dank evening and uneasy welcome had given him a great thirst. He lowered his voice and wished that Taggy would follow his example. "No pleasures, Madam Taggy, but some information. It is a man I seek."

"A man?" Taggy folded her arms and her lips disappeared into a thin line. "Well, you will find no hedgecreepers in this house, Mister Paycocke, no tale-tellers. A man's business is his own."

"You will not find me ungenerous."

Her dark eyes widened a fraction. "How generous?"

Thomas covered his mouth with his hand. "A royal if I do find this William Spooner."

Taggy's eyes were prised apart at the thought of the ten shillings, but she betrayed no knowledge of the builder's name. "William Spooner, you say?"

"Aye, an ox of a man." Thomas held out his arms, spreading them as though he were measuring cloth. "A fellow so long that he would stand in this room only with great discomfort, but with a fine calf to his leg all the same. A goodly man; a Coxhall man."

Taggy took her apron in her hands and wiped her fingers, although there was no dirt that Thomas could see. It was clear she was evaluating him and that there was no doubt but that she knew William. Still she did not answer. Thomas turned to Robert and urged him to drink from the sticky tankard. Robert looked pale, out of his depth in this low place. The older man resolved to leave as soon as they could. He should not have brought Robert with him.

Taggy made to leave their table and Thomas stayed her with a single gesture, the wave of a finger, the mark of a man used to having his own way. "And a royal for Spooner if he will meet with me. It is a matter of some import, Madam."

The woman scanned the room. The low murmur still prevailed, but Thomas knew they were being watched. "Here. On the morrow. After dark," she said. "I promise nothing."

Thomas stood up and left his half-finished ale on the table. "Then there is no more to be said. I thank you kindly for your hospitality."

They hurried back up Rose Alley. The smell was stronger than ever and time and again their flat shoes skidded on the damp cobbles for want of grip. Paycocke wished to be back at their lodgings. As far as he was concerned you could keep London, with its putrid air and broken people. He wondered what had ever possessed a sane and godly man like William Spooner to have come to this foul heathen place.

He looked about him. They should have reached Cheapside by now. The walls of the buildings, crouched together like monstrous black sheep, reached far over their heads so that the leaden sky was scarcely visible. Their footsteps echoed around the filthy abyss and disappeared into the night. They must have taken a wrong turn; he did not recognise this alley.

Thomas stopped. "Robert." He spoke in a whisper, even though there were none to overhear them. "My thoughts were elsewhere. We have mistaken our way, methinks."

Robert was a shadow beside him, a trompe l'oeil on the dank walls. "I know not, Thomas. I think… I think I do smell the river." He hesitated. The silence was punctuated by a distant noise. "Listen, Thomas, is that the sound of oars I hear?" Robert sounded younger than his years, the confidence that flowed from him at home in Coxhall had subsided.

Thomas felt much the same, and his stomach seemed to rise up inside him. It could have been the slap of oars on the Thames, it could have been a bucket of water sluicing down the rank cobblestones. "If we are by the river then we have taken the wrong direction. Let us retrace our steps to Taggy's and begin again."

"I do not much care for Taggy's." There was a tremble in Robert's voice. Thomas was glad he could not see the lad's face, but could picture it wan and touched with fear.

"Nor I, but it is a simple bawdy-house, no more. God forgive me that I should have brought you…"

"A bawdy-house?" At least the astonishment in Robert's voice drowned his fear.

"Aye, lad," Thomas said. "Bawdy-house, brothel-house, what you will. 'Other pleasures' indeed." They stood at a junction of alleys. "Right or left?"

Robert shook his head.

"Then right it is." They headed from darkness to darkness. "Aye, Taggy is none but a brothel-keeper. 'Tis a fair profession, to be sure, but not for the likes of us."

"Shall we be burnt with disease?" A different edge slipped from Robert's words.

Thomas laughed. "Fear not. That is a pox you do not catch

through breath alone." He stopped again. "Do you still hear the river?"

Robert cocked his head. "It is further away now."

"Would that you yourself were further away, Paycocke." The voice was sturdy, deep and full of hatred. It boomed around the narrow alley. Thomas turned, but could see no one. "Paycocke." The word was spat out onto the air.

That voice, William Spooner. It was William, who had cradled him as a boy. A tall silhouette of a man stepped out from the desolate shadows. He stood but fifty feet from the clothier and his companion, stood high, but no ox of a man was he, but a thin and decrepit creature, spare of leg and wild with ale. "William? William Spooner?" said Thomas. "It is I, Thomas Paycocke."

"Thomas Paycocke, son of John? You three-inch fool, you had better stayed away."

Thomas held up a hand. "I mean you no harm, William."

"Then that is less than I mean you, you quailing hedgepig."

"I wish only to talk."

"Talk? I have no need of fine Paycocke talk. I live in Hell from your Paycocke talk." Spooner stepped towards them. "You see me? You can see me now?" In the disappearing light Thomas saw that the master builder's fine muscle had wasted away. His flesh draped from his skeleton like folds of cloth, his face was ravaged, a field of scars and pox marks. "Look at me, shadow of a man that I am. This is your father's doing, Paycocke, your father's curse."

"But how so?" Thomas held up his hands to try and placate Spooner. He had no idea what the man was talking of. He looked at Robert by his side. "Step back, Robert, I must do this alone. Speak to me, William, I beg you."

"Truth needs not many words, Paycocke. Look at me. Your father destroyed me, with his vile will." Spooner moved towards them and Thomas could see that he carried a large cudgel. He tapped it on the ground; it splashed in the puddles like an oar. "Yet I have strength enough left for you, Paycocke. And for your slitgut knave."

"I do not wish to fight." Thomas's bravery was of a different kind; he had no experience in this dirty arena. He stepped back. "Away, Robert, run."

"Puny milk-livered bum-bailey."

"But I do not understand, William. What did my father do? What was it that was in his will? William, speak to me."

"The lying scut. His 'most faithful friend' indeed. May he rot for his deeds, and I too for being party to his stinking bequest." Spooner edged forward, but Thomas stood his ground, though his heart raced. His knife was still at his belt, tucked ready in its sheath, but this man had been his father's most favoured friend. How could he use it against him?

The crazed man before him had no such reservation. Spooner raised his weapon and swung at Thomas's head with a force that belied his skeletal frame. The merchant ducked, feeling the cool wind of the cudgel wash his cheek. He held his hands aloft and tried to plead with Spooner. "William, please."

Spooner drew the cudgel behind his head, ready to unleash a blow that would make a duck's egg of Thomas's skull. "Begging will aid you not, Paycocke. All of you ought die, all Paycockes. I curse you for what you have done to me. Look upon me well, Paycocke, for this is the last face you will ever see."

"No, William." Thomas at last drew his knife, his hand trembling, but as he pulled it out it caught on his leather belt and jerked from his grasp, clattering to the cobbles. He bent to reach for it, but lost his footing on the wet stones. As he fell the cudgel combed his hair with another reckless blow and thudded into the house behind him with the deep jarring thud of oak on seasoned oak. Thomas scrabbled for grip on the damp ground, the stench stronger down there amid the puddles of human waste. It was so dark that he could not see his blade.

"'Tis Hell for you now, Paycocke." Spooner loomed above him, pausing, struggling for the breath which came in racking gasps. "And there we will be well met." He snarled and raised his cudgel once more. Then Robert was upon him. He leapt upon the big man and rode him piggy-back fashion, wrapping his arms around Spooner's neck and trying to bring him to the ground. Spooner roared and circled, wanting to shake Robert off, but the younger man clung on. The builder's strength was deep-set in his bones; he dropped his weapon and reached behind him for

Robert's arm. With one movement he ripped the young clerk from his back and hurled him to the ground. Robert landed awkwardly and his head jerked back, thumping against an unyielding oak corner-post. He slumped forward, motionless.

"Robert," screamed Thomas.

"Pray your end is as quick." Spooner looked around for his weapon but it was lost in the black shadows. His veins stood out like ropes on his emaciated arms as he turned to Thomas.

Paycocke faced the man. Could this be the end? He threw a punch at Spooner, a punch that was merely a memory from childhood scraps, one made soft by easy living. It caught Spooner on the chin and his head snapped back, but no more than an inch. Spooner laughed at Thomas's puny effort and grabbed him with both hands, forcing him back against the wall. "And when this is done I shall have your fine red coat too," he said, spitting in Thomas's face. "A plague upon your name." He put his enormous hands around Thomas's neck and started to squeeze. Thomas beat against Spooner's sinewy arms, but it was like fighting the tide. It was all over. His arms were growing weaker and he felt his legs betray him as he crumpled to the ground. Still the vice of Spooner's fingers continued to crush Thomas's life. "I curse the day I ever met your father. I curse him and you and the testament that brought me naught but ill. I curse your sons and your sons' sons." The grip grew stronger with each word, "Paycocke, swagbelly whoreson wretch."

The air seemed to grow thinner as Thomas's struggles subsided. He felt his eyelids give up the fight. *I will be with Margaret.* Spooner's laugh came from all about him, echoing in this last dark alley, booming in Thomas's head. "I do see it now. It is *your* face. It is. It is yours. Kees, where are you?" The laugh magnified until it was all that was left of Thomas's world, and then it was gone.

"Master Paycocke." The voice came from above; it was God, no, an angel above him. He heard its rhythmic and fearsome breaths and then knew he had been cast down to Hell and was in the clutches of a demon. He could feel William Spooner's hands still about his throat, but their grip was loosened and then he realised it was he himself who was gasping, he who was retching for breath. He inhaled the putrid and vile air as though it were nectar.

"Master Paycocke."

He opened his eyes, the night flooding his vision and he started to lose consciousness. He fought it, wanted to be alive. There was a weight on him, as if he were lying under a dead sheep, and he rolled the carcass away. The black night receded and he saw a young woman in a goose-turd green kirtle. She held a knife, Paycocke's own, and it dripped dark blood onto the body, where it joined the blood oozing from a gash in Spooner's side.

"Ann Cotton," she said, almost curtseying in the half-light. "We must away."

Chapter 14
Buttercups

Sparrow was often there in those embryonic Hampstead days, putting the finishing touches to projects or planning some major coup before he crossed the Atlantic. He chipped away at Simon's resolve, made him laugh on those bleak days when the highlight of his afternoon had been stepping barefoot on a piece of Lego.

He made a habit of turning up at their place when Robin was out at work, agonising over pastels and off-white emulsions that all looked the same to Simon. The two men went for walks on the Heath with Cassie and Alex, Martin flashing ever more ludicrous business proposals in front of Simon. The last time he came, Sparrow had an airline ticket in his bag, a United one-way to Boston. He had sold his Kensington penthouse, his Range Rover and the yacht, the last shredding Simon's Isle of Wight memories of Sparrow flirting with his wife.

Sparrow stood in the doorway of the Chances' terrace and pointed to his carpet-bag. "It's all in here. My new life."

"All of it?" Simon's voice lengthened with sarcasm. "I don't believe you. You've got more suits than Rumpole."

"Well, I have had one or two other bits and pieces shipped out." Sparrow's eyes sparkled in the spring sunshine. Honeysuckle dripped its fruit salad colours down the wall to where seedlings spotted the flowerbeds in perfect geometric patterns.

"Want to come in?" Simon said.

Martin seemed unnerved by the idea and scrunched up his mouth. "Fancy a stroll?" He reached into his bag and brought out a bottle of Bollinger and two flutes. "We should celebrate. For old times' sake. For new times' sake."

Simon couldn't stem the laugh. There were times when he thought Martin's bluff was just a veneer, when the public schoolboy had grown up, but those times were not often. "Let me get the girls ready."

They sat on the grass near Kenwood House, the breeze cancelling out the efforts of the early season sun. Cassie and Alex had an argument about what to do. Neither would give in, so each played in her own world, Alex darting through the trees pretending to be a butterfly and Cassie sifting through the grass, looking for suitable daisies and chin-ripe buttercups.

"Here's to the States." Simon raised his glass.

"Cheers."

The champagne was colder than it had a right to be, infiltrating a filling in one of Simon's canines and making him gasp as it touched a nerve. He took another swig as anaesthetic.

"I'll miss you guys." Martin's hair bristled in the wind like corn.

It was about as open as Simon had ever seen him. He didn't know what to say, was uncomfortable with the new persona that Sparrow was allowing him to glimpse, had never had any idea that vulnerability played a part in the man's character. "You're the one that's leaving," he said.

"I have to."

"Have to?"

"It's one of those things, Simon. If I don't go, I'll always regret it. You know that poem, 'The Road Not Taken'?"

"Robert Frost?"

"Yeah, well it's like in the poem, I've come to a fork in my life. I can go either of two ways, but whichever path I choose, I'll leave something behind that I haven't done." The alcohol was making Sparrow expansive. "But I have to take… what does Frost call it, the road less travelled by, something like that, I think." He paused, staring into his champagne flute as though it were a crystal ball. The sound of swifts and yelping girls filled the crack of silence between them. "I have to take that path."

"'And that has made all the difference.'"

"Huh?"

"That's how it goes on. 'I took the road less travelled by, and that has made all the difference.' You're doing the right thing, Martin. You'll never forgive yourself if you don't give it a shot."

Sparrow nodded, looked around him at the new leaves,

sprigs of candles erupting on the horse chestnuts, the bright green of the early season painting the trees with optimism, an optimism destined to darken as summer took hold. "I'll miss England, too."

Simon wasn't sure he was ready for ex-pat melancholia even before Martin had stepped onto the plane. "There's always Boston Common," he said. "Feed the squirrels. They eat from your hand there."

Martin refilled their glasses.

Simon shuffled the conversation along on the same track. "When I was in rooms in Cambridge, there was a squirrel on the Backs which used to come up to my window. I would feed it nuts, bread, Rice Krispies, whatever I had handy. Robin loved it. She named him Voltaire."

Sparrow gave an idle laugh. "No."

"Yeah. But I got my own back. At her place she used to put crumbs out for a thrush." Simon smiled at the memory. "I called it Candide."

Martin fell back onto the grass, mouth creasing with laughter.

"Daddy, daddy, daddy, do I like butter?" Cassie held a buttercup under her chin and the soft yellow glow was reflected there like a watery sun.

"You most certainly do, sweetie-pie, a whole packet at a time." Cassie giggled. She snuggled into his arms, her frail body melting into his hug.

"I'm tired, Daddy."

Simon looked at his watch. "It's time we were going, anyway." He picked up his glass. "Where's Ally?"

"I don't know."

Simon sat up. "Was she not with you?"

Cassie yawned and shook her head. "I haven't seen her for ages."

Simon dropped his daughter and got to his feet, scanning the Heath. "Where is she?" A flame of panic kindled within him when he couldn't see her. "Bloody hell, Cassie. You were supposed to be keeping an eye on her. Martin?"

Martin Sparrow was still lying on the grass, chuckling. Simon gave him a kick. "Hey, watch it," Martin said. "Nearly spilt the fizz."

"It's Alex. I can't see her." He called out for her. "Alex. Alex. Ally, where are you?" He tried to make it sound light-hearted, like he would have if it had been a game of hide-and-seek, but the words came out brittle and scared.

Sparrow sat up quickly, knocking his glass over. A stream of champagne flowed out into the grass. "She can't have gone far. When did you last see her?"

"I don't know. Cassie?"

"Ages ago. Where is she, Daddy?"

"I don't know. I don't bloody know. No, no, where is she?"

Martin put his hand on Simon's shoulder. "Take it easy, old chum. We'll find her. Don't panic."

"I'm not panicking." Simon spat out the words, then took them back. "Sorry."

"Hey, it's OK, don't worry. Look, what was she wearing?"

Simon tried to think; his mind had been wiped out. "I don't know, Martin, I can't remember. Look, I have to find her."

"It'll save time if we know what she was wearing. Dungarees, wasn't it?"

Martin's words triggered the memory of getting Alex dressed that morning, the annoying straps of the dungarees coming undone. "Yes, that's right. Blue and white striped dungarees and... a red pullover."

"No, Daddy, the blue one." Cassie tugged at Simon's sleeve. "The one with the boat on it, remember. She spilt milk on the red one and you got cross." Cassie giggled.

Simon was too worried to be irritated. "Yes, yes, that's right, the blue one." Alex was missing and he and Sparrow had been laughing and drinking. How long had she been gone? He had only known for two minutes and already his stomach was turning inside-out. And they'd just been sitting there drinking.

Martin took over. "We'll split up. You go with Cassie... no, on second thoughts I'll take Cassie and go down by the house, you take that stretch near the trees – she'll pick up on your voice more easily."

Simon nodded. His heart seemed as though it would burn through his chest. His face felt furnace hot.

"We'll meet back here in ten minutes."

What if she had been abducted? What was she feeling now, lost and alone? Simon fought to regain control of his emotions and ran towards the trees, shouting Alex's name, struggling to keep the fear from his voice. As Martin and Cassie went down the hill he heard their voices echoing his, "Alex, where are you? Alex. Ally."

Simon had stopped believing in God many years before, but still prayed that he would find her, find something that would indicate where she was. He looped through the sycamores at the edge of the expanse of bright grass – surely she would not have gone further into the woods? Already he had established a useless pattern: calling her name; stopping to listen, hoping that each sound in the undergrowth might be her tiny trainer, but hearing only the whispering heartbeat of the trees. He waited for the 'Daddy' that would save his world, but it refused to come and he started the desperate cycle once more.

The ten minutes ached. He was almost senseless with loss and trudged down the hill to meet with the others. Searching, calling as he went, looking in places he had already been, behind trees in case she was playing some dreadful game. Then the stark walls of Kenwood House were looming up at him, and there, coming out of its doors hand-in-hand, were Martin, Cassie and Alex.

Simon's vision blurred and he blinked to restore his focus. Alex, it was Alex. He ran to them, picking up his daughter and hugging and squeezing her, burying his face in her dungarees, inhaling her warm young smell. "Ally, Alex. Oh, thank God, Alex, you're all right."

She wrinkled her nose. "Daddy, you smell of wine," she said. "Yuk."

"Oh, darling, where have you been? I've been so worried. Oh, darling." The relief that had swamped him ebbed, revealing a guilty anger. "Why did you go running off? Why didn't you tell anyone where you were going? Where were you? Alex, you must never do that again, never."

She smiled. "I goed to see the pictures." Her eyes were wide blue pools of stating the obvious.

Martin melted the ice with his light-hearted tone. "She was just sitting on the floor, happy as a sandboy, gazing at all these Vermeers like she was the Times art critic. I almost expected her to give me a talk on Dutch aesthetics." He put his arm around the two of them. "Let's get you guys home, eh?" For once in his life Sparrow had become the sensible one.

Simon sighed, shaking his head. Never again. He held his daughter in his arms and thought he would never be able to let her go. He looked across at the man he still fell short of calling a friend. "Thanks, Martin. Thanks. I owe you one."

*   *   *

Sparrow blocked out the light coming from West Street, casting an even murkier darkness into Paycocke's entrance hall. He put the box down on the floor and gave Simon an unexpected bear hug.

"Simon Chance, you old son of a gun, how in the world are you?"

The schadenfreude Simon had been planning had rebounded upon him. Sparrow's hair had exposed an inch of his temples, sure, but his blond highlights were just as Simon remembered, as though the man had combed his hair with sunshine. He wore a royal blue cashmere jacket and a white open-necked shirt. Simon was sure he could smell money.

"Good to see you, Martin. It's been a long time."

"You've done well for yourself." Martin looked around the entrance hall and Simon had the sudden feeling of the light fading, almost imperceptibly, like someone holding a palm over a candle flame.

"Well, it's not ours..." Simon started to explain.

Sparrow grinned. "I know. National Trust and all that. You going to invite me in properly?"

Sparrow helped him unpack the shopping, examining each new item with excitement. "HP sauce. Rice pud. And Marmite.

Years since I had Marmite." He tossed the jar to Simon, who caught it on the second attempt. "Mainly because I always hated it, I have to say." He laughed. "It's been a long time."

"How was the States?"

"Big. Everything is big. From the buildings down to…" he picked up a packet of Wotsits, "…the Cheesy Doodles." He shook his head. "Boy, it's great to be home."

"You're back for good, then?" Simon was busy loading the fridge with the perishables.

"You know how it is. Whatever it's done wrong, England's home."

"You mean the income tax rates have fallen enough for you to come back?"

Sparrow thumped him on the shoulder; it hurt. "You old cynic."

Simon got to the point. "So, *Artes*, what's it all about?"

Martin opened a packet of biscuits. "Only place in the world you can get decent shortbread."

"Well, here and every duty-free shop on the planet. So, the book, Martin. *Artes, De Medicina*?"

"Hold your horses, good buddy, plenty of time. I heard a rumour you could finally get proper coffee in this country?"

Simon was beginning to lose patience; he had a hundred things he needed to do, or could invent doing, that would be more interesting than being party to Martin Sparrow's idea of building up the suspense. His sigh was a hint that even Sparrow couldn't miss. "Thing is, Simon, it's good to be back and all that, great to see you, and this *Artes* thing is really going to take us places…"

"But?"

"Well, I'm in a bit of a hole right now, funds in short supply…"

"Don't look at me. I'm broke."

"Perish the thought, old chum. I'm not looking for a loan, more… let's say, an investment."

"An investment?"

"And a place to stay." He put his hands on the warm range. "Nice Aga."

"Hold the bus, Martin, what do you mean? I thought the States was going to make you rich."

"Well, yes," Sparrow switched to a cowboy drawl, "it sure did, pardner." Then he shook his head. "It's staying rich that's the problem. It won't be for long, a few days, couple of weeks at most..."

"A couple of weeks?"

"Definitely less than a month."

"A month?" Simon shrieked.

"Absolutely gone by Christmas. Promise. OK, then, Easter." His snigger gave the game away. "Only having you on, Simon. A few days, that's all. It will give us a chance to work on *Artes* together."

Simon held his hand in front of his face. "I've got a lot on my plate right now."

Martin looked sideways at him. "Tell me you're not interested, and I'll leave."

Artes, the missing volumes, unseen for almost two thousand years; how could he not be interested? Simon bit his lip. Temptation flooded reason. "A few days."

"Yip, yip, coyote." Sparrow mimed throwing his hat into the air. "I'll go and fetch my stuff."

"It's special, Simon." Martin picked up the box and placed it on the Jacobean table in the dining-room. He took out a white paper parcel, opening it to reveal a ream of A4. "And this is part of it. Of course you remember there were eight *Artes* volumes?"

Simon nodded.

"I'd always wondered why the medicine book survived the Dark Ages and none of the others did. After all, it was an encyclopaedia, right? A *group* of works. And where do you keep the individual parts of an encyclopaedia? Together. It never made sense to me why the *De Medicina* volume surfaced in Bologna in fourteen something, but the others were lost. No, I didn't buy that." Simon winced and Martin apologised. "Sorry, force of habit. No, there was a reason why the others didn't show up – someone didn't want them to."

"Go on."

"You have to remember that this was a dodgy time in Bologna, nobility versus Papacy. And yeah, the Pope took it on away goals in the end, but at that time, the unveiling of a controversial manuscript could have made the whole pot boil over."

"Makes sense." Martin had not lost his ability to make the wild seem plausible.

Sparrow looked up at the fireplace, plaiting his thoughts into a cohesive string and admiring the linen fold panelling. He rubbed the end of his nose with his finger, then pointed at the wall. "You know your panelling is upside-down, don't you?"

Simon took a deep breath and gave Sparrow a grim smile. "Yes, thanks. Carry on."

"So, they allowed the medicine volume to come to light, but not the others."

"And you believe the rest is still in Bologna?"

Martin puffed out his cheeks and expelled the air in a 'who knows' gesture. "I don't think so. The city was very volatile in the second half of the fifteenth century. Whoever had it knew of its worth – he would have smuggled it out of the country."

"So what you're saying is it could be anywhere in the world?" Simon was beginning to smell the aroma of wild geese.

"Not quite. Let me jump to the twentieth century. OK, by now it's accepted that only *De Medicina* survives. One day this summer I happened to be in Philadelphia on business. Well, the Historical Library of the College of Physicians there is one of the only places in the world to have all four 15th-century editions of *De Medicina*, including the 1478 *editio princes...*"

Simon pursed his lips in professional appreciation. "Mmm, the first printed edition, nice."

"Yes, it's exquisite - beautifully decorated, sumptuous Florentine penmanship. Anyway, they allowed me to examine it, even to copy some of the pages." He tapped the box. Simon wondered what credentials he had shown the curator, or whether Sparrow had done it through charm alone. It was possible. "And what do you know, there were a number of famous autographs of former owners scribbled in there. 'This book belongs to...' sort of thing, just like a fifth form Greek primer." He laughed.

"And?"

"Giorgio Vespucci."

"Ah?"

"Uncle of Amerigo, the founder of MacDonald's and Coca-Cola. Uncle Sam's grandpa."

"So?"

"Giorgio was Amerigo's tutor, very learned man, taught Amerigo all he knew, brilliant scholar and intellectual… and collector of rare manuscripts."

Simon smiled at the detective work. "So you think he was the one, the one who hid the other volumes."

"Well, he's got the MO, and he lived in Florence, just down the road. And no alibi."

Simon's heart pulse louder with the excitement. "Wow." His mind flitted around the possibilities.

"And I think he passed on the knowledge in those other volumes to the young Amerigo, knowledge which had been lost for centuries. Things like," he rubbed his chin to prolong Simon's agony, "ooh, the location of America, for example."

"But Columbus…"

Sparrow held up his hand. "Amerigo became good mates with Chris, didn't he, when he was sent to Seville by the Medici boys? I think the knowledge in those missing volumes…" he paused, "…changed the world. And I also think it still could."

A key sounded in the lock and the massive front door swung open. Cassie stood in the doorway, in a black tracksuit and breathing heavily. Her hair was tied back into a severe chignon and she appeared sullen and out of sorts; but then again, that was her default look these days. Her eyebrows formed a brief V as she looked at Simon and Martin, then they relaxed with a guarded recognition, settling on Sparrow's holdall loitering by the staircase. The late afternoon sun angled in through the front door, reflecting on her necklace and casting the faintest of yellow glows on her chin, like the wan reflection of a buttercup.

"Hi," she said.

"Cass, you remember Martin? Martin Sparrow."

She nodded. "How could I forget?"

Chapter 15
Pillows

She had never expected to see Sparrow again, to look into those filthy eyes, so dilated with deceit. It made her problems with Roach insignificant and unworthy.

Cassie had hidden the Trypholine under her pillow, somewhere Dad was sure never to go. You could trust him to trust you, you could say that much. Each morning she counted the black and orange pills, the little tigers, moved them around on the table, making patterns and luxuriating in their number. The ritual of swallowing the tiger was wonderful, surged through her, except that it was accompanied by the flicker of panic that meant there was now one pill fewer, one pill nearer the end of the supply. The euphoria of a full pot was a slippery feeling.

She weighed herself at the same time every day, before breakfast, before the pill, monitoring her body fat and body water in an Excel spreadsheet. Who said that Alex was the organised one? The Trypholine box got a kiss for every hundred grams lost; how could they have banned it? Bloody nanny state. What could be wrong with wanting to look good? She moped around her room when there was a tenth of a percentage point gain in body fat. What had she done? What had she eaten? She skipped breakfast and searched her memory for the illicit ginger nut that might have caused the blip.

Cassie had forgotten to call Roach, forgotten to settle his bill. How was she to know 'end of the week' meant Friday? Roach was hardly a nine-to-five sort, was he? And she for sure hadn't expected to see him in Coggeshall that morning, inhaling the fresh clean air and taking in the views like a Sunday tripper.

"Cass, babes. What's up?" In the daylight Roach's black leather jacket looked rough and faded, like his face. Darkness suited him better. He scratched two day old bristle.

Cassie had been for a run and was out of breath. "Hi, Roach."

"You didn't call me." Roach dredged up an apology of a smile. "I was worried."

"No problem." She exhaled the words, hoping this pain was doing some good.

"I like to keep in touch, know what I mean?" He looked around at the gaggle of listed buildings fronting onto Market Hill. "Nice place."

"You've never been here before?"

"Yeah, sure. A while ago, mind. I don't get out this way much these days." His eyes laboured to being half-open. "But I like to make a special effort. For you."

"Thanks." He didn't mean it, she could tell he didn't mean it, but the humour under his expression told her that he knew she didn't believe him. And that meant that he did mean it. Why else was he here?

"So you didn't call?" he said, smiling.

"I've been busy."

Roach nodded. "Yeah, busy, busy, busy. World's a busy place, isn't it? No time to relax. You need to relax, Cass, chill a bit." He pointed at his boots. "Me, I like to walk."

"You walked from Colchester? That's miles."

"S'good. Gives you time to think. You should try it, come along sometime."

Cassie looked Roach up and down. "And there's me thinking you abused your body."

Roach looked at her from the side. "Pots and kettles, babes. Pots and kettles. How's the Tryph?"

"OK." Cassie nodded.

"Got some cash for me? I might take the bus back home."

"Not on me, I've been out for a run." She gestured at her tracksuit.

"I can see, babes, I can see. Looking good on it." Roach shrugged, his jacket creaking. "Anyway, it's not important, Cass. Whenever you've got it."

"I'll go home now if you like, Dad will…"

"Yeah, I'd like to meet your Dad. He sounds cool."

"Believe me, he is the antithesis of cool."

Roach laughed. "The anti-freeze of cool. Yeah, like it."

"You don't want to meet my Dad, Roach."

His eyes narrowed. "In case I tell him what a naughty girl you've been?"

She tried to calm down, to stop Roach lifting the lid on her fragile mood. "It's not a big deal."

"Sure, whatever you say. So he knows about the Tryph?"

Cassie bit her lip. "No, of course not. But it's nothing, why would I mention it? It's an appetite suppressant, Roach. That's all. It's nothing."

"It's a drug, babes. So drugs are nothing. I'll go along with that. Look, I'd best be off, unless you fancy walking back with me. We could find a haystack on the way?"

She shook her head. "Another time. I'll get the money, Roach, don't worry."

He laughed. "I don't, Cass. I don't worry." He rubbed his bristle again, then reached into a jacket pocket and brought out a box of Trypholine. "Brought you a pressie. Since I was coming anyway."

Cassie snatched at it and hissed at him. "Roach, what are you doing? Anyone can see."

"But it's nothing, Cass," he grinned.

She snatched the pills from him and thrust the box into her tracksuit pocket. It bulged awkwardly against her thigh, advertising its presence. She grappled for her composure. "Thanks. Thanks, Roach."

"S'OK, babes. Any time."

"I can't pay you right now."

"No worries. You can owe me. I'll see you soon." He looked around him. "Yeah, nice place." He put his hand behind Cassie's neck and drew her face towards him. "You smell good, Cass." He kissed her, his rough stubble scratching her so that she wanted to pull away. He tasted of Extra Strong Mints and subliminal sausages. "Mmm," he said. "That's *amore*." She felt his strong wiry arms envelope her, holding her to him for a small second, then the pressure was gone just when she wanted it to linger. "Look after yourself, babes. Don't do anything I'd do." He strode up the hill without looking back.

Cassie stood confounded in the doorway to Paycocke's. Sparrow. Martin Sparrow was with her father, both of them smiling. He made Simon look shabby, his faded olive cords drifting without shape over scuffed brown oxfords. Sparrow was in good shape, too, whereas the only place Dad would see 40 again was on his waist measurement. Still, she was tugged by a twitching loyalty to her father. What was Sparrow doing in Coggeshall? She hadn't seen him for so many years, not since she was a kid, eons ago. Her hand reached down to hide the bulge of the Trypholine box in her tracksuit trousers. Sparrow. The wanker. So Sparrow was back. She felt she might lose her breakfast, felt the nausea of emptiness tightening her stomach. What was he doing here?

"Hi," she said.

Her father looked up from the table where they had spread out some papers, his sad eyes seeming to strain in the poor light of the hall. "Cass, you remember Martin? Martin Sparrow."

The blond man smiled. It was a nasty flirting grin, the one that she remembered so well.

She nodded. "How could I forget?"

"Boy, have you grown," Sparrow said, the smile never leaving his tanned face. His eyes seemed to swallow her and she felt overwhelmed by a sudden heat. "You must have been eight or nine. Now look at you." And he did look at her, couldn't take his eyes off her. She just hoped she was too old for him. But then, it had never been Cassie he had preferred. "How's Alex?" he said. "I can't wait to see her."

She bet he couldn't.

*　　　*　　　*

He had been hanging around the house again. All those months, before he went away to America, when she had hoped he was gone forever, he had been in and out of their home. She could never understand why Dad had put up with him for so long, but then he had never seen the way Sparrow looked at Alex, always watching her, always creating opportunities to hold her hand or to play 'Round and Round the Garden', to touch her soft skin and to 'tickle her under there'.

It all came to a head that day on the Heath, the day Alex got lost. Dad went into his usual bull-in-a-china-shop routine the moment something went wrong, blaming everyone but himself for Ally going missing. At least you could say something for Sparrow; he got his act together that day.

They had walked home, her hand tucked into Daddy's. He was carrying Alex, slumped across his shoulders in a trusting heap, fast asleep. Cassie could almost feel the guilt coming from Daddy. He knew it was his fault, whatever he liked to pretend. Grown-ups didn't always know best. His breath was sour from the wine he and Martin had been drinking and Cassie bet he wished Mummy wasn't home yet.

Every now and then his hand trembled, as though he were imagining how it might have turned out. Cassie was never worried, even though Mummy was always telling her not to speak to strangers in the park. 'There are lots of bad men about.' Since Mummy and Daddy never worried about Martin, who was just about the worst man she had ever known, what was there to be worried about?

Martin followed them into the house. "I'll make a pot of tea," he said.

Alex was still asleep; it was time for her afternoon nap. Daddy slumped back in the old flowery sofa and kicked his shoes off, those big brown leather ones with the holes in, the ones that Cassie thought were like boats. She wanted to sail them in the pond and wondered if Daddy would get angry.

Martin ("don't call me 'Uncle Martin', that makes me sound so old," he said, twinkling those spangly eyes of his) came in with two mugs of tea. He didn't bring one for Cassie, but looked at Ally asleep. "Aah," he said. "What a sweetheart. Shall I pop her upstairs?"

Cassie's father nodded. "Cheers, Martin. I'm wiped out."

"Take it easy, old chum. I'll see to Alex."

He took Alex in his big brown arms with their fleece of

golden hairs and climbed the stairs, whispering to her little sister. "Who's a lovely girl, then? Who does Martin love?" He was so engrossed that he didn't hear the padding of footsteps on the thick navy carpet as Cassie followed him up.

She heard Alex's whimper as he put her onto her bunk. "Ssh," he whispered. "Let's take these clothes off, eh, my little sweetling?"

Cassie inched closer, her steps muffled by the deep shag, and melted into the wall. Her heart beat like a tambourine and her face felt hot. She pulled her sweater tight to her body, as if it were her Martin was undressing. Part of her wondered what he was doing, but part of her already knew. She willed Alex to wake up or to cry so that everything could be normal again.

"One armie, two armie, off we go. Now the trousers. What a sleepy little one." Cassie closed her eyes and clenched her fists. "Let's have a good look at you." Alex gave a dreamy murmur. "I'm going to kiss you all over, you lovely little bunny."

Cassie felt glued to the wall outside Ally's bedroom. The bravest thing she had ever done was to have an injection in her mouth when she had a tooth out. Well, the dentist said she was brave, but she hadn't felt like it. She had been scared, so frightened of the horrible needle coming down out of the air like a mean old hawk. She wasn't brave. The dentist said it wouldn't hurt, but it did, and she had been so scared, too scared even to cry. People lied when they said it wouldn't hurt. Grown-ups always thought it was OK to lie to children. She heard the kisses, each one like a can of Coke opening, and she stepped into the doorway, her chin trembling. No, she didn't feel brave at all.

Martin was on his knees at the edge of the bed, his face next to Alex's naked body. He had his lips on her tummy-button and looked as though he were blowing her up like a balloon. His back was to Cassie so he didn't see her at first, but then he stopped kissing Alex, just stopped and raised his head, a bit like he was a lion sniffing the air for prey. He turned around and Cassie wanted to scream, to run, to be anything but brave, but she was locked in her position, no more able to scream than one of her teddies. Martin sprang over to Cassie, grabbing her by the shoulders. The physical contact broke her paralysis and she started to yell. He clamped a big brown hand over her mouth; it was damp and smelt of grass and earth, but also of Ally, her delicate perfume shining through.

Martin hissed at her through clenched teeth, white and square like piano keys. "What are you doing? Why are you watching? What did you see? You brat. I'll…"

She could see that he badly wanted to shout at her, badly wanted to shake her to bits, but didn't dare. Daddy was downstairs. Then a light slowly turned on in his eyes, like an old television set coming to life, and he smiled. "Cassie." He stroked her hair and smiled again, although his breath was coming out in sharp, rancid bursts that made her want to turn her face away. The softness in his voice was a mirage. "Cassie, hey." She stared at him, did not dare to drop her gaze.

He assumed a good humour. "We were only playing, Alex and I." But there was a crack in his words, a chink through which Cassie could see what he was really up to. "Just playing. Don't shout, you'll wake her up." He lifted his hand from her mouth and her chin felt cool again. Martin's grin didn't waver, but he swallowed hard. His Adam's apple bobbed up and down.

"It's all right, Cassie. There's nothing to worry about. It was just a game, a funny little game that we play sometimes. You like games too, don't you?"

Cassie looked at him.

"Hey, don't look so worried. It's only a bit of fun. There's no need to tell Mummy and Daddy, is there?" Martin was fighting to hold the splinter in his voice. "We're buddies, aren't we, Cassie, hey?" He gave her a big wink and a punch on the shoulder. "No need to mention anything to Mummy and Daddy, is there? It was just a game."

Cassie felt small, like Alice, as though the world were growing huge around her and leaving her behind. She wanted her Mummy, wanted to be held warm and snug and tight. Where was Mummy?

"I'm going to America soon," Martin said. "Shall I bring you back a present? A cowboy hat? Would you like that? Or a baseball?" She didn't know what a baseball was; he was confusing her. "Well, that's all sorted, eh? Let's tuck Ally up for her nap and then we'll go downstairs and see Daddy. All sorted out, and I'll bring you something brilliant back from America. Just a funny old game."

Cassie pulled the quilt up around Alex's perfect chin and kissed her on the forehead, like she had seen Mummy do. She followed Martin down the stairs. She wanted to say something, but she didn't know what she could say, and who would Daddy believe, anyway?

Martin went to the States several days afterwards without saying goodbye. A few weeks later they got a postcard of the Paul Revere house in Boston, 'Hi there, pardners, sure is mighty fine here in the U S of A! Love, Martin.'

"Did you bring me a baseball?" Cassie said.

The October half-light could not hide the recognition in Sparrow's eyes. He saw that she remembered and his lips disappeared. She gave what she hoped was a welcoming nod.

Simon invaded the silence. "Martin's going to be staying for a few days, we have a… we're working on a project together."

Cassie took a deep breath. Staying for a few days? Was it going to start all over again? Sparrow winked at her and she saw where the sun had creased his eyes.

"I need to learn some lines," she said.

"Cass, wait a sec," Simon called as she ran up the stairs.

"I'll speak to you later." She slammed the door to her room and threw herself on her bed. She felt the box of Trypholine dig into her thigh, tore it from her pocket and hurled it at the wall. What was the use?

Chapter 16
The Entrance Hall

I ran into the garden, my scarf trailing like bunting, but Conrad Noel had already left. I was mortified. Gussie raised an eyebrow at my return, which meant that he was not best amused, and I was in the doghouse for the remainder of the evening. I sat alone in my tiny room as the sun went down, fiddling with Edward's key and wondering what on earth it could mean. I put it under my pillow and lay sandwiched between the cool, crisp sheets, waiting for sleep to come, and wondering whether it would indeed be sleep or the terrible shrieks of Paycocke's spirits. I was almost disappointed to awaken the next morning rested and refreshed.

Conrad's card arrived to thank us for the hospitality. It spared me from an icy breakfast as it invited us to be his guests at Thaxted at the coming weekend, thus giving me an early opportunity to make amends for my rude departure.

Gussie was greatly exhausted from the previous afternoon, and his spirits were low. He turned the card over and over. "Decent of Noel, of course," he said, "but I am feeling so dreadfully tired at the moment and my arm gives me more pain than ever. I am not sure I am up to driving, I should be afraid of causing an accident..."

"Then I shall drive," said Iso, lining up her knife and fork like soldiers on her plate and rolling up her napkin.

I must have looked startled, for Gussie laughed at my expression and said, "Your mother is a most accomplished driver. Indeed she drove lorries in the War. I shouldn't be surprised if she could manage one of those confounded Big Willies, too." I had a sudden bizarre image of my mother piloting a tank across the fields to Thaxted, her golden hair trailing in the wind. I laughed too and we were on good terms once more.

My father waved Conrad's note in my direction. "Ah, Imogen, this reminds me. In your absence the dear Reverend asked me to give you a message - he would be much obliged if you could find for him the carver's self-portrait at Paycocke's. Quite what he means I have no idea. He said it came to mind when he saw you speak to the young lad beside the fence yesterday afternoon. Conrad knew the boy from the restoration of the house. Carver's self-portrait? Perhaps the notion holds some significance for you?"

I shook my head. "I have not the slightest inkling. Self-portrait?" Conrad could be so infuriating sometimes. He was fond of cryptic little puzzles and even fonder of teasing me on the path to their resolution. "Could it be connected to one of the carvers of Paycocke's - perhaps he means a photograph?"

"We shall have to wait until Sunday."

Maddening, maddening Conrad.

And maddening, maddening Edward, too. I still had his key, tucked under my pillow. It was the first thing I saw when I woke up, cold and shiny, with its heart-shaped cut-out hinting at lovers' trysts or clandestine rendezvous. As I sat on my bed brushing my hair, I was overtaken by the shocking feeling that perhaps that was the nature of his intent too, passing the key to me as some kind of love token. My cheeks burned at the very thought, and I determined to disabuse him of the notion the next time I saw him. Dear sweet Edward, with his stumbling words and too-earnest smile, it could not possibly be so.

The days ticked by, oh, so slowly. Edward had seemed so urgent when I left him, as though his news could not wait to such a degree that he needed to blurt it out to me as I ran back to Paycocke's. And yet I had heard nothing from him. I did not know where he lived, or I should have knocked on his door with a bold request that he should divulge everything. What a queer fish he was. I passed the time pleasantly enough, sitting in the garden drawing the beautiful rear elevation of Paycocke's and inking in the wisteria with pale lilac. How the wisteria lived up to its name in those dragging days. It dripped down the white walls in forlorn profusion, as though its very existence were the most melancholy thing on earth, and indeed it transferred some of its mood to me. I became restless and impatient.

Nor could I find any clue as to Conrad's 'self-portrait', although I searched the whole house, even the cavernous loft, which was consumed by the dust of centuries. It seemed that I was condemned to wait. Then I had a sparkling piece of luck. An acquaintance of Iso's had passed to her a recent copy of the *Country Life* magazine, and, what do you know, inside there was written an article on the subject of Paycocke's House.

How strange it felt, to be so famous and to have our extraordinary house leap from the pages of a magazine. It was not at all like Gussie's fame, for he was part of the furniture and not at all grand, just my darling, lovable father. The article was much taken with the restoration of Paycocke's and went into great detail about Conrad's contribution in conjunction with the estimable Buxton. I laughed to have such splendid ammunition with which to tease the Reverend at the weekend, for he emerged from the pages of *Country Life* with no little credit. Much of the magazine's story I already knew, but it was so romantic to see it in print: how John Paycocke had given the house to his son Thomas and his wife Margaret on their wedding day; how he had had their initials T. P. and M. P. carved on the rafters; how Margaret had died childless. How terribly tragic it was that such sadness should be visited on a place of such astounding beauty.

I went into the entrance hall and looked up at the ceiling to see the carved letters once more. They might have been hewn yesterday they were so fresh. Dear Thomas, dear Margaret. I examined the other carvings: the merchant's mark which looked much like a clover leaf; the flowing vines; and the tiny roses dotting the perfectly formed leaves. Truly exquisite.

I almost missed it, my gaze flitting from flower to flower, but there, exactly the size of an acorn and nestled in amongst the roses with the greatest of discretion, was a tiny carved head. I stood on a chair for a closer look. He had a long, sad face with large lips and eyes that looked like marbles bulging out of his head. He appeared altogether glum and I hoped that he had not been so, for he had produced the most blissful work. I, however, was now far from glum, as I had solved the great Conrad's puzzle and so could now rib him on two counts. Hurrah. What a lark it would be.

The tapping nearly made me fall off the chair, so engrossed was I. It came from the window looking out over West Street and had an urgent, pressing nature to it. It sounded just like a pebble or a coin being rapped on the glass, as though someone badly needed to attract my attention.

"Wait a minute," I called. It must be Edward. I picked up my skirt to stop it catching on the back of the chair as I climbed down. I must have wasted precious seconds doing so, for when I went over to the window, the tapping had ceased and there was no one there. I looked out of the oriel window up and down West Street. There was no one to be seen; perhaps I had imagined it. I shook my head and went back to my chair, placing it underneath the table once more. Picking up the copy of *Country Life*, I opened the door to the garden. What fun I would have with Conrad.

The tapping started again and I swivelled to the window. Again it stopped. "Hello?" I said. Once more there was no one there. My heart began to beat faster. Suppose it were the ghost, the same ghost that had wailed below my room. Perhaps it was trying to send me a message. How utterly thrilling it was. I crept to the front door and opened it slowly. It creaked as though it belonged in an Edgar Allan Poe story, sending shivers through me. I stepped silently into the street and there was Edward, with a small canvas knapsack on his back, reaching for the knocker.

"Oh, it's you." I was disappointed not to be confronting an émigré from the spirit world.

My sense of disappointment mirrored in his face, which dropped in a fraction of a second. "Hello," he said. His shyness seemed to have taken over again and the tops of his ears were blooming roses. He thrust his hands into his pockets as though he was not quite sure what he should do with them, then took them out again and folded his arms.

"I am sorry, Edward. I didn't mean that. I just thought the tapping was a ghost." I gave him a bright smile and he seemed to recover.

"What tapping?" he said.

"The tapping at the glass." I pointed at the sedate oriel

window. "When you were tapping there, a minute ago. I thought it was something else."

"But I weren't tapping," he said, confusion dulling those brilliant green eyes and swamping them with hurt that I should have imagined him so forward.

I led him to the window. "But look. There are your fingerprints." There was a small arc of finger marks on the panes.

Edward shook his head. "Not me. I never went near it."

The shiver rippled through me again. "Well…"

"I promise. Cross my heart and hope to die." He was so sincere, I was convinced he was telling the truth. It must have been the neighbours' children, or… I shuddered to think.

"That won't be necessary, silly." I thumped him on the shoulder and his face caught fire again. "I've been wanting to see you anyway," I said. "Where on earth have you been these past few days?"

"Working," he said, incredulous and holding his hands up for me to see. "I was working. I told you I'd come back." He was pained that I should have doubted him.

"Yes," I said. "Now, I want you to tell me everything."

Edward looked up at the forbidding timber-framed frontage of Paycocke's, its jettied upper storey looming out into the street as though it might reach down and take him prisoner. "Not here. Will you take a walk with me? We can go up through Vicarage Fields. Nice up there. Nice and open."

"Righty-ho," I said. "I'm game."

"Do you have the key?"

I fetched the key and placed it solemnly in his palm. "Let's go," I said.

Coggeshall is situated in a bowl, so that whichever way you walk out of the village you are going up a hill. We looped through the fields and trees to the outskirts, and settled on a slope from where we could see everything spread out before us like on one of those Ordnance Survey maps, with its roads and woods and churches and houses, each in its proper position. Edward opened his knapsack and took out a small tartan rug. He spread it out on the baked ground and bade me sit down. He himself squatted on the grass close by and ferreted around in his bag, pulling out a black tin box, which he placed ceremoniously on the ground between us.

"This is all very intriguing," I said, resting my chin on my hand.

"You hungry?"

I smiled and shook my head.

He held up an impossibly green apple. "Do you mind if I...?"

"Not at all."

He polished the fruit on his shirt sleeve and gave it a large crunch. He was being so jolly infuriating that I reached over, grabbed his apple and took a bite out of it myself. He laughed, on more solid ground up here on the hill. Paycocke's seemed to unnerve him. Even so, there was something else: he was fidgeting with nerves and would not meet my eye.

"Can I show you my box? There's something I'd like you to see." He tapped the tin box with the heart-shaped key.

"Yes, but I want you to tell me about Paycocke's first. I have been dying to know and I simply cannot wait any longer."

"Well, can I tell you something first?"

I pouted. "If you must..."

"See that over there?" He pointed across the fields to where the ruins of a long low building were silhouetted like a skeleton against the blue sky. I shielded my eyes with a hand. I could not say whether it was painted black or overgrown with ivy. "J. K. King's seed warehouse, that is. It burnt down a few years ago. The black you can see is charred timbers. If you go closer you can still smell the fire."

"What happened?"

"Nobody knows. Thing is, J. K. was the biggest seed grower in England at one time. But family, they can be the best people in the world and the worst in the world. You just never know how it will turn out." He looked into the distance as though he were thinking of someone specific, someone other than one of the esteemed Kings. "Well, old J. K. fell out with his grandson, and the boy swore he would take over the old man one day and ruin him.

He opened up his own business, E. W. King's Seeds, right here in town, and they've been fighting each other ever since. Their men won't even drink in the same pub." Edward had finished his apple and was picking at long blades of grass. "I don't believe it, mind, don't reckon it's true, but there's some say as how it was E. W.'s men torched that warehouse."

"How dreadful, but what does it mean?"

"Family," he said. "It shows how bad family can be to each other. Blood don't mean nothing. Anything." He plaited the blades of grass together, but they sprang apart the moment he let go of them. "The Paycockes were the same."

I adjusted my position. The ground was beginning to feel hard and lumpy beneath the woollen rug. "What happened to the Paycockes?"

"Something bad, I know it; I feel it. There's something inside that house wants to get out. It's trapped. Billy knew it, too."

"Billy?"

"Billy Howes, sort of an uncle, I suppose you might say. He was Ernest Beckwith's apprentice, and he did a lot of work on the Paycocke's restoration. Well, at first he did, anyway."

"What do you mean?" I stared at Edward but he would not, or could not make eye contact with me.

"He left halfway through, right out of the blue. One day he was working in the panelled room, in the evening, it was, wanted to finish a job on the fireplace before it got dark. He was rummaging in his tool bag and heard a sound behind him, like wind whistling through a crack in a window. He thought nothing of it; houses like Paycocke's have more draughts than the Forth Bridge.

"Anyway, he took up a chisel, and started to tidy up a bit of carving. There's a name on the fireplace, the name of 'Paycocke' that Billy was working on. Well, no sooner did the tool touch his name than it flew out of his hand across the room, and buried itself in one of the panels opposite. There was no one else there, but he heard footsteps, like they were in the room, like someone was walking on the panels.

"Well, I would have been out of there like a bullet, but Billy goes to get his chisel back, right expensive they are, and on turning back to the fireplace to get his tool bag, he sees a child come out of the panelling, and he can see through him, right through to the panelling on the other side, and the child is holding out his hand, like he wants Billy to come inside the panels with him."

Edward was shaking. I held his hand, cold despite the heat of the afternoon.

"How do you know all this?"

"He told me himself. I was only little. Lord, and I didn't sleep properly for weeks after. He told me never to go inside Paycocke's House. That Thomas Paycocke had done something evil, and that the house was possessed. He told me that, then he was gone the next day. He took his tools and left without even saying goodbye. And he's not been seen in Coggeshall since." Edward put his head in his hands, letting out huge gasps like a steam engine. "No one else knows. No one. Until now."

He turned away from me, but his shoulders were quivering.

"Oh, Edward." I pulled him towards me and held him, ruffling his hair. It smelt of fresh sawdust.

"I... I had to tell you, Imogen...because I want... I want you to be safe." He looked up at me, his eyes red and pained.

"I am safe, Edward, you mustn't worry. Oh, dear, dear Edward."

He blushed. "I'm sorry."

"No need to be sorry. It is done. It is out now. Your worries are over."

Edward's tears subsided but he sighed. "I wish they were." He relaxed, safe in my arms. So Paycocke's was haunted after all. How positively ripping. It was like something from *The Detective Magazine* and I shivered with excitement. It had not been my imagination after all. I couldn't wait to get back home to check the panelling and I started to formulate a plan: I would wait until everyone had gone out, and then I would entice the ghost out. How fearfully exciting it was, to have our very own spiritual resident. I so hoped he would be friendly. Or perhaps it was a girl; I had not thought of that. A gyroscope of possibilities whirled inside my head.

I felt Edward's fingers brush against my linen sleeve and gently made him sit up.

"I'm sorry, I didn't mean…."

"Do stop apologising, Edward."

"Sorry." He smiled.

"That's better. You should smile more often."

"If it makes you happy," he said. He looked up at me and his eyes were bright, but the smile was only pasted on his face, as though it were a veneer on a deeper sadness. "There's something else."

"Yes?"

He turned his attention to the small black tin box, its clasp held securely with a padlock, small but sturdy-looking, with the strange word 'Dalab' embossed on its shiny silver front.

He put the heart-shaped key in the lock. It sprang open at once and he placed the padlock on the rug. He paused as if it were Pandora's Box and looked at me, deliberating whether he could truly trust me. He lifted the lid. There was a strange collection of objects inside: a cat's eye marble; the skull of a small animal; an old rusty horseshoe; and other things I did not recognise. He tipped them all out onto the grass and laughed, not with happiness, but with a profound resentment.

"What is it, Edward?"

"Why?"

"Why?" I was confused.

"Why did I ever save any of this? All this. It… it's just rubbish." He gestured at the contents of the box. "There's no point. Nothing matters."

"But what's wrong? Please, Edward, you're scaring me." I took his hand and it seemed to lift him.

"You save all these things, and what for? You keep your life in a box, instead of living it. What's the use?" He picked up each item in turn and hurled it into the trees. "I used to think those things were important. I saved them in this box, my treasure chest, it was, but there comes a time when things lose their meaning. There's only one treasure and I can't save it."

I was baffled; surely he did not mean me? "But I will be safe, Edward. No ghost frightens me."

He smiled at my misunderstanding, shaking his head. "No, it's not that. Not just that." He delved into a pocket of the knapsack and took out a parcel small enough to make an island in his palm. "Mammy gave me this today." He took a breath as deep as the ocean and unwrapped the tissue paper to reveal a brooch in the shape of a golden hand holding a ruby heart. He looked at the brooch and turned it over in his delicate fingers, before passing it to me.

"It's beautiful, Edward."

"It was my grandmother's. It gets passed down through the family. She gave it to my mammy on her wedding day, said it would mean she was always safe and loved."

The brooch was cold in my hand and its red heart pulsed in the sun. "But why…"

"…did she give it to me?" He swallowed and closed his eyes. "She's dying, Imogen. She'll never see her own grand-daughter now."

"Oh, Edward, I'm so sorry." I did not know what to say. What can one offer but warmth and compassion? Empathy was impossible. I tried to peek through the curtains of my emotions and imagine how I would feel were I threatened with the loss of Iso or Gussie. I could not contemplate it; the thought was too horrid.

"Will you take it?"

"Edward?" I was shocked and tried to pass the brooch back to him.

He clasped his hands together and looked at the brooch, then at me, his bright eyes clouding with sadness. "Will you take it? Just for now. If I keep it, you see, it means that I accept she's going to… she won't live. It's the sugar sickness."

I held my hand to my mouth. Edward closed his eyes to shut out tears.

"Take it, just for a while. Keep it safe." He wrapped the brooch back in its tissue paper and put it in the box.

I nodded. "Of course."

"I don't want it," he said. "I don't want her to die. I'm no King."

Chapter 17
Medicine

"So that's it." Cassie folded her arms and looked at Simon, daring him.

"Cassie, do you know what you're saying?"

"Dad, I wouldn't make this up. I couldn't." Her lips drew together.

They sat on Cassie's bed. The sheets needed changing; they were creased up into ridges, giving away his daughter's restless nights.

He shook his head. "I can't believe it. You were, what, only eight, it can't be… you must be wrong. What you saw…" He plucked at the rippled sheet. It smelt sour and old, uncared for.

Cassie's eyes hunted him down. "I know what I saw, Dad. He's sick. Sparrow is sick and he's after Alex again."

"No, I just don't believe it. We're working on something together, that's all, that's why he's here. He needs my help…"

"He needs your daughter."

Simon placed his palm on her wrist. "No. There has to be a reasonable explanation."

Cassie broke free of her father's hand and stood up. "There is – he's a cradle-snatcher. A sick pervert."

Simon looked down at his hands and worked some dirt out from under his fingernails. "OK, I'll keep an eye on him."

"Oh, come on, Dad." Her voice was getting louder.

"Ssh, he's only downstairs."

"I don't care. I know what he did and he knows I know. Did you see the way he looked at me?"

"We can't just jump to conclusions…"

"Will you jump off your fucking fence for a minute, Dad?"

"Cassie, please…"

She pointed a finger at him, challenging him to defy her. "He'll be after her again, you watch."

Simon tried to placate her. *What was she up to?* First there was the business with the printer, then the lies about the audition. *Why she was being so secretive?* "I'll watch him. Don't worry, Cass. If anything happens, I'll be the one to tackle him. OK?"

Cassie took a deep breath through clamped teeth.

Simon put his hand out to her, inviting her to sit down beside him. He put an arm around her shoulder, the very act reminding him that he had not done so for years. "I'll handle it."

"Don't wait too long." Her voice hummed with intensity.

Simon smoothed out the hills and valleys of Cassie's sheets. "Are you all right, Cassie?"

"Yeah, why shouldn't I be?"

"I just wondered. Are you sleeping OK?"

Cassie snorted.

"Is it this thing with Mom?" he said.

Her reply was too quick. "Yeah, that's it. I *am* worried, Dad. Worried for you." She sighed. "First Mom, then Sparrow and now all this stuff with the house. I've been meaning to ask you about that. Everything's been a bit freaky. It must be tough for you."

Simon shrugged, trying to compensate for the suspicion he felt. Her concern felt wrong, out of character, and he tried to read between the lines. "Yeah. It is. It's like being widowed, except almost worse, because there's no finite end. She's still there, her life going on without me, and I feel like the dead one."

Cassie put her hand on his knee. "It'll take time, Dad."

"What's this?" Simon was plumping up the pillows and had found the box of Trypholine.

Cassie took it from him as though she hadn't known it was there. "Oh, nothing." She held it in both hands, so he couldn't read the label. Tryn-, or Tryp- something.

"What do you mean, nothing?"

"Just some stuff." A rose blush appeared on her cheeks.

"What is it, Cassie?"

"Oh, health pills, Dad, vitamins, that sort of stuff."

"Doesn't look like vitamins to me." He tried to peer through her fingers at the box, but couldn't decipher anything. "Can I have a look?"

"It's nothing, Dad. Girls' stuff. It wouldn't mean anything to you. It's something Mom got me into, you know what a health freak she is." Cassie rattled the box and laughed.

"Yeah." He smiled. The bathroom cabinet was still full of the chemical compounds that Robin used to tank up with every day. He wondered how she was managing without them.

"It's not a problem, Dad." Cassie shrugged, her smile too fixed. *What was going on?* Maybe Alex knew. He forced himself to drop it for now. She was almost twenty – he had no cross-examination rights.

"Hey, Simon, what's happening, old chum?" Sparrow's voice climbed the stairs.

"Go, Dad. I don't want him in here."

Simon stood up. The bed still looked a mess. "OK."

"And keep your eye on him."

"Yeah. I will."

"Thought you'd packed up and left." Martin had spread out the title pages of *De Medicina* over the Jacobean table and had fetched the atlas from the sitting-room bookshelves. It lay open at Italy.

"Bit optimistic, aren't you?"

Martin looked at him out of the corner of his eye. "That's me. Half-full."

"So?"

"Now, where were we?" Martin said. "Yes, so Uncle Giorgio is a monk and he doesn't get out much, but Amerigo, well, he's here, there and everywhere, loading up the Air Miles."

"So you think he smuggled the manuscripts out?"

Martin nodded. "The Vespuccis were first and foremost businessmen and Amerigo's dad wanted him to join the family firm. Would probably turn in his grave to see what the boy's spawned today. Amerigo compromised, took a Business Studies 'A' Level or something, and started handling the family's finances. He went to Spain around 1480 and was headhunted by the Medici clan, working for them for most of the rest of his life. Now, if these manuscripts were as controversial as I think, he wouldn't have taken the risk of offending the Medici boys."

Simon huffed. "Come on, Martin, this is all speculation."

Martin Sparrow was only warming up and held up his hand to ward off Simon's negativity. "Intelligent speculation, though. Luckily for us, Amerigo proved to be a bit of a pen pal. I tracked down a letter from him to his dad in 1476. There's a lot of guff in there about his studies and how much he respects his Uncle Giorgio and how he's the most learned man in the world, blah, blah, blah. But he talks about Uncle G's manuscript collection and you can tell by his phrasing, reading between the lines, that he knows about the hidden *Artes* books."

Simon folded his arms. "I didn't realise you had such a spectacular knowledge of Renaissance Italian."

Sparrow grinned. "Latin, old mate. Public school education had to come in handy one day. Even more, I think the plan was already in motion. And by 1478, Amerigo was living in Paris, working for the ambassador. So, if I'm right, I think the volumes were smuggled out sometime between October 1476 and 1478."

"Phew. It's a big 'if'."

Sparrow rocked his hand from side to side as if to challenge Simon's scepticism. "A medium-sized 'if', and it all falls into place, Simon. My guess is the plot was hatched late 1477. They wouldn't have wanted to waste any time."

"So what was Amerigo up to that year?"

"I don't know. Travelling, learning, disposing of priceless manuscripts, I don't know. That is as much as I have. Well, that and a hunch."

"Yes?"

"Well, 1477 – think about it, you're the bookworm."

Simon didn't have time to think about it. The telephone rang, Vivaldi's autumn leaves bouncing around the ground floor.

"Paycocke's, this is Simon."

"Dad, where are you?"

"Alex?" Then Simon remembered. "Bloody hell, sorry, Alex."

"You were supposed to be here half an hour ago."

"Oh, no. I'm sorry, Al, I'll be there in fifteen minutes."

Martin peered around the door to Simon's study. "Problems?

"Alex – she had a hockey game this afternoon; I promised to pick her up."

Sparrow wagged a finger. "Kids today."

"What would you know about it?" Simon realised what he had said and flinched. "Be back in a bit."

"Can I come?"

Simon's antennae waggled and he hoped he gave the illusion that he didn't care. "No, it's OK. I'll just whizz off." *Easy-going, nonchalant – see how easy it is to lie?* "Make yourself at home." He needed to speak to Alex first.

*   *   *

Simon pulled the Citroen into the school playground and saw the two girls standing beside their bags over by the science block. As he drove across the tarmac he tried to see Alex as Sparrow might, as if it were for the first time, and not as a father. She was slim and athletic, and, yes, attractive, the bright streaks in her hair pointing at a mischievous and anarchic nature. Maybe that was why he liked her so much, and maybe why Robin had always favoured Cassie.

"Daaad, you made it," she shouted. She ran across and gave him a hug.

"How did you get on?"

"3-0."

"You score?"

"No, but Julia did." She nodded to her friend. "Penalty flick. Have you met my Dad?"

Julia gave Simon a shy smile that revealed the shiny scaffolding of a brace. "Hi."

Simon waved a hand in Julia's general direction, just ambiguous enough that it might be confused with a general invitation to shake hands. "Hi, Julia… er, congratulations on the goal."

"Thanks, it was nothing."

"Yeah, you're supposed to score from a flick, Dad."

Alex veered to one-upmanship when her friends were around,

never afraid to have a dig at Simon's expense, but he didn't care. She was fifteen. You owned the world at fifteen. There was time enough to find out that the world owned you.

"OK, let's go. Nice to meet you, Julia."

"Dad, the thing is, I was wondering if Julia could sleep over…"

"Well, it's kind of a bad time right now, with, you know, Mom, and…"

"I already said it was fine. Her folks are out at some do or other. It's not a problem - I'll dig out the air-bed…"

Simon did not need this. He struggled to extricate himself from the tangles of Alex's little finger. "Alex. You could have checked with me first. What are mobiles for?"

"Saying no?"

Simon had to laugh; he was definitely going to get her to negotiate his contracts. "All right. Hop in, Julia."

The traffic was backed up on the A120; roadworks again. Alex and Julia were talking in low voices in the back, in a slang that made him feel more than his age. As the car crawled forward he kept putting off talking about Sparrow, rolling possible words around his head. They pulled up at the red lights and he looked into the rear view mirror where the girls had their heads together.

"Alex?"

"What?"

"You remember Martin Sparrow?"

"No. Should I?"

"He was an old…" an old what? Mate, acquaintance, git? "…an old family friend from when you were small."

"Oh, right."

"He's come to stay for a few days."

"Yeah, whatever."

"You don't remember him?"

"That's what I said."

"Blond hair, tanned, went to the States?"

"Friend of Mom's?"

"Yes, well, no, both of us, I suppose."

"Never knew you had any friends, Dad." The girls laughed.

"Well, I expect you might recognise him when we get home."

"I wouldn't bank on it."

The lights greened and Simon edged forward. It was nothing, Cassie must be wrong. Whatever Martin Sparrow was, philanderer, con merchant, used car salesman in cashmere, he was not a... a...

"Watch it, Dad." A scream came from the back seat.

Simon's heart bungee jumped as he missed the oncoming Transit by inches. He swerved back over to his side of the white lines, bumping the kerb. "Sorry." It could not be true, couldn't be. But what if it were? If the bastard had been... had so much as touched... Simon could not bear even to think about it. His hands gripped the steering wheel as though it were Sparrow's neck. But no. He relaxed his hold. He would have seen something; Robin would have. Except she had always been taken in by the louse's public school accent and outrageous flirting. She wouldn't have noticed if he'd had 'paedophile' tattooed on his forehead. *Come on, get a grip. It can't be true.* All the same, he would watch the man. And if he put a foot wrong, then...

Simon swung the Citroen into West Street and found a space forty yards up the road, out of range of creeping double yellow lines. Alex and Julia jumped out.

"Can you bring my kit bag, Dad? Thanks."

Julia was taller than his daughter, with spiky dark hair still glistening from the showers. Perhaps Sparrow would like her more than Alex. Simon rubbed his temples; what was he thinking of? He took a deep breath and hauled the girls' bags out of the boot.

They were waiting by the front door, ringing the bell. "Forgot your key again, Al?

Alex laughed. "It's in my bag, Dad. Dur."

Before Simon had a chance to get his own key out, the oak door swung open, and Sparrow stepped out into the late afternoon. There was a pause and Simon's heart all but burst from his chest as he saw that Cassie was right; he saw it in the man's lust-dilated eyes. A tightness gripped him when Sparrow smiled, the coy smile he used to give Robin. *It was true. How had he been so blind?*

Martin Sparrow inclined his head and twitched an eyebrow. "Hello, Alex." He seemed to taste her name, as though it were a succulent truffle to be kept on his tongue while it melted. He put out a manicured hand and Alex took it. "Alex. Martin Sparrow. I don't suppose you remember me. I... knew you when you were...," he smiled and curled a finger and thumb into a C-shape, "...very small." Simon noticed that his accent had acquired an extra veneer of sophistication, that his voice had dipped a few notes.

"Hi," said Alex. "No, I'm sorry, I don't..." She laughed, not sorry at all. She seemed so unconcerned; perhaps the slime was not getting through to her.

Sparrow laughed. "That's OK. Now, I'm going to have to say it, but, gee, how you've grown." He winked.

Alex laughed too.

Simon was fighting a losing battle to contain the urge to drag the man away and thump him, when Sparrow let go of his daughter's hand at last and turned to Julia. "Not another Chance you've been hiding away, Simon?"

"This is Julia White," said Alex. "My best friend."

"Hi." Julia reddened a shade.

How could they be taken in? Simon clenched his teeth, his pulse rate taking off. "Shall we go in?" The anger wanted to overflow, but he still felt seized by claws of doubt. *How could it be true?*

Martin ushered everyone into the entrance hall with a largesse that would have made a bystander believe it was his own home. "You look like you could use a drink, Simon, old pal."

"No." Simon was short, but, damn it, he did need a drink. "Yes. Near miss on the A120."

Martin poured out two glasses of Jack Daniels. "Cheers. Here's to *Artes*." He clinked the tumbler with Simon's.

The drink soothed the acid of Simon's temper at once. "Where did this come from? I didn't realise there was any bourbon in the house."

"Never travel without Jack the Lad." Sparrow raised his glass. "And it's Tennessee whiskey. Bourbon's Kentucky."

"Huh?"

Martin ignored Simon's question and winked at him. "There's something you're not telling me, old chum, isn't there?"

Simon flushed. Had his suspicions been so obvious? He put his glass down and started to tidy up his desk, displacement activity to avoid confrontation, shuffling pens together and tucking the spaghetti of cables behind his laptop. "No... look, Martin, it's about... we need to get something straight..." He picked up the brown wrapping paper left over from the Thomas More book and bent down to put it in the wastepaper basket.

Sparrow read the name and address. "Mark Fitzwarwick? Clacton?" Not the King of Clacton, surely?"

"You what?"

"You know, Mark Fitzwarwick, the boxer, don't you remember? Made a big splash in the Olympics a few years back. They used to call him the King of Clacton. They loved him in the States. Been a while since I heard his name. Whatever happened to him?"

"No idea. It's just some bloke. He bought a book from me."

"Oh. Anyway, what was I saying? Yes, Robin called." He paused, waiting for Simon to respond. "I know you've split up. She told me. I'm sorry, Simon, really sorry. She is some lady; I don't know what made her hook up with you in the first place, mind." Simon felt his gorge rise again. "Only kidding, pal, you were really good together. I'm looking forward to seeing her again. What's the White Hart like?"

"What?"

"The White Hart? I didn't mention it, sorry. I said we'd meet up for dinner at the White Hart, my treat."

"Martin! For heaven's sake."

"It's OK, don't worry, I'm not completely broke."

"No, it's not that..."

Martin Sparrow held up a hand. "Say no more. Seven-thirty in the bar." He held his glass aloft. "It's been a long time."

Simon knew he had to face Robin sooner or later. Maybe it would help, neutral ground and a referee. He looked at Martin, the drink mellowing him, confusing him. *Was that what Sparrow wanted?*

"So Robin's a free agent, eh?"

"No," Simon said, then changed his mind, giving a sigh he hoped sounded heartfelt. "But, in a way, I suppose you could say she's free now."

Chapter 18
Rings

'The big Russian takes another right to the body, and it's hard to see how he can come back now. I score Fitzwarwick at three ahead, two rounds to go, but surely it's not going to go the distance. Kalin is rocking. He ducks, he dives, evades the Fitzwarwick jab again and takes refuge on the ropes. His eyes are glazing over. He's praying for that bell. Kalin is a beaten man. The belt is on its way to Essex.

'Oh, and look at this, would you just look at this, Mark Fitzwarwick, the King of Clacton, he's backing off. He's dropping his guard and turning to the crowd. I have never seen anything like it. He is orchestrating this Albert Hall crowd, and, my word, its acoustics have never been used like this before. They love this boy.

'But has he made a terrible mistake? The Russian's coming forward. He leads with the left, jabs. Fitzwarwick sways back, and Kalin meets fresh air. Oh, and I could swear the King is smiling. He's loving it. He rocks back, counters. Kalin is off-balance and Fitzwarwick takes him with a jab, a second, oh, and a glorious right cross. Kalin is reeling and oh, my word, Fitzwarwick is switch-hitting. He's changed from orthodox to southpaw. He's got more tricks than Paul Daniels, this boy. A thudding left to the body and Kalin doesn't know what day it is. The referee must step in, surely. A tremendous uppercut and he's down. Kalin is down, and he'll be feeling the whiplash from that one. He's taking the count... two... three... there's no way back now... five... the crowd is going wild. Seven... they could give him a hundred and he'd still be on the floor... nine... ten... that's it, it's all over. Mark Fitzwarwick has tamed the Russian bear. He is the new European Champion and they'll be partying in the streets of Clacton tonight.'

The video clunked to an abrupt halt as Fitz pushed the remote control. He stared at the blank television screen as though the fight were continuing. He didn't want to watch the rest of the tape; didn't want to see the Russian unable to get up, the seconds tumble into the ring, the medics arrive in a flurry of white, his night ending in chaos. Not that he felt bad for Kalin. The Russian knew the risks when he climbed through the ropes, just as Fitz had. Fitz had always known it would come to an end one day. And it had, that night under the lights. He had put his gloves in the attic the day after the fight when it was clear Kalin would not be boxing again, would not be doing anything much again. Fitz knew he had lost his focus, and when that happened, you would be the next one to fall, the next one contemplating life from the wrong side of a coma.

"King of Clacton, my arse." He smiled at the mute television. History. Ancient history. But history could be rewritten, *should* be rewritten when it was wrong.

He raised himself from the lotus with his arms, lifting his whole body clear of the carpet by a few inches. He held the pose for five seconds, then lowered himself back to the floor. Good. He was still strong, still fit; no time was wasted. Seeing himself in the ring now was like seeing a man more foreign than Kalin had been, with his steel grey eyes and alien way of looking through you. All show, that's all it was, all everything was, show. But now that Fitz had learnt to see through that show, it all became clear, like wisps of grey mist lifting from dormant fields.

Poor old Simon didn't even have any show. Fitz liked him, in an odd way, as though he were a spaniel, eager and affable but with not much going on between the ears. Sloppy, too. He could use a haircut and a trip to Boss. How could you respect a bloke who didn't respect himself? 'Oldmanbooker'. Fitz laughed. Chance had a way with words, all right, but no common sense, no nous; Fitz would run rings around him. Simon Chance: slim chance, fat chance, it all meant the same – no chance. He just had to be careful. Softly, softly, catchee monkey. Or catchee about 10,000 monkeys, more like: five million, yeah, Paycocke's might be worth that. His, all his. The letter had made that clear: the house was ' the one bequest he might claim.' The thought made him light-headed. Was this too big for him? Maybe he should get someone else in? He crunched the doubt. No way. In the ring it had just been him; that's how it would be now.

The house was stunning, everything he had expected. It was the right place, for certain, for sure, one hundred percent diamond. The photographs hadn't lied. The merchant's mark was bang on, the ermine tail that looked just like a funny little clover leaf or a shamrock, maybe. A shamrock for luck. He smiled; luck - no such thing, you make your own luck. He was a bright spark, mind, old Paycocke, knew the value of merchandising. You had to respect him. But what did it all mean?

Fitz went over to his desk and pulled an album out of a drawer. He looked at the black and white shots for the thousandth time, levering them out of the photographic corners and taking them over to the window. The ones of the people he hadn't fathomed, seemingly random shots of strangers in a garden somewhere, sometime in the 20's, judging by their dress. That's all he'd been able to work out. But the pictures of the house were different. They seemed to be a deliberate series, to have been taken especially for him. And anyway, the letter had only mentioned the house, 'the place to which you should go, the merchant's house in which you will discover your heritage... once in this great house you will be led to the truth.' A few of the Paycocke's photographs were half in shadow, the light sucked out of the frame, and it was easy to believe – that house was as dark as a priest's hole, and no less secretive. A couple were blurred; this was no David Bailey at work. But a pricey camera, he could tell that, even though his knowledge of photography was sketchy. The edges of the snaps had dulled now, lost that sharpness that you could use to clean your fingernails. He had handled them so much over the last two years that they had softened in the warmth of his fingers, aged before their time. Mind, they had a lot of catching up to do.

There was one of the entrance hall, which was a lot less vibrant in monochrome than it was in real life. There were a couple of the ceiling, but the carving was lost in the darkness of the picture. That carving had been amazing. He smiled at the unknown photographer who had been unable to do it justice, the intricate detail lost, although now that he knew what he was looking for, he could pick out the Paycockes' initials and the ermine tail on each beam. There was another photograph of a trapdoor, he hadn't seen that. It was somewhere in a beamed ceiling, although that didn't narrow it down. He curled his lip, wondering what its significance might be. There were three of the dining-room, taken from different angles. One was so dark it was practically worthless, the sharp vertical lines of the linen fold reduced to smudged shadow on the image. Another was marked by a pale cloud of cigarette smoke. The photographer must have exhaled at the instant he released the shutter, leaving the picture blemished by the captured smoke, obscuring the panelling behind.

Fitz put the photographs down on the desk and rearranged them into different orders, hoping that a certain juxtaposition might prove inspiring. They were a jigsaw he could not piece together. Now that he had found Paycocke's after so long, their importance seemed to be fading. If only Granddad was alive. He must have known something more about the camera. But he had just given it to Fitz on his twelfth birthday, with a toothless smile and a wink, saying it might be worth a bob or two. He hadn't mentioned the film inside, perhaps hadn't even known about it at all. Fitz himself had left it undeveloped at the back of a drawer for years before having it processed out of curiosity, ending up with the blurred, shaky snapshots of someone else's crummy old house. Only when he had found the note hidden in a slit in the lining of the camera case had he started to wonder, started to chase old shadows and dig into the family history. Only then.

The geezer was about as good a writer as he'd been a photographer, nothing clear, the whole letter full of ambiguity, but some things shone out: 'the merchant's house in which you will discover your heritage' – Fitz liked the sound of that. But some of the rest of it sounded downright bloody creepy. The guy must have been losing his marbles. Fitz had better watch his footwork. He wouldn't be surprised if Chance was one of those Masons. Things could get tricky; never drop your guard.

And now it was gathering pace like a slalom skier, twisting this way and that. He'd have to fight to keep control, but that was good. The magazine had arrived this morning, the *Country Life* she'd found, dating all the way back to 1923, the year Grandad was born. Funny, that. The article rubber-stamped everything he knew about Paycocke's, beautiful, beautiful Paycocke's. He was on the right track - it was just a matter of time. And Mark Fitzwarwick could wait, oh, yes; he was patient, a quality sharpened by his years in the ring, biding, watching, picking the moment. He had waited so many years already; what difference could a few weeks longer make? But the visit to the house had posed as many questions as it had answered and Fitz knew he would have to go back to Coggeshall. He had to look at the panelling again. And that trapdoor? Where was it? What did it mean? The carvings, too: the photographs didn't show enough detail. And the letter, it hinted at so much. 'Wealth untold.' Was it just the house, or was there more, something buried there maybe? He was so close, so close. He tucked the snaps into a creased grey envelope and put them into his shirt pocket.

Right now he needed to get out, needed to feel the wind in his face and the air fill his lungs. The sun was shining and the wind had dropped for once; no need for a coat. He closed the front door behind him and the frosted glass rattled in the frame. Damn. The rotor arm was still indoors, still in his parka pocket. The car was never going to start without the rotor arm.

Good job the breakdown bloke hadn't looked in the distributor.

Chapter 19
All Truths Are
Not To Be Told

They travelled through the night, resting the horses often, for they were three and the two animals had not yet recovered their strength from the journey to London. Though both were weakened by the brawl with William Spooner, Robert and Thomas took turns to walk, with Ann silent and reflective on the bay. They stopped for water and food as the sun poked over the eastern horizon and blinded them with its early morning brightness. They ought not rest for long. Gangs roamed this countryside and they were too soft a target.

Ann slept. Robert draped his cloak over her still body and tucked it up close to her chin. Her long russet hair had fallen out from her coif over a cheek and it rippled in the lightest of breezes. Robert plucked the hairs away from her face. She did not stir at his touch. "Will Ann live, Thomas?"

Thomas picked up on the use of the girl's name in Robert's question. His throat felt like fire and his voice could manage only a harsh croak. "Aye. 'Tis no great matter, the green sickness, I have seen it ofttimes before. It will cure, if well fed. And that is the smallest service we can offer her."

Robert sighed and shook his head.

The clothier smiled. *Oh, to be youthful again.* He put his hand on the younger man's shoulder. "You had great fortune, Robert."

"If great fortune be a lump like a hen's egg, then that be so." Robert rubbed his head. "'Tis thanks to Ann alone that we are here today."

"Aye, indeed. We both of us had great fortune. In truth she risked her own neck in the saving of ours." Thomas took his bloodied knife from its sheath and examined it. Its edge was dulled and it was speckled brown with the taking of William Spooner's life. He poked it in the stream and then wiped it on the lush grass, restoring its lustre. He looked at his tired and old reflection in the blade.

"She is a brave woman," Robert said.

Thomas nodded and looked across at Ann, whose body rose and fell like a sleeping calf. But she was thin like no calf ever was, her tinged skin stretched over her high cheekbones. She was moving her rose-coloured lips as she slept, muttering a prayer or lost in some dream. Thomas hoped it was a good dream and trusted in God that it might be some recompense for the nightmare they had escaped.

Robert wrenched his gaze from the sleeping woman. "And what now, Thomas?"

"I do not know." Paycocke's eyebrows buckled at the memory of Spooner's anger. "Why did William rage at the Paycockes so? What reason…"

"He was without reason, Thomas."

"Nay. I mean that something did drive him to his wrath. Some great anger at my father, God rest his soul. William Spooner was a fine man; he built my very house with his own hands, and a finer house there never was. And my father trusted him like no other. Wherefore was he so beguiled?"

"Mayhap the bequest?"

Thomas shook his head. "Whatever it was, it rendered him mad. Made him leave Coxhall, his kin and friends. 'Tis a piece of knowledge he takes to the Lord Almighty."

"If indeed that is where he has gone." Robert scowled.

"The Lord has infinite mercy, Robert. Infinite. There is room in Heaven for William Spooner."

Thomas's face was heavy with sadness. The loss of Margaret followed so swiftly by the death of William Spooner, a man upon whose knee Thomas himself had bounced. The end of friendship is a terrible thing, a betrayal. But how was it that John Paycocke had himself betrayed his oldest friend William? He had trusted him, left him as guardian of some object or some piece of knowledge that had destroyed the man's sanity. What was it, that curse?

Robert sat still, his hands together as if in prayer. Thomas Paycocke looked away, into the slow-running waters of the stream. He would never disturb a man at peace with God.

"It was not immediate, was it?" Robert spoke through his fingertips and Thomas turned away from the hypnotic waters.

"How so?"

"His leaving of Coxhall and his descent to madness? It was not immediate upon the death of your father?"

"Indeed not. My father died in the year of Our Lord 1505 and Spooner did go about his business for some time after. Only after the building of Paycocke's House four years later did he leave Coxhall. Soon after, and he was still as fine and hale a man as ever was."

"Soon after?"

"A matter of days, methinks. I know not the precise time." Robert fell silent and Thomas prodded him with the handle of his knife. "What ails you, friend?"

"Perchance naught, but does it not strike you strange that he should build your house and leave for London so abruptly? Was there a paucity of work in Coxhall?" The young man's eyes were bright with intelligence, ideas roaming like wild boar around the forest of his mind. Thomas thought him in that instance wasted in the cloth trade and that he should have been marked for higher things.

"Not at all. Business was good. Many thought him a fool to trade Coxhall for London."

"So why leave?"

Thomas shrugged. "Were I to know that, then happen I would have an answer to the questions that have plagued me these years."

"Then happen that answer might lie in your house."

Thomas stared at Robert Goodday. His was a reputation for few words but wisely spoken. It was not like him to speak out of place. Such a pronouncement was the result of much deliberation. Still, Thomas was confused and concerned. "The Paycocke House? My own very house? How so?"

"John's legacy. I believe William broke the terms of the bequest. He could not live with the responsibility that your father had bequeathed him. Somehow, he left it buried in your house and he escaped to London, thinking that he might also escape the clause of your father's will. But he could not. The legacy hunted him down and turned his mind."

Paycocke turned the notion over in his mind, gave it length and strength like a good yarn. "There is an old saying of my father's: there is no wool so white that a dyer cannot make it black."

Robert nodded. "Aye, indeed. There was no escape for William Spooner. His guilt followed him like an arrow and brought him low just as swiftly, addled his head to a great degree. And whatever he has left behind in Paycocke's…"

"…is there still." Thomas put his hand to his face. Of a sudden he felt unclean.

There was a stirring beside them.

"Ann awakes. We should talk later, Thomas."

"Aye, indeed."

Robert turned to the waking woman. "Will you take some water?" She stretched her thin arms out from her and the folds of her sleeves dripped from her like honey. She took the cup from Robert and sipped at the icy water.

It pained Thomas to see that her clothes were swamping her. Still she did not speak, just stared ahead of her with eyes which looked too large for her face. He must persuade her to eat. He fetched a linen parcel in which he had saved some hard cheese and offered it to her with a hunk of black rye bread. His own hunger rendered him ashamed of his large belly. He had taken for granted the good living given him by his trade and the comfort which had accompanied his married state.

Paycocke smiled. "There will be better repast when we are at Coxhall."

A question flitted across her eyes.

"'Tis where I and Robert live. It is a small town but a few more hours from here. Eat now, Ann, you have need of strength."

Ann nibbled at the cheese like a field mouse, not taking her eyes from him. Not for the first time, Thomas marvelled at her power in dispatching the crazed Spooner. Yet her feat seemed to have sucked the life from her, she was so grave.

Robert refilled the cup from the stream. There was a lamb-like quality to his demeanour, undimmed by the events of the evening and the hasty escape from Cheapside. He looked innocent and guileless in the early morning light. Thomas was uneasy. The day was yet quiet, but who knew what friends Spooner had acquired in his time in London? To judge by the company at Taggy's, not such as would invite the two Coxhall men for a friendly game of dice, that was certain. He rued having left his name and that of his town behind at the bawdy-house and hoped his fears were groundless.

"Good morrow, Ann." Robert offered the cup to the young woman and Thomas could scarce recall ever having seen the boy so light of heart. "Thomas and I wish to thank you for your kindly intervention this night."

Ann shook her head. "'Twas naught." Those were the first words spoken since they had left William Spooner lifeless in the Cheapside alley, his blood draining into the filth of the London cobbles.

"Then it was the largest naught I ever have seen. I thought you were Our Lady of Barking come to save us."

To see Robert jest was a new experience, but Thomas was glad of it, for it lifted the moment and brought a ghost of a smile to Ann's sombre face. Even so, he had to know whether they would be followed. The words hurt his throat, but he knew he could not leave them unsaid. "You knew William Spooner?"

Ann looked away, to the west from where they had travelled. "Aye. I knew him."

Thomas allowed himself to wonder at her presence in the bawdy-house, that such a wan girl should have been a slave to such debauchery, that she should have sold her... No, he must not think it. Ann had saved their lives. God would wish charity to be shown. He clenched his fists behind his back, but the girl had seen his awkward movements.

"Nay, I cry you mercy, but you misunderstand. It is not as you think. William Spooner took my aunt for a lover."

Robert gasped.

"Taggy was my aunt," Ann said. "She gave me shelter after the death of my parents. I might not condone the nature of her business..." she blushed rose and her words tumbled out unchecked "...but I played no part in its doing, that I swear."

Paycocke held up a hand. "There is no call to swear, Ann

Cotton."

"Her heart was true to me, that I might say, if not to others."

Thomas did not wish to dwell on imagined events in Cheapside. "Aye," he said. "I am sure of it. But as for William Spooner...?" How to phrase the words? "Was he respected... much-loved in the... alehouse?" Thomas grimaced at his own clumsiness and wished Margaret were there to translate for him. A life in the company of men had left him ill-prepared for such emotional conversation.

Ann gave a meagre laugh, seeming to find humour in his question, though none had been intended. "Aye," she said, realising his worst fears. "Aye, but only when he was heavy with coin. Then he was... as you say, much-loved. That apart, a hated man, bitter with life, and with no friends save those he might purchase with ale. He will not be missed, have no fear. There is only Taggy whom you have offended – she crossed you as soon as you were gone, sending a lad to Spooner's house. She would sell you for a greater prize than your royal." The girl smiled and it gave her cheeks substance and colour for the first time.

Then they would not be pursued. Paycocke was grateful for this respite, but still the journey to London had achieved nothing but the death of his father's best friend. Thomas felt the burden of Spooner's demise and prayed that God would forgive him for that untimely taking of a man's life. None the less, he was no closer to unravelling the tangled yarn of the conundrum. "Did William... did Spooner talk of the Paycocke name, of my father John?"

Ann folded her tiny hands together and they sat like a small sparrow on the lap of her kirtle. "Indeed. Each day when he was in his cups he cursed your father's name to all who would listen."

Robert could not contain his impatience. "And did he mention the Paycocke House? That he did bury something under Thomas's home?"

Thomas wrinkled his brow at the younger man. "There is naught but oyster shells and the Romans' fine road under my house. No space for treasures."

"Nay. He did not speak of any house, just that the name

of Paycocke was all that was evil and that he was cursed by that family's name and unable to escape its long reach. He was a damned man, Master Paycocke. I knew he would try to kill you. It was in his eyes, it has always been in his eyes."

"But why did you come after us? You owe us naught."

"I hated him. I hated him." Her dark eyes hinted at more than she said, dwelling on some inward heaviness, but Thomas did not press further. He picked at the last crumbs of bread and cheese, wasting nothing, rolled up the linen and packed it away.

So it was over. John's secret had died with William Spooner. Thomas would never be able to reconcile his nightmares, never be able to save his father's soul. The clothier bowed his head in prayer and asked forgiveness for whatever it was his father had done. He prayed too for the tormented soul of William Spooner.

"Will you return to London?" Robert's words were almost off-hand, but the cheerfulness was so thin that Thomas wondered at the tone of concern beneath.

She shook her head. "There is no life for me there. Naught but fear and death. I will make my way to Suffolk where I have some kin."

Thomas held up his hand to deflect her. "You will travel with us to Coxhall."

"It is not…"

"Until you are well. You will stay at Paycocke House as my guest until you have recovered your health to some measure."

"I accept no charity." For the first time Thomas heard spirit, verging on anger in her voice.

He sought compromise, his merchant's skills put to good use. "Can you spin?"

"Does a fox chase a coney?"

"Then I shall find you labour in my workshop and we shall hear no more of it." Thomas stood and shook dew from his cloak. He looked at the rising sun, now shedding the earth's grasp. "There is no time for dalliance. We ought not tarry, for there is still far to go." He held out a hand to Ann to help her rise. She looked up at him, her face calm but stubborn, fixed and resolute. She took his proffered hand, but Thomas made no move, just stared at her face, at her wide eyes. Her face. A face. Spooner. What had he said? Thomas had clutched at life like a drowning man and Spooner had said something about a face. "A face." The words had drifted through his semi-conscious state and he was not sure if he misremembered or not. A face? What was the meaning of it?

"Thomas?" Robert was at his arm. "Are you well?" He had helped Ann to her feet but Thomas still held her hand, cold and tiny. She came to his shoulder, frail as she was, and when he put his woollen cloak about her it trailed in the damp grass, gathering apple blossom and last year's fallen leaves.

"Aye, Robert," he said. A face. "Aye."

Chapter 20
Steps

How could Dad not have believed her? And what was Sparrow still doing in their house? Why hadn't Dad kicked him out or called the cops? Or anything?

Cassie heard footsteps pass her room. "Dad?" She opened the door, but it was only Alex, Alex and one of her boring hockey mates. "Oh, hi, Al, what's up?"

"Not a lot." Alex smelt shower-fresh, bloody health freak, although she could do with losing a few pounds. "This is Julia." She gestured at the friend. "I'm just showing her around."

"All right?" Cassie nodded at Julia. "I have to talk to you, Ally."

"Yeah, we're just…"

"It's sort of urgent."

"Can't it…"

Cassie grabbed Alex's wrist. "It's Sparrow."

Alex wrinkled her nose. "Huh? What?"

"Watch him."

"But…"

"Just fucking watch him."

"What are you talking about, Cass?"

Cassie's mouth went dry and she felt dizzy as though she had stood up too quickly. She leant against her bedroom door and it swung inwards, making her struggle to maintain her balance.

"Cassie?"

"It's all right. I'm OK."

"Cassie?"

Alex held out a hand and Cassie's temper snapped. "For Christ's sake, Alex, I said I was all right, OK? Leave me alone." She knelt on all fours, waiting for the dizziness to pass. Her head pounded.

"OK, whatever." Alex turned to Julia and mouthed, 'Period.'

Cassie watched them draw away and float up the stairs. She wanted to be sick. Sodding Sparrow. If she could just stay here for five minutes, she would be fine. She rested her head on the cool floorboards and the nausea began to fade. The floorboards, that was the obvious place for treasure, wasn't it? She'd read Conrad's book again; he said the treasure was *buried*. She had to find it before Dad. He'd insist on handing it over, when she needed the money, needed it so badly. But the floorboards weren't that old, were they? So where could it be? She felt so sick, so confused. She couldn't do this on her own. Where was Roach when you needed him? If only Roach was here, he'd know what to do. Footsteps passed by her, clattering on the wooden stairs on their way to the public bedroom. Laughter bounced off the walls and into her head.

"Alex, stop laughing, stop it." Cassie looked up; there was no one there. The motion of her head made the banisters surge away out of focus. She reached out to steady herself, then heard the footsteps again, not Alex's usual clomping elephant, but light and quick like a child's, chasing each other around the top floor and up and down the stairs. An archipelago of sweat islands broke the surface of her forehead. She felt so hot. What was happening? Where was Alex?

The laughter started again, children somewhere. Cassie tried to filter the sounds, but they kept getting jumbled up inside her head. Why would nobody listen to her? It must be next door's kids. Yeah, it was next door, the laughter of a game of Hide-and-Seek floating through the wattle and daub. Why couldn't they keep the noise down? She felt so thirsty; if only she could get to the bathroom. She needed a glass of water.

Cassie sat on the steps and hauled herself up one by one. Her dank blonde hair straggled over her face and her lipstick tasted like lard. One step, rest. One step, rest. From the public bedroom the bleeping started, like a reversing lorry. At first she thought it was out in West Street, but it got louder and louder. She knew if she turned around she would barf. Louder and louder. One more step. The laughter and the beeping noise swamped the room; why couldn't Alex hear it? Dad was just downstairs; even that bastard

Sparrow – why could none of them hear it? She crawled into the bedroom and rested against the wall. It was one of the theft alarms on the Staffordshire dogs. She started to cry. Why would anyone want to nick one of them? Ridiculous things holding their stupid flowers. Why? She held up a hand and reached out towards the spaniel to try and turn the alarm off. Her hand was blurred before her eyes, blurred and shaking. The alarm stopped and silence invaded her. She closed her eyes and slumped against the timber studs.

*   *   *

Simon and Martin walked down to the White Hart as rain was spotting the pavement. Simon's heart felt like a large piece of dough lodged in his chest. All the way from Missouri to Coggeshall, the scenic route, he just a bit part player in her story. It dawned on him that he had stopped feeling sorry for himself and now felt sorry for her, growing up in a vacuum with four brothers in small town America, an alien planet of Dairy Queens and baseball, bullets and guns and Hershey's Chocolate Kisses. Robin suddenly seemed the smaller of his problems. He wondered if he should tell her about Cassie's suspicions, put her on her guard. Maybe she had noticed something ten years ago. But wouldn't she have mentioned it? He should at least broach the subject with Sparrow.

The two men broke the silence at the same time.

"Sorry, you first," said Simon.

"Shame Alex didn't want to come, that's all," Sparrow said. "Cassie too, of course," he added.

The mention of Cassie seemed to be a suffix, an add-on to throw Simon off the scent. Damn – why was he so suspicious? And Cass? Those vitamins she was taking; he wasn't convinced. That was another thing he should speak to Robin about. "She hasn't been herself."

Martin nodded and looked up at the sky; the rain was getting heavier and a crack of lightning decorated the sky. "Er, I think we'd better run for it." Simon felt his ankle whine as he jogged the last twenty metres, coming in a poor second. Sparrow already stood in the doorway of the White Hart, grinning, while Simon felt short of breath, short of most things. Bloody Sparrow. As he shook the drops from his clothes he looked out into the street, where rivers were collecting in the gutters. As the rain slid off the porch, a waterfall formed in front of them, and through it Simon could see two people dashing across the flooded street, strobe-lit by lightning. They were screaming and laughing as though it were a Disneyland ride, one voice the epitome of the Shires, the other a soft 'Misery' accent. Robin. Abby looked like Batman, a long dark cape flying behind her. Batman and Robin – they belonged together.

The women crashed through the cascading water hand-in-hand. Abby's ankle-length Driza-Bone had left her relatively unscathed, while Robin in wool had been a sponge and her blonde hair lay flat and mangled across her flushed cheeks. Mascara leaked from her lashes and she looked like a muntjac caught in the storm.

Simon managed a smile. "Robin." He held out a tentative hand, feeling like a toddler making his first tottering steps. She looked down at the outstretched hand and ignored it, instead taking him in her arms and hugging him. He could smell her perfume, Hermes Rouge, diluted by the rain, soft and warm and if 'red' had a smell, that was it. "Simon," she said. "Honey."

They held each other, their shared life clutched between them in a second, and then let go.

"I think we should go inside. It's bloody freezing." Martin rubbed his hands together and opened the door.

Simon laughed. "You've been in the States too long – this is England, mate."

Robin sat nearest the fire and started to steam. She hadn't fixed her hair, had barely mopped up the debris of her make-up with a tissue. She must be squelching in her suit, he thought. She laughed at the incident, toasting it with kir and holding her left hand out of sight beneath the table. Simon imagined her fingers curling into Abby's as they fed off each other's warmth and happiness. Her eyes caught his and he saw pity in them. Yes, he loved her, had always loved her, but for her to be true to herself and be happy, that was more important. But how had he not known?

"Hey, why so quiet?" Martin waved a menu in front of Simon's eyes, breaking the spell.

"Oh, sorry."

"What do you recommend?"

Simon scanned the menu, knowing well that whatever he recommended, Martin Sparrow would avoid. "Um… I had the tagliatelle the other day, that was good…"

"Scratch that, then." Martin laughed and the women laughed too. Simon couldn't believe that Robin and Abby would go along with his tired routines; they should know better. "Only teasing, Simon. What do you fancy, Robin?" They established eye contact and Robin looked at him over her menu, licking her top lip.

"Something hot," she said.

Simon turned to Abby and she winked at him, composed and sure. "Abby?"

Abby swirled malt in a tumbler. "The tagliatelle looks good to me," she said. She was as groomed as Robin was bedraggled, a mirror for the slick Sparrow. She dropped her voice. "Where did you find him?" she said, flicking her eyes at Martin.

"He found me, I'm afraid." Martin hadn't changed at all. He was all over Robin, doing his maple syrup impersonation, but this time Simon could let it go. They ordered a bottle of Sancerre and its flowery notes started to react with the harsher Jack Daniels. Simon began to feel gently at home. "Tell me about your snake."

Abby smiled. "Alfie? I've had her for a couple of years, now."

"Alfie's a she?"

"Yeah, there was some confusion when I got her. She's a Burmese python."

"What? A python? Aren't they dangerous?"

"Not really. The Burmese are really sweet…"

"We have a different definition of sweet."

"She was a touch jealous when Robin, you know, moved in, but other than that she's adorable. Loves company, and, OK, she's no guinea pig, but I've got her wrapped around my little finger."

"As long as she's not wrapped around your throat."

Abby laughed. "Honestly, it's not like that. If you handle

them from young, they just get used to it. It's a matter of building trust."

"Right. I think I'd prefer to build a six-foot wall. How big is Alfie?"

"She's still quite small, only four, five feet long."

"Hey, I'd hate to meet a big one."

"They can get up to twenty feet."

The thought of Robin living with a twenty-foot python left Simon astounded. It must be love. Then again, just ten days ago the thought of Robin living with a five foot four woman would have astounded him even more. The wine started to talk. "You're OK, you know. Really nice." Nice. He blinked at his banality and wondered where the main course had got to.

Abby put her hand on his. "So are you."

In another world, in another life, he thought. But he was stuck with this one, with its confusing signals and its secrets and lies.

"Oh, Simon, we moved too quickly. I'm so sorry."

He squeezed her fingers. "I know."

"Whatever we can do to help you…"

"It's OK. I'll live. I just need to let go."

"What will you do?"

Simon stared into his glass of Sancerre, saw in its depths a blurred and smoky reflection of himself, straining to be noticed. Life would not always be like this. "I need to stick around until Alex and Cass get sorted, off to Uni or what have you. Then, I don't know. I used to look at life in terms of… well, that it would be for life, for the rest of my life. I expected to be leaving Robin in a box. I took too much for granted." The alcohol was making him maudlin, he knew. "I thought I would have Robin always. I suppose I never had her at all."

There was a moment of silence in which they could hear Martin and Robin's animated conversation on the other side of the table, pulling out musty, forgotten anecdotes from long-closed drawers and dusting them down. Robin's accent moved further across the Atlantic as she laughed at Martin's tales.

Simon and Abby looked at each other and snorted simultaneously.

"He really has no idea?"

Abby shook her head, her lips bulging with the effort of containing the laughter. "No, none, not at all, not an iota, not a single solitary cocktail chipolata."

"You've made her very happy," he said.

"So did you, Simon, so did you. Don't forget that."

He nodded at Robin. "But not like this."

"I had a head start."

"Yeah."

"We're both lucky to have known her."

"You're right. I should see things in terms of half-lives. Start again." *Where?*

"He is a prat, isn't he?" Abby laughed.

"He's a dying breed."

"Put him in a zoo, then."

Yeah, behind bars, a caged sparrow. Cassie's warning still haunted him. He had to speak to Robin, alone.

The waiter filled the gap with clams and monkfish and Sparrow ordered another bottle of white wine. Simon's head was beginning to feel fuzzy and he played with his food, spearing penne cylinders on the tines of his fork and creating pyramids of pasta on his plate. His appetite had gone AWOL. Robin excused herself to go to the toilet. This was his chance. He wolfed down some unwanted food to make it look good, then scrunched his napkin on the table.

"Can you excuse me? I need to powder my nose," he said, scraping his chair on the floor.

Abby laughed. "You mean siphon the python?"

They both sniggered and Martin joined them, in ignorance. "As long as you can trust the two of us alone," he said, smirking.

"Mmm, let me see..." Simon said as he left the table.

Good timing. As he closed the outer door to the dining room Robin was coming out of the Ladies. "Hi," he said. "You look great."

"Gee, I'm a wreck," she said.

"No." And she wasn't. There was a glow in her eyes he couldn't remember ever having seen.

"Martin tells me he's living with you. Boy, you're a fast worker, Simon."

Simon held up his hands. "What? What are you talking about?"

"Joke, Simon. You know how you're always saying Americans have no sense of humour. I figure the British are rubbing off on me at last."

"OK, OK. No, he's just staying for a few days. We're working on something together."

"I'd forgotten how much I liked Martin. He's a fun guy."

"If you like that sort of thing."

The conversation stalled and Robin moved towards the door. "I guess I'd better be getting back."

Simon had to stop her. How the hell could he bring this up? "Abby. She's... she's very... nice."

Robin smiled, a you've-been-drinking-but it's-OK sort of smile. "I know."

"I like her."

Her fingers rested on the door handle, opening the door a crack. "Is this where I say, 'Stay away from my girl?'"

"Have you got a minute?"

She closed the door and looked at him. "What is it?"

"This might sound crazy, probably is crazy, it's something Cassie told me, about the old days, about Sparrow. He..."

"Yeah?"

"Sparrow and..." He could hardly get it out.

"I'm waiting."

"Alex."

Her face went white. Simon was horrified. Whatever he had expected it was not this. His heart plummeted like a lead weight. *She had known all the time. My God, she had known all the time.* "You knew. That pervert was...touching our daughter and you knew. You knew."

Her expression changed and leached incredulity. "No, you're wrong, Simon. You've got it so wrong."

Simon twisted out of her grasp and made for the door back to the dining room. "I'll kill him. I'll fucking kill him."

"No." Robin's scream stopped Simon dead. His wine-powered fury struggled to be unleashed.

"What?" Simon was shaking.

"It's Alex."

"I know…" He wrestled to control his breathing. "I know."

"No, no, no, Simon, you don't. It's not that." She placed a hand on each of his arms and massaged his biceps with her thumbs. Her green eyes flickered and she stuttered as though her whole body were undergoing a power cut. "Alex." Robin swallowed and a tiny tear leaked out. The smell of Hermes Rouge was overpowering in the small space. "Alex. She's Martin's… daughter."

Chapter 21
The Staircase

We walked back over the fields in silence. I held Edward's box and its precious cargo under one arm, and tucked my other through his. Dear Edward. He held onto me as though I were his lifeline. His poor mother. I knew little of the sugar sickness save that of its pernicious and unforgiving nature, sucking the life and strength from a soul and leaving a tired and withered husk. Not, of course, that I mentioned this knowledge to Edward. The doctors would hold little enough hope for his mother. I resolved to find out what I could about the illness so that I could comfort Edward in the coming weeks.

We parted by the Hitcham School. "Thank you, Imogen," he said from the crater of his silence.

"I have done nothing." Truer words never spoken. What more could I say? "Give your mother my..." My what? Best regards? "...my love," I said. "If there is anything I can do..."

"You're already doing it." He smiled, but it was shallow and I could see the great sadness lurking behind. He lumbered down West Street, his dry boots kicking up clouds of dust behind him.

Sad though I was at Edward's plight, my excitement had been fired by his talk of Billy Howes the young carver. Goodness, had he been scared away by a ghost? So it was true, Paycocke's House had a real, live ghost. Or a real, dead ghost. I shivered with delight. I simply had to explore the dining room. The answer lay there, I was convinced of it.

Iso was waiting for me, a frown scarring her perfect white brow.

"Imogen, where in the world have you been? We are expected at Orchard House in one hour."

I had completely forgotten that we had been invited to take dinner at Doctor Phipps's. My heart sank. We should not be back until far too late.

"Oh, Imogen, you have grass stains on your sleeves. Whatever have you been doing?"

"I'm so sorry." I was suddenly struck by a peach of an idea and clutched my head. "I have been… I feel rather unwell." I feigned slight dizziness and clutched at the doorframe, and with a master stroke missed it, stumbling into the house.

It had the desired effect. "Imogen. Are you quite well? Sit down, darling." Having seen the lasting effects of Gussie's nervous tension in the preceding months, my mother was remarkably sympathetic. I felt a stab of guilt at my deception.

I managed a feeble reply. "I… the sun was rather hot."

"Goodness. You simply must wear your hat, Imogen. What are we to do with you?"

"I shall be all right." My wounded soldier impersonation, all bravado and selflessness, had done the trick.

"You must lie down. We shall present your apologies."

"I do have the most infernal headache," I admitted.

I was helped up the stairs at a great test to my acting skills and lay on my bed until I heard the huge door close. I waited another ten minutes until I was certain that the house was empty, and only then did I creep downstairs. A creak on each step warned me of my folly and that I was sure to face certain doom in the dining room. I trembled with a heady melange of excitement and fear.

Stopping halfway down the stairs, I listened, but the old house was utterly silent and grave-like. I shuddered; my own thoughts were frightening me. But what a delicious sensation it was, to be scared and excited at the same time. I felt so safe and so happy in Paycocke's that I was sure it would never allow its ghosts to harm me. Surely something so beautiful could not harbour evil. I was on the verge of continuing my downward journey when I heard footsteps on the red brick path outside. Oh no, my parents had returned. How could they be? What could have brought them back? Supper must have been cancelled. I froze, awaiting the key in the lock, but none came. It must have been my imagination, or perhaps it had been a deer clopping up the path. Iso had seen just that the other evening, a young doe munching at the trailing leaves of the dogwood. That must have been it. I should have loved to have seen it, but I apologised as I took the rest of the stairs two at a time.

The dining room was quiet, too. The beautiful linen fold panelling stretched from floor to ceiling, not part of Conrad's restoration, but rather installed by Paycocke himself. I wondered if it was Thomas or perhaps his father John who stalked the corridors of Paycocke's House.

"Hello," I whispered. "Thomas? John? I don't want to hurt you, just to thank you for your glorious house, and if you should like to meet one day, I should consider it an honour. My name is Imogen. Imogen Holst."

It was something of an unorthodox introduction, although in my defence I do not recall a chapter in any etiquette manual on 'How To Converse With A Ghost.' Unfortunately, my efforts, though well-intended, met with failure and the house retained its silent and imposing aura. I saw the name of 'Paycocke' carved on the bressumer beam above the fireplace, so fresh that it might have been carved yesterday. Of course I had seen it many times before, but after Edward's grisly tale I looked at it anew, with a different fascination. Billy had touched the name, and then his chisel was wrenched from his hand. I stretched out my own hand, and curled all but a single finger away from the name, as though a spark of electricity might arc out and seize me. I did not know what to expect and brushed a mere fingertip against the 'P'. Nothing. I sighed, a mixture of relief and disappointment. I touched the letter more firmly, and its response was the same.

I stroked the name. "Oh, dear Mister Paycocke, won't you talk to me? There is so much I should like to know." Paycocke still slumbered and I was beginning to doubt the truth of Edward's revelation. Then it dawned on me that Billy had not touched the carving, but had taken his gouge or his chisel to it. Perhaps that was the key. Metal; I needed metal. I looked about me, but there was nothing that might suffice. I brushed my hair away from my eyes and felt a hairpin, that trusty accomplice of Poirot and Holmes. I unlatched it from my hair and held it to the wood, willing it to be torn from my grasp, yet nothing happened. How sorely trying it all was.

I decided on a different approach. Now, when (I had persuaded myself long ago that it was a 'when' and not an 'if') Billy's tool had flown across the room, Edward described it as having stuck in one of the panels opposite. I set myself the task of finding the evidence of the incident, and I described the trajectory it might have taken. The dining room is long, some fifteen feet, with the lintel upon which the name is carved standing at about four feet and six inches. Therefore, unless the force were supernatural, the mark on the wall must have been quite low down. (I ignored for the moment the idea that the force was very well supernatural.)

Since Paycocke's faces to the north, the dining room is usually rather dark. The wall was in shadow, so I was forced to kneel down and feel the panels. They were smooth to my touch, like stroking clouds. Yet, they were perfect in every way, no blemish or flaw. I welled up at the craftsmanship. The excitement I had inhaled from Billy's story began to wane; it had never happened at all, was an exaggeration or the culmination of decades of gossip.

The sun moved around to the front of the house, illuminating it with its brief evening glare. A finger of sunlight stretched in through the window and then I saw it, a slice of darkness in that light, a half-inch groove into which my fingernail slotted perfectly. Billy's mark. I tingled with excitement. So it was true after all. This was where his tool had landed after it had been torn from his hand. I turned slowly back to the panelling, having the feeling now that I was being watched. It was not altogether pleasant and for the first time I had the sensation that all was not well at Paycocke's House. I struggled to reassert my earlier sense of excitement, but I then had the most horrid epiphany: perhaps the reason Billy had never been seen again was that he had been sucked into the linen fold to a nether world from which there was no return.

I started to sing to myself to keep my spirits high, and crept towards the door, not taking my eyes from the panelling for a second. "Please do not be angry," I said, speaking the words slowly so that the Tudor family might understand my modern speech. "I wished only to help, to understand. Thomas, Margaret, John, is it you? Please let Billy go. He did not intend any harm."

The silence seemed complete, yet I was sure I could hear the pistons of my own heart thumping away.

"I shall leave now. It is so kind of you to share your house with me."

In answer, the room went as dark as if an electric switch had been turned off. Of course it was only the sun disappearing behind a tree, but the whole room seemed to me to shift. My qualms were becoming harder to suppress and I clung to the knowledge that at least Thomas had not thrown a chisel at me.

Another noise outside made me come alive again - footsteps in the carriageway. It must be Gussie and Iso, back already. I dashed out of the dining room and up the stairs, hurling myself fully clothed into bed, pulling the blankets over my head. I waited for the footfalls of my parents. I waited and waited, tucked inside my bedclothes like a hermit crab until tiredness and the heat overwhelmed me and I succumbed to sleep.

*   *   *

Iso swung the Bullnose around the corners with a verve that had been far from Mister Morris's intentions, but rather exhilarating and hat-holding none the less. When one approaches by automobile, the view of Thaxted is like no other, with the mighty spire of St John the Baptist's piercing the sky like a giant needle. Standing high on the hill commanding the landscape, it somehow feels closer to God. Seeing John Webb's windmill standing beside the church I was taken by a pang of nostalgia for childhood summers spent playing in the mill and its field. It seemed to have been overtaken by the years, falling into disrepair and wearing its age poorly, and I wondered whether it had always been so, or whether my mind might be playing tricks on me, as it has taken to doing these past few days.

I had put my experience in the dining room behind me, blaming my own prolific imagination. I was convinced that the Paycockes could not wish me harm. However, I determined to wrench some information out of the charismatic but infuriating Father Conrad. To this end I had with me the evidence of the

Country Life magazine article that had so eloquently listed his achievements with respect to Paycocke's House.

We arrived in time for the last service of the day, so my interrogation had to wait. Conrad gave the most rousing sermon from the pulpit and I was all but driven to applause. The interior of the church bristled with William Morris, admired as much by Conrad for his politics as his designs. His wife Miriam had filled the chancel with flowers and tapestries, and light flooded in through the clerestory windows, scorching the nave with colour. This was surely how He had intended it to be.

We walked together back to the vicarage. Conrad blushed at my praise and the wings of his curly hair seemed to fly even further away from his head. "I did nothing but allow that which was already there to be seen."

"You are too modest."

"Now, I have a small surprise for you," he said. I was disappointed, for it had been my own intention to surprise Conrad with my resolution of his carver conundrum. We strolled down Newbiggin Street and he refused to hint at what the surprise might be, practically dancing with rapture at my ever more outrageous guesses.

"Frances." I clapped my hands in delight as his sister opened the front door. "How wonderful." I turned to Conrad and he winked, holding out his arms as if to disclaim all responsibility, as mischievous as ever. "Dear, dear Frannie, how are you?"

We sat under the canopy of the old walnut tree as I pumped Frannie on the famous people she had been photographing. What an exciting and glamorous life she led, travelling all over the country. She was at pains to assure me that it was far from exciting and that she should like nothing better than to rest her head in Thaxted each night. Oh, to be a slave to one's art.

The best was yet to come.

Conrad went into the house on an ostensible errand for a jug of cream (and I thought men of the cloth were not supposed to tell lies) and came back instead with a small parcel, which he produced, magician-like, from behind his back.

"Happy Birthday," he said, handing me the package.

"Birthday?" I was confused, as my birthday had been some months before.

"Somewhat belated, I fear, but my reasoning is sound." He smiled, as well did the whole company, since it was clear that they were part of the conspiracy.

I tackled the gift with as much restraint as I could muster. How I adored presents. I untied the ribbon and placed it on the grass beside me. I trembled with anticipation as I unpeeled the wrapping paper from the box. Looking up I saw a forest of grins. It was a camera. "I... I... thank you... oh, thank you... it's glorious... my goodness..." I looked around at those responsible, aglow with smiles at the success of their subterfuge.

Conrad inclined his head. "I had to avail myself of Frannie's advice, which explains its rank as 'belated'. My sincere apologies."

"No, no, you mustn't, it's perfect, it's absolutely perfectly perfect." My words fell over each other like infants racing to their mothers' arms. "Goodness."

Frannie showed me how to operate the machine and I took some photographs of the assembled group. We played croquet on the sweeping lawn and I captured Conrad in mid-roquet. Gussie demonstrated some surprising skill at the game and I was left hoops and hoops behind. Still, I had the consolation of my fabulous birthday present.

The afternoon cooled and we retired indoors. The Noels had impeccable though eclectic taste, with a house full of fascinating odds and ends. I had always found it a wondrous Aladdin's cave when I was a girl and many of their possessions now tugged at childhood memories. We sat down before the fire and played charades.

Conrad romped around like a spring lamb and still no one was able to recognise his heartfelt gorilla. He flopped beside me on the long settle, carved in a linen fold fashion much like that at Paycocke's. He was laughing fit to burst.

"So how are you enjoying Paycocke's?" he said, mopping his brow.

"Truly splendid."

"And did you find the carver's portrait?"

In the excitement of my birthday present I had completely forgotten the carving. I could not resist the temptation of playing Conrad at his own game, and I contorted my face into a theatre of disappointed abandon. His eyes lighted up with triumph, then I said, "Oh, yes, and what a dear, sweet little face he has."

The vicar's look of failure would have been too much to bear had I not known from the Conrad Noel of old that he was teasing me. "Do you think the same carver might have worked on your church?" I asked. There were gorgeous carvings at his parish church: feathers; horns; roses; and angels flying so high I used to wonder that they did not burst through the roof. In private, though, I preferred the carvings at Paycocke's – they seemed so much more intimate, so much more tangible.

Conrad thought, wrinkling his brow. "Perhaps. It is possible. The buildings are more or less contemporary, well, given that the church was one hundred and seventy years in construction." He laughed. "And of course the carver of the day was very much an itinerant, following the work around the county. Yes, it is possible. Maybe it was he who left the carvers' coat of arms."

I was puzzled and Conrad laughed.

"I must show it to you, carved on one of the ceiling bosses, a set of crossed chisels, finely executed and very amusing."

I was instantly reminded of Billy Howes and his flying chisel and probed Conrad further. "Was there much carving done during the restoration of Paycocke's?"

"Some. To the exterior in the main. The front elevation had weathered to a degree."

"But inside?"

"The beams are as they were. You look at honest work crafted more than four hundred years ago."

I continued to press. "Did you know a carver called Billy?"

He looked away, and I could not see whether it was because he did not want me to see his face, or whether it was an aid to thought. "Billy? No, I don't think so." He shook his head.

I feigned not to know his surname. "Billy...what was it? Billy Horton? No... Billy Howes, yes, that was it."

"Howes?" He rubbed his chin. It was most unlike Conrad to

aver so. Either he knew something, in which case his memory was as sharp as a new razor blade, or he did not, and if that were so he was ordinarily happy to admit his ignorance. I felt sure he was hiding something.

"It is just that I recently heard a story about Billy, about how he saw a ghost in the dining room."

"A ghost at Paycocke's? The only ghost with whom I am familiar is the Holy Ghost."

This coyness was most unbecoming and I swiftly told him the full story. Upon seeing what I knew, he was forced to recant, albeit reluctantly.

"Howes, you say it was? Mmm, so many craftsmen worked at the house in those years. Howes? Yes, I do remember now, a young local lad. Oh, Imogen, such a junior carver would not have been permitted to work on the Paycocke name. That would have been the responsibility of Ernest Beckwith alone. You must be mistaken." His eye contact was devastating. "If I recall correctly, he was dismissed. Mister Beckwith found him idly carving his initial on one of the panels. Doubtless the incision you saw was the vertical stroke of the 'B'. This story of a ghost was nothing but a… ah… a smokescreen."

"Then what happened to Billy?"

Conrad laughed. "It is more prosaic than you imagine, Imogen. He left Coggeshall for Ipswich." For someone who claimed not to have heard of Billy Howes two minutes ago, Conrad was very well informed of his whereabouts.

"But…"

He put his hand on my knee and pretended to light-heartedness. "There are no ghosts at Paycocke's. I would not have it."

Could it be so? Was Billy in Ipswich? My theory of his being absorbed by the panelling did seem fanciful, but was there nothing more to it than a bored apprentice being shown the door?

Iso snapped me out of my thoughts. "Imogen, you are monopolising the Reverend. And more to the point, it is your turn for a charade."

Chapter 22
Beckwith's Room

Dire, utterly dire. Something was wrong, yet I did not know what. Why did Conrad Noel… no, lie is not the word… why did he… evade my questions? It was clear that all was not as it should be at Paycocke's House.

We went home exhausted. The evening did take a happier turn with more charades and an uproarious game of throwing-cards-into-the-hat, a pastime at which Iso excelled. I wondered if I had been rude to Conrad, but he was his usual charming, funny self, so I drew that he had taken no offence. Indeed none had been intended. Yet there was a void where my equanimity had been.

Paycocke's House felt cold on our return, as if it had disapproved of our absence. The door to the dining room was closed, and I felt that the room was hiding from me. I went to bed but slept only fitfully, feeling a sense of anticipation, a waiting for something (or someone) that never came.

I was awoken by the gentle bickering of mallards in the courtyard. The house was silent. Although the sun was making inroads into the day, it was still rather cool in my eyrie, so I put on a dressing-gown. I was torn between my nonsensical notion that Billy Howes had been abducted into the panelling and the even more chilling idea that the room still held some other dark secret to be revealed. I wanted to look at the chisel mark again. Waiting at the top of the staircase for the sound of stirring, when none came I took the first step slowly, expecting the usual rifle-crack of a creak as the stairs awoke from their slumber. I was spared; it seemed that the steps themselves were conspiring with me in my attempt not to awaken the rest of the household. Once in the entrance hall, I paused. Goodness, the floor was cold to the soles of my feet.

The dining room door was open now. Perhaps Gussie and Iso had had a nightcap, I thought, simultaneously knowing that it could not be true. The room was quiet. A vague scent of damp earth wafted through and I no longer wanted to be there. How attractive my nest upstairs seemed. I padded over to the window and looked for the mark. A 'B', Conrad had said. But surely if Billy had wanted to leave a mark, then why would he do so here? I felt the groove. Billy, though young, was experienced with wood; had he been carving his name then the cut would be more even and of a regular depth. The scar that was there was anything but. It looked like it had been the result of an accident, or a tool thrown at the panelling from a distance. Conrad was wrong, and he had known it too, trying to put me off the trail with his talk of vandalism. Such a slur on Billy Howes did not seem fair and I determined to speak again with Edward. Or perhaps the master carver; he might know more. I wrestled with my memory. What was his name? Conrad had mentioned him. Ernest, yes, that was it, Ernest... Beckwith.

"Imogen?"

I turned to see Gussie in the doorway. I felt my face catch fire. I had not heard my father at all.

"What are you doing down here so early?"

"I... I couldn't sleep."

My father put his hand to his head, adjusting his spectacles. "Nor I," he said. "I heard your footsteps." And I thought that I had been so quiet.

I moved towards him. "Is it the headaches again?"

He nodded and sighed. "It does not appear to be working."

I must have looked puzzled.

"This." He gestured around the room. "The peace, the quiet. It is not working. Oh, nothing seems to work. I feel useless, Imogen. My talent is deserting me." He slumped down on the bottom steps of the staircase and put his head in his hands.

I sat down beside him and put my arm around his bony shoulders. "No, no. It is not so. My dear sweet father, you are the most talented man alive and I love you more than the sun. It is just your fall. It takes time to recover."

My early morning exclamations brought some life to his cheeks, but he did not stir. "It is no use." He was so listless and looked so thin that I was brought to mind of Edward's description of his mother, she who could no longer bake cakes. Surely he could not be afflicted with the same illness. Not my father, no, not Gussie.

I took his hand. "You are so cold." His fingers were almost transparent. They wound around my own.

"Am I?"

"You must not walk around in your pyjamas." I chided him with a note of gentle reproach.

"I don't know what is wrong with me, Imogen. My will has been sapped, my motivation gone, my creativity shrivelled up. This new symphony - I look upon it as though it were Cantonese."

I paused, taking a deep breath to calm my nerves. Maybe I should not mention the illness. Perhaps he knew already that his time was limited and he wished only to spare Iso and me the terrible hurt. Yet not knowing was a hurt worse than Hell itself. If I knew my enemy then I could face it. I struggled to form the words. "Do you know of the sugar sickness?"

He looked bewildered by my question; confused, or acting confused. "The sugar sickness?"

"I think it goes by other names, but that is…"

"The sugar sickness," he repeated, then to my horror he nodded. "Ah, yes, diabetes mellitus. It means 'honey', you know, 'mellitus' in Latin. Strange that I should remember that."

I started to sob and it dawned on him why.

"Oh, Imogen, dear lamb, do not worry." He pulled me to him and I buried my damp face in the blue and white stripes of his pyjama jacket. In an instant the comforter had become the comforted and Gussie resumed his paternal role. "It is not that, do not fear. It is, as you say, my fall in Reading which plagues me still. And perhaps the fact that I need to accept that my time in the limelight has passed." He lifted my chin, looked into my eyes and smiled. "It is not diabetes mellitus, Imogen, I promise you."

"But you are fading away…"

"My talent is fading, that is all." He put up a hand to stop my protests. "But this talk of the sugar sickness, from where does it come?"

I told him about Edward's mother. He nodded and gripped my hand. "You have not been yourself these past days. It is such a burden, such a burden on one so young. You must not harbour such dreadful thoughts. The diabetes: yes, it is a terrible, terrible thing," he said.

"Will she die?"

He dropped his sad eyes. "It is likely. Your friend Edward must prepare for that. Oh, there have been great medical advances in the last twenty years, but maybe insufficient for Edward's mother."

In the tranquil early morning I wanted to tell him about the ghost of Thomas Paycocke, about Billy Howes and his chisel and about the weird blood-curdling screams I had heard on that night which now seemed so long ago. Something stopped me. It was perhaps my fear of ridicule, perhaps the knock to my confidence from Conrad's rebuttal, perhaps it was Paycocke's House itself.

*   *   *

Tilkey Road runs up the hill out of Coggeshall, a continuation of Stoneham Street, where the market takes place and the hunt gathers. It was where I would find Ernest Beckwith.

The street held rows of pretty pastel cottages in the East Anglian style. Everyone knew Ernest, who lived with his wife and children in a pale blue terrace. I was not quite sure how to begin.

"Good morning. Mister Beckwith?"

"Beckwith'll do, Miss." He had a pre-war air of deference, a deference I would normally have taken pains to make plain that was undeserved and unwarranted. However, that was not my charge. He kindly invited me into his home and I asked him about Paycocke's House.

Ernest Beckwith cleaned out his pipe with an old knife. "Paycocke's? Fine house. None finer. Some of my best work is on that house. Have you seen it?"

I reddened and confessed that I did not know which was his craftsmanship and which belonged to the original building of the house.

"Good. That's how it's meant to be." He pointed his pipe at me. "It's not about me, you see, it's about the house." He went back to scratching at the bowl of the pipe. The smell of old tobacco filled the small room, comforting and soporific. He stared at the pipe in rapt concentration and I could see how this might translate to his work, worrying away at the detail, always seeking perfection. His face was lined and cracked like old leather, but he was not old himself and I wondered if his work had dried up his features so, and turned him into one of his own perfect carvings.

"Now then," the carver said.

"Well, I was wondering if you could tell me a little about the Paycocke's restoration."

The man nodded, settled back in his worn chair and pondered, as though it were a question of great political significance. "What'd you like to know?"

"Not so much about the work itself, but, well, I have been... I think... well, did anything... untoward happen while you were working there? Were there any unusual incidents?"

"You mean is Paycocke's haunted? Did I see any ghosts?" He tossed his head back onto the antimacassar and laughed. I felt a touch humiliated that he should consider my query so amusing. Perhaps I was indeed making a fuss about nothing.

"'Course," he said, still smiling. "Of course it's haunted. It wouldn't be right for a house like Paycocke's not to be haunted." I felt a tickle of anger rupture inside me; he was making fun of me. He must have seen my expression change, because he made a calming motion with his pipe. "It's all right, miss, I'm not teasing you. This village is as full of ghosts as a barrel of apples. Hardly room for any more. Almost every house here has its own ghost. That's what I mean. You name it: Cradle House; the White Hart; the Abbey; they're all haunted. And Paycocke's is the jewel. Oh yes, Paycocke's is haunted all right. And the little white cottage next door, too."

At last I was making progress. I inched to the edge of my seat. "And you have seen these spirits?"

"Don't have to see to believe," he said. I waited for him to elaborate, but he just explored his mouth with his tongue.

"Are you acquainted with a man by the name of William Howes?"

"William…?" he laughed again, but this time his laugh deteriorated into a plundering cough and he dropped his pipe onto a what-not beside him as he alternated between mirth and his alarming expirations.

"Are you quite all right? May I fetch you a glass of water?"

He waved one hand at me to sit down and tried to control his escaping cough with the other. Eventually it subsided.

"'William Howes' indeed. Not even his old ma would have called him William." He sniggered again, careful not to let it overwhelm him this time. "William, eh? So what of young Billy, then?"

"I am told that Billy had a strange experience at work one day."

"It would have been a strange experience for Billy to be at work at all," Beckwith said, his sense of humour still much to the fore. It was not a promising beginning. If Billy were well known as workshy and untrustworthy, then his testimony on which I relied would be deeply flawed.

I continued to press. "But you know of the incident of which I speak?"

"I do at that."

"And you think it unlikely?"

He picked up his pipe again and stared into its bowl, as if looking for an answer there. "Lazy? Yes. Unreliable? That and all. A liar?" He shook his head. "No, not Billy Howes. He saw what he saw." He paused. "Whether he saw right, now, that's another matter. But there's strange goings-on in this town, as can't be explained by no chaplain or politician."

I did not understand. "But you dismissed him?"

A spark of anger flitted across his eyes. "Now where would you get a tale like that, Miss?" He jabbed his pipe in my direction and I could see that I had been mistaken in my earlier appraisal of deference. I moved to apologise for my assumption, but he brooked no interruption. "I'll dismiss no man up to the job. And whatever else he was, let me tell you, Billy Howes had flair. Best woodman of his age I ever seen. Green oak was putty to him. Could carve an angel out of a tanner."

So he had not been sacked, as Conrad had said. But where did the truth lie? I was no closer to an answer than before. If only I could speak to Billy Howes myself. "But he left Coggeshall before the restoration was complete?"

Ernest Beckwith nodded.

"Do you know where he is now?"

"It just so happens that I do." He opened a drawer in the Welsh dresser and took out a sheaf of envelopes. "Had a letter not a week ago from a certain Charles Townsend in Ipswich, asking after Billy's skills. Restoring a house in Silent Street, he is, and Billy looking for work on it. I said it like it is: he may be lazy, he may have a mouth on him, and the Lord knows what a mouth like his would do in a place called Silent Street, but his carving is the best I ever seen."

There seemed to be no more to say. I thanked Beckwith for his time and stepped out into the warm air of Tilkey Road. A light breeze threatened my cloche as I walked down the hill. Once or twice I had to put my hand up to my head as I felt my hat begin to lift, and that was why I did not see the human cannonball that crashed into me. I tumbled to the ground and grazed my hand on the kerb.

"Edward!"

*   *   *

Edward had walked home in despair. Now what would she think of him? Pouring out his troubles like an old water pump, with no thought for what was there to catch the water as it fell. He had disgraced himself. Imogen would never want to see him again. He kicked at a pebble, sent it a few yards down the pavement, caught up with it again and booted it into the road. It crossed the street to the other side and neatly slotted into the drain. Goal. Two-nil to West Ham and Edward Daynes has won the Cup. But they had lost, hadn't they, two-nil? You couldn't rewrite history. It would always be Bolton 2 West Ham 0.

191

At least she liked his story about Billy Howes. He thought she would, after that first day, when she had asked him all those questions about ghosts and Robin the woodsman and the mad friars. And it was all true, as true as he was standing there. Almost, anyway. Some embroidery around the edges, that was all, just made the tale a bit more interesting. Imogen's eyes had been as big as saucers, and it was him that had made it happen. He hugged himself with delight.

His mood swung like a pendulum to despair again. The brooch. Had he done the right thing? What would his mother say? Worse than that, what would his father say? Edward was not so old that he couldn't take a fine six across the backside. Best to leave things unsaid.

He pushed open their front door and took his boots off, carrying them through the front room into the kitchen. The house smelt of cabbage-water and old cigarette smoke, smells of decay. Mammy would still be in bed, then.

"Where have you been all day then, fellow me lad?" Albert Daynes was sitting on the back step, peeling vegetables. He did not look up, just flung a peeled but grey potato into a pan of murky water.

"Not all day, pa, just..."

"Less of your lip, son. She's been asking for you, the Lord only knows why."

Edward heard a simmering menace in his father's voice. "Sorry."

"Get up there. See your mother. What good it'll do her." He nodded up the stairs. "And when you're ready, you can finish off these." He flung the peeler into the pan of potatoes. Water slopped onto the kitchen floor. "There's cabbage and all. I'm off down the Grey." The Yorkshire Grey, he meant, for six pints worth of peace and quiet, the price of forgetting. He got to his feet and his dusty boots made dark brown puddles on the linoleum where the potato water had sloshed. Edward looked down at the mess. "And mop that up too."

"Pa..."

"Don't you pa me, out gallivanting all day..."

"But…"

Edward's father squared up to him, crossing his thick arms and lowering his scowling face to within inches of Edward's own. Edward could smell the Grey on him already. "But what, you little runt? Get to it, or you'll feel the back of my hand. Bad enough your ma's dying of the pissing evil, without you playing the high-and-mighty." He made as if to push his son, but when Edward flinched, his father sneered and walked past him.

Edward trudged up the narrow stairs, where the handrail was coming loose from the wall and shook in his hand. The world had stood still when mammy'd got sick. Drifts of dust had settled on the skirting boards, the windows wore an opaque film of grime and the steps went unscrubbed. The house smelt of neglect, and even though Edward spent his Saturday afternoons playing catch-up with the chores, there were always more to do. His father couldn't cope, and it wasn't only the 'women's stuff', the washing and cooking; he couldn't cope with watching Ida die. Everything went unfixed, Albert Daynes most of all.

"Bert, is that you?" On another day, Edward might have thought his Nan was paying a surprise visit, the voice was so frail. As he neared the bedroom door the smell of sweet urine made him gag. "Albert."

"It's me. Edward," he said, trying to pitch some hope into the words. He paused by the door, not wanting to go in, not daring to see the latest deterioration. He swallowed, thought of Imogen, and entered his mother's bedroom smiling.

"Come closer, love, I can't see you properly."

She looked so fragile, buried in pillows and with the blankets cruelly draped over her emaciated legs, emphasising every bony contour. Her hair had lost the sheen he loved, and it stood out from her head, grey and thin and scared.

"I'll get up soon, love. I'm a bit tired this morning."

"That's all right, mammy." Edward did not want to correct her, to remind her that the day was nearly done. The dying sun would do that for her soon enough. It hurt so much. This woman had held him inside her body, nourished him, made him live. Why could he not do the same for her? He sat on the edge of the bed, the soft mattress giving way with his weight, and took his mother's hand. He injected a note of levity into his voice. "What have you been doing with yourself, then?"

She looked up at him, sleep still crusting her eyes. He would wash them in a minute. "You're a good lad, Edward. You mustn't mind your father."

"It's all right, mammy."

"He's afraid, is Albert."

Edward squeezed her hand. There was only a slight increase in pressure in return. "I know."

"Don't you be afraid, Edward."

"No, mammy."

"He does love you, you know, but it's harder for men. You know what I mean."

She struggled for breath and Edward shushed her gently, "Now, now, mammy, I know. I do know. It's all right."

He stroked her fingers; they felt like pencils, hard and lifeless.

"It will all work out in the end, Edward. It's God's will."

How could she speak of God? If this was God moving in his mysterious ways, then Edward would rather he didn't move at all. "Don't talk like that."

She closed her eyes and relaxed the slight grip she had on his hand. The blankets rose and fell with her shallow breathing. *Please, God, please don't take her. I do believe in you, I do. I'll do anything, but please let her live. Let me die instead, please.* His thoughts chased each other in circles until he could bear it no longer. He placed her fragile hand back on the coverlet.

"Edward?"

She was not asleep. He turned to the window so she could not see his tears. "Yes?" The smallest of words to disguise his fear.

"Can you get me the po, love? I need the po."

Edward reached under the bed for the pot. A scummy film had settled over a stagnant pond of urine. He turned his face away from the smell which he had unleashed into the room and wondered when his father had last emptied the pot, whether he had even been upstairs all day, whether he could face the sight of his dying wife.

"I got to empty it first."

"Be quick, son, I'm bursting."

Edward picked up the pot and urine sloshed over the brim, dribbling over his fingers. He wanted to be sick. Do it for mammy, do it for mammy, he repeated to himself.

Halfway down the stairs he heard the thud and groan behind him. He put the chamber pot down on a step and dashed back up to the bedroom. His mother lay on the floor in a tangle of bedclothes.

"Mammy?"

"I needed the po, love."

"I'm doing it, I'm doing it, mammy." He picked up his mother, a fragile fading butterfly and put her on the bed. He held her face close to his own and could not stop his tears. Her breath smelt sweet, almost fruity and he wondered what she had been eating. He had not seen her eat anything for days.

"I'm sorry, love, I'm sorry."

So was Edward; his tears fell on her cracked face. "Nothing to be sorry for, mammy, nothing." He felt her bladder open as he held her, flooding the bedclothes and overpowering the room. He held her close to him and stroked her hair. There was no rush for the pot now.

She seemed to look through him, beyond him, as though there was someone else in the room. Her eyes struggled to focus. "Your father said it was a good job he wasn't called Downes."

"Mammy?"

"Then I'd be Ida Downes." Her brittle laugh echoed in the dank room.

Edward tried hard to smile, in case it was the last thing his mother ever saw. She raised an arm an inch above the bedclothes, but it was like she was lifting an iron girder and her hand dropped, twitched and stopped moving. Edward felt the small resistance fade and she fell back into the bed and closed her eyes.

"Mammy. Wake up, mammy." He felt her cheek, cold and papery. She couldn't be dead. "Mammy, no, mammy, please wake up. Don't... don't..." He put his head on her chest and could not sense any breathing. "No." Then a bubble escaped her dry lips and her chest rose a fraction. "I'll get the doctor." He held her hand to his mouth and kissed it; there was a feeble response.

He had to get Doctor Phipps. He kissed her again and pulled the blankets up around her. Taking the stairs two at a time he caught his heel on the chamber pot and sent it flying down the steps, spilling its wretched contents on the carpet and the worn wood. There was no time to worry about that now. He left the front door wide open as he tore into the road, crossing without looking and making a cyclist lose his balance. His arms pumped fire as he reached the corner with Stoneham Street and he collided with what felt like a brick wall.

"Edward!"

Imogen.

Chapter 23
Flowers

Simon didn't know where he was. He opened his eyes to be assaulted by the dazzling white swirls of a textured ceiling. The bed was a single and the room's walls were uninterrupted by beams. Daylight forced its way through a slit in the rose paisley curtains. Kit Carson? Cat Kitson? Cath Kidston. Simon had a sneaking liking for the designs, although Robin had spurned her for bleak monochrome and harsh minimalism. Today he was inclined to agree that it was altogether too much flora for a morning after. He gripped the bridge of his nose where the worst of the throbbing had collected and angled his head towards the invading daylight. He felt like he had been through a liquidiser. His jaw pounded and he put a hand up to his face, feeling an unrecognisable melon shape, skin stretched tight. He moaned. What had happened?

Sparrow. Martin Sparrow had happened, of course. He remembered tearing himself from Robin's grasp and storming into the dining room of the White Hart, a fork-stopping moment as all the couples watched him rip Sparrow from his seat and give him a bloody good hiding. He wished.

The element of surprise is overrated. The element of the right hook is not. Simon had lashed out at Sparrow, pummelling him with all he had, screaming whatever came into his head. Sparrow had taken the hits like a pillow, but one of the pebble-dashed blows must have found its mark, because Simon remembered the explosive retaliation of a concrete fist in his face, and falling back onto their table into a car-crash of pasta sauce. The remainder of the evening was hazy: milling waiters; screaming; laughter; the taste of blood; Eleanor. Eleanor?

"Good morning." Eleanor Simmons stood in the doorway. "I've brought you a mug of tea. Paracetamol if you need them."

He tried to utter thanks but his jaw felt unattached to the

rest of him. He rotated it in its socket. "Ow. What happened? Where am I?"

You may well ask. It's not what you think, so don't get your hopes up, Mr Sad-Eyes. Anyway, you've a talent for scrapes, I'll give you that much.

Eleanor drew the curtains and the sudden light made him turn away. "My place," she said. "Up the Tilkey Road." When his eyes had become accustomed to the brightness she was sitting on the bed beside him, and he registered that he had no trousers on. Her hair was tied up and she wore a red and white pullover with a design of Chinese characters upon it. He blinked to restore his focus. "All a bit of a mess, really. You came out of the loo breathing fire and went for your mate. Abby tried to calm you down, but you were past reason. It was only self-defence, to be honest; he knocked you cold with one blow."

"Self-defence?" Simon was astounded, would have dropped his jaw had he been able.

"It was very clean, very quick." She laughed.

"Great." He took a gulp of tea. Must be about eight sugars. He winced and swallowed. "I'm still a bit out of it. Where do you fit in?"

"Well, I happened to be having a drink with the deputy head…"

"Oh, you and he…?" That twinge he felt, was that disappointment? It couldn't have been.

Don't look at me like that. So trusting. I don't want you to trust me. So don't trust me, all right? Look, it's Jack first, Jack second and Jack third. Everything else comes after. I'm sorry Simon, but that means you. So don't trust me. And don't look at me like that.

"Get away, would you?" She laughed, too loudly, and hit him on the knee. At least that part of him didn't hurt. "I thought it wouldn't be wise for you to go back to Paycocke's, so I brought you home, put you up in my spare room."

"And Sparrow?"

"Sparrow? Oh, your mate."

Mate? Simon shook his head. "You must be kidding."

"I think he went back to Robin and Abby's."

"Oh." He stared into the mug and wondered if he could face another sip.

"You don't have to talk about it. I'll make you some bacon and eggs and take you back to Paycocke's." Eleanor smiled at him. Above one eyebrow there was a tiny scar that creased when she smiled.

Simon felt ill and wanted to stay in bed for a while longer to avoid the responsibilities and recriminations. He took a deep breath; it was going to be common knowledge soon enough. "That guy, the one I thumped, well, the one who thumped me. That was Martin Sparrow, Alex's..." He could hardly believe it; his whole world had imploded. Robin leaving had devastated him, but this, how could he ever recover from this? His chest felt constricted, as though breath had deserted him. "Alex... is Sparrow's daughter."

Eleanor frowned as she grappled to understand what Simon was saying. "Alex? Your Alex?"

He nodded. "Not, as you say, *my* Alex."

Her eyes gaped in shock. "Oh, Simon."

"Yeah."

"You never suspected?"

"Oh, he used to flirt like mad with Robin." He thought about the previous night with bitterness. "Still does; you might have seen him?"

"I wasn't paying much attention."

"No, no reason why you should. I never imagined... never in a million years would have thought... Alex..."

"Does Alex know?"

"No." At least he thought not. Yet. A flicker of panic stabbed at him. He had to tell Ally before she found out from someone else. Unless she already knew. Damn it, there had been so many years of secrets. He spilt the whole story to Eleanor, from Cambridge to Coggeshall, the long way.

Why are you telling me all this? I shouldn't know. This is not what I got into this for, Simon. I don't want to know. Look, I'm not going to feel guilty about this. I'm not. It's a sad story, but I'm not involved. This is as far as I go. I can't get involved. Change the subject, for God's sake change the subject.

"Maybe he's not a bad bloke, Simon. Perhaps he went to the US to put some space between Alex and himself. To leave her to you and Robin. It might have been a noble gesture."

'Noble' and 'Sparrow' didn't go together. Sparrow would always do the best for Sparrow, but Simon had to admit that it must be a sacrifice to leave your child, one he could never have made. His memory pinpointed incidents from their shared history: Sparrow putting Alex to bed; Sparrow walking behind her bike with his hand on the saddle to stop her falling; Sparrow playing peek-a-boo. No wonder Cassie had suspected him of abuse. No wonder. The wonder was that Simon had seen nothing. How had he missed it? They even had resemblances, with their easy tans and affability. Oh, Alex. No longer even Alex Chance, but Alex Sparrow. "Oh, yes, that was it," he said.

"What is it?"

"Her middle name."

"What?"

"Edie. Short for Edith. Robin said it was her grandmother's name."

"And?"

"Edith Piaf: 'la môme piaf', the little sparrow." He looked up at the ceiling and followed the spiral patterns until he lost his place.

Damn those sad eyes. Get the Plan back on track.

*   *   *

Simon was glad that Eleanor had hushed his protests. Strength in numbers and all that. "I'll come with you. Jack'll be all right on his own for a bit." She passed him his trousers and fleece. The sleeves were still damp despite having been on the radiator and Simon didn't ask Eleanor whether she had undressed him.

Large puddles lay witness to the previous night's rain. One of the bay trees outside Zebra had fallen over. Simon picked it up and put the sodden earth back in the pot. At least the wind had dropped. They turned the corner into West Street where Paycocke's stood silent and it struck Simon that he was afraid to go in. For the first time he had the feeling of something wrong. Was this the catalyst that had spurred Robin to leave? He stopped at the front, played for time, patted pockets for keys, although he knew where they were.

"Are you all right, Simon?"

"Yeah, it's just… I don't know, Eleanor. I don't know if I'm all right or not."

"Take your time."

Simon inserted the key in the lock. It turned, but the door didn't move; the bolt was across. "Oh, damn," he said.

"Is it worth going around the back?"

"Knowing Alex, she'll have locked up the house like the Tower of London. What time is it?"

"Quarter past ten. They must be up by now."

"I wouldn't bank on it. This is still the middle of the night for Cassie." He yanked on the bell. Footsteps came from within and the bolt was pulled. Simon was surprised that the girls had surfaced so early, but it was Robin. Behind her, keeping his distance, stood Martin Sparrow. Simon felt Eleanor's hand on his back, giving it a brief rub.

Sparrow tried a smile. "Morning, Simon."

Robin turned and gave him a warning glare.

Simon was speechless; he couldn't understand what they were doing at Paycocke's. He looked from Robin to Sparrow and back again. Sparrow was doing his best to submerge his default smirk and Robin looked sad and over-tired. In fact they both looked exhausted, up-all-night worn out.

"We came back here last night," Robin said. "I… we… needed to explain."

Simon stood in the open doorway as though he might need a quick escape route.

"We waited for you."

"I think I should go," Eleanor whispered in Simon's ear.

"No." The word was sharp, but he hadn't meant it to be. It had just shot out like a misfire. "No," he softened his voice. "Please." He didn't introduce Eleanor, didn't stop to wonder whether they had all met the previous night.

"Like I said, we wanted to explain."

"Are the girls up?"

"Not yet. We had to speak to you before we told Alex. Told both of them."

"That's good of you." Simon was beginning to find his words again, no longer so many fathoms out of his depth. "So she doesn't know?"

"No."

"Doesn't know what?" Alex stood on the landing looking down at them, her eyes red-ringed with tiredness. She still wore her faded poppy-sprinkled pyjamas and clutched a ragged pillow. She looked so much younger than fifteen.

Simon gazed up at her, his daughter; no matter who the father was, she was his daughter. Bloody hell, he loved her, he would die for her. He held eye contact with her, stretching out the last few precious seconds of their old relationship. A figure emerged from Alex's bedroom, yawning. Julia. He had forgotten about Julia. "Oh, Julia, I... There's been a bit of a... I'd better run you home."

"Let me," Sparrow said. Robin gave him a set of keys. "Simon..."

Simon turned away. Now was not the time. He waited in silence as Julia fetched her bags and the giant front door echoed throughout the house as the two left.

There was a slight pressure at his elbow. Eleanor. Simon nodded, biting his lower lip.

The silence between Robin and Simon grew bigger, as though it had taken the place of Sparrow and Julia. Alex sat on the staircase, her bare toes drawing patterns in the dust, watching her parents spar.

"Simon, I never meant it to happen like this."

"How did you mean it to happen, Robin? With a six-gun salute and fireworks? A deathbed confession?" His voice dropped into bitterness. "Or maybe a chorus of *Je ne regrette rien* would have been more appropriate? You even named her for him, damn it."

Robin stepped forward, trying to bridge the chasm between them. Her eyes were wet. "I... am... sorry, Simon. We both are."

Alex yawned, quite obviously. "Will someone tell me what's going on?"

"Not now, honey, your Dad and I... You go get dressed, OK?"

"No, I think now would be exactly the right time, Robin. Will you tell her, or shall I?"

"Be careful, Simon," Eleanor whispered.

"I don't want to be careful," he said. Eleanor squeezed his arm. "You really have taken everything from me, haven't you, Robin? Our marriage, Alex, everything I ever believed in, it's all been lies, deceit, secrecy. What else have you been hiding from me? What about Cassie – is she an alien love-child?"

"It was over before it had begun."

"It'll never be over now." Simon looked up at Alex, trembling. "Alex, I'm not your father."

Robin screamed. "No."

"Dad? What are you saying?" Alex's voice fragmented. "Dad?"

Eleanor put her arm around Simon and it felt as much a gesture of restraint as of solidarity.

Alex looked from one parent to the other. "Mom? Dad?"

Simon stared at Robin. How had he ever loved her?

"Your father's right." Robin went over to the oriel window and looked out into the street where leaves had piled up in the gutters and the slate sky held the promise of more rain.

"Mom?"

"He was kind and thoughtful. He made me feel like a woman again. After Cassie was born, I felt like my whole world had imploded. I lost sight of myself in the tidal wave of Cassie's needs, Cassie's wants. All Cassie, Cassie, Cassie. I needed to be me."

"But you weren't even that, were you? Not until Abby came along." Simon fought the urge to shout, and moved to the stairs, holding out a hand to the quivering Alex, staking a territorial claim.

"I'm not trying to defend what we did, Simon. But you don't know what it's like to struggle and to hide, to hide from the world and hide from yourself. To deny everything that you are and pretend to be someone you're not. An endless charade, an endless pretence."

Simon gripped Alex's hand, feeling that if he let go now, he would never be able to get her back again. Alex drew his hand up to her face. Her cheek burned against his palm.

"One summer," Robin said. "One summer, that's all it was. He wanted me to leave you. Martin forced me to choose." She looked down at the floor and the decibels of her voice wasted away. "I chose you. You are the dearest man I have ever known, Simon."

He refused to be derailed. "Why? Why couldn't you tell me?" The answer was hidden in the question and Simon didn't wait for the reply. "Oh, Robin."

"I didn't love him."

Simon laughed. "Well, of course I know that now, don't I?"

"He may be Alex's father, but she's your daughter."

Simon sat on the steps and put his arm around Alex. She nestled into his embrace like a fledgling, vulnerable and uncertain.

"Listen." Robin held up her hand.

Simon looked up. "What?"

"Footsteps. You hear them?"

Simon cocked his head but could hear nothing.

"Outside, in the yard, footsteps on the path." She went to the back door and looked out of the window. Simon ruffled Alex's hair. If this was an avoidance strategy, it was in poor taste. Robin had spent so long evading the truth it had been good to be feeling fresh, clean air between them.

"Simon, can you really not hear them?"

He shook his head. He glanced at Eleanor and she shrugged.

"Alex?"

"I don't know. I thought…" Alex looked at Simon and he offered a pursed-lipped scepticism. "I don't know, Mom, it's probably just the wind banging the wisteria on the wall."

"This place…"

"…gives you the creeps, I know."

"And it's so cold."

"It's October, it's autumn…" Simon paused, subconsciously waiting for her to correct him.

"Fall," she said, and put her head on his shoulder. Alex sneaked between them and wound her arms around them both. Eleanor stepped into the shadows.

Chapter 24
Keys

The day felt distant to Simon, as though he was watching it through a cloud of smoke. Sparrow returned and they all sat around the table like bridge partners bidding for a contract. Robin made coffee, irking Simon that she felt she still had some rights at Paycocke's. By chance she had the robin mug and Simon wondered if their memories were coinciding. He had the wren. Wasn't it the North American wren that built dummy nests? He stared into his coffee. Paycocke's was the biggest dummy nest of all.

He realised that Eleanor had gone, had melted out of the morning without him knowing. He should thank her; he would go over with some flowers later.

Cassie surfaced, looking haggard, fitting in well, and they were five together for the first time in more than a decade, bound in silence by their new ties.

Simon wondered where there was to go. Sparrow avoided his gaze and Simon had to get his hands dirty. "That was quite a punch."

"Yeah, I had a good boxing coach when I was at school. I was useful in those days, could have gone to the Olympics. That's how I knew your Clacton King chum."

Simon remembered how Fitz had accounted for the guy in the pub. "We should match you up sometime." Fitz would take care of Sparrow. Simon was sure that Martin's inclination to fight dirty would not extend to abusing the Queensbury Rules.

"I've been a bloody fool," Sparrow said.

Simon nodded, still wary of his one-time rival. "I'll go along with that."

"I... I couldn't help falling in love with Robin, I'm sorry, Simon, but I'm not going to apologise for that."

Robin drummed her nails on the kitchen table. "Can we gloss over that right now?"

Martin held up his hands in surrender. "It's OK for you. You're reborn, you've found yourself, whatever."

"It's more complicated than that."

"Sure, I understand. If I was a woman, I'd be a lesbian, too."

"Martin, for Pete's sake."

"Sorry. Where do we go from here?"

Simon was still riled. "How about back to the States? Alaska, this time, maybe?"

"No can do, big buddy. The fact is, I'm... not quite as welcome there as I once was."

"So there's no difference between here and there, then?" Cassie was acid, still unforgiving that Sparrow had not turned out to be a paedophile.

"Funny."

"Cass has a point."

"I'd like to build some bridges, old chum. We... I screwed up badly and I want to make amends. I know it can never make up for what I've done, but I'd like to cut you in for half of the Celsus manuscript deal."

"Celsus?" Alex perked up.

"Just some book stuff your Dad... your... Dad and I have been working on."

"Wasn't he some random Roman philosopher boff?"

Martin gave Alex a light thump on the shoulder. "Hey, you're a chip off the old block, eh?" Simon stared at him.

"We've just been doing Pliny..."

"Anyway, we're getting away from the point here." Simon could see that Martin was swinging the conversation back to the bait of *Artes*, and found himself unable to resist the lure. Sparrow had failed to solve the riddle, otherwise he would never have come back to England for help. And Simon had to admit that he was intrigued; to be the discoverer of such a unique piece of work, it just confounded belief. Simon didn't care about the money, or the fame come to that, but to hold *Artes*, read its secrets, he felt alive just thinking about it, which of course was exactly what Sparrow was relying on. Damn, back to the point. "This is not the time, Martin."

Sparrow launched a pre-emptive strike, rubbing his hand over his sandpapery golden stubble. "Yeah, I know. Maybe I should just get back to London this afternoon. I've caused too much trouble already."

"No." Simon hated himself for his abrupt interruption. He knew he was making a fool of himself, but *Artes* was more important than that. "Look, perhaps I'm being selfish, I'm sorry, but, well, we're all grown-ups, aren't we? I think maybe you should have the chance to see more of Alex."

Robin caught his eye and he knew he was behaving at odds with the person she knew, this sudden display of adult behaviour in contrast with his tantrum of the previous night. He wanted to redeem himself. "You're a complete arse, Martin, that's taken as read, but we need to extricate ourselves from this." Simon glanced around the table and received a favourable nod from Cassie, at least for the 'complete arse' part. "Maybe we should all just take it easy for a few days while we work out what's best?"

Martin nodded. "OK, if you're sure. Sounds good to me. Robin?"

Robin shrugged, clearly still suspicious of the way this was going. "Yeah, sure."

"I'll find a place in the village."

Simon looked from Martin to Alex, searching for their reaction, wondering what emotional links they were creating, grieving at the loss of his paternal status. Alex showed no sign that anything had changed; she was more well-balanced than any of them. He didn't dare unlock the part of his heart where he kept his love for her, didn't want to see whether it had altered.

Martin stood up. "I'll just go and get my things together." He paused, and Simon wondered whether he was waiting for someone to offer him a bed. Well, he could wait.

"I'd better get moving too." Robin pushed her mug away from her. "I have a ton of stuff to catch up on." She gave Alex an extended hug. "Come over tonight, honey, we'll talk more."

Alex smiled. "You don't have to if you don't want to. If you're not ready for it."

"Jeepers, are you the Mom or am I? I *have* to." Robin fingered at the suggestion of a tear in the corner of an eye. "I *want* to. I'm ready." She turned to Cassie. "Cass, your skin looks terrible."

"Thanks, Mom."

"Are you getting enough sleep?"

"Come off it, Mom." Cassie rolled her eyes.

"Green tea, OK?"

"OK, whatever."

Simon needed to speak to Robin. "I'll walk back with you. I need to get the Sunday paper."

They strolled down West Street and Robin put her hand in his, something she hadn't done for years. "How's it going, Simon?"

"I'm still in a state of shock, I suppose. First you, now this. Would you ever have told me?"

"I don't know. I wanted to at first, but Martin said no, and the more years that passed, the harder it became. Then it got so I thought it would kill you to know, so I kept quiet. That's my excuse, anyhow."

"Keeping secrets must have become quite a habit," he said. His bitterness had a depth that surprised him.

"Oh, Simon." Robin absorbed the verbal pummelling, lost in thought. Then she spoke, her words soft, but considered and measured with care. "When I was growing up, I used to go hunting with my brothers all the time. Me and four redneck guys in plaid shirts and beanies camped upstate with only the beavers and woodchucks for company. Sounds like the Waltons, huh?"

"Goodnight, Robin-Bob."

She stopped and sat on a wall. She still held Simon's hand and played with his fingers, turning the wedding ring that still sat on his second finger, dormant. "Yeah, well, I must have been about thirteen when we were pitched up in the Ozarks one time. The night was black as tar and I was lying awake in my sleeping bag thinking about the stars and trying to figure out what in tarnation I was going to do. All of a sudden I heard the zip on the tent open, real slow, and I knew that no bear had evolved that sense of cunning yet. I was about to scream when I heard my eldest bro's voice, whispering to me. Jim was twenty-eight, so as far as I was concerned he'd always been an adult and not someone you'd mess with either – he was built like a pick-up truck and just about as intelligent. He snuck into the tent like a grass snake and by God, I wished I'd screamed when I had the chance."

Simon could guess what was coming. "Oh, Robin, your brother."

Robin stood up and walked away, her voice cracking. "He clamped his hand over my mouth and swore he'd rip my face off if I said anything. And I felt so goddamned used and dirty I vowed I would never tell anyone." She stopped with her back to Simon, and her head dropped. "So you see I had an early introduction to keeping my mouth shut."

Simon went up behind her and placed his hands on her shoulders. She reached up and squeezed his fingers and they walked on to Stoneham Street. Robin's face was empty of emotion, as though it were someone else's tale she had told.

"But your father? Couldn't you tell your father?"

"Tell *him*? They were his boys, Simon. They could do no wrong. How could I tell him? I'd be the slut, the whore, the sinner. So I vowed to leave Missouri as soon as I could, before I went bad too."

"And you couldn't even tell me?"

"You least of all. I'd gotten used to hiding and lying from a very early age."

"Does your family know about your... your..."

"My 'homo-sex-you-alitee' as my Daddy would have said? Heck, no. They'd probably come across the Atlantic in a convoy and tear me apart." She smiled. "I'm done with them, Simon. You can't choose your family, but you can sure as hell choose your friends."

"You're the best friend I ever had, Robin." He fought to control a tear, a tear that should have belonged to the woman opposite him, spilling the pain of growing up alone. She hugged him.

"You, too. I should have told you about my childhood, I should have told you about Martin, most of all I should have told you about my lesbianism." The last word whipped Simon across the face.

He tried to be light. "Not even bi?"

"I loved you, Simon, as a dear sweet wonderful friend and the father of my daughter, but it was all a lie. It sounds like a cliché, but that's what it was. I'm sorry."

"And Cassie. So at least *she's* mine?" Everything he had held as true was up for grabs. Everything.

Robin nodded, a sadness appearing in her eyes at his question. "I'll never lie to you again, Simon. She's yours, she's ours." She smiled. "Talking of which, Cassie doesn't look so great."

"Yeah, I wanted to talk to you about that."

"She's taken it bad, Abby and I, I mean?"

"No, I don't think so. She was pretty easy about that. There's something else. She's been so, I don't know, secretive."

"Runs in the family."

"And I found some pills in her room."

"What sort of pills?"

"I'm not sure. Before I had a chance to look at the box she snatched it away, said it was nothing, vitamins that you'd given her."

Robin twisted her lip. "I don't remember... maybe it was zinc or some echinacea."

"No, it began with T. Trip-, Try- something like that. Mean anything to you?"

"You got me worried, Simon."

"Yeah, me too. I thought you'd have the answer."

"You've got to find those pills. We need to check them out."

"Should I have it out with her?"

"I don't think so, not right now. It might be nothing. Let's find the pills first."

"OK, leave it to me."

They walked up the hill past the newsagent's. "Didn't you want to pick up a paper?"

Simon scratched his ear. "Oh right, I'll get it on the way back."

"You don't have to chaperone me, you know, I'm old enough now."

He smiled. "Yeah. Listen, I'm sorry about last night, Robin. I overreacted."

"You reacted exactly how I thought you would. There's nothing to be sorry about. It was my fault. Mine and Martin's."

"Do you mind having him around for a few days?"

"Do you?"

Was this one of those strange Latin questions that demanded the answer 'Yes'? His guilt at the priority he was according *Artes* flashed to the front of his mind. "I suppose not."

They kissed at Abby's door. "Want to come in?" Robin offered.

Simon shook his head. "No, not yet. I'd like to meet the snake some time, but I need to get back. Give Abby my love."

"Sure."

The pavements were still wet and plastered with leaves as he went back down the hill, picking his way with care. His ankle still didn't feel a hundred percent and the last thing he needed was to go over on it. He didn't see Martin Sparrow coming towards him.

"Hi, I saw you go by."

Simon nodded.

"I was in the White Hart, checking in. They're taking me in for a few days, obviously not too put off by last night's antics." Sparrow laughed.

Simon grunted.

"They had one room left. They hoped I wouldn't mind that it was haunted."

"Oh yeah?"

"Yeah, some old girl topped herself about a million years ago. A little bird tells me you've got some ghosts of your own at Paycocke's."

Simon had just about had enough of little birds. "Who's been telling you that?"

"Robin, last night. I get the impression the place freaked her out."

"I don't know." Simon just wanted to get home, stoke the fire and have an afternoon nap in front of the Spurs game. "I've never seen anything."

"You believe in ghosts?"

"No, not really. You?"

"The question is: do they believe in me?"

Simon smiled without much enthusiasm.

Martin put his hand on Simon's arm. "It's never going to be the same, Simon. I wouldn't have come back if I'd known Robin was going to tell you. Alex *is* your daughter, Simon. No amount of blood tie is going to take that away. But, you're right, there's no going back now. It's done and we have to deal with it. Like you said, we have to move forward."

Simon didn't recall saying that at all, but he let it pass. He couldn't think about that right now. "What about 1477?" he said.

"What?"

"1477? *Artes*? You remember? 1477?"

"Oh. Oh, yeah. Call yourself a book man? 1477 was the year Vespucci smuggled the manuscript out of Bologna, the year Thomas More was born, the year Edward IV was on the throne and the year," he paused for effect, "William Caxton printed his first book."

"Caxton?"

"Think about it: you have this priceless and controversial manuscript. It's unique, too unique, so you'd like to make a few backup copies. Mr Xerox hasn't invented the photocopier, but you hear of this Billy-boy Caxton in merry olde England and you think maybe you could do a deal. The manuscript's here, Simon, I'm convinced of it. It's here in England. Caxton is the key."

Caxton. Could Sparrow be right? Would the Vespuccis have trusted *Artes* to an Englishman? It seemed so tenuous, but so enticing. Where could the manuscript be now? Was Caxton the key?

Chapter 25
Money

"Can you lend me some cash?" Cassie fiddled in her handbag as though she had only just noticed she was running low. This stupid business with Alex had stopped her tapping Dad for more, so Alex owed her. Dad was drifting from crisis to crisis. "I've got an audition this afternoon. In London; I've got to catch the 12:15."

Alex shot Cassie a dubious look. "An audition? What for?"

"What do you mean, 'What for?'?" Cassie snapped back.

Alex held up her hands in surrender. "Whatever. Take it easy, Cass."

Cassie tried to calm herself down. She felt on edge all the time, couldn't control her temper. Like Dad, she thought. Someone said Dad had gone for Sparrow at the pub last night; good for him. Except that judging by the size of Dad's jaw, Sparrow had returned the punch with interest. What a massive outcome: so Alex wasn't Dad's kid at all. Cassie was glad she didn't have that smarmy bastard for a father – he'd more likely be borrowing money from her than the other way around. "It's for a mobile ad."

"Oh, yeah, where's it all happening?"

Cassie could tell Alex didn't believe her. The stupid thing was that this time it was true. She was trying out for the sassy one, the fast-living model with her life entrenched in her mobile. Yeah, she could do it standing on her head. "Some studio in East London. Wapping way."

"Many up for it?"

"I won't know until I get there. A few."

"You might want to fix yourself up a bit - you look kind of tired, Cass."

Cassie prickled. Was she going to make her beg for it? "Want to come up for the ride? We could take in a show or something after."

It seemed to crack the nut. Alex sighed. "Wish I could. Revision to do. I've got a module coming up."

Cassie wanted to say, 'Loosen up, pull a sickie, Dad'll never know,' but the notes weren't in her hand yet. "Too bad. So, what's the score? I could badly use a loan."

"OK, then. I've got some cash upstairs."

Cassie was dazzled by the tidiness of Alex's room. When she had had sleepovers her bedroom had been trashed for days afterwards. With Alex you'd never know there had been one at all.

"Can you manage fifty?" It was always better to pitch high; that way you got what you wanted.

"Where would I get fifty quid? Babysitting's not all it's cracked up to be."

"Yeah, whatever." Cassie knew she had it, it was just a matter of playing the game. "Listen, I'm sorry about the business this morning. Must have been quite a shock."

"Yeah." Alex had her back to Cassie and was unlocking one of the desk drawers. Cassie wondered why her sister felt the need to keep everything locked away. Alex liked to keep herself locked up too – you were never sure what she was thinking.

"What about Sparrow? You won't believe I thought he was a paedo." Cassie scratched her thumb impatiently as Alex counted out the tens.

"Yeah. Well, we'll just have to get used to it. I feel sorry for Dad more than anything."

"By 'Dad' you mean…?"

Alex rolled her eyes. "What do you think? Martin Sparrow is no more my father than Marilyn Monroe. He's just a guy, and not even a very good one at that."

"He's a wanker."

Alex shook her head. "He's just not important."

"If you say so." Cassie caught sight of a wad of notes in Alex's hand, fleeting promises of purple and brown. Damn, she hadn't had a chance to looking for the buried stash yet. The house was always so bloody busy, either Alex with her stupid hockey mates, or Dad and that shit Sparrow. Maybe she could get rid of them all for the day, have a good poke around. Anyway, where did Alex get so much money? Hell, if she wasn't her sister… Alex locked the money back in the drawer. Cassie tried not to be tempted to look where Alex stashed the key.

She felt that Alex didn't trust her, that the lock and key precautions were done for her benefit. But then again, of course you never knew with some visitors to the house, they looked upon the 'Private' signs as a challenge, although most of the time anybody breaching the private rooms would just be confronted by a pile of washing-up or a stack of mouldy books.

Cassie folded the notes and tucked them into the back pocket of her jeans. "Right, thanks, cheers for the loan, but I need to be out of here."

"You going like that?"

"Like what?" Cassie challenged her. Just because Alex was bankrolling her, she didn't have the right to get all maternal.

Alex backed off. "Nothing. Just, you know, maybe like a shower or something."

"No time."

"Cass?"

"What?"

"You sure you're OK? I mean that stuff with Mom and all, and now Martin? You look, like, wasted."

"I'm fine, right?"

"You're so thin."

Cassie flipped it into a joke. "That's the nicest thing you've said to me all day."

Alex held her with her gaze until Cassie escaped by reaching for the door handle. "I'm just worried about you. So is Dad."

Cassie turned back to her sister. "So that's what it's all about, is it? Dad's got you spying on me. He doesn't believe me himself, so he gets his little KGB to work on the case. Is that where all your money comes from?"

Alex tinged red. "No, Cassie, come on, it's not like that."

Cassie opened the door. "Look, I got to go, OK?" She felt her back pocket to make sure the cash was still there and tried to put a lid on her irritability. "Thanks for the loan, Al. I'll pay you back at the end of the month."

"Whatever."

*   *   *

The train rumbled through the no man's land of outer London, blackened walls giving way to tags spray-painted in garish colours, neon reds and oranges blazing up the sidings. Her reflection admonished her as the train went through a tunnel. She hadn't realised she looked so tired. Pulling a compact from her tote bag, Cassie tried to mend the red crescents under her eyes, and touched up the tiny craters of wear and tear on her complexion. She wished they had never left London; she had been happy there. Not at school, no, that had been lousy. But, at some point she had been happy. She strained to remember the good times sieved from the bad.

'This train is now arriving at Liverpool Street. Please check you have all your belongings with you as you leave the train. This train is now arriving at Liverpool Street.' Cassie checked in her bag. She still had the Tryph. She was sweating.

The studio was a walk and a few stops away on the Docklands Light, the carriages deserted with everyone else going into town. She followed her A to Z to a barren brownfield site near Canary Wharf, where a lot of small industrial units were clustered together. Maybe she would give Joanne a call, meet up after the audition and dump some of Alex's cash in that new bar in Angel. There was a short guy standing by the entrance to Unit 7A, wearing a leather jacket and Police sunglasses, pointless in the bleak afternoon. He held a clipboard.

"Hi," Cassie said. "Cassie Chance. I'm here for the mobile ad."

"Oh yeah?" He sniggered. Looking at his pad he put a tick against her name. He waved Cassie inside. "Go see Mike, second door on the right. You got some competition, I'll tell you that for nothing."

Mike perched on a table, holding court to half a dozen women, none of whom looked like they had travelled by rail. He wore a marsh green Paul Smith jacket with a black turtleneck that picked out his two day growth. He stopped talking as Cassie walked into the room. Everyone looked at her.

"Yeah?" said Mike.

"Hi, I'm Cassie Chance, here for the audition."

"You what?"

Cassie was overwhelmed with confusion. The guy at the front had had her name; the audition was here, wasn't it? "Are you Mike?"

"Yeah."

"The guy on the front door said to see you. I'm here for the mobile audition."

He smiled. "You're having me on."

A titter snaked around the room. The other women looked impossibly elegant for a Sunday afternoon in East London. Cassie had never felt less sassy in her life. "The audition's not here?" She clung to the frail hope of misunderstanding.

"Look, darling, look around you."

Cassie looked at the other women for support, but they looked through her, not wanting to side with her against Mike, the string-puller. There was a mirror on his right, ringed with bulbs like in a theatre dressing-room, a mirror designed to expose flaws. She saw herself, not slim and glamorous, like the other reflections, but scrawny and tired, her dank hair matted and dead-looking. For a second she thought it was someone else.

"Let's not waste your time, eh, love?" He turned his attention back to the group of women again and resumed his extravagant gestures and big voice. "Now what I want is pure sex appeal, über-confident, in your face sex. You're in control, but you're mad for it. You call the shots. Guys want you, but you're in charge, and..." Mike registered that Cassie still stood in the doorway, too stunned to move. He wasn't even going to let her audition. "Do you mind? I'm short of time as it is."

"I..."

"Come on, girl, win some, lose some. Rick," he called to the guy in the leather jacket. Rick came in, still wearing his sunglasses.

"Rick, mate. See..." Mike clicked his fingers.

"Cassie." Rick helped Mike out.

"Yeah. See Cassie out, would you? Better luck next time, darling."

Thunder sounded like stones on a tin tray as she walked back over the waste ground to the station and she didn't notice the marbles of rain start to splatter from the sky. She needed that job, needed it, and they wouldn't even let her audition. How could she have failed? She didn't want to call Joanne any longer, just wanted to be in her bed, where it was safe and warm and there were no Mikes to reject her. She needed Roach.

The carriages were packed with steaming people this time, all seemingly aware of the failure that spiralled from her, their laughter mocking her. Their bodies swayed with the movement of the train, jostling her and making her feel sick. The air was fetid and sour and each breath made her want to vomit. Sweat started to run down her neck. Westferry, Limehouse, Shadwell, when were they going to get there? The carriage stopped just before they drew into Bank, the dim glare of the platform lights tantalising but unreachable. People pushed against her, as though they could leave the train before the doors opened, and she was squashed against a pole. She felt a tug at her handbag and she clutched it to her. The train juddered forward and edged into the station. The doors opened with a shake and people pushed to get onto the platform.

Cassie lost her balance as she fell out backwards and that was when the Stanley knife flashed across her and sliced through the strap of her tote bag. She didn't even see it happen as she fell to her knees, just the silhouette of fingers drawing the bag away from her and her own flailing hand clutching at air. She screamed but her weak voice was lost in the crowd, and no one responded. When she got to her feet she just saw a milling throng of long coats, no one running, no one with her black bag, just a thick wall of laughing, chatting people.

She sat down on the steps and started to cry. She had no ticket, no mobile, no money, no job and no life. And no pills.

Chapter 26
Room

Simon needed room to think. And time. He had put Sparrow off until tomorrow. Another day. Was it always just another day, or the same one - one more day, crawling by?

Alex was clacking away at her keyboard when he got in; for her it was another day, another essay, always on time, not like Cassie. Why had he loved Alex more? He sat on the staircase and put his head in his hands, listening to the rhythmic typing upstairs. Did he love her because she was everything he wasn't? Organised, purposeful, fit, in control, whereas Cassie was another version of him, insecure and cracked? He owed Cassie.

He owed Cassie because there was something wrong – she was disintegrating; he had to find those pills. He knocked on her door and when there was no reply he pushed it open. There was no end to the chaos; there was not even a beginning. Alex's typing drummed through the thin ceiling above him and he felt like a burglar in his daughter's room. Cassie's curtains were only half-drawn and the room was all shadow. Simon built an excuse for his furtiveness if he was interrupted by stripping her bed and putting the dirty washing in a heap in the floor, joining the other heaps dotted around the room like molehills.

Where would she hide pills? Everywhere he looked there was anarchy. Thinking that there must be some kind of order to the disarray, Simon put everything he moved back in its disordered home. Cassie had been so touchy lately that she would erupt if she knew he was searching her room. OK, so on the one hand, tough, but he needed to get her on his side if he was to get her out of this mess. Robin was right – they had to find out what she was on, then they could take it from there. Obvious places revealed nothing: the wardrobe; her chest of drawers; the bookshelves.

He checked in all the drawers on her desk – nothing but piles of old notes, envelopes and papers. Looking further, he saw that tucked away in the corner of the desk was a curling Post-It with the message 'Call Roach' written on it beside a Colchester number. Was this progress? Roach. Who was Roach? Memories of Cambridge evenings tempered by mellow spliffs of Red Leb flickered in his head and he dismissed them. They knew what they were doing back then, and the stuff wasn't cut with God only knew what. Roach. Simon copied out the telephone number onto a scrap of paper and put it in his pocket.

He stopped, his subconscious registering that Alex was no longer typing above him. He heard her laugh, light and breezy, and wondered where she could find the humour after all that had happened. What did they call it? Bouncebackability – whatever it was, Alex had it. Again he was struck by his closer similarity to Cassie. Hers had been a teenage apprenticeship with which he had empathy: sullen, moody and rebellious. At thirteen she had wanted to paint her bedroom black and learn to play bass; at thirteen Alex had wanted tennis lessons and a filing cabinet. Her laugh drifted down through the ceiling again, or maybe she was coming downstairs, he couldn't tell. She was finding something funny in Much Ado. That was fine. While she was engrossed in her homework she wasn't finding him at it.

Simon opened the curtains wider, knelt down and rummaged through her bedside cabinet. There was a small army of pill bottles there and his heart hit the accelerator pedal. He couldn't be certain, but he didn't recognise the one she had snatched from him the previous day. On the floor months of dust had drifted up against the skirting board. Something had disturbed the dust, making a track like jerky footprints disappearing under the bed. Simon followed its path with his hand, feeling into the dark void. He could see nothing under there, and swept his hand in a blind arc, picking up a dropped ballpoint, a pound coin and an uncapped mascara, wizened and dry. He swept deeper and touched something else which skittered away from his fingers. Hauling himself further under the bed he covered the floorboards with his palm and ran into a large splinter.

"Bugger." Simon drew his hand away and it bumped into the recalcitrant object again. It rolled a couple of inches away from him before he trapped it and curled his finger around it. Clutching his prize he moved back and cracked his head on the underside of the bed as he came out. "Damn." Leaning against the side of the bed he opened his hand and stared at the small black and orange capsule. It had some writing on the side, but Cassie's room was so dim that he couldn't make out what it said. He put it in his shirt pocket and patted the small lump it made.

The laughing had stopped and he could hear Alex's keyboard tapping away in the distance again. He had better get out while the going was good. Picking his way through the minefield of Cassie's cast-off clothes he paused at her door, listening for Alex. Now there was no sound at all and he was easing the door open when he remembered his alibi, the bedclothes. He went back for the bundle and came out of Cassie's room, whistling 'Oliver's Army' in open innocence. He might as well do Alex's washing while he was at it.

With exaggerated clumping he went upstairs, calling, "Alex?"

"Yeah?"

"Just washing the bedding, Al. Can I come in?"

"OK."

Alex was slumped at her desk.

Simon dropped Cassie's sheets and put his arm around her. "Are you all right, Ally?"

She raised her head. "Yeah, I suppose."

He ruffled her hair. The red streaks were fading, or maybe he was just getting used to them. "Is it Martin?"

She looked up and sighed. "No, Dad." She gestured at a textbook, open at a page of mystical hieroglyphs and formulae. "It's organic chemistry."

Simon laughed.

"Dad?"

"Yes?"

"I love you, Dad."

He hadn't noticed its disappearance, but he couldn't recall exactly when she had stopped telling him that she loved him. Sometime between learning to ride a bike and catching the Tube by herself there had been an unstoppable surge of independence which had flattened the words in its path. He smiled. "I love you too, Al."

"It doesn't matter. Martin, I mean. He doesn't matter. You're my Dad, only you."

Simon went down on his haunches and hugged her, feeling his eyes start to give way. "Oh, Alex."

She hugged him back, pressed herself into his embrace. She seemed five years old again. "I'm so sorry, Dad."

"I know."

Simon started to strip Alex's bed. Unlike Cassie, who had always bitten the feeding hand, Alex gave affection without price. Maybe she knew something; perhaps she was closer to Cassie. "Al?"

"Yeah?"

"About Cassie?"

"What about her?" Alex was buried in her chemistry textbook again.

"I don't know. She's been behaving oddly lately."

"Lately meaning the last fifteen years?"

"You know what I mean." Simon centred the sheets and pillow cases in the duvet cover and rolled it into a ball. "She's been so moody, so secretive, so..."

"So?"

"So... I don't know. Well, you know her better than I do."

"I wouldn't bank on it."

Julia's bedding was folded up neatly on the air bed. It looked so pristine that Simon wondered if he could get by without washing it and just put it back in the airing cupboard. Robin would have laundered *him* for taking such a short cut. He had to ask Alex; he couldn't keep it in. "Look... do you think she might be on something?"

Alex caught his eye contact and maintained it. "You mean on drugs? Hard drugs, Dad?"

"Well, yeah, any drugs?"

Alex shook her head. "She wouldn't. She's not that stupid." There was something in Alex's expression that made Simon doubt the last part.

"But?"

"I don't know, Dad, she has been acting weird lately. I caught her crying in the bathroom the other morning."

"Over what?"

"I don't know. She wouldn't say. Maybe she's got some kind of boyfriend hassle."

The thought pricked Simon. "Do you know someone called Roach?"

"Roach? As in…"

Simon nodded. "Yes, as in."

"No. I'm sure I'd remember if I'd heard the name, but, no."

"You haven't seen her with any strange pills." He debated whether to show her the black and orange capsule.

"Dad, all pills are strange." At odds with his own teenage years, Alex trusted her body to get along without any help.

"Yeah. Maybe you could keep your eye on her as well."

"Talk to her, Dad."

Simon waved his arms in exasperation. "I've tried."

"Try again."

"Talking doesn't always work with Cassie. She's not you."

"Good job, too."

The phone rang.

Alex jumped out of her seat and hared downstairs. "I'll get it. It's probably Julia."

Simon picked up the parcels of washing and negotiated the narrow door, only to hear Alex pound the steps on a return trip. She brandished the handset at her father.

"It's Cassie. She's reversed the charges. I think you'd better have a word."

Chapter 27
You Cannot Catch Old Birds With Chaff

Ann perched on a stool in the courtyard, raising the nap on the wool with long, delicate strokes. She had a natural way with the teasels, using their stiff and prickly spines to separate and straighten the fibres without tearing them. It was a skill not readily acquired, but one for which her born talent was clear. It had been a chance meeting of some fortune, Thomas reflected, both sparing their lives and giving him a fine worker. Not that the fortune had been in just the one direction. In three weeks Ann had grown healthier on good pottage and flesh, losing that greenish tinge which had so concerned Robert. She was still gaunt, but with a pleasant flush arising from work well done.

Thomas noted that the development of Ann's prowess with the card and comb had been accompanied by a singular change in the opposite direction where Robert was concerned. Around Ann, his wise and measured words descended into farce as his tongue tied, and last Friday he had walked into a pail of water, sending it flying across the yard. The man became boy once more in her presence.

The business continued to prosper, but the failure in London harried him, gnawing at his thoughts. He and Robert had searched the house but found nothing that might indicate William Spooner's hand. It seemed that the riddle was not to be solved and that his father would remain in purgatory. The killing of the builder lay like an anvil on Thomas's conscience and his sleepless nights returned. He awoke sweating in the dark, reaching for the comfort of Margaret next to him and finding her gone before he remembered the truth. The dread recollection stabbed at him and sleep eluded his grasp as he stared into the dark until dawn offered peace.

Some respite was gained by taking Ann into their confidence in the hope that she might throw light onto the sombre secret.

She was sympathetic. "Your father was a good man, was he not?"

"Aye, indeed, none better."

"Then you cannot doubt the workings of the Lord. Surely he is gone to Heaven."

Thomas looked about him at the walls of his house. Once they had seemed so grand, yet now they conspired to cage him, the close-packed studs like bars. "What you say is true, yet I fear that something passed which was not of my father's making, but which embroiled him in its terrible consequences. He was a party to some design against the Lord's will, and now is being punished for it." He sighed and looked down at his bowl, the fat beef cooling untouched. "As I am." He pushed his food away and picked up his spoon, turning it about. Ash wood; he had carved the delicate pattern on it himself in idle moments many years before. It did not compete with the carving on the ceiling above his head, but gave its own rudimentary pleasure of achievement. His knife he found hard to use after its devilish work in Spooner's end. He blamed himself still.

"Thomas?" Robert looked up at Paycocke and the clothier saw himself twenty years before, full of hopes and dreams, a confidence and self-belief that he thought could never be extinguished, but which had burnt low somehow, like a candle for which only the stump of tallow remained, with a weak and wavering flame.

"Aye?"

"William Spooner follows you still?"

The older man nodded. "Each night."

Robert put his hand on Thomas's arm. "Mayhap if you seek confession with the abbot, it will spare you the dreams."

Thomas looked away, unconvinced.

"The better man was saved that night."

"I am none so sure."

Thomas could feel the heat of Robert's exasperation. "Well enough, Thomas. But if there is to be resolution to this sorry tale, then it rests in your own hands." He thumped the table and turned his face away.

The clothier was unaccustomed to being spoken to in such a fashion and was about to start at Robert when Ann intervened, reaching over to touch him on the hand. "Be not angry, Master Paycocke." He saw her as for the first time, still waif-like and as transparent as a fairy, but her skin bright and her eyes dark pools in which he could see himself, bitter and lost. "Robert speaks true."

Thomas nodded. He knew in his heart Robert was right. All his life Thomas had controlled his own destiny and been master of his fate, bowing only to the Lord. To be like a leaf in the wind ailed him. "Aye, perchance so. I will seek absolution this day."

Robert sought out Thomas's gaze. "And then there is no more to be done."

Thomas sighed and forced himself to agree. "We have sought the answer in all quarters of this house and found naught. There is in very truth no more to be done."

His clerk laughed. "So eat."

Thomas laughed in return. Robert was his wisest ally. The beef, though cooled, was fine and tender. "We should not tarry overlong. I have much else to do this day, bales to deliver, a new loom to install, and weavers who complain of tardy spinners who render them idle."

Robert looked at him in mock horror. "The weavers complain of idleness? Then that is a new tale."

"Time lost is pennies lost." Thomas began to feel more like himself. Perchance it was possible to leave this wretched episode behind him.

Ann was pensive. She had her hands together up to her mouth as though she were praying, and her head tipped to one side so Thomas could see her white neck, wisps of her plaited ruddy hair trailing from her coif like strands of fine wool. She would make Robert a fine wife, were he able to curb his clumsiness in her presence. And he would make her a fine and lusty husband. What childer they might have.

Ann raised her strong and stubborn chin – something of which Robert would be wise to be wary, he thought. "If I might be so bold?" she said.

"Aye?" Thomas wondered what was afoot.

"When you looked at me just now, it did bring to mind that day by the stream, on our journey from London…"

"Aye?"

"You did look at me then, and told something of a face. What meant you by that?"

Thomas rubbed the callous tips of his fingers. "Aye, a face. I do not rightly know, but it was your own face at that instant, thin and worn, your eyes too large for that comely space, and it recalled to me William Spooner's final moments of life, indeed the moments that I believed were my own last. Spooner stared at me, his eyes ablaze, and laughed at my impending death. The life was draining from me, my lips feeling no more my own, my eyes wanting to escape the dying husk of my body, and Spooner said something about a face. I know not if I misremember, but he said, 'I was the face' or 'the face was mine.'" He shook his head with his inability to fix upon the scene. "I do not rightly know."

Robert leant forward with urgency. "But you think it of import?"

"Mayhap. But his senses were lost to him. A man imbalanced in his humours might say anything that came to his mind. And Spooner was as choleric a man as any I have known."

Ann smiled. "But William Spooner was not so imbalanced that he could not see the reason for his downfall. See it more clearly than day."

Paycocke's brow furrowed. "What is it you say, Ann?"

"The face, I am convinced, is the key. Whose face it is, we have yet to determine. But I am persuaded that in this tale there is another character with the knowledge to unlock our mystery, and his face is the one so pertinent at the time of your demise."

It was novel to be enlightened so by a woman. Thomas was disinclined to accept what she said, but had to contend that her idea had merit. She spoke with good counsel and equity, as he had become accustomed. As far as William had been concerned, it was the hour of his vile enemy's death, so the symbol of the face might have had some great significance for the man. But how? Thomas had all but erased the foul memory of that night, the stench of Spooner's breath as he choked the life from him. He shook his head. "I do not have the answer."

Ann contradicted him with a force that made him draw

back. "I believe you do, Master Paycocke." He admired her vigour. "You have buried the memory, and will fain resurrect it."

She had some strange design in her head. "So?"

"We must draw it out."

"And how, pray, shall we do this?" Robert's scepticism was clear. Thomas could see that the boy was affronted that he had not himself conceived of this plan.

Ann placed her palms on the table. "We shall revisit that night."

"I have not the time to journey to London," Thomas said.

Ann smiled. "Nay. We shall not leave this room."

"Then?"

"I propose that Robert take the part of William Spooner and we relive the night's events."

"And you, Ann?"

"I shall watch. I shall observe and I shall see. Robert?"

"I am no strolling player but game nonetheless. Thomas?"

Paycocke's mouth was dry in recall of the incident. "I know not."

"Be of good cheer, my friend. What harm might it do?"

"Very well."

Ann looked at the two men. "So, how did it come to pass?"

Thomas stood. "We were lost in the maze of alleys that is Cheapside. This much you know. We stopped, the better to discern our way. Then, out from the darkness stepped Spooner. At first he was content with hurling insults..."

Robert smiled and raised his smallest finger. "He called you a three-inch fool, if I am not incorrect, Thomas."

"If I am not incorrect, I believe 'twas nine, Robert, and a vast underestimation at that, if you value your position as my clerk."

"Tush, gentlemen." Ann grinned at Paycocke's humour. Thomas's spirits lifted at the sight of her. It might be well in time.

"He wielded a large club and proceeded to attack me."

Robert looked about the room and picked up a staff resting near the window. He approached Thomas with menace, assuming his role with great verve. "You puking maggot-pie, Paycocke. You pox-marked canker blossom."

Thomas Paycocke retreated against the wall, some of the fear of the Cheapside night entering him anew. He held up his arm in front of his face as Robert aimed blows at him, missing and striking the walls. For a brief moment the fear was real, such looked the anger in the younger man's eyes, then Robert stepped aside as though someone had jumped on his back. He flung the invisible assailant to one side, in the process losing the staff. "A pox on you, Paycocke," he screamed, and put his hands around Thomas's neck.

The pressure was real, and it seemed to Thomas that Spooner's hands lived again in the form of Robert, crushing the life from him. Robert brought his face down to Thomas's and Paycocke could smell the meat on his breath. "The face. Whose is the face?"

Thomas gasped, and looked at his clerk. Robert would play his part too well. The clothier started to feel light-headed and wanted this foul game to be over. Nothing would come of it, nothing.

Robert squeezed harder. "The face, Paycocke. My face, your face, the face. The face. The face."

Thomas stared into Robert's eyes, as black as honeybees, and he saw again the anger and hatred that had possessed Spooner. Then he saw past Robert into his own reflection, saw his bulging eyes and his lips screaming for breath.

"The face, the face, the face." Then Robert tossed back his head and laughed, in doing so relaxing his grip.

Thomas surged at the air, gulping a huge mouthful and screamed, "Kees."

Robert took his hands away and held Thomas in his arms. "Thomas?"

The clothier heaved back and forth, taking in the precious air. "Aye. My face. It was my face. And Kees. It was Kees whom Spooner would tell. The carver Kees."

Chapter 28
A Little Pot is Soon Hot

"Who is this Kees?" asked Robert.

They sat in the garden as Thomas recovered his senses. Pale and gentle doves swooped over their heads into Margaret's dovecote. Thomas's throat was reliving his agonies at Spooner's hands and as he talked he wondered if it were of true necessity for Robert to have gripped him so. Indeed so, or he would not have recalled Kees's name, lost in the hidden corners of his memory. It had been a cunning idea of Ann's. "Kees," he said, "was a Dutchman, a carver of wood and a fine one too. He spent a single summer in Coxhall at work on this house." He gestured at his home.

Robert could not conceal his excitement. "And how does he look? How is his face?"

Thomas put his head in his hands and stared into the distance of his memory. His words were measured. "I do not recall. There were many carvers, some from Coxhall and Lavenham, but others from France and the lowlands. The house was built in one single season."

"And this Kees?"

"He had a fine way with wood - that I do remember. He arrived with a master carver by the name of Gijsbert, but it was plain from the beginning that Kees's work outranked his master's. He was but a journeyman and I did not speak with him over much. Indeed he did have a mode of speech most injurious to the ear." He laughed at the memory. "Happily, William Spooner as master builder busied himself with such detail as there was to discuss. Nonetheless, I do know that it was this Kees who was the carver of my Margaret's 'M' and my own 'T', so I have cause to thank him for this legacy."

Robert was puzzled. "But why, Thomas, did foreign craftsmen come to be in your employ?"

Thomas smiled. "Now that I can answer. Look about you in Coxhall, in Bocking, in Halstead, Colchester even. Do you see a house as mine own? Carved with such beauty, such a wondrous feat of craftsmanship? On our brief journey to London, did you see anything to rival the Paycocke House?"

Robert admitted to the house's uniqueness.

"I desired a house fitting to the name of Paycocke, to revere my father, a house such as none other would possess. I have been to France, Flanders, The Netherlands even, for trade, for mark my words, Robert, there is much coin to be made for the adventurous trader. Aye, it is not for naught that they do speak of the Merchant Adventurers. And in those lands I have seen beauty such as which an Englishman may only dream upon. Their carvers, their masons and builders have methods far in advance of our own and I saw a home for such splendour here in Coxhall.

"In the few years after the death of John Paycocke, God rest his soul, I set about devising this house, and sent word to my trading partners that I sought the finest craftsmen to work upon it. It would be a fitting tribute to my father and the place in which I would cherish Margaret and our children." He swung his head from side to side, sighing. "A place for my sons to inherit."

Robert was silent. Thomas valued his clerk's disposition and placed a hand on his shoulder.

"Ho there, gentlemen." Ann came from the house carrying cups of ale. "'Tis thirsty work, the actor's life, is it not? I have brought sustenance. But wherefore so quiet?"

Thomas took the ale and drained half of it. Ann was right, it was thirsty work. The drink tackled its labour at once and lifted Thomas. "I am telling the tale of how my house did come about."

"Aye? Then an interesting tale it must be, for never have I seen such a place." Ann sat on the long grass beside them. Her kirtle rose a few inches and Thomas could see her thin ankles, as white as the doves, delicate and fragile. She should have a care lest she raise the blood in Robert.

"As it should be, for I did spend upwards of forty pounds on its building."

Ann gasped at the inconceivable amount of money that one man might have that he would spend so much on his dwelling.

"And Kees, tell her of Kees, Thomas."

"Aye, in good time, Robert, but it boots not to think too much upon Kees, for I know not where he might be found, even if he is still in this land."

Robert told Ann of Kees's prowess as a carver and his involvement in the construction of the house. She turned to Thomas, the same light in her eyes as she put the same question as Robert, "And how did he look, this Kees? How was his face?"

Thomas laughed. "Would that I could remember. I houstered so many craftsmen and builders in Coxhall at that time that they all become one in my mind. Oft did I share a tankard of sack with William Spooner of an evening to talk of progress on the house and would see the group of carvers at another table, supping their pennies, but one Dutchman is like any other, and they did not drink long, for hard-earned money is soon spent, and these lowlanders are wise with their coin."

"Think, Thomas, think on it." Robert urged Paycocke to dig into his memory. "Were they to be seen at church?"

"Nay. It is my belief that we pray to the same God, but the Dutchmen held to a different doctrine and I saw them not at St. Peter's. They prayed together, but apart from us, as indeed they did everything: eat, sleep, drink, everything apart."

Robert winked at Ann. "Then perchance we have need of a second play, this time set at the inn. We might drain a firkin or two in pursuit of Thomas's recollections."

"I would sooner that Robert run a course or two of jousting for his sport than make merry at my expense." Thomas laughed but shook his head. "In truth it is no use. I have a picture in my head of the men, but no more. And indeed were I to know the face of Kees, what then?"

Robert had no answer.

"Know you where the band of carvers went after that summer?" Ann pulled her cloak about her, for the evening was cooling. It fell over her bare ankles and Thomas smiled to see the flash of disappointment cross Robert's face. His enthusiasm for the pursuit of Kees the carver was a fair screen for his enthusiasm for the pursuit of Ann Cotton.

"Perchance Lavenham, for I heard tell of much work there on the church at that time. But years have passed. I doubt but that any of the Dutchmen are still in this country." Thomas shrugged.

"Thomas, how can you be so…"

"There is no more to be done at this time. I will send word to my trading partner in the lowlands that I seek word of Kees and happen something will arise in time."

"But months may pass…" Robert protested.

Thomas raised his hand. "Hush, Robert. You would be over the stile ere you came to it. This is my busiest season of the year. I have no time to chase rainbows."

"Mayhap…"

"Enough, now. The sky grows dark and there is much to be done on the morrow. I have waited many years for to cleanse my father's soul. If it be God's will that it be done, then I am ready to wait until the end of time."

Robert stared into his cup of ale. "What you will, Thomas. What you will."

Still, Thomas could not stop himself thinking of the Dutch carver and he fell asleep that night with the name of Kees on his lips. For once he slept long and well.

*   *   *

The following day dawned clear. A packhorse arrived with a cargo of pins, girdles and other trifles and Thomas called for Robert to unload and catalogue them, but the clerk was not to be found. Goodday's bed was empty and his shoes gone; no one had seen him leave. The whole day was full of irritations, each of which made Paycocke curse Robert's absence, and even the light-hearted banter of Ann at dinner could not pierce his foul mood.

The day was growing old when Thomas watched Robert Goodday stroll up West Street as though he owned it. "Robert, where have you been this day? I sought you at first light and discovered you had been up betimes and gone. I had great need of you, with a packhorse of supplies and wool arriving from Suffolk, and sorting to be done for the combers. The weaver's boy, idle slugabed, did not come to work this morning, one of the looms has split a warping peg, and John Fuller has broken a finger and is with the barber-surgeon. I ought to have remained a butcher like my grandfather. A pox upon this day. And you, trim mate, were nowhere to be seen."

Robert smiled and Thomas's mood slipped further. "Damn you, Robert. Know you well that idleness is the mistress of vice. Where the devil have you been?"

"Colchester, Thomas."

"Cease with these riddles, Robert Goodday. My wrath is but an inch away."

Robert dropped his good humour and looked down at his shoes, grey with the dust of the road. "I have been to Colchester, Thomas, for there is a quarter in the town that has been settled by the Dutch. Many did come here for work, as far back as the reign of the third Edward."

"And?" Thomas wondered where this was leading.

"It was something you said, Thomas, about the nature of Dutch craftsmen, and how they kept their own company."

Thomas turned his back on Robert and walked over to the house. He wanted the day to be done. "We have talked on this…"

Robert persisted. "I have ofttimes heard tell of this small group of Dutch families that live in Colchester, and it did occur to me that your own Netherlanders might have sought them out in the summer your house was built, if only to hear their tongue and taste their vittals."

Thomas stopped, but did not turn around.

"Thomas, they knew of Kees."

The clothier looked up at his house, at the ermine tail merchant's mark carved on the fascia by Kees's hand. His anger evaporated like the dew. He could not help but love Robert, who would give his life for him. He turned to face his clerk. "Aye, now, did they?"

Robert smiled, his eyes wide with delight. Again, Thomas

saw himself in the boy, before the strains of business had sapped his energies, before Margaret's illness had sucked the joy from his life. "Aye, Thomas. They do call him Kees Visser, a Hollander from Amsteldam. They knew him well."

The clothier could almost not bring himself to ask. He approached Robert, his voice dropping. "And… his face… how is his face?"

Robert laughed. "A fine handsome face, strong of chin with full ripe lips. His hair is of a light brown, like straw, they said, so I do not understand why the sight of you reminded William Spooner of Kees Visser."

"And I not, but he is the only Kees I have ever known, and I'll wager the only Kees known to William, so he must be that man. Oh, Robert, each day we add to our knowledge. Could it be that the Lord will have mercy on my father? He lies with a fair stone over him at St. Peter's, but my heart is heavier still. Can it be that I might free him of his burden? Yet with each day we also add to the mystery. What is it to be?"

Robert grasped Thomas by the shoulders. "The good tidings do not stop there. Kees Visser was not much taken with England. He did go, as we thought, to Lavenham, where he worked for one season, but thereafter he was stricken by sickness for home. He declined to settle in Colchester with his countrymen and returned to Holland."

Thomas's shoulders drooped. The good tidings had been chased by bad. There was no solace to be gained.

"But all is not lost, Thomas. Far from it." Robert opened the pouch at his belt and pulled out a much-folded piece of linen paper. "One amongst the Dutch had his letters, and I did persuade him to write down for me the whereabouts of Kees's family home." He passed the paper to Thomas, who opened it with care. He read the scrawled words, which meant nothing to him, save for the name of the town, Amsteldam.

"Know you Amsteldam, Thomas?"

"Amsteldam. I know of it, in the north of Holland. So far north I have not been. Leyden, Utrecht, aye, for there is an exceeding fine linen to be had in this province, but this

Amsteldam I have not seen. It trades in the main in fish and grain."

"It is on the sea?"

"Aye. I hear there is a fine harbour."

"Then a ship might sail there from Gippesvic or Orford?"

Thomas laughed. "Aye, it might."

"Then?" Robert's eyes widened.

The clothier gripped his clerk. "You are a good man, Robert Goodday, none better. What should I do without you?"

"It is I who could not bear to be without you, Thomas. Then we might leave for Amsteldam?"

"Such a voyage is not made in a day." Thomas fought to restrain Robert's enthusiasm. He struggled to contain his own, even though he knew that Kees might no longer live, or might have taken his craft elsewhere. The life of a journeyman was hard. Yet if he had suffered from homesickness then he might have stayed with his kin in Amsteldam; he might be there still. Already Thomas was building plans. After harvest they could go, he and Robert, when the heavy work of the year would be done. They could take a wain of his best broadcloth, and make some fair trade to finance the venture. It had been a while since he had been to the lowlands. Aye, it would be a fine adventure, and with Robert by his side, yet more than that. Robert Goodday, the son he would now never have.

"Amsteldam." Thomas went to his knees before his house, mindless of the dust on his hose. "Amsteldam, my father." He put his hands together. "Amsteldam."

Chapter 29
Ida's Room

Doctor Phipps came with us at once. I had the rather unpleasant notion that his eagerness to accompany us drew some origin in the fact that I, a Holst, was with Edward Daynes, but perhaps I was being uncharitable. He was a short, plump man with a baldness that he tried to disguise by sweeping the sparse remaining hair across his shiny pate.

The doctor leant over Edward's mother, brushing her fine hair aside and prising open her parchment eyelids. It was all I could do not to scream out, for she was more ghostly than any spirit I might have imagined emanating from the panelling at Paycocke's. Her face was the colour of milky porridge, grey and apathetic, her skin stretched across her bones like a drum. Suddenly my appetite for ghost hunting was much diminished.

Doctor Phipps was not in the slightest alarmed by Mrs. Daynes, but took her temperature and her pulse. He was altogether something of a cold fish, although I expect that is what is required in the medical profession. I gathered that he has been a physician for more than thirty years, so there is little he has not seen. Yet he was so matter-of-fact, almost dismissive, that I wanted to cry for Edward's sake.

"There is no real change since last I saw her. In fact she is holding up quite well." He removed his round spectacles, the better, I had the impression, to avoid looking us in the eye. He lowered his voice. "I do not need to tell you, Edward, that your mother is dangerously ill. I have seen a number of cases of diabetes and your mother's is amongst the worst." The doctor curled up his stethoscope and put it back into his black bag, burying his attention in his instruments. "The next stage is likely to be a diabetic coma. You should prepare yourself for that, my boy. Chin up. In the meantime, make sure your mother has plenty of fluids and try to keep her comfortable."

How I hoped Edward's mother was not able to hear him. I could hold myself back no more. "But is there nothing you can do?"

The doctor held his spectacles up to the light, as if searching for smears that might be blurring his vision. "Miss Holst. There is, unless you wish to enlighten me, just the one physician in this room. If *Mister* Daynes wishes for a second opinion..." He made it clear that he expected no contribution from me.

I looked at Edward. He stared down at the quilt. "Edward?" I said, but he was lost somewhere in his memories.

Doctor Phipps made a show of consulting his pocket watch, then put a hand on Edward's shoulder. His fingernails were perfect white new moons against Edward's faded charcoal jacket. "All right, my lad. I shall call again in a few days."

Edward did not move as the older man left, just looked down at his mother, and we heard the doctor picking his way down the stairs through the frayed carpet and the broken stair-rods. With the panic diminished I became aware of the smell of urine fogging the air with its rank and acrid presence. I closed my eyes to steady myself against the foulness and was swamped by the dignity Ida Daynes had lost. *I must not cry. I must not.* I counted the stripes on the wallpaper until my eyes lost their place in the confusing pattern and the moment passed. My stomach seemed to grow with every second, as though it wished to escape from the confines of my body. The wallpaper, the cracks in the window panes, the noise of a passing horse in the street, they all assumed the role of an anchor, mooring me to reality.

"Mammy." Edward's voice was small and fragmented. I held out my hand to him and he curled his fingers around mine. He came alive with an immediate vibrancy. "This is Imogen Holst. I told you about her. Remember?" Although his eyes were shrouded with sadness, it could not diminish those brilliant emerald pools. He held my gaze and I wondered what it was he was looking for. My heart skipped as I realised that it was what he was showing me that was important. I was gripped by the awful mosaic of emotions within him: despair; fear; hope; and a flash of desire, all flickering in those green depths. It must not happen, for his sake. His thumb stroked the back of my hand and his eyes mesmerised me; I could do nothing to break their hold.

"Edward." Mrs. Daynes said her son's name without moving her lips. It crawled from her mouth, a mere mumble, and fell. She did not open her eyes.

Edward turned to his mother and the spell was broken. I shivered at its passing. "Mammy?" Ida's mouth twitched into a raw smile. "Can I get you anything, mammy?"

"Imogen," she said.

"Good afternoon, Mrs. Daynes. It is a pleasure to meet you." I reddened at my own crassness, but the twitch that I had seen fledged and grew and a real pleasure bloomed.

She forced her shaky eyelids apart and I could see Edward's eyes in the slits, but darker and mistier, like bottle glass. "You *are* very pretty," she said, as if confirming her own thoughts.

"Edward." A man's voice, simmering with rage, accused him from below. "Where are my cigs?"

"Pa." Edward looked around the bedroom.

"Edward." The voice was louder. His father was at the bottom of the stairs. "Edward, what the fuck is this?"

I was shocked by his father's language and drew back into the room, tucking myself into the curtains. Edward choked and gestured at me to be quiet. "I'm coming, pa," he called from the door.

His steps were light and were accompanied by a heavier footfall going up the stairs to meet him. "I want it cleaned up, you rat's arse. And you've not finished the spuds yet, neither."

The chamber pot, of course. I remembered seeing it as we dashed into the house, but hardly registering it with the urgency throttling us. Edward must have dropped it as he left the house to fetch Dr. Phipps. The stench of urine rose into the room to confirm it.

"Where are me Gallahers, Edward?"

"I don't know, pa."

"What do you mean," his father raised his voice into a squeaky imitation of Edward, "'I don't know, pa?' I'll give you, 'I don't know, pa,' smoking all me fags."

"I didn't, pa. I never touched them."

"Don't give me that, you whelp. What you need is a good hiding, and I've half a mind to give it you now."

I looked over at Ida. Despite the noise, she had drifted off into a leaden sleep again. I tried to place the blame for Edward's father's temper on his love for his dying wife, but I could only clench my fists at the cruelty of the man. He thumped around the two rooms of the ground floor, slamming cupboards and drawers. I heard cutlery fall to the floor and more curses. No sound of Edward could be heard, only his brute of a father. I imagined my friend curled into a ball, rendering himself as small as possible to escape harm. I prayed Edward would not do anything silly.

"Did you look on the mantelpiece, pa?"

"Of course I looked on the..." The ranting stopped. "Who put them there?" I heard the crackle of a new packet of cigarettes being opened and a match strike and then silence followed as he inhaled the tobacco. "I suppose you want this, do you? 'British Birds', pah, I don't know why you collect these."

"Pa?"

"Ask nicely." Edward's father sniggered. "Go on, then."

"Please, pa."

There was a sound of tearing and Edward gulped back a cry.

"Waste of bloody time. Better if they took a ha'penny off the price of the fags." Edward's father laughed, a deep guttural roar. It was the first time I had heard his temper ebb, lubricated by the vindictive act of ripping up Edward's cigarette card. I simply had to step in, to stand beside my friend, and I took the steps with a thundering heart. He was astonished to see me, his concrete jaw hanging open in surprise. "Who the hell are you?"

"This is Imogen Holst, pa."

"Imogen who? You the nurse, then?" He gestured up the stairs.

"Pa, they live at Paycocke's. The Holsts." Edward was having trouble manipulating his voice to more than a mumble.

Daynes tipped his head as recognition sifted through. He nodded and stroked the harsh black bristle on his chin. "You're them Germans, aren't you?" I opened my mouth to contradict him. "I had enough of you Jerries in the war." He spat on the kitchen floor.

"They're not German, pa. They're…"

"German name, ain't it?"

"I am English," I said. "I was born in Richmond." I was determined not to let him bully me.

There was no resemblance between Edward and his father, whose eyes were empty, past feeling. He was heavy and lumbering, a sour man. Unkemptness hung from him, his black matted hair curling past his ears to his stubble. I thought he had been drinking, for a visible aggression rose from him. He stared at me. "Oh, aye," he said, folding his arms. "What you doing here, then?"

"Imogen is my friend."

The big man turned to his son, his eyes livid with hate. He raised his hand across his face as if to give Edward a clout. Edward drew back and I could see this was no idle threat. A half-scream escaped my lips and his father stopped, instead scratching the hairs on his chin. "Is she now? Is she?"

"Yes, pa."

"Perhaps I should go, Edward." I did not want to leave Edward to the cauldron of his father's unpredictable temper, but I was an unwilling catalyst for the man's ire.

Edward moved his head just an inch from side to side. His lower lip was clamped between his teeth, as though he could not trust his mouth to follow orders and might let slip some incriminating phrase.

His father nodded. "Aye, go," he said. "Better that you don't come back here and all. You're not for the likes of us. Get back to your Paycocke's House. See if you can find some happiness there." He turned away, but I heard him laugh under his breath. "You'd be the first."

"Mister Daynes…"

He sniggered and gave a beer-stained belch. "That house is jinxed."

"What do you mean?" Edward tugged at my sleeve to warn me not to take this conversation any further, but I was compelled to. Even if he were to strike me, I had to find out what he knew.

Daynes locked me with his eyes. They did not have the bright intensity of Edward's, but even so held a wild force of their own. "No one stays there for long," he said. "Have you not noticed?" He raised a thick arm and leant against the door jamb. His grubby shirt cuff slipped down and I could see each individual black hair carpeting his forearm. "They all scarpered: Charlie Pudney; that Buxton feller; and your red vicar. Mind you, he knew more than he was letting on. You'll be the same, believe you me. I give you six months."

"But I don't understand," I said. "What is it?" Edward's tugging became more frantic.

"It's evil is what it is. You'll take my advice and leave that house before Robin comes for you."

"Robin?"

"Aye, Robin." He jerked a nod at Edward. "And I'll not have my lad in there neither."

"But, Mister Daynes..."

"That's all I'm saying. I'm off." He put the packet of cigarettes in his pocket and lurched through the front door.

Edward picked up the pieces of the cigarette card. He placed each of the torn scraps on the dresser and fitted them together like a jigsaw puzzle to reveal a robin, its red breast scarred for life by Edward's father.

"I didn't really collect them anyway," Edward said.

"Edward, what did he mean by Robin coming for me?"

"Can we go for a walk?"

"Yes, but..."

"I'll just check on mammy."

Robin was the woodcutter, was he? Edward had told me his story the first time we met: Robin who had carved the Christmas angel which had disappeared during the dissolution of the monasteries. He had been searching for it ever since.

We walked in silence down East Street, in the opposite direction to Paycocke's. Edward led, but looked down at the pavement, his hands thrust into his pockets. The quiet seemed to intrude between us, and I knew that he was embarrassed that I had met his father. His awkwardness contaminated me.

"How is your mother?" I asked.

He shrugged. "You can get used to anything, can't you?"

I put my hand on his shoulder.

"He wasn't always like this, you know." Edward stared into the distance to where the road tailed up the hill. "He used to play for the Seedgrowers. The football team," he added. "He taught me to how to trap the ball, how to head it with my eyes open. We would stay out until dark smacking that old piece of leather and I was the happiest lad in the world. And I would be West Ham and he'd be Ipswich and some of the other lads would come down with their brothers and their dads and we'd have a right old time. Some nights you would hardly be able to see the ball and we'd walk home back up Stoneham Street arm in arm and we'd have missed tea and mammy'd be in a right state." He looked away from me. "And then she got ill and it was never the same."

I did not know what to say. We walked further.

"We were in the Cup Final this year, did you know that? West Ham?"

I shook my head.

"Lost to Bolton 2-0 at Wembley. Jack and Smith scored and there were all those thousands of people and there was that copper on the white horse, and the King presenting the Cup. Times were that was all I could have wanted in the world, was West Ham in the Cup Final." He kicked at the dirt on the road. "Now it's just dust.

"I love him. I think I still love him. It's just that the pa I know has gone. He's hidden himself away and I don't... I don't know where to find him anymore. He's lost. And I'm lost."

We stopped at a point in the road where a small stream ran. "It is never too late, Edward," I said. "There is always hope. Hope for your mother and for your father too." My heart pounded. I knew it was a lie.

Edward took a deep breath and his thin shoulders heaved. He pointed at the stream. "This is Robin's Brook."

"Robin the woodcutter?"

He nodded. "I don't know if it's true or not," he said. "Some stories get bigger the more they're told. I grew up with him. There's some truth in it, I suppose."

"Your father believes that Robin is haunting Paycocke's?"

"I don't know what he believes these days. Some say as how they've heard Robin's axe chopping in the distance. West Street, East Street, Stoneham Street, he's been heard all over." Edward turned to face me. His cheeks were streaked with grime and he looked much younger, but his eyes still held hope. "Don't be too hard on him, will you, Imogen?"

I wanted very much to be hard on the odious man, but relented. "I should go, Edward, it is getting late."

"I'll walk back with you. But I mustn't be long. I don't like leaving mammy alone."

We left Robin's Brook with its impenetrable secret dappled in the afternoon sunshine and made our way back to Paycocke's. The sun had not yet come around to the front of the building, so the studs and the rusty bricks were enveloped in shadow.

"Imagine getting this house as a wedding present," Edward said.

"Mmm."

"Beats a clock, don't it?"

"Will you come in?" I wanted to tell Edward what I had discovered from Ernest Beckwith. I wanted to look in the dining room at the panelling and imagine once more that I was Billy Howes. I wanted Edward's opinion. More than anything I wanted not to be alone. For the first time since we had moved into Paycocke's House I felt the eeriness that others had mentioned. I felt it upon my shoulders as heavy as the world, weighing me down and seizing my happiness with its giant claw. It had been an absolutely vile day. Perhaps I would feel more optimistic in the morning.

Edward looked up at the jettied first storey, jutting out into the street, looming over us. I could tell he had the same feeling of trepidation as I. The beauty of the carvings on the flying beam at the front taunted me. They knew something I did not, the recumbent king and queen, the mummer and the fool, even the leaves and flowers mocked me, and for a brief second I had the impression that it would always be so, and that I would never discover what lay beneath. "No," he said. "Not this time. I need to get home."

A breeze set a horse chestnut branch tapping against the timbers of a house across the street and the dull sound reminded me of Robin's axe, forever chopping, forever searching for his angel. Children's laughter carried on the breeze, perhaps a gentle game of 'Ring-a-Ring-a-Roses' or hopscotch, pastimes long gone for me, in a childhood that seemed decades old.

Chapter 30
Silent Street

Paycocke's House,
West Street,
Coggeshall,
Essex.

August 12th 1923

Dear Mister Townsend,

I trust you will forgive me for writing to you, but I have no other option. As you will see by my address above, I live at Paycocke's House in Coggeshall. You are perhaps familiar with the house, since I understand you have recently undertaken a restoration of a similar timber-framed house in Silent Street in Ipswich.

Paycocke's is a remarkable example of early sixteenth century architecture, embellished with the most beautiful carvings I have ever seen in my life, yet there is something strange about the house, which seems clouded in mystery. We have lived here but a short time, yet already I feel an unease that seems not in keeping with the beauty of the surroundings. Unusual noises and inexplicable incidents colour our days and nights, and I am most anxious to delve further into the history of Paycocke's in order to assuage my troubled feelings.

I shall come to the point. A number of years ago, Paycocke's house was the subject of a major restoration itself. Perhaps as a connoisseur of historical houses in this region you might recall it, for I believe that it did cause something of a stir at the time. The restoration lasted several years and was overseen by the Reverend Conrad Noel of Thaxted, who was resident in the house at the time. One of the craftsmen, a certain William Howes, is reputed to have had a strange experience in the house, and it is this that I wish to pursue further. There is much gossip in the village as to what he did or did not witness, and the story has accumulated a great deal of substance over the years, but I cannot be certain of what is fact and what fiction. For this reason I wish to speak to Mister Howes myself.

I am told by Mister Ernest Beckwith that Mister Howes, whom you might also know as 'Billy', has recently worked for you in Ipswich, and I would very much like to ask you whether you have knowledge of his current whereabouts. I should be most grateful to be put into contact with Mister Howes, as I believe he might be able to shed light on the aspects of Paycocke's House which trouble me.

I am respectfully yours,

Imogen Holst

Miss Imogen Holst

*   *   *

Edward walked home. His head pounded. Why could he not tell her how he felt? Why did the things he loved elude him? It was like chasing a dragonfly, the pearly blue insect flitting tantalisingly close, so you could rejoice in its beauty, then darting out of reach just when you got near enough to see its markings. And he was afraid, afraid to get close to Imogen, in case he might destroy her the way he would kill a dragonfly were he to catch it.

His father would still be at the Yorkshire Grey, sinking pint after pint, each one a step further away from his son. Albert Edward Daynes. Edward had been named for his father, but that was the only thing they shared. That and Ida Daynes, but she was not much longer for this world, and Edward knew it now. Everything had withered away. Perhaps it was his father who had been the wiser one, for he had known it almost from the beginning, and had begun the process of distancing himself from the hurt, hiding his feelings.

When had that started? They had always been so open with each other. So when had they begun to lock their true feelings away, to revel in the secrets that split them apart? Was it just a part of growing older, growing up? Was it inevitable that you had to guard those secrets and never let anyone in? Would it always be this way?

He stood on the doorstep of their house. The fading paint on the front door peeled off as he touched it, revealing grey oak below, scarred by age. He supposed that it was inevitable. There was no sound from his mother's room, and he was grateful that he did not have to face her just yet, with his shaky grasp on the secret of her impending death.

Chapter 31
Trains

They sat in the 19:47 to Kelvedon and Simon watched London recede. He wanted to give Cassie time, but was not sure how much time they had to spare. He had never seen her so gaunt and afraid. Her face was streaked with decaying make-up and her fingers fidgeted.

She had looked like a homeless person, huddled on the wire bench at Liverpool Street, her knees hunched up against her chest, her arms wrapped around her legs, rocking herself back and forth. It was a wonder she hadn't been moved on. Her face was blotchy and worn, her eyes dull and without focus. And she looked so thin. Simon stood under the departures board and took the blame. She saw him and he held out his arms.

"Dad. You came," she said. It was the smallest of voices.

"I'll always come for you, Cassie. Don't ever worry about that. I'll always be here for you." He took his daughter in his arms and stroked her grubby hair. She hugged him back with a strength that belied her thin frame. "Everything's going to be all right." He bought her a single and they held hands as if she were still five years old.

Cassie traced the pattern on the train seat with a fingernail. She had protested against reporting the theft so violently that Simon had given in. He had called the emergency number and stopped her bank cards, and the rest was only money. The loss of her mobile seemed to pain her the most.

"What will I do, Dad? I've lost all my numbers. What am I going to do?"

He looked out of the window at the lights flashing by, streetlights, car headlamps, and lives in embankment houses framed in lit windows. He wrestled against recrimination; that was the last thing she needed.

"You don't keep anything written down?"

Cassie shook her head.

"Have you got an old SIM card?"

"Somewhere, I don't know."

"Then maybe we can restore some of your address book."

"Maybe." Cassie lolled against the window and her head vibrated with the movements of the train.

Simon leant forward and took her hand. Her fingers slotted into his and her mouth creased into the glimmer of a smile. "Cassie, what's wrong?"

"Nothing, Dad." Her voice sounded so weary. "Nothing. Everything. Nothing."

"You haven't been yourself, Cass. You're drifting." Her eyes met his, then fell away with the effort. "Please, darling. I want to help." He rubbed the back of her hand and took a deep breath. He searched out her blue eyes, fogged by some distant thought. "Are you on something?"

Cassie's lips tightened and she looked down at her lap.

"It's OK," he said. "We can deal with it. Is it dope? Speed? Ecstasy? It doesn't matter, Cassie. We can deal with it." Cassie was silent, just picked at a loose thread on the hem on her shirt. "Talk to me, Cass. Is it crack?"

Cassie gave a snort. "Thanks, Dad. I've got more sense than that."

"Please, Cassie."

She looked at him square in the face. "It's nothing, Dad. I don't do drugs." The constant unwavering eye contact was too much.

He had seen it before in a ten-year-old Cassie, with dimples like miniature pudding basins and long golden hair that reached to her bottom. Skimble had bounced onto their bed that Sunday morning, upsetting the milk jug over the crossword.

"Skimble, get your butt out of here," said Robin, trying to dam the stream of milk before it reached the duvet.

The two girls giggled from their perches at the end of the bed and Simon grabbed the cat in both arms and scratched him under his chin to calm him down. It was then that he noticed the whiskers.

"Robin?"

"Uh-huh?" Robin turned away, putting her mug on the bedside table.

"Have you seen Skimble?"

"Seen him? He nearly drowned me."

"No. His whiskers." Simon tilted Skimble's head towards Robin.

"Simon," she said. "What in the world has happened to his whiskers?"

Simon shook his head. All of Skimble's fine curled white whiskers had been trimmed to tiny stumps. Simon and Robin looked at their daughters.

"Do you guys know anything about this?"

Alex looked terrified. "No, Mommy."

Cassie stared at her parent with unwavering, challenging blue eyes. "No."

"Cassie?"

Cassie's lips were glued together, her eyes fixed beyond her parents. "It wasn't me."

"Please don't lie to us, Cassie. Did you cut Skimble's whiskers off?"

"Why is it always me? You love Alex more than me. She's the favourite. Why is it always me?" She ran from the bedroom in tears.

They found the whiskers laid out like corpses in a drawer in Cassie's desk, a pair of scissors beside them.

Robin was furious. "You're grounded."

Simon felt in his shirt pocket and found the black and orange pill. He held it up between thumb and forefinger.

Cassie closed her eyes and took a deep breath. "It's not what you think, Dad." She told him about her constant struggle to stay thin. "I'm not like Alex. I can't do all those stupid sports. I started to take supplements and stuff and... OK, drugs, Dad, I started to take drugs and... they helped."

"But Cass, you look great. You looked great."

"No."

"Yes." Simon put his hand up to his face and massaged his brow. "No, you're right. You don't look great, you look awful. But you don't look overweight, Cassie."

"You don't understand, Dad."

"Then help me understand."

"You can't ever know what it's like, Dad, to be rejected."

Simon reflected that rejection had paid him a couple of harsh visits in recent days, but said nothing. "Look, I'll get an appointment with the GP tomorrow and we'll sort it out."

"No. Dad, please." Cassie grasped his hand with the pill and squeezed it.

"Darling, I don't know enough to help you."

"I'll tell you everything, everything I know. Please, Dad, don't tell anyone, please. Not yet."

"What about Mom?"

"Please, Dad."

He crossed the gangway between them and sat beside her, holding her to him and feeling her panic ebb as she folded into his firm embrace. "OK, darling, just for now. We'll see how it goes, eh?"

She nodded.

"We might have to get help if you and I can't sort it, though. OK?"

Cassie smiled. "Just you and me, Dad."

"Yeah."

She told him everything, from elation to desolation, how she had taken more and stronger pills as time had gone by. He felt the barriers that the years had created come down.

The house was brush-stroked with shadow when they got back. Simon put Cassie straight to bed, smoothed her forehead and kissed her goodnight, ten years old again. Poor kid, she was exhausted. He stood outside her bedroom door for a second and there was no sound; she was already asleep. Creeping downstairs he poured himself a large shot of Scotch, sat down at the kitchen table and drew his fingernail across the grooves Skimble had once made. Roach. Who was he? He swirled the whisky around the tumbler.

Cassie folded back the quilt and swung her legs across the mattress. She knelt on the floor and reached under the bed, sweeping with her hand in long fluid movements, just in case there might still be a stray pill lurking in the darkness.

*   *   *

The smell of bacon wafted through the house. The red LCD on the clock radio showed 07:46; damn, he had forgotten to set the alarm. A quarter to eight. He started. Alex. Damn. School. He stumbled up to Alex's room, putting on his dressing gown as he went. One of the sleeves was inside out and he was still half-naked when he knocked. There was no sign of life from within and he pushed open her door, padding over to the bed. Her prone figure lay pulsing beneath the duvet cover. Simon put his hand on her shoulder and rocked it. "Alex," he whispered. "Alex. Time to get up. You'll be late for school."

Alex stirred and grunted.

"Ally." Simon raised his voice a notch. "It's ten to eight."

She opened her eyes, crusted with sleep. "Huh?"

Simon tapped his wrist. "Hey, sleepy-head, time to get up. Sorry, darling, it's my fault. I forgot to set my alarm."

"Uh, Dad?"

"Come on, Al, no time for messing around."

"Dad." Alex yawned and rolled over.

"Don't go back to sleep, Alex."

She faced the wall. "Dad, it's half-term."

With everything else that had been happening he had completely forgotten. Alex was right. It was half-term. "Oh, darling, I'm sorry. Go back to sleep."

"Is that bacon I can smell?"

"Yes, I think Cassie's started without us."

Alex opened her eyes wide and blinked twice to clear her vision. "Cassie?"

"Yeah, turn up for the book, isn't it? Go back to sleep if you want..."

"I'll be down in a minute."

Cassie wore a striped apron over her top. Her hair was damp and tied back and her face flushed from the shower. "Morning, Dad. Bacon sarney?"

The table was laid for three, pressed napkins lined up at their places. Simon realised that they had not eaten properly together for several days, in fact was so unused to seeing the table laid that it seemed as though a place setting was missing, Robin's. "Yeah, that'd be great."

Cassie piled four slices of back onto a hot plate with a toasted muffin. "I need to get my head in gear, Dad. Everything we talked about last night. It can't go on."

Simon nodded.

"It's not like I'm addicted to Tryph, you know, Dad. It's more like a crutch, something to shore up my confidence. So what I'm going to do is just kick the pills – I don't need them, right? – and join a gym, get into shape."

Simon took her hand across the table.

Cassie smiled. "Only, since I lost all my cards and that last night, I am, like, short."

Her father laughed. "OK, I'll sub you for the gym membership. It's the least I can do."

"It's just until my new cards come through."

"Yeah, OK." Why he could trust her now, after all that had happened, Simon wasn't sure, but he had to give her another chance.

She squeezed his fingers and lowered her voice. "Alex is coming down. Can you not mention… all this?"

He returned the pressure.

Alex bounded into the kitchen. "Bacon, yay."

"Sorry about waking you up, Al."

"S'all right." Alex piled the remainder of the bacon onto a plate and sat beside them.

"What are you up to today?"

Alex spoke through a mouthful. "I thought I'd go over to Julia's, do some Chem revision."

"What about you, Dad?" Cassie looked at him.

He looked at them both. Coggeshall was so claustrophobic right now. Everywhere he went he was faced with failure, running the risk of bumping into Robin or Abby or Sparrow. "You're right, I think I'll get out for the day." There was nothing urgent that couldn't wait. Maybe he would stick his boots in the car and go for a walk on Orford Ness. He had been meaning to do that ever since they moved out this way. The sea air would help him to think, get his mind around his battery of problems.

*   *   *

Simon pulled up the Citroen by the newsagent's for a Guardian. Even if it was too windy he could just sit in the car, struggling with Araucaria's clues and watching the waves break on the shingle. Realising he was on double yellow lines, he looked back at the car again as he went into the newsagent's, to make sure the warden was nowhere about, and collided with a customer coming out of the shop.

"Oh, sorry," he said. "I'm ever so... Eleanor."

He's pleased to see me. He's only pleased to see me. What am I doing? This wasn't meant to happen.

The teacher smiled at him.

"Simon, how's things?"

"Um... you know, I don't know. Everything happened so fast that I just can't seem to take it in. Thanks... thanks for the other night." Flowers, he thought. He had meant to give her flowers.

"That's all right," she said. "What was I going to do, let you get plastered by Martin?"

"I was plastered enough to begin with," he said. They both laughed.

"You've a lovely laugh, Simon."

"I haven't had much use for it lately."

She put her hand on his upper arm and gave it a light squeeze. "What are you up to today?"

"Nothing much. I just thought I'd go for a walk and get some fresh air."

"On your own?"

Was she fishing? And that flash in her eye, what did it mean? It was so many years since he had been single that Simon had forgotten all the subtexts and signals he had ever known. "Yeah. Alex has gone over to a friend's for the day, and Cassie's out looking for a gym. The last thing they'd want to do is go for a walk with the old man."

This is it. This is what it's all about. It's all for Jack. Don't forget that. Get him far away from Paycocke's and then the Plan can do whatever it likes. It's all for Jack. I am not going to feel guilty. But God, those eyes of his. He trusts me. He doesn't deserve this.

Eleanor smiled. "I know what you mean."

"And you?"

Eleanor waved her hands in the air. "Freedom."

"Freedom?"

"Half-term."

Simon laughed; he had forgotten again. "Of course."

"I've got a pile of projects to mark, but I'm in a procrastinating mood. I thought I'd go out for the day too."

"Anywhere special?"

Eleanor shrugged.

A train of thought was getting up steam in Simon's head. "You're welcome to come along." He waved at his car in what he hoped, believed was a nonchalant manner. "I'll bore you with the story of my life."

"Great, I love repeats."

"Oh, yeah, I forgot you knew it all."

She laughed. A gust of wind caught her hair. She put her hand to her head and adjusted the clip. "Only kidding, Simon."

"I'll just pick up a Guardian."

"Snap." Eleanor waved a rolled-up newspaper at him.

"Well, jump in."

This is it. One call and it's done. This is what he wanted from the beginning, Paycocke's to himself. Would you look at the way his hair flops over his eyes? I want to touch it, brush it back. Stop it. Stop it, just make the call.

"Can I phone Jack first and tell him what I'm up to?" Eleanor rummaged in her handbag for her mobile as she climbed into the car. She dialled. "Jack? It's Mum…. Listen, something's come up… Aye, that's it… Right… And there's plenty in the fridge for your dinner… That's the one… I'll do my best. OK, see you later."

There was a pause while the back of the Citroen hauled itself into the air like a camel standing up. Simon's left hand rested on the gear stick. As Eleanor put her handbag down by her feet he changed into first to move off and his hand brushed hers, sending a tiny amount of static through him. He looked towards the road ahead.

Chapter 32
Sideshows

Simon wasn't sure how they had ended up in Clacton. He had thought he wanted isolation and the endless skies of the North Sea, and then Eleanor had said something amusing about childhood holidays in Scarborough and Skegness, and suddenly the windswept Suffolk coast had lost its allure, the sea an October grey and the sparse grasses quavering from the onslaught. His torpor needed an antidote of candy-floss and rock, the kindergarten colours and comfort eating of a seaside resort. Neither Frinton nor Walton-on-the-Naze would do. It had to be Clacton.

Eleanor had a talent for navigating conversation, for knowing where the rocks were and where to find the smooth channels. They talked of the merits of pebbled versus sandy beaches, the irritation of wet sand between your toes and the breakdown of love.

Simon parked the Citroen a couple of hundred metres up from the centre, the lack of cars on the Monday lunchtime an indicator of the late season, and they walked down the red ribbon promenade towards the pier. Their shoulders touched, his ragged Barbour and her bright North Face alibis for them both.

I like this man. I like the way his hair, too long, is snatched by the wind. I like the way he cares so much about everything. I like his vulnerability, the way he isn't scared to be open. What have I done? What's happening at Paycocke's right now? I've tricked him, tricked my way into his home, and... worse.

"You didn't fancy going back to Yorkshire?" he said.

Eleanor didn't answer and he wondered if his question had been lost in the wind. She stopped and looked out to sea. The murky brown waves crashed into the concrete breakwater, which looked like sharks' teeth bared against the sea. A single ship strolled the horizon. "There didn't seem to be much point. Jack was settled here in school. The only thing waiting for me back there was a life I'd long since abandoned. Memories. Better to move on." She zipped her jacket up another few inches around her neck.

"Cold?"

"Not cold, exactly…"

"Shall we get a cup of tea?"

He could feel the light pressure of her arm through the waxed sleeve, resting a moment longer than necessary. There seemed to be no urgency about it, no hidden agenda, but at the same time it leached a gentle affection. She bent her head to his shoulder, butting him lightly.

"Why not? There used to be a café on the pier."

The arm of the pier stretched out into the sea, a folly that could never be built today. Wooden shacks lined its length just as shops once had on the old London bridge, and from behind these a paratrooper ride surged out.

"Looks like there's some life, at least," Simon said.

They passed closed ice cream concessions with their faded primary bunting, the silence between them light and wind-blown.

Eleanor went back to his original question about Yorkshire. "There's a point of no return, when you're away so long that to go back is to notice the changes. And to disapprove. The new shopping centre that sucks the life from the town, the roundabouts that you don't recognise, the shopkeepers' faces that never used to be lined. You want everything to stay the same, to return and find it as you left it, and it always betrays you."

Like I'm betraying you. I can't do this. I feel sick. I've got to say something. I've got to do something. God, I'm shaking. I can't look at him. He must know something's up.

Simon persisted. "But the scenery, the people, don't you miss all that?"

Eleanor coarsened her accent, but her voice quivered in the wind. "Aye, 'appen I do, lad."

Simon could smell the ghost of a fairground at the entrance to the pier: engine oil and doughnuts and rides, fistfuls of two pence pieces hot and coppery in your hand, primed for the Penny Falls, but the paratrooper was in operation for maintenance only and all the sideshow shacks were shuttered up, rattling their padlocks in the wind. The smell was of excitement tinged with loss.

"Shall we go into town?" Simon said.

Eleanor looked down towards the sea. "Can we go to the end first? It's ages since I've been on the pier."

"OK."

The palmist, the tattooist, the haunted mansion and the bucking bronco, they all stood waiting for better times. Only the lifeboat station was restless and alert, the one sign of life the loitering fishermen, their rods defying the wind.

They stood at the end of the pier and watched the boiling sea. The ship on the horizon had made no progress. The wind pulled at their faces and dragged at Eleanor's hair. It flailed about like a loose sail and she leant forward over the rail. Simon put his hand on her arm to steady her and she turned to him, her eyes the colour of hazelnut shells, a warm and comforting brown. She put her fingers up to his cheek and drew him to her, and he felt her lips on his, strange lips, the first new lips in almost twenty years, soft and yearning.

He drew back, his heart yelling. "I... I'm not sure about this," he said. "I don't know, Eleanor. I'm just not sure."

NO. Hold me, Simon, hold me tight. Come back.

She looked down at the churning water. "Nor am I, Simon."

They walked back down the pier and Simon could see grand houses on the shoreline, wealthy Victorians and Edwardians muscling in on the best views. Something had changed. The kiss was a barrier between them and now he noticed the silence. The houses on the front became slot machine arcades as they walked inland, screaming neon at the few passers-by. They found a deserted café and shared a pot of too strong tea.

Simon tried to pull things back to where they were, before the kiss. "It's not that I don't like you, Eleanor. I do, I really do."

And I like you. Already more than I should. What have I done?

"I know. You don't have to explain."

But he did. "So much has happened. I feel like I've been in a hurricane."

Eleanor put her hand on his. It was warm. "I shouldn't have... kissed you. It wasn't fair of me."

They sipped their tea and Simon added more milk than he liked, both to temper the strength, and to cool it down so that they might leave, shattering this threatening intimacy.

"We should do this again," he said, in the tone of someone who expected that they would not.

Music blared from the Golden Nugget gaming arcade and Simon took Eleanor by the hand. He needed noise. "Let's go in," he said, conspiratorially. They salvaged their burgeoning friendship by losing heavily on the slot machines and the misnamed Roll-a-Penny, which consumed ten pence pieces by the bagful. He bet on blue at 2-1 on the Donkey Derby; green came in at 4-1. He bet on green and the winner was red. Eleanor put twenty pence on white and it won at 10-1. They laughed. Maybe it could be all right.

Daylight was fighting a losing battle with the dingy clouds as they went back into the street. "We should get home," Simon said. "I think it's going to rain."

Eleanor gestured down a side street plastered with wet leaves. "Do you think if we nip down here it might be a short cut?"

She put her arm through his and it felt comfortable. They zigzagged back to the car through the residential streets, terraced houses with names like Windermere and Blake's, and for the first time since they had arrived it struck Simon that people were here all year around. Whole lives were played out in this town. Nestling between the harsh neon and the leaden sea, people were born, they lived, loved and died. Fitz lives here, he thought, wondering why he should think of the ex-boxer. Fitz, the King of Clacton.

*   *   *

Fitz picked up the phone. "Fitz here... Eleanor? Yay, great stuff... Paycocke's, you mean? Empty? What, now? Monster, Eleanor... The fridge? What do you... oh, yeah, yeah, I'm with you, Chance is there, right? Can you keep him busy for a while? Good. Nice one. Cheers, El, appreciate it."

What a result. Good old Eleanor. Trust her to come up with

the goods. She could take care of oldmanbooker for the day, leaving him to have a good poke around the house. He hadn't expected an opportunity to take a gander around Paycocke's so soon, and with the place empty he could have a really good butcher's. He fetched the photographs from his desk and threw his toolbox into the back seat of the Escort. Contradiction in terms, that old car. E90 MPH the number plate said, and it wouldn't go over 60. He wondered what he'd get next. A Merc? A Porsche? A Ferrari? Why not?

The outside of Paycocke's House was as serene as ever, its dark oriel windows harbouring the secret that Fitz had to crack. He stood outside and admired the carvings again. Stunning. And if everything panned out the way he hoped... You just never knew.

He had already thought about getting in, hopping the fence at the bottom of the garden from the pub next door, but first he would ring the bell, just double check no one was home. Teenage girls were likely to change their minds at a second's notice. He tugged on the bell-pull, waited ten seconds, then tugged again. Great, the place was his. He started to walk up the street, when the voice called him back.

"Hello?" The owner of the voice stood in the doorway of Paycocke's House, a girl of about nineteen in a black hoodie, slim with blonde hair, Simon's daughter at a guess, although she didn't look a whole heap like him. Maybe the eyes were the same, just a little bit nervous, darting, diving, just like her Dad's. Would it be Cassie or Alex? Cassie, he'd bet. Good old El, right on the button. But she must have got it wrong, both girls hadn't gone out. Attractive and slim, this Cassie was; cracker, in fact. Who would have thought it of oldmanbooker, eh?

Switch-hitting, over to southpaw, change of plan, sweet as a nut. "Hi, Mark Staines. I'm with the Trust." Not the 'National Trust' but the 'Trust'. Familiarity. Affability. "Buildings and Maintenance. Annual inspection." He held his toolbox aloft. "Is Simon about?" Fitz smiled.

"Um, hi," Cassie said. "No, no, Dad's not here, he's gone out for the day."

Fitz pushed a hand through non-existent hair and rubbed his

chin as if in thought. "I called a few days ago to fix it up. Is there a problem or did he just forget I was coming?"

Cassie nodded. "That sounds like Dad."

"Yeah, when I spoke to him it seemed like he had a few things on his mind. OK if I come in?"

"Er, yeah."

"I won't get in your way or nothing. Just need to give the old place its MOT, you know."

"I suppose…"

"If it's a problem I can make another appointment…" Fitz took a step back, as if he didn't care either way. He saw the doubt disappear from the girl's eyes.

"No, no, that's OK. I expect Dad'll get back before you're finished."

"Lovely stuff, that'd be great. I'm sorry, I didn't catch your name?"

"Cassie." Cassie held out a hand and Fitz put down his toolbox to shake it, little that it was, disappearing into his own fist. She waved Fitz into the house. The entrance stalled his breath; it was still unbelievable, so much better in the flesh than in all the pictures. He couldn't resist the urge to look up.

"Lovely, isn't it?" she said.

"Yeah, every time I come here, I'm just blown away."

"Come through. Fancy a cup of tea?"

Paycocke's House, a stunning bird and tea as well. Storming.

As he thought, she had better things to do than chat with some geezer from the National Trust, leaving him alone in the entrance hall with a mug of tea and some ginger nuts. She had even found him a stepladder in the utility room. What a girl. Absolutely wicked.

Fitz put the ladder up, careful not to be too quiet to reinforce the impression that he was expected to be here. The lighting in the room was poor, and Fitz marvelled at the carving close up, the intricate whorls and swirling tracery delicately hewn from the wood, the initials of Margaret and Thomas Paycocke picked out in several different styles. He matched the photograph in his pocket with the beams above and examined every inch of the carvings, finding nothing. The initials, the merchant's mark, the carver's head, they were all fantastic, but what had made the photographer shoot that particular piece of the ceiling?

In the silence he could feel his heart beat; the gloom seemed to press in on him and he felt light-headed. The breathing he heard, was that his? The house was closing in, it would take him, devour him. He gripped the stepladder hard and wiped his brow, his fingers coming away damp with the sheen of sweat. 'There are forces at work about which we know little.' *Get a grip, man.*

Fitz stepped down from the ladder, leant back on the wall and took a deep breath. Focus, he just needed focus. It was only a house, right? Take five, have a blow back in the corner and come out fighting. That was better. He felt calmer on the floor. He made a square with his thumbs and forefingers to replicate what the photographer would have seen. It didn't make any sense. There was something there; he just couldn't see it. Blimey, this was some place. He examined the beams again. Man, looked just like diminished haunch joints; he hadn't thought they were around when this place was built. Ahead of his time, old Paycocke. If he had a hat he would have doffed it. Fitz fished in his pocket for his digital camera and took a few photographs of his own.

It was turning out to be a waste of time. Fitz scratched his head. Was he looking for an excuse to leave? No way. No way was a house going to freak him out. He took out the letter, looking for clues. 'The house will know you belong there, Mr Fitzwarwick...' Holy crap, was that what he'd felt? 'It will draw you in and take you...' His heart raced. No. No, it was begun. There was no backing out now. It was just a house.

There was nothing in the entrance hall he didn't already know. Fitz shuffled through the other photographs: the dining room, yeah, he would have a good shufty in there, and that trapdoor, if he found nothing else he would track down that trapdoor. He carried the stepladder into the dining room and compared the photographs with the panelled walls. It was the panelling above the fireplace, he was sure of it. One of the photographs was so obscured with the cigarette smoke, you just couldn't tell, but the other two, yeah, it looked like the spot. If only the letter had told him where to look.

He heard children laugh. Was it in the carriageway? Or out at the front? It didn't make sense. He went over to the oriel window and looked out into West Street. There was no one there and he heard the laughter again, words as well, that he couldn't make out. It seemed to be behind him, in the house this time. Unease pricked at him. Suddenly he didn't want to be alone in this room.

"Shit," he spoke aloud and it was as though a bubble of uncertainty had been burst. It was OK, as long as Simon didn't come back. He was meant to be here. Didn't the letter say that he belonged here? There was no need to panic. Probably the laughter was the other daughter back with some of her mates. He should have checked with Cassie. He stood in the centre of the room waiting for the sound to come once more, cocking his head so he could get a better pin on its location. All that he heard was the sound of a lorry reversing in West Street. He shook his head; now he was imagining stuff.

The sitting room in the east wing was a long low-ceilinged affair. But this part of the house was more recent; the mansard roof gave it away in any case. And the beams too - it was all recycled timber, bits and bobs nicked from other houses or ships, maybe, and no trapdoor. Paycocke didn't build this wing, he had too much class for this, only virgin forest for him.

Simon's study he had been in already, so he passed through on the way to the kitchen. Again recycled timbers, evidence of old mortises and pegs; still no trapdoor, nothing for him here. He went upstairs, not worried about the creaking steps.

The bedrooms were not much to write home about, either. Lovely roll moulded carving on the ceiling beams, mind, although judging by the black holes all along them someone must have nailed plaster laths up there at one point. Where the hell was the trapdoor? There had been no photographs of the upstairs rooms, so they had to be irrelevant, still… He took out the photographs again and sat down on an old Queen Anne leather chair opposite the bed. He started to flick through the pictures when he noticed the dimple on the counterpane, as though someone had recently sat on the bed. The room was cold and Fitz began to feel uneasy again, as if he were being watched by the Staffordshire dogs. Downstairs would be better; it was bound to be downstairs. As he moved towards the door, one of the alarms went off.

"Fuck me," he said, under his breath. He held his hands out as though it might calm the dog down, and Cassie appeared from her bedroom.

"They're always going off," she laughed. "You've only got to step on the wrong floorboard and it sets the alarm going. Cassie picked the spaniel up and the beeping from the mechanism increased in volume. She fiddled with the base, then put it back on the oak chest. The alarm stopped.

"Cheers for that," Fitz dragged out a smile. Floorboards bollocks. You didn't get to be European champion without having control of your toes. Indian braves had nothing on him. Poxy dogs. He wanted to get outside, breathe again.

"How's it going?" Cassie asked.

"Yeah, pretty good. Almost there. She's looking in good shape." *And so are you.* When she laughed, it was like a warm breeze blowing through the house. He had a feeling that he didn't recognise. The way she looked at him gave him a pit in his stomach, distracted him from the business in hand. He didn't want to be distracted, but at the same time he wanted it more than anything.

"I'm off in a minute," she said. Her blue eyes were searchlights in the dusky light of the bedroom. Wherever he turned he could not avoid them.

"Right."

"Can you let yourself out?"

"Yeah, sure, don't worry about me. I just need to finish up in the lace room and I'm done."

"OK, I'll hang on and set the burglar alarm after you."

Good. Did she not feel it?. Was it just him? Fitz went down into the lace room, breathing heavily. Nothing, but he was hardly looking any longer. He had to get a hold of himself. It was this house, it was affecting his judgement. The trapdoor, the trapdoor, where was the bloody trapdoor? He folded up the ladder and carried it into the utility room. On his way back he met Cassie in the study, the room too narrow for them to pass each other.

"I've put your ladder back," he said. "Cheers for that." He curled his fingers against his palms. They were ice cold. She smiled. Bloody hell, it was like lightning passing through him.

"No problem," she said. "Can I get by? I need to set the alarm." She pointed at the panel behind him.

"Sure." Fitz squeezed back against the desk, looking up as he did, and saw the trapdoor, right there above him. It was here, here all the time. He swallowed his frustration. The number of times he had passed through this room; he couldn't believe he hadn't noticed it. What was going wrong with him? How the hell had he missed that? Sloppy, careless, amateur. How long would he have lasted in the ring? Blown it, he had blown it.

Fitz took a deep breath. It was too late. Step back, quit while you're ahead. Don't push it. It's not blown. We can come back to this. He watched Cassie set the burglar alarm: 1977. Good year, easy to remember. She set his heart racing but he still had time to think, 'What a mungo. Fancy setting the alarm in front of a stranger.'

They stood in the street, waiting for the alarm to finish setting. "Can I give you a lift anywhere?"

"If you're going Colchester way?"

"Yeah, sure, hop in." Even if he'd been going in the opposite direction he would still have been going Colchester way.

Shaky. This was too shaky. Fitz knew he was making a big mistake, but could not help himself. Cassie was a magnet, pulling him away from his goal, complicating things beyond reason. He was powerless to resist, didn't want to resist.

Chapter 33
Signals

Simon and Eleanor were stuck on the A12, sandwiched between two once-white vans. Radio Essex warned them as they waited: 'A jack-knifed lorry has spilled its load of toothpaste on the A12; there is a six-mile tailback.' The traffic simmered in the dwindling daylight, the eastbound vehicles on the other side of the dual carriageway roaring past them, leaving the west's fading glow behind. Simon turned off the engine and the Citroen sat down in the middle of the queue. He was grateful for the background radio broad-brushing the silence.

Eleanor left him to his thoughts, and he was aware that he had said little during the return journey. She was engrossed in the Guardian, filling in the sudoku, her eyes flashing up and down, left and right as she tracked possible solutions. The scar above her eyebrow was more visible from the side angle and Simon wondered what had caused it, a straight white blemish that burrowed into her brow. Perhaps it had been a broken bottle that might have taken out her eye; perhaps a teenage accident on the dodgems or a flying swing when she was a toddler. He wanted to know more about her life. He wanted to touch the tiny white crease but resisted the temptation. Eleanor inked in a single number and Simon realised she was aware of his presence, his looking at her, and she smiled without turning her face. The way her eyes stood still betrayed her, no longer criss-crossing the grid, but staring through the newspaper. What was she thinking of? He wished he had not disturbed her; he just wanted to sit and watch her doing the puzzle, slowly making progress, number by number. It was all too soon, wasn't it? This was crazy.

Progress. Robin, Sparrow, Cassie and now Eleanor, although this last was a progress he could only look at out of the corner of his eye.

He's watching me. He knows I'm not doing it properly. How can I? How could I concentrate on anything?

Her gaze switched again, a deliberate change of focus and there was a subtle shift in the way she was holding the newspaper so that it was angled towards him. She still did not look across at him, but continued to scan the sudoku, seemingly at random filing a number in one of the blank squares. Her pen rested still in her long fingers and Simon became aware of the sound of the radio, an interview with a politician about the London Olympics.

"It's about finding a pattern," she said.

"Sorry?" Simon's automatic reaction was to pretend he had been listening to the radio interview.

"The sudoku." She didn't challenge him and he was grateful, although he knew she was aware he had been watching her. He smiled.

"Oh, I've never tried them. Are they good?"

"I don't know why I do them. You don't learn anything; all you get is a daft little sense of achievement when you slot in the last number." Simon liked her short 'a' in 'last' and 'daft'. It was no-nonsense, a huge bound away from Robin's American 'a', long, drawn-out and deceptive. "I suppose they're quite therapeutic," she said. "Everything has its place; everything fits into a pre-defined order..."

"Like life?"

Eleanor laughed, and her scar twitched. "Definitely not like life," she said. "That's probably why I like doing them."

Simon raised his hand to his own eyebrow. "How did you get your scar? If you don't mind me asking?"

She touched the mark as though she had forgotten it. "Stupid. I had my eyebrow pierced when I was fifteen. It went septic. Did you think it was Alan? Hit me with a broken milk bottle?"

"No. I don't know what I thought. I was just... interested."

"No one hurts me, Simon. There's no room in my life for more hurt." It sounded like a warning and Eleanor's eyes seemed to recede to another time.

"I'm sorry. I didn't mean to intrude."

I want to touch him, even if it's only this once.

She took his hand and stroked his fingers with her thumb. Her hand felt dry and rough.

A horn sounded behind them and then another, and Simon looked up to see the traffic disappearing ahead of them, leaving them stalled at the head of a queue.

"Bloody hell," he said, and laughed, turning on the ignition and holding a hand of apology up for the following cars.

Eleanor squeezed his upper arm. "I'll finish the sudoku," she said.

*   *   *

It was dark when they arrived back in Coggeshall, the streetlights showing through the spidery horse chestnut branches opposite Paycocke's. The house stood in shadow, midway between two lights. One flickered as they approached, casting a strobe-like glow on a man walking towards the village. The man passed through the spotlight of the second street lamp as they drove by, his hair appearing bleached in the glare, but he was hunched forward, staring into the distance, so Simon could not tell if it was Sparrow or not. He hoped it was. The man could wait.

Eleanor put her mobile back in her handbag.

"Everything OK?" Simon asked, as he pulled in to the kerb.

"Yes. Jack's going to pick up some fish and chips." She peered at her watch. "I can't be long, Simon."

"One drink, I promise," he said.

"I'm not usually this bad a mother, you know."

He turned his key in the Yale and pushed the giant door inwards. Immediately the burglar alarm sounded an urgent repetitive screech that would give him 45 seconds to deactivate it. He scrabbled for the light switch. "Bugger, bugger." He hadn't expected this. Where were the girls? He tripped over the drugget in the hall and went flat on his face. "Bloody hell."

Eleanor put out her hand to help him up. "Are you all right, Simon?"

"Yes. Got to turn the alarm off." He dashed into the study to where the alarm panel was, its red light winking in the darkness. The alarm's siren stopped and Simon sighed, slumping against the wall. Eleanor stood by the study door laughing.

"What's so funny?"

Eleanor's shoulders heaved.

"One day I'm not going to make it, you know," he said.

Eleanor tossed her head back, the wave of her hair catching the small amount of light in the room and holding it captive.

"And it's directly connected to the police station. If the alarm goes off we'll have Essex's finest thundering through the house within minutes."

She held out her arms, laughing.

"It's not funny." He moved towards her. "The fire alarm's the same: light a match and, bing, there's a big red Dennis on our doorstep." He stopped in front of her and lowered his voice to whisper. "So stop bloody well laughing."

He makes me laugh, this lovely, funny, sad man, makes me laugh so much. And I've fucked it up. I've deceived him. I've betrayed him. And still he makes me laugh.

Eleanor took his hands and smiled, one that broadened her face. Her eyes still sparkled with amusement.

"It's... not... funny, Eleanor," he repeated. The air between them had grown heavy, as though he had to wade through it to reach her. Her smile twitched, a small dimple pooling on her cheek. Simon drew her to him and they kissed.

When he opened his eyes the room seemed darker, as though they had adjusted to a different reality. Simon held Eleanor in his arms, exploring the contours of her head with his fingers, and allowing her hair to trickle through his grasp. It smelt of honey and flowers and he kissed it. A warmth flowed through him. He wondered what to say, or if he should say anything at all. What was next? Chess moves. Simon had forgotten the rituals of courtship years ago. She took his hand and laid his palm on her cheek. It was warm and cool, soft and unflinching at the same time. "You're one of the good guys," she said.

The compliment fell through his fingers like a dropped catch, so unused was he to hearing them.

I have to make things right. Somehow.

Eleanor smoothed his eyebrows with her fingertips. "You've got more grey hairs there than on the rest of your head."

Simon laughed and kissed her hair. "No excuses, I'm afraid. No traumatic piercings, just age."

"You've worn well."

"You're having me on."

She looked puzzled. "You look good, Simon."

"Do I?" He had never thought of himself as handsome or desirable, not beside guys like Sparrow.

"Yes, of course. Not in the obvious way, but then again, you're not an obvious bloke." She looked deep into his eyes, her pupils wide and straining. She smiled, nipping her bottom lip with her teeth. "Yes, you're extremely lovely, Simon, a slow-burning, calm, deep lovely. Do you really not know it?" She held him at arm's length, and the distance suddenly felt too great to him.

"There's no accounting for taste," he said, feeling a flicker of embarrassment. But when had Robin ever called him attractive to his face? How was it that he had never noticed that? Uneasiness swamped him in the face of the flattery and he turned away to where a light on the answering machine blinked, trying to catch his attention.

"You have two new messages. Message one: received today at 16:23: 'Hi, Dad. It's me. I thought I'd stay over at Julia's, yeah? You can reach me on my mobile if you need me. All right? See you tomorrow. Love you.' Message two, received today at 19:48: 'Dad, it's Cassie. I won't be back tonight. Don't worry, I'm not going off the straight and narrow. I just met this girl at the gym and we got talking and we're going to this party tonight. I wouldn't be back until really late, so Karen said I could kip at hers, yeah? So, well, I'll see you in the morning. Probably quite late, OK?' She laughed and there was background noise of scuffling and giggling as she put the receiver down.

Too much information? She didn't need to explain. Simon cursed himself for being so suspicious, but couldn't put the handset back on the base. He felt Eleanor's arms curl around him as he dialled 1471. It was a Colchester number, the same one, he was sure, that was written on a scrap of paper in his pocket, Roach's number.

He turned to Eleanor and she smoothed the furrows on his forehead. "Problem?"

"I don't know." Maybe he was wrong.

Eleanor rested her head on his shoulder and her hair tumbled down his shirt. She looked at her watch. "We have twenty-five minutes."

I have to make things right.

Chapter 34
Imogen's Room

Mason's Hall,
Silent Street,
Ipswich,
Suffolk.

August 15th 1923

Dear Miss Holst,

There is nothing to forgive. I thank you most kindly for
your warm and intriguing letter, and it is I who must beg
your forgiveness, for I fear I can shed but little light on your
conundrum.

You are correct in your assumption that I know Paycocke's
House; indeed I have done so for many years, as Coggeshall
is directly on my path from Ipswich to London. If I am not
mistaken, Paycocke's stands on Stane Street, the old Roman road
between Colchester and St. Albans, and I doubt that the two
thousand years that have passed have witnessed a more handsome
resident of that street. I have often admired the house, whose
now restored front elevation is, I believe, without parallel. I recall
most well its dowdy aspect in the latter years of the last century,
and rejoice that such a jewel has been so sympathetically restored
to its finest. As you write, it is most remarkable.

My own restoration is rather modest by comparison, and I am
sure I might learn much from that of Paycocke's House. As
you rightly assume, Billy Howes is one of the craftsmen in my
employ, and I have spoken to him on your behalf. I had not
realised that he had worked on Paycocke's House itself, only that

he had worked in Coggeshall for Mister Ernest Beckwith, whose craftsmanship and opinion I greatly respect.

Howes is a taciturn man, yet well skilled in his profession. I am fortunate indeed to have such a person involved in the restoration of my home. However, his conversation was much strained when it came to the subject of Paycocke's. He wished neither to relate that which came to pass there, nor to have any contact with you on the subject whatsoever. He has led me to believe that he suffered a great ill within the house and indeed had you seen the fear in his eyes when I brought up the topic then I am sure you would agree with me. His only words were that Paycocke's House was possessed. All else he declines to discuss.

For this reason I think it unwise to pursue matters with Howes. Nevertheless, I have myself had in my time some little experience in matters spiritual, and if I might be so bold, I should like to offer my services to you in that regard. It has been my fortune to inhabit a number of houses with ghostly residents and I flatter myself that I have accrued a little knowledge in the field. I should be honoured if you would allow me to assist you in your quest for the resolution of the mystery of Paycocke's House.

I am at your service,

C Townsend

Charles Townsend Esq.

*   *   *

I turned the letter over in my hand. It was dispiriting to hear of Billy Howes' unwillingness to talk, but whatever the nature of the truth, it was clear that something had happened at Paycocke's to render him unspeakably afraid. Charles Townsend was right: it would not be fair to burden Billy further with the goings-on at the house, which the intervening years had transformed into a dreadful talisman for him.

But what of Mister Townsend? I knew little of him, but already was drawn to the notion that he might be able to provide an answer. It was most forward of him to propose an involvement, yet I have long spurned such ridiculous niceties. However, the involvement of a stranger was much to be preferred when considered against that of my own family and friends. How could I speak to Gussie of my concerns, when he himself was at such a low ebb? As for Iso, she was utterly tied up with my father's deteriorating health. Conrad Noel? It seemed to me that he was part of the problem, and knew more than he was prepared to reveal. Perhaps Edward? Edward, my dear sweet Edward, who would do anything for me, I knew. I baulked at the idea that he should be laden with yet more troubles, but he was the one person whom I could trust. It had to be Edward. I would give him the chance to help me and if we should find nothing then I would consult Mister Townsend. Now, it would have to be now. Gussie and Iso had gone to the vicarage for supper and the house belonged to me.

I folded up Charles Townsend's letter and tucked it inside my pillow case. I started to go downstairs when I had second thoughts: suppose the maid should strip the beds in the morning? I returned to my room and made the hiding place under the rug. Again I changed my mind, for the rugs were regularly beaten. I settled on Edward's black tin box, which had successfully guarded many secrets in its short life. I opened it and saw the brooch once more. Poor, poor Mrs. Daynes, who would not see her Edward grow, fall in love, marry and have her grandchildren. I had to close my eyes to fight the tears. I blinked them back and mumbled a prayer for her. Still, the box was an excellent place for Mister Townsend's letter, so I placed it next to the brooch, locked the tiny padlock and pushed the tin box far under my bed.

I had to loiter outside Edward's house for fear of incurring his father's wrath once more. Not that I cared one jot, but I feared that Edward would bear the brunt of any reprisals, and Albert Daynes had the largest fists I had ever seen. Edward must have seen me in the street, for he appeared from an alleyway and bade me walk with him towards Market Hill.

It took some persuading to have Edward accompany me back to the house. I told him about Mister Townsend's letter and how it appeared that Billy's story was true.

At this Edward raised an eyebrow. He was clearly not of an inclination to enter Paycocke's House. "I don't know, Imogen. Strikes me that bad things have happened there," he said.

I appealed to his masculine vanity. "But you're a man, Edward, you're not afraid."

"There's things we don't understand, Imogen, stranger things than you or I have ever seen. You can't fight a spirit, and you can't shake hands with him neither."

"So you do believe in ghosts?"

"I don't say yes and I don't say no." His eyes looked anywhere but at me, as though I were Medusa and that to look at me might mean complete capitulation.

I put my arm through his. "Will you come back to Paycocke's with me, Edward? Now? Please?"

He looked away.

"Edward?" I was ashamed of myself for asking, for trading on his love for me, a love that I could never return. "I cannot do it without you."

He turned to me and I could see in his eyes that he had lost. His bright green irises seemed to become swallowed up by his pupils as he looked at me and he tendered a weak smile. How could I not reward him? I gave him a brush of a kiss on his lips and I thought he might swoon.

Paycocke's House was bathed in evening sunshine. Facing north, there is such a brief window of the day when this side of the house sees the sun's rays, but when it does so it is at its most striking, looking composed and serene. We stood outside in West Street, still arm in arm, and I could feel him shiver despite the warmth.

I felt guilty. "You may change your mind if you wish, Edward," I said.

"When I say I'll do something, I do it. And I will do it, Imogen, I will."

We opened the front door and I was sure I could hear his heart beat. Stepping into the entrance hall, he gasped for breath.

"Are you all right? Edward? What is it?"

"It's fine. I'm fine. I just never thought I would ever... I don't know... ever..." He looked up at the ceiling. "It's grand, ain't it?"

I felt proprietorial. "Let me show you the initials." I pointed out the 'M' and the 'T' and the merchant's mark and the funny little carver's face that I had found.

"It feels... nice in here," Edward said. "Not like I expected. I thought I'd be afraid this time, but I'm not. It's like walking into a warm bath of friendliness."

I knew exactly what he meant, for I recalled having the same feeling about Paycocke's earlier in the summer when we first moved in. I tried to pinpoint when those feelings had metamorphosed into ones of unease and anguish, but it eluded me.

"Did you know, Edward, that we are standing on a Roman road?"

He shook his head.

"This was Stane Street. Imagine Roman centurions marching where we are standing now."

"I should rather not," he said, in the tone of one who was afraid that the said centurions might materialise at any time from the walls. "Some folk say as how they *have* seen Roman soldiers walking up East Street."

I held his arm. My imagination sometimes gets the better of me, and was in all likelihood the reason for my current predicament. I promised myself that I would try to curb its excesses. "You are right, Edward. It does feel friendly and kind." I crossed my fingers behind my back, and my heart thumped with the lie, because the house knew I was doing it, I was sure. I sent out a mental apology to Paycocke's, while thinking that it was probably the fault of my wretched imagination that it no longer felt friendly.

The dining room seemed to radiate, to draw us in. I put my hand in Edward's. He appeared to be not the slightest part scared, but on the contrary invigorated by my touch. This was not happening as I had imagined, with Edward taking the lead and I trailing in his wake. I do not know why, but my voice dropped to a whisper, "This is the room where Billy…"

Edward squeezed my hand. He walked around the room stroking the panelling. "Beautiful." He himself did not feel the urge to whisper. I showed him the mark made by Billy's chisel and he knelt down, felt it with his fingertips and nodded slowly.

"What is it?"

"It's… it's just as I remember it." Edward's gaze was glued to the mark Billy had made.

"What?" I hissed in confusion. "What do you mean, 'As you remember,' Edward?"

"I didn't tell you the whole truth, Imogen. When I told you the story about Billy, I mean. I suppose I was trying to impress you. I never thought you'd go following it up the way you did with Mister Beckwith and Mister Townsend and all."

I was confounded. It felt as though the room were watching us and I drew Edward towards the door. He was captivated by the panelling, staring at it as though it might give up some secret, or yield to him some long-lost memory. "There's no peace here," he said.

I dragged him out into the entrance hall, where the air was lighter and I could speak normally once more. "Edward, please tell me what this is all about."

He smiled at me and his eyes softened. "May I have a drink of water?"

"Yes, yes, of course. Are you all right?"

He nodded and I led him through the wide passageway into the kitchen. Gussie had lined this area with his books and sometimes sat there of an evening, writing letters at his roll-top desk. It was a strange little place, too wide to be a corridor and too small to be a room in its own right. The wall adjoining the entrance hall must have been the outside wall of the house at some point, for it was still decorated with attractive pargetting. Edward stayed in this ante-room, examining the spines of Gussie's books, while I fetched him a glass of water. He did not want to come further into the more private areas of the house and I did not press him. He sipped at the water and his eyes lost the dark quality that they had possessed in the dining room. Edward was being infuriating and my patience was scrabbling for purchase. I wanted him to tell me what was happening, but he just gazed around the tiny room.

He looked up and his eyes narrowed. I followed his stare up to the ceiling, about four feet above our heads to where a trapdoor was recessed. "Funny place for a trapdoor," he said.

I shrugged. "I've never noticed it before. It cannot be important. I expect it is a... "

"It's just that you never see trapdoors on the ground floor of a house – they usually go up to the attic, don't they?"

He looked at me for confirmation. I said I supposed he was right. "But the dining room, Edward, what happened..."

He put his finger to his lips and stared at the ceiling. "Can I go up there?"

*   *   *

It was meant to be. It was all meant to be. This was his destiny. Back in Paycocke's for the first time since he had been a toddler, and it all felt so right. Edward looked down at Imogen below him, holding the ladder as he hauled himself up into the darkness. Her eyes burned with questions, and could you imagine it now, that Edward had thought once that it was *she* who would have all the answers. And it had turned out that he had had them all along, or at least knew where to look for them. Funny how things turn out. Not that she didn't look beautiful down there, framed by the trapdoor in a shaft of light, her golden hair full of promise and the dust motes careering around her as though they did not dare to touch her. She was so lovely that it made his heart somersault.

He withdrew into the trapdoor, feeling the darkness embrace him. Imogen reached up to hand him a candle and he felt the merest touch of her white wrist on his thumb. Better that he had told her than Billy. Poor Billy Howes.

Billy used to carry him everywhere. He was a neighbour, one of those men you grew up calling 'uncle', and it had been years before Edward had realised that he hadn't been a relation at all. He remembered being on Billy's shoulders that day, walking down West Street, the jigging man between his legs singing, 'It's A Long Way To Tipperary.' Edward forgot why he was there, but Billy was always doing favours for a pint or a packet of smokes. Billy put him down in a corner of the panelled room with a little wooden horse to play with. Edward had forgotten all about the horse; he wondered what had happened to it. And such a horse too: Billy had carved it himself, and he had such an eye as could pick out each muscle, each curve, so that the toy horse lived. In the meantime Billy worked, teasing life from the oak lintel above the fireplace, carving a scroll of paper that looked as though it might crackle when you touched it.

"This is the life, eh, young Eddie, my lad?" Billy whistled a rambling tune with no beginning and no end, just variations on the same theme, over and over again. From the flat plain of wood grew delicate letters from Billy's touch. Hours passed with the carver engrossed in his task, and he did not see the infant lurch over to the tool bag and find Billy's sharpest blade, then return to his perch by the window and start to whittle at the horse. And if you could change the way the horse looked with one stroke of this scintillating tool, then maybe you could do the same to yourself.

Billy turned to see Edward raise the knife to his face and he hurled his chisel at the boy. "No," he screamed, and the chisel split the air and dashed the knife from Edward's hand. The tool embedded itself in the panelling at Edward's shoulder and the infant burst into tears at his lost plaything. Billy tore across the room and picked Edward up, rocking him with relief. There was no blood. Edward squirmed in Billy's grip, the carver shaking with the shock of what might have happened, and then Edward saw the cloud over his shoulder. A mist it was, obscuring the panelling with its light grey tendrils. Billy just stroked Edward's head, not seeing the fingers of smoke curling towards them.

Edward pointed over Billy's shoulder and he heard the laughter, children's laughter, jolly and mischievous. Edward saw the boys through the mist, beckoning him to come and play. "Eddie want play," he said.

"Sh, it's all right, Uncle Billy didn't mean to make you cry. It's all right, little Eddie."

"Boys want play. Eddie play."

Billy turned and saw them too, shimmering behind the grey curtain. "Fuck," he said, backing away. The laughter increased, as though centuries of boys had been released. Billy backed towards the door with Edward in his arms. "Fuck this." His eyes danced with sudden terror and he sidled from the dining room into the fresh clean air of the hall. Billy slammed the door and Edward reached out to try and claim the boys.

"Want play. Want boys." He started to cry.

Out in the street Edward howled in Billy's arms. The carver leant against the brick nogging and sank to his haunches, the crying boy snuggled in his arms until he fell asleep, thumb in mouth.

As far as Edward knew, that was the last time Billy Howes had entered Paycocke's House. Certainly it was the one and only time he himself had been inside, and one he had scarcely remembered in its entirety until now. He could not even be certain whether he recalled it true, or whether the intervening years had made the memory run wild. He had massaged the story for Imogen's benefit, but now the time for deception had passed.

The candle flickered in the small space; there must be a draught somewhere. He wished he had an electrical torch. The meagre flame was so vulnerable and only threw a small illuminated pool ahead of it as Edward crept further into the confined area. Beyond was blackness. The room might stretch for miles or might end inches from his nose, he could not tell.

"Can you see anything, Edward?" Imogen's voice sounded distant, as though it belonged in another world.

"No." He reached forward and caught his hand in a mesh of spiders' webs. Feeling a scuttling down the back of his hand, he drew back. He waved the candle forward and it caught several threads of silk, melting them. A large spider faced up to him, holding its ground before edging into the darkness. Now that he was up here, his curiosity had diminished, his bravado eroded. He was not certain how much longer he wished to spend in this nest.

The space was not high enough for him to crawl with ease, so he pulled his prone body along by his elbows. His face caught another huge web spanning his path, its silk soft and dusty on his skin, trailing across his cheek. More spiders crawled around him and he reached up to swat one from his forehead.

Edward looked over his shoulder at the small square of light that was the trapdoor. Surely he had not crawled so far? And suppose a beam gave way under his weight? He could crash down with the ceiling and heaven knew what else. The space around him seemed to shrink. Although his eyes had become accustomed to the darkness he could still see only a hand's span ahead of him, his nostrils choked with dust and cobwebs and his mouth dry. Why had he come up here? There was nothing in this crawlspace but dust and decay.

"Edward?" He jolted at Imogen's voice. "What are you doing up there?" There was a touch of irritation in her voice, impatience too. Edward had lost track of time, cocooned up here in the darkness, draped in spiders' webs and the soft dust of decades. Maybe it would be good to stay here, safe in this impenetrable place. His candle loomed at him; surely it had been much brighter? And it was half an inch shorter than when he had climbed in through the trapdoor. There was nothing here, he was sure, but there was a peace that began to soothe him and hold him in its arms. It was so quiet, so calm.

"Edward?"

"It's all right," he called. "I'll be down in a minute." Just a few seconds more to savour this tranquillity, to bask in the absence of light. His candle flickered again and he wanted to blow it out, to be at one with the darkness, as though he might once again become part of his mother, cherished and safe. As the candle wavered it flashed across something pale, something he could only see out of the corner of his eye. Pushing the candle stump ahead of him, he dragged himself further into the net of webs waiting to trap him and keep him, a willing victim.

The pale object grew in the dim light he offered, took shape and became something.

"Holy Mary, Mother of God," he said. "It's a shrine."

Chapter 35
The World is a Book

"…And those who do not travel read but a single page." Thomas looked out at the port of Amsteldam becoming solid through the mist. There was a fluttering in his breast, as though a moth lived within.

Robert crossed himself. "'Tis a strange place, Thomas." Their ship lurched onward. All manner of boats loomed into sight in the harbour, then shrank back as they were covered once more by the mist's sombre veil. "You do not find it so?"

Paycocke laughed. "Aye, indeed, Robert. But then Holland itself is unlike any other place in the world."

"How so?" Robert drew his cloak about him. The sun would force its way through this grey blanket in time, but for now the chill found the two men's very bones.

"Ask any Dutchman and he would say, 'God made the earth, but the Dutch made Holland.'" Thomas smiled.

"That has a blasphemous air, Thomas."

The clothier shook his head. "In very truth, I mean exactly what I say, for these cunning lowlanders did rescue their land from the sea, by means of mills."

"To hold back the sea…" Robert gazed through the mist to the south. They lumbered past a set of huge wooden gates, the ship rocking in the swell. From behind the gates surged a defence tower of brick, watching over the entrance to the city.

Thomas pointed at the gates rising from the salt water. "That is the dam, a most sly device, is it not?" he said. "And, if I am not mistaken, behind it is the Amstel river."

"Amstel… dam. Indeed they are cunning, Thomas."

"Aye. What secrets do those gates hold, Robert, my friend?"

"And wherefore do they exist: to protect men or to cage them?"

"Men such as Kees? We will find him. If it is God's will, we will find him, and my father's soul may then rest."

Robert put both of his hands on Thomas's arms and the older man reciprocated, the two men holding each other in a fast embrace. Thomas wondered if his clerk was thinking of Ann at all.

The ship sailed through a series of locks and moored at the side of a wide moat that curled to the south around the city, like a protecting arm. All around were waterways, small and large, some seeming to lead nowhere, others carrying larger ships than their own, low in the water with grain and timber. Thomas wondered that the city did not slide into the still dark depths. He spoke with the captain. Though Thomas owned one twentieth part of the vessel, he had no say in its business. A tiny surge of panic whispered within him when he learnt that the captain had now decided to make for Hamburg within two days, to take advantage of favourable tides. Their link to home would be gone. Thomas inquired after the whereabouts of Pieter Janszoon, a Dutch cloth trader known to him through a business partner in Utrecht.

The captain had his boy fetch a small cart, on which Thomas and Robert loaded their cloth and the two men pushed their way through the alleys, following the captain's directions. Robert fell silent, intimidated by the harsh guttural voices around him. They negotiated the cart through the narrow streets, with tall wooden buildings hemming them in on both sides. Thomas tried to raise Robert from his introspection.

"The tongue is not so strange," he said. "I have traded in Ypres and Gaunt, even as far north as Leyden, and many of the words are similar."

"It doth sound like a flock of geese in a storm," Robert grumbled. "How is it that you understand these people?"

"All men are the same in the eyes of God, Robert." Thomas could see that Robert's confidence had been strangled by their unfamiliar surroundings. Words so easily spoken in Coxhall had shrivelled like an old walnut upon arrival in Amsteldam. "I will teach you some of their words, but it is wise to remember, Robert, that a smile and a goodly handclasp do go a long way in business."

They laughed together as Robert attempted to master the Dutch for 'Good morning' and 'Please', his tongue stumbling over them. They passed the New Church as the captain had directed, into an open space of light and bustle. Stalls clustered in the open square, pastry makers, apothecaries, tinkers and all manner of traders. Thomas could not help but assess the clothing of the men around him.

"In truth there is occasion for us here, Robert." Thomas whispered, as though those around him might take offence at his words. "There is evidence of much coin about this place. Look at the wares for sale. Yet the quality of cloth I believe we can master." He tapped the samples on their own small cart. Amsteldam might be more renowned for other commodities, but of all things, man would always need clothes.

They skirted the throng and crossed the river. "The Amstel," Thomas said. He pointed towards the north. "Look. There is the defence tower we saw from the boat. It is part of the city wall. And there the gates, holding back the sea." On the other side of the river a mound ran both south and north as far as they could see. "The Zeedijk. Janszoon lives just beyond."

The Dutch draper welcomed them into his house like a brother. He was a tall and angular man, his hair a light golden colour as though bleached by the sun, his beard clipped short around a square chin. He had some English, so Thomas was spared Robert's attempts at the language. "Sit, sit, my friends, you must be weary after your journey. Will you drink some beer?"

Robert looked at Thomas. Thomas smiled; traders were the same the world over. First drink, then talk, the tongues loose and the minds addled in favour of a skewed transaction. "Aye, indeed, that would be most well."

Pieter left the room.

Thomas leant over to his clerk. "Do have a care, Robert. This beer of which he speaks is no small ale. He would have us in our cups and so strike a better bargain. It is as it ever was." He laughed and looked around the room. It was a similar size to his own parlour, with painted cloth hung on the walls, illustrated with a design with which Thomas was not familiar. The room was furnished simply, but with pieces of great quality. The cloth trade had clearly been good to Janszoon.

The Dutchman returned with a large pitcher and three tankards. He filled them and raised his own. "Welcome in Amsteldam."

Thomas raised his own beer and returned the toast. "I thank you kindly, Pieter." He took what he thought looked like a deep draught of the drink. It was much stronger than the Coxhall ale and tasted sharply of hops. Thomas licked his lips.

"Good, ja?"

Thomas nodded. "Aye." He must take care not to be seduced by this drink.

"Ja, those Hanse men must be good for something, I think."

"Hanse men?" Robert asked.

"Ja, ja, those boys of Bremen and Hamburg. They try to tell us what to do, this Hanse League, where we can, where we cannot trade. Who could believe that our little country could fight against them and win? It is like the story of David and Goliath, you know." He laughed, thumping his tankard on the board. "It is not wise to think small of Holland." He raised his drink once more. "Still, their beer is good."

In spite of the big man's good temper, Thomas could see the warning implicit in his words. Pieter's humour lay like a simmering kettle that might boil over at any moment. It would be well to be wary, for such a man should not be readily crossed, and he and Robert might need an ally in this city. "Aye, indeed, Pieter, my friend. But who might think small of a city whose achievements are so great?" He waved an arm in the direction of the Amstel.

They got down to business. Robert and Thomas laid the cloth on a board at one side of the room. He had brought the best examples, the finest weaves and the most beautiful hues. Pieter Janszoon examined them in silence, the bluffness of his mood eradicated. It was well, better than a false good humour. He ran the cloth between his fingers, closing his eyes the better to let his sensitive touch determine its worth. Janszoon opened a bolt up to the light, inspecting its grain and letting the carnation red material flow down his arm. Had he hoped to disguise his feelings by his silence, he had failed, for Thomas could see that he was most impressed by the English cloth. Paycocke smiled.

Janszoon smiled too, and nodded. He offered Paycocke a sum in excess of what the clothier had expected. Thomas did not let his surprise show, but asked for a higher amount, and the two men settled on a figure in between the two. Thomas speculated that Amsteldam might make him a good market. His purse heavy with florins, they might now embark upon their true business in this country. As Janszoon poured out another tankard of beer, Thomas unfolded the paper on which the Dutchmen of Colchester had written the name of Kees Visser's family home.

"Know you this place, Pieter?" He passed the parchment to the Dutchman, who held it at arm's length. "It is the home of one Cornelis Visser, although some do know of him as Kees."

The blond man rubbed his chin, as though deciding whether to share his knowledge. "The corner of the six laughing herring?" he said. His face brightened with recognition. "Ja, ja, the six herring, naturally. It is not so far. It is close to the Schreyhoeckstoren. This Kees, I know him not, but his father Jacob, he was... how do you call that, he works with the wood?" Janszoon mimed gouging the board with a chisel.

"A carver?" The excitement in Robert could not be suppressed. Thomas smiled to see the clerk recovering his confidence.

"Ja, ja, a carver, a builder, also. It was not always so. Jacob's own father was a fisherman, but years ago in my father's time there was a great fire in Amsteldam. Three houses of four were destroyed. There was much work to be done to rebuild the city and much coin for a man willing to turn his hand to that trade. In principle the town council no more allows houses of wood, but, ja, a man must live." Janszoon shrugged. "And so the Vissers are no longer vissers." He laughed. "A 'visser' is a 'fisherman'," he explained at Robert's blank look.

"And this Schrey...?" Thomas stumbled on the word.

Pieter laughed again, and beer slopped over the edge of his tankard. "Schreyhoeckstoren. It is on the city wall, beside the Amstel."

"The defence tower that we saw from the boat?"

"Ja, this is the one. Schreyhoeckstoren..." Pieter pondered

the translation. "Sharp... angle? Ja... sharp angle tower, but Amsteldammers do call it the Tower of Tears."

"The Tower of Tears." Thomas was intrigued by the name. "Wherefore?"

"It is there that women stand to bid their men farewell when they leave for sea. None know if they will ever return." He sighed at this revelation. "Ja, the Tower of Tears."

"And the corner of the six laughing herring?" They were so close, Thomas could feel excitement lapping at his insides.

"Close by. Only one, two... ja, two steegjes. Steegje, how do you call it, it is a very small street?"

"Alley?"

"Ja, alley. It is the second alley to the north. The house is on the corner, naturally. But you will see the sign of the six laughing herring on the wall. Look up at the house on the outside and there you will see him: six herring, tied in a small bundle. And they are laughing," he added. "Come." He gestured that they should walk outside, and he pointed up to his own gable where a plaque was fixed. "See. The sign of the golden cloak. All who know Amsteldam know the sign of the golden cloak. It is how to find Pieter Janszoon." He laughed.

Thomas and Robert thanked the Dutchman and promised to visit him once more before they returned to England. Paycocke thrust aside the stirrings of mistrust that brewed within him. It was just his business sense.

The two men found the sign of the six laughing herring with ease. It was just as Pieter had described, although the plaque was much more weathered than Janszoon's own. The herring did not seem to laugh so much as scowl, although Robert pointed out that 'the six scowling herring' might bring in less trade. Thomas laughed and knocked on the door.

It was opened by a surly round-faced man in a dirty linen shirt. His dark beard was striped through with grey like a badger. "Ja?" he said.

"I seek Cornelis Visser," Thomas said in Dutch. "I am called Paycocke."

"Cornelis?"

"Aye."

The man stared at Thomas and at his clothes. "English?"

Thomas nodded.

The man smiled, but there was no humour in his expression. "Kees is dead." He switched to English. "Kees Visser is dead," he repeated.

*   *   *

He should have been prepared for this. They had come all this way, had trusted in God that Kees Visser was the answer to their prayers. Thomas's faith was shaken. How could it be so? How could the Lord allow him to feel such pain after such hope? He had sinned, that was clear. He had not deserved to free his father; he had not been worthy and now he was being punished.

It had been Robert who had led them from the Vissers' door in the shadow of the Tower of Tears and found them lodgings at a monastery nearby on the Oudezijds. Thomas's spirit had deserted him and he knelt in the bare cell and prayed the whole night for forgiveness.

The dark, brooding man was Johannes Visser, Kees's brother. Kees had returned from England with his health in ruins and had perished shortly after. Johannes folded his arms as he related the tale, standing in the doorway. His initial rancour did not fade as he spoke, and he offered them no hospitality, no hope. Thomas could see that he had blamed the English for his brother's death.

As first light glanced through the slit of a window in the stone walls, it caught Robert. He still slept. The peace of the young, Thomas reflected. Robert's eyelids flickered and Thomas wondered if he dreamt of Ann. The young clerk rolled away from the light and his jerkin shifted on him. As he had promised that day soon after Margaret had died, God rest her soul, Thomas had given Robert several ells of cloth for new clothes. He had created a new colour from walnut and camomile, a delicate light brown that exactly matched Ann's eyes, and had had the dyed cloth made into a jerkin for Robert. When the two stood together they looked perfect. Ann had embraced Robert on the quay at Orford so fiercely that the boy had flushed.

Guilt gripped Thomas: blame for his father's sufferings; sorrow at Spooner's unnecessary death; sadness at Kees Visser's demise. It was the Sabbath; they could not leave on this day. He held his head in his hands. *What is my penance? What must I do? Please, Lord.* The shafts of sunlight grew stronger. If he left now he might meet a monk on the way to lauds. He must needs find a church, pray for guidance, and thereafter might they leave, forget this quest – all was lost now. At least he might say that they had tried.

Thomas smiled down at the sleeping clerk. He could leave the boy for now. In truth he would likely have returned by the time Robert awoke, and in truth this struggle was his alone. He drew Robert's cloak over his prone figure and left the cell.

There was indeed a church close by; the monk called it the Old Church. So there was both an Old and a New Church in this city. It was apt. Perchance he might take leave of these old gnarled thoughts, pray for resolution in the Old Church, and then begin a new life, putting his failures behind him. He resolved to pray later that day in the New Church also, to begin anew, to set in motion a spiral of hope that would leave the old ways behind. Aye, that would be well.

The Old Church, the Oude Kerk, was as cold as midwinter, its stone walls shielding him from the fires of Hell. They were building side chapels for God's glory, but it was yet too early for the masons to be working, and Thomas wandered alone in awe of the magnificent church. He found a corner in shadow where the cold was at its most biting and knelt down to make his peace with God.

Thomas did not know where he was when the hand shook him, at first a tender touch, light on his shoulder, but then more rough, and he heard a whispered voice in a foreign tongue. In his dream he had met his father and begged mercy for his failure, but his father had turned his back on Thomas and walked away, melting into the distance.

"Father," he said, opening his eyes. The day was older and sun streamed through the high windows of the Oude Kerk, splashing the flagstones with great puddles of light and warmth.

"Nee, nee. Vader niet." A man stood beside him, his clothes sprinkled with grey dust and a hammer in his left hand. A stone mason. He must have fallen asleep at prayer. Thomas's bones ached as he rose. The man let forth a torrent of Dutch, the dialect too coarse for Thomas to pick up more than one word in three. He saw the confusion in Thomas's eyes and gesticulated. Work was beginning here. Thomas must move. He was in danger. The mason smiled.

Paycocke stood and thanked him, nodding. A great church was always a work in progress, always changing, always moving forward. He left its cavernous womb and walked outside, looking about him. The place appeared different in the brightness of morning and he was not certain from whence he had come. All manner of folk scurried about on their business: a brewer with a cartload of firkins; a pedlar with a tray of aiglets, thongs and charms; a smith's boy with a sack of nails. Thomas realised he had lost his bearings. He looked up at the sky; he had come from the north, north and perhaps east. He made his way through the crowd of people, smiling and nodding. Some stared at him, knowing his clothes marked him out as no Amsteldammer, but a foreign trader. Others tried to sell him their wares, but he waved them away. He felt a hand slide towards his purse and pulled his cloak about him and jostled through the wall of people, no longer paying any attention to the direction in which he was walking, just desirous of leaving this melee behind. The crowd thinned out and he found himself at the entrance to a narrow alley. Looking behind him the throng seemed thicker and he did not want to return that way. The sun shed no light into this dark tunnel, but Thomas pressed forward nonetheless. Amsteldam was not so great a city, and so bounded by water was it, surely it was impossible to get lost.

It was a maze, nevertheless. All the alleyways looked the same and the canals too. Time after time he came across a place he was sure he had passed but moments before. It was as though he had circled the same area constantly. When he did reach a larger square where he could see the sun, it was not where he expected in the sky, and he had to alter his course to one which he thought not possible. He felt hunger ravage his belly. It must be late. Robert would be asking himself what had happened. He trusted that his clerk would have more sense than to go looking for him in this strange city, knowing none of the tongue. Where was he? He emerged again from a dark lane to bright sunlight, to a place he again recognised in part, but it did not make sense.

"Thomas. Thomas Paycocke, my friend."

Paycocke turned. It was Pieter Janszoon.

It is not easy to succeed in trade without knowledge of one's fellow man, and Thomas's business had prospered on the back of his insight. Yet Janszoon eluded him. He had a casual demeanour and a dubious sincerity that suggested a mean streak lurking within, but he had yet treated them with kindness and affability, and had not attempted to take advantage when trading Thomas's cloth. Perhaps there was less to him than met the eye; perhaps he was just stupid. Even so… Thomas shook his head and smiled. "Pieter," he said, holding out his hand. "This is most well."

Janszoon gripped his hand with both of his own, wrapping them around Thomas's fingers. "You are an explorer, perhaps?" The blond man waved his arm at the canals, laughing. "There is much to see in Amsteldam."

This was a time for truth and honesty. Thomas held up his hands. "I am lost."

"Then we must make you found."

"All does look the same, and the sun plays such tricks upon me that I begin to doubt my own eyes."

Janszoon looked up at the sky to where the sun was now sheltering behind a lonely cloud. "Where is it that you will go?" He looked sideways at Paycocke, pursing his lips.

Thomas felt himself being assessed, and was again gripped by a sense of unease in the presence of the larger man. He would be well advised not to underestimate the Dutchman. Yet, for now, he must trust him. He had to return to Robert. "The monastery of Saint Gregory."

"Then you are far from home. Walk with me awhile and I shall set you on the right path."

As they took turn after turn through the labyrinth of alleys, Pieter spoke of Thomas's fine cloth and what he hoped to make of it. There would be great demand for such quality, he predicted. Amsteldam was a growing city; many wealthy merchants had chosen it as their home. Despite the fires of the last century, despite the floods that constantly threatened its walls, Amsteldam was destined to be one of the richest cities in the world. Thomas would share in that wealth by virtue of his fine English cloth, which had no parallel.

Thomas said little, but tried to follow their winding route. He could not but help be reminded of Aesop's tale of the fox and the crow, the wily animal distracting the bird with flattery, the better to steal the cheese. Janszoon prattled on beside him, the very soul of amiability, his arm around Thomas's shoulder, now relating the story of Amsteldam's coat of arms. What did he seek to hide? It was no use, Thomas felt himself more lost than ever, and kept his hand to his purse, his trust on the wane.

They emerged beside Janszoon's house, the golden cloak on the plaque winking down at them in the sunlight. The Dutchman clapped his hands. "There. All is well, is it not?"

"Aye indeed. I thank you kindly, Pieter."

"Will you come in?"

Thomas shook his head. "It is most kind of you, but I must needs find Robert. Our business here is done."

Janszoon smiled, nodding. "I trust it will not be your last visit to Amsteldam."

Thomas held out his hand. "Indeed not. What you say has great merit, Pieter. There is much coin to be had for a wise trader." The clothier spoke the truth. Personal feelings would not interfere in Paycocke's transactions. Thomas saw a great opportunity opening up for him and pledged to return.

"And to come first to the house of Pieter Janszoon."

"Aye. We are well met." And better, he reflected, to have Pieter Janszoon on his side of the board.

"Farewell, Thomas Paycocke."

"Farewell, Pieter Janszoon."

"And have a care whither you wander." The Dutchman laughed.

Thomas laughed too, but as he turned his laugh dropped from his face. Was the last a warning?

Their cell was cool and silent as he walked in. At first he thought Robert had already left, and he cursed his ill luck should Robert become as lost as himself in this infernal maze of a town. Then he saw the clerk slumped in the corner of the room, cocooned in shadow, neither asleep nor awake.

"Robert?" he said, his voice betraying his growing alarm. "Robert, are you well?"

He reached over and put his hand on Robert's shoulder. The boy slid down the wall, his face angled towards Thomas, bloody and beaten.

Chapter 36
Light

The light looked as though it had already been used, greying light sold at a knock down price. It dribbled through the glass and lay in dappled shadows on the carpet. Simon lay still and struggled against the gloom, action eluding him. He felt so bloody tired.

The sheets on Robin's side were crumpled where Eleanor had lain. *Robin's side?* Simon picked up an Ian McEwan, drifted through a couple of pages, then put him back down again, bookmark rigid in its original place. He would have to go back to it.

Eleanor. There was something there, he knew, had known it when they kissed on Clacton Pier, when he had thought that the buffeting came only from the wind. He thought of her soft skin, clear and pale but with the collateral damage of age, the tiny wrens' feet at the corners of her eyes and the septic piercing, one of those scars that life inflicts in passing. What would it be like if she occupied the space next to him? He rubbed his eyes and breathed out. It was too soon. It had been a mistake. It must be too soon.

The house was silent - of course, no girls. How long before it was always this silent, bereft of all life but his own, as though it were waiting? He would call Eleanor later. No, he would go around. It was not a matter of explaining. She had been through much the same thing, but her hurt had healed. Time heals. And Sparrow, Martin bloody Sparrow, they would talk too. No doubt about work.

1477. Vespucci was in Paris with the manuscript, assuming they were right. Assuming, assuming; you go through life assuming so many things, and eventually they turn around and bite you on the backside. He made coffee, clearing away the dirty mugs from the work surface, each in its own state of decay. And Caxton, well, where was Caxton? He stared into the too-full dishwasher. It could all be bollocks, anyway, and maybe Uncle Giorgio had used the damn manuscripts to light his fires. Maybe? Probably.

But what if? And how could he not try? He ferreted in the bread bin for a muffin. Best before yesterday, it was dry and hard; still, it would toast. Had things really been best before yesterday, before last week, when he had lived so unknowingly surrounded on all sides by secrets, by a wall of lies?

So, Google William Caxton. Born 1422 in Kent, printed his first book at Westminster in 1477, *Dictes or Sayengis of the Philosophres*. So far so good. He travelled a bit as a diplomat to the king, moving in high circles. Interesting. Fluent in Latin, Dutch and French and translated a good many of the books he printed. Even more interesting. Chances are he might well have bumped into Vespucci. Simon surfed on, allowing himself to get pulled in by the idea that Sparrow had launched. A real connection; if only he could see a hint of a real connection between the two men, something to imply they had met.

He pressed on, chasing Caxton as he went to Cologne to learn the art of printing, following him down blind alleys in Bruges, pursuing links that went around in circles. Maybe there was a glimmer of something there, something that flickered in the corner of his eye, but jumped out of range the moment he got it in his sights. Maybe, just maybe.

"I'm back!"

Simon jumped from his chair as though nudged by a cattle prod. "Hell's teeth and bells, Alex." His daughter had her fingers around his eyes, and he pulled them away, squeezing her fingers gently. "What are you doing?"

"What are *you* doing, Dad? It's gone eleven and you're not dressed."

"I thought that was my line - you're the teenager."

"This is no time for lazing around, Dad."

Did she know about Eleanor? How could she? And, in any case, why should it matter? And yet it did. He gazed up at Alex. Her hair was shower damp, her skin clean but flushed. Probably she had been for a run already. Bloody kids. Just when he should have been expecting her to start smoking dope, there she was, training for a marathon and insisting on organic. He stroked her hair and smiled up at her. But what about Cassie? The telephone number glowered at him from his cork notice board. What about Cassie?

"You making coffee?" Alex looked down at his half-empty mug on the desk, long cold.

Simon looked at his daughter, oozing health. "Isn't it bad for you?"

"Yup."

"Be there in a sec. I need to make a quick phone call."

He closed the door behind her as she went out to the kitchen, perpetrating an elaborate mime of fetching the telephone directory so she wouldn't think he was shutting her out of his study. Deception – he felt guilty that it all came so naturally.

Simon punched in the Colchester number, his heart rising to meet his throat. It rang at the other end, again and again. He relaxed as the possibility of it being answered faded. It was probably nothing. The ringing stopped.

"Yeah, Roach?" The man was laughing.

Simon held the receiver away. *Why did I not plan something to say?*

"Hello, who's that? Monkey, is that you, mate?"

Simon's words stumbled out. "Oh, sorry, I think I have a wrong number, sorry." Sweat beaded his forehead; he wasn't sure why, he was not in the wrong here. Maybe it *was* time to let go completely. But how were you ever supposed to know when was the right time? He looked up in despair; he could no more fathom Cassie than the stupid trapdoor. Everything was nailed shut to him. Was he doing the right thing? Cassie was almost twenty, for Pete's sake. He just didn't know any longer.

"Dad, where's the coffee?"

"Where do you think?"

*   *   *

The shrill phone pierced Roach's bedroom. He rolled over, reaching for the handset and knocking over the card that sat on the bedside table. Even though his birthday had been three months ago, he had left Cassie's card next to his bed. She knew it was inertia rather than sentiment.

She chased him across the bed, not wanting to lose his warmth, and saw her home number filling the display on the telephone. "Oh hell, it's Dad."

Roach shook the handset at her, grinning. "Your Dad?"

"No, yours, fuckwit."

He mimed answering the telephone, putting on a posh voice. "Good morning, Mr Chance, and how are you this fine day? Would you like to speak to your daughter? She is right beside me, for we have just shagged something rotten..." He burst out laughing.

"Fuck off, Roach." Cassie tried to wrestle him for the receiver, but Roach held it at arm's length over the side of the bed, and held Cassie back with his free hand. "Give me the phone. Give me the bloody phone, Roach. No, no, don't answer it. No, Roach." Cassie cut her own voice off as Roach hit the talk button.

"Yeah, Roach?" He could hardly contain himself. Roach put the phone onto loudspeaker mode. There was silence. Cassie glared at him and made a throat cutting gesture. Roach's face reddened as he fought to check his laughter. He shoved the phone deep into the folds of the duvet and let out a vicious snigger, then twisted his expression into something serious. "Hello, who's that? Monkey, is that you, my old mate?"

Her Dad's voice came through, crackling and unsure. "Oh, sorry, I think I have a wrong number, sorry." He hung up.

Roach curled his lip. "Oh, poor Daddy, he's vewy sowwy."

"Don't you diss my Dad, Roach, don't you fucking dare."

"Come here, babes." Roach held out an arm. Cassie slumped against the headboard, sulking. "Come on, Cass, I was only kidding."

"Kid this," she said, and ripped a pillow out from behind her, pummelling the unsuspecting Roach.

Roach held up his arms to fend off the blows, still laughing. "Hey, hey, Cass, stop it."

Cassie drew away, holding the pillow to her chest. It smelt of Roach, indefinable traces of aftershave mingled with forgotten sweat. It was good, but dangerous.

"What about breakfast?" Roach said.

"I'm not hungry." When Roach was around she found it hard to maintain a level mood, her frame of mind surging from one extreme to the other. Why could she not just calm down?

"How about a blow?" Roach turned to the bedside table where he kept his tin.

"You know I don't touch that stuff, Roach."

He nodded. "Yeah." The crisp note of the crackling Rizla erased the silence. "I know." Roach shredded the tobacco evenly along the little paper furrow. "You want to know something else, Cass?"

"No." She hugged the pillow to her and drew her knees up to her chest. The speed with which she had defended her father surprised her. His love tugged at her and she wanted to go home. She remembered how she'd thought of telling Roach about the Conrad treasure, had thought he would help her. What had she been thinking of? He would take it all and then leave her behind in a heap and not look back. And shit, worse than that she still loved him. "No. I don't want to know."

Roach ignored her and carried on rolling the joint. "It's better when you don't come off stuff so quickly."

She dropped her chin onto the pillow.

"No, really, babes. Your body is like an oil tanker, you know? It needs time to adjust to a change in direction." He held up his hands in a shrug. "You know, who am I to say what you can and can't do with your own body, Cass?"

"Spare me. Just put a sock in it, Roach. Put a pair in it. Put your whole fucking sock drawer in it."

"I don't have a sock drawer."

"You know what I mean."

"What I'm saying is, you're wired, babes, you're sparking. Your body doesn't know what's hit it. Don't try and do too much at once. Cut down the dosage, yeah?"

Cassie felt as though she was sinking into the mattress, becoming smaller with every second. "I want to get right off it, Roach."

"Yeah, and that's OK, I respect that. Man, how many times have I told you, you don't need that stuff anyhow." He put the finished joint on the table and took her chin between his thumb and index finger. He turned her face slowly towards him. She resisted, but met his eyes. "You're beautiful sometimes."

"Sometimes?"

"Sometimes."

Cassie twisted her chin out of his grasp.

"Sometimes you're together and sometimes you're apart," he said. "It's like you're trying so hard to be two opposite things at the same time, babes. It's like... there are words that mean two opposite things, you get me?" He stroked her cheek and she felt a tear begin to well. "Like... like 'sanction', you know, to authorise, to allow, and then again it's punish. And... there's other words like... 'cleave' – you can cleave things together or cleave stuff apart. Do you get what I'm saying?"

Cassie nodded, twitching her lips.

"And that's you. You're opposites at one and the same time. And sometimes I just can't work out which one of you is the stronger. And I don't think you can, either, can you, babes?"

Cassie slumped sideways into Roach's arm.

"You got to look after yourself, yeah?" he said.

She swallowed hard.

"What I'm gonna do is find you some other stuff. It'll help you kick the Tryph. It's different gear and it's not addictive. It's stronger, OK, but you take it in smaller doses. I appreciate what you're trying to do. I just want to help you, yeah?"

Cassie bit the inside of her lip. Why was this so hard? All she wanted was to be normal. Why couldn't she be normal? She looked at Roach. His eyes were plaintive, very trusting. "Oh, Roach," she said.

"We'll get you over the hump, and then it's all downhill, yeah?"

Cassie nodded.

They made love as the morning dissipated. It was tender and harsh at the same time, cleaving her, she thought, splitting her and putting her back together again. As she sank into the bedclothes, Roach kissed her forehead and crept out of bed. Did she love him? Could she love him? Could she love anyone?

She heard him downstairs, the kettle straining to boil, mugs rattling. What did she know about him? He was the friend of a friend who was a friend no more. He was a dream peddler, promising heaven in a tab or twist of powder. Was there nothing he wouldn't sell? She sat up in bed and pulled the curtains open. Light rain spotted the window pane. Its pure drops gathered on the glass and funnelled downward, not taking any of the grime with them.

Weed, grass, cheeba, leaf, hash, ganja. Ask and you shall receive.

The drizzle was still coming down.

Heroin, acid, roofies, GHB. GBH, more like. Was there nothing he couldn't get?

She heard Roach's footsteps on the stairs. Something in his way tumbled down a few steps, there to remain until the next time he noticed it.

Snow, smack, skag. What was she doing here?

"Special K?"

Cassie opened her eyes, felt tears breach the gap. Roach rattled the cereal box at her. "It'll be OK, babes."

Chapter 37
Robins

Simon picked up the phone, wondering if it was displacement, whether he was calling Eleanor to put off seeing Sparrow. What did it matter? At least this time he knew what he wanted to say. "Eleanor, it's Simon, I..."

"Mum's not here. She had to go into school for some stuff."

"Hi, Jack?" Simon said. There was no sound from the other end.

"Can you tell your Mum I called?"

"Yeah."

"Simon Chance."

"Yeah, all right."

So it was done. Half-done. Begun, then. Strange things, beginnings. Lumps in the throat and sweaty palms of uncertainty, snatched phrases that overlap with the other person's, each word considered, yet vulnerable and ambiguous. Then, at some point the need for deliberation evaporates and the other's words are an old winter scarf, plain but warm. Was that good? Simon couldn't decide.

He thought he might walk up to the school, peer in through the darkened windows like Snow White and see all the tiny furniture laid out for the infants. Eleanor glowed, the newness of her just glowed in his memory. Simon snatched at it, savouring it, rolling its sweetness around his mind. One way or another it would soon be gone. Had it been like this with Robin?

Crossing Market Hill Simon saw the two of them in the distance, Abby and Robin, laughing like sisters, Robin's head bent down to Abby's to share a moment. Not sisters; of course not sisters, but lovers. She was still beautiful. How had he stopped noticing that? Not that it would have helped, would have mattered, could ever again matter.

It was overcast, ashen clouds in the east threatening rain, but shafts of sunlight seemed to follow the two women as they walked down the hill. Simon didn't want to be seen and tucked himself into the doorway of an estate agents, watching their reflections as they passed on the opposite side of the road. He hurried up Church Street, wanting to catch Eleanor while she was still at the school. Then he saw her fifty yards ahead of him, running for the shelter of the church, a bunch of pastel files under her arm.

"Eleanor," he called, waving to try and attract her attention. She hadn't heard him, or worse, she had. He ran up the hill and stopped at the entrance to the churchyard. She stood in the porch, the drizzle between them, then put down the files and walked out into the rain to meet him. He moved towards her, his heart going for broke. No compromise this time, no secrets. They kissed in the rain. She pulled away and took his hand, leading him to shelter. The rain looked like tears on her face; they dripped from her chin and she made no effort to brush them away.

"There's something I have to tell you," she said.

He tried to be light-hearted. "No, not more secrets."

"That's just it, Simon," she said. "I don't want any secrets between us."

He brushed her hair from around her eyes. "Then what? What is it, Eleanor?"

"Oh, Simon, I've done something awful."

*   *   *

Cassie and Roach walked up the hill into town, sharing an umbrella. She looked at him and wondered when he shaved, since he always looked three days past the most recent razor. His arm curled around her shoulders, holding her close to his body, sheltering her from the drizzle. He would take care of her, he always had so far. That's all she needed, that and some time and space. They stopped by the cashpoint.

"How much?" she said.

Roach made an expression as though he were calculating a debt. "Two hundred."

"What?"

"I can't give you credit forever, babes."

"How can I owe you that much?"

"The new stuff is pricey, Cass."

There was no way she had that much in her account; no way it was even in the black. She put her card in the slot and it was sucked away: 'Please consult your branch.' A wave of despair passed through her. "No. No. Roach, what am I going to do?" She thumped the cashpoint machine, yelped at the pain and Roach drew her away.

"What am I going to do? I haven't even got the bus fare home."

Roach's dark eyes twinkled, teasing her. "Didn't you get a return?"

"No... No, some bloke gave me a lift."

Roach tilted his head and a sourness flitted across his voice. "Who's that? What bloke?"

"Just some Trust geezer. Some National Trust bloke. I don't know. Some guy, Roach. Don't look at me like that. He gave me a lift, that's all."

Roach smirked. "Yeah, OK, Cass. I'll go for that." He drew her into the doorway of a department store, relaxing his grip on her arm and stroking her cheek. His fingers smelt of soap and old tobacco. "Look, I'll lend you the cash, Cassie. Last time, yeah? I can see you're desperate. But you got to start paying me back, you know. It's not good to have debts." He smiled, but there was a darkness in his eyes that nagged at her.

"Yeah, OK, I know. But I've got no money."

"Tap your Dad?"

"No, I've already..."

"He can afford it."

"No, Roach."

"Then how's about something on account?"

"What do you mean?"

"Sort of like interest, you might say." He nodded at the window of the department store where there was a display of DVDs.

"I'm not with you, Roach."

He gestured at the display. "A little present, just to show a bit of... ah... commitment, babes, you know what I mean?"

"No, Roach, I can't afford it. I haven't got a penny."

He ignored her and stared into the window. "Look at that: a limited edition boxed set of 'Kill Bill'. With a T-shirt."

"But, Roach, I haven't got any fucking money."

He swung his head from side to side, smiling at her as though she were a difficult pupil. "I wasn't asking you to pay, babes."

"Then…" Her voice dropped as she realised what he wanted. "Shoplifting? I can't steal it, Roach. No." Panicking, she backed away from the window.

"I suppose it depends how much you want the gear, doesn't it?" Roach's voice descended to a monotone whisper. "I bet you could give Uma Thurman a run for her dosh. Tell you what, I'll give you the T-shirt."

"No. No, Roach, you can't make me do it, you can't."

"I won't make you do anything, love. It's just, you know, a simple choice." He held out his hands as if they were scales, dropping one hand suddenly as if it were holding a ton weight.

"But it's theft," she hissed.

"Nah, not really. They'll thank us for exposing the flaws in their security system. It's all insured anyhow, so who gets hurt? Come on, babes, here's what you do. We go in separately, browse for a minute or two. You stick a copy of the DVD in your handbag, Christ knows it's big enough. Then just carry on looking through the other movies. I'll pick up another DVD, all nice and open, like. We both go to the exit at the same time, you walking through the door and me holding the DVD up to the light as though I'm looking at the small print. Of course the alarm goes off when you go through, but Security thinks it's me and I go back all sheepish and apologetic. Think you can do that?"

"I don't know. I don't know." Cassie shook her head.

"Let's have a quick walk around the block, blast of fresh air and all that. I'll see you in the shop. Five minutes later we're done and dusted. Roach is happy, Cassie's happy. What could be simpler?"

"I…" Cassie tried to take a deep breath to quell her panic.

"You won't let me down." He chucked her chin and kissed

her on the lips, his stubble scratching her as he withdrew. "Will you?" The way he framed it, it didn't sound like a question.

*　　*　　*

Simon walked the long way around to the White Hart, cutting through the nature reserve up to where he could hear the traffic on the A120. The drizzle had eased off, but the grass was heavy with raindrops and broad blades leant over the greasy footpath. Simon's cords soaked up the drops and flapped around his ankles. He himself was anything but calm. What was happening? Who *was* Eleanor? Did it matter? He had already gambled and lost; why *not* flip over another card? What more could there be to lose? But there had been something else, a shadow across her eyes that he could not quite penetrate in the badly lit porch of St. Peter's.

She had taken a deep breath, which should have warned him. It was unlike her; at least the Eleanor he had seen so far, the crisp forthright teacher in command of every situation. It was as though her self-assurance had cracked and something else was leaking out. Did he like it? Did he trust it? He just couldn't tell.

"Oh, Simon, I've done something awful." She turned away and he couldn't see her expression.

"What is it, Eleanor?" His heart beat away the rain that trickled through his shirt, not noticing it until its cold fingers reached his stomach.

"Last night…"

"Last night was… good," he said. He touched her shoulder and felt her collar-bone through several layers. She did not respond to his touch, just looked up at the darkening sky.

"I know," she said at last.

"Then?"

God, how can I say this? He'll hate me and he'll be right to hate me.

She shook her head.

"What did you mean, 'something awful'?"

Eleanor sucked in a breath. "I've gone too far, Simon."

He was defiant. "What do you mean? Eleanor, I don't understand."

"I can't expect you to," she said. "I... I'll betray you." She turned her face from him, examining the huge chunks of cold stone, fingering a piece of ancient carved graffiti. She darkened the grey masonry with her damp fingertips. "I already have."

"I'm not with you, Eleanor."

She breathed out through her nose. "That would be the best thing." Her words were muttered so low that Simon questioned whether he had heard them at all.

"If it's Robin, or Jack, or whatever, we can work things out, Eleanor." Suddenly he needed her. After a few tender hours together he needed her. If he was objective he could look at his behaviour as a straw-clutching response to the first bit of affection tossed his way. Well, what the hell, he didn't want to be objective. Maybe it *was* too soon, maybe it *was* just the knee-jerk reaction to Robin walking out. Who cared? However short-lived, he just needed Eleanor now.

"You're such a sweet man, Simon." She faced him and when her eyes fixed on his he knew she was hiding something. Secrets. More secrets.

Simon pulled her towards him, knowing that she wanted to in spite of her resistance. Were there people watching? Was that it? Would they be gossiped about in the Post Office queue? He didn't care and he wanted to show her how much. His lips found hers. Some of the drops on her cheeks were salty and warm and the dispassionate part of him was eroded. He held her to his chest. "It's OK," he said.

"Oh, Simon." He could almost see the sigh.

"It's OK."

"I... don't know."

"It *is* OK."

"It... I should have... I need to..."

"There's no 'should have', no 'must', no 'need to'," he said, brushing her tears away. "There's here, there's now, there's tomorrow." He smiled. "There's last night."

"I'm afraid, Simon."

"Don't be."

"I'm afraid..."

How can I tell him about Fitz? How can I? And risk everything?

She kissed him and he lost sight of her eyes. Now he felt scared. There was a chasm in his stomach waiting to swallow him whole. "I'm afraid, too," he said.

He looped back down towards the village, following the path of Robin's Brook. There was such a thin line between gossip and legend, rumour and folklore. Did people care enough to talk about him and Robin, him and Eleanor? Were they all creating folklore right now? Was this a story that would be repeated in Coggeshall in the years ahead, gathering pace and sensation with every repetition? Was this the effect of Paycocke's? He wondered whether there had ever even been an Angel of Christmas carving, with odd stories accumulating to explain away a quiet and hermit-like woodsman. The chopping cut through his thoughts, the unmistakable thud of axe on wood. He laughed out loud.

The path veered away from the brook and the sound of chopping faded. How easy was it for something to acquire the status of truth? It was all a centuries old game of Chinese whispers. He came out by the old Hitcham school, just up from Paycocke's, his tan oxfords muddy and darkened from the wet grass. Best nip in and change. The key was in the lock when he changed his mind. Sod it. He had to see Sparrow, now. Kicking off the worst of the mud he strode down to the White Hart. The sky was clearer, small patches of blue appearing in the east.

"Martin Sparrow?" he asked.

The receptionist looked at the day's register, then flicked back a page or two. "I'm sorry, sir," he smiled. "There's no one of that name staying here."

Chapter 38
There is No Pack of Cards
Without a Knave

Robert stirred beneath his touch and Thomas thanked the Lord that he still lived.

"Robert, my boy, who has done this to you?" The clerk's face was covered with his own blood, some now drying and cracked like red clay on his cheeks, but a small brook still flowed from a cut above his eye. One side of his face was swollen beyond words. His eyelids flickered as Robert recognised Thomas's voice, but they would not open. "Hush, lad. There will be time. Time we have, my dear friend."

Why had he left the boy? Thomas clenched his fist at his selfishness. He had known that something was amiss, yet he had left Robert alone to pursue his own aims. Was there to be no end to his punishment? Who else would suffer for his sins?

As he stepped back towards the door he saw that Robert's jerkin and cloak were gone. All he wore was a crumpled linen shirt, islands of dark crimson stains testimony to the blood he had lost. There was no purse at his belt and his knife had been taken too. Who would do this? Thomas knew he should fetch help, but was loath to leave his charge alone once again. He stroked Robert's forehead and his hand came away red and sticky.

Fighting the panic that burned within him, Paycocke located the still room and beseeched the herbalist through a mixture of English, Dutch, Latin and frantic gestures to accompany him back to their cell. The monk was silent, showing no surprise at the state of the young clerk. He touched Robert's face and cheeks, rolling his fingertips over the boy's injuries and feeling the beating life in his neck. He bade his novice fetch some water to clean Robert's wounds. Then he turned to Thomas, his fingers arched together like a great steeple in front of his lips. "He will live," he said in

311

English. "He has lost a deal of blood, but God willing he will live. It is not so grave."

"I thank you most kindly." Thomas sighed with relief.

"There is nothing to thank."

"That such a thing should happen within these walls…"

"There is evil all about us, my son."

"Aye indeed. Then all will be well?"

The monk tipped his head to one side as if unwilling to concur. "I will make a poultice of comfrey for his face. His body is young and strong. There is nothing broken. But he is weak and the risk of infection great. He might not be moved, not for several days."

They must remain in Amsteldam? The thought was like a knife in Thomas's heart. He wanted to be home in Coxhall, where the air did not bristle with threat. He wanted to hold his brothers to his breast and to take ale once more with his friends. And of course to see Ann. What would he tell her? He had let her Robert fall from his protection; he had failed to find Kees. Everything had ended in chaos and failure.

The days limped by. The swelling would not settle at first, remaining a fearful red, and Robert burned to Thomas's touch. The monk brought feverfew but Robert did not respond. Thomas feared the worst and did not dare leave the boy, save for medicine and water. Robert grew delirious in the night, screaming for his mother and for Ann, "Do not let them take me, Ann."

Sleep eluded Paycocke, ever on the brink of wakefulness should Robert need him. He had so much time to think and yet so little inclination to do so. It was over. If only he could bring Robert back to England in some health, he would consider the battle ended. In those critical hours, a small victory was perceived when Robert would take a spoonful of gruel or the littlest sip of caudle, grimacing at its sweetness. The very grimace would lift Paycocke's heart that all might be well.

The sun spilled its light through the narrow doorway on the fifth morning and Robert's eyes opened fully for the first time.

Thomas lay beside him on the cusp of sleep, but still watching, still on guard. He smiled, raising himself upon an elbow. "Robert, you are with us once more. God has been merciful."

"What has passed?"

"Would that I could tell you, lad. You were attacked, some five or six days ago."

Robert looked down at his filthy sleeves. "They took my jerkin," he said. Those words hurt his jaw and he put a hand up to his face. The swelling had subsided, but one cheek was ravaged by a field of purple and yellow. There would be scars, one above his eye, another snaking across his chin.

"Aye, they took your jerkin. Your purse too. But a small price for your life, methinks. A second jerkin is easily made, a second life not."

Robert looked away. It was clear he was thinking of Ann Cotton and her eyes, the same light honey brown as his lost jerkin. "How do I look?" he asked.

Thomas smiled at Robert's vanity. The boy would heal. "Well enough. Well enough, Robert. Do you recall what passed upon that morning?"

"I awoke. It was light, but there were shadows across the doorway." Robert put his hand to his face, feeling its strange contours, wincing as he found an area of unexpected pain. His tongue probed his cheek where he had lost a tooth. "The men were Dutch. I believe they were Dutch, for I understood not a single phrase they uttered. I knew them not, but they knew me, or us, for the one word I deciphered was 'Paycocke'." He started to shake although it was not cold.

Thomas put his arm around the clerk. It was his fault. He had drawn the attackers to their lodgings where they had torn Robert apart. What manner of place was this?

Robert rubbed his head. "'Twas as though I was a pig's bladder in a game of football," he said. "They cared not if I died."

"They said nothing?"

"They said much, Thomas. But I understood nothing. They asked questions which I could not comprehend and beat me further for my lack of answer."

Thomas looked down at his knees. There was nothing to be gained here. "I will have Janszoon make you up a new suit of clothes, then we will leave on the next tide. This city is too costly for me."

The light returned to Robert's eyes. "But what of Kees?"

"Kees is dead. There is naught for us here. We have failed."

"Think you not that Johannes knows more than he says?"

"Perchance. And perchance he was responsible for the thuggery that near cost you your life."

"Then all the more reason to stay, Thomas. If my life was threatened for some grave purpose, then we ought know what that purpose is."

"I feel the Devil's hand at work here, Robert. There is naught but ill for us in Amsteldam. The sooner we make for England, the merrier I will be."

Robert's anger was clear and his words leaked out through clenched teeth. "This is coward's talk, Thomas."

Thomas held up his hand. Robert's spirit was in great measure, but that counted for little when weighed against his ill-developed common sense. "Mayhap so, but there is a time to fight and a time to withdraw. It is God's will that we leave now. He has sent us this sign. We are not meant to know more."

"Thomas..."

"I will hear no more."

"But Thomas, this is folly..."

"Then so be it. You will see. It is for the best."

"We are so close..."

"We are as distant as we have ever been, Robert."

Robert was close to tears, weakened and frustrated. "Nay, it cannot be so."

Paycocke played his final card. "Ann would not want it thus."

Robert rolled away from the clothier, his mouth set in fury. Thomas put a gentle hand on his arm and felt only tension. Robert would see. In time he would see. The fever had unbalanced his sanguinity. He would see it was for the best. There was silence between the two men.

Thomas sighed. "It seems there is much merit in the English cloth."

*　　*　　*

"I did not expect to see you so soon, Thomas." Janszoon smiled and ushered them into his house. "You have more wares for me?"

Thomas noted the lack of surprise on Janszoon's face that the Englishmen had not yet left the country. "Indeed, Pieter, this time I come coin in hand to purchase your own wares for my friend Robert here."

Robert stood beside Thomas dressed in an old hessian habit borrowed from the monastery. He bore a sullen expression as of a sulking child.

Janszoon laughed, his face assuming its naturally cheerful disposition. "And there was I thinking you had taken the vows."

"He has need of new clothes, as quickly as they might be made."

"Aye, aye, that can be done." The Dutchman measured Robert with his hands and eyes. "I think we might help you, lad." He left the room and came back with a small bundle. "These were my son's. If they do not fit I will have the seamstress render them worthy."

"But your son?" Robert accepted the clothes.

"He has no need of them at this time."

Thomas put his hand to his purse. "This is most kind, Pieter."

Janszoon waved his hand away. "I accept no coin from you, Thomas. This is a gift, offered in recognition of our friendship."

Thomas did not want the obligation of a gift, but bowed under the pressure. On return to Coxhall he would parcel up his own gift to Janszoon and the debt would be paid, with no more to be said. "Most kind."

"But what became of your fine cloak?" The blond merchant's eyes sparkled as though he were teasing Paycocke. Did he know of the attack?

"Robert was set upon by some vagabonds. His purse and clothes were taken and he was fortunate to escape with his life."

315

"You must think poor of our city. I hope my small gift can persuade you otherwise."

"It is most generous, but in very truth the coin in my purse is yours. I would…"

"A gift most happily given. We were indeed well met, Thomas."

"Aye, Pieter. To my very great honour." The two men clasped hands and their eyes locked together that instant longer than Thomas would have liked, although the Dutchman's smile never wavered.

Janszoon turned to Robert, holding out his hand. "I will keep an eye sharp for your lost clothes, Robert Goodday, for such quality and colour is not oft seen in this land."

Robert could scarcely manage a muttered thanks, so keen was the loss he felt for his favoured jerkin and so harsh Thomas's decision to leave Amsteldam.

Thomas and Robert crossed the city, passing the New Church once more. Thomas remembered his resolution to pray there, to divorce the old from the new path, but found that he had lost his will to do so. He just wanted to leave, to be rid of the ill luck that had dogged them in Amsteldam. All manner of boats were moored in the Singel; one of them must be bound for England.

This time their fortune was good. A large vessel was at anchor in the IJ to the north of the city and would be leaving at first light for London with its cargo of timber and furs. A paying passenger was always welcome.

Thomas felt the pang of a job of work ill-judged and poorly done, and he wished heartily that they had never embarked upon this mission. Robert for his part hardly spoke to his employer. They found an inn and supped in silence to while away the hours. Thomas tried to raise his clerk's spirits with a game of dice, but the younger man just shook his head. He was still in pain, still suffering. It was as though the heart had been sucked from him.

As dawn played upon the streets they left for the harbour. New flotillas of boats sailed up the Singel, low in the water with their loads of spices, soap and grain, charged with optimism for deals to be done. It had been just a week before that they had been on such a ship themselves, fresh and vibrant and the best of friends. Folk stood on decks just as Thomas and Robert had, anticipating the smells and sounds of a new land. Thomas turned his back and the two men trudged down to the churning grey waters of the IJ.

Their ship was loading supplies. In a few days Amsteldam would be a bad dream. Thomas shuddered to think of the bad dreams that had brought him thus far. Would those dreams ever end? He looked down at the reclaimed land; how had the Dutchmen kept the sea at bay? Surely no man could battle against the will of God? What indeed *was* the will of God?

"Thomas." Robert's hand tugged at his sleeve. "Thomas, look."

Thomas raised his tired eyes and squinted at the shore. "What is it, Robert?" At least the boy was talking to him.

"The tower. The Tower of Tears."

Thomas looked towards the Schreyhoeckstoren, the forbidding tower frowning at them behind the huge dam on the Amstel. It was he who felt the tears coming, not those left behind.

"Thomas." Robert hissed his name, pointing with urgency. "The man. The man on top of the tower. He wears my jerkin."

There was indeed a man atop the tower. Robert's eyes were keener than his own, but the jerkin he wore, Thomas admitted, might be a similar colour, a light beeswax hue. It might be camomile and walnut. It might not.

"It is mine, Thomas. We must go back."

"Nay, Robert. It has a similar air, that is all."

"We must go back," Robert repeated.

Thomas grabbed the younger man's arm and pulled him out of the way of a mariner with a barrel on his shoulder. "Wherefore? What is there here for us? What is the use? It is done. We must away."

Robert pulled away, almost in panic. "It cannot be…"

Thomas turned Robert to him in fury, grasping him by both shoulders, oblivious to the younger man's injuries. "It is done, Robert. It is over, damn you," he shouted. "Over."

"Nay." The scream came from the shore. "It is not over. It is but begun."

Robert and Thomas both turned to the gangway and their jaws fell as one. "Ann."

Chapter 39
Doors

"Simon, wait up." Sparrow's voice hurled down the corridor.

Simon could do without the long-lost friend act. "Martin, what's going on? Have you checked out?"

Sparrow put his arm around Simon. "You heard of the saying, 'One door closes…'"

"Another one slams in your face." Simon scowled. "Yes, thanks. Now will you…"

"Come on, let's go for a drink." Sparrow hugged Simon to him and walked him out of the door. He lowered his voice. "Actually, at the White Hart they know me as Martin House."

"House? Martin House? You're having me on. Martin House?" Simon looked away in astonishment. Raindrops clung to sycamore leaves, themselves clinging to the tree. It was a fair wager which would fall first, the leaf or the raindrop. You held on by such a slender thread sometimes, so afraid of the drop, then when it happened you wondered why you had been scared, that perhaps to fall was the best thing that could have happened.

Sparrow's lips spread out in the parody of a grimace. He was enjoying the subterfuge. "Not so loud, eh? Yeah, Martin House. Housemartin. Nice, eh?" Simon blew out a breath and rolled his eyes. "Look, I hadn't expected to need an alias." Simon now glared. "It was the first thing that came into my head."

"Martin, you're *off* your head. And what's this alias stuff?"

"Truth is, old pal, I haven't been quite straight with you."

"Well, there's a surprise."

"I left the States… in some disarray. There are a few folk over there who would like to see me again, and well, it just makes sense for me not to use my own name while I'm here."

"Bloody hell, Martin, what have you done?" Simon lowered his voice, mired in a new conspiracy.

Sparrow shrugged. "It's a long story. You don't want to know."

Simon's lips became a slit. "I think you owe it to me, Martin."

Sparrow had the temerity to look hurt. "OK, yeah, I'll give you that. Can we go back to your place?"

"Paycocke's?" Simon was playing for time.

"Yeah. I can't talk," Sparrow looked around him, "out here."

"What the hell is it, Martin?"

"You worry too much, old pal."

"With good reason."

Simon pulled the giant oak door shut and the darkness of the entrance hall closed in on them, barely illuminated by the single sixty watt bulb. "So?"

Sparrow looked around. "This place is really special," he said.

"And so are you, mate. Now spill the beans."

"I'm wanted."

"That's hard to believe."

"No, really, Simon. I'm wanted in four States."

"Oh, piss off, Martin."

"This is serious."

"When did you ever take anything seriously?"

"When I nicked the *De Medicina* book."

Simon's jaw locked in mid-riposte. "What? You... you stole it?"

Martin nodded. "That's why I need to lie low."

"Lie low? Maybe you just mean lie?"

"No, honestly, Simon. I swear. On my mother's life."

"You never had a mother, Sparrow. You were invented."

"Please, Simon." The gloom of the hall seemed to have sapped Sparrow's self-confidence. "I'm in the crap. Please."

Say no. Turn your back. Call the police. Say, 'Bugger off, Martin.' Say, 'Tough, it serves you right.' Say, 'Just fuck off out of my house and never come back.'

"Please, Simon."

Simon crossed his arms and looked at Sparrow, his eyes awash with uncertainty. He took a second to enjoy the moment. "Go on."

"I swapped it for a pile of old Hemingway jottings. You'd think they'd be pleased."

"What?"

"They twigged it was me, I don't know how, but they knew. Pretty quickly, I'll give them that."

"Let me see... Fingerprints, perhaps?" Simon said.

"Yeah, maybe, but whatever it was I found myself having to move sharpish. I headed north to Massachusetts and hitched a ride on a yacht at Martha's Vineyard. Plenty of rich folk around there wanting to get richer, no questions asked. Sailed across the pond in no time. Nice bloke, the skipper. Rich industrialist, philanthropist, would have thought they were a contradiction in terms, eh? Fleming Land, his name was."

"Get on with it."

"Well, anyway, the trouble is, I had to leave most of me behind in the States. All I escaped with was what was in my case at the time: my laptop, my ID, some papers, some cash, a few clothes. It was a snap decision."

Simon laughed at the thought of Sparrow being chased across the United States.

"It's not funny. You don't know what happens in US jails, mate, I don't want to spend the rest of my life in some Guantanamo Bay, thanks. It's not as if I was Butch Cassidy. But when I saw *De Medicina*... well, I just had to have it. I thought it was the key, I really did."

"And it's not?"

"I've been through it and been through it again. I thought there might be cross-references, hints, indications as to where I might start looking for the other manuscripts, but... I just don't know, Simon. I couldn't find anything."

"Then send it back."

"No." Sparrow backed away. "No, I can't. Not yet. There might be something. Something I've overlooked. I can't give it back, not yet. Anyhow, they'd have my guts for whatsits."

"For heaven's sake, Martin, it's stolen property. I don't want to know. I don't want it here. Damn it, I thought you only had a copy."

"It's in a safe place."

"And, hold on, there's one thing I don't understand. Why haven't I heard anything about this? A priceless manuscript stolen? Books are my business. I would have heard about it on the grapevine. Why has there been no publicity?"

"Search me."

"I just might do that."

Martin Sparrow spread his arms. "Maybe they were too embarrassed to take it to the Feds, I don't know."

Simon sighed. It was all just so exactly Sparrow. It all added up, well, almost. A small detail niggled at Simon. "If you had no money, how did you pay the skipper of the yacht for taking you to England?"

Sparrow winked. "With my body."

Was there no end to the man? "There's something else about you I don't know?"

Sparrow laughed. "Not that, pal. I mean I sailed the damned dinghy over for him. Most of these guys couldn't sail a paper boat across the Serpentine."

"Hell, Martin. You are crazy."

"I know."

"Well, I don't know what to do."

"We'll give it a couple of weeks, how about it, old buddy? See what we can find out. If we get nowhere, I swear we'll send the manuscript back. Take a day-trip to Prague or Moscow and post it back from there."

"But there'll be a watch out on your passport."

"Actually, when I said 'we' I meant you."

"Why am I not surprised?"

*   *   *

"The rest of the story is true."

Simon looked at Martin across the dining room table. They spread the copy of *De Medicina* out on the polished surface. Simon's Latin was rudimentary compared to Sparrow's; he could hardly follow the text at all. Still, he had to agree with the younger man: if there was a clue in there, it was buried too deeply for them. "There's nothing else?"

"Nothing."

"Are you sure?"

"Hey, what are you saying, Simon? Why would I lie to you?"

Simon gave his benevolent parent look.

"All right, all right, I get your point," Martin added.

The two men worked in silence. Simon brought his laptop through and tried chasing down some of the Caxton leads that had promised so much. The dim light gave him a headache as the afternoon gave way to evening and the room descended further into gloom. "Let's call it a day, yeah?"

Martin bit his top lip, a gesture Simon had never seen. It was unlike Sparrow to be so low on ebullience. "OK."

"The trouble is that we don't even know what we're looking for. It could be a few dozen pages or it could be... I don't know, you remember Yung Lo's Great Encyclopaedia from fourteen hundred and something?"

Sparrow laughed. "Oh yeah. Over eleven thousand volumes? Well, at least we could hardly miss it."

"Yeah. It could be anywhere, Martin. Anywhere, or nowhere. Maybe we're wrong. Maybe it no longer exists. Sleep on it?"

Sparrow twisted his upper lip in frustration. "Yeah," he said, shuffling some papers into an ordered pile. He rubbed his chin. The tan was already fading, assaulted by a British autumn, and the low light could not disguise the dark circles appearing under Martin's eyes. Simon pondered on how well his friend was sleeping, and how well he was managing to submerge the consequences of his actions in the States.

Simon shut down the laptop. "1477," he said. "1477. So the Wars of the Roses have finished, right?"

"Well, just about coming to an end. It's pretty peaceful on the whole. Henry VII still has to give Richard what for at Bosworth, but, yeah, things are going OK. What of it?"

"The Hundred Years War has been over a while, too?"

"Right. Can't say exactly when off the top of my head,

fourteen-fiftyish, something like that, but yeah, it's been done and dusted for a while. What are you getting at, Simon?"

"Everything is quite stable. We're on as friendly terms with the French as we ever are."

"I expect they hadn't forgiven us for Agincourt. Then again, they never have."

"So we're trading with them again, right? The manuscripts would have come in to the country as part of a shipment, agreed? What you have to remember is that they were really hot on import taxes then. There would have been an inventory of every shipload of stuff coming into England, and there are records of these things – cargo manifests, customs logs."

"What are you saying?" Martin rubbed his chin and swirled Jack Daniels around his glass. It caught the light and for an instant looked like an amber dreamcatcher. "Sheesh, Simon, you might have something." The glint was back in Sparrow's eye.

"I don't know where they'd be, but… it's a long shot, Martin."

"Well, nobody ever calls it a short shot." Sparrow pointed at Simon's laptop. "Get that thing back on again."

*　　*　　*

"Dad." The whisper infiltrated Simon's dream like a spy. There were children laughing, Cassie and Alex, but it couldn't be them, they were grown. "Dad, are you OK?" The laughter seemed to grow louder, seemed to be all around him, then inside him, taking him over, lulling him. "Dad." Someone shook him and the laughter stopped as though it had been turned off with a switch.

Simon raised his head. His right eye quivered as if he had developed a nervous tic. He blinked hard. "Cassie?"

"It's four o'clock, Dad."

He peered out of the leaded window into West Street. It was completely black, the streetlight out of action again. Bloody hell, he had fallen asleep. The laptop screen in front of him was charcoal and mute, it too in hibernation. "Martin?" he said, rubbing his neck and hearing ominous cracking sounds.

Sparrow was stretched out on a seventeenth century settle, his chino-ed legs dangling through the bobbin turned arm supports, his head cushioned by a small rolled-up rug.

"Oh, hell." Simon yawned. The tic started up again and he rubbed his eye.

"Go to bed, Dad."

Simon registered that his daughter was dressed, although something did not seem right. "Yeah, I should." The background hum of parental responsibility gave him a nudge. "Have you just come in?"

"Yeah." She was little more than a silhouette in the night.

"Where have you been?" Simon yawned again and his eyes watered.

"Clubbing."

"Oh." There it was again, in the distance, children laughing a long way away. The more he tried to home in on the sound the more it faded.

"Go to bed, Dad. Come on." Cassie took his arm and led him up the stairs. He lay down on Robin's side, on top of the duvet and felt Cassie peel off his shoes before he went under. There was no more laughing.

*   *   *

"Christ on a bike, man," Sparrow said. "What time is it?"

"Half-nine. Drink this." Simon held out a mug of black coffee, the wren mug, Simon had made sure of that. "Sleep OK?"

The circles had deepened under Sparrow's eyes. "No thanks." He sat up, crouching over his coffee like a praying mantis and Simon could see dents in his clothes where the hinges of the settle had dug in to him. "Not at all."

A little bit of schadenfreude never hurt anyone, Simon thought. "You were snoring away when I went up," he said.

"Blimey I had some weird dreams." Sparrow ran his fingers through his hair. It spiked up, irking Simon that it showed few signs of receding. "I dreamt that there was fog everywhere, and noises in the fog, voices, laughter. Maybe it's my subconscious taking the piss."

"Laughter?" Simon remembered his own fractured night and scratched his head.

"I don't know. This place is odd, Simon." Martin looked around the room.

"What do you mean?"

"I feel uneasy. I don't know how to explain it, matey, but there's something out of kilter. It feels fine when you first come into the house, but after a while, you feel as though you're looking at things through net curtains, as though there's this blurring of reality. Know what I mean?"

"No." Simon laughed. "I have no idea what you're talking about."

"Methinks he doth protest too much."

"Honestly, Martin. Maybe I'm defending Paycocke's because so many other people have a problem with it…"

"See, it's not only me…"

"Hang on. I mean, no one has ever seen anything, and there's no evidence that anything terrible has ever happened here. Thomas Paycocke was a good bloke."

"If you say so."

"Oh, come on, Martin. You're not telling me you believe in ghosts?"

"I keep an open mind. On everything. Now where did we get to?" The debris on the dining-room table was an answer to the question - not very far.

Simon shrugged, shaking his head. "I don't know."

A key turned in the front door and Alex came in, panting. She leant forward with her hands on her knees and drops of sweat dripped from her face.

Martin looked away. "Grief, Alex. Isn't it a bit early for this sort of thing?"

Alex gulped down deep breaths of the stale Paycocke's air. "This early? Come on, Martin, I've been up for hours." Simon made a mental note that she still called him 'Martin'. Whether deliberate or not, he thanked her. She unclasped a tie from her hair and let it fall loose, sleek and unfettered. Simon wanted to touch it and draw her near to him. "So, what's up?" she said.

"Oh we're still working on this Celsus thing." Simon gestured at the chaos on the dining-room table.

"Needle in a haystack, huh?"

Martin drained the rest of his coffee, wincing. "If the haystack is the size of the world, and the needle is the size of a... a needle." Simon found Sparrow's pessimism demoralising. He had always been so positive, always the one to get things moving and to keep them flowing. Did age do this to you, sapping your enthusiasm, milking you until you no longer cared?

"It sounds like that Raiders of the Lost Ark," Alex said. "You know, at the end, where Indy's found the Ark of the Covenant, and it's like one of the most important artefacts in the history of the world, and the American government like just sticks it in a box and stores it in this massive warehouse with millions of other things, so that no one knows where it is or will ever be able to find it."

"Thanks. You're a right little spark of joy, aren't you, Ally?" Simon frowned at his daughter.

Sparrow put his head in his hands. "Yeah, it's like trying to find your favourite grain of salt."

"Hey, shut it, the both of you." Simon touched the mouse pad and the laptop lurched into action. Of course, he hadn't shut it down properly the night before. He clicked to re-open the windows. How much time had they wasted last night? He didn't even recognise the windows that were open: three from the National Archives; several County websites; one from the London Records Society. 'The overseas trade of London: exchequer customs accounts 1477' – he didn't remember that. "Martin?"

"Huh?" Sparrow was still listless, stretching his arms out to loosen them.

"Look at this."

"What is it, Dad?"

"I don't know." He read the text, "'Petty custom accounts of imports to and exports from the port of London by alien and denizen merchants. Records vessels and masters and details of cargo.' Do you remember this, Martin?"

Sparrow stood up, yawning, not fixing on Simon's curiosity. "What?"

"Look."

Sparrow shrugged, shaking his head. "No. But that doesn't mean a lot – we went down so many dead ends last night..."

Simon paged down. "It's a list of shipments. This is the sort of thing we were after: '2 Oct from the ship of William Johnson of London, Peter Morse: 3 packs flax, 3 lutes, 1 timber mink, 1 doz. candlesticks, 2 doz. squirts...' whatever a squirt is. There are pages of it, all the ships that traded, where they were from, exactly what was on them. This is a goldmine, Martin. If it's there, we'll find it. Look at this one..." Simon scrolled down, "... 'Robert Longfellow: 1 pr kempster's combs.' If it goes into that level of detail, Martin..."

Sparrow peered over Simon's shoulder. The aroma of coffee clung to his breath but could not disguise the staleness of his night on the settle. "Go down a bit." Simon scrolled the page further. "A bit more." Simon could sense an excitement brimming in Sparrow's voice. "Bit further. Oh, oh, look. Look, Simon. 'Amerigo Vespucci: 6 priceless manuscripts.' By God, we've found it."

Alex burst out laughing, her shoulders heaving.

Simon stared at the screen. "Very funny."

Martin put his arm around Simon's shoulders. "Let's have something to eat. Bacon sandwich would go down a treat. What do you say?"

Simon was reluctant to leave the laptop. "We're so close."

"Simon, compared to this, Pluto is close, pal. Look, we can come back to it." Sparrow scrolled to the bottom. "There are over two hundred ships on this page alone. And how many pages are there, forty, fifty? Let's have some brekkers and come back to it, old chum. If it's there, it's there, and it's not going anywhere soon. Coming, Alex?"

"No, not for a minute, I need to warm down. I'll catch you up."

The two men went into the kitchen. The bacon spat in the frying pan and they said nothing. Without the laptop and *Artes* there was a brooding silence splitting them. Simon turned the back over with a spatula and it sizzled even more strongly. A spot of fat jumped from the pan towards Martin, hitting him on a white shirt-tail.

"Damn," Sparrow said.

"Sorry."

"No. It's me who's sorry. I'm really, really sorry, Simon."

The apology hung between them.

"Dad, come here." Alex's voice came through the house. "Dad," she shouted.

Simon left the bacon and rushed through to the dining room. "What is it?"

She pointed to the laptop. "Look." She positioned the cursor over shipment 238. "Look at this."

Simon stared in amazement.

"Well, what do you know?" He read the item, "'John Paycocke…'"

Chapter 40
The Study

Edward was up there for ages. His boots slid through the gap and it was as though he had been eaten by the gaping hole in the ceiling. I wondered how I should explain his disappearance to his parents were he to be swallowed by Paycocke's. I pulled myself together.

"Edward," I called. "What are you doing up there?" I was beginning to become rather cross. Not only had he pulled the wool over my eyes with his tale of Billy Howes (and how foolish did I feel now, having written to Charles Townsend about the episode?), but he did not even have the decency to tell me what was happening in my own home. "Edward."

"It's all right," he called. "I'll be down in a minute." The scraping of his boots on the floor of the crawlspace seemed to get further and further away. How could he possibly be down in a minute? He sounded miles away, although I knew that he could not be. I was starting to worry about Gussie and Iso coming home. What on earth would they think? It was bad enough that I had invited a stranger into our house, but that he should be creeping about its innards like a death watch beetle - oh, it did not bear thinking about.

A minute passed which felt like an hour. I gripped the ladder and made sure it was steady. He should have one last chance. "Edward." There was no reply and I began to climb.

At the trapdoor I peered into the darkness. It was as black as tar and I could not see a single thing in those inky depths, not even the vaguest shadow of my friend. A panic seized me and I felt my cheeks grow hot. Edward had gone. This could not be so. My knuckles whitened as I gripped the top rung and I stared into the chasm, praying that he would appear. I only dared whisper, "Edward," and I felt the tremor in my own voice. A dreadful heat overcame me and I slumped forward against the ladder, feeling the coolness of its wood and metal frame against my burning cheeks. Oh, dear God, what had I done?

I looked up once more, a horrid fear lining my stomach and then the Stygian mist seemed to part inside the hole, a tiny flicker of light appearing in the distance. I could not tell how far away it was, since I had no single point of reference for it. Everything else was completely obscured.

The vestige of light was eclipsed by something moving across it and Edward's voice sprang both from nowhere and from everywhere, filling the void. "Holy Mary, Mother of God," he said. "It's a shrine."

I almost lost my grip on the ladder.

"Look," he said.

I could see nothing and said so. He seemed silent for an eternity.

"Come in." His voice was urgent, pleading.

How could I? It was not that I was in any way squeamish about the spiders and other wildlife that might frequent such a place, although I suspected that they were legion, but more that it simply would not be seemly to squeeze myself into such a place with only Edward Daynes for company. Furthermore, I have to say that my trust in him had taken a severe pummelling after the Billy Howes revelation. "No, Edward. You come out." There was silence, a war of the wills. Then the shadow moved and pushed the flicker of light before it. It seemed that I had won the battle.

Edward brought back some artefacts: a miniature of the Sacred Heart; a small statuette of the Virgin Mary, looking rather less than immaculate, I had to say, with tendrils of long vacated webs garnishing the folds of her robes; and a dish, which I presumed had once held holy water. He handed them to me and I climbed down the ladder. "What can this mean?"

He peered from the trapdoor; he was gruesomely filthy and clouds of dusts swirled around him. "It's a shrine, or an altar or something," he repeated.

"Yes, I know, but…"

"There's a bible up there too, and some other stuff."

"Who would have done this?" I laid the holy objects out on the table and stared at them. "And why?"

"Mind out. I'm coming down."

Such a Catholic collection, but was it part of an exorcism, or had some bizarre sacrifice taken place behind the trapdoor? I shivered and tried to rein in my imagination before it went completely out of control. Nevertheless, by now I was utterly convinced that Paycocke's House was haunted; there was not a scrap of doubt in my mind. So taking things a step further down the path of strange ritual did not feel odd in the slightest.

Conrad Noel. It must have been Conrad. The Noels had lived in the house for a number of years while the restoration was taking place. He had seen the ghosts, had witnessed for himself their malign influence on the house, the pallor that they cast over all who entered. He must have built this shrine to protect future residents of Paycocke's. It all added up. Moreover, his interest in all things Catholic was well documented, although often frowned upon by his peers. It must have been he. I shuddered to think that a man of such charisma and power was unable to exert any authority over the supernatural beings in his house. What hope had I of getting to the bottom of Paycocke's secret? It was no wonder he had been so shifty when I tackled him about it at Thaxted, changing the subject, making jest of my questions and avoiding me. He who had always spurned the spiritual. It must have been quite the shock for him to meet the ghosts of Paycocke's.

I determined to confront Conrad now that I had a clearer picture, but first I would write to Charles Townsend. I would invite him to Paycocke's that he might add an impartial opinion as to the goings-on. Armed with this knowledge, I would go back to Thaxted and see whether the Red Vicar might become the Red-Faced Vicar.

"Imogen." Edward's whisper behind me felt like a puff of dust. I had forgotten he was there, but suddenly I felt his emerald eyes burn into the back of my neck. Although he said nothing but my name, something had changed, something had happened to him in that tiny attic room. It was as though he were possessed. I turned to face him and he repeated my name. Oblivious to the state of himself, dripping cobwebs and dust, so grimy that he looked more like a chimneysweep or a Tommy fresh from the trenches, he took my hand and put his other around my neck, pulling me to him.

"Edward," I said. "No, Edward." I tried to turn my face away, but I was magnetised by his eyes as they came closer to my own, drawing me in and when he kissed me it felt like the most romantic thing in the whole world.

*   *   *

The tremor of Edward's hands sent the candle's jerking light skittering across the darkness. He stared in awe. "Holy Mary, Mother of God," he said. "It's a shrine. Come and look."

A shrine, Edward thought, a holy place, a holy place surrounded by night. How could this be? The candle wavered in front of him and its light seemed to be sucked away by a minuscule draught. He cupped a palm around the frail glimmer, not wanting to be left alone in the dark hole. The blackness gathered around him like a soft woollen blanket and he heard the voices, not sure if they were there in the darkness with him or in his head. 'Be not afraid, Edward. Join us. It is meant to be.' Soft wisps of shadow draped over his shoulders, pulling at his arms as he tried to move, covering his face like a mask. He felt uneasy, not scared or threatened, but wanted and desired. He fought to control the uncomfortable feeling, taking deep breaths that tasted of damp and decay. 'Stay, Edward, stay.' He brushed his palms about his face and cobwebs fell away, a spider scuttling from his hand for more obscure parts. He must go back. He must go back. 'Stay. Join us.'

Edward closed his eyes and a flash of light assaulted all of his senses. Imogen. He opened his eyes again and the light was gone. Perhaps it had never been there. Imogen. His love. She would bring light. She would *be* his light. The voice in his head argued. 'No. Stay, Edward. You must stay.' Of course he could stay. It would be warm here in this bed of darkness, warm and safe, and with Imogen a haven of love. At this moment he knew how much he loved her, as much as all eternity. Beside the shrine he had had his own epiphany. What he had felt for her hitherto was a boy's infatuation. "Come in," he called.

"No, Edward. You come out."

Edward was torn, the darkness holding him, the sound of Imogen's voice pulling him towards the light. The candle was growing weaker; he did not have much time. Looking behind him he saw her head framed against the light in the trapdoor opening, a halo around her. She beckoned, a silhouette against the day that invaded the crawlspace. He had to go to her. His heart ached for the darkness, for the lost spirits who needed him here, but he had to go to Imogen. Taking some of the objects from the shrine, he crawled back to the trapdoor, trying not to hear the moans that pursued him, begging him to stay. He would be back. His feelings were whirling around like a kaleidoscope and he fought to stay in control, passing the objects to Imogen. Her fingers touched his, sending a surge through him and he struggled to retain his focus, trying to concentrate on drawing in breaths of fresh air. She put the objects onto the table, turning each one over in her hands.

"It's a shrine, an altar," Edward said, every syllable a labour of Hercules. "And there's more. A bible. Some other stuff." She had her back to him but he could see her every tiny movement as she inspected his gifts to her.

"I'm coming down," he said. Imogen seemed not to hear him, so engrossed was she. He climbed down the ladder, with each step leaving behind the dark abyss which called to him, its voice growing ever fainter. When he planted a foot on the wooden floor the final tie was broken. What had he been thinking of? The darkness had had some kind of hold over him, mesmerising him and stealing his thoughts. Down from the ladder he felt free again, free to exist and to love. He whispered her name; it felt like a breeze on his lips. He said it again, relishing its sound.

"Edward," she said.

He pulled her to him and kissed her, his heart pulsating with longing and relief. Neither heard the front door.

"Imogen. What on earth is the meaning of this?"

Chapter 41
Imports

"John Paycocke. Well, I'll be damned," Simon said. "This is some coincidence." They clustered around the laptop's screen.

"It's bloody spooky," said Martin. He folded his arms and looked at the screen from the side.

Simon rolled his eyes. "It's not that weird. Paycocke would have done a lot of trade with the continent, probably had shares in a number of ships. It would be strange if we found *no* mention of him here."

"Still, the first page we look at…" Sparrow brushed a hand through his hair. "Alex?"

She looked up at her blood father, shrugging. Simon searched for signs of a connection between the two of them, but saw nothing. Alex pointed at the screen; the fonts were so small that the men had to bend their faces close in to the laptop.

"This is the site you were looking at before. I just scrolled down. I was looking at all the lists of stuff: 'a fardel with 2 dozen skins of cordwain; 3 puncheons; 1 pack of stockfish.' There's stuff here I've never even heard of. It's like a different world."

"So what was Paycocke into?" Simon asked.

Alex ran the cursor alongside Paycocke's entry in the records. "Several different sorts of cloth: Brabant; Flemish; Osnabrück; Ghent."

"Makes sense," he said.

Martin Sparrow was shaking his head. "Not to me it doesn't. Something's not right."

"What are you on about?"

"It's all too much of a coincidence. We're looking up import records for something completely different and all of a sudden we happen on Paycocke? No, it's not right."

Alex scowled at Martin and Simon cheered inwardly. "Well, what do you reckon then?" she said.

"I just don't remember being on this website. Simon?"

"Well, no, but…"

"It was there, this morning, when you switched the laptop on again."

Simon felt uncomfortable. "I'm sure there's an explanation." He gestured at the empty tumblers on the dining room table. "We downed quite a bit last night, Martin. And we were both knackered by the end. We went down a lot of dead ends; maybe one of them was not that dead."

"I don't buy that, Simon."

"And?"

"Look," Sparrow said. "Someone… or something reset that web page. They wanted us to find this site. There is something on this URL that we're meant to see."

"Oh, come off it, Martin. What's all this 'someone or something' Hollywood crap?"

Sparrow turned away and looked around the room, where the linen fold panelling crowded them in on all sides. He raised his voice in exasperation. "Why do you think it's always so bloody cold in the hall? Why do those dog alarms keep going off? Don't deny it, Simon, I see it in your eyes. Robin told me. What was the laughter I heard? There's something wrong here, Simon." He thumped the linen fold. "You just can't see it. Why don't you open your eyes, Simon? Why can't you bloody well see what's going on right in front of your face?"

Sparrow stopped, realising what he had just said. He clasped his hands behind his head and looked up to the roll-moulded ceiling. "I'm sorry, Simon," he said at last. "I didn't mean that."

Simon acknowledged his apology with a nod, but did not answer.

"Hey, what's up? What's with the noise?" Cassie stood at the bottom of the stairs.

Simon stared at her. "Cassie. Your hair." It was black.

"Oh yeah. You like it? I fancied a change."

"I… It's…"

"It's wicked, Cass," said Alex. "That's what Dad was going to say. Right, Dad?"

"Oh… yeah. Hey, thanks for getting me to bed last night, Cass. I was a goner."

"S'OK, Dad. No worries. I thought you must be a bit out of it when you didn't mention my hair."

"What time was that?"

"Not that late," she said. She fingered her hair. "It was School Disco night down at The Raven."

"School Disco?"

"Yeah. I borrowed a mate's tie. It was like nostalgic."

Simon laughed at the idea of a nineteen year old doing something for the sake of nostalgia.

"Anyway, what are you all up to? It looks serious."

Simon bit his bottom lip. "Did you touch the laptop before you went up last night?"

Cassie's face hardened. "I didn't touch anything, OK? It wasn't me." Alex put her hand on her sister's wrist.

Simon held up his palms in a calming gesture. "I'm not accusing you of anything, Cass. Just wondering if maybe you did a bit of surfing before you went to bed, chased a few links, you know? It's not a problem. It's just that when I turned it on this morning there was a website I didn't recognise."

Cassie looked at him sideways, still suspicious. "Porn?" She cast a glance at Sparrow.

Simon laughed. "No, of course not. A list of fifteenth century shipping manifests."

Cassie's eyes widened and she drew back her head in astonishment. Then her mouth creased into an unaccustomed smile and she laughed. "How sad is that?"

"Just asking."

"No, Dad. Just to clarify, I didn't come back from a night's clubbing, sit down and investigate fifteenth century shipping thingies."

Simon looked at Martin. "I don't know. It must have been us…"

Sparrow shook his head.

"Then…"

Out of nowhere, the fire alarm went off. Simon leapt towards the kitchen. "Oh, no, hell, the bacon, it's the bacon. It's set off the bloody alarm."

*   *   *

The fire engine arrived ten minutes later, the kitchen still choked with smoke. Once the firemen had left, Simon and Sparrow's impetus was gone. Cassie had disappeared; the embarrassment of the fire brigade had proved too much for her. Alex was sitting at the laptop, playing pinball. Maybe Sparrow was right. Simon couldn't see what was happening in front of his nose: Robin; Cassie; Sparrow himself; Simon couldn't even make a sandwich without it developing into a crisis. He had spent so long on his blinkered path he had missed the world turning around him. Robin. He had to speak to Robin.

"I'm popping out… I'm going for a bit of fresh air," he said.

Martin uncrossed his arms. "Yeah, all right."

Simon gestured at the laptop. "You carry on."

"Wait up, Dad, I just need to finish this ball."

"It's OK, Alex," Sparrow said. "I'm whacked. I think I'll nip back to the hotel and get some shut-eye."

"You can crash in the spare room if you like."

Martin smiled, shaking his head. "Thanks, mate. It's better if I get back. Get cleaned up, you know what I mean. We can catch up with this stuff later. Give me a call this afternoon."

"Sure."

"And it's 'House', don't forget."

"House? What do you mean, 'House'?" Alex glanced up from the laptop, the briefest of looks before switching her concentration back to the game.

"I'll tell you later," Simon said.

Simon was halfway down the street before he realised that he should phone. Robin was his wife on paper only; he couldn't just walk in. He was taking for granted the fact that she would be home and that she would even want to see him. How long had he been taking things for granted? He stopped and sat on a bench in the small memorial garden and dialled Abby's number. He had wanted to call Robin so many times in the last couple of weeks, to ask her what had happened and why, although of course he knew why. What if Abby picked up? He examined his feelings, wondering if he could feel his heart racing or detect any nervous tension. Just when he expected to be channelled to the voicemail, the phone was picked up.

"Hello?" Robin.

"Oh, hi, Robin." Too nonchalant. He bit his lip. "Hello, Robin, it's Simon."

"Hi, Simon." Her voice was bright, brighter than when she had picked up the telephone. Was it faked, or was she really pleased to hear from him? "How are you today?"

"Yeah, OK. I was wondering if I could come over? To see you? Just to talk?"

"Now?"

"If it's convenient."

"Is it Cassie? Is there something wrong?"

Simon felt a sudden stab of hurt that she should assume his visit was only connected with their daughter. "No, not at all." Although maybe there was. That story about the school disco had an air of concoction about it. What was that about? "I just wanted to talk, that's all."

"Oh."

"If you're busy…"

"No, no. Abby's at the shop. I have a meeting in town this afternoon, but right now I'm all yours."

Simon clamped his eyes shut at the last words. She was not all his, would never again be. *Had she ever been his?* He hadn't thought his nerve endings were still so sensitive, had begun to believe that his developing affection for Eleanor was soothing his wounds, but it wasn't so easy to paper over a twenty year relationship. "Great," he said. "Is now a good moment?"

"I'll put the kettle on."

"See you in a minute."

Their house was the one with the clean windows, the one with the new paintwork crisply cut in against the sash frame.

There was a doorbell next to which a white card proclaimed 'A. Williams & R. Chance' in a bold traditional font.

"Simon. Hi."

He felt an awkwardness between them, a first date-like invisible wall that governed how far each was expected to go.

Robin ushered him into the kitchen. She was beautiful. He could see that, as though he were looking at her from a distance. How long was it since he had thought of his wife as beautiful? Beautiful and now untouchable. "How are you… settling in?" he said.

"Good. We have the same taste in drapes." She laughed so that Simon would know it was not a serious point she was making.

"And Alfie?"

"She's upstairs right now. Sleeping, I guess. She does a lot of sleeping."

Simon looked up to where the bedrooms must be, to where Robin and Abby themselves must sleep.

"Yeah, it's kind of weird living with a snake, but she's OK. Little bit jealous now and again, but who isn't?"

"I'm sure you can get used to it."

Robin poured the coffee, not asking whether he wanted milk. He appreciated the intimacy of the assumption.

"Your things?" he said. "I wondered if you wanted to come and get some of your things."

"Yes, sure, although…"

"Although?"

"There's not too much I need. This is sort of a fresh start, Simon. I've stopped running away. You know what I'm saying? You know how you can get weighed down by possessions?"

Simon knew. He knew it every day: pieces they had chosen together, presents they had given each other. He tested himself for bitterness and felt none. He wanted to say, 'I'm thinking of a fresh start too, you know,' but he just agreed. "Well, whenever you want. It's not a problem."

"Thank you." Such politeness.

"I'm sorry I didn't see it coming."

"I hid things pretty well. Practice." Robin put her mug down on the work surface and rubbed his upper arm. "Don't beat yourself up, Simon."

"It's like a lot of things. Sparrow said…"

"Oh, Sparrow." Robin laughed. "You don't want to listen to him. He's full of it."

"Yeah, but he spouts so much crap he has to get it right once in a while. I just don't seem able to open my eyes. Like you, like Cassie, like Sparrow and Alex, like the ghosts…"

"Ghosts?"

"Well, I don't mean ghosts, Robin. I don't believe in any of that. But so many people have been going on about Paycocke's that I wonder if there's something in it, something I've missed. It's even got Sparrow spooked now, and you know what he's like."

"It's a sad house, Simon. Something happened there. I guess we'll never know what, but something happened. I felt… uneasy at Paycocke's, Simon. I don't know how to describe it exactly, but it's as though I was never alone there, as if there was always someone watching me. I would hear noises in the public rooms, footsteps or laughter, and when I went in the room there would be no one there. Sometimes those little security alarms would go off for no reason, and, Simon, it got so gosh-darned cold, even in the height of summer."

"I… I like the house."

"Maybe it likes you."

"What should I do?"

"You're asking me? Maybe you should leave, too. In the last few months it got to me so much that I thought something terrible was about to happen."

Simon resisted the urge to say something terrible *did* happen. He nodded. "I'll think about it."

Robin faced him once more. "I want to be your friend, Simon. I love you. In the best way that I can, I love you."

Simon ached for her, felt the tears coming and pulled her to him in a tight embrace, running his fingers through her new hair, inhaling its clean fresh smell.

A key sounded in the front door.

"Abby," Robin whispered, without moving. Simon took this as a cue that he too did not need to end their hug, did not need to draw away with guilt.

"Hi, honey, I'm back," Abby called from the front door in the worst American accent Simon had ever heard. He and Robin both grinned. Abby walked into the kitchen and saw them together, but her embarrassment was only there because of her appalling greeting, that was clear.

"Simon!" She put her handbag on the kitchen table and gave him a hug and he wondered what he and Robin looked like, tear-stained and dishevelled. "Staying for lunch?"

"Thanks no, I need to get back," he said. One step at a time.

Abby seemed so young, her face so unmarked by life. Why did he feel so careworn? "You're always welcome here, Simon."

He blinked. "Thanks." She *was* so young, that was the reason, only a few years older than Cassie. "Hey," he said. "Do you know the Raven, Abby? In Colchester?"

"The club? I've been there once or twice."

"Do you know if they have a School Disco night?"

She winked. "Are you asking me out, Simon? I've still got a gymslip in the attic, you know. Or is this for some more nefarious purpose?"

"No, no. I just wondered."

"The Raven? Disco Night? Could be."

"On a Tuesday?"

She narrowed her eyes at the question, furrowing her eyebrows together so that they looked like a child's drawing of a bird. "Don't know. Seems like an odd night of the week for it. Why?"

"No reason. Just wondering." *'An odd night.' Oh, Cassie, not again.*

Chapter 42
Games

Fitz pulled up outside Eleanor's house and watched her boy leave on his mountain bike. *No helmet. What sort of a mum let her kid go out without a helmet?* He swung himself out of the Escort, leaving it unlocked and strode up to the front door, rapping on the glass.

Eleanor's silhouette appeared through the crazy paving of the frosted pane, some fragments of her shape seeming larger than others, other parts blurred and obscure. *Nice legs.* She opened the door and filled the entrance. "Oh, it's you," she said. "You'd better come in."

"Ta very much. Just passing. House clearance in Earls Colne," he said. Let her think he hadn't made a special trip. It was good to lie, good to keep in practice. He followed her through to the lounge, sitting down in one of the armchairs without being asked. "Your lad?" Fitz jerked a thumb towards the street. "On his bike?"

"Yes." Eleanor looked at him sideways, as though trying to read between his lines. "What of it?"

Fitz smiled and spread his arms. "Shouldn't go out without a helmet is all." He was getting hostile vibes from Eleanor. Something wasn't right. She was up to something. Read the opponent, predict his next move, pre-empt, counter. It never left you, that.

He mustn't see I'm scared. Not of him, not anymore. But losing Simon, that's something else. It's all so fragile. I've got to keep control.

Eleanor rubbed her hands together. "Oh, Jack. If I've told him once…"

"Kids. Who'd have 'em?" Fitz nodded, sympathising. "Now…" He leant back in the armchair and laced his fingers behind his head.

Tell him. I have to tell him. I have to take that risk.

"Something's happened, Fitz…"

"I like it when something happens," he said. "Tea?"

"What?"

"Are you going to offer me a cup of tea? It's a drive and a half back to Clacton, you know."

She was blunt, unsmiling. This was better. "Do you want tea?"

Fitz wrinkled his nose. "No thanks, not for the moment, but ta for offering. Oh, thanks for the mag, by the way, smashing, appreciate it. Absolute treat. I love *Country Life*, me. Did you read the article?"

She shook her head.

He clapped his hands once. "So, what have you got for me this time, El?"

Eleanor sat on the arm of the sofa, as though not wanting to come any closer. She would not look him in the eye. "Nothing. Look, Fitz, it's over. I can't do this anymore."

He smiled and made his words sound friendly, a quiet laugh underpinning each syllable. "Come on, Eleanor, do me a favour. Please?" He ran a finger over the maroon leather. "Nice," he said. "New?"

She nodded.

"I guess I paid for it then." He laughed. "Look, who looked after you when your old man left you, Eleanor? I'm surprised at you." From the coffee table he picked up a small bronze sculpture of a cat cleaning itself. He weighed it in his hand; heavy, lovely piece. He placed it back precisely in the same spot it had occupied. Eleanor had the guts to face up to him, good girl. Truth was, it was all bark; he wouldn't hurt a fly. "I'm not going to ask why, Eleanor. Your business is your business..."

"I... I can't pry into his life anymore, Fitz. He doesn't deserve it."

Fitz saw through the blind. "The old son of a gun. You've fallen for him, haven't you, doll?" He flung his head back on the sofa, laughing. "You've only gone and fallen for him?" He could see from her reddening face that he was right. "And his wife only just walked out. The old charmer, eh? Well, fuck me sideways, who would have thought it? Not so simple Simon."

"Fitz, please..." Eleanor fidgeted with a small string of beads around her neck.

Fitz was hurt that she was pleading. It was as though she thought he was simmering with menace and might boil over at any second. That really hurt. He tried to inject calm and reason into his voice. This was so much harder than boxing. Man, no one knew how hard. "Look. It's a good thing. I'm pleased for you, both of you, honest I am. He's a lovely geezer, Simon. I've said it before and I'll say it again: champion bloke. Just do me a favour and take him shopping for a decent suit. Diamond. I hope you'll be very happy." Fitz meant it too. He hoped it would be a happy ending for all of them. Especially him.

"In any case, there's nothing more I can do."

Fitz pondered that one and couldn't resist the urge to tease her. "Mmm, not strictly true, especially now that you and he are courting."

A fire sparked in her eyes. "Fitz, no. This has gone far enough. You've got what you wanted. I've done my share, paid off my debt. Don't you think?"

Nothing more she could do? Yeah, she was right. Now that she had fallen for Chance, he couldn't expect any more reliable information. Best to quit ahead of the game – a points win was worth just as much as a knockout. Still, he had had the cream. Be grateful. He had to give it to her – she'd more than paid off the debt. She had been the one to tip him off about Paycocke's, the one to get him inside the house. She had done her part, good girl. "You know what? I think you're right, El." But had he got what he wanted? Not yet. Not by a six-foot chalk. He stood up, shaking the creases out of his trousers.

She looked surprised.

"Cheers, Eleanor," he said at the front door. "You've been great. Just one thing: it might be best if you don't mention our friendship to old Simon, eh? He might take it the wrong way." He squeezed her upper arm. "Look after yourself, girl." He might need her again, who knew. Best to leave on good terms. "Give me a call if you're ever down Clacton way." Like hell she would.

Like hell I will. I want you gone, Fitz, out of my life, gone. All I want is a chance with Simon, however slim.

He drummed his feet on the floor of the car, a tapping on the rubber mat that soothed him. He had never expected this, not in his wildest dreams. How about that, old Simon Chance, dark horse coming up on the rails? Maybe he had underestimated him. Not like the Clacton King, that. Still and all, Eleanor had been worthwhile, very worthwhile. But it was best to let her go, move on. What could she tell Chance? She didn't know anything. And look at it this way: if she did tell him, the poor guy might crack, all these women ganging up on him. And bang would go her chance to play happy families again. Yeah, it was storming. He put the car into gear and headed east out of Coggeshall.

So many complications. And that Cassie, was she a complication too far? What a cracking girl she was. Spirit, she had. Sweet, like her Dad, but with more balls. He pulled out at a roundabout in third and the gearbox complained as the car chugged out into the traffic. An old BMW 7 series sounded its horn at him and he let it pass. "Whoo, what's up with you, mate?" He stared at the road ahead and tried to do some breathing exercises. They'd helped in the ring and they would help now. Cassie was a distraction - there was time enough for that when the job was finished, when he had what he wanted, what he had been waiting for all these years, what his granddad should have had. He wondered if Cassie would be interested then.

Fitz was losing control of his feelings, he knew that. It was a new one on him. He pulled the car out onto the A12 on autopilot. Cassie, eh? He liked the sensation of whimsy with which she filled him. Life had always been so full of planning, careful meticulous planning, squeezing out the unpredictable from every situation. Cassie made him feel spontaneous, gave him a hollow feeling beneath his sternum where his nerve endings tingled. The thought of her name made his insides flip. He laughed and his mind went wandering off on strange fantasies: they could buy a farm somewhere, Scotland or Yorkshire, maybe, somewhere remote where he could have her all to himself. He thought of the guy who had come to the door in Colchester when he had dropped her off. *Slime. Yeah, remote was best, keep her away from scum like that.* His hands tightened around the steering wheel. *A farm would be nice.*

They could raise pigs or sheep maybe, have hens running around the yard. Cats all over the place, slinking in and out of the barns. She liked cats, he knew. And kids, yeah. Three, maybe, two boys and a girl. A lorry bellowed at him as the Escort straddled the white lines and he pulled over into a lay-by as the traffic screamed east. *Whoa, man, got to calm down.* What was doing this to him, Cassie or Paycocke's? The strange feelings had begun the day he went to the house. ('It will draw you in and take you in its heartfelt embrace, change you and all that you know...')

He pulled the old *Country Life* from the glove compartment, opening it at the Paycocke's feature. Reaching inside his parka pocket he felt the envelope of photographs: the ones from his grandfather's camera; and now, nestling against his heart, the new ones he had taken at the house. It wouldn't hurt to have another look, take his mind off farmhouses and idyllic domestic scenes.

Before and after; before and after. The house hadn't changed much over the decades. The monochrome of the old photographs seemed crisper, the chiaroscuro defining the pictures, assaulting him with their sharp contrasts of dark and light. How many times had he looked at these? His own photographs, by comparison, were washed out and soft around the edges. He would have to get a better digital camera; perhaps Cass would buy him one for Christmas. *Hey, stop it.* He shook his head to batter away the distracting thoughts. Paycocke's. Get back to Paycocke's. He'd done his research, knew as much about the house as any man alive. But did he know as much as any man dead? *Shut up, would you, shut the fuck up.*

Flicking through the pictures, he held them up to the light, comparing them with the professional photographs commissioned by the magazine. Paycocke's had hardly changed at all, no more than a granite pebble on a beach, washed endlessly by the tide, would alter with the passage of time. The carvings retained their timeless beauty, the panelling its delicate yet severe lines, the folds of the linen very much as Paycocke would have commissioned them. Or were they? Fitz put the *Country Life* on the passenger seat and held the photographs of the dining room next to it. For an instant he wondered if he was holding them the right way around, because there was no furniture in the frame by which he could orient the pictures. But they must be right. There, in the magazine photograph, was a fragment of the bressumer stealing across the bottom of the shot; in his photo he could make out the flying hearth on the ceiling. But the linen fold wasn't right; they didn't match with the magazine. Had the panelling been replaced in between? That didn't make sense. Everything Fitz had read about the house indicated otherwise – that it had been in place since the sixteenth century. Then how could they be different? He rotated the photograph, changing the angle at which the light hit it, and it became clear: the panelling was upside down. The bloody panelling was only upside down. Turn the snap through 180 degrees and the two pictures matched exactly. At some point it had been removed and replaced, upside-bleeding-down. Why? Fitz put a hand up to his mouth. Why?

*   *   *

Simon strode back home via the Tilkey Road, the air cool and thin as though it could be sliced. He debated whether he should call in on Eleanor and loitered behind a grimy Ford across the street from Eleanor's door, his heart skipping in a schoolboy fashion he had almost forgotten. He had a puerile urge to trace her initials in the dust on the car's boot. The unknown quivered inside him, standing on the threshold of the second half of his life. He checked the time; he should be getting back. There would be other chances. Lots of them.

No regrets. How could he have regrets about the years he and Robin had shared? Not to mention their daughters. Their daughter. No, their daughters, the plural was right, deserved. Regrets for Robin, yes; how could he not? He still loved her, had always loved her. There would always be a Robin-shaped place in his heart.

But what about the School Disco? Was this more of Cassie's fabrication? Did she lie for fun? He stopped off at the newsagent for a copy of the Standard. There would probably be an advertisement for the Raven inside.

Sparrow had gone by the time he got back to Paycocke's. The sound of the heavy iron latch echoed around the entrance hall and he wondered if anyone was home at all. Those girls never set the alarm. Martin would be back at the White Hart by now, sleeping off their altercation. Simon could use a nap too, wishing he still had that teenage ability to stay up all night without repercussions. 'Sorry' hadn't sat too easily upon Sparrow's lips and Simon was glad he was gone.

There was a sound of footsteps from upstairs. "Anyone around?" he shouted from the bottom of the stairs. The footsteps stopped, an abrupt guillotine of the noise. Simon's internal organs were not obeying him these days and he dismissed the goose pimples that rolled across his forearms. "Hello?"

There was no answer, just a silence that hung in the stale air. Simon walked around to the kitchen which still reeked of charred bacon. He threw open the windows onto the courtyard; he should have done it earlier. Everything had a musty feel to it, as though it were a house where nobody lived. Dust carpeted the window sills; the place could use a spring-clean. In the spring.

"Dad." Alex poked her head around the door that led to the west staircase. He hadn't heard her come down.

"Hi, darling."

"Have you got a minute, Dad?" She stepped away from the door, but held onto the knob as though it would somehow earth her.

He should get on the *Artes* case. He should check his email. He should check his eBay store. People would think he had stopped trading. He should have a nap. "As long as it's not organic chemistry."

"It's about Julia." Alex's hand rested on the door handle, twisting it open, then closed, then open again.

"If she wants to stay again…"

"No, it's not that, Dad." Alex paused, looking at the floor. "Julia, well… Julia and I, really, we …If it's a bad time, Dad…"

"No, no, it's not a bad time at all." Simon yawned and scratched an ear. "Well, it is really, I suppose. Damn it, Alex, everything has spiralled out of control. It's been one thing after another."

Alex stepped away from the door and padded across to her father. "I know, Dad." She opened her arms out wide to him. It reminded him of when he and Robin had taught her to walk, opening their arms to her as she staggered her first steps towards a reward of a parent's hug. Now the roles were reversed. He was so tired that it was just about all he could do to totter into his own daughter's arms. That wasn't how it should be. "It'll be OK, Dad. Don't worry."

Alex's arms felt warm and strong around him, stronger than he himself felt. Her hair smelt faintly of the swimming pool, as though the slightest dusting of chlorine had been applied. "I don't think I could take much more," he said.

She put her hand to the back of his head. As his chin flopped on her shoulder he saw the Standard he had dropped on the kitchen table. Alex might know. "Al?" Simon yawned again.

"Yeah?"

"Do you know the Raven?"

"Quoth the raven 'nevermore'?"

"No, it's a nightclub."

"Oh. That Raven."

"Do you know if they have a School Disco night?"

Alex drew her face back from his. "Aren't you a bit old for that?"

"Oi."

"Only kidding, Dad."

"I was... just wondering."

"Well, don't ask me. It's out of my league." She nodded down at the newspaper. "Should be in the paper. Or Cassie would know – that's her idea of fun."

Simon picked up the paper, nodding. "Mmm." He flipped through, looking for the entertainments section. There it was, a quarter of a page: 'The Raven, Colchester's Hottest Spot. Mondays – Alien Night; Tuesdays – School Disco...' He dropped the paper back on the table, suddenly tired beyond words, sick and tired. *Great, she wasn't lying after all.*

Chapter 43
Sleep

Simon awoke, confused. A grey light shafted through the window, but the insipid sun looked all wrong. He opened his eyelids, dislodging crusts of sleep, and yawned. It wasn't morning; that's what was wrong. The LCD on the bedside clock flashed 16:13; he had slept for hours. Pushing the duvet back, he was assaulted by the sour smell of his own body. He groaned; he always felt more tired after an afternoon nap.

The telephone's shrill 'Autumn' fired up downstairs. "Damn," he said. "Sparrow." He jumped out of bed and clouted his head on a ceiling beam. "Agh, buggeration." He put his hand to his temple and flopped back on the bed. The ringing cut out. "Bloody bugger." A quail's egg appeared on the top of his forehead. It must have been Sparrow.

"Dad." Cassie. "Dad." Louder.

Simon grunted. "Yeah, I'm here."

Cassie leant on the door frame. In the dim light she looked Transylvanian, her pale colouring even more washed out by the contrast to her dyed black hair. "You haven't banged your head again, Dad?" She was trying, but not at all hard, to suppress a grin.

"Sod off."

"Aaah. Shall I kiss it better?" His daughter bent over him like a vampire, her jet tresses falling over his face.

Simon turned away and was rewarded by a fiery burst from his temple. He rubbed the swelling. He flinched. "Who was on the phone?"

Cassie shrugged. "Don't know."

Simon rubbed his eyes, picking at flotsam of sleep crusted to his eyelashes. "Did you not answer it?"

Cassie shrugged again. "If it's important they'll ring back. Fancy a cup of tea?"

He yawned. "No. No thanks, Cass, not right now. I need to get cracking."

"OK." She turned to go.

"Cass?"

"Uh-huh?"

He was about to ask her where she had been this afternoon. "Never mind. I'll see you downstairs in a minute. Pasta OK tonight?" Why could he not get off her back? He felt guilty at the corroding suspicion that had been eating him away these past few days. If only he had been able to take her assertion about the Raven at face value. She was turning over a new leaf, of course she was. It's just that this sort of behaviour usually meant she wanted something, was digging, worming inside him to get what she wanted. He hated himself. Of course he had to believe her. Who else would?

"Yeah, sure. I'll make a salad." At least she was in a good mood. She ducked back out of the door frame and he heard her footsteps fade.

There was no flashing light on the answer phone, so no message. Simon dialled 1471 but the caller had not left a number. The White Hart, maybe? He tapped in the hotel's number.

"White Hart?"

"Can you put me through to Martin... House's room, please?" *Idiot.* 'Martin House' indeed.

"Just connecting you..."

There was a click, followed by a second's silence on the line before some music kicked in. *My Way.* There could not have been a better choice for Sparrow's room. 'And now the end is near...' Simon hummed along. Sparrow must have gone out. Sinatra crooned on. 'Regrets, I've had a few...' Now that wasn't like Martin at all - regret was just not in his vocabulary. It should be *No Regrets*, the Piaf one. Simon knew he shouldn't go down that route.

"Martin." The voice on the other end of the line sounded like his own ten minutes before, worn and bleary.

"Hi, Martin. Did you just call me?"

"Do I sound like I just called you, mate?"

Simon was impatient to get moving and took the handset

into the dining room where his laptop lay dormant on the massive Jacobean table. He still had not shut it down and wiggled the mouse to reactivate it. "Look, are you coming over?" he said.

"Give me a chance, old pal. I need to take a shower and grab a sandwich at the bar. I'll be with you in… an hour or so. That all right?"

"Yeah." The screen came to life again, half a dozen programs active. "Oh, Martin?"

"Yes?"

"Could you bring the *De Medicina* original with you? There, I don't know, there might be something you missed."

"I've been over it, Simon. There's nothing." Sparrow was blunt, as though he were now very much awake.

Simon wanted to look at the centuries-old text, to hold it in his hands and feel its pages, run his fingers across the ancient words. "You never know."

There was silence.

"Well?"

"Yeah. Well I… I haven't got it right now, have I?"

"Haven't you?"

"No. It wouldn't be safe. I had to leave it behind… in London."

Simon wedged the handset between ear and shoulder and started to alt-tab between the windows. "Where?"

"King's Cross."

"King's Cross? What do you mean?"

"Left luggage."

"For heaven's sake, Martin. A priceless manuscript and you put it in the left luggage?"

"I was in a hurry."

Simon's thumb and little finger paged through the open windows. The bump on his head was making him irritable and so was Sparrow. And where was the website? "You are a twat sometimes, Martin. Look, are you coming over or not?"

"Dad?" Cassie appeared at Simon's shoulder.

He struggled to contain his brusqueness as he tried to cope with Sparrow, Cassie and the laptop. "Yes?"

"I'm off out."

"Out?"

"Yeah, you know. Out."

"Clubbing?" He winced inside. He hadn't intended it to be an accusation.

"Maybe." She knelt down and kissed him on the forehead. "Love you, Dad."

"Simon, everything all right, mate?" Sparrow's voice pounded in his ear like a pneumatic drill; he should get some paracetamol.

"Look, Martin, are you coming over or not?"

"Yeah, yeah, what's the rush?"

Simon must have missed it. Here was the National Archives page; here was the Suffolk County site; there were a couple of Word documents open, a PDF, the calculator. Then he was back to the National Archives. Again. The imports page had gone.

"Simon?"

"Uh?"

"You still there, mate?"

Simon's heart felt loaded with omen. Where was the website? "Did you touch the laptop, Martin?"

"Now how in hell would I have touched the bloody laptop? I've been akip all afternoon."

Maybe it was Alex. "It's the imports website. It's gone."

*   *   *

Cassie felt great, on top, in control. She felt good about Dad, no longer felt she was deceiving him. She was on the right path. He had been right - she had lost her grip. Sometimes you don't see these things until it's too late and you're floundering in a Wapping studio with mascara leaking down your face and you're wondering who you've become. It would be better now. She stopped to look at her reflection in a shop window. Hell, her hair really was black. Better that than being caught. And if they had spotted her, they would have come for her by now, surely. Their CCTV would show a shifty blonde girl.

You never knew with Roach. He could be so tender, so

generous, so open, and yet at other times mean and sadistic, with a taunting humour that winkled its way through her fragile defences. He hadn't seemed to care that her heart was pumping like a steam hammer when they left the shop, that she was petrified she had been seen. He seemed more interested in the DVD and the extras that might be on it; what the director's commentary might say. She should sack him, she knew. She didn't love him. How could anyone love him?

A horn beeped on the other side of the road. The window of a red car rolled down, a driver looking for directions. Cassie braced herself to say she didn't know the area, hadn't long lived here, when she recognised Fitz. "Oh, hi." *What was his name again?*

He seemed to read her mind. "It's Mark," he reminded her. "We met at your house. I thought it was you," he said. "Not a hundred percent, but…"

Cassie laughed. "Oh, the hair. Yeah, I thought it was time for a change."

"Well, you know the thing with hair?"

"What?"

"It grows on you."

"That's terrible."

"I know."

There was a second of silence, then they both spoke together.

"Sorry," she said.

"No, after you."

"I don't suppose you're going into Colchester?"

"Didn't your Dad ever tell you not to accept lifts from strangers?"

"Yes."

"Hop in, then."

The tattoo on Fitz's arm rippled as he changed gear.

"Does it hurt? Having a tattoo done, I mean?" Cassie asked.

"Nah." Fitz laughed and the skin on his scalp creased. "Well, yeah, actually. It does hurt."

"I was thinking about getting one done."

"It hurts quite a bit."

"As bad as the dentist?"

"Well, it's not as bad as the dentist, but then again, I'm no extractor fan."

"No extractor fan?" Cassie shook her head when she got it. "Mark, those are the worst puns I have ever heard in my life."

"Oi, now that hurts. Quite a bit," he said.

How long was it since she had known someone who made her laugh? Maybe it had something to do with having blonde hair and always attracting creeps and losers. Perhaps she would keep the black. This was a fresh start. She would pick up the new pills from Roach and start again.

Cassie and Fitz talked about what it was like to live at Paycocke's, about his job with the Trust and all the other old buildings he took care of. Cassie had done a lot of boning up on the house and timber-framing so she could give the spiel, but Fitz genuinely loved it all, going wild about soffits and cantilevers and sill plates, and running off at delightful tangents. It was weird. He looked like a football hooligan or an arc-welder or something, with his tattoo and shaven head, but he was knowledgeable and funny and, she thought, a bit shy, tossing out those outrageous puns as little defence mechanisms.

Fitz dropped her off at Roach's, pulling away with a small wave. A sweet guy, a sorted guy. Roach's front door opened before she had time to knock. He was smiling.

"Babes, fancy seeing you here."

"You knew I was coming." Roach seemed manipulative after the easy banter in the car.

"Yeah, I know that. I'm just pleased to see you."

"Are you?"

"You're my best customer." Lies upon lies. "Who was that?"

"A friend."

"Right." He waved her through the door with a Walter Raleigh-like obsequious bow. "Good film, wasn't it?"

She hadn't thought so. Violence. So much violence, exquisitely put together, but, still, there was a limit to how much beauty there was in grisly death. "No. Not for me, Roach."

"Woo-hoo." Roach backed off, making a mock cross with

his index fingers. "What's up with you today, babes? Forget to take your pill this morning?"

She smiled. It felt empty, as hollow as Roach's charisma. "Let's just do this, Roach, OK? I want to pick up the new tabs and get moving, yeah?"

Roach pulled away, fixing her with his small blackcurrant eyes. He put his hand up to his mouth and stroked the bristly groove under his nose. "Yeah, OK," he nodded. "Whatever you want, babes."

They walked up the hill in silence and Roach stopped outside Colchester Castle. "Weird to think it's been here for hundreds of years," he said.

Cassie shrugged.

Roach put his hand on her arm. She felt nothing, only a strength to resist him. He was part of her malaise. She had to get away from him. But first she needed the new pills; they would be her passport, the first stepping-stone. "We've come a long way too," he said.

"Have we?" Cassie looked into his eyes and could fathom nothing in their blackness. Did he really give a toss? And what did she know about him anyway? Failed musician, failed songwriter, failed man. Oh, a successful dealer, yeah, let's not forget that. Weed, grass, oil, shrooms, coke, smack, there was nothing Roach couldn't get you. E, G, H, X, the whole fucking alphabet. And yet there was so little she knew about him, so little, and what she did know, she no longer cared about. Maybe the reason there was so little to know was that there was so little there.

"Yeah," he said. "We have." His lip curled as though he was debating what to say next.

When they first arrived in Coggeshall, Cassie had been told to check out 'this cool guy'; well if cool was a synonym for lost, then she had found him only too easily, and it was time to find herself before she got lost too. Everything was a sham. Her relationship with Roach, the Tryph, even that stupid business with the Conrad Noel treasure. What was she thinking, that it was going to drop into her lap? There *was* no treasure. Stuff like that didn't happen, not to her at least. The only one who was going to make Cassie's life better was Cassie. There was no point in hoping for miracles. She had to take control. "I think we're through, Roach, aren't we?" she said.

"Through?"

"End of the line, the last stop, the terminus."

"What are you saying?" His old leather jacket creaked as he put his other hand on her arm.

"You don't get it, do you, Roach? You truly don't get it."

"I just want the best for you, babes."

"That's sweet of you. And don't call me 'babes'."

It was the first time she had seen confusion on his face. It looked out of place, as if it had landed there for the first time and was bewildered by this new landscape. His eyes darted from side to side and his tongue explored the crevices of his mouth. Then the confusion vanished, suppressed. Roach's lips tightened and he found Cassie's eye contact once more. He smiled, with as much sincerity as he could muster, then leant forward and stroked her cheek. She saw softness in his dark eyes and wondered how real it could possibly be. "Cassie," he said. "I love you." It had the air of a last card being played, a joker, a wild card, maybe even a marked card that he knew all along he would need to produce one day.

"Do you?" she said.

"You don't believe me?"

"Let's get going, Roach." Cassie started to walk away.

"We need to get your pills."

She stopped and turned to face him. Could she manage without the new pills? Could she look in the mirror without them? Could she look in the mirror with them? Who would she be? Cassie walked back towards Roach and he grinned.

"See. It all comes down to one thing, doesn't it, babes?" He laughed. "Oops, sorry, I didn't mean to say 'babes', force of habit, you know what I mean. Force of habit."

Cassie looked at him. There was a hole under the arm of his leather jacket that she had never noticed. His stubble was a day too long. In the distance a bus pulled away up the High Street. It was where she should be. "I quit, Roach, in all senses of the word."

She walked straight past him and cut through to where shoppers thronged the pavement. This time he followed her.

"Cass, you don't know what you're doing," he said. He had to jog to keep up.

"Yes. I do."

"But..."

"I know exactly what I'm doing," she said.

"Shit, man. Hell, Cassie..." Roach tried to laugh.

"It's too late, Roach. I can see you." She slipped through a gap between two dawdling teenagers and hit open pavement, striding away.

Roach stepped into the street and a taxi swerved to avoid him. "Wait, Cassie, wait for me."

"What for?" she said as he reached her side again.

"Look, I'll do anything."

"You already do anything." Cassie broke away and headed into the department store.

"What are you doing?" he said. "Why are you going in here?"

Cassie fiddled with the clasp of her handbag. "First up I am going to give the cashier twenty quid for the DVD I nicked yesterday, and then I am catching the bus home. Don't follow me, don't call me. It's over, Roach. I'm sorry." She was not sorry.

"You'll be back, babes," Roach muttered as Cassie weaved through the electronics section to the nearest cash desk. He dropped off. *Yeah, he wouldn't want to be seen there, would he?* He turned away from where the assistants were gathered and pretended to be interested in the CD players.

Cassie stood in the queue at the till. What would she say? It was all very well offering to pay for the DVD, but supposing they pressed charges? Surely they wouldn't. She was being honest. But then again she had swiped the thing in the first place. They might well just make an example of her. Brilliant - it was one thing to be done for the shoplifting, but something else to take the rap when you were trying to put it right.

There was only one person in front of her now; she had to make a quick decision. The queue behind her was growing and she was jostled by someone pushing through. Then she saw the NSPCC collection tin on the counter. Cassie smiled to herself, took out two ten pound notes from her purse, folded them into four and stuffed the wad into the narrow hole. It wasn't designed for notes, she thought. Pity. The assistant's mouth dropped open when she saw what Cassie had done. "Good cause," Cassie said, and turned away.

Now she could get on with her life. She headed for the nearest exit, hoping that Roach had gone. Gone for good. She looked around her but saw him nowhere.

A weak autumn sun cast shadows on the entrance and as she passed through she felt the hand on her shoulder. Damn. Why could Roach not take a hint?

"Excuse me, Miss, would you come with me?"

The man was about six feet four, with a navy uniform that reflected her pale face with its black thatch in each of its buttons. "What?" she said.

"Would you please come with me?" he repeated.

"I don't understand."

The security guard sniggered, barring her way out of the store. "And you don't have an iPod in your handbag, I suppose?"

Chapter 44
The Parlour

How could I explain it? Edward's kiss was something beyond explanation. I could not tell my parents how I felt, for I did not know how I felt myself. Gussie was shocked and turned his back on me, a thing he had never before done. Iso led me through into the small parlour so that we might be alone. Such matters are best dealt with by women. I do not know what became of Edward on that day, save that he was well castigated for his stolen kiss.

Indeed it was stolen, but not entirely unexpected, for I admit that I had toyed with his affections over a period of weeks. I was ashamed of myself and told my mother so. "Please do not hold Edward responsible."

Her tone was hard but fair, dear sweet Iso, who held the power to raise or dash my spirits with but one breath. She gathered her words together like a spray of violets, with a great care that each should be seen to its best advantage. "It is most unseemly, Imogen, that you should behave in such a fashion. Gustav and I have brought you up in an atmosphere, we have hoped, of love and trust. Your father is most distressed."

It was the phrase 'we have hoped' that hurt me most, a stiletto in my heart. I felt as if I had betrayed my parents, squandering both their love and their trust. To have them think that I cared not a fig for their feelings plunged me into a trench of despair. I closed my eyes, hoping to prevent the tears from finding their way out, but my emotions were too strong and I felt the salty dew trickle down my cheek.

Iso's voice softened, not so much that she was yielding in any sense, but so that I should see that she had some empathy with my position. "It is clear, Imogen, that this boy does not know how to behave. Just how the two of you have become so close during recent weeks escapes me."

"We are not close." I eked out my words in a tiny monotone.

"Not close? A kiss is not close?"

"We are only friends."

"Heaven forfend that one should have such a friend who would take advantage in so cavalier a manner."

I said it was difficult to explain. Every effort I made to persuade Iso that the kiss was not iniquitous was met with a stark disbelief. How could there not be anything underhand, I could see her thinking. I have always known my parents well, yet on this occasion I found myself stymied. I looked about the parlour for inspiration. It was a small room, a good deal longer than it was wide, and indeed of such a narrow width that we found it of little use. With just the one window it was a poky place, well suited to its current use as a centre of inquisition. It seemed insulated from the rest of the house, as I myself was. Yet this small oasis did not provoke in me the same sense of unease that had begun to characterise my relationship with the rest of the house.

"Imogen?" I had been away longer than I thought.

"I beg your pardon. I was elsewhere."

My mother frowned. "I am not at all convinced that Paycocke's has been an overwhelming success," she said. "Your father has achieved little thus far on the new symphony and is most out of sorts, complaining of constant headaches and fatigue. Your behaviour seems to have reached unfathomable depths, and…"

I sought not to defend my case, but the pause gave me hope enough to transcend my hitherto resigned meekness. "And…?"

"I do not know." A furrow appeared in Iso's pale brow. "There is something about this house, something I do not like. It is as though… as though we are being watched." She folded her hands on her lap and played with her ring. "Manipulated."

I gasped. So Iso had felt it too. I took her hand and squeezed it.

She raised her chin and looked down her nose at me, one of her gestures that is not redolent of any high-handedness, but of a piercing search for answers. "You sense it, Imogen?"

I nodded, biting my bottom lip. "The house wants something." I mumbled the words in embarrassment, expecting, not derision, which I had never heard from Iso's soft lips, but more an outpouring of common sense. I should imagine that that was what I roundly deserved.

Iso stroked my fingers, saying nothing, just drawing my hesitant gaze. "Yes." She put her face closer to mine, as though we should share a great secret. In that instant a surge of love rushed through me. "I hear things." She looked about us for fear we might ourselves be overheard.

"I too," I said. I shared my experiences: the eerie screams; the tapping on the glass; the footsteps; the echoing laughter. I left out certain parts, such as the story of Billy Howes. I did not feel ready to divulge anything related to Edward. This time she reacted with a quizzical stare, her finger up to her lips as if she were forcing herself to keep silent against her own will.

"Voices? Do you hear voices?" she said.

I shook my head. "Only the laughter. Bright laughter, but with a cold sadness that lingers behind. And the voices?"

"They are not distinct. I hear no precise words, only the outline of sentences, the rise and fall of pleading, of desperation." Her blue eyes filmed over. "I am a mother," she said. "I hear this because I am a mother."

I loved her so much in that moment that my heart stopped me speaking.

"Do you know why I brought you to this room?" She looked around the parlour, where the evening light now cascaded in through the leaded glass, creating a criss-cross pattern on the fireplace tiles like a snakes and ladders board.

I raised my eyes in query.

"Because there is peace here. It is not like the rest of the house. I sometimes come here to sew. It is as though this is a place where the melancholy does not reach. Do you understand, Imogen?"

"Yes, yes. I can feel it now. We are alone here."

Iso smiled. "One is never alone. But, yes, we are as alone as can be. The entrance hall, the dining-room, the bedrooms too, they are all places of great turmoil. There is no peace there."

"Edward said the very same thing."

"Ah, Edward, yes. We have become a trifle sidetracked, have we not?"

"I did not mean…"

"Of course not. But tell me though, Imogen, do you harbour feelings for Edward?"

I did not have to lie, for that I was most grateful. When I was a little girl, Iso always said that a light came on in my eyes when I told a fib. Part of me will always believe that. "No. He is a dear friend, very dear. I cannot imagine what possessed him to behave in the way he did. He is such a sweet and gentle boy, much distressed by his mother's illness. But I do not care for him in that way."

"And he?"

This time I toyed with the untruth, and for a second it seemed that the parlour brightened with an incipient glow from my eyes. "I think he does hold a secret infatuation for me."

At this my mother laughed. "Not such a secret, I believe."

"No." I smiled an apology.

"What are we to do?" She did not wait for an answer. "We ought to speak with his parents."

"No." I blushed at my interjection. "No, please. It is just that Edward's father… he is," I tried to be kind, "much embittered by his wife's illness and takes it out on Edward." I sighed. "He is a terrible bully. And Mrs. Daynes is so ill. Doctor Phipps says she will die."

"This is the diabetes?"

"Yes."

Iso nodded, drawing her lips together. "Mmm. I do have some reservations concerning the good Doctor Phipps."

I bristled at the memory of that arrogant little man. "He simply does not care."

"No, I will not have that, Imogen. It is unfair and most unlike you. A medical man must by nature become inured to illness and death, otherwise he should spend his life in the shadow of grief. And yet…" She was thinking of something specific, weighing up whether or not she should tell me. "Should we leave here, do you think?" Iso said at last.

Difficult though things had become, I was not ready to leave Paycocke's House. A bubble of panic stirred within me. "We must not leave yet. Paycocke's needs us."

"Then what to do, Imogen?"

I recalled Charles Townsend and told Iso of our correspondence. She was surprised at my revelation, but I thought I could detect parental pride at my ingenuity. "He says he has some experience in matters spiritual. It may be that he is well positioned to offer us some advice."

"I seem to know the name," Iso said. "Perhaps he has connections in the City. I shall speak to your father." Iso held up her hand to stay my protests. "I do not wish to take over, Imogen. However, it seems that your behaviour of late has taken a rather alarming turn towards the forward." Her blue eyes sparkled. "Writing to strange gentlemen, kissing boys in the study…"

Although I knew she was teasing, I still bridled and thought to put the record straight. "I did not kiss him. Edward kissed me."

"Indeed. I shall invite Mister Townsend to call next week and we shall see whether he might be able to assist us."

I wished that the Buxtons had had the telephone installed so that we might not waste time in contacting Mister Townsend, but I was sure Iso would forbid this course of action anyway, as she always insists on 'behaving properly'. I struggled to contain my impatience. "And Edward's parents? Must you tell them of his… aberration?"

"If I might have your assurance that it will not happen again."

I felt my cheeks on fire. "I shall do my utmost." Poor Edward.

*   *   *

Charles Townsend was not at all how I expected. I had imagined a small rotund fellow with spectacles dripping from a florid nose and unruly hair like Einstein. Instead we opened the front door to a rather severe looking man with a handsome chiselled face and a beard that looked as if it might have been carved from his chin. He wore a plain mackintosh and his countenance was entirely proper, yet there was something about him that made me want to shrink away the instant I met him. As befitted a man of his station he was an extremely gracious guest, dropping compliments like confetti and charming my parents beyond the call of duty. It was a rare occasion that he addressed me directly, save to offer another of his honeyed phrases upon the subject of my scarf or my hair. And as I would with a surfeit of honey, I grew tired of his ministrations and the interminable small talk. I longed to discuss the haunting of Paycocke's and was thwarted at every turn by my parents' insistence on the formalities of hospitality. Gussie was terribly quiet, clearly preoccupied with something. He had done hardly any work at all on the new composition in recent days and I wondered if Iso's fears about Paycocke's were becoming reality. Perhaps we should leave this house. We were finding no happiness.

At last the conversation turned to the spiritual world and Mister Townsend became more animated, although he avoided my questions concerning Billy Howes with a politician's skill. "I felt it at once," he said. "No sooner than I stepped through the door was I gripped by a sense of some malevolence. A great ill has occurred in this house."

I could not believe his words which were utterly opposite to my own experience. I recalled being wooed by the splendour of the house and it was some weeks before I became attuned to its angst. Iso, I know, felt as I did, and we exchanged a glance but said nothing.

Townsend continued. "With your permission I should like to see more of this quite marvellous abode." He boasted a Cheshire Cat-like grin and looked jolly pleased with himself, as though he had burrowed his way deep into our confidence.

Iso showed him into the entrance hall. Gussie declined to join us, professing a slight headache, and although he had become prone to such maladies of late, I was more struck by the feeling that he wanted little to do with this supernatural goose chase being initiated by the women in his life. Townsend stood in the centre of the hall, insisting on complete quiet. He raised his arms and muttered a strange incantation to the beams. "I sense it," he said. We waited for more. "There is evil here."

"No." That I could not believe. Whatever ill had been

perpetrated in this house, I felt no malicious intent, only sadness.

The spiritualist looked down at me and raised an eyebrow. "I must tell it as I sense it. You would have it otherwise?" He smiled in the most obsequious way and I began to regret consulting him. Iso continued to offer him the greatest of courtesies as we gave the man the Grand Tour of Paycocke's. In each room he found something new over which to exclaim. Even the parlour, hitherto the most innocent of rooms, was not spared his scathing inspection. He professed to hear noises, to experience sudden changes in temperature and to smell strange odours. I myself could sense nothing of the kind. In fact it was quite to the contrary - I felt that the house was lying dormant in the presence of Townsend, not wishing to reveal itself in any way. Nevertheless, any eavesdropper to our exchange would have been convinced that Paycocke's House was the most iniquitous place in England.

I was unsure whether Iso felt the same way as I. Although my mother is always an astute judge of character, she also has the ability to behave with the greatest of decorum no matter what the circumstance, without giving the slightest clue as to her true feelings. However, I could not believe that she was being taken in by this charlatan. Nothing he said tallied with our own experience, and I began to find him so loathsome that I determined to say nothing of the shrine we had found in the small crawlspace above the study. There was nothing we could learn from Townsend. I had made a monstrous miscalculation and with every passing minute I found the man more and more absurd.

We walked through to the dining room and my only thought was that I wished to be rid of Charles Townsend. He paced around the room, touching the linen fold panelling and at least having the grace to comment upon its beauty. Needless to say, his eyes did not alight on the chisel scar left by Billy Howes. Townsend knew nothing of this house. What his true motive was in coming here I did not suspect, but when Gussie called from the sitting room, Iso left me with the vile man.

"Do you feel it, Imogen?" he said. It was the first time we had been alone. We stood shoulder to shoulder, and all I felt was a shimmering unease at being in his presence. His large hairy hand hung prone by his side, and brushed my own. I would have assumed it an accident except that it happened again as he turned towards me, his thick fingers touching mine. "Do you not feel it? A stirring of emotion in the air."

"No," I said, stepping back. "I feel nothing." I wanted to be sick. "Please excuse me, Mister Townsend, I must go and see where my mother is."

Townsend put his hand out to stop me and I gasped. As he took hold of my forearm, a small vase toppled from the armoire and crashed to the floor. He dropped my arm like a hot stone and pulled away from me, putting welcome fresh air between the two of us. He gave what I can only assume was intended to be a laugh, but came out sounding like a nervous whine.

Iso returned at the crash and stood at the door. "Oh dear," she said, looking at the remnants of the vase.

Gussie was by my mother's side, grimness personified. He ushered Townsend into the entrance hall, brooking no objection. "We must thank you kindly for your time, Mister Townsend, but alas, we have a luncheon appointment." He opened the front door. I struggled to recall seeing my father behave in quite so rude a manner and I rejoiced in it.

Gussie closed the heavy oak door, his face etched with a grave expression. "I knew I had seen him before. He is well known in town. A man of great business acumen he might be, but I will have nothing to do with a disciple of Aleister Crowley."

I gasped.

"I will not have such a fellow in my house," he said. "These are... unpredictable times, Imogen." Gussie had never spoken a truer word, although we may have differed in our interpretation. However, there was something only too predictable about my persistent failure to get to the bottom of the Paycocke mystery. I turned to go. Perhaps it was not meant to be known.

"Imogen." Gussie called me back, his face grave. He licked his lips and swallowed hard, as though he had something wretched to impart and wished to defer the moment as long as possible. "There is something I must share with you, Imogen, something which has greatly troubled me, and I can wait no longer," he said.

"I had hoped to spare you this sorry news, but I have been thinking upon it these past few days, and I hope that it might provide you and your friend Edward with some little comfort."

I did not understand and looked at Gussie with confusion.

My father blinked hard. "It is about Conrad."

My bewilderment deepened. What on earth could Conrad Noel have to do with Edward?

"Conrad Noel has the diabetes."

Chapter 45
Compost

Simon raked the fallen leaves into piles. Whatever else happened, there was no way to stop the blasted leaves from dropping. He lost count of the barrow loads he wheeled down to the compost heap. How long would it take for them to mulch down? How long before they could be recycled, reused, turned into something new? He forked another pile onto the heap. Perhaps some small animal would make its home there this winter.

The phone call from Colchester police station had felt surreal. Cassie shoplifting? Impossible. Even when he went down there to pick her up, he half expected there to have been a case of mistaken identity.

Cassie looked as if she had been days without sleep, sitting on the wooden bench with her elbows on her knees and pushing her fingers through her blue-black hair time and time again. A ticking guilt went off inside her father. He should have prevented this. Whatever had happened had been because of his short-sightedness. Cassie raised her head at the sound of his footsteps, registered his presence in her dull eyes, then sunk her gaze back into her lap again.

Simon took her limp hand. She had been biting at the skin beside her fingernails and a small curl of blood had dried by one cuticle. "Cassie, darling," he said. "Whatever's wrong, we can sort it out."

Cassie shook her head. Simon sat beside her, took her cold hand in his and rubbed it. There was no response.

A WPC brought them mugs of tea.

"Good cop, bad cop?" Simon said when she had left, trying to generate a smile. Cassie just sighed, staring into her drink. He looked around. The room was bare, stark white walls unblemished. The single table looked out of place, a desert island in the centre of the sparse room. There was one small reinforced window, which let in so little natural light that it hardly merited its place. There was no escape from the harsh neon overhead. "It's not much, but at least it's home," Simon said.

"Oh, Dad."

"Do you want to talk about it?"

She held up a hand to show him her stained fingers. "They fingerprinted me."

He kissed her fingers one by one. "It's their job, darling."

"They swabbed me, Dad." She started to cry and he pulled her closer to him. "They swabbed me for DNA."

"It's OK, Cass, it's OK."

"They took my things."

"We'll get them back, darling."

She buried her face in his pullover, mascara inking the Arran wool. "I didn't do it, Dad. I didn't do it. Please believe me. Please."

Simon hesitated. Cassie's lies had become so commonplace in the past couple of years that he no longer knew where trust began. He closed his eyes and slapped down his doubts. "If you say you didn't, of course I believe you, Cass. But if you did, don't be afraid to say it. I won't love you any less."

She looked at him, fixed him with her wavering eyes for the first time since he had entered the room. "You don't believe me." It was not an accusation. Simon could see that the heart had been sucked out of her. "It's what I deserve," she said, dropping her head. He looked around them. The room was so bare, so oppressive. He wrapped his arm around Cassie's shoulder. Whatever cry wolf episodes she had been party to in the past, this was not one of them.

He put his hand under her chin and made her look at him. "I do believe you, Cassie. I do. Do you want to tell me what happened?"

She stared at the ceiling as if the memory might be persuaded to evaporate. "I was in this shop, just looking, just browsing. Early Christmas shopping, you know. Then I went to leave and there was this iPod in my bag. I swear I didn't know it was there. I swear, Dad. The security man caught me as I was going out, and put his hand on my bag. I thought he was going to snatch it and then I saw his uniform, and... oh, Dad, what am I going to do? I only wanted to make everything be all right. What have I done?" She shrank back into the bench, smaller than ever.

"Hey, hey, Cassie, it's OK. Drink some tea." She took the mug and cradled it in both hands, but did nothing more than inhale its steam. He forced her to drink and her quaking shoulders subsided. "Do you think it was planted?" he said.

"It must have been."

Simon's doubts nagged at him. "But why, Cassie? Why?"

She shook her head. "Maybe someone who wanted me to take the risk and then pinch the iPod back from me in the street, I don't know." She looked at him, her eyes so earnest, so lost under the mass of tangled dyed hair that he knew this was not right. "It wasn't me, Dad, honest."

He squeezed her hand, trembling inside, wanting so much to believe her. "Trust me, Cassie. Trust me, darling," he said. "Was there someone else there?" She looked away and fiddled with her hands, digging dirt out from underneath her fingernails. "Was it... Roach?"

Her hands stopped moving. She stared at her fingertips.

"I can't help you if you won't tell me, Cassie."

"You don't know him, Dad," she said under her breath, as though they were being bugged.

"We need to tell the police..."

"No!"

"Cassie..."

"No, Dad. It'd make things worse, don't you see that? This is his revenge. He'll be happy now, he'll let me go."

"No, he won't, Cassie. He won't. He'll always come after you. If you let him do this to you, he'll never let you go."

"Please, Dad, please. He will. It's over, Dad. It's all over. Please."

How could he deny her? She was the daughter who had always been the less favoured, the one who had turned out to be his only true child. How could he say no? "I'll speak to them," he said.

What could he say? He filled out a stack of forms, repeating the same information over and over. No, she was not prepared to admit guilt. The iPod was planted. No, she did not know how it had got into her handbag. No, she did not suspect anyone. The officer's initial helpful mood dissipated when he saw that this was not going to be resolved immediately. The statement of the security guard indicated she had been caught red-handed. It would have to go to court, unless the store was prepared to drop the charges. The policeman shook his head; that was unlikely.

They gave Cassie back her bag, uncannily tidy now, and the two of them left the station. Simon looked at his watch. *Should still be open.* Instead of walking back to the car park, he headed for the High Street, Cassie tugging his arm. "Dad?" He could feel a tremor of panic in her grip.

"We need to know," he said.

"No, Dad, not today, please. Not now." She tried to drag him to a halt and they stopped outside the department store.

"Trust me, Cass," he said. "It'll be OK."

They walked into the shop, Simon wishing he felt as confident as he sounded. They found the security guard in kitchenware. He recognised Cassie immediately and grinned. "No hard feelings, love," he said. "Only doing my job." Simon could see his daughter was holding back the tears. Maybe this was a mistake. The man's uniform was sharply pressed, his black boots gleaming; ex-copper. His breast pocket bore a badge: 'RightWatch – Kevin Lewis'. Lewis stared at Simon and crossed his arms. "Brought in the big guns, have you?"

"I'll be straight with you," Simon said. "She didn't take the iPod."

Lewis laughed. "That's what they all say."

"Look, is there somewhere we can talk?"

The man smirked and pointed towards a door on the far side of the room. It was a compact store room, walled with shelves of paper, till rolls and stationery. Lewis closed the door.

"So?" he said.

"She didn't take the iPod," Simon repeated.

"It was in her bag. In fact the box was half hanging out of the bag. She was asking to get nicked."

"Exactly. That's why it wasn't her. Look, did you see her take it, put it in there?"

Lewis chuckled. "I don't need to."

"Someone else put it there."

"Oh yeah? Her fairy godfather, maybe?"

"Check the tapes," Simon said. "Your CCTV. They won't show her stealing it. And there won't be any of her fingerprints on it either." He hoped that was true and looked at Cassie. She seemed bewildered, a rabbit in the headlights. She wouldn't remember whether or not she had touched it at all.

The security guard nodded, humouring them.

"It'll be thrown out of court. Please…" Damn, he was begging. He could sense the man sniggering at his weakness. "There won't be a case."

Lewis put his hand on the doorknob. "If you've finished?"

Simon sighed. There was no persuading him. The man was half outside the door, his broad back filling the space between them. "Two hundred," Simon said.

Lewis stopped and turned to them. "What?"

"Two hundred. Call it a bonus. The case will never hold. It's a waste of everyone's time. Cassie did not do it, I swear. You have my word." Lewis snorted and Simon ploughed on, reckless now that he had the guard's focus. "Three hundred, get the charges dropped."

Lewis stared at Simon, twisting his lips. "And what do you expect me to say?"

"You'll think of something."

Lewis smiled, not dropping his eyes from Simon's. He nodded. "Five."

Simon winced. Hard come, easy go. "Four."

"Done."

"I'll need to go to the cashpoint."

"Whatever." Lewis opened the store room door and ushered them out.

In the street Simon felt the cold air dry the sweat on his forehead.

Cassie squeezed his hand. "I am never, ever, shopping there again," she said.

*   *   *

Simon forked another barrow of wet leaves onto the compost heap. Would he still be here next year to do the same? Who could ever predict what lay ahead? A month ago the world was a different place: he had Robin, two daughters, no Sparrow, had never even heard of Roach. Should he pay the man a visit, or would he be getting ever further out of his depth? He laughed and his breath came out in great grey gusts. He would be out of his depth in a paddling pool.

Physical work was good. You became stale sitting at the computer all the time with no fresh air, nothing to energise you. He wondered how Alex was getting on with the laptop. 'Footprints,' she had said. 'The web page might have left footprints.' She might still be able to find a hook to the Paycocke site lurking somewhere in the system directories. Well, better her than him.

Cassie was in bed, exhausted. He would let her sleep. Opening up in the car journey home had taken the last out of her..

"I've lied to you, Dad." She stared out at the traffic in front, as though she were driving, as though that were her excuse for avoiding eye contact.

"You wouldn't be the first."

She put her hand on his thigh. "I know. I haven't made things easy for you, Dad, but that's going to change."

They stopped at a red light and Simon looked across at Cassie. "It's part of being a parent," he said. "I just want you to be happy, Cass. Whatever you do, I just want you to be happy."

"I know."

"And Roach?" The question was tossed into the air like an idle afterthought, but it was what he most needed to know. Roach was the answer to a lot of questions and maybe the key to how things would go. A car beeped behind them before Cassie had time to reply. Simon stalled the Citroen as he tried to take off in third gear. "Bugger."

Cassie smiled. "I don't know. Like I said, Dad, it's over."

"Were you sleeping with him?" Simon's eyes were on the road again. "Sorry," he said. "That's a real 'Dad' kind of question."

She laughed. "Yeah. Yeah, it is a real 'Dad' kind of question, and yeah, I was sleeping with him. What did you think, Dad, we were playing Twister?" There was no sarcasm or malice in her voice, only humour and, was that protective love?

"I know."

"He was cool, Dad."

"Yeah, I can dig that." Simon smiled and felt his daughter's glare.

"Dad, I'm warning you."

"OK."

"He was cool in more ways than one. He would never show his feelings, but fuck... sorry, Dad... he took care of me, made me feel wanted."

"He got you stuff?"

"How do you know so much?"

"I'm your Dad. I'm paid to know. It's in the job description."

"I'm not proud, Dad, but this is a wake-up call. I've really screwed you and Mom around and this is it now. It's all over. Fresh start."

Simon pulled off the A120 into Coggeshall, slowing down as he drove into the village. "I'm here for you, Cassie. Whenever you need me." He drew to a halt at the zebra crossing to allow a few people across. A light rain spotted the windscreen and he flicked the wipers. A woman on the crossing turned to acknowledge his stopping for them; it was Eleanor. She waved and walked towards the Citroen. Simon opened the window, but before she reached the car she noticed that Cassie was in the passenger seat and she abruptly turned, mimed a telephone at him then waved and walked off.

"What was all that about?" Cassie asked.

Simon shrugged.

"Dad?"

"Yeah?"

Cassie smiled. "What's the score between you and Eleanor?"

Simon blew out a lungful of air. "Nil-nil I think."

He parked up the road from Paycocke's and they walked back to the house, arms hooked, heads bowed against the thin drizzle.

"I need to get into the garden, rake the leaves," he said.

"It's almost dark, Dad."

He looked up at the leaden sky. "There's a half an hour."

"Whatever. I'm knackered. I might go and have a nap."

"Yeah, you do that." He fiddled in his pocket for the front door keys. The wind blew Cassie's hair in front of her face. She looked so monochrome in the fading light, framed by grey sky. He put a hand up to her cheek.

"Thanks, Dad."

He shook his head. There were no words he could think of to illuminate the moment.

"I love you, Dad."

"I love you too, darling." Simon smiled, stroking her face. "What about your hair, Cass?"

She touched a damp curl. "I guess blonde is the new black," she said.

*   *   *

Rain battered the roof and the wind tore a small branch from the hornbeam, sending it skittering up the garden into the courtyard. The security light came on, the dazzling halogen finding the curtain Simon had forgotten to close and spilling its glare across his pillow. In a second he was wide awake, yanked from his dream, his T-shirt damp.

02:13. He closed the curtain and got back into bed, but the incessant percussion of the rain would not lull him. Why was he here, alone in this empty cold bed, with shadows eating up the room? Should he take a chance with Eleanor? He drew his legs up to his chest, hugging them. The silence was a blanket on the whole house, but from its depths he heard a regular dripping noise. A leak.

He put his dressing-gown and slippers on and followed the sound, down the corridor and past the spare room. The bathroom. The noise became louder, a sharp irritating plop on the floor. Pulling the light cord he saw a puddle gathering near the window, some of it draining through the gaps between the floorboards. He looked up but could see nothing, no tell-tale rivulet, only the persistent one-two-three drip, one-two-three drip. The flashing on that side had been replaced the other week; maybe it had something to do with that. He put a bucket under the leak and immediately the sound was amplified as the water bounced onto the plastic. He would have a proper look in the morning.

The house was silent, silent and cold. He had never seen it at this time of day, sleeping. The stairs whined with his every step and he sat down halfway, gazing into the gloom of the entrance hall. The streetlamp light barely reached the house, casting its glow only as far as the sill of the oriel window where the Nankin vases sat like guards of the darkness within.

A car went by on West Street and its headlamps created a pool of light that flashed into the hall, grasped at the gloom, then retreated. Were there ghosts? Was there really such a thing? The cold seemed to rise up from the hall to meet him, icy fingers that made him draw his dressing-gown closer about his chest. And if there were ghosts, could they read his mind? Would they, even now, be berating him for his lack of belief? In her talk, Cassie told the punters that the house was haunted; she said that it was mentioned in letters written by Imogen Holst to her school pals. The public liked all that, especially the kids, the idea that they might see Thomas Paycocke in the abyss of the night wailing for his late Margaret.

So here he was; it was truly the dead of night. His eyes were accustomed to the blackness and he stared down into the pit of the entrance hall, willing Thomas to appear. The shadows seemed to have shadows of their own, swirling about in the room, but there was no movement, no presence. He edged down the stairs and stood in the middle of the hall. "Thomas," he whispered. "I mean you no harm. Whatever happened in this house, I'm sorry." There was no reply and only the steady fall of rain acted as a backdrop to the unending silence.

Simon sat down at the table. As the rain eased he became aware of the metronomic ticking of the grandfather clock, so regular, so soothing, washing over him. He felt drowsy and fought against it, shifting his position in the chair so as not to fall asleep. The grandfather clock chimed three.

"Dad."

Simon's neck hurt. Why did it hurt? Where was he? He put his hand up to his eyes, massaging the sockets with finger and thumb.

"What are you doing down here?"

He opened his eyes. Alex. "Alex?"

"Dad, what are you doing down here?" she repeated.

He twisted his head from side to side, wondering if she could hear the horrible creaking sounds his neck was making, or whether they were in his mind. "I don't know," he said, yawning. "I couldn't sleep."

She took his hand. "Dad, you're freezing."

"It's OK, it's OK. What time is it?"

"Seven."

"Bloody hell. Bloody bloody hell. I must have fallen asleep."

"I'm just going out for a run."

He yawned again; his bones ached with cold and he shivered. "Are you mad?"

She smiled. "Probably. Want to come with me?"

"Now you are mad. Give up my nice warm… chair?"

"Just what on earth were you doing down here? Have you been sitting there all night?"

"Not all…"

"Well…"

"It seemed like a good idea at the time."

"What did?"

Simon felt vaguely ill. "I don't know. I was just thinking about how everyone talks about Paycocke's being weird, saying it's haunted and I wondered… I thought I would just… sort of… you know, check it out." It sounded very limp in daylight.

Alex laughed. "And?"

"Like I say, it seemed like a good idea at the time."

She bent down and kissed the top of his head.

"How is it that you got all the common sense?" he said.

"Huh?"

"The rest of this family is all screwed up: Mom, Cassie, me, all trying to achieve some semblance of normality, whereas you, you're fit, healthy, organised, sorted. How did you get all the common sense?"

Alex turned away, touching her toes. "Well, maybe I didn't," she said. "What you see is not always what you get. WYSIWYG."

"Whizzy wig?"

"It's an acronym: What You See Is What You Get. Computer jargon. Which reminds me, I had a look at your laptop."

"And?"

"Nothing. It's like the page you had up there never existed. I can see traces of the other stuff you were looking at, the National Archives pages and so on, but the shipping page, there's nothing. I don't understand."

Simon shook his head, but hadn't expected anything else. They would look at it again later. He would get Sparrow in and they could try to recreate the setup. If he could persuade him to come over – it seemed that his enthusiasm had completely run out. *Left-luggage, my arse.* Simon itched to see the *De Medicina* book.

"I'm off, Dad." Alex opened the front door and a splinter of wind rippled through the gap.

"OK, sweetheart. See you in a bit."

"Take it easy," she said, closing the giant door.

He had a moment to think to himself. 'What you see is not always what you get.' What was that all about?

Chapter 46
A Man of Straw is Worth a Woman of Gold

Robert held Ann in his arms, cradling her as one lost. She exclaimed at his injuries, for half of his face still raged with the colour of a beet. She laughed at his attentions but did not thrust him away, allowing his fingers to curl between hers. Thomas smiled at the two young people and marvelled that she should have made such a dangerous journey on their behalf. She was indeed a brave woman, a wondrous woman, a woman of more than gold, and no matter what the old saying might tell.

Ann turned to Thomas and curtseyed. The clothier put his hand up to his mouth to hide a grin at the formality. "Aye, I cry you mercy, but it is in very truth only now begun, Master Paycocke."

She would say nothing more, looking around her as though the harbour walls might curse her for her knowledge. They went back to the quayside together and found lodgings for a few days. If it was God's will that they stayed here, then stay they would until the work was done. Thomas found that he trusted Ann's judgement as he had done Margaret's in happier times. It was not until the three were alone that Thomas voiced his question. "So, wherefore all this ado?"

"I flew here not without reason." She had fetched cheese and fish and a jug of beer, reminding Thomas of his empty belly. In truth she would make Robert a fine wife. Not a humble wife, nay, Ann Cotton would never be a woman demeaning in all things, but a wife of great spirit, such as would make a husband proud. She bustled about the two men, making sure of their comfort and he pondered upon her role at Taggy's in Cheapside. There were some things that were better left unsaid; more they did not need to know. He was glad they had rescued her from that situation, then he remembered that it had been she who had rescued the two men, and he laughed to himself. Aye, a fine wife she would be.

"I could not sit a-spinning and think of the two of you gone," she said. "So I resolved to discover all that I could that might aid you, aid us, in this quest."

The cheese was good, the herring young and soft, like melting butter. Thomas relaxed and nodded. Robert had fallen silent and gazed up at Ann as she continued her tale.

"I wished to speak with Gijsbert, the master carver. I had heard tell that the band did journey to Lavenham, so by your leave I took your second-best mare and rode up to that town."

How many summers had she? Thomas was awed at her confidence. It would be a great pity for her to leave his employ for the sake of Robert's hearth. She might have a great future in trade, and who could say that she might not add much to his business. Margaret, God have mercy on her soul, had been a great asset, to be sure, but Ann had a deftness of mind and a sharpness of wit that he had never before seen in a woman.

"To my surprise, Gijsbert was still in Lavenham. He was much taken by a local maid and was wed some months after arriving. He is also a fine stone mason, and the church there is being rebuilt these past years, so there has been work aplenty for him. Indeed he was much pleased to settle down to a wife and family after many years tramping the ways in search of labour."

Thomas nodded. Good ale, good food, good company. It was well. He found that he had missed Ann's lively presence. She should have accompanied them from the beginning. He could see that Robert thought likewise, his clerk not able to avert his eyes from her person. She wore a man's apparel, likely to facilitate her journey, Thomas thought, although surely no one could have thought her a man, with her soft pale skin and delicate hands. Her face was grimy and her jacket and hose rough and much patched, doubtless to draw attention elsewhere. It was clear she did not have a purse worth cutting.

She sat down. "Gijsbert remembered Kees well, although it was by now some years since they met. A quiet and godly man, he said. But when I told him that I came in the service of Thomas

Paycocke, Gijsbert grew silent and I had to press him to say more. He told me that Kees had been much troubled by something that had befallen him there and proclaimed Paycocke's House a place of damnation. I cry you mercy for this revelation, but I tell only that which I have heard.

"Oh, it does become warm." Ann took off her brown woollen helmet and laid it on the board. Her hair tumbled about her shoulders and Thomas wondered that any sailor had ever mistaken her for a young lad. "Gijsbert knew no more. He had tried to persuade Kees to stay in Lavenham and work alongside him, but Kees Visser was an only child and wished to return to Holland for his parents' sake."

Thomas and Robert exchanged confused looks and the clothier held up his hand. "I understand not. You say that Kees was an only child?"

"Aye, Master Paycocke. In truth, I know not but what Gijsbert told me, but he would have no cause to make free with the truth, methinks?"

"Then I am much bewildered, for we have these past days made the acquaintance of Kees's brother, one Johannes Visser."

Ann held Thomas with her dark eyes, which twinkled like berries catching the afternoon sun. "Do you remember how Kees looked?"

Thomas waved his hand, not understanding the question. "I know not that I ever truly saw the man."

"How can that be so?"

"I was busy with other affairs. The house was but a few months in the building and all was handled by William Spooner. Whom he chose to employ on my behalf was a matter of trust. I did not need to be met with all of his men. You must understand that Spooner was a man I trusted as my father had before me - I had no reason to suspect that there would be aught amiss." Thomas raised his tankard and took a deep draught of the beer. Pieter Janszoon had been right – the Hanse men were good for something after all. Perhaps this beer was the reason for Kees Visser's homesickness.

"Then might it be that Johannes and Kees are one and the same man?"

Thomas put his drink back down on the board. It had not yet addled his head, in truth it had made him see more clearly. Was Ann right? Was Johannes Visser the carver Kees? He thought of the broody man's countenance and removed the beard in his mind. Mayhap he did recognise the man, one amongst many working on his house, but the Dutchmen had all seemed to have the same countenance. He could not be certain. Thomas stared into his beer, becoming more sure by the moment that Ann spoke well and true. He felt himself to be the man of straw. How had he been so blind? He stood up, pushing his drink away from him. "The runabout, the dog. We must act."

"Tarry a while. We ought not act in haste. There is but one more scene to my tale."

"How is that?" Thomas was impatient and he could see that Robert too was on his feet, ready to join him, ready to avenge the beating he had taken.

"Visser swore he would kill any Paycocke on sight. That is why I am here."

*   *   *

Robert proclaimed he would comb Kees Visser's head with a stool. He did not recall anything of his attackers, but was convinced already of Visser's guilt. Thomas and Ann had to combine forces to quell the anger in the young man.

"What good will it do if we take blood for blood, Robert?"

"It will do me good, Thomas. The man must make amends. He has wronged you."

Paycocke laughed. "And you are King Arthur who would right all wrongs?"

Robert thumped his hand on the board. "Better Arthur than Merlin, Thomas. Sooner actions than words."

Ann took Robert's arm and gave it a soft squeeze. "Then that would make us no better than he, think you that not? Did you come to Amsteldam to seek violence and retribution, or on a quest for knowledge from a man perchance as burdened with life as you might yourself become? What is our true aim, Robert? What is our true aim?"

They stood in an alley several doors away from the sign of the six laughing herring. It seemed as though Ann's eyes could calm an angry ocean, such were their power, and Robert fell into a placid silence, smiling at his love. A good wife makes a good husband, thought Thomas. As soon as they returned to Coxhall, he must see the two young people betrothed. It would be right.

Although there was still light in the sky, it struggled to penetrate down between the tall buildings, and there was plenty of shadow to obscure them as they waited for Visser to emerge. At the moment they had the upper hand, for he would think them returned to England, so would be vulnerable to surprise.

"Unless of course it was he whom we spied upon the Tower of Tears," Robert argued.

"How so?"

"Visser was desirous of seeing us leave. Be sure that he himself would shed no tears at our parting, but he would have wished to see us in the act of departure, gone in failure. He would have waited until our ship was left and we two aboard."

"Then we must act with great care. It is not without possibility that he has accomplices, and we are in this city without friends."

"What of this Pieter Janszoon?" asked Ann.

Thomas scratched his chin. "I know not if he is to be trusted. The only allies we have in this place are one another."

Wind funnelled down the alley and the warmth of the day was fast disappearing. Robert shivered in his new clothes and Thomas all but smiled to see the quality of the Dutch cloth challenged and found wanting. Yet waiting did not sit well on Thomas's shoulders and he said so. "What is to be gained by this vigil?"

Robert concurred and only Ann pressed the need for caution. "If he is within, we know not the forces he can muster, and we are but three, one of whom is weakened through injury," she nodded at Robert, "and another who is but a maid."

Thomas snorted. "You would do well to remove the 'but' from your assertion, Ann, for never have I come across a maid of your like." He saw Robert move closer to Ann, both to emphasise the point Thomas had made, but also, it seemed, to press some proprietorial rights. Thomas grinned to himself, sure that his expression could be seen in the deepening shadows. Robert whispered something to Ann that he did not catch. "Come now, my friends," Thomas said with an air of mischief. "It is not well for there to be secrets between us." He could almost feel the waves of heat from his clerk's cheeks.

"Wait." Ann held up her hand. Footsteps sounded in the adjacent alley, then from the brooding darkness came a figure. The silhouette passed across the cobbles where the moon splashed more light between the crouching wooden buildings and Thomas saw an illuminated jerkin, the colour of camomile and walnut. It was Visser, and alone. They moved behind him with care as he approached the sign of the six laughing herring, Thomas ahead and Robert and Ann a few yards behind, each hugging one side of the alley. Thomas stopped Kees at the door to his house, putting his hand on the Dutchman's shoulder. "So, Kees Visser?"

Visser did not turn around, but stiffened under Thomas's touch. Thomas could see he was weighing up the alternatives. He was not a big man as William Spooner had been, but he looked as though he would be strong and able in a tussle. He spoke without moving, just stared at the door of his house. "The English ones?" he said, malice in his voice.

"Aye." Thomas would not pursue a path of violence while there was any chance of a peaceful resolution. He softened his voice. "We wish for information only, Kees Visser."

"There is no more Kees Visser." The man spat out the words. "You have killed him."

Thomas felt Ann and Robert move closer, flanking him for support should Visser go for his blade. "No," he said. "I cannot believe…"

"You do not believe. You are ungodly, unclean, a… a… a heretic." He whirled around and caught Thomas with a granite working-man's fist. Paycocke's head snapped back and he fell against Robert, the two men tumbling to the ground. Visser raced away from them towards the Zeedijk.

"Quick, Thomas, after him." Robert was to his feet, but Ann had already begun the pursuit, moving like lightning in her men's hose. Thomas knelt on the ground watching the couple turn the corner. He stood up, his head spinning, and ran to the junction in time to see his friends disappear around another bend. He chased them to the next alley, but lost sight and he stopped to catch his breath by one of the small canals. Life had been too good, he thought, as he bent over the water, struggling for air. There had been too many fine meals and strong ale and he could not match the stamina of the younger folk. On all fours he panted like a wild dog. They had not handled it well. He should have realised that a man capable of attacking Robert so viciously and with so little qualm, such a man would not be open to an approach of reason. They ought to have tackled him with force while they still had the small element of surprise on their side. Now the carver would escape and have time to assemble his forces and then it would be the Coxhall three who were the hunted. They would be fortunate to escape Amsteldam with their lives.

Thomas looked about him. It was ill that they were separated thus. He more than the other two knew the maze of these city streets, and he knew them only to such a sparse fashion that he recognised himself lost again. The day was fading rapidly now, the moon's glow fast becoming his only source of light. Footsteps echoed from a nearby alley, but it was hard to tell from which direction they came. Thomas pressed himself into a doorway as the sound of the running steps grew louder, accompanied by a harsh and breathless cursing in a guttural tongue. Kees. The footsteps stopped and Thomas heard the man throwing out great animal breaths; Visser's condition seemed no better than his own. He listened for the pursuing footfalls of Ann and Robert, but there was nothing. Visser would believe himself free.

Thomas crept from the shadows, this time with his knife from its sheath. He was no murderer, but even so, he kept his blade well ground and it would serve the purpose. He hoped that the darkness would disguise the tremor in his hand.

The Dutchman knelt by the water as though he were admiring his reflection. He looked spent and Thomas was grateful that he had not expended all of his own strength on the chase. His thin leather soles made no sound on the cobbles as he edged towards Visser, and by the time the carver realised Paycocke was there, the knife was at his throat, its keenness teasing a small drop of blood from the man's neck. That had not been Thomas's intention, but all well and good, it would serve to alert Visser to the dangers of underestimating him.

"So kill me, English," the Dutchman said. The moonlight drained all of the colour from his cheeks. Again, he would not look at Thomas and stared down into the canal.

Paycocke relaxed the pressure on his blade, but stood ready for any sudden movement. "I do not wish to kill you."

"Then I…" The carver turned to face Thomas, a thin trickle of blood trailing down his neck. He made no attempt to wipe it away.

The canal stank of dead animals and human waste, but amid the foulness ran the scent of blood. Maybe it came from the small cut he had inflicted on Kees Visser, but maybe it was Thomas's own, rising within his gorge. He wondered if it could be his father's, searching him out from beyond the grave, seeking resolution from his purgatorial torment. It was imperative to keep a clear head. He tightened his grip on the knife, but even though it was he who held the weapon, Thomas felt the vulnerable one. He sensed fear grasping him with its cold fingers. Paycocke knew he could never willingly take a man's life and he struggled to prevent that knowledge showing in his eyes. He wished that Robert and Ann were there.

Kees got to his feet, even though Thomas's knife hovered an inch from his throat. He smiled. He could see the cracks of weakness in Thomas. Paycocke inched forward, desperate to hold his position. "The face," he said. "What does it mean?"

Visser smiled and opened his palms as if he posed no threat, spreading his arms wide. He took a step backwards to evade the point of Thomas's knife. "I know not what you mean."

Thomas pressed forward, not taking his eyes from the Dutchman's. "Aye, you know it well."

The light dimmed as a cloud wandered across the moon. Visser's eyes dropped to his side and Thomas prodded him with the knife to hold his attention. The carver took another step back and lost his footing, reaching out as he fell, but clutching only air.

Thomas heard a vile crack as Kees's head hit the side of the canal wall and a loud splash as the waters surged up to envelope the Dutchman, releasing a foul stench as his body broke the surface. There was no cry for help.

Seconds passed and Thomas could not see where Visser had fallen. The cloud that had eclipsed the moon moved on and he saw Kees's form, now drifted to the other side of the canal, bobbing for an instant on the surface, but then being pulled down as though by some terrible sea monster. Thomas threw aside his cloak and dived in, reaching Visser in a few strokes. His heavy woollen clothing dragged at him and Visser was like a dead sheep in his arms. The Dutchman did not stir at his touch and Thomas held his head from the water. He clutched on to an iron mooring post with one hand and held Visser's lifeless body out of the water with his other. He looked down at the Dutchman's face and gasped. By the Lord, it was the carving brought to life, the cheeks bloated and the eyes large and round, bulging from their sockets, the lips horribly swollen.

The effort of holding on sapped his strength and he did not know how long he could go on in this manner. He called for help but his words were lost in the void of the canal. What more could he do? If Visser recovered consciousness he would kill him; if he was already dead then he would shortly drag Thomas with him. The merchant realised he would be responsible for yet another death. Mayhap there truly was a curse on the Paycocke family, that deceit and death should await him at every turn of his life. What was it that his father had done to deserve this?

His arm ached and his grip on the mooring cleat loosened. Still Visser did not stir. Thomas groaned with the effort of staying alive.

"Thomas, is that you?" Robert's voice descended from above.

"Robert, aye, my friend. Be quick."

"Where are you?"

"Here, in the canal." The words rushed out on a single breath. Thomas did not know how many more he could spare. "I have Kees."

"Give me your hand."

"I... I might not let go. Kees will drown."

"Then give me his arm. I will take him first."

"He is too heavy, you cannot..."

"But we are two." Ann's face appeared above him, moving across the pallid moon.

Ann and Robert pulled the unconscious Visser from the water and laid him down at the side of the canal. The weight of Visser's body still told on Thomas's arm, and he could hardly move. His friends took hold of his screaming muscles and wrenched him upwards and he lay panting beside Visser, scarcely more living than the prone Dutchman.

"By the heavens," Robert said. "His is the face."

"Move." Ann pushed Robert out of the way and pressed again and again on Visser's stomach. Water dribbled from his mouth. She pulled away as Visser choked back to life. "He would carve his faces in Heaven if we did not show a care."

Thomas looked up at her. Her hose were torn now and one sleeve of her jacket had become detached and was wrinkling down her arm. She had lost her hat in the chase and now her hair was escaping its ties and flowing down her shoulders. Thomas smiled at the results of combat. "You make a fine man, Ann."

She looked down at her clothes. Robert put his arms around her. "But a finer woman still," he said. "And I would sooner see you attired as such, if it would please you."

Thomas winked at the two of them. "I do know a good clothier in this city."

Chapter 47
Truth Needs Not Many Words

Kees opened his eyes, those eyes which belonged on the carving in Thomas's house. He said something in Dutch, although his words were mumbled and Thomas could not even tell in which language he was speaking. His breath was ripe with decay and with the foul smell of rancid onions; he would be a stranger to toothsoap and all that was clean. Thomas turned his face away.

So blessed was Ann with a sense of direction that she had led them back to the house of the six laughing herring within minutes, Thomas and Robert carrying Kees Visser between them. The journey warmed the three even though the night was growing cold. Visser's home was small, only two rooms downstairs, and there was no sign of any other occupants. It smelt musty, as though fresh air had passed by this place and all life allowed to become stale there. The clay floor had not seen a broom in weeks, and breadcrumbs, filthy grease and fragments of chicken bones nestled into the damp reeds scattered there. No herbs were strewn across the floor to disguise the foul smells; the occupant of this house had lost heart. A mouse scuttled for cover as Paycocke laid Kees out on the floor, peeling off his soaked clothes and covering him with Robert's dry cloak. Ann lighted a rush torch so that they might have some illumination.

Thomas was no surgeon and could not tell how the blow to the head had affected Kees. He might die; he might wake up with no ill consequence. In Thomas's experience it was impossible to predict. They found some rough candles and set them about the room. It spoke of hardship and poverty. Some of the woodwork was decorated with carved foliates and tracery, but it looked ill-judged, as though Kees had perhaps been practising his art. There were two three-legged stools and a board set upon uneven trestles, but no more furniture. In one corner was an ark, with an end of hard carter's bread within, and next to it was a stout wooden box containing some of Kees's tools. They looked to be in poor condition, lacking use, the tips of his chisels bleeding rust. The window held no glass, only a flapping oiled cloth stopped the worst of the wind penetrating the mean barred opening.

Thomas kept his voice low, as though Visser were a sleeping babe they dare not wake. "Methinks the Vissers have fallen upon difficult times," he said, looking around.

Robert nodded, although he pursed his lips as if to say that difficult times were merited by such a blackguard. In the wan light Thomas could not read his clerk's expression, but he knew well the direction of Robert's heart.

Ann smiled across at Paycocke, meeting his eyes in the candles' smoky gloom. "Aye. It is a wealthy enough quarter, that is true, but this dwelling is no better than a hovel."

"There is not the coin in carving that there once was," offered Robert.

"Or happen that Kees Visser is not the carver he once was." Everything seemed to be Thomas's fault. He bent his head and silently asked God to forgive his sins and relieve him of the guilt he felt.

Kees Visser stirred and again muttered something they did not understand. They watched him strain to open his eyes and focus on them. "You English," he said finally, heaving with the effort of breath.

Thomas put his hand on Kees's shoulder. "Easy, easy."

Visser closed his eyes; he seemed to be remembering. "I fell," he said.

Paycocke nodded. "Aye, you did, and fortunate was it that there was help at hand, for you did take a mighty blow upon the head."

"I am wet."

"Indeed. We pulled you from the canal."

Visser's eyes receded and he closed his eyelids for a long time. "So you saved me," he said at last.

"Aye." There was nothing more to add.

"Why?" Visser tried to sit up, but the pain was too great.

"Be still now," Robert said, coming around the table to join Thomas in the half-light.

Kees recognised Thomas's companion. "And you, naturally."

Robert turned his face so the Dutchman could see the extent of his injuries, deep purples tinged with yellows on his face. "Robert, not now," whispered Paycocke.

Visser raised a hand. "Nee, nee, it is good. I have done by you a great wrong, I see, that is clear."

Robert stood grim-faced, although it was not obvious to Thomas whether his rancour stemmed from the beating he had taken or from the loss of his favoured jerkin. They must find dry clothing for him and for Thomas too, and he shivered, as though he were only now aware that he stood dripping in Kees's dank parlour. He held up a hand. "What is done is done." He wished that that were true, yet he would sacrifice much for the greater good.

Ann built a fire and Visser pointed them in the direction of clean apparel. In truth there were little more than rags, and it was no surprise that Visser had been unable to resist stealing Robert's fine clothes.

"So," Visser sat before the flames, cradling a hot posset, "you have me at a disadvantage."

"That was not my intention." The cloak that Visser had found for Thomas was of a poor quality, thin and torn, its inadequacy putting Thomas rather than the Dutchman at the disadvantage, he felt. Still, it was dry and had been offered in peace. "I swear that I know naught of your trials during the building of my house at Coxhall. Pray, believe that." He took a deep breath; this was more difficult than any negotiation for cloth. He held out a hand. "I would that we might begin our acquaintance anew, Kees Visser."

Visser looked up at Paycocke, whose outstretched hand trembled at this possible point of no return. Just when it appeared that he would ignore the approach, he put out his own hand, a tentative offering. "Ja, so be it, Thomas Paycocke. I owe you my life. So be it."

It was begrudged, to be sure, but at least he was not trying to kill them. Thomas introduced Robert and Ann, and began the delicate process of prising information from the stubborn Visser.

It was like trying to open the most recalcitrant oyster, but once breached, Kees gave his knowledge as though in a confessional.

"It was Gijsbert who found the work. He was the talker. I only carved, following Gijsbert from town to town, a year here, three months there, you never knew. Coxhall was a town like any other and I had need of the money for my family."

Robert looked around at the empty Visser house. "And where is your family now?" Suspicion edged his words and Thomas had to put a hand on the younger man's arm.

Kees did not pick up on Robert's ill-feeling and just continued to stare into the flames. "Dead. All dead. Cursed."

"So you followed Gijsbert to Coxhall?" Thomas did not want to lose the thread of Kees's tale.

"Naturally. As I say, Coxhall is a town as any other, but Paycocke's," he shook his head, "a house not like any other. That was clear from the start. We worked for William Spooner, a hard man to please. Always faster, faster he was wanting things done. Change this, change that, he was never pleased. But I work not for Spooner but for God, and it was God who made my carving in the green oak: dragons and crowns; the leaves of spring; your Paycocke ermine mark; flowers so delicate that you could almost smell their fragrance."

"And the face?"

"Ja, ja, I come to this." He took a long draught of the cooling drink and it seemed to lubricate his voice. "It was my best work, but upon such a place." His mouth drooped in sadness. "You must never build on a Roman street," he said. "Every day I worked on this house I heard the steps of Roman soldiers around me, crushing the oyster shells laid betwixt the road and your house. They were trying to stop this profane building, but none would heed their cries. I was but a carver and my voice counted for nothing, but never before did I have the feeling of doom that I had then. And that was before Spooner…"

The firelight dimmed and Ann stepped forward with another log. It would be elm, thought Thomas, for it smelt like mould in a graveyard and the warmth it provided was poor. Robert made as if to hurry Kees in his story but Thomas stayed him with a gesture.

"Mad was Spooner, mad, working like crazy to make this house in two months, like he was holding a hot ember from the fire. And then, it was almost at an end, the men were making the linen panels and he took me to one side. I never spoke with him before. It was always Gijsbert. He said that he watched me, that I was the most skilled carver, and also the most silent one. I knew at once that it was the second quality that was the most important in his eyes. He wished for me to make him a special carving, and to make it at night, so that no one would know it was there. I would be well paid for this." Visser sighed. "False coin - the coin of the devil.

"He wanted a carved face, a face to watch over the panelled room, to guard it so that none should escape from within. I made this face, sculpted it from the oak as though it were cheese. My own face, that I should have been such a fool as to use my own face as a model for this carving, it is unbelievable. I was a proud man then." He looked around him at the stinking, dingy room and shook his head. "Mayhap you do not think it now, but I was proud of my life. Aie, aie.

"It was night. I lay on my back up to the ceiling and fashioned the face he wanted so, that small face with a little of my own likeness within. And while I carved Spooner was busy in the panelled room behind me. He was alone, but making such a noise that there might have been ten men with him. He cursed and cried and swore all night on the name of John Paycocke."

"My father."

"Ja, and it seemed that he would lose his mind, one moment laughing, the next eaten with anger."

"What... what was Spooner doing?"

"I did not know and I feared to look about, that I would be turned to stone if I faced the evil that was in the panelled room. I knew I had to leave, but when my carving was complete I saw that I had left part of myself in that house for all eternity, looking at the devil's deed of Spooner. I changed my carving at the last moment, so that the eyes appeared shut." Kees closed his eyelids and his eyes bulged outwards, just as in the carving. "That way, I would not have to look upon the evil for all time."

"And then?"

"Spooner looked upon my carved face with great happiness. He became a different man, his shoulders lifting like a mule when you have removed a burden. I could not see what had happened in the other room, nor did I wish to know. I only knew that something of monstrous ill had passed, and that I was damned for being a part of its execution. I left for Lavenham the next day. I did not stay to see the finished house. The name of Paycocke rang in my ears and I swore to kill any man of that family who should find me."

"You did not stay in Lavenham?"

"Nee, the curse followed me. I fell ill, many things went wrong. It was clear I was still too close to the source of the evil. I came back to Amsteldam, but might not escape Paycocke's. My father died of the sweats, my mother poisoned by foul water, I could not find work. My friends turned their backs on me. All I have is what you see." Visser put his head in his hands.

Thomas felt a curious mingling of sympathy for the accursed Dutchman and excitement at the discovery of what had passed at Paycocke's House. They must return. He put a hand on Kees's shoulder, but the carver hardly seemed to register his presence. Even though he had tried to murder Robert, this was still a man on whom God would show mercy. "I knew nothing of this," he sighed. "You have been ill-used, Kees Visser, and the Paycocke name has not proved worthy. But I swear to you that I knew nothing. It was Spooner's doing and he alone." Yet it had not been Spooner alone; the master builder had in some way acted upon John Paycocke's instructions. Spooner had only been a conduit. It was Thomas's own father who was responsible, his father who now languished in purgatory, paying eternal penance for a deed that could never be forgiven. "Did he say more about my father?"

"More?"

"Aye. Spake he of a legacy, a will, of some act that my father would have Spooner do after his death?"

Kees Visser rubbed his beard. He shivered, even though he was the closest of them to the fire. "My English was not so good at this time, and, remember, I did not want to be a part of the sorcery in that room. I tried hard not to hear. He talked of John Paycocke indeed, cursed him with his every breath. I understood but one word in two. But, nou ja, as he finished in the room, as he came into the hall to see my work, he said something, what was it?" He closed his eyes and dredged up the memory. "He said, 'What you have... left to me, John Paycocke, I leave ... to your son, your true heir, Thomas Paycocke.'"

Chapter 48
Land

It was cold in the hall, colder than it had any right to be. And there were no ghosts, no ghosts at all. Simon laughed to himself as he stretched his fingers to get the circulation moving. It had all seemed so plausible in the middle of the night.

He stoked up the wood burner. How Fitz had been able to tell the difference between the wood amazed him. Sure, they were different, but... He held up a couple of logs, one having a thin smooth bark that looked like camouflage, the other having a tough ridged outer skin that rasped against his fingertips. Wood was wood. Funny, really, when you considered that he made his living from it in a sense, and he himself couldn't tell one piece from the next.

The fire drew immediately and it blazed hypnotic yellows and reds while Simon watched. He didn't hear the tapping at first, so locked into the fire was he, but its insistence broke through his concentration. When he drew his eyes away, the after-image of the glow was stamped on his retina. He turned towards the light, towards the persistent sound, like tiny hoof beats on the window pane. Sparrow.

"So where the hell have you been? Call me up like your backside's on fire and then you disappear."

"Couple of things to sort out." Simon didn't elaborate, but ushered Sparrow into the hall. Cassie was none of his business. Nor Alex for that matter. Especially Alex.

Martin pushed his fingers through his hair and strode up to the wood burner to warm his hands. "Nice fire."

"What do you know about wood?"

"Not much. It burns."

Simon held up one of the logs from the basket. "What's this?"

Sparrow turned. "Um... is it plane?"

"Search me."

"No, no, no, that was my modest way of saying, 'It is plane.'"

"Modesty? You?"

Sparrow spread out his arms, smiling.

"Anyway, how on earth do you know that?"

"I don't know, mate. Too many forays into the Savernake Forest with the town girls, I suppose. Some things stick."

Simon opened the wood burner and put the plane log inside. He held up the more gnarled faggot. "And this?"

Sparrow's grin drooped in apology. "Oak, old pal."

"How is it other people know so much more than I do?"

Sparrow shrugged. "What's up, Simon? You look a touch ropey. Not sleeping?"

"Not great. It's... I don't know... I seem to be running on the spot, getting nowhere."

"I know how you feel."

"Do you?"

"I've been thinking."

"About?" Simon turned back to the fire. He gestured Martin to sit down in the other chair.

"About *Artes*..."

Simon puffed. "Yeah, I wanted to speak to you about that..."

"I think we've exhausted all the avenues, all the streets, all the cul-de-sacs, even. We should send the original back."

Simon woke up. "What? What are you saying? We've only just scratched the surface. We've got websites to chase up. I want to visit the National Archives, dig up some documents in the county repositories. Those import manifests - we're just getting somewhere, Martin."

Sparrow scrunched his lips together. "Well, we're not really, are we?"

"What do you mean?" Simon prodded the fire, stabbing the oak log so it dropped onto the flames, dousing them temporarily. "Of course we are." He stared at Martin.

"It's all conjecture, isn't it? You said it yourself."

"No. It's… intelligent supposition. Look, don't back out on me, Martin. This is the one bloody positive thing that's happened to me in the last few weeks. I'm not giving up that easily."

"Well, that and Miss Simmons."

"What?"

"You know. Another positive thing?"

"What the hell has that got to do with you? And it's nothing, anyway, we're…"

"…Just good friends?"

"Bugger off. Anyway, I want to see the original. You can't send it back. It's… it's my passport to Prague."

The oak log had knocked out the flames and sat on fiery embers. Simon poked at it, cursing, nothing happening. Then Martin picked up the poker and levered the piece of wood so that air could pass beneath it. He leant forward and blew at the base of the log. Flames sprang from behind it at once. Martin Sparrow was the most annoying person in the world, Simon reflected.

"I think we're wasting our time," Sparrow said.

Simon sighed. "I have plenty of time to waste."

"It's all guesswork."

"I want to see the original."

"We need to let this go, Simon."

"I want to see the original."

"You can't."

"It's in London. I want to see it. Today." He stood up. "Come on, let's go. We can catch the next train and pick up the wretched thing. It's not over. No way."

Sparrow shook his head. "It's not that simple." His fringe flopped in front of his eyes and he pushed it back. He would not meet Simon's stare. "Simon, we have to drop it. My life's in danger. Yours, too." He looked out of the window onto West Street, as though right then someone might be there. "I'm being followed."

"What?" Simon couldn't believe what he was hearing.

"It's Land, Simon, Fleming Land. He's at the White Hart. He's after me."

*   *   *

Cassie stared into the bathroom mirror. The voices of the two men below echoed through the house, her father's more animated than she had heard for a long time, the ebullient Sparrow now the subdued one of the pair. Sparrow - now there was a proper target for hatred. Roach was behind her now, small and insignificant. She was sure he would not follow up on his sneaky parting gesture. What she was not sure of was why she hadn't grassed him up. Did she care about him? Could she see Roach again and care less? Her heart beat faster – best not go down that road just yet.

Her face looked bleak and unloved, her skin washed out beside the awful black hair. She would have it done soon; perhaps Dad would cough up for it. How many weeks, months even, had it been since she had slept so well? She didn't look any better on it, she thought, but at least she had turned the corner. Thanks to Dad, her own Get Out Of Jail Free card. Who would have thought it, Dad bribing the security guard? Her eyes filled up at the thought of what her father had done for her. Unquestioning, unconditional loyalty.

Cassie stepped back from the mirror, as though distance might improve her reflection, and stumbled into a bucket. It wobbled and fell, sending its contents splashing over the floorboards. "Shit," she said. "Who put that there?" The water seeped through the cracks between the boards. She turned the bucket the right way up but made no attempt to clean up the mess.

Pulling out the scales she stood staring at the zero reading as though she was taking a step into the unknown by testing her weight. She put her feet onto them, watching the black digital readout creep up, way past the last time she had weighed herself. No, it couldn't be. She took off her light cotton dressing-gown, hung it up on top of one of her father's shirts and weighed herself again. She had put on nearly two kilos. Stepping off the scales, she let the readout die back to zero and tried once more, in case there was some kind of fault with the machine. The result was the same. Two kilos: a bag of sugar or a sack of cat food carried around her middle. She sat on the side of the bath, almost faint with the thought and fighting an urge to be sick. How could it have happened? She hadn't been watching things, hadn't taken enough exercise. Taking slow, deep breaths, the feeling of sickness dimmed and she felt the cold enamel of the bath comforting against her skin. She stood up and examined her profile in the mirror, lifting her nightdress to inspect her bulging tummy. It didn't look *so* bad. She had caught it in time. All she needed was a new regime. She reached for her dressing-gown, lifting it from the hook, and her father's shirt peeled away with it and dropped to the floor. She picked up the soft chambray and something toppled out of its pocket, spinning onto the floor in a tiny whirl of black and orange – a Trypholine pill.

A light slick of sweat appeared on her brow as she reached down to pick up the capsule, her breathing becoming faster and shallower. Would one pill count? Just one for today, only for this lousy day, then tomorrow she could make a fresh start. It had been such an awful week and yesterday had been the worst day of her life. Who could blame her for one pill? What difference could it make? She turned on the cold tap and the water lurched from it, filling her glass.

"Hi." Alex spoke between gasps. "Cass."

Cassie spun around, her fingers clamped around the pill. "Alex! You nearly gave me a heart attack." She was aware of a false, almost guilty quality radiating from her voice, and tried to relax. "Been for a run?" Why did she say that? She never asked about Alex's training regime.

Alex blew hard. "Yeah. OK... if I... have a... shower?"

Cassie took a drink of the water she had poured. "Oh, yeah, I'm nearly finished." She slipped the small capsule into her pocket.

Alex looked down and saw the scales, the digital readout still on. "Everything OK?"

Cass smiled. "Yeah, sure."

Alex closed the bathroom door, guillotining the sound of the men's voices below. "Cass?" she said, her tone flat.

Cassie could not tell whether an interrogation was coming and she instinctively clammed up. "Look, can I catch you later, Al?" She needed that pill, just the one. "I'm like up to my eyes in crap at the moment. I gotta run." She opened the door and heard

Alex's sigh trailing her as she sought the sanctuary of her room. What the hell was up with everyone? God, they didn't know they born – she'd trade problems with them all, any day.

*   *   *

"Land? What do you mean, he's after you, Martin?"

Martin Sparrow licked his lips. "He knew something, I could tell. All the way over the Atlantic, he was asking these questions. Where had I been in the States? What was I going to do next? Where had I learnt to sail? What did I do for a living?"

"Oh, come off it, Martin, reasonable questions to ask someone you're trusting on board your boat."

"You don't understand – you weren't there. It was relentless, an inquisition. And one night I went back to my bunk and my bag had been rifled." Sparrow folded his arms. "I think he knew about *De Medicina*."

"How could he? You said yourself it didn't make the news."

"I told you, he's a philanthropist or something. Maybe rare books is a hobby. I just know that he's followed me here. He wants the book."

"So why didn't he take it and dump you overboard?"

Martin scratched his head. There were heavy crescents under his eyes. "I don't know, mate. There were other crew around and he would have had to get the book off the boat while the place was crawling with the Old Bilious. I don't know."

Simon had never seen his old colleague look so lost and forlorn. Was this Land some kind of shadowy underworld figure? Maybe he was a manuscript dealer and had spotted *De Medicina* in Martin's luggage. Such a thing would never be for sale on the open market, but there were collectors who would pay anything for a unique work, stop at nothing to have it in their hands, absolutely nothing. He shivered, despite the roaring blaze two feet from their noses. "Where is he now?" he said.

"I saw him in the foyer of the White Hart. He's obviously snooping around."

"Hence the 'Martin House' business?"

Sparrow looked away. "OK, OK, maybe that wasn't so clever."

"Did he see you?"

"I don't think so, but…"

"You're sure it was him?"

"Look, Simon, a guy follows me halfway across the country to kill me, I think I might recognise him, yeah?"

Simon stared at Martin. "Kill you?"

"This is serious, mate."

"You been screwing *his* wife too?"

"Oh, come on, Simon, that's cheap." Sparrow took a deep breath and chewed his bottom lip. "You've got to help me. Land means business. He wants the book, and he doesn't care how he gets it."

"So what do you want to do?"

"I need to lie low, very low, just for a few days. Maybe he'll lose the trail and move on."

Simon took the hint. "Stay here? You've got a nerve, Martin."

Sparrow stared into the fire. The oak log shifted in the burner, but the flames were as steady as ever. "I know. Who else can I turn to, Simon?"

Simon clenched his teeth. "OK, a couple of days, no more. I'll go to the hotel and check Land out, try and find out what he's up to, keep tabs on him. A few days, Martin, that's all."

Sparrow smiled. "Cheers, Simon, you're a real friend."

No, I'm not. "Look, let me make you some coffee, Martin. You look out of it."

"Thanks, old pal. I could do with one."

Simon walked through the study and looked out into the courtyard where the rain was falling again. Land kill Sparrow? Some bloody philanthropist. This was Coggeshall, not New York. How could he say no? He had never seen Martin so shaken. Perhaps they could make a deal with Land. What was he thinking? What they should do was go to the police, although first he'd have to convince Sparrow. Maybe the guy was right: lie low for a few days and see what happens.

The Cleaving of Paycocke's

A raindrop splashed on Simon's head. He brushed it away, smoothing his hair and looked up at the ceiling. A thin trickle of water darkened a beam above his head, running in a tiny groove towards the middle of the room, where it collected by a knot and fused into a large drop blooming on the surface of the oak. As he watched, it grew bigger, becoming large and swollen, before the water broke again on his forehead in a thick droplet.

The leak. He had forgotten the bucket; it must have overflowed. Now he would have to get that trapdoor open.

*   *   *

Cassie stared at the pill in her hand. She would have taken it had Alex not barged in, she knew that. Alex had saved her, she owed her one, because one moment of weakness would be all it took. And then where would that lead? Two, three, four more moments, then a lifetime of weakness. It couldn't happen. She would not allow Roach to reel her back in. No one could be strong all the time, but she was going to make sure she was damn well strong now. She opened the window, ready to chuck the capsule out into the street, then had a vision of herself on her knees in a couple of hours, scrabbling in the gutter to find it.

"No," she said. "Fuck you, Roach. This is really over." She lit a match and held it to the last of the Trypholine. *Everything changes. Everything.*

Chapter 49
Edward's Room

Edward had kissed her; he had truly kissed her. The strength to do so came from nowhere in that second. He had held her in his arms as though nothing mattered, streaking her fresh white blouse with his grimy fingers and putting his lips to hers, gently at first, like a butterfly landing, then firmer, more insistent, as his obsession drove him to a new level. And did she resist? Perhaps at first, aware of her upbringing, the impropriety of the moment, but she had melted, her lips like sweet marshmallow.

And nothing did matter. The world became trivial beside his love for Imogen. He stared at the walls of his bedroom, the wallpaper to which he had woken up every day of his life, a pattern of fading roses curling through an endless trellis. There were small rips where strips met, when his infant hands had been unable to resist tearing the lifting paper. Edward saw it as if it were new, its crimson flowers alive, each winding tendril of the bush protected by sharp green thorns. How he would protect Imogen, protect and adore her. Nothing else mattered.

He looked over to his bedroom door, guilt stirring in his stomach. Across the landing his mother slept, as she did for most of the day now, taking food and water only when forced. She was giving up. Edward closed his eyes to let the feeling of desperation wash over him and when he opened them again it was to the drab and peeling room that had been his prison for sixteen years. He must let go. His mother was ready to join the Lord, that was becoming clear. There was no return from the sugar sickness, the pissing evil. It was time to release the past and look forward, and it was a good time, the right time, his mother leaving him as Imogen joined him, even if his breath lodged in his throat as he contemplated his mother's death. As for his father, what was he? Who was he? Nothing, a destroyer of dreams. They would leave, Imogen and he, and start a new life. Nothing could stop them now.

There was a faint noise coming from his mother's room. Edward opened her door and peeked in through the gap. The curtains were half-drawn, but the dirty nets prevented much of the sunlight filtering through. "Mammy?" he whispered. There was a subtle shift in the shadows, his mother's tiny body moving on the bed and sending the frail light spilling elsewhere on the eiderdown. Edward did not want to go into the room; it pulsated with sickness and he fought the urge to close the door and turn his back. Everything he did, he did for Imogen – that was the way it would be from now on. He pushed the door open and some of the landing light illuminated his mother's bedroom. Still he hesitated.

"Edward?" His mother did not move. "Is that you?"

"Yes."

She raised a skeletal hand a few inches above the covers. "My boy."

"How are you?" Edward cursed himself for his stupid question, but what else could he say? He struggled for words. "Do you need anything? How about a nice bit of porridge?" *Please. Please eat, mammy.*

Ida Daynes smiled, a weak smile that only existed in the twitched corners of her mouth. "No."

"Do you want me to fetch the doctor?" He took refuge in the practical, wanting to smother his emotions until this awful moment was over.

"No doctor. No use for me. No point."

Edward willed his tears to come and prayed for release, release for his mother and release for himself.

"I love you, Edward."

"I love you, too, mammy." The affirmation was helpless, feeling like a stock response. Guilt over his love for Imogen nagged at him and he wrestled to keep it under control. "I love you."

She turned her head to face him, her eyes so far back in her sockets that they seemed to peer from distant tunnels. "It's the end, my little Eddie," she said. "The end for me."

'Eddie', when had she last called him 'Eddie'? Now the tears did start to come. "No, mammy. I won't have it."

Ida tried to hush him, but the sound came out as a strangled wheeze. "It is, son. Look after your father. Look after your girl." Edward's face grew hot. He said nothing, not wanting to promise to look after his father, anything but that. But Imogen, yes, for her he would make any pledge. His mother placed her hand on his, her flaking fingers rasping against his own. "I know, son. I was a girl too... once... a long time ago."

Edward smiled through his tears. "I'll look after her."

"Be happy, Edward."

"I will."

"Do the right thing."

"I will, mammy."

His mother closed her eyes and sank back into the pillows, her breathing settling into a steady rhythm.

But what *was* the right thing?

The front door slammed and glass shook in the windows. "Edward. Get your arse down here. I know you're home." The voice came closer. Edward shut the bedroom door and stood at the top of the stairs, heart thumping like a battering ram. "Don't make me come up there." He saw his father's face, dark with rage, appear at the bottom of the stairs and he started down in silence. He said nothing to his father, just stared down at the steps. *I do this for Imogen. Everything I do, I do for her.* How many times had he climbed these steps in his life, in joy, in fear, in anger? How many more times remained?

"So, what's this I'm hearing?" Albert Daynes pushed Edward through into the kitchen. "Sam Trotter says he saw you, the two of you, you and that natty madam, out walking. In a field." There was a glaze over his father's eyes and his breath smelt of ale and cigarettes. "What have you got to say for yourself, you little bugger? You just wait." He fiddled with his belt buckle. "It'll be the belt for you, my lad. You're not so big as you couldn't take a good hiding."

Edward looked down at his shoes. How many more days? One, three, ten, fifty?

"Look at me when I'm talking to you, you brat." Daynes spat the words out and a few drops of spittle flew through the air and landed on Edward's face.

The kiss, the golden kiss. Things could change. Not everything was pre-ordained. *Everything I do, I do for you.* He put two fingers up to his cheek and wiped his father's spit off onto the tips.

"Is it true? After me telling you? You little bastard." Daynes gripped Edward by the shoulders and shook him. His father was by far the stronger and Edward could not move in the vice of his thick hands. "She's too good for the likes of you, she's nothing but a posh tart."

"No." Edward made his voice as big as he could, but even then it seemed as if it had not yet broken, a quivering reed in the gust of his father's anger. How many more days at home?

Albert Daynes laughed and let go of his son, putting his hands on his hips. "No? The fucking posh tart?" He repeated the words, as though savouring their taste in his mouth. "Posh... tart?" He pushed Edward through the door. The boy stumbled but kept his balance, squaring up to his father. *Everything I do, I do for you, Imogen.* Daynes pushed him again, repeating his mantra and laughing in Edward's face. "Posh... fucking... tart. Tart... tart... tart..."

His father's voice grew louder and louder, filling Edward's head. *No more. No more. No more days at home.*

"Tart."

Edward snapped back his head. "No," he screamed, leapt in the air and planted a bullet-like header onto his father's nose. There was a crack as Daynes's nose broke, and he staggered back into the kitchen, putting one hand up to his face, blood spurting from between his fingers. He flailed at the door jamb with his free hand, but lost his footing, fell backwards and cracked his head on the dresser.

Daynes lay still.

Edward stood over him, his breathing steady. There was a dull ache on his forehead where he had butted his father. He put his hand there and felt a small lump and a few spots of blood which he wiped off with his fingers. Daynes did not move, but bubbles of air spluttered from his nose with the blood.

"No more," Edward said, and walked from the house.

Chapter 50
Conrad's Room

I caught the omnibus to Thaxted, no easy journey, I must say, for we were stuck for aeons, first behind a motor-lorry and then a dawdling steam-tractor. At least those hours of motoring gave me a great deal of time to reflect on what I would say to Conrad Noel. It was well that I used this time wisely, for I alighted in front of the old Guild Hall on Town Street in a much steadier frame of mind than when I had left Coggeshall, the spirit of intrepid adventure and confrontation somewhat subdued by the interminably slow progress of the vehicle across Essex.

It was ironic that I should leave the omnibus in front of this beautiful building, for it was again one in whose restoration Conrad Noel had taken a keen interest. Some yards away from the Guild Hall of the Cutlers was our old house 'The Steps'; memories of our own happy times at Thaxted flooded through me: parties with the Noels at the Vicarage; carol-singing through the streets; the Whitsun Festival at the church, where Gussie would make the organ sing. Thaxted was buried in my heart.

I walked up the hill to the Vicarage. Conrad was not expecting me, but when he opened the door he showed no surprise. "Ah, Imogen, my dear," he said. "You are just in time for tea."

He held my hand in his and led me into his kitchen, where he himself filled the blackened kettle. I did not understand. Conrad Noel had diabetes, the sugar sickness? Yet the difference between our old family friend and Edward's mother Ida was that of different worlds. He was not weak as a new-born kitten, nor thin and wasting. I did not understand. I held my hands pressed to my lap so that they should not give away my discomfort, but I was torn between love for our old friend, curiosity as to the queer goings on at Paycocke's, and the gravest of concern for Conrad's condition. I did not know where to begin. Picking up a set of Morris dancing bells from the sideboard, I jangled them to fill the silence.

Conrad smiled at my effort to break the ice of the moment, but said nothing, just tipping his head to one side and arching one of his unkempt eyebrows. He poured the tea into delicate bone china, whose gold leaf rims had worn thin with the countless cups of tea served to his parishioners. A humbling feeling surged through me. Surely Conrad Noel could not be guilty of any subterfuge? If there was a man alive as open and good as he, then that man had already booked his passage to Heaven. He swirled a silver spoon around his cup. "Now, then, to what do I owe the honour of your visit, Imogen?"

Dear, dear Conrad. I took a deep breath. "I have heard… I am led to believe…" I cursed myself for my formality. I had practically grown up in the Noels' house, playing in their garden, eating Miriam's cakes and taking part in impromptu choir practices. "Conrad?"

"Mmm?" He took a sip of his tea.

"Do you have diabetes?" I bit my lip. *Horror of horrors, what have I done now?*

He laughed and his longish curls bounced on either side of his head. "Why, yes." He saw that I was not much amused at his boundless good spirits and he tipped his head to one side as an apology for the levity. "Yes, Imogen," he said, in a tone that was much more serious. "I do indeed have diabetes."

A lump came to my throat and I wished I were not holding a cup of tea. How could he be so calm? "Will you die?"

"We all must die, Imogen. If it is God's will, I shall live to carry on his work. If not… well, he has honoured me greatly up to this day."

"But I do not understand. I have a… a friend…" Was I correct? Was Edward still a friend, or was he now more than that, having shared a kiss? Or had it made him somehow less than a friend now? I had pushed him away as though it might grant me some sort of alibi, but his grimy kisses loitered on my lips. I could still taste him there and I did not know what to make of it. I supposed he was a friend, an accomplice even. "I have a friend whose mother also suffers from the illness, and yet… and yet she is near to death. It has run through her body taking all that is good. She is capable of little more than sleep now."

Conrad held his palms together as if praying, the gesture looking odd despite his ecclesiastical station. Indeed perhaps it seemed odd *because* of his vocation, for I am sure that Conrad Noel is constantly at prayer, seeking guidance and blessing from the Lord, and as such has no need of physical gestures to underline the prayer in his heart. He gave tiny nods, as though bidding me to carry on.

I faltered. "I see no such signs in you."

"I have made a small study of my condition," he said at last. Of course I might have guessed at this fact, for never have I known such a glutton for knowledge as Conrad Noel. As other men breathe, he reads and dissects. "It seems that there are a number of different types of diabetes, or the sugar sickness, if you will; it has a number of names, some less than decorous." He chuckled and I blushed. "It manifests itself in various guises, and while it is never less than serious, it need not always be life-threatening in such a short space of time. It seems, alas, that your friend's mother is afflicted with the most onerous of its forms."

"And you?"

He spread his arms as though it were nothing. "I am, I believe, fortunate. The Lord still has need of me."

"Then you will not die?" I clapped my hands, then thought better of my gesture, clasping my fingers together in a large fist and burying it in my lap.

Conrad smiled. "Not today, I hope. But of your friend's mother, is there truly no hope?"

I launched into a tirade on Doctor Phipps, how little he cared, how offhand had been his manner with Ida Daynes, and how dismissive he had been of her hopes. Conrad shushed my protests and to my indignation defended the horrid doctor, talking of the difficulties of facing illness and death on a daily basis. I felt my temperature rise.

Conrad stood and turned his back on me. "I do believe we have some macaroons," he said, and rummaged in a cupboard.

I could not contain my anger. "This is a matter of life and death and you talk only of macaroons?"

He passed me a plate on which sat one of his wretched

confections. I put it on the table; I was in no mood to humour him. He waved a biscuit at me. "Look how crisp is the shell, how firm and solid." Then he broke it in half and took a bite. His eyebrows wrinkled with pleasure. "Mmm. Miriam tells me that I should not eat them, but the denial of all pleasure is not possible, do you agree?"

I folded my arms, determined to have nothing to do with macaroons.

"So crisp and firm, yet inside so soft, delicate and succulent." He stopped in mid-bite, holding up the biscuit as a priest might raise the Host in a service. "Things are not always what they seem, Imogen."

"How so?"

"There *is* always hope."

I sighed. "Ida Daynes is dying."

"I know."

"How can there be hope?"

"There is..." Now Conrad chose his words carefully, as though they were blackberries, examining each one for its size and ripeness. "There is some research that has been in motion these past few years into the condition of diabetes, conducted by two Canadian scientists of good standing, a Doctor Banting and a Professor Macleod, if memory serves me. Now, you understand that the problem is one of excess sugar in the blood and the urine, hence its nicknames?"

I nodded.

"This sugar acts as a poison on the human body and as I say, in its worst cases is invariably fatal."

"But surely everyone eats sugar in one form or another?"

"This is true, but under normal circumstances there is a certain hormone in the pancreas, called insulin, which controls the metabolism of these sugars. An individual who is lacking in this insulin," he smiled and waved at himself, "will experience the sugar accumulating in the blood and then excreted in the urine."

It all seemed so hopeless. "Then without this insulin there is nothing to be done?"

Conrad took another bite of his macaroon. "The two Canadian gentlemen of whom I spoke appear to have developed a method of isolating this hormone, such that it can be injected into the diabetic, where it replicates the function carried out by the pancreas."

"Then it is a cure? Diabetes can be cured?"

Conrad Noel held his hands up in front of his face to stay my excitement. "Not so much a cure as a treatment, Imogen. Little is known of the reasons for the failure of the pancreas, but it seems that it will be possible that its deficiencies might be compensated for in some way by this application of external insulin."

My face must have exploded with delight. Conrad Noel was right - in the darkest corner there might be light, there might be hope. Edward's mother might yet be saved.

The vicar's expression grew as grave as mine was happy. "I tell you this to give you hope, Imogen, but be aware that it might yet prove too late for your friend's mother. Banting and Macleod have carried out a great many experiments on dogs, but their trials on humans have been limited. It may be some little time before the procedure becomes commonplace."

"But why has Doctor Phipps not spoken of this?"

"A general practitioner is concerned with the here and the now. I should not expect him to have knowledge of all research in all medical fields. That should be a burden too far."

"But there is hope, a small hope, for Edward's mother?"

"Perhaps."

"And for you?"

"My life is in God's hands," he said.

I did not understand. "But the new procedure will benefit you. You will be able to inject this insulin and keep your diabetes at bay?"

Conrad Noel shook his head. What did he mean? "It is for each and every man to decide what is and is not acceptable to him. I cannot go down that path."

"But…" Tears sprang to my eyes. How could Conrad be so prepared to sign his own death warrant?

"The procedure has been tested on animals, and that is something of which I cannot approve."

"But your own life…"

"'All creatures great and small,' Imogen," he said, smiling. "What right do I have to live at the expense of others' suffering?"

"No." He had raised my hopes to the stars only to crumble them like his soft macaroon.

I became silent at the enigma of Conrad Noel, that he should offer hope with one hand and despair with the other, and yet still remain the most magnanimous man I had ever met. A lone tear trickled down my cheek. I was overwhelmed with admiration for him. And yet, even as I wept for the hope that he had given me for Ida and for his own suffering yet to come, an uneasiness swept over me. This was the man who had covered up his knowledge of the strange happenings at Paycocke's House, who had in some way been responsible for its unhappy state. I fixed my eyes upon his and he knew at once that I had come upon a different mission.

"You are troubled, Imogen," he said. "Although your concern for Edward's mother is laudable, it is not the uppermost thing in your mind. Am I right?"

I gave the slightest nod.

"Of all the sheep in the Lord's flock, you will never be one who follows blindly. Do you wish to talk of the matter?"

"It is why I am here," I said. "It is on the subject of Paycocke's House."

He looked at me with his soft brown eyes. Oh, how I believe that he could not stop the twinkle even if he wanted to. "Everything exists for the glory of God," he said. "I seek not to evade responsibility in this matter, Imogen, but to pursue a greater goal." He looked about him. "May we talk in my study, Imogen?"

Conrad's room seemed to overflow with books. Two large bookcases struggled to cope with their load and they spawned piles of volumes at their feet. It was hard to know where to step. Conrad sighed. "So many things to know, Imogen. So many things." He moved some papers from a leather armchair and bade me sit down. He himself sat at his mahogany desk in a hard chair.

"When we first arrived at Paycocke's," he said, "it was in a most sorry state. You know from the *Country Life* article that it had been divided into three cottages. The oak carvings languished under several layers of paint and there were match board walls and plaster lath ceilings hiding the beautiful fluted beams upstairs. Everywhere there was neglect and disarray. Yet there was something about the house that drew me. The first moment I stepped over the threshold was one of joy and excitement, a schoolboy's thrill of an adventure to come.

"Of course, it was terribly uncomfortable, living constantly with dust and rubble about the place, but the wonder of each new discovery more than made up for the inconvenience. We lived there, as you know, for several years, mostly in a state of upheaval. Then, one day, Ernest Beckwith and I decided that we had to know what lay behind the Georgian fireplace in the panelled room. Dear Miriam had had enough of the tiresome reconstruction by this time, but was kind enough to indulge me. We pulled out the Georgian work and revealed the most marvellous carved Tudor bressumer beam over a deep fireplace. It had suffered some damage, but still bore intricate carvings of a lion and other animals, and also the name of Thomas Paycocke. A most splendid piece of work. But, alas, it is from that moment that I date my anxieties."

"Anxieties?"

Conrad's brow knitted. "It was as though we had released something in Paycocke's. Our life was not to be the same thereafter. Small things happened, each explicable in its own right, but taken together indicative of a greater malaise. Once a small piece of Meissen was knocked over when there was nobody in the room. Another time I was convinced I heard footsteps in the hall yet no one appeared, and on a third occasion my daughter Barbara heard laughter in the panelled room. And all this time there was a prevailing sense of unease, as though something were watching us, watching and waiting."

I saw that it bestowed a sense of unease upon Conrad merely to remember his time at Paycocke's. "Do you believe in ghosts?"

He did not smile as I expected, nor dismiss my question as he had once before. "I wish to be honest with you in every way,

Imogen. Prior to moving to Coggeshall I had never entertained the notion of ghosts. Never. But in our latter years at Paycocke's my belief was much tested."

"But now?" I bit my lip in an effort to contain my excitement.

"I am always at pains to avoid laying stress upon that which lies on the other side of the grave to the exclusion of the concerns of this life. The Lord indeed does promise eternal life, but... the shape which that takes only He knows. I tried hard to ignore the signals which I felt the house was giving me.

"Then, one day, Beckwith and I came upon a chamber at the rear of the house, in the area that joins the east and west wings. It is accessible through a small trapdoor in the ceiling."

"I know it." I waited for him to say something about the shrine, but he merely raised an eyebrow.

"It was a place beset by dust and spiders and must have been so for hundreds of years. And yet it was infused with life, to such a degree that I was led to question my own core beliefs." Conrad took the largest breath I have ever seen anyone take. It was clear that I was the first person with whom he had shared this knowledge.

"I would not have Beckwith climb into so small and dark a hole, so I took it upon myself to crawl into the space. It was night in that cave, and though I carried a candle ahead of me, it shrank before the dark and only illuminated a few inches all about me. In the beginning I felt as if I were in my own coffin, so suffocating was the grim light, but after a few minutes that feeling began to fade and the dark seemed to welcome me as an ally, enfolding me in its embrace. It is the only time in my life I have ever thought myself returned to the womb, and what a gentle sensation it was, comforting, drawing me further into the body of the house.

I heard Beckwith call me from the sanctity of daylight. I heard voices too, voices that seemed both all around me and at the same time in my head, telling me that he no longer mattered and I ignored him. The sounds were soft whispers, the tone that of a mother speaking to a small child, words of love and tenderness. 'Come within,' they said. 'Let us comfort you, soothe you. You belong here.' And I felt as though I did belong, that I was home, and that none should ever harm me while I rested in this place, deep in the heart of the house."

Conrad gripped the arms of his Windsor and closed his eyes. The memory seemed to sap him of his strength. Never before had I seen him so moved. "But what then?"

"Forgive my arrogance, but I knew that this was not the will of God. I questioned my own sanity but not that of the Lord and I knew in my very soul that this was not my destiny. I wrestled with the voices while they tempted me and I knew I must not give in. I repeated the Lord's Prayer over and over again, trying to still the voices in my head, and it was made worse by the fact that I knew that this was not evil that was trying to tempt me to its lair, but innocence. There was no malign influence at work, only a gentle and tender yearning within the house. Never before and never since has my love of God been tested so. I turned back to the pinpoint of light that was the trapdoor. It astounded me that I had crawled so far. As I made the return journey I felt myself clawed back by the darkness again, not in any malicious way, but in the desperate manner in which the poverty-stricken might reach out to me and beg of my help. It tore at my heart to refuse the pleas, but I knew that I must if I was to live.

"Once down again I blinked hard in the daylight to rid myself of the feelings I had experienced in that confined space. I tried to explain it away as mild claustrophobia, but I could not suppress the vestiges of guilt I still felt at leaving those behind me. Beckwith was troubled and asked me what I had seen up there that had rendered me so pale. God forgive me, but I lied and said, 'Nothing.' Well, there was nothing *tangible* in that space, nothing except the terrible sense of loss.

"It plagued me over the following days. I felt as though an opportunity had been missed to put right a great wrong. I could not concentrate on my work and Miriam had constant cause to cajole me. Even Barbara said I was far from myself. I knew I would have to go back to that place and attempt to bring it peace."

Conrad's tale made me shiver and I was not at all sure whether I wanted to return to Paycocke's House. If a man of his faith and integrity felt compromised by the strange goings on at Paycocke's, what chance could I possibly have? I was beginning to regret having opened such a Pandora's Box. "Were you not scared?" I asked.

Conrad smiled. "Oh, yes. Very much so. More scared than I have ever been and more scared than I ever shall be, for I feared for my very soul. The temptation to embrace the darkness had been so great that I doubted my ability to withstand it a second time. And with that doubt I questioned my faith and everything I had ever lived for. Oh yes, Imogen, I was truly, truly scared."

"Then why go back?"

"Because there are some risks that must be taken, if a life is to be called a life. Part of me believed that God was leading me, but to where, I did not know. I placed my trust in Him and wished that He himself would speak to me in the way that the voices had, to guide me to His will, but there was only silence. Yet I knew I could not leave the desperate souls locked in the house to their endless torment, and so I decided to take up some items which might help to watch over them in my stead."

"The shrine?"

Conrad laughed. "Ah, so you are aware of the shrine? I should have known it. You are such a resourceful girl, Imogen. A resourceful woman, I should say, no longer a girl. Yes, the shrine. As a boy I had been much taken by Catholic artefacts of prayer, and often busied myself creating all kinds of altars and shrines, from the like of which I derived great spiritual peace. In my heart I felt that such an arrangement might also pacify the beleaguered spirits of Paycocke's House."

"So you do believe…"

Conrad held up his hand to deflect my question. "I believe in God's love, in that above all things, and I took the symbols of His love up into that attic space. There I organised them so that they might be of comfort to the pleading voices. Still they tugged at me, begging me to release them with my presence. Truly, they were like the sirens of mythology, hypnotising and mesmerising me with their kind and gentle voices, whispering thoughts of eternal happiness to me and telling me that it was indeed God's will that I should stay with them, care for them, look after them. It taxed my own will to its extreme to push those thoughts from my head. The whispered pleas became more urgent, but after a short time they could sense that I was not to be swayed in my mission and assumed a more persuasive air. They begged me to liberate them and they talked of a 'face', a 'face that would be the key to salvation'. I talked to myself in Latin as I worked, trying to distract myself from the words which were pounding inside my head. The voices were hushed by my actions, realising that I brought peace, but this did not quell the sense of unease within me, and the guilt was still with me when I came down." He wet the end of an index finger and traced it around his small plate, then put it in his mouth, sucking the sweet remnants of a macaroon. "The guilt is still there," he said.

"Oh, Conrad," I said, my heart filling for his plight.

"It was only when I was down again that I was able to think clearly. I saw that I had brought hope where there had been none, that I had perhaps instigated peace for those troubled spirits, and that they would be watched over. I closed the trapdoor and resolved never to go up into that space again, for I did not think I would be able to resist its lure a third time."

Conrad Noel grew silent after this great catharsis. He looked about his room as though surprised to be there, as though some part of him still remained at Paycocke's, watching over the unfortunate souls who had suffered in the house. The quiet devoured us. Finally he spoke. "The face of which they had spoken was that of the carver, hewn from one of the main cross beams in the hall. Of course I had known it well, since those beams had been painted white when we moved in, and Beckwith's men had painstakingly scraped off every last inch of paint, and in doing so found this marvellous little self-portrait. Yes, I had known of its existence, yet not realised its significance. When I examined it at close quarters I saw that the eyes looked directly into the dining room, resting upon a certain piece of the linen fold panelling. The instant this came to me, I heard the laughing, children's laughing, and a mist appeared in front of the oak panels. 'May God have mercy,' I said. I stood down from my perch and closed the door to that room." Conrad drew his hands together in that steeple gesture of which he was so fond.

I prodded him to continue. "And then?"

He looked away. "There is some presence in that room that ought not to be disturbed. This I feel most keenly, Imogen. Some great ill has befallen Paycocke's House..."

"And its secret lies behind the oak panelling?" My love of adventure was once again beginning to outpace the fear I had earlier experienced.

"There are some secrets that are better left untold," Conrad said. "Sometimes the past is better left alone."

"So you did not remove the panelling?" I was astonished. How could Conrad not have wanted to know?

He pre-empted my inquisition. "It was God's will that I take this no further. I felt that most strongly, and I defer to Him in all things."

"Then..."

"I urge you too to take this no further, Imogen. You do not know the forces with which you deal."

That stung me like a hornet. "And you do?"

He fixed his eyes upon me, and for once the smile had dropped out of his gaze. "I want what is best, Imogen, for us all. I want what is right. Some things are better unspoken."

"No." I stood up and went to the window. The spire of Conrad's church scratched the clouds. How dare he lead me to the brink of this knowledge and forbid me to take it to its conclusion? How dare he? He in his grand ivory tower.

His tone softened. "Do you know, Imogen, I am thinking of purchasing a wireless."

I looked at him and there seemed to be an impenetrable sadness clouding his eyes.

"It could be a great tool of knowledge. There is so much to know, and I have only skimmed its surface. I seek wisdom in all its forms, you see. You yourself are wise, Imogen, wise beyond your years. I do not attempt to order you, only to guide and advise you." He picked up a book from the floor, examined its flyleaf, and then placed it on his desk. "Yet sometimes wisdom alone is insufficient."

I faced him, sitting there in his chair, dressed in black as though mourning some great loss. During the course of our conversation Conrad seemed to have aged, had assumed some great new burden at which I might only guess. In that moment I bore him a great affection, this man of astounding intellect who gave so much to so many and stood up for causes others would have deemed lost. He was no coward, as I had thought before. If he had walked away from Paycocke's House, then it was for a good reason, a reason of faith. Conrad Noel was always true to himself and true to his God.

I, however, could not walk away. I would now seek to know what lay behind the panelling. I would attempt to discover the secret of Paycocke's House.

Chapter 51
Leaks

"Martin," Simon shouted. "Can you give me a hand?" He heard a slow ironic applause filter through from the hall. "Come on, Martin, get your backside in here, now." Rain battered the leaded windows, driven by a merciless autumn south-westerly.

Martin's face appeared at the door. "OK, OK, what's the panic?" He folded his arms and leant on the jamb.

"Look." Simon pointed up at the dribble of water edging across the beam.

"I bet it always does that. House as old as this, it comes with the territory."

"Can you get me a bucket while I try and find out where it's coming from?"

"Yeah." Sparrow disappeared into the kitchen.

Simon climbed onto his desk and traced the flow of water across the beam. Finding his finger the flux grew more persistent and ran down his hand and into his sleeve. The water seemed to be flowing from the rim of the trapdoor. It must be coming from the leak in the bathroom, pooling in the middle section of the house and then finding a path down into the study. Damn. "Hurry up," he shouted. "I'm getting soaked."

"This do?" Martin held out a white nappy bucket that Robin had bought when Cassie was born. They had had such plans for their first baby: home-made food; no dummies; cloth nappies. How long had those resolutions lasted? The incessant crying had sent Robin resorting to the comforter; the towelling diapers leaked; and operating the blender with a baby in one arm sent half-liquidised food flying against the wall. Plans change.

"Yeah."

Martin put the bucket under the leak while Simon wiped his damp hair, his hand grimy and sticky. God only knew what filth had accumulated up there over the years. They went upstairs.

He saw where Cassie had kicked the bucket over. "Why do I bother?" How much water had collected in the space between the bathroom floorboards and the trapdoor was anyone's guess. "I'm going to have to get in there," Simon said. "See if there's any damage."

Martin looked at his watch. "I was sort of hoping..."

"What?"

"Well, you know," Sparrow continued, "what with Land on my tail, I wondered if you could check me out of the White Hart and move my things over here?"

Simon looked at the ceiling. The tick-tock of drops had slowed. "Oh, come on, Martin, I need to get this sorted now."

"Please, mate. It could be a matter of life and death. My death."

"Come off it, Martin. You're being melodramatic."

"That's fine for you to say. You're not at the bottom of the Thames wearing concrete boots."

"Is it really that bad?" Simon stared up, counting the seconds between drops. Yes, it was definitely better than it was.

Sparrow sighed. "Look, I tell you what, you nip down to the pub, get my stuff, and in the meantime I'll fish the ladder out and hoik the nails from the trapdoor. Can't say fairer than that, can I?"

Simon looked at Sparrow, wondering what his angle was.

"Oh, come on, mate, I can't go back there. Please."

Simon rolled his eyes. "All right, all right."

"Keep an eye out for Land. He's about six foot four, similar width, cropped steely hair, looks a bit like Ironside."

"Who?"

"Never mind. Where's your stepladder?"

*   *   *

Sparrow's room was low-ceilinged and oak-beamed. It wouldn't have looked out of place at Paycocke's. He had said something about it being haunted, hadn't he? It looked normal to Simon, innocuous even. He stuffed Sparrow's few possessions into a Nike holdall with room to spare. It looked like he had quit the States in a hurry.

There were several people in front of him at reception, and Simon wandered through the lobby and bar, looking for Land. No steely-haired men to be seen at all. Sparrow was imagining things; it wouldn't be the first time.

He handed over the room key and settled up. As he was offering his Visa card to the clerk it occurred to him that maybe that was what this was all about - Sparrow stinging Simon for his hotel bill. The receptionist swiped the card through the reader and there were a few seconds while it registered. "Perhaps you can help me?" Simon said. "I've been expecting an old friend from the US. I wonder if you can tell me whether he has checked in yet? The name is Land, a Mr Fleming Land."

The receptionist parsed the day's bookings, then the previous day's, and shook her head. "I'm sorry, sir, there is no Mr Land staying with us at the moment."

"No reservation at all?"

She flicked through the coming days' bookings. "No, sir."

The credit card machine printed out a receipt. Simon signed. "Do you have any Americans staying with you at all at the moment?"

The girl checked his signature against his card, licking her top lip. "Not that I know of. Wrong time of year, really."

Simon tucked the receipt into his wallet, puffing at the size of Martin's bar bill. Even when he was broke he didn't have the first idea about economising. That was Marlborough for you. Well, Sparrow would have another bit of education when Simon slapped the bill down in front of him.

As he turned to leave, he saw him. Land. It must be him, he was just as Sparrow had described. Simon didn't have a clue who Ironside was, but the man's hair was iron grey and cut short, a short-back-and-sides. He was dining in the restaurant, so it was not clear how tall he was, but the table looked like it belonged in a junior school, so dwarfed was it by his large frame. Land looked up from his plate, directly at Simon. The moment's eye contact between the two men continued, until Simon broke it by hurrying out into the street. He hoped to hell Land did not connect him to Martin. It was too late, of course. Land would make enquiries at the desk, discover Sparrow had checked out, and it wouldn't take long for him to piece together a link between Simon and Martin. Bloody hell. What next?

"Simon?"

He looked up. Eleanor.

"Oh, hi," he said, forcing a smile. "Hi, Eleanor. I've been meaning to…"

"Um… me too." She gave a nervous laugh.

"It's…" Simon felt his stomach churn. He had forgotten this adolescent feeling of insecurity. Surely the decades should have taken care of this? "It's been really busy, I'm sorry."

"It's OK. Me, too. Busy, that is. Marking. School work. That sort of thing."

"Great," he said. Of course things had changed since he had been a teenager: then you went through weeks of nervous chatter which might eventually lead to sex; now the sex came first and the nervous chatter followed.

Simon didn't want to let her go. There were things he needed to say. "Fancy coming back to Paycocke's for a coffee?" He waved in the general direction of West Street.

Eleanor looked at her watch and nodded. "That'd be nice."

And I want you to hold me. I want to push my fingers through your hair.

"I'm afraid Martin's in the house, Martin Sparrow, you remember?"

"Your nemesis?" She laughed. "Sorry, I shouldn't."

They walked back to the house, a sliver of daylight between their dangling hands. Simon kicked at a horse chestnut husk which skittered across the pavement and hit the wall, its sea urchin casing splitting open. A conker popped out from the perfect velvet interior. Simon knelt down and picked it up, giving it to Eleanor.

"Thank you," she said, rolling it in her palm. "I love them when they're shiny like this."

"It won't stay like that for long," Simon said. Not for long; no matter how bright something was when new, the lustre inevitably faded. But maybe that was good, the fickle and superficial giving way to reliability and strength. Was that how it would be with Eleanor? His stomach flipped. What was he thinking about? They had only just met. He laughed.

"What is it?"

"Conkers," Simon said, picking another up from the pavement. "Do kids still play conkers? When I was that age, you would never have seen so many lying on the ground."

"Aye, us too. In fact, the conkers would never get a chance to fall; we'd be chucking sticks up at the tree to knock them off, or climbing up there after them."

"Never had you down as a tree climber."

Eleanor looked at the pavement, kicking through some dry brown chestnut leaves, curled inwards like talons. "There's a lot you don't know about me, Simon. Maybe..."

He looked at her and his heart turned over. "Maybe?"

"Maybe we... How did *you* harden them?"

"We always used to try and leave ours in the back of a drawer for a year, but we could never find them the next autumn. So then we'd bake them in the oven."

She gave him an incredulous look. "The oven? That makes them dry out, go brittle. Vinegar's what you want. Soak them in vinegar."

Simon looked at her in disbelief. "Vinegar? Bollocks."

"No, it isn't."

"Complete bollocks."

"Want to bet? I'll pitch my vinegar-soaked conker against your oven-baked one any time."

"All right," he said. "You're on. Tonight."

Eleanor knelt down, brushing her hands through the crackling leaves to find more conkers. She sat on the brick wall with a handful, holding them up to the light, checking for flaws, pressing them between finger and thumb. Simon sat beside her. She had him worried.

"When Alan left," she said, "I was only working part-time. He walked out, leaving me with the mortgage and a stack of unpaid bills." She tossed one of the conkers to the ground. "I had no money of my own and he'd raided all the savings in the joint account. Gambling."

Simon shined a conker on his trousers as though it were a cricket ball.

"I had to sell some stuff: an antique sewing machine; some of my Nan's jewellery."

"I'm sorry."

"It's all right. I hardly remembered her. So anyway, I called this antiques bloke in. He gave me a good price, did me a big favour, as it happens. I was scrabbling around for a new pair of school shoes for Jack, it was that bad. A bit later though, he called in the debt." She threw another conker to the ground.

Simon put his arm around her, feeling her head fall onto his shoulder and her hair ripple across his cheek. "It's OK, Eleanor, it's done now, isn't it? You don't have to say any more. It's all right. It's going to be all right."

I want it to be all right, more than anything. But how can it?

Eleanor smiled and squeezed his knee. Simon could see she wanted to say more, and wondered what else there could be to say. The past was done, over; to have it hang between them was unnecessary. He turned her face to his, brushing a strand of hair from her cheek, and allowed his hand to rest on her face. "It *will* be all right."

The wind whistled through the dying leaves, shuffling them up to their feet.

"I've got mine now," she said at last.

"Your what?"

She held up a bright conker; it was the one he had first given her. "Race you to Paycocke's. Last one back's a ninny." She leapt from the wall and sprinted up the street, her coat flying behind her like a superhero.

Panting, Simon caught up with her at the giant front door.

Martin was in the study, the stepladder reaching up to the trapdoor, where an open black space gaped down at them. There was a pile of bent and rusty nails on Simon's desk. Sparrow grinned. "Easy as pie."

Simon looked up. "Great. Have you been up there?"

"Are you kidding? With these trousers?" He gestured down at his chinos, which meant nothing to Simon. "Oh, hi," he said, seeing Eleanor at Simon's shoulder.

"We've had a bit of a leak from upstairs," Simon said. "I just need to go up and make sure there's no damage." He dropped Martin's bag on the floor. "There's your stuff."

"Cheers, mate. I'll... I'll pop it in the spare room, shall I?"

"Yeah, you do that," Simon said.

Eleanor raised an eyebrow. "I'll just put the kettle on."

Simon unzipped his coat and threw it over the back of his chair. He gestured her into the kitchen and realised he was still holding his conker. "Right. This'll sort you out." He put the conker into the bottom oven of the Aga. "Coffee's in the larder," he called. "And when you're finished you can come and hold the ladder."

The aluminium stepladder creaked as he climbed, settling into a safe position. Simon poked his head into the square of darkness. Hell's teeth, it was black; he couldn't see a single thing. The gloom seemed to come down to meet him, to welcome him. "Eleanor," he called. "Could you pass me a torch? On the shelf over the washing machine." She brought him the thick rubber torch and he played its light around the entrance of the hole. The thin glow was sucked into the solemn chamber, not lighting more than a few feet ahead of itself.

Simon saw where the water had trickled through the bathroom floor and down the wall. It kept to the beam, pooled on the floor of the attic and found a crack in a rafter from where it dribbled through to his study. He felt the timbers and surrounding plaster; they were only slightly damp. Playing the torch around the dark space, he wondered what it could have been used for. Storage, maybe? He hauled himself in the last couple of feet and knelt in the oppressive silence. Curiosity overtook him and he started to crawl into the void.

The torch sliced through the darkness but not much more, its weak beam struggling to penetrate the obscurity. Simon raised dust as he moved and he coughed under its powdery assault. He felt as though he were crawling in the intestines of the house and he could see no end to the chamber. Looking behind him, his study light glared in the distance like a sunrise through the trapdoor. He hadn't realised he had come so far.

It felt warm and he loosened his clothing. He must be close to the chimney stack where the hall fire was burning, or was he over by the dining room? It was impossible to tell and he had lost all sense of direction. Curtains of webs hung across the beams, catching in his face as he moved forward. There was nothing here. The warmth fingered him, travelling down his spine and making him shiver. No, there was nothing here. "Nothing."

'Everything.' It was not a voice, only a hint of a thought or an echo, but it had not come from him. 'Everything is here.' He pushed his hand through his hair, feeling the wispy mesh of old webs in his fingers. He shook his head, releasing a little snowstorm of dust that made him sneeze.

The torch flickered and Simon shook it to maintain the steady stream of soft light. A million dust motes swirled in the narrow beam as he watched. Things could live and die up here, and nobody would ever know. 'Nobody would ever know.' Here in this womb of the house, he would be safe, always safe and warm. There would be no more problems; the house would always be here for him. He blinked, shaking away the thoughts, and tracked a spider trying to escape from the torch light. What was he doing? Looking for something. But what was it? Would he even know when he had found it? He crawled further into the darkness, trying to focus against the onslaught of dust that blurred his thoughts. It would protect him when the light went, when the batteries died. Yes, he could stay. 'Stay.' Then it would all be over. It would cocoon him in its soft embrace and he could rest. How he so wanted to rest. The torch flickered again and he shook it, blinking in the darkness. The light recovered and it trapped something in the periphery of his vision, something draped in cobwebs. 'Stay. Yes, stay.' Simon crawled around, his eyelids heavy, hypnotised by his own thoughts. He pushed the torch forward, feeling himself rocking on his knees, and saw the beam play over something dark and square.

'Stay.'

He pulled himself forward, his arms feeling numb. It was a box, a small metal box, the persistent acne of rust eating away at the corners as though trying to find a way in. A padlock rattled on the front. Simon passed the torch over it. 'Dalab', it said.

'Stay.'

He pulled his head back and banged into a rafter. His knees buckled from under him and he lost consciousness.

*   *   *

"Simon, Simon, wake up."

He opened his eyes to see Eleanor's white face hanging in the air like a theatrical mask. All around her it was night.

She put her hand on his cheek. It felt hot, as though it might brand him. "What?" he said.

"You've been gone ages," she said. "I came up to see where you were."

He tried to raise himself onto his elbows, but the weight seemed too great and his head was spinning. Images flashed in front of his eyes. Were they dreams?

"What happened? Did you crack your head? You must have knocked yourself out or fainted. It's so hot up here."

Simon nodded, unsure whether she could see him in the darkness.

"Come on, Simon, we need to get you down."

He held onto her shoulder and hauled himself up onto his side. She had come to get him, to save him. Save him from what? He had only half-memories of what had happened before he had passed out, memories which danced out of reach when he tried to grasp them. Nothing seemed real.

"Take it easy. Stop there for a second. I don't want you blacking out on me."

"It's OK," he said. Had there been voices? Was that what he remembered? Or had it been his conscience leading him on? Simon listened in the darkness and heard only his breathing. He reached out for Eleanor's fingers but his hand caught against something sharp. "Aah."

"What is it?"

The box, how had he forgotten it? It was the last thing he could remember; the only thing he remembered. "It's... I don't know what it is. Some kind of a box." He sucked the back of his hand, tasting his own blood. "Let's get out of here, Eleanor."

Eleanor crawled ahead, lighting the way, and in less than a minute they were at the trapdoor. Simon had thought that the darkness had stretched for miles. Eleanor climbed down first and he passed her the box, dappled with orange rust. Doubtless leaks and damp had visited the attic before. Simon felt Eleanor's arm curl around him, her thin fingers massaging his shoulders. It was a good sensation, a sense of belonging. "You know, I think I have the key to this," he said. "I can't be certain, but I recognise that name." He pointed to the embossed letters on the lock. "I found the key a couple of weeks ago in the dining room. What the hell did I do with it?" He turned over piles of papers and invoices. Damn, he really needed Alex to organise him.

Steps hammered on the west staircase. "Sparrow," Simon said. "I don't want him to see this." He shoved the black box behind a collection of Jiffy bags, took Eleanor in his arms and kissed her. Her startled reaction evaporated and she returned his urgency as Sparrow walked through the door.

Martin put his hand up to his face, as though shielding his eyes. "Oh, sorry, you guys. Didn't mean to... that is... well... great, yes, great."

Simon smiled at his friend's embarrassment. He didn't think he had ever seen Sparrow like this. He would apologise to Eleanor later. Or maybe he didn't even need to. He looked at Martin, Eleanor still in his arms, both of them smiling.

"Did someone mention coffee?" Sparrow said.

Simon waved a hand towards the kitchen. "Be my guest."

Sparrow disappeared and Simon inclined his head to Eleanor's so that their foreheads touched. They both laughed. He put his hand up to her face and saw that his fingers were besmirched with dirt and dust. "I'm just going to wash," he called out. "It was filthy up there." He took the box up to his bedroom and shoved it under his pillow.

*   *   *

"I never planned this," Eleanor said. *Not this part.*

"Sometimes it's better not to," he said. Her head dimpled the pillow and she stared up at the ceiling. Simon lay on his side, admiring her profile, thinking that this was a sight he could get used to, her lovely face beside him.

Eleanor pulled at his arm, yanking him towards her. He fell into her kiss as though into a warm bath, but stopped, distracted. The key.

"The box." He whispered it as though hoping to keep the secret from the walls. "I remember where I put the key." He swung his legs out from under the covers. The air was thin and cold. "I'll be back in a minute."

Rain machine-gunned the roof as he crept downstairs. Yes, he'd tossed the key into the in-tray, now he remembered; it was gathering dust with all the other things he was supposed to have done in the last two weeks. It felt cold in his hands, cold and unused. He padded back up the stairs, stopping at every creak.

"Got it?" Eleanor's face peeked from the covers, turning towards him.

He climbed in beside her, holding out two closed fists. "Take your pick." She tapped the left one and took the key from his palm. He kissed her. "Good choice."

"I'm known for it."

She turned the key over in her hand in the shallow light of the bedside lamp. Simon reached over and pulled the black box out from under his side of the bed.

The key turned stiffly in the padlock and he had to draw the U of the lock from its nest by hand. Opening the lid the smell of old paper spiralled upwards from the box. He unfolded a yellowing document and turned to Eleanor. "My God," he said. "It's a letter. From Imogen Holst."

Chapter 52
Panelling

Thomas put his hand in Ann's, small and delicate inside his huge fist. He bade Robert take her other hand, and Thomas himself took hold of Robert's free right hand so that they formed a circle. The bruises were now pale yellow on Robert's face, but Paycocke needed no reminder of the service his clerk had done him.

"God have mercy on us," Thomas said, the panelled room echoing with his voice. He bowed his head and recited the Pater Noster; the others did likewise, taking solace from prayer. It was not too late. They might yet leave this room unbreached, leave its secret untarnished, but at what cost?

Thomas saw that Robert's thumb touched upon Ann's pale wrist. He himself felt the cool pressure of Ann's other hand in his. He raised his head and let go of his friends' hands with reluctance. "It is time," he said.

*   *   *

Who else could I turn to but Edward? My mother, though a staunch ally regarding my beliefs in the supernatural forces at work within Paycocke's, would never countenance the tearing down of its beautiful linen fold panelling. Conrad Noel had made his feelings quite clear. There remained only Edward. I felt awful, as though I were trading on his feelings for me, but who else might I ask? He came to Paycocke's House with a readiness that tore at my heart, slipping in through the carriageway door lest he should be seen. My parents had gone to town to see some friends in Hammersmith, Iso's eyes searching me as they left, and a tide of betrayal swept over me. Yet how could I not take this opportunity? Already at breakfast, she and Gussie had started to talk of taking another house in the autumn, perhaps moving back to Thaxted or to London. All would then be lost and I might never know what lay at the heart of Paycocke's House.

I let Edward into the house through the back door. It was quiet and still, yet with the feeling of a leaf trembling in the wind, that a great change was imminent. It was as though the house knew that Edward and I would be the architects of that change, and it lay silent and waiting before us.

"Hello," he said, his eyes looking everywhere but at mine.

"Edward."

"I… I'm sorry if I got you into trouble."

"It doesn't matter."

"I'm sorry… I didn't mean…" He bit on his tongue, then finally found my eyes with his, those green orbs alive with sadness. "I'm not sorry," he said. "I love you, Imogen."

I could see what those words had cost him and he seemed to deflate before me. I dared not bridge the small gap between us. He sensed my unease and stood in the doorway, nervous to proceed further. What does one say in reply to those three words: 'I love you'? I can only hope that I do not live to say them to one who does not reciprocate my affection, for an unrequited love is the saddest and most desolate of all things. "Edward…"

He held up a hand. "You don't need to say anything."

I ushered him in, his face the epitome of melancholy, despair etched there as though it would never lift. I determined to raise his spirits and told him of Conrad Noel's revelations concerning diabetes. "Do you not see, Edward? There is hope."

He smiled, but a smile so wan I thought it might fall from his face, it drooped so. He looked down at the floor and shrugged. "Maybe."

I told him more about the vicar's experiences at Paycocke's and about the attic space that had captivated him so, and the story brought an unaccustomed glow into Edward's eyes. He probed me about Conrad's tale, as if it might cast light upon his own time up in that darkened chamber. I pointed out the carver's face in the entrance hall, and the way it looked so propitiously through the dining-room door and upon the panelling. I took a deep breath. "There is something behind those panels," I said.

Edward stared at the panelling. "I feel nothing," he said.

"There is something there," I repeated.

"I know." He looked at me. "What tools do you have?"

*   *   *

Simon and Eleanor felt yanked into the past, into 1923. The perfect copperplate was dated and faded to a dim blue, the language certainly formal, but dense emotion simmering between the words. Imogen's letter spoke of great injustices and a fearful dilemma and of assuaging her guilt with this act of writing. She would find a way to put right the wrongs of centuries past, but she knew not how. The letter talked of the attic chamber they knew, of its hold over them, of the carver's face and the way it watched over the panelling in the dining room, guarding its secret. She wrote of spirits trapped within Paycocke's House, of their desolation and yearning, and at this point her writing wavered, as though she had not been able to keep her hand from trembling. He finished the letter and flipped immediately to the first page, reading it through again.

"What do you think?" Eleanor asked.

Simon frowned. "I don't know… it's… there are no real details, Eleanor. A lot of imaginative ramblings about spirits and secrets and great wrongs being done, but no names, dates or concrete facts, as though she were somehow afraid and didn't dare mention them. And there was someone with her. She talks about 'us' and 'we'. Who could that be?"

"I can't imagine. Gustav, maybe?" She held his right hand in both of hers, stroking the hairs in the wrong direction, then stroking them back again. "What do you want to do, Simon?"

He squeezed her hand, pulled it up to his lips and gently brushed her fingers. "The panelling. I want to see what's behind the panelling. I want to take it down today."

She nodded and then smiled. "I'll help."

"But no Sparrow. I don't want him there."

"And the girls?"

"No." he laughed. "Don't ask me why. I just… I don't want them there, in case…"

"Ooooo…" Eleanor gave a quavering impression of a ghost.

"I'm not sure that's funny."

"You're not really serious, Simon?"

"I don't know. I just do not know."

"So no Cassie or Alex, no Martin... But me... I'm expendable?"

"No, no, no, I didn't mean..."

She winked at him. "Just teasing. I'll be here." Her pressure on his hand was tender. "How will you get rid of Martin? He seems... at home here."

Simon thought, chewing his bottom lip. "He can bloody well go to King's Cross."

"King's Cross?"

"It's a long story."

Martin complained over breakfast, reckoning that Land might follow him down to London, but Simon wasn't having any of it. "I'm running you down to Kelvedon in twenty minutes, so you'd best get ready. And don't come back without the book."

"Oh, Simon, mate, do me a favour."

"I'm bloody well doing you one."

Alex and Cassie ambled into the kitchen, arms hooked. Simon did a double-take; he didn't remember seeing them so pally since... since... ever. "Did someone mention going up to town?" Cassie said.

"Oh, yeah, Martin's going to pick up a book for me."

"Mind if we tag along? Alex and I fancied doing a bit of shopping."

Simon stared at his daughters. It was no surprise that Cassie would compromise on her hatred of Martin for a ticket to London, but since when had Alex liked going shopping, and with Cassie at that? "I thought you didn't have any money."

"Alex is subbing me until my next cheque comes through."

Martin grinned, his languor of the last few days disappearing. "Hey, girls, yeah, that'd be cool. I can show you a few of my old haunts."

Cassie and Alex looked at each other and burst out laughing. "What did I say?"

Gift horse, thought Simon, when he got back to Paycocke's.

Eleanor was standing in the entrance hall, looking almost ethereal, arms held out to him. He went to her and buried his face in her neck. Neither spoke.

"They didn't blink," she said.

"Huh?"

"The girls. Seeing me there at breakfast."

"It's something to do with being young," Simon said. "Remember that?"

"Vaguely."

He took her by the hand and led her through to the dining room. "I read Imogen's letter again," he said, staring up at the panelling.

"And?"

"Changes. She talked about changes." Simon brushed Eleanor's hair away from her eyes, leant forward and kissed her. She held him close to her, more tightly than he had ever been held. Her tongue probed his mouth and she bit his bottom lip, sending his heart into overdrive. "Changes," he said again.

She smiled and put a hand up to his face. "Changes," she repeated, drawing his mouth to hers.

Above them the spaniel alarms went off.

*   *   *

Thomas stood on the long oak board in the hall, his face close to the carvings rendered there by Kees. The Dutchman had been most discreet with his self-portrayal, most discreet indeed. Paycocke's hand hovered by the initials that the carver had chiselled from the beams. What would Margaret say if she were alive? How she had been his right hand, a well of advice from which he could draw without fear of it ever running dry. She had surely gone to Heaven, dear Margaret; her soul, unlike his father's, rested secure. Would she have him set aside this ridiculous quest? He thought not. She would have him finish what he had begun; always bring a task to its true completion, for good or for ill.

He followed the line of sight of the carved face through the door of the panelled room, where it rested upon the south wall.

Kees had spoken well and spoken true. Thomas prayed that he could bring to an end the torment of souls other than his father's, for Kees too had suffered much. It was too late for William Spooner, he reflected with sorrow. Much too late.

"Is this well, Thomas?" Robert called from the other room.

"Aye, well enough."

As he stood down from the board he heard Ann's laugh ripple through the silence like a small hand bell. "No, Robert," Thomas heard her say. "It is not seemly." He smiled at Robert's impatience, at the completeness of his love for Ann Cotton. Such had been his own feelings for Margaret, those innocent fumblings of the early years transforming into a deep and beautiful love. Ann was worthy of Robert's love, more than worthy. The two young people stood by the panelling, eyes bright with the hope of youth. What he would give to recapture that lustre.

"My friends," the clothier looked at the two young lovers, standing apart, as though some unspoken decorum ruled them in Thomas's presence. He wished that it were not so. He did not feel a father to these two, someone to be respected and held at a distance, a person whose very feelings should be coddled. Paycocke struggled to define his relationship with the pair, only knowing that there was a closeness that bound all three that should never be sullied. Even so, his heart fell at the thought of them together, for they would make a life betwixt them that would exclude him. As it should be. Thomas forced his spirits up. "The panel on the left," he said. "This is the one which should first be removed."

*   *   *

I gazed upon the panelling as though it were for the last time. Such things had it seen in its four hundred years: such merriment, despair, poverty, riches, happiness and misery. I ran my fingers up and down the perfect lines of the oak. So true was it that my fingertips could not discern a single flaw. I was flayed by doubt: suppose Conrad were right, that we should leave this alone and trust in the ways of the Lord? I looked at Edward for help, but knew that he could offer none. It had to be my decision. I gazed at the panelling, feeling rather like Howard Carter must have done when standing on the threshold to Tutankhamen's tomb.

"Listen, Imogen," Edward said.

"What is it?" I cocked my head.

"It is nothing," he said. "Only silence. It is a…"

I laughed, and my chuckle bounced around the panelled room. "Yes, you are right, Edward. There is nothing." Nothing but the silence. It was as though a… a peace had descended on the house, like a soft cumulus which breathed its way into every pore. The sense of unease that had been with me for weeks had gone.

Edward's brow wrinkled and he swallowed hard. "It knows," he said. "It knows we're coming."

I reached up for the leftmost panel, and felt the head of a large iron nail in its side. "We shall start with this one," I said. "Pass me the pliers."

*   *   *

"What is the National Trust going to say, you tearing down the panelling?" Eleanor tied her hair back into a pony tail. She had become a different person, the schoolteacher he had met two weeks ago at the door.

"Um… I was hoping they weren't going to find out," Simon said. "We don't open until next April. It should give us… well, I mean me, plenty of time to put it back how it was."

He removed the last nail holding the section of linen fold so that it rested on the bressumer beam above the fireplace. The panel felt loose, as though a small push from within would send it tumbling into the room. Simon held his hands against it, keeping it in place. Was he doing the right thing? Maybe he should leave well alone. What could be gained from this, other than the satisfaction of his curiosity? If only Imogen had said more in her letter, if only she had hinted at the secret lingering behind these ancient panels. Then perhaps he would be spared this step into the unknown. Or would he have taken it anyway? It was impossible to tell. He looked up at the section of panelling quivering to be released, then down at Eleanor. She smiled at him and mouthed something. She didn't say the words, just breathed them, but the shape of the syllables on her lips said more than he could imagine. How could he not step into the unknown? "Take the other end," he said.

*   *   *

Robert stacked the sections of panelling against the east wall. Behind them was brick. Kees had not spoken of brick, but then, Kees had not seen the efforts of William Spooner, and he could not know (or had not wanted to know) the workings of the builder's mind. To have used brick on an interior wall, and even then cover it with the sumptuous panelling, that was extravagance beyond anything Paycocke had commissioned. It was little wonder the house had cost him so much coin to build. But wherefore did Spooner make this wall?

Thomas's heart beat faster and he called for a thick chisel. Ann fetched him the tool and a blackened iron hammer. "'Tis no mason's chisel," she said, passing it to Thomas.

"No mind. It will do," he snapped, reaching down for it.

Ann did not let it go immediately, and for a second the tool acted as a conduit between the two. "Softly now, Master," she said.

Her eyes caulked the impatience leaking from him. "Aye," he said, and starting chipping away at the lime and sand mortar with less abandon. It was heavy work, although the mortar surrendered with an ease suggesting that it had been applied in haste. Sweat ran from Thomas's brow and his linen shirt was soon damp. His lungs heaved with the effort of breaking through Spooner's wall.

"Thomas." Robert's voice seemed distant.

At last one of the thin bricks showed signs of movement. It might be that the mortar at the centre had not yet taken. Paycocke had heard that this might be so, that it ofttimes was tens of years before the mortar might set true.

"Thomas."

The clothier scraped at the brick with his chisel and his fingers.

"Thomas, I beg you. I would be of some help."

"It is almost done, Robert."

"Aye, and so are you, my friend. I would work in your stead for a time. It is heavy labour and I have years over you."

Thomas shook his head, but he struggled to release the words, so exhausted was he. "It is my labour, mine own. What I begin shall I end." He leant forward and his forehead touched the cool brick. Life had certainly been too kind to him. He was weary indeed. It would be good to rest.

"I wish only to aide you in that goal, Thomas."

"Robert is right. Take your ease for a while. I will fetch you some small ale." Ann held out a hand.

Thomas astonished himself by taking her offered hand and stepping down from the wall, where he could see now from a distance how little progress he had made, compared to how much was still to be done. He passed the tools to Robert. "I thank you kindly, Robert."

"There is naught to thank." Robert clapped Thomas on the shoulder and rolled up his sleeves.

*　　*　　*

I held Edward's hand in mine, the silence screaming in my head. It was now too late, the panelling was down and before us was a brick wall, but no wall which would bring any pride to a builder's heart. The bricks were slotted together, but without mortar and in a haphazard fashion that suggested no care had been taken in its construction. None of the lines was straight and there were gaps between some bricks, hinting at a lurking darkness beyond.

"This is not how it was," Edward said.

"How do you mean?"

"You can see that this wall has been taken down before." He pointed to the black cracks of shadow between the bricks. "Taken down and then put back together. There is cement or mortar on some of the bricks. It has been put back together all right, but it's like a jigsaw where the pieces don't fit."

Edward was right. I stood back from the wall, examining

its shabby imperfections. It seemed to me that the daylight was diminishing outside, although it was still mid-afternoon. Long shadows licked at us where we stood, the brick wall in front of us challenging us to go further, challenging us with its very frailty, for it looked as though a single push would topple it.

"So?" he said. "What do you want to do, Imogen?"

I had no choice. We had come too far to turn back now. The panelling was removed; dust and detritus carpeted the floor beside the fireplace like a light fall of snow. The bricks beckoned, the cavity called me. I started to pull at the first one and it shuffled in my grasp.

* * *

"It weighs a ton," Simon said. "How on earth did they manage in the old days? They were only half the size we are."

Eleanor grunted. "They didn't spend all day in front of a laptop."

They rested the last section of panelling against the wall and stared at the gap the panel had opened behind it. It had once been a brick wall, but over the years it had collapsed inward, leaving a gap-toothed hole of darkness in its place. It exuded a smell of damp earth, of long-dead mould, of years of quashed longing for light.

"Blimey," Simon said. Eleanor put her arm round him as he stood there.

"Can you fetch me the torch?" he said.

She left the room and he was alone. Trees whispered in the breeze out in the street, yet the soft noise sounded as though it were inside the room with him, inside the hole in the wall, then inside his head like white noise. He felt light-headed and reached forward for something solid, feeling a loose brick with his right hand. He then groped with his left hand and the wall met him. Simon closed his eyes to steady himself while the world swam, and he tried to take a deep breath, but only inhaled dust and decay. Then Eleanor was beside him again, her hand on his shoulder. She arced the torch into the hole and cried out.

Simon gasped and turned away, his back to the cavern they had so easily opened. There were skeletons, two small skeletons. Children, just children. They looked as though they were pleading.

Chapter 53
Corrosion

Was this what love was like? The thought of Cassie ate at him, tore at him; this couldn't be right.

Fitz stared in the rear-view mirror and saw someone else. The eyes were different, softer, as though a glaze blurred their hard edges. His insides writhed. He parked the car in the Dutch Quarter and got out.

The rain was no more than a fine mist; the granite sky promised more to come but it would hold for now. He felt fresh, new, washed, but burnt alive by his feelings for Cassie. Chrissake, he hardly knew her. This was not what he had meant to happen. He closed his eyes and in his mind saw her turn towards him and laugh, her hair taking off in the wind. Her black hair, what was all that about?

The Escort had put in some mileage between Clacton and Coggeshall in the last few days. He had turned down jobs so he could be near her, breathe some of the same air, watch her from afar. He felt like a stalker, knew that she had really screwed him up. Or was it Paycocke's? Was the house doing this to him?

Fitz banged on the door of the squat terrace, and picked paint from the frame, peeling off like dead skin after sunburn. There was the thud of footsteps descending stairs and the door opened.

The guy was short, with dark hair so greasy that it was probably a couple of shades lighter when it was clean. He wore a cracked leather jacket over a black T-shirt that he must have slept in. More bizarrely, he was wearing a pair of bright yellow rubber gloves. "Yeah?" he said.

Fitz smiled and shook his head. "You shouldn't answer the door barefoot," he said, dropping his chin and taking Roach out with a jab. The punch corkscrewed from his shoulder and slapped through Roach's jaw like a whipped towel. Roach crumpled to the threadbare carpet. "That's for Cassie."

He stepped over Roach's prone figure into the house, pulling the door closed behind him. The place stank as though the air had been imprisoned there, beer, cigarettes and stale grease all mingling with the waft of lavender air freshener. Fitz wanted to be sick. He knelt down and opened Roach's right eye; there was no sign of life. Probably wasn't much when the guy was awake. He looked for signs that Cassie had been there, knowing all the time that she had, that she had spent time with this toerag, slept with him, loved him even. The thought shuddered through him and he went upstairs.

There was a birthday card on the bedside table, a picture of rabbits in a field. 'To Roach, love Cass.' He took a deep breath and clamped his eyes shut, letting the air escape in snatched bursts. It hurt. It wasn't supposed to hurt. 'Roach', the card said. Must be short for cockroach. A mug stood on the floor with a half-inch of liquid in the bottom. It might have been tea, but there were islands of powdery green mould rising from the surface. A crescent of dried red lipstick decorated the lip. Cassie's. Jealousy burned through him again and he wiped the stain from the mug, as though he could wipe Cassie from Roach's life. She deserved more than this. Picking up an old tobacco tin from the floor, Fitz opened its lid and snorted. Fixings. He tossed it down again and opened the top drawer of the chest. Fishing through some socks he felt something plastic, a small packet or bag. Careless, so careless, and so predictable. He held the clear bag up to the light: they looked like they might be uncut diamonds or something you would buy by the quarter at an old-fashioned sweet shop, dusty white rocks of crack. Nasty. He picked up Roach's mobile and called the police.

Fitz knew it wouldn't stick, not with his fist printed on Roach's jaw, but what the hell, it wouldn't hurt to give the man a little scare. He stepped by Roach on his way out, prodding him with the toe of his boot. Cold. Fitz smiled. He still had it. He still had it.

He felt good as he drove out of Colchester. Action energised him. Yeah, he could have both: Cassie and the house. Why not?

It was time to play his cards. He pulled over and dialled the Paycocke's number.

*   *   *

"What?" Eleanor was the first to speak, as though what they had seen had drained all the words from the both of them. "Who are they?"

Simon stared into the void, shaking his head. He stroked Eleanor's hair, twisting it between his fingers and kissing it. "They are Paycocke's secret," he said.

"How long…?"

"Who knows?"

Simon approached the skeletons' resting place as he would a sleeping child, creeping forward in case he woke them. They lay side by side in the darkness, the torchlight spilling through the opening, reflecting the stark whiteness of their skulls. So this was it. This was surely the reason for the sadness that shrouded the house. Death had watched over this room for, who knew, centuries maybe, begging for release. The sounds he had heard: the laughing; the footsteps; the alarms. A strange sensation gripped him, like a sexual awakening. It was the realisation of something new, an unexpected area of life that had hitherto lain dormant. The house had brought him to this place, holding his hand like a small child, leading him to this moment. He reached inside the hole, red brick dust falling from the jagged edges and sprinkling down like cayenne pepper.

"Simon?" There was a worried edge to Eleanor's voice, as if her lover were about to leave her. She moved forward and put her hand on his shoulder.

He said nothing, just held his palm over one of the skulls. Sadness radiated from it, pulling him towards it with its desperate power. As his fingers touched the bone he felt an awareness surge through him, something he could not contain or define. He closed his eyes to dam the tears. "They're children," he said. "Just children."

"But how…?"

"And why?" Simon shook his head, opening his eyes. He no longer tried to stem the emotion. "I don't know, Eleanor."

"We should call the police," Eleanor said.

His heart waged war with his head. "No. No, not yet. I want to understand."

She pulled him back from the opened tomb. "Simon. You shouldn't touch anything. It might be the scene of a crime."

Simon nodded. "It must be. I feel it. Something very bad has happened here." He threw off her hand and touched the other skull. It was cold and hard, yet so frail and exposed. He stroked the cranium and felt a purring in his own head.

"What are you doing?" Eleanor's tone increased in urgency. "You can't do this, Simon."

Simon splayed his fingers and rested them over the tiny bones of a child's hand. They felt so fragile they might crumble to dust, but wasn't that true of all young children? A tiny trusting hand, so delicate that one wrong move could spell the end. One's own children, forever a vulnerable, endangered species. You never escaped the feeling of exposure that having children gave you. He had tried so hard not to let his daughters down, but in the end failure was inevitable, wasn't it? "Please," he said. He saw confusion in her eyes, that she was seeing a Simon she had not known, that she was not sure if the 'please' was directed at her or at the child. He moved to calm her. "It's all right, Eleanor, it's all right. It's just that... I feel I've lived with these children since I arrived. They have a story to tell me. It's why I'm here. I've been sent here for this."

Her confusion morphed to concern and he took her hand, trying to offer a reassurance that he did not feel. "If you're sure...," she said.

He looked into the hole, staring intensely. "They still need me, Eleanor."

The sound of the telephone hacked through the silence between them. Simon looked towards the source of the ringing, without making any move to suggest that he would answer it. Eleanor frowned and started to go to the study. Simon held up his hand to stop her.

"It might be Jack," she said, and picked up the receiver. "Hello?" She flushed and passed the handset to Simon. "It's for you."

Simon grabbed the phone and stormed back into the dining room, closing the door and leaving Eleanor out in the entrance hall.

"Simon, mate."

"Hello? Who is this?" Simon stared into the opening they had made above the fireplace. *Who were they? Who were the children?*

"It's Fitz. Mark Fitzwarwick? Don't know if you remember me?"

"I…" *How did they get there? How long had they been imprisoned behind the linen fold panelling, behind the crumbling brick wall? How long had they been waiting?*

"I bought a book from you, the Thomas More, on eBay it was?"

"What? eBay? Oh, yeah, yeah, sorry… Look it's a bad time right now…"

"You're telling me. Look, I've got to speak to you, Simon."

"Now…"

"It's about Cassie."

"What?"

"I got to talk to you about Cassie, Simon. It's urgent. Life and death, mate."

"What the hell…? Is this something to do with Roach? Are you…"

"Roach? That fucker? Excuse my French, mate. He's out of it."

"Then what…?"

Fitz's voice was insistent and aggressive, but with a shade of uncertainty loitering in the background, a wavering something that Simon had not seen the first time they had met. "Look, fuck this for a game of soldiers. I got to see you, Simon."

Simon stared around the dining room. Brick dust was settling on the Jacobean table, the panelling leant against the wall, and beyond the lip of broken bricks lay the skeletons of two children. "I'm sorry, Fitz. Now is a *really* bad time. Later on, maybe.

Tomorrow." *Any time, just not now. What on earth did Fitz have to do with Cassie?*

"Three?"

"Three?" *What the hell did he mean?*

"Yeah, three o'clock - it'll still be light. I'll see you then, mate."

He was gone, Simon left holding the buzzing handset with questions on his lips.

Eleanor knocked on the door and pushed it open. "I'm sorry, Simon, I didn't mean…"

"It's OK…"

She took the phone from him. "I thought it might be Jack…"

"It's OK." He put a hand on her arm. "I'm sorry I snapped at you."

Her smile didn't look as though it belonged, apologising for its presence.

"We don't really know each other, do we?" he said, drawing her to him. "It's all been happening so fast, I forget that I don't actually know you yet."

No, you don't know me, because if you knew me…

Eleanor took a deep breath. "We can work on it, Simon." She looked through the open door behind him. He felt protective of the room, of the secret that Paycocke's had held and he couldn't move from the doorframe, as if guarding it from Eleanor. He knew he was being irrational, but he could not let her hand this over to the police. Not yet.

"What do you want to do?" she said.

"Give me some time, just today, a few hours. I want to know… to find out what happened here. Then we'll report it."

Eleanor put the phone back on its cradle. "Who was that, anyway?"

Simon looked at her, wondering why she asked. "Just some guy. He bought a book from me a while ago. Why?"

"Oh, no reason. I just thought I recognised the voice. Must be a school parent or something."

Since opening the panelling Simon had felt a barrier between them, a force field stopping him from sharing with her what he felt. He didn't want that and held out his arms. Eleanor kissed him on the forehead and he brought her face to his, sensing a resistance but doing it anyway, finding her lips with his and feeling a surge as they touched. He took her hand and they went back into the dining room.

A father had lost two children. Had he known the loss? Had he come home one day and found his children missing? Had he known of their deaths, or had they simply disappeared and never been found? Maybe that unknown father had spent the rest of his life in a desperate, futile search for them. Or had he seen them dead, and in that way suffered a lifetime's torment of guilt, rage and helplessness? Or maybe he had been their killer, walling them up behind the panels. Would the truth ever be known? And what of their mother? What did she know?

Simon hugged Eleanor close to him. He wondered if he could really bear to look again at the skeletons, the thought terrorising him that this might have been Cassie or Alex. Cassie *or* Alex. He loved them both, equally.

"Simon. Go back." Eleanor let go of his hand and peered into the hole, staring inside. "The… the one on the left. Go back."

He played the torch where she pointed and looked into the hole. "Where? I don't see anything."

"By the… ribcage. Maybe you can't see it from your angle. There's something there."

He moved behind her, looking at the bodies from her vantage point, and pierced the swarm of dust motes with the light. Something winked at him from the cage of the child's bones. "It's a brooch," he said. "A brooch or a pendant or something."

Chapter 54
The Dining Room

Suddenly the laughter was all around us: in the room; coming from every wall; in my head; everywhere. Absolutely everywhere. It was as though I were walking through clouds, soft white wisps caressing my cheeks. The panelling somehow receded from me and I fell.

"Imogen, Imogen." Edward. His fingers were on my cheeks, icicles burning my face with cold. He shook me. "Imogen. Wake up."

I opened my eyes to see his face inches above me, his own eyes red-rimmed and damp. I saw my flickering reflection plunged in their green depths, two small, pale versions of myself. "Edward." I felt so incredibly weak.

"You fainted," he said. He was bending over me, concerned, but unwilling to touch me, as if he dared not trust himself.

"Did you hear them?"

"Who?"

"The children," I said. "They were so happy."

He pulled away from me. "What children?"

"They were so happy," I repeated. I gave him my hand. Edward looked at it with cowed eyes, almost expecting it to bite. He chewed his bottom lip and helped me up. "Did you not hear them?"

"You've had a bit of a fall," he said. "When you took that brick out, the rest just collapsed like a mortar shell had hit the wall and they fell into the hole. There was a cloud of dust as though death itself were climbing out. I turned my back, choking with it, but you just walked straight into the cloud, and then you fell, just slumped to the floor."

"And the laughing?" I leant back against the table leg, struggling for focus.

Edward shook his head. "There was no laughing, Imogen.

Leastways, none I heard." His mouth was set in a grim slash and he worked with a thumb at the tiny crescents of dirt underneath his fingernails.

I put my fingers to my temples. My head hurt; I must have knocked it when I fell. I looked at the wall over the fireplace. Fortunately the bricks had fallen inside the wall rather than into the room, otherwise the disarray would have been much greater. Out in the entrance hall the Westminster clock chimed five times. The effort of opening up the panelling had taken us much longer than I had expected; my parents would soon be home. Dust still rained over the chasm.

Edward held my hand, but not tenderly. He tried to pull me back from the hole. "Imogen," he said. "We should not have done this."

"It's all right, Edward." My heart careered around my chest as I took a step forward, displacing the dust particles that whirled around my face. When I saw the bodies I was not shocked, not surprised even. It was as though I had been prepared for this moment, that every second of my existence had been spent in waiting for this confrontation. There were two small forms, lying side by side, each covered with a sheet or a cloth, and although it was not clear what they were, I knew. I just knew. "We have found them, Edward."

He shuddered. "What is it, Imogen?" He dared not come closer. His face was streaked with grey smudges, but it was so ashen that it was hard to tell where the dirt ended and his fear began.

"We must be quick, Edward. We have only an hour at most."

I lifted the cloth, and there was a child, or rather the bones of a child, white and innocent, dead years or hundreds of years it was impossible to tell. "I am sorry," I said. "I am sorry I did not come sooner." Dust puffed up from the cloth and settled again, like sleep after a long journey.

"What are we going to do, Imogen?" Poor Edward stood back like a small child. I pulled the cloth from the hole and held it against my heart. "We will do what is right, Edward. We will do what is right." I shivered, trusting in God and my heart to let me know what was the right thing to do. "For now we must put the panels back. My parents must not know. For the moment this shall be our secret, Edward."

Edward could not put back the linen fold fast enough. He worked with a fever and a robustness that I had not hitherto imagined he had. Yet he would not look into the hole. It was as though he expected something to escape from it at any second, escape from this vault and taint him. It was impossible to mend the fallen wall from without and in any case we simply did not have the time, but I did not see that as important. We would come back to this when I had solved the conundrum, when I discovered what would be fitting. Once the panelling was righted, I kissed Edward on the cheek.

"Thank you, Edward. This means more to me than you will ever know."

He blushed through his grime. "Me too," he murmured.

"You must go. It would not do for my parents to find you here. I shall see you tomorrow, tomorrow evening."

"When?"

"Um… Eight o'clock, at St. Peter's. Rain or shine." I tried to be light-hearted, although I felt anything but.

He left through the back door without looking at me, steeling himself so that he would not have to see my face. I wrestled not to show the pity I felt.

I brushed away the dust and debris from the wall so that it looked as it had. I no longer had the sense of unease that had been my companion during these last few weeks, but something did not look right. The oak panelling that Edward had replaced - it looked as though it had been disturbed, as though it had been the source of major upheaval. I touched it, promising the spirits within that I would procure peace for them. The piece of cloth I had taken from the body was fragile, like rice paper. I held it to my cheek and smelt its decay. I had time only to put it under my bed when I heard my parents at the front door. The cloth poked out from under the hanging quilt and it was then that I saw the mark on the corner of the material, faded to a shadow, but still recognisable and unique: the ermine tail merchant's mark of the Paycocke family.

*   *   *

Edward trudged up the hill, seeing every crack in the path, every pothole, every flaw. His father would be at the Grey by now, taking anaesthetic to prepare for another night beside his dying wife. Edward wished he had something to dull the amputation of his heart. The house would be quiet, as quiet as death. And maybe that would be the truth. Perhaps he would find his mother gone. It would be good. Then he could leave – there was nothing for him in Coggeshall now.

Imogen had kissed him on the cheek. He rubbed the place and imagined he could still smell her cool clean scent on his fingers. Edward sighed. The kiss meant nothing. How could it? It was something she might give to a child or a maiden aunt. Her hug on leaving was even worse, a pretence of proximity that had stolen his dignity. He would leave tonight. He was no more than a clockwork toy to her, something to be wound up to do her bidding. Love? What use was love? What was the point of it?

Edward had seen nothing in Paycocke's House, nothing but the bones of a past long gone. What good would it do to resurrect that past? Imogen was busying herself with the dead when she should be looking to the living. Dry dust, forgotten people, there was nothing in Paycocke's but memories, and his own had turned sour, like milk left too long in the sun.

There was a light on upstairs in the house, a small, dim light that turned the red curtains gold. It looked as though the sun were setting in his mother's bedroom. What had Imogen said? Something about research in Canada. He closed his eyes, batting the flutter of hope away. Nothing would change. Nothing ever did. He would leave tonight, just pack a few things and go. To meet her tomorrow at the church would achieve nothing. She had never loved him and she never could. The house had come between what might have been. To see her one more time would only deepen the hurt and make everything harder. He had to forget her.

Edward looked in on his mother for the last time. He knew it must be by necessity the last time. She took up so little room in the bed, her silhouette like a broomstick, without substance, with no more life than the bodies he and Imogen had seen walled up behind the panelling.

She opened her eyes, smiled at him. He could not bear to smile back. "Edward," she said.

"Mammy."

"Come here, son."

He faltered at the door of the room. The air was foul and used up, as though his mother's illness had tainted it.

"Been with your girl?"

Edward nodded, not wanting his mother to feel the burden of an outright lie.

"She's beautiful. Imogen, isn't it?"

He wanted to stop the warmth that spread through him when he heard her name. *Would this feeling ever stop?* He held his mother's hand hanging limp on the eiderdown.

"Really beautiful."

He nodded, feeling the tears of hopelessness start to come.

"Don't cry, son."

Guilt stabbed him because he was not crying for her, but for a dying love. He forced a smile. His mother sank her head back into the pillows and lay still for an age. Edward stroked her hand, the skin loose and grey. He knew that he had to meet Imogen tomorrow, had to see her.

"I love you, mammy," he said.

*   *   *

I had not seen my parents in such good spirits for many a week and it soon became apparent why. They did not seem to notice how grubby I was from our exploits in the dining room and talked only of one thing.

"London would be so bright for Christmas."

"I might get this wretched symphony behind me."

"It is imperative that we leave before winter. Conrad said the garden floods after heavy rain."

"I might take up my teaching post at St. Paul's once more."

They would not speak of the unease that they had felt at Paycocke's House, of the melancholy of the place that was driving them away. I wanted to shout out that I had discovered what lay behind its desperate sadness, but I could not, not until I had solved its mystery.

"But what of Paycocke's?" I said.

My mother winked at me, a sly gesture that spoke of something known only to the two of us.

Gussie stepped in. "Old Buxton has different plans for this place," he said. "I do not mind admitting that I have never truly settled here. In spite of its beauty, it is not wholly comfortable. Of course that is part of its charm, but when one is trying to create…"

The sentence hung in mid-air, as though it did not know which way to turn. I was pleased that my father had a hook on which to blame his lack of productivity, and that he might now continue to pursue the greatness of which he was capable. However, I was saddened to perceive Paycocke's in such a role as scapegoat. "But what is Buxton to do?" I felt a pang of worry assault me. Suppose he were to demolish the house? What would become of the souls that had resided here for so long? I simply had to get upstairs and examine the shroud; it might hold some key to the conundrum.

Iso saw straight through my worry. She was my mother, after all, the closest person in my life. "Do not fret, Imogen. The house will be in good hands. He has decided to pass Paycocke's on to the National Trust."

"The National Trust?"

"A fine institution," said my father.

"Then it is to be a museum?" A horror came over me. Paycocke's was not meant to be a museum. The house needed love and compassion.

"I do not know the precise details. However, the National Trust has a worthy record in assuming responsibility for buildings of national importance. I have no doubt that they will take the best possible care of Paycocke's."

A panic washed over me. "But when is this to happen?"

Gussie rubbed his hands together. "We will leave within a fortnight."

*   *   *

The house echoed with activity over the following days. Friends and tradesmen passed by to give us their best wishes. Others, I have no doubt, were pleased to see us depart, those such as Edward's father who had always equated our Germanic surname with the heinous enemy, and who sought to ally Gussie with their absurd stereotypes of German soldiers. There was no opportunity to be in the house alone, to examine the panelling and its secret room once more. The cloth I had taken from the child's body remained the only link I had. It had once been a rich cream, but the dirt of centuries had infiltrated its weave and broken down the delicate threads of colour. In the evenings after bidding my parents good night, I painstakingly rubbed at the layers of filth. The Paycocke's family merchant mark became clearer, its three round pins astride the forked ermine tail. I was awed to be holding a piece of Thomas Paycocke's cloth. The children could not be his, as he died without issue, so the question remained: how had they come to be interred behind the oak panelling? And who were they?

If only, if only Edward had not left, if only our last meeting at St. Peter's had not been so fraught, so charged, he might still be here now, and I might not carry the burden alone. Are we always to be held hostage by our decisions, always to rue an action we have taken and wonder whether a different outcome might have ensued? The thought burrowed into me and would not let me sleep.

It was two days later that I noticed the orientation of the linen fold panels. I was in the room with Gussie, packing the best china. He was staring at the linen fold above the fireplace, wrinkling his brow.

"Something is different, Imogen. I do not know what, but something is different."

458

I scanned the floorboards, looking for evidence. We had cleaned up jolly thoroughly, but I could not help but inspect and re-inspect our handiwork. It must be how a murderer felt, going back to the scene to check for bloodstains when he knew he had already cleaned them up. It could not be the spirits' presence that disturbed my father, for if anything there was no activity in the room, nor indeed had there been elsewhere in the house since I had opened the panelling. It was as though Paycocke's and its inhabitants were awaiting my next move. Yet Gussie was right. Something *was* different.

"What do you think, Imogen?"

I tried to be non-committal, shrugging my shoulders.

He shook his head, frowned, and wrapped another saucer in paper.

Then the sun rose on my thoughts. No, it could not be. My eyes were magnetised to the panelling and I almost dropped the cup I was holding. Edward had replaced the panels upside down, I was sure of it. I dared not go closer with my father in the room, but I scrutinised their orientation. Yes, the fluted edge now lay at the bottom, with the flat edge at the top. It was all I could do to stifle a gasp.

"Imogen, my dear, are you quite all right?"

"I just feel a… a little dizzy." I averted my eyes from the panelling in case he guessed what had happened.

He took my arm and led me into the entrance hall. "Perhaps some fresh air." Dear Gussie, how I ached with the pain of deceiving him, when all he offered in return was tenderness and love.

"Yes, yes, thank you." I sat in the courtyard and breathed the cool air, the first autumn air.

I had to speak to Edward; he would know what to do and how to put the panelling right again.

Edward was not to be found and it transpired that he had left Coggeshall immediately after our meeting. No one knew where he had gone. Not wanting to risk the wrath of his father, I went to see Doctor Phipps, since he visited the Daynes' house regularly. He had no idea of Edward's whereabouts and was about to make a house call, if I would permit. He stared at me, remembering the perceived professional slurs at our last meeting. I asked after Mrs. Daynes.

"As well as can be expected. These things take time."

I struggled to control my anger at these platitudes. What he meant was, 'She is taking her time to die.' "Have you heard of Banting and Macleod?" I said.

He sniggered. "Music hall?"

"The physicians. Great scientists," I said, assuming a greater height than the doctor.

"Indeed." He moved forward as if to pass me, but I blocked his way. "Miss Holst…"

"They have been working on a cure for diabetes."

His mouth drew together as though he sucked upon a lemon. "A cure?"

I relayed what Conrad had told me. It is only in romantic novels that the odious remain so, unable to be touched in their hearts. I believe everyone has good within and in that moment saw the decent side of the doctor, a man struggling only to care for folk.

"Well, well, well," he said. "Insulin, you say?" I nodded, and he mirrored my nod, his mind ticking away in the distance. "Well, upon my word, this is quite some news. Banting. Macleod. This may have a discernible impact. Goodness me."

I had never thought to see him smile and I could not return his humour, for my thoughts were strangled by the loss of Edward and more immediately by the fate of his mother. How would she manage without him? How could he possibly have left her? "Might Mrs. Daynes be helped by this development?"

"She still lives," he said. "Against my judgement she still lives. And while there is life…" He inhaled a sharp breath. "But I do not think so. I do not deal in false hopes, Miss Holst. As wonderful as this discovery is, my professional opinion," he lowered his spectacles, and peered over the top of them at me, "which I am aware you hold in scant regard, my professional opinion is that it will be too late for Mrs. Daynes." Phipps clasped his hands together and brought them up to his chin, his eyes filling with sympathy. In that second he became a bigger man than I had thought possible. How must it be to be able to set the greater good of mankind against the death of people you know, have seen born and grow and wilt? "Yet, you never know." He was not so callous that he would not drop a small scrap of hope. "I will see what might be done."

Oh, Edward. It was hopeless without him. Where on earth had he gone? Yet I knew in my heart that I had driven him away, and that the awfulness of our final meeting would always plague me.

With every passing hour I felt the cloud of despair descend on me and on Paycocke's House. How could I put right the panelling without him? We were to leave the house in a matter of days and still nothing was resolved. It felt as though our shared experiences had torn us apart.

The spirits seemed to sense my burgeoning unease and the euphoric peace that had accompanied the opening of the panelling was replaced by a simmering unrest. I heard whispers in the dining room and took to avoiding entering alone if I could help it. Once in the entrance hall with Gussie, I heard a plaintive cry that tore at my heart. My father did not even react and I took the wail as being intended for me alone. Was it to be my fate to suffer for my inertia?

My labours at the ragged piece of cloth had revealed a royal coat of arms: three lions passants quartered with fleur-de-lys. The patterns had almost faded to obscurity, but I could still pick out what once had been vibrant golds and reds and blues. Excited as I was by the discovery, when I looked it up in the encyclopaedia I found that not only did it represent the arms of Henry VIII, king at the time of Thomas Paycocke's death, but it was also that of a clutch of the other Henrys, as well as an assortment of Edwards, with the odd Richard, Mary and Elizabeth thrown in. There was still no clue as to what had happened in Paycocke's House.

There was no alternative. I would have to pass on my discovery. The footsteps of authority would resound throughout the house. It would become quite the tourist attraction, yet another ghost tale for the Coggeshall collection. Still, it was the right thing to do: the bones might be buried in consecrated ground and there would at last be peace in the house, even if the riddle were never solved.

I sought out Gussie. He had been so much more animated since the decision to leave Paycocke's House had been made that I was filled with happiness for him. Whatever the truth of the matter, he was convinced that the house was draining the talent and soul from him. A fresh start would allow him to flourish. I just wished that I had more time. He was in his study, packing books. I took a deep breath – so be it. Gussie would know what to do.

"Why, Imogen, have you come to offer assistance?" He winked at me.

"Yes, of course." I smiled, wondering how best to turn the conversation to my ends.

As is usual with books, they might sit upon the shelves untouched and unobserved for many years, but the minute they must be moved, each assumes a singular importance.

"Why, *De Profundis*." Gussie brandished an old grey volume at me. "Wilde, you know, in gaol – you simply must read it, Imogen. Startling. Poor chap." I had to wrest it from his grasp on pretence of interest, so that I could pack it and keep the momentum alive. However, it was only minutes later that 'Practical Herb Growing' suddenly captivated my father. He almost had me sold on the properties of rosemary before I was able to house the book with its fellows. It seemed there was to be no easy entrance for me.

Gussie sensed my disquiet. I have always found it difficult to suppress my feelings from those who know me well. "Imogen, there is something amiss." He passed me another volume and I opened it at random, the better to avoid his eyes when I launched into my plea.

"Not amiss, exactly," I said.

He raised my chin. "Come now. I know this upheaval is a nuisance, but it is the right thing to do in the long term."

I nodded.

"It is the house, is it not?"

"Yes, I…"

"I saw you fall in love with it on the day we moved in. It was such a bright and happy day that I thought I myself might explode."

I remembered the day clearly, the dreamlike qualities of discovering Paycocke's, exploring its labyrinth of rooms and marvelling at the wonderful carvings. If only I could have that day again, when anything seemed possible and the weeks stretched ahead, warm and endless. I looked down at the book he had passed to me, stroking the morocco binding so that my father should not see the foetal tear growing in my eye. I flicked through the foxed pages, trying to distract myself.

"Do not fret, my little princess. All is for the best."

"'In this, the best of all possible worlds.'" I finished the Voltaire quotation. It was one that I had shared with Gussie ever since I was a tiny girl, a small tie that bound us whenever things went wrong. "Yes," I said.

"Thomas More," he said, looking at the book I now held. "That was written about the time this house was built. Incredible to think, isn't it?"

Words floated from the page: 'Kyng Edwarde of that name the fowrth, after that hee hadde lyued fiftie and three yeares, seven monethes, and five dayes...'. I turned the pages. I did not know why, just that I must. My father receded from my focus and I scarcely knew that he was there. I heard voices in my head, soft whispers encouraging me and urging me on.

And then I knew; in that moment I knew precisely what had happened. The enormity of it flooded me and I felt as a drowning man must, reaching upwards for help and finding none. I dropped the volume. It could not be, I thought. Yet in my heart I knew it was so and the whispers inside my head concurred, urging me to accept it.

I had solved the mystery, and in solving it, had made my predicament worse than ever. How could I now reveal the secret of Paycocke's House to the world? Those poor children. Those poor, poor children. What could I do now, for them and for myself?

Chapter 55
Relics

"What is it?" Eleanor held out her hand.

Simon felt a pull from the object, as though he could not let it go. It was warm in his palm, at home there. It needed him.

"Simon?"

"Oh, sorry, Eleanor. I was just... just wondering what it was." He smiled, but knew there were secret thoughts chiselling away at the trust between them. He passed her the piece of jewellery, masking his reluctance with chatter. "I've never seen anything like it. It looks like it's gold. Lord knows when it's from. Any ideas?"

The piece was larger than he had thought, a diamond shape, or was it a rhombus, about two and a half inches wide, too large to be a simple brooch. Eleanor rubbed at the edge with her thumb. "I think you're right," she said. She held it up to the light. "There's an inscription around the edge. I can't see what it is exactly. We'll have to get a magnifying glass. What about the stone?" It was not the gold that had glinted at Simon from its hiding place inside the skeleton, but a large blue oval gemstone set into the apex of the diamond. "Is it a sapphire?"

Simon felt the stirrings of a sense of possession. He had found the piece. He lived there. It was he who should be holding it. He needed to examine it in peace, by himself, alone. It was his.

"Simon? Are you OK?"

He was breathing heavily and he felt small trains of sweat roll down his cheeks. Bloody hell, what was he thinking of? "Yeah, I'm fine." He tugged at the neck of his shirt. "I'm just a bit warm."

"Warm? You're having me on? It's freezing." She put a hand to his face and he saw that she was right, her fingers were icy.

Simon tried to be calm. "Yeah, it does look like a sapphire, doesn't it?"

"You know what, Simon? I think it's some kind of box. Look at this edge. A snuff box maybe, something like that." She held it out to him and Simon almost snatched at it. Eleanor showed it to him closely. "Look." On one side Simon could see a primitive hinge mechanism. "It won't budge," she said.

"Let me try."

"Just a sec."

"Eleanor." He could not control the edge that crept into his voice.

"All right, all right." Her eyes were fiery, glinting orange in the dim light. What was happening to them? She gave him the box and with it came calm and reason. He kissed her cheek.

"What was that for?"

He laughed. "I don't know. Does there have to be a reason?"

"No," she said. "Of course not." Eleanor glanced at her watch. Her wrist looked impossibly slim and fragile. "Look, I need to get back and fix some dinner for Jack. He'll be home soon. I don't want him to think...."

"Sure. I'll see what I can find out about this." Simon turned over the small box in his hand. It was too flat to be a snuff box; it looked more like a cigarette case for midget Sobranis. He struggled with his feelings, realising that he was glad she was leaving, that he would be left alone with the case. He bit his lip. No, that was wrong. It was all wrong. That was not how he felt. He took a deep breath. "Pop back after lunch if you can."

Simon kissed her at the door, a perfunctory kiss, the kiss of the long-married. Something had changed. He was worried.

The house was silent, as though he now existed in its vacuum. Only he. Was this what the house wanted, him alone? He shook his head to dislocate the thought and took the golden case through to the breakfast room where the Aga simmered. He had wanted her to go. Why? For the same reason as he had not wanted his daughters there when he opened the panelling. Was it to protect them, or to protect himself? He couldn't tell. He placed the box on the table in front of him and stared at it. If it was as old as the house it would be worth a fortune. Treasure trove. Not that he cared. Money had meant nothing to him his whole life, as the girls reminded him when he forgot to pay their allowances. It wasn't money that drove him on, but knowledge. In front of him was something that might not have been seen for centuries. It sparkled under the halogen spotlights as he wiped it with a damp cloth, revealing the enamel lettering which ran around the rim. He would have to report it, both it and the bodies, that was clear. Absolutely clear. No Question. Not a shred of a doubt.

But not yet. No, not yet.

As he removed the dirt from the case, working at the black fissures with a soft toothbrush, a picture emerged on the front, the crucifixion worked into the gold. Who had put this with the bodies? Why had they been walled up there, a secret never to be told? What he would give to keep this piece. If only he had been alone when they had found it, it would be his. He put it back on the table, trying to organise the rush of thoughts which threatened to overwhelm him. What would he really have done had Eleanor not been with him? He dreaded to think. The legacy written on the outer edge of the artefact became clearer: 'Ecce agnus dei qui tollis peccata mundi.' Simon's Latin was no match for Sparrow's, but he had picked up a word or two over the years: 'Behold the Lamb of God, who taketh away the sins of the world.' What was it?

Simon remembered the letter, Imogen's letter, perhaps there was some clue hidden in there. It had made little sense when they had read it together, he and Eleanor, when it had not crossed his mind that they should *not* do it together, stumbling over the faded blue words, trying to piece together the Edwardian ramblings. Simon opened the thick pages once more, and re-read the long paragraphs.

So Imogen Holst had taken down the panelling, too. It read as though she had had some help, although no other accomplice was mentioned by name. Simon could believe it, though – that oak had weighed a ton. She must have seen the bodies, but had elected to do nothing about them, leaving them entombed. Why? He read on, a little more sense filtering through to him now that he himself had seen what lay behind the linen fold.

'Upon reflection I wish that I had never disturbed the panelling, for it has brought me only the misery of dilemma, and I shall spend the rest of my life debating whether I have done the right thing. In truth it is what I have not done that causes me the most grief. I have denied souls their right to peace and salvation and their laments shall pursue me for the rest of my life. I pray that what I have done has been for the greater good, to avoid war and the deaths of thousands.'

'To avoid war.' 'The deaths of thousands.' What did she mean?

The upside-down panelling, that had been Imogen's work, of course. She must have put the panels back the wrong way around and somehow she had not had the time to correct her mistake. Or she had not wanted to take down the linen fold a second time, having discovered the secret of Paycocke's House. Simon thrust her letter down on the table. And she wouldn't tell him, damn it, she wouldn't tell him.

She wanted to do 'the right thing.' Who knew what 'the right thing' was? Who ever knew? He picked up the case again, felt it tingle at his touch, come to life. It must be a trick of the light. As he turned it over between thumb and finger, his nail caught on a sharp jagged edge, encrusted with dirt. He fiddled at it with a toothpick, urging the tiny crust of filth out, and in doing so released a minuscule pin. The box sprang open and inside was a small splinter of wood, so dry and insubstantial that it looked as if it might crumble to dust if he tried to pick it up. *My God. Yes, my God, absolutely.*

The telephone rang. Simon glanced up, but ignored it. After half a dozen rings he heard his own voice kick in on the answer phone, telling the caller about Paycocke's opening times. The beep sounded.

"Simon, it's me, Eleanor. Please pick up. I think I know what it is."

Simon interrupted her message. "It's a relic case, isn't it?"

"Yes, I think so. How…"

"I opened it."

"And…"

The sound of her voice on the telephone washed through him. Yes, he did want to share this with her; he wanted to share everything with her. "Can you come over? Now."

*   *   *

Eleanor took the reliquary from him. "It's incredible," she said. "You've cleaned it up beautifully, Simon."

"Open it. The tiny pin at the back."

Her delicate fingers sprang the catch and she saw the splinter of wood. "Is this...?"

"Even if it isn't, whoever put it there thought that it was. I don't dare touch it; it might disintegrate."

"What was it doing in there?"

"I think it was a talisman. Whoever laid it with the bodies wanted God to protect their souls."

"The murderer?"

Simon shrugged. "We can't be sure that they were killed, but it is suspicious. Maybe it *was* him." He closed the case and pointed out the inscription. "It shows up a lot clearer now, 'The Lamb of God, who takes away the sins of the world, have mercy on us.' It could be that the killer was making a desperate attempt to have his sins forgiven."

"Or maybe an act of contrition?"

"Who knows? It would have been quite a sacrifice to conceal the relic - a piece of the true cross. I bet it was worth a fortune even then."

"If it was real?"

Simon snorted. "If? Yeah, if you added up all the wood that was supposed to have come from Christ's cross, you'd have a whole forest. But whoever put it there was convinced that it was the real thing. It's an article of faith. It's non-negotiable."

Eleanor put the golden case back on the table and walked over to the window, staring out at the courtyard.

Simon could feel her probing him, asking him to let go, but not wanting to look at him, not wanting to force his hand. He had to say something. "Who put it there? I just wish I knew who put it there."

"Imogen Holst?"

He shook his head. "I don't think so. It doesn't feel right. Not when you read her letter. It just doesn't seem like the sort of thing she would do. I think she didn't see it. Imogen opened the panelling, that much is clear, but she had to put it back in a hurry and ended up missing the case." Simon sighed. "She didn't bloody well miss the meaning of what had happened, though, did she? I think she knew exactly. There must be some more clues. Anyway, how come you know about the case? You had some kind of epiphany?"

"Nothing much, really. We've been doing Tudors with Year 6," she said. "That's why I thought it was a reliquary. That's why we're coming to visit you next week."

"Heck, I forgot all about that."

Eleanor laughed. "I'm not surprised. You've had other things on your mind. Anyway, I've been doing some background reading to stay ahead of all the daft questions..."

Simon approached her from behind, putting his arms around her and laying his head on her shoulder. "There are no stupid questions, only stupid answers."

"I think the case dates from that period, maybe even earlier."

"Paycocke?" The thought surged through him like mescaline. He suddenly found the house oppressive. "You think Paycocke put it there?" he repeated. If it were true, the skeletons and the talisman had been there for nearly five hundred years. "I need some air," he said.

Simon opened the back door and walked out into a maelstrom of spinning leaves; they crunched underfoot and caught in his hair. He sat on his haunches at the top of the garden and examined the lavender. It had grown leggy, too woody, it would have to be replaced or severely pruned. Of course they would have to turn this thing over to the authorities, should have done it already. It was not a part of their past, nor their future. They could not allow it to come between them.

He felt hands on his shoulders. He didn't turn to see her; he didn't need to. It was her, he knew that; it could only be her. He reached up and touched her cold, slender fingers. "I love you," he said.

"I love you too, Dad."

Chapter 56
Everything Hath an End
and a Pudding Hath Two

What had his father done? Thomas stepped back from the ruined wall, horrified. What torment had John Paycocke visited upon him? And in very truth, it was his own father who must be culpable, for did not his own merchant's mark, bright as a new groat, mock him from the folds of the cloth?

There was a hand at his elbow. "Master Paycocke?" He felt Ann's weight upon him, and was not sure at that instant who supported the other. This was no sight for a maid.

Robert joined them and they were once again a triumvirate, although it did not escape Thomas that Ann had not clung to her lover at that terrible moment of revelation, but to him as one might seek strength from one's father.

Robert Goodday broke the silence with slow, measured words. "What manner of blasphemy has occurred here?"

Thomas shook his head in resignation. All his life he had believed his father to be the most worthy of men, one whom he had been proud to emulate, one in whose footsteps he had been honoured to walk. To have a faith shattered in such a way drew the heart from him.

Ann admonished the clerk. "It is William Spooner's doing, Robert."

"Nay, Ann. Robert speaks true. A great blasphemy has been done, and in very truth in the name of my father. It may not have been his hands that mortared these walls, but it was done at his bidding."

"I will not have it. You beat yourself with briars. Whatever sin your father committed, you are not doomed to repeat. It was not John Paycocke, but William Spooner who did place these bodies within your walls."

"Cease with this, Ann. It is I who will not have it. My father was guilty of a grave crime, 'tis not to be denied, but the graver sin was to will his knowledge of that deed to Spooner. Poor William."

Robert folded his arms and grimaced. His ill humour shone through like a torch. "'Poor William' would stove in your head with a staff, Thomas, and not think twice upon it."

Paycocke could not rein in his temper. "But he was not well used in this matter, Robert, see you that not? It was not for my father to bequeath such a responsibility to an outsider. It should have been left to me or to my brothers. All that Spooner did was to try to right that wrong." Thomas turned away from the hole as though the air within were poison. He thought that he heard laughter, a child's laughter. It echoed in his head and he put his hands up to his face, feeling tears stain his fingers. What had they done? What had they released?

He felt arms around him and he shook himself free of their attentions, staggering to the north wall of the room, where he heard life continuing apace in the busy street outside, lives without hindrance, without burden. How could he have known that when he built this house he would be building a prison for himself? "What am I to do?" He screamed at the window. "Father, what would you have me do?"

Thomas sensed Ann's proximity. There was no touch, but the scent of lavender burned the air with its pungent freshness. As Margaret had, she made her own soap from woodash and animal fat, but where his wife had impregnated the soap with rose petals, Ann did so with lavender. She was at his shoulder, her cheek an ell from his own. "What are we to do, Thomas? What are we to do?"

Calm pricked his anger and deflated it. He heard the word 'Thomas' on her lips for the first time. When he turned to face Ann she was looking in the other direction, at Robert standing beside the door, shock contorting his face.

"I cry you mercy, Robert. I fear I have used you most ill." Ann's voice cracked in a way Thomas had never heard. Something had passed which was out of his ken. He stared at the pair of lovers, a wall of silence between them. "It is Thomas I love."

The blood pounded in Thomas's head. What was it she said? Words were strangled in his throat. Thought would not come to him. He could neither move nor speak.

"No." Robert screamed. "No. It cannot be so. No. I will… I cannot… No. Ann. No." The clerk grasped his head. "No, no." He slid from anger to pleading and back again. "Ann, I beg of you. You might not do this, Ann. Take back your words. Ann, no."

He looked at Thomas, held him fast with his gaze. Paycocke was not sure whose shock was the greater, but he saw no anger in his friend, only desperation. Goodday pleaded with him. "Thomas. I beg of you."

Paycocke was still paralysed, could only shake his head at the younger man, a gesture not intended to deny Robert, but to voice his incomprehension, his utter confusion. Ann loved him? It was he that she loved. Ann loved him. How could this be? He had not known it, had not guessed at it. Yet, now, how could he *not* have known it?

She touched him softly and he felt her warmth through layers of linen and wool. She loved him. How could this be? Ann loved him.

The reality of loss sank into Robert's eyes, true fear encapsulated there. He gasped out his breaths as though each might be his last. His voice quivered, and all at once Thomas was reminded of how young the man was, how young and innocent. "No. It cannot be. I love you, Ann."

Thomas could feel Ann's presence bite into his own, so that he no longer knew where he ended and she began. Her love had surprised him, as if waking him after a long sleep. It stirred something within him, something that he now realised he had always known, ever since that first fleeting moment in Cheapside, when he had seen the ailing young woman in the green kirtle. Thomas loved her too, he knew that. The admission lifted him, made his heart fill. He loved her, aye, in very truth, in more than truth. He had always loved her. He knew it now. How blind had he been? He loved Ann. He would always love her.

"No. You will not have her." Robert rushed at them, taking refuge in his anger. Paycocke stood before Ann and took the younger man's blows on his forearms. Goodday was strong but fuelled by rage, his fists wild and inaccurate.

"Robert, I…"

"You have betrayed me, Thomas. Ann is mine, I tell you."

Thomas stood firm. "Ann is of Ann, and of Ann alone. Robert, my friend, I beg you, think upon…"

"No. No. A thousand times no. I served you, Thomas. I loved you. You who have transacted a thousand falsities against me, I who loved you. I would have done anything for you, given you anything. My life, anything." The tears came and Robert sank to his knees, falling to the floor like a dog. "Anything… but… this."

Thomas laid his hand on Robert's shoulder but the slumped man shrugged it away. The clerk stared down at the wooden floor and put his head in his hands. He bellowed out his breath in huge uncontrolled gasps.

Thomas felt overwhelmed by gentleness and compassion. "Robert."

"No."

"Robert?" Ann was crying for her part in Robert's downfall.

The clerk clamped his hands over his eyes. "No," he said, his voice less than a whisper. "Go. It is done. It is ended. I can look upon you no more." He stood, unsteady, but pushed Thomas's hand away when he moved to help him. "No. I wish nothing from you." He felt his way to the door, his eyes cast down, averted from Thomas and Ann. He stood in the frame of the door, his back to them, raising his head to the ceiling. "I loved… I love… you." He staggered from their sight and they heard the giant door slam.

*　　*　　*

Robert had disappeared, had not been seen in town these past two days. Thomas had closed the door on the panelled room, though the wall still remained breached. Its secret had to be hunted down, but after he had breathed in the wondrous presence of his new love. The unaccustomed hunger for life that Thomas felt could not disguise his anguish at the fact that he had lost his dearest and most trusted friend. The rift between them could never be mended. Love might bring folk together, yet at the same time might divide them. Love was a cleaver of hopes, a cleaver of dreams, both creating and destroying.

As much as it pained Paycocke to dwell on it, it had been the best thing for Robert to leave; it was a price that had to be paid. A friendship for a love. That was a bargain well made. Still, it lay heavy on his heart. And how his heart sang when he looked at Ann. He questioned himself at length. Why had she fallen in love with him? Why not Robert? What was within him that had inspired her so? The answers remained out of reach. It was enough that she loved him.

Sometimes answers are not necessary, yet oft an answer must be sought as far as the end of the earth, no matter what the outcome, no matter what the cost. For two days he had allayed the fears that awaited them in the panelled room, but now it must be revisited, and this time without Robert at his side.

Thomas took Ann's hand and they entered the room together. He had destroyed the wall in his efforts to clear the space behind the linen fold, and dust and debris lay all over the oak floor. Traced in the dust were small footprints, indeed only the shadows of footprints, and seen in a different light they would be altogether missed. Thomas knew that he had locked the room and none had entered since. He sighed. What had he done? Who walked within his walls?

He held a candle at the entrance to the tomb, his heart pounding a sonorous, almost tangible beat. Ann seemed to sense his trepidation and stayed close to him, adding her strength to his. A task insurmountable became possible with her by his side. What might they not achieve together? Her love for him was plain, scriven upon her face, as must be his own for her. The sun shone for Ann, his love, the winds blew clouds across the sky for her, birds sang so that she might hear them. He was sure that God had sent her to him.

"Afore we begin, Ann, there is something I would ask."

"Speak, Thomas, I am your vassal." She winked at him, a delicate, almost imperceptible movement of the eyelid, not as when he himself tried the gesture and half his face collapsed in the effort.

Her beauty was indeed divine, and the spirit of youth that she possessed made him feel twenty summers younger than his age. She wore a kirtle of his finest worsted, such as would not look out of place on the highest of gentry. She wore it well and with dignity, but then she had done the same in a low bawdy-house frequented by knaves and vagabonds. She lighted up Paycocke's House like a thousand candles, lighted up his life like a thousand more. Thomas gazed at her, but the words would not come. He had spent most of his life cultivating the spoken word, knowing when to praise, when to jest, when to castigate, when to tease the best from a business proposition, and, of the greatest import, when to be silent. This, above all moments, however, was not the time to lose his tongue, yet the words stopped in his throat, too bashful to be heard.

"Thomas? Are you well?"

He felt the colour rise to his cheeks. "Aye, most well. It is… a different ailment that afflicts me, a most uncommon ague for which I know but a single remedy."

"Aye?" She teased him with her eyes, held him at arm's length so she could scrutinise his face. "Then it is a complaint for which we ought seek a cure."

Thomas thought he might explode like a keg of gunpowder if he did not make his feelings known soon.

I shall count to three and then I shall say it.

One, two, three.

Thomas hesitated, waiting for the words.

What if she were to laugh at me? She says she loves me, true, but it is soon, too soon. How can I be sure? The way she looks at me makes my heart rise up to Heaven, but mayhap I am mistaken. Wherefore would she love me so? This is madness.

He quickly nodded towards the gaping hole in the wall. "We must to work," he said.

"Aye." Ann made no move towards the wall, just looked at Thomas, her skin as pale and beautiful as winter.

"There is much to be done."

"Well enough. Well enough."

I shall do it this time. I shall count to three once more. Then

I shall take a deep breath and swear not to take a second until it is said.

One, two, three.

He sucked in the room's stale closed air and held it. *I shall do this now, on my God, on everything I hold true, on everything in which I believe.* "If it would please you, Ann..." Thomas closed his eyes.

"Aye, Thomas?"

"If it would please you..." his heart threatened to escape his chest "...I... I would have you as my wife." Done. It was done. It was said and might not be unsaid. Whatever the consequence, he had spoken the words and gladly so. He opened his eyes.

Ann laughed, her voice filling the room like Sunday bells. "Oh, Thomas," she said. "Thomas, my love. It would please me greatly. It would please me greatly indeed."

He held her to him. What was this strange thing that was love, that it could demolish and rebuild him within a second? It was a feeling that could create a new world for him, diminishing all others. They kissed, a moment of perfect synchronicity, something rare in a lifetime. To love and to be loved in equal measure, and for that love to be as great as the sky, who might ask for more?

The dark hole beckoned him. Whatever wonders the future held, there was one obstacle to overcome. They approached the wall together, hand in hand. "Heavenly Father above," Thomas said, "be my guide, help me to do what I must, show me what I should know."

Thomas lifted the small, frail bodies and unwrapped the cloth from them, holding the corner where the Paycocke ermine tail mark was stamped in gold. Shorn of their shroud the bones gleamed raw and innocent in the candle's mean light. Here was purity. As he peeled back the cream linen from the skeletons he prayed for the salvation of these poor souls. The motion of the cloth wafted the candle and Ann held her hand to the wick to safeguard the precious light. As it flickered, it played upon the reverse of the material. Words. There were words written there.

"What is it, Thomas?"

"I know not," he said. "And I know not if I wish to know."

He pulled the cloth out from the tomb with a gentleness that suggested he might have been uncovering a sleeping child. The material had a fine, tight weave, yet was as soft and delicate as cobweb in his hands. Paycocke acknowledged that he had learned much from his father. What now was he about to learn? They spread the cloth out on the long board, and Thomas traced the pattern of the first letter, its maze of curlicues descending into the margin of the material. The ink had faded, though not overmuch that Thomas could not read it, and its once dark hue had spread tiny tendrils where it had bled into the linen. "'In the name of God, Amen'," Thomas read. He made the Sign of the Cross and looked to Heaven. Ann moved closer to his side and put her hand at the back of his neck, massaging the muscles. He scanned the text ahead; his stomach felt like churning milk and his voice dropped. "It is my father's confession," he said.

It was the year John Paycocke died, some two months before the illness claimed him. Yet he had known his demise imminent from the day of the first cough. He had known that God was to take him when he wrote these letters. "'Here I confess in the sight of the Almighty, that which I have done and which I now regret with my body and soul. May the Lord in his infinite wisdom grant me the mercy that I do not deserve.'" Thomas felt Ann's cool fingers snake around his neck, his firm touch drawing his head to hers. He was shaking.

"Fear not," Ann said. "When it is done, it is done, and then you might live once more."

Thomas drew his lips together, nodded and carried on. "'It was not I who killed the boys, but I am as guilty as if I stole the last breath from their mouths, took it and claimed it as my own. My loyalty to the King is as unquestioned as my faith in the Lord, as I showed Henry at Bosworth. To deny his request would have been to seek an audience with God, yet when he asked of me this commission, I should have chosen Death.'"

Paycocke closed his eyes to prepare himself. "'I knew not of its invidious nature, or I might have readied myself for damnation. To keep safe that which Henry asked seemed simple enough, yet when that secret is the sovereignty and all upon which it rests, then it is a burden to break the heart of a stronger man than I. In very truth, my soul was forfeit when I broke the seal upon his request and found that Paycocke was chosen to be the eternal guardian of Edward and Richard.'"

Ann gasped and she put her hand up to her face. Thomas trembled, felt as though gripped by fever. The words seemed to lose their focus, rising from the linen and swimming in front of his eyes. He felt Ann's touch and he leant into her for support.

It was she who finally spoke. "They are the murdered princes, Thomas. Paycocke's House harbours Prince Edward and the Duke of York, the Princes from the Tower."

Chapter 57
Burdens

In the kitchen, Sparrow was chatting to Eleanor and Cassie. He was making those expansive hand movements Simon remembered from their Cambridge days, the incline of his head to Eleanor's creating a sense of both intimacy and conspiracy. Cassie no longer sparked with animosity towards him; it was as though she had changed overnight, or at least was trying hard to do so.

Martin had seen the reliquary. Simon let him hold it, though he watched over him carefully. "This is incredible, Simon," he said. "Eleanor was just telling me." The sapphire sparkled under the lights. "Where did you get it, mate? Eleanor," he winked at her, "is being a tad coy."

Simon took the case from him and walked through his study. He turned to make sure Sparrow was following, enjoying the confused look on his friend's face. He twitched his head in the direction of the hall and went through to the dining room.

*   *   *

"Bloody hell," Sparrow said when Simon had finished. "Bloody, bloody hell. So who are they?"

Simon shook his head. "We don't know." Eleanor was behind him, her head resting on his shoulder, and he felt her warmth through the wool of his marl sweater. She twitched at the word 'we'. "We think Paycocke had something to do with it."

"Thomas Paycocke?"

"Yeah, it must have been. John died in 1505 and the house wasn't built until four years later."

"I thought it was built in 1505, that John gave it to Tom and Marge as a wedding gift?"

"All bollocks," said Simon. "The dendrochronology dated the house at 1509. John can't have had anything to do with it. I don't know where the 1505 bit came from, maybe some old wives' tale gathering pace over the years until it became gospel."

"So Paycocke killed these two kids and walled them up over the fireplace? Or the other way around: walled them up, and then…" Sparrow made a strangling gesture to his own throat.

"That's enough speculation, thanks Martin," Simon interrupted.

Cassie looked inside the hole, where darkness muffled the shapes of the two skeletons. "And you found the case in there? In there, inside his ribcage?" She flinched. "You actually put your hand in there?"

Simon nodded, grinning.

It looked like she was going to be sick. "Oh, man, gross. I can't deal with this." She left the room.

Sparrow took the prime viewing position. "So what are you going to do about it, old mate?"

"There's only one thing to do," Simon said.

Martin shrugged. "Sell tickets?"

"Get out of it."

"Come on, there's got to be a way of making some folding out of it."

"I don't want to make any money out of it. I'm going straight down the police station to report it. It could be a crime, for all I know."

"What about this little fellow, they would hardly miss this, would they?" Martin rubbed the sapphire on the reliquary.

"Give it here," Simon called to him. He grabbed at the case and Sparrow stepped back, keeping it out of reach. "Do you want to give it to me?"

Sparrow held up his hands in mock affront. "OK, OK. Only kidding, Simon. Only kidding."

They would take flak for touching the reliquary, but, what the hell. Simon put the case back where he had found it and locked the dining room door behind them. Eleanor looked at her watch and then moved to the front door. "Jack," she said. "I absolutely have to go."

Simon followed her out into the street where the wind blasted them.

"Thanks," Simon said.

"For what?"

"Everything. Thanks for being here. Thanks for helping me get through this."

She put her hand to his face and he felt her soft fingertips scrape against his bristle. "It will be all right, Simon."

Maybe it can be all right. Maybe he'll never know and we can just get on with our lives. I love him. If I lose him, I lose everything. A lie has to be worth it. I can live with that.

He smiled. "Yeah, I'll call the police tonight…"

"No, not that." Eleanor kissed him. A shiver gripped his neck, paralysing him for a second. He did not want to let her go, not now. "That," she said, and then left.

He watched her walk down West Street.

"Close the door, Simon, mate. It's bloody parky out there."

"Light a fire, then."

Martin opened the wood burner and put a firelighter at the bottom. He selected some small sticks and built a pyramid. It lit first time. "Simon?" he said.

Simon's back was turned. He was gazing out of the oriel window towards where Eleanor had gone. She would be home by now, building her own fire, or getting tea on for Jack. Simon wondered what the boy was like, wondered what it felt like to have a son, or even a stepson. He shook his head. Stupid. He shouldn't think that far ahead.

"Simon?"

"What?"

Sparrow stood back from the fire, as though admiring the blaze. "I was on the Heath today."

"What?"

"Hampstead Heath. First time in God knows how many years."

"Oh, yeah?"

"It hasn't changed. Hardly at all. Even the kids still look like the same ones as when… when we used to go down there."

"Yeah." There was a space, a space where Eleanor had been, and for the first time he registered her absence. A few weeks ago he had not even known her, even known she had existed. And now? She'd been gone five minutes and he missed her already.

"You remember that day?"

"What day?"

"That day, on the Heath? We were there, you and I, Alex and Cassie. I don't know where Robin was, working, probably, always the puritan."

"What of it?"

"I knew where she was all along." Sparrow said. "Alex, I mean. You remember, she got lost?"

"Yeah, I remember." It was so long ago, a lifetime, a whole other lifetime ago, when he was with Robin, when Robin was with him. But she had never really been with him, had she? "What do you mean, you knew where she was all along?"

Sparrow stared into the flames. "I watched her walk down the hill. Didn't take my eyes off her. Never could."

Simon nodded.

"She toddled into Kenwood and I wanted to be there, with her, hold her hand, pretend... pretend that I was her Dad, pretend that I deserved her. Just for a minute."

Simon stared at him. It was a long time ago. A month was a long time ago now, a very long time. The emotion this confession would have stirred in him then was a well forgotten one. Maybe he *had* changed, had evolved somehow. To be a parent was the greatest gift you could have. How could he deny Sparrow the smallest taste of it? "It's all right, Martin. Don't worry about it."

The late afternoon washed the hall with its darkness. There was a cosiness about the big room that Simon had never noticed before, or perhaps it was just that Martin knew how to light a better fire. Sparrow smiled up at him. "Cheers, Simon," he said. "You're my best friend, you know that?"

Simon supposed he was now. It would never have occurred to him before to think of Sparrow in that way, but it seemed that the things that should have split them apart had brought them together. Apart and together, at one and the same time.

There was a moment when Simon thought Sparrow might

actually hug him. They sat opposite each other in front of the wood burner, cheeks on fire from the light.

"Thanks."

"Yeah. No sweat, Simon."

"Hey," Simon had a sudden thought, "what about the *Artes* book?"

Sparrow nodded. "Oh, yeah. The *Artes*. Right. *Artes. De Medicina*. Yeah, well... I don't have it."

"What?" Now Martin had his complete attention. He stared at his friend, feeling frustration ferment within him. "What do you mean, you don't have it? It's what you bloody well went to London for. What happened? You got off at Liverpool Street and took a wrong turn on the Circle Line?"

Martin tried to laugh off the question. "Look, it's a long story, Simon."

"No, no, no. *War and Peace* is a long story. You going to London and forgetting to pick up the thing you went there for is not a long story. It's a joke. A bad joke." Simon got up and walked across the room.

"Oh, come on, Simon, it's not that simple."

"It's not as simple as you are, that's for sure."

There was a knock from outside, the iron ring shuddering the massive oak door.

"For heaven's sake, who's that?" Simon swung the door open.

"Hi, Simon, what's happening?"

Simon was wrong-footed, his rage at Sparrow still smouldering. "Hi... this isn't a good moment right now. I thought you were coming tomorrow?"

Fitz?

Chapter 58
Photographs

Fitz leant against the oak doorframe, his huge hand resting in the gap. He knew Simon wouldn't close the door on his fingers; he was too nice a guy for that. Some things you could rely on. "I'm sorry, mate. It couldn't wait." *Just in time, something was up.* The feelings of unease he had felt when last at Paycocke's had dissipated, diluted by the others in the house, or maybe it was that the house knew Fitz was home now.

"Well…" Fitz saw Simon sneak a look out of the corner of his eye in the direction of the dining-room. So he had been right. He had been right all along. The dining room. The panelling. That's where it all was. The photographs had been right, had pointed him in the right direction all along. It was like solving the last clue of the crossword.

"Can I come in?" Fitz nodded inside the room, as though he were going to come in whether Simon liked it or not. Nice. "I won't be a minute." *It will take as long as it takes. It all ends here. It all begins here.*

Simon sighed. "Yeah, OK, come in." He ushered Fitz into the entrance hall.

Fitz nodded at Sparrow sitting by the wood burner. "All right?"

"Mark Fitzwarwick," Simon introduced them, "an old friend of mine, Martin… House." Sparrow smiled and nodded his head in recognition. Fitz forced down the automatic scowl that surfaced when he was remembered as the King of Clacton.

He lowered his voice. "Can we talk?"

"If it's about the More…"

"No, it's not the More. Great stuff, mind. Paid a bob or two over the eight, you know that, course you do, but it was worth it in the end." It certainly was. The book had been his passport to Paycocke's, to that pivotal moment when he walked through that

484

door for the first time, a door that would soon be his. "Thing is, Simon, me old mucker, I think you've got something of mine."

"Huh?"

Fitz grinned at Simon's confusion. All the degrees in the world couldn't buy you any common sense, could they? He waved an arm around the entrance hall. "This place."

Simon's face crumpled. "I'm not with you, Fitz," he said.

You had to laugh. Poor old guy probably never knew what hit him. To be honest he looked like he walked around with his eyes half closed most of the time anyway. Couldn't see what was going on right under his nose: Cassie and Roach; his missus, too. Hadn't lost any weight since the old lady left, either. "If you're not with me, you're agin me," he said. "Nah, only kidding. It's like I say: I do believe, me old mate, that this house belongs to me." He reached inside the pocket of his parka and drew out a sheaf of photographs. "Any chance of taking a butcher's in the dining room?"

"I don't understand."

"You will, mate, you will." It was clear that Chance hadn't a clue what Fitz was on about, and while that was the case, he was hardly going to let him look at the panelling. With Cassie at stake, too, it was softly, softly. He opened the packet of photographs and placed them on the table in the centre of the hall. The glow from the fire crept over the pictures, filtering them with its soft reds and yellows.

"About twenty years ago," Fitz said, "we were living in Romford – I was just a kid, didn't know my arse from my elbow. There was me, my Mum and Dad, and my Grandad. Lazy old tosser he was. He used to spend all afternoon watching the nags, but sometimes he'd throw me a couple of quid if I'd go down the bookies for him on pension day. More often than not he'd just glue himself to the racing, take his teeth out and suck on these pear drops. That's my childhood, played out to the smell of pear drops. Don't see them much these days, do you?"

Simon leant on the newel post at the bottom of the staircase, drumming his foot on the last step and picking at a threadbare eyebrow. He said nothing.

Fitz carried on. "Anyway, that's beside the point. But, like I say, about twenty years ago, someone sent him this old camera through the post. We had no idea who sent it. Nothing. Never found out, neither."

Simon sighed. "Where is this going, Fitz? I don't see what it's got to do with me. It's all very interesting, but right now I'm..."

Fitz held out a hand, as if preaching calm. He smiled. "Hold your horses, mate, I won't be a minute. What I mean to say, is that when the old geezer pegged out, he left me the camera. He'd never done anything with it. It had just sat in the bottom of a drawer for years, then it, well, emigrated to the attic. He always said it might be worth a bob or two, but he never did anything about it, never had it valued or nothing, he couldn't be arsed. Just like Grandad. So he left it to me.

"You know, and stupid tosser, me, too, I did nothing about it for years, either. Thought, 'Yeah, that's nice of Grandad,' but I was too busy doing other stuff. Fighting, mainly." He laughed. "You know what I mean, 'arry?

"All right, nearly there. Anyway, when I did get around to checking it out, it was obvious that my old Grandad hadn't even looked at it. Beautiful, it was, all shiny black and chrome like an old car – made things properly in those days, didn't they? And in the case, tucked inside the lining, was this letter, written anonymously to Grandad, telling him that this camera was his legacy, his birthright." Fitz snorted. "My Grandad never even read the letter, never even knew it was there. Stupid sod."

Sparrow leant forward, tapping his fingers on the table. "So what's this bit about the house being yours, then?"

"Yeah, yeah, yeah, I'm getting there. Well, it didn't make sense to me neither, until I took a good shufty at the camera and realised there was still a film in it." He pointed at the photographs on the table and Simon moved away from the stairs, bait finally taken. "It was some weird type of film I'd never heard of, but I took it to a bloke in town and got these developed. He said it was a while since he'd seen a camera like it. As I thought, worth a bit and practically brand new. He dated it back to the twenties, and I could tell he was right, there were a few snaps of some people from around that time. But, anyway, feast your eyes on these." Fitz gestured at the photographs.

"It's Paycocke's," Martin said, flicking through the pictures. "Look, Simon, there's the merchant's mark. There's the panelling. There's the carver's head." He picked up one of the pictures, the one with the cigarette smoke obscuring the panelling, and held it up to the light, as though it might be able to pierce the grey cloud that hung over the linen fold. "Photographer's a bit shaky, but it's the house, all right."

"Took me a while to find that out, I can tell you," said Fitz. "I had some help, mind, but if it wasn't for the merchant's logo there, I never would have twigged it."

"But why would the photographer have made such a big secret of it? Why didn't he just take a photo of the outside of the house?" Sparrow was beginning to show an interest for the first time.

"Because it's the panelling that's important." From a deep pocket Fitz pulled out a magazine. "Check this out. *Country Life*, June 1923. Your house was featured." He smiled. "*My* house was featured." He opened the magazine to an article about the Edwardian restoration of Paycocke's. "The story I'm sure you know, but it's the photographs that are interesting. Look." He passed the old magazine to Simon and Martin stood up and peered over his shoulder. There was the standard photograph of the front of the house, with its carved frieze and lime washed studwork, another showed the linen fold panelling in the dining room, while a third showed the rear elevation.

Simon shook his head. "I don't get it," he said.

"So the magazine pictures were taken early 1923, late '22, maybe." Fitz said. "Whereas the pictures that came from my camera," he waved at the snaps spread out on the long table, "are later, a year at most."

"And?"

"Spot the difference," said Fitz.

"All looks the same to me," said Sparrow.

"Simon?"

Chance shook his head.

"The dining room?" prompted Fitz. He picked up the loose

photograph of the linen fold panelling and placed it directly under its brother in *Country Life*.

Simon looked back down at the photographs.

Well, fuck me sideways, he knows. He knows it's upside-down. The crafty old so-and-so. Fitz could almost see the wheels turning, Simon's eyes looking towards the dining room, then darting back at the photographs, maybe deciding on the story he was going to spin. *There's something more. He knows something more.* He grinned. At last. It had taken years, but at last he had found out what it all meant. The house would be his, he saw it in Simon's face, the filmy gauze of doubt lingering there like net curtains over his eyes. Chance was still saying nothing. Fitz would have to help him out. "The linen fold panelling," he said. "It's upside-down in the second photo, isn't it? But you knew that, didn't you, mate?"

Simon nodded, then stared again at the two photographs. Of course, he couldn't lie, could he? Fitz knew that. Chance was too good for his own good.

Fitz carried on. "So, whenever the journalist got out here to put the article together, the panelling was the right way up. Within a year, it had been taken down and put back up again, the wrong way round."

Simon took a deep breath.

Sparrow passed the magazine back to Fitz. "I don't understand. What does this prove?"

Fitz waved the copy of *Country Life* back at Martin. "Well, Martin House... nice name, mate, where did you get that one, Tesco's? I'll tell you what that proves, Martin. Someone, it might not have been the bloke who took these photographs, I don't know, but someone was up to some monkey business with that panelling. There's something behind it, something important, something that proves my Grandad's legacy. Whoever took the photographs found it out and that's why they sent the pictures to the old man. But you already know that, Simon, don't you? You already know that this house belongs to the Fitzwarwicks."

"Simon?" Sparrow looked puzzled and for the first time Fitz wondered whether the two friends were in cahoots at all.

Simon shook his head. "You're wrong, Fitz."

Fitz tossed the magazine down on the table and two of the loose photographs fluttered to the floor. "I'm not wrong, Simon." Chance was obstructing him. What did he have to gain by it? It wasn't his house, he just rented it. Unless... unless he had opened the panelling himself, and found something there, something he wanted to keep for himself. "There's another thing. Thomas Paycocke had a son."

"What?" Simon turned to Fitz and for the first time maintained eye contact.

"Didn't know that, did you?"

"There was no son. The house passed to Thomas's nephew when he died. It was 1518. He and Margaret never had any children."

"She died first," Fitz said. "And he married again." He looked up at the ceiling, where Thomas and Margaret's initials were carved. "The new missus didn't get *her* initials up on the ceiling, though."

"I know. Ann it was. Ann Cotton. She was much younger than him, but we don't know a lot about her."

"She gave him a kid."

"She was pregnant when Thomas died. We don't even know if the child survived."

"It was a boy."

"This is crazy, Fitz. You don't know what you're talking about. The house went to his brother's son, John Paycocke. And when John's son died, that was the end of the Paycockes."

"No." Simon was talking crap, he just didn't know it yet. "Ann's son – he was my ancestor. This house was rightfully his. There *are* Paycockes still. I'm one. And the proof," he prodded a finger in the direction of the dining room, "I'm betting, is behind that panelling." He strode towards the dining room and tried the door. "Simon?" His patience was wearing thin.

"No, Fitz, you've got it all wrong." Simon spread out his hands.

"Where's the key? Come on, mate, do us all a favour."

"Fitz..."

"You've been in there, haven't you?"

Simon sighed. "Yes."

Sparrow came up behind Simon.

"The key, Simon," said Fitz. "I won't ask you again."

"No, Fitz, please…"

Fitz clenched his fists and could feel the crescents of his nails cutting into his palms. He badly didn't want to have to do this by force.

Sparrow stepped in front of Simon. "Right, Mark… Fitz, whatever the fuck you call yourself," he said. "Get… the fuck… out of Simon's house." He swung a right. Fitz snapped his head back in a fraction of a second, then cut through Sparrow's guard and connected square on his chin. Martin crumpled to the floor.

Fitz was completely calm, completely in control. He turned to Simon and smiled, holding his palms up in front of his face and shaking his head. "Sorry about that, Simon, mate. I really am. Now, have you got the key?"

Simon stepped back and looked down at the fireplace, seeking out the poker. Was nothing what it seemed to be? What was he going to do?

"Mark? Is that you, Mark?" Cassie's voice floated from the stairs. "What are you doing?"

"Cassie?" Simon looked up to where his daughter stood. She knew Fitz? He didn't understand.

"Cassie." There was something new in Fitz's voice, a hairline crack of nerves. Simon looked at the man who had just laid Sparrow out. He seemed smaller in his dark green parka, the shadows of the fire licking over it, turning it to camouflage. "Hi." He smiled.

"What's going on?" said Simon.

"What do you mean, Dad?" she said, her trainers clomping on the stairs and echoing through the hall. "It's Mark, you know, Mark… I'm sorry, I've forgotten your last name?"

"Fitzwarwick." Fitz raised his hand in a half salute and gave his crease of a smile once more.

"Yeah, Mark Fitzwarwick, the Trust guy."

"What trust guy?" Simon felt as though his sense of logic had gone AWOL. There was some connection here he was failing to make. How on earth did Cassie know Fitz?

"Dur, the National Trust, Dad. Remember. The National Trust that owns Paycocke's House. Mark's in charge of the buildings maintenance department or something. That's right, isn't it, Mark?"

"He's what?" Simon looked at Fitz. *What was Cassie talking about? And why the bloody hell was the guy staring at his daughter like a sodding lovesick schoolkid?* He felt a bucket of snakes writhing in his stomach. It couldn't be. It just couldn't. She had only just freed herself from Roach's tentacles. She couldn't be seeing Fitz, could she?

Fitz stroked his head. "Er, no." He took a tentative step towards the bottom of the stairs. "I'll be straight. I'm not part of the NT, Cassie."

"What has this guy been telling you, Cass?" Lies and deception were everywhere. He had no idea what Fitz was talking about.

"I bought a book from your Dad, that's all. A couple of weeks ago."

Simon nodded. "A Thomas More. Two hundred and seventy-five quid. Paid cash. I thought you were mad."

Fitz gave a wistful smile. "Sterling stuff, money," he said.

Cassie gave a snort of laughter.

Simon turned his head and looked at Fitz from the side. "You *are* bloody crazy, Fitz." He had to get him out of the house.

Cassie backed away from Fitz and Simon. "So you don't work for the Trust?"

Fitz shook his head. "I'm an antiques dealer."

"Then what were you doing in our house?" She stared at Fitz.

Simon saw the lightning flash of confusion cross Cassie's face and felt a mirror image on his own. "What? What do you mean, '*in* our house'?"

"I can explain." Fitz raised his arms in a gesture of surrender.

Simon didn't trust him. He looked down at Sparrow, still unconscious. 'Martin House' – what a prat.

"He's OK," Fitz said. "He'll be OK." There was a shred

of doubt in his voice and Simon knelt down by his friend and touched his cheeks. Martin stirred. "I pulled the punch."

"Martin?"

Sparrow's head moved. He opened his eyes and seemed to look beyond Simon, his pupils struggling for focus. He grunted.

"Anyway," said Fitz, "like I say, I can explain…"

"Yeah, I think you'd better," said Simon.

"I had to see the house, Simon. I had to be sure."

"But you saw the house when you came around for the book."

Fitz moved closer to Simon. "Yeah, it wasn't enough, mate. It was like a taster. I couldn't be sure. I knew it was the right place, but I just had to get in. I had to check it against the photographs. I had to have the evidence."

"You broke into my house?"

"No, not as such…"

"You really broke into my house?"

"Simon, I…"

"I think you'd better leave, Fitz." Simon's heart clattered. If the guy lost it he could kill them all.

"Please, Simon." There was no trace of menace in Fitz's voice, only a desperate pleading, ill-fitting on his heavy frame.

"Dad." Cassie's hand was on Simon's arm. "Let him speak. It's all right."

"Look, Cassie, maybe you should go back upstairs."

"Dad?"

She stared at him, his daughter. How many times had he looked into her eyes and not known what lurked behind them, what subterfuge she was planning, the games she was playing? Her eyes were clear this time, as clear as a bright winter morning that stretches for miles, as open as the great, yielding East Anglian skies. He nodded. "Go on," he sighed, looking at Fitz.

Fitz looked over at Cassie and smiled a thanks. Simon saw something pass between them, a look, a mere glimpse stolen from the shadows. Who was he to argue? He who had fallen for Eleanor in a sharp gust on Clacton pier. He who had fallen for Robin without question, without doubt. There would always be a path not taken, always, and who knew if that was really the right one? He felt in his pocket for the key to the dining room. Fitz should know.

Martin moved on the floor, hauling himself onto one elbow and holding his jaw.

"Come on, Martin," said Simon. "Join the party."

*   *   *

Fitz was silent. He stared into the void behind the panelling. He felt himself reach in, be pulled in, not by his hands, but by his thoughts. The confusion that had enveloped him these past weeks melted and he was left only with truth. There were two children and he held their hands like an uncle, to reassure them. Their clean slate of innocence passed to him. They merged with him, became him. 'Wealth untold. The riches of resolution.' "Who are you?" he whispered.

"We are you. We are of you."

"And I am of you," he said. "I am with you. I see. I am no Paycocke, but it is of import no more. What is done is done. Debts are paid. We are all freed."

Other voices penetrated from afar, parting the fog in his head. "Fitz, are you OK?" Fitz held the small hands, gripped them tighter in his own, but felt them fade from his grasp as the voices grew louder. "Fitz. What is it?" And then they were gone.

"Fitz. Are you OK? What happened back there?"

Fitz pulled himself away from the panelling, aching with loss. Already it was just a dream, the knowledge the boys had passed him slipping through his fingers like fine sand, fine golden sand. He struggled to keep hold of the shining memory as it flitted out of his grasp, but Simon's words were too strong, hauling him back into the room. Yet those moments *had* happened – he knew they had, but all he had left were thin wisps of recollection. "Simon, I was wrong," he said eventually. The path that had brought him to Paycocke's had vaporised.

There was nothing else there. The two skeletons gazed out at them, their skulls winking in the glare of the torch. "I think so," Simon said. "Whatever happened here, I don't think it's to do with any legacy. The Paycockes died out in 1584. You're no Paycocke, Fitz. But what happened back there? You seemed to have... gone. What the hell happened?"

"Nothing. Everything. I don't know. I really don't know. I'm not a Paycocke, I know that. But... the camera? Why did he send me the camera? The photographer? I don't understand. It doesn't make any sense."

"Have you still got the letter? The letter from the camera?"

Fitz felt in his breast pocket and pulled out a piece of folded paper, taped at the crease where it had worn through. He passed it to Simon. With it, he felt as though he passed the burden of truth. He could let go. It would be all right.

"I think it was a she," Simon said, scanning the handwriting. There were similarities between it and the letter from Imogen's box. He couldn't be certain, but the author seemed to be the same. "Hold on a sec. You said there were some pictures of people as well?"

Fitz fished in his inside pocket and gave Simon a few more black and white images.

The scene was genteel, a long ago summer afternoon's croquet captured for always. "It's Gustav," Simon smiled. "Your letter writer was Imogen Holst. Whatever happened here, she found out. She opened up the panelling and discovered the bodies. And for some reason she didn't report it, but just walled them back up again. Imogen Holst took the photographs and something convinced her to send them to your grandfather. What, I suppose we'll never know."

"I've been chasing my tail." Fitz turned away.

"Who knows? I'm turning it over to the police. It's worn me out, Fitz. Maybe they'll find something. Track down the DNA."

Fitz was deflated. He turned over the old photographs, shaking his head. "Six years," he said. "Wasted years."

"You can't say that," said Cassie. She moved up behind Fitz and put her hand on his shoulder.

Fitz looked up at the linen fold panelling. "It's still stunning, whatever happened. And there's something... something I know deep down... I can't remember... something happened to me..." He stared at the ceiling. "It's no good, it's gone." Simon followed his gaze up to where the Paycockes' initials were carved. "Thomas? Margaret?" Fitz called out. "What's it all about, eh? What's it all about?"

"I'll probably get a report back from the police at some point," said Simon. "I'll let you know how it all pans out."

Fitz nodded. "Cheers, Simon." He turned to Sparrow. "Sorry about the punch, mate," he said.

Sparrow grimaced. "Don't worry about it. Any time."

Fitz opened the door. The last of the weak autumn sun split the dark clouds and picked out the carpenter's mark on the stud beside the doorframe. Fitz touched it, running his fingers over the contours of the ancient carved notches. "Knew what they were doing, those boys," he said, and stepped out onto the pavement. "See you around, guys." Fitz started to walk down West Street towards the village.

"Mark, wait," Cassie called after him.

Fitz turned, as though he had forgotten she was there. But when Cassie stepped into the street, snatching at her hair flailing in the biting wind, he grinned and held an arm out. "Most people usually just call me Fitz," he said. "But you can call me Mark."

Simon and Martin watched on, for a moment transfixed.

"Well, that's that," said Sparrow. "Can we go in, it's bloody freezing? Packs a punch, that Fitz."

"They didn't call him the King of Clacton for nothing."

"Don't I just know it?" Sparrow rolled his jaw.

They both went inside, where the fire had now died down. "So, anyway," Simon said, poking at the remnants of the fire and releasing waves of heat, "before we were so rudely interrupted..."

"Oh."

"So what about *Artes*?"

Sparrow's eyes looked like empty caves in the gloom of the hall, the firelight picking out tram-lines on his forehead and ageing him. "I'm sorry, Simon," he said. "I've screwed up, haven't I?"

Simon sighed. "Yeah, well, who hasn't?" Fitz had left some of his photographs on the table. Simon picked one up. It was the linen fold panelling, partially obscured by the smoke. As he looked at it, the grey veil seemed to lift, the oak carvings becoming sharper, more in focus. It must be a trick of the light. He put it down on the table again; Fitz would be back for them.

"It's not just that, Simon, it's everything." Sparrow knelt by the fire and picked logs out of the wood basket. He sized them up, looking for the perfect addition to the dying fire. "There... there is no *Artes*."

"What?"

"It was all bollocks."

"What do you mean?" Simon felt a flicker of panic, reminded of Martin's betrayals.

"You know what, Simon? I wanted to be you. You had everything: fabulous wife, wonderful home, beautiful kids," his voice sank, "one of them mine. Everywhere you went people liked you: good old Simon, witty, charming, clever. I wanted what you had, but no matter how hard I tried, it was always out of reach, something I couldn't trade, couldn't buy."

"I don't understand..."

"Of course you don't. People like you never do. I don't mean that badly, mate. It's just that when you have everything, you don't know it."

Simon shook his head.

"At first I loved you, and then I tried to hurt you."

"What?"

"No, not that kind of love, you idiot."

"Oh."

"I went after Robin. I admit it. I chased her until she gave in. I wanted what you had."

"You don't need to say this..."

"Yeah, I do. It was like a coke high. I thought I'd done it, cracked it finally. But she left me, went back to you, with my child inside her. She loved you, Simon."

Simon nodded.

"All I had were glimpses of happiness. Alex just made it worse, seeing her grow, but not being with her, not feeling her tiny hand in mine, not seeing her last thing at night and then first thing in the morning..."

Tears glistened on Sparrow's cheeks. Simon put his hand on his friend's shoulder.

"I had to leave. I couldn't bear it. I thought that time and distance would heal the wound." He looked up at Simon, making no attempt to corral the stray tears. "It doesn't, you know. It makes it worse. It's a scab that keeps opening, every time you see a child. In trying to hurt you, I'd only succeeded in making it worse for myself."

"Hey, it's over, Martin. It's over."

"It'll never be over."

"Hey, hey..."

"I had to come back. My child is a drug. I couldn't live without seeing her. So I made up the story about *Artes*. It was all bait. There are no other volumes. Well, maybe there are, but God knows where. There *is* a copy of the *De Medicina* volume in Philadelphia, that bit's true. I even went to look at it, to give credibility to my story. But I never had any original."

"So what about the theft?"

Sparrow smiled. "You really think I would be capable of pinching a book like that? I'm no Raffles, old chum. Nothing that romantic about me. I wouldn't have had the guts to nick it."

"And what about Fleming Land?"

Sparrow's laugh echoed around the hall. "The famous around-the-world yachtsman? There *was* no Fleming Land. I flew the red-eye from Boston."

"I saw him. In the White Hart. I saw him."

"Oh, Simon, you're so sweet, so bloody gullible. That was just some salesman from Blackburn, I expect."

Simon was angry. It was like catching fog, and the more he tried to snatch at half-truths, the more they slipped through his grasp. So there was no *Artes*. It had all been a lie. "You used me," he said.

"Some of it's true," Sparrow continued. "The fact that I came back broke and a failure. Yeah, that's true. I went out there with hopes that things could be different, leaving the old Sparrow back in England, build a new life, become someone else... I swore to Robin I wouldn't come back, promised her I would keep this secret. And I meant it. I really meant it, Simon. But it's like a dam: the emotions wear away at it over the years and cracks begin to show. Then one day you give in. It bursts, everything spills out when you least expect it." He put his head in his hands.

Simon crouched down beside Sparrow and put an arm around him. "Hey, it's OK, mate. It's OK. Let it go." Martin's shoulders heaved. "We'll work it out." It felt as though he were seeing the real Martin for the first time. He was fragile and vulnerable. "We'll work something out," he said.

Simon stood up, feeling a sudden dizziness. Was this what happened when dreams were dashed? He had wanted the *Artes* story to be true, wanted it so much. Of course Sparrow would have known that from the beginning, weaving his web of deceit to best advantage. How could he kick the guy, down as he was? He clutched at the final straw. "So everything was a ploy? The book, the story about Vespucci, the imports website?"

"The website?"

"You dangled that in front of me too, only to spirit it away before I could get a closer look."

Martin's forehead creased in confusion. "No. I don't know what that was about. It must have been Cassie or Alex."

Simon nodded, disbelievingly.

"You're a good mate, you know that?" He stood up without waiting for an answer. "I need some time to think," he said. He picked up his jacket from the carver.

Simon held up his hand. "Hey, it's OK. Why don't you stay by the fire? I need to go out anyway... don't forget Land's still looking for you."

Sparrow laughed and threw his jacket back down. "If you're sure?"

"Yeah, there's something I have to do."

Chapter 59
Wind

Simon walked out into the wind, stuffing his hands into the pockets of his old Barbour. It needed re-waxing, yet another thing he had allowed to slip by the side of the road. No more. Sharp gusts found the cracks in the jacket, chilling his skin. He wished he had worn gloves.

He knocked on Robin's door, Robin and Abby's door. She was lucky, his wife, she had discovered the secret to her happiness before it was too late. To live without regrets, that was all you could ask for. He had no regrets about their time together, none at all. He stood on the doorstep, tucking himself in to the tiny porch. Maybe she had gone shopping. Just as he turned to go, the door opened a crack and a wave of tropical heat escaped.

"Hi." It was Abby, pleased to see him. "Come in," she said. "It's snifter time." Simon wondered if Abby harboured any secrets, if she would ever deceive anyone.

"Thanks." He stepped into the safe haven of the warm house. He had forgotten what central heating felt like and shucked off his waxed coat.

"Who is it, honey?" Robin.

"Simon." Abby kissed him.

The sitting room was decorated to Abby's taste, but he saw a few of Robin's things dotted around the room: a small Moroccan copper bowl he remembered; a marble sculpture of a woman with Henry Moore holes piercing her; a watercolour of an autumnal Hampstead Heath, Kenwood a pale shadow in the background.

"Robin," he said.

She smiled, held out her arms and hugged him. "Jeepers, Simon, you're freezing." She rubbed his arms. "So, how's it going, big buddy? You'll stay for a drink, huh?"

He smiled and nodded.

Abby put her delicate hand on his. "Scotch, Simon?"

"That'd be good, thanks."

"Paycocke's is freezing, I'll bet?"

He fought his natural inclination to defend the house. "Not too bad."

"Yet." Robin laughed.

"How are you?"

"Good, real good."

She looked it. There was a spark in her, a real vibrancy. He took her hands.

"You're cold, Simon," she said.

"Cold hands, warm heart."

"I know." She looked at him, her eyes soft and misty. "You have the warmest heart of anyone I know. Any man, at least."

Abby came in with the drinks. He took a sip of the malt.

"Cheers," he said.

"Bottoms up," said Robin, affecting an English accent.

"Where's Alfie?"

Abby laughed. "She's around. she's a bit shy; doesn't usually show up when there are strangers about. There's part of her, though." She pointed to the sofa. From underneath poked a replica of the python, down to the holes for the eyes.

"May I?" He knelt down to take a closer look.

"Don't worry about it, I have them by the dozen. And Alfie doesn't need it anymore."

The snakeskin was a perfect mesh of overlapping scales, translucent and practically weightless in his hand. Simon had never seen anything like it. He stroked it, rough and smooth at the same time. How satisfying it must be to shed your skin at will, to take on a new persona, a new life and leave the old one behind. He caught Robin's eye. Maybe it wasn't so difficult for people to do. They both smiled.

"With skins you don't usually get to see them so intact," Abby said. "Pythons like to find a good rock to rub against when they're ready, so the skin normally comes away in smaller chunks. No rocks in here," she smiled. "No hard places."

Simon nodded. "It's great," he said.

"You can have it if you like."

"I think it might freak Cassie out," he said, putting it back in its hiding place under the sofa.

"How's Cassie?" Robin leant forward in her seat, her hands cupping the glass.

"Good. I think she's turned a corner."

"And the pills?"

He smiled. "She's got her head screwed on. We never needed to worry."

"Worry? That comes with the territory, Simon."

"Yeah." He laughed.

"Will you stay at Paycocke's?" Robin asked.

He hadn't thought about it. His life had changed, that was certain, and Paycocke's had been a huge catalyst in that. He owed the house. "For now, we'll stay."

"The reason I ask is because...," she looked across at Abby, who took her hand and squeezed it, "because we're leaving Coggeshall. Not immediately, but next year, in the spring, we think." She paused to let the news sink in.

Simon nodded. What happened when the old skin was left behind? You couldn't leave all of it scraped on the rocks. Some of it always went with you. "I'm sorry." He meant it. "I really am."

"I need... we need a fresh start, somewhere where nobody knows us. I tried so hard to make us work, Simon." She looked down at her lap. "But I failed."

"No," he said. "You would have failed if you'd carried on as we were, if you'd spent the rest of your life wanting what you couldn't have."

Robin smiled and squeezed his hand. "I have one specific memory, you know, Simon. You remember our first place in Hampstead? There was a Christmas – we didn't have any money for decorations, so we wrapped matchboxes in scraps of wrapping paper and hung them on the tree."

Simon remembered. There was a scattering of snow outside; they lit a fire and decorated the tree. He drank sherry; she mulled wine.

"I opened your present, the robin cup."

Simon smiled.

"In that moment, I loved you. I loved you as much as I ever could. I thought it could work, Simon. I really thought it could work."

"Oh, Robin, my darling. I loved you, too." There. He had said it, said what he had come here to say, love in the past tense. Now he could let go. "You're doing the right thing," he said.

"When do we ever know what's right?"

He nodded, and left soon after.

There would be a frost tonight, the first severe one of the season. He crossed Robin's Brook on the way back home. Poor old Robin. Simon wondered if the woodsman had ever found his carving. He thought he heard the thud of an axe on the wind, but maybe it was just a car door slamming.

When Robin had ended their relationship, he thought it destroyed, but she had really only pollarded it, trimmed off the long spindly branches. It would be stronger now, stronger than it had ever been. Even when she moved away with Abby, there would be a bond between them. They had grown together, evolved together. Of course he loved her; of course she loved him. That would never change. She would always be a part of him, no matter how far away she was.

Eleanor. The thought of Eleanor sent a ripple of expectancy though him. Who knew what would happen? Who knew? For the moment, he enjoyed the uncertainty.

*   *   *

Alex picked the Wollstonecraft book from the shelves, and turned to the title page. 'To my own Vindication, love J.' She smiled, hugged the book like a memory, tight to her pullover. Secrets. Everyone has to have secrets.

There was a knock on the bedroom door. *It must be Dad. Only Dad ever knocks.*

"Alex." Cassie.

"Hi."

"Just wanted to know how you were."

"Yeah, good. I saw you go off."

"I was just walking Mark back to his car."

"Are you seeing him?"

Cassie gave an expression that looked how Alex felt: bashful with a hint of excited. "I think so."

"You either are or you're not."

"Then I am. We're going out tonight."

"What's he like?"

"Not how he looks. First impression you think: tough; aggressive."

Alex waved the Penguin at her sister. "Never judge a book…" She turned to the window and looked out on the back garden. The trees were almost naked now. It was hard to believe that spring could ever come. "Do you think it's serious with Eleanor?"

"Does it matter?"

"I suppose not, so long as Dad is happy."

Cassie sighed. "It's all change around here, isn't it? All of us."

"Change is good."

"Sometimes. Sometimes it's nice when things stay the same."

"You old reactionary."

Cassie threw a tube of lip salve at her sister. "Watch it. How about some respect?"

Alex picked up the tube from where it had fallen. She unscrewed the top and sniffed it. "Cherry," she said. The smell sparked a memory that she held inside her. She closed the tube and the scent of cherry faded. "I knew. I knew all along."

"Knew what?" Cassie moved closer.

"About Martin. About Martin being my real father."

"Alex…?"

"He told me when I was a kid. Not in so many words, but then I always was a precocious little brat."

"Still are."

Alex stifled a laugh. "He didn't need to spell it out. But then he wrote from the US later and told me everything. He's the type of man that usually you would dismiss ninety-nine percent of what he says as bollocks. But this time… this time I knew…"

"Why didn't you tell Mom and Dad?"

"You're kidding? And break Dad's heart? He should never have had to know. I'm sorry he found out."

Cassie put her arm around Alex and the younger girl reciprocated. "Hey, you could have told *me*."

"Could I? We never really got on that well, did we?"

Cassie sighed. "No, you're right. I probably would have blackmailed you."

"Don't be too hard on yourself."

"If I'm not, who will be? Dad?"

They both laughed.

"Martin used to send me money from the States."

The older girl snorted. "I used to wonder why you were always so flush."

"And little things, tokens, the sort of things a father likes to give to a daughter. I felt sorry for him."

"He's still a wanker."

"It's funny. It's normally the folks who hide the parenthood from the child, not the other way around." Alex twirled the lip salve between her fingers. "But sometimes truth isn't the only option."

"I know what you mean."

"What are you going to do now?"

"I'm sick of secrets, keeping them and telling them, Ally. It's all over. I just want to be happy."

"Don't we all?"

Alex moved away from the window. A couple of the lights were cracked and a draught streamed through. It would be a cold winter. "There's something else. While we're telling secrets, I mean."

"Mmm?"

"You remember Skimble's whiskers? When they got snipped off?"

Cassie nodded.

"That was me. I did it."

"I know."

"And I let you take the blame. I wanted you to take the blame." Alex hugged herself. She had four layers on but still felt cold. "You knew?"

"Who else would it have been?"

"And you didn't grass me?"

"I'm your sister."

Alex looked out of the window. She had to see Julia. It was getting dark outside and the wind was firming up. The past was done, over; there was no changing it. The best you could hope for was to learn from it. The future was different. She could either shape it or let it fly away. She put on a coat and scarf. Cassie hugged her, not the brief hug one might expect from an older sister, but one that might be from a lover, firm and hot, her hands tugging at the folds of Alex's woollen coat. Alex hugged her back, gripping fistfuls of night-black hair.

"I love you, Ally," Cassie said.

"I love you too."

Alex went to the door. She had one more thing. "Cass?"

"Yeah?"

"You won't tell Dad, will you? Tell him that I've always known?"

"Depends."

"Depends on what?"

Cassie laughed. "On whether you make it worth my while."

Chapter 60
A Bow Long Bent Grows Weak
1518

"It is time," Thomas said. The bed felt ever softer, ever warmer. It was a good place to bid one's life's farewells.

"Say not such things, my love." Ann leant over him. He felt her cool fingertips caress his cheek and he opened his eyes. Three years they had been together; the shortest of years, but the longest also, time stretched, seemingly endless like the clouds in the sky. Aye, it had been three years since they had met, and now he saw her as though for the first time. Their lives had fused together like molten iron, forever intertwined. Time had passed and there was a single grey hair that defied her youth, the result of harsh winters and tough business dealings. There was also the child she carried; his child, straining the wool of her kirtle.

By the Heavens, she was beautiful, vibrant as a lamb, bright as a smith's well-stoked furnace. The fever burned deep within him, but it felt like love, a love branded on his heart. "I might not dare to dream of life when there is no more to be had," he said.

"Oh, Thomas." Paycocke's wife took his hand. He wanted to squeeze it but the strength was not there. Even his hands no longer obeyed him.

"I love you, Ann," he said.

"My dear husband."

There was silence between the two, the sort of silence that only exists between lovers, filled with nuance and understanding. It had not been a bad life, one he would willingly have chosen, yet there were regrets. He had not seen Robert alive since the day he stormed from the panelled room downstairs. Some said he had gone to London; others that he had taken a post aboard a trading vessel and had sailed east. Thomas would never know, not

506

in this world at least. He prayed that the time would come when he would meet his young clerk in Heaven and atone for the wrong he had done him. Yet that wrong had not been intended. Thomas's love for Ann had arrived like a flash of lightning in a clear sky – wild and unforeseen, but so omnipotent. The boy had deserved more; he had been a true and loyal friend. Thomas wished he had followed him into West Street on that day, brought him back to the house and showered him with the love he felt.

And as for the Princes? What else could they do? He had not felt cursed by them since their discovery. Indeed, life had been good to him. The final question was: had he deserved the life he had been given? Only the Lord could decide, but that day was now near at hand. "Ann?"

"Aye my love?" She sat on the bed and he could feel her pregnant belly warm against his thigh. Was that a kick he felt, or merely Ann adjusting her position, seeking comfort in these last weeks, her burden soon to be shed for a greater one? A life that he feared he would not see. He raised his anvil-heavy hand and placed it on her stomach. Ann covered his fingers with her own. Hers seemed the larger of the two hands now. How had that happened without him noticing? Yet to see his wife go with child, and know that he would not live to see its birth, that hurt more than to be torn apart by horses. His child, it was. Their child.

Ann read his thoughts. "This will be the most wondrous child who ever lived, for he was created with a powerful, powerful love," she said.

Thomas smiled. "It might yet be a girl," he said. And what a girl she might be, a miniature, angelic version of Ann. What a glory it would be to see such a child grow. In his heart he knew it would be a girl, but it mattered not. Such a girl would be a treasure beyond price. William Spooner was right - the Paycocke family would always be cursed, there would be no more boys. And in very truth there had been no male births in the family since Spooner uttered those desperate words. Perchance it was merited then, the true Paycocke inheritance of his father's folly. Yet who could have acted in another manner? To go against the wishes of the King? Without divine intervention it was impossible to conceive of.

John Paycocke had been trapped. In making his choice he had sought to remove the burden from his children, but in the end had only made it greater. Aye, the sins of the father had indeed been visited upon the son.

"It might be a girl," Ann agreed, stroking his hand, and with it their unborn child.

Paycocke struggled for breath, forced his lungs to pull in the thin air. "My love," he said.

Ann bent forward and kissed him, not on the forehead, an invalid's kiss, but full on his lips, the passionate kiss of lovers. She tasted of honey and spices and her neck was scented with lavender, the smell of sweet summers past.

Thomas looked into her eyes and lost himself there. She still made his heart rage, even after these few years. He sighed out the laboured breath he had taken and asked silently for too much, for more time with Ann, for a chance to see his child, to hold her, if only for a few vital seconds. God had granted him many things already; it was selfish to ask for more. Yet still he prayed, begged for another month, a week, a few days, even. Ann stroked his face again, and this time it was her warmth that touched him and he became aware of a creeping cold invading his insides. Was his fever on the ebb? Could it be that the Lord might answer his plea? In the face of his sins, could it be so? *Please, Lord, grant me a little more time with my Ann, that I might serve you the better once I am called. Please, o merciful Lord.*

"Ann?" He had to force the word from his mouth, so reluctant was it to be spoken. He shivered.

Ann pulled the linen covers up around him and moved closer. "My own Thomas. My true love."

"Did we do right? Did we do well?" The thought had plagued him these past few years. There had been a dreadful period when he realised what his father had done, and that had been coupled with his own indecision. Together they were concentrated into a single formidable foe that would not let him rest: self-doubt. Aye, he doubted if he would ever know what was right.

*   *   *

"The Princes? The lost Princes? It cannot be." Thomas shrank from the panelling. No, no, it could not be true. He closed his eyes, wishing for this to be gone, but the truth would not leave him in peace. He knew it was so. "The boy who should be King."

Ann moved to his side and Thomas felt her strong arm around him. "The fifth King Edward," she said.

Paycocke lowered his voice to a whisper, as though the walls might be eavesdropping on their words and damn them for their conspiracy. "It would seem... nay, I will not... I cannot..." He sank to his knees. "How could the Lord have permitted this?"

"Some things are done with no clear reason," Ann said, "no reason that is apparent at the time. It was God's will. It must have been so, else it would not have passed as it did."

Paycocke nodded. "So it was King Henry's father. It was he who killed the Princes when he took the throne. I had heard tell that it was Richard of Gloucester who had them murdered. But the seventh Henry? He with no right to the throne save that of conquest?"

"Mayhap we shall never know, Thomas. Whether it was their uncle Richard who killed them that he might usurp the crown, or whether it was Henry who took the throne by force, it matters not to those boys. For both men it was a secret that might not be allowed to see daylight. Henry would have needed a man he could trust in order to safeguard his monarchy."

"Aye, indeed. And I do recall that Henry did make an Easter pilgrimage to this region in the year of 1487, the year of the pretender Simnel. His reign was under threat, despite papal support." He laughed sardonically. "My father and Henry would have been well encountered at that time."

"Aye, and was not John Paycocke a man who could be trusted?"

Thomas nodded. His father's integrity was legendary. "Indeed, with one's very life."

"What was your father to do? A life is a high price for a principle. And there is no way to know whether other lives than his own would have been placed at risk had he refused the request."

There was no gainsaying Ann's words. Which man would be able to refuse with his children's lives at stake? What would Thomas himself give for a child? The question was a false one. What would he *not* give? He understood his father's motives now. There could be no blame, no recrimination. He had done what he had believed necessary to protect his kin, and there was little shame in that. The Lord was all-powerful, it was true, but at the same time possessed of a mercy unparalleled. He would surely forgive his servant John Paycocke. "Then what are *we* to do?" John Paycocke had surely never imagined placing his son in such a position. He looked to the ceiling. "Help me, Father," he said. "Help me, father."

Thomas felt a hand upon his shoulder, then a second. He looked up. "Listen well, Thomas," Ann said. "There is but one thing we might do."

Paycocke shook his head. "No, Ann, no. It would be unjust. I must not err on the side of caution as my father did. I will..."

"Sacrifice? You would sacrifice all that we hold dear and yet still be wronged. For that is what would surely come to pass. You think King Henry will hear of your tale and believe you misguided? A man so strong and puissant you would cross at your peril, Thomas. He would end this family afore it had begun."

Thomas looked at the floor. "Think you that he knows of this?" He waved his hand at the princes' tomb behind his own bricks.

Ann shook her head. "I cannot believe so, for he would have come a-visiting before this time, so that he might be sure of the family's loyalty to him. He was not even born when the princes were killed. No, I cannot think but that he rests innocent of this knowledge."

Paycocke held his head in his hands. Ann was right. The eighth Harry was shaping England, taking her in directions his father's generation would never have foreseen. But there remained something of an enigma about him; he was not a man to whom one could swear loyalty lightly. The consequences of crossing the King would, as Ann said, be devastating. Thomas was sure that Henry would bear no supplication on the issue, and even should he reach another man of influence with this story, the results could be catastrophic for England. Henry Tudor had brought stability, prosperity and peace to the country when he defeated Richard at Bosworth, that could not be denied. To throw those gains like chaff to the wind… "Then…"

"The future of England might now rest in our hands, Thomas."

"And what of Spooner's curse upon my name? What if there should be no heir to guard this secret?"

"I care not for Spooner's curse," Ann spat out the words. Thomas was shocked; he had never seen her thus animated. "We can allow this to rule our lives or we can act. I will have your children, Thomas, I promise you this, promise you it with all my heart. God willing there will be Paycockes in this house always. In hundreds of years our descendants will revere our memory. There will be Paycockes."

"Then we have no choice. I will do this for my sons. I will do this for England. May God help me." Thomas stood. He stared into the cavern where rested the remains of the princes. "I cry you mercy," he said. "With every bone in my body, with every beat of my heart, I cry you mercy for what I am about to do." He picked a brick from the floor and placed it at the bottom of the opening. "Would that I could do otherwise."

The clothier stopped and prayed for the souls of the boys, that they should rest eternally in the embrace of the Lord. "There is one thing I might do."

"Thomas?" Ann was by his side.

Thomas realised greatly how he had come to rely upon her these past months. He was but a shadow in the presence of her wisdom. He smiled at her and Ann's berry-black eyes sparkled back at him. Opening a drawer, Thomas took out a small parcel wrapped in a rich carnation-coloured woollen cloth. He unfolded the material and held in his hand a golden case, edged with a royal blue enamel. He nodded. "Aye, this is worthy."

"What is it?"

"The most precious thing I do possess," he said. He opened the small case, and showed Ann the splinter of wood that lay within. "'Tis a piece of the True Cross. It is all I can offer to watch over the boys on their way to Heaven."

She placed her fingers on his cheek, cool against his burning flesh. "It is worthy, Thomas, most worthy."

Thomas placed the reliquary within one of the skeletons and said a silent prayer, folding his cloth over the princes. He took Ann in his arms and kissed her. "I truly love you, Ann. More than life." He then leant over to pick up a brick and began to reconstruct the wall.

*   *   *

"Aye, we did well, Thomas," Ann said, her hand taking his. His grip loosened and his hand fell away, the warmth gone.

She closed his eyes, at the same time feeling the new life in her belly, squirming to be liberated, as at last Thomas was set free. He had not deserved a life tainted so, imprisoned by the house he had built, ever striving to atone for the sins of his father. It was John who had blighted Thomas's life, he who set the events in motion, he who should bear the burden within Paycocke's House, as if he had built it himself. *Aye, and why not? Why could he not have built it? Why not yet let history deem* John *to have constructed Paycocke's?* The idea swirled around Ann's head, gaining size and momentum. She would slowly circulate the notion that the house had been built not in 1509 by her husband, but four years earlier, in 1505, by John before his death. In time the talk would be truth, as was the way, and after a generation it would never be questioned. The story might be embellished: she would even say that John had given the house to Thomas and Margaret on their wedding day – who would not wish to believe such a romantic tale? Aye, it would be well, and in time none would know the truth of Thomas's involvement. Everything would end with John, and it would be right that it was so. John himself would have wanted it and he might then rest in peace also.

She touched her husband's hand, lying stiff on the coverlet. It had begun to grow cold. Yet her love would never grow cold, for she would keep it burning bright and alive, both without and within.

Chapter 61
The Street

Edward walked down the narrow lane, south east he could tell by the sun, but only when he could bring himself to look up at the sky. It was a sheet of blue without a crack in it, one of those early autumn days when you could not believe rain would ever come. On either side of him maize danced in the wind, their drooping cobs gap-toothed where husks had been stripped away and plundered. The plants' leaves all pointed west in the breeze, a field of signposts pointing in the opposite direction to which he was walking.

Despair. Total despair. What was the use? She would not even speak to him now. What was the point in anything? It was as though she had appeared in his life like a genie at the start of the summer, had offered him three wishes, but granted him none. There was only one wish he wanted, the one single wish that could never be granted.

Imogen would be packing now, laying her fine things in trunks, anticipating parties in London, dances at the Palais and recitals with her father. It was over for her. She would not need to remember him and their short interlude together. He stopped and screamed at the sun, "Why? Why?"

The miles ate the soles of his shoes, so thin that he could feel every contour of the road, each sharp piece of gravel. He wished it would rain, to pour yet more scorn on his misery. Why had he been so blind?

Soon they would be leaving, disappearing up West Street without turning back at Coggeshall or at Paycocke's House. Would she look for him as she left, seek him out under the horse chestnuts, in the shadows where he belonged? Would she be disappointed that he was not there, that there was to be no final wave goodbye? Or was it all just another episode in the Holsts' lives, a meagre chapter in their adventure, a biography in which he would not rate a mention. He kicked out at a stone and caught it so fully that it hurt his toe. The stone flew into the undergrowth. A cock pheasant screeched out of its hiding-place and flapped by like a mechanical toy. He did not deserve a mention.

How stupid he had been. "Why did I fall in love with you?" Love – at least he could say it now. Yes, it had been love, that leech of sanity, that destroyer of souls. Her face would not leave him as he walked, haunting him with her presence. He would never see her again. 'Forget me,' she had said. 'Forget me.' Edward would as soon forget to breathe. That would be easier. He fisted his hands into his pockets, and felt the coins clinking there. Pulling out a penny he tossed it to see which way he should go. Not that he cared. Holding up the copper he saw just how thin the dividing line was between heads and tails, between love and hate. He knew he would always love Imogen, always love her and always hate her. His life was sullied now; who could touch him and live? She had rendered him bright for a while, made him exist for a short summer, but the leaves were falling now and the colour dropped from the sky with each day. He rubbed some carpenter's chalk from the penny and shined the coin on his sleeve. The King's head gleamed. Love and hate, like chalk and… a different kind of chalk.

Edward reached the sea. There were no cliffs here, just flat land that segued into water, grey and churning. He looked out to the horizon and could not tell where sea and sky met, where one thing became the other. If only life were as seamless. Was there a time when he would have been able to see the difference, a time before the spectre of Imogen had tormented him? Had she made him blind to everything? He had reached the edge, the edge of his world, and sat down on the pebbles, picking at them one by one and hurling them into the water. Go on? Go back? What did it matter? His father might kill him if he went home and there would be no point in resistance this time. No point. It would be best to let his blows land, one after the other until he fell. His mother would die soon, today, tomorrow or the next day, each lingering hour a further torture. How could she live? Why would she live? It was just like Imogen to try and set a spark of hope within him. All this research, all this book learning, maybe it would help someone, some day, but it would not be him, it would not be his mother. No, that was not the way things worked. It was too late; it had always been too late.

How far had he come? Twenty miles? Thirty? He took off a shoe and held it up to the light. The sole was so thin that he could see the silhouette of his thumb through it. It was the ghost of a thumb, a wavering shadow, and that was all he was himself now. And if he did die at the hands of his father, would she care? Would she come and hold him in his last moments, whisper her remorse to his crushed face, wipe away his last tears? Would she remember their kiss, the moment by which Edward defined his life? Would she remember what they had shared? Would she? He shook his head and flung another stone into the sea. It was swallowed whole with a watery belch. Just one more pebble. He looked around at the thousands of stones on the shoreline. He was just one more pebble, unremarkable. Imogen had been his sea. What he would have done for her. What would he not have done for her?

"Why did I ever meet you, Imogen?" he screamed at the sea. "Why?"

*   *   *

Downstairs the noise of change thundered around Paycocke's house. I sat on my bed, packing the last of my things: my clothes; my pencils and sketchbooks; the camera Frannie and Conrad had given me and which I had hardly touched; Edward's black box of treasures and his mother's brooch.

I had wanted to tell Edward what I had discovered, indeed he was the only one I could tell, but in that final instant I was not able to share my knowledge, and, if truth be told, I think he did not want to know. It would be my secret and mine alone. So much had changed; so much had indeed changed because of a single kiss. Why, oh why had he kissed me? Why did he love me? Why had he not been able to hold back his feelings? I thought again of my last moments with Edward, the two of us sharing stumbling words out of character with our previous friendship.

We had met in the fading light behind St. Peter's church as arranged. I remembered him walking me up the hill to this very place on the first day we met. I had not been used to love, had not recognised it in his emerald eyes. Love at first sight – that is what they call it, is it not? I had no sense of it. My naivety was overwhelming.

I had to sneak out of Paycocke's after supper. Iso was supervising some packing; Gussie was resting. How pernicious the house had been to my father, dampening his inspiration and boxing his talent. My mother loved him dearly, would have done anything for him, but I wondered if his self-belief would now ever recover. As for me, Paycocke's gave me the horrible feeling of my own unfinished symphony, a half-built bridge to a place I dared not imagine.

Walking up Church Street I was assailed by the thought that he would not be there. I had made him suffer for his love, and then turned him to my own ends, using his talent and muscle to open up the panelling. Why would he come, to be the object of yet more humiliation? But there he was, his clothes hanging loosely from his frame as though they had outgrown him, almost hiding in the shadows of dusk behind the church, leaning against a gravestone, he as perfectly grey and sombre as it.

"Hello," I said.

"Imogen."

"I have some bad news."

"Oh."

"We are to leave Coggeshall."

Edward gave no reaction. Perhaps it did not matter to him whether or not we stayed, for he knew now that I could not return his love. He spoke little to me, passing some pleasantries more suited to folk who had not had the experiences that had passed between us. In the dying light we became strangers to each other, each floundering in the bewildering complexities of the other's life.

I took out his mother's brooch and offered it to him. He made no move to take it, but turned his face away, as though the cold words on the gravestone held the greater attraction.

"Please take it, Edward," I said. "It is your mother's. It is yours."

He raised an eyebrow. "I don't want it. I don't need it. You keep it, Imogen." He laughed, but it was a sour sound that pierced my heart. "Something to remember me by."

"It will all be well in the end, Edward," I said. "You will see."

"S'all right for you to say. You don't live here."

His sullenness hurt me; we had been such friends. He had said that he himself would do anything for me, anything. And now bitterness and vitriol inked the air between us. If this was what love spawned then I wanted none of it. Yet of course he was right: I was leaving Coggeshall, he was staying, staying to fend off the whispers and cupped hands. "I know," I said. "Edward?"

He looked up and the hope in his eyes stung me. I could not hold his glare and looked away to the dull grey sky. When I turned to him again the sheen had gone from his gaze. His eyes were like marbles now, the colour still there but lifeless, the emerald spark doused. I knew that I would prise little more from him. He avoided my searching look and his eyes sought the shadows as though they wished to be lost there.

How had I given rise to such a love in him? I had not intended it or wanted it. What was it that he had seen in me? I was not beautiful or kind or gentle. And worse, why me, who could not return his feelings, who must condemn him to his unrequited love? Who is worse off, the lover or the loved? What is this emotion that it hurts so much those whom it brushes? "Whatever it is I have done, I did not mean to do," I said. "I meant you no harm."

"It isn't what you've done, Imogen." Edward dropped his head to the ground and I could scarcely hear the words. "It's what you haven't done."

"I have to follow my heart."

"You have no heart." I flinched. It pained me. He tossed his head back, clamping his eyes shut and gripping his temples with both hands. "I'm sorry, I'm very sorry, Imogen. I know you do... have a heart. I know that." His next words lay unspoken, but we both knew they were there: 'And so do I.' He had followed his heart into uncharted waters and been utterly shipwrecked in the attempt.

"You will meet another girl." I cursed my platitude even as I uttered it.

"No."

"You will love again."

"Never."

Tears pricked my eyes and unfolded down my cheeks. "Edward, I cannot love you."

"I know," he screamed. "I know." He ran from me, out of the church gate. As he left I wondered to myself why we had met here at all and I knew that he must be asking himself the same question.

"Edward," I called after him, but he did not turn around, shrinking to a small dot as he neared the village. I had been selfish. I had wanted to plaster over the difficulties between us, to leave with a whitewashed conscience, and Edward, in his tortured love, had not allowed it. He was right, of course. I had encouraged him. I had led him on. I had been so driven by the desire to fathom Paycocke's secret that I would have taken any risk, involved my friend in the darkest subterfuge, if it would aid me in my quest. To leave with our friendship shredded was perhaps the least that I could have expected, and I still came out of the affair more whole than Edward. Would I ever see him again? I closed my eyes, and the rain started to leave the clouds. I sat on a gravestone and allowed the first drops to dampen my hair, trickle down my neck and across my cheeks, mingling with my own warm and salty tears. Leaving. Everyone was leaving, I most of all.

*   *   *

So Edward had gone. To where no one knew. I held his mother's brooch in my hand, and it glinted from within at some memory of happier times when it had graced young Ida's wedding gown. It deserved a better fate than incarceration in Edward's black box. I would take it to their house and return it to his mother. It was not what Edward wanted, but then, I could give him nothing that he did want.

My new camera, so sleek and modern, enchanted me, and

I thought to lift my spirits by taking some photographs of the house: the wonderful carvings in the entrance hall; Thomas and Margaret's initials; the delicate little carver's face. I am mistaken when I say that I knew nothing of love, for if I speak true then I should admit that it was love at first sight between Paycocke's House and me. Its beauty enthralled me, its sense of lives lived penetrated my very soul, its beautiful sadness tugged at me.

I was drawn to the dining room one last time. The room was cold; there had been no fire there for several days now, and dust had begun to gather on the linen fold panelling. I drew my finger along the grooves of the bottom edge. How careless that we should have replaced it upside down. Perhaps no one would notice now, now in its new guise. The room had called to me, called to say its goodbyes, and I closed the door so that we might do so uninterrupted. I hesitate to say 'in peace'. I took a photograph of the sumptuous panelling, then another, and then the dust that lay there seemed to gather in the air, obscuring the oak panels with the finest of smoke. It hung there, challenging me to take another picture, accusing me of deeds undone. I took one last snap and let my head hang. "I am so sorry," I said. Guilt surged through me. It remained within my grasp to reveal the story of the Princes' fate, but to a Commonwealth still struggling in the aftermath of the Great War, to a country whose future felt uncertain? I dared not take that responsibility. I truly believed the monarchy might not survive.

I turned my back and left the room. I put my heart into a letter, which, upon re-reading, made insufficient sense. My love for the house and guilt at leaving the story untold shone from the lines, but that was all. Though I wanted to tear up the pages, I could not do so. These words were the smallest legacy I could leave to Paycocke's House. I placed the letter in Edward's box, turned the key in the small padlock, and kissed the cold black metal; there was no more fitting place for the box than here, where it might provide wisps of comfort to the desperate spirits.

I climbed up to the trapdoor. It moved easily inwards, and I saw what Edward and Conrad had seen: blackness that might be an inch or a mile deep. I crawled into the space and it enveloped me, both caressing me and moving through me, as though I were the ghost and it were solid. I felt the spirits' need in that dark abyss, felt it more keenly than ever, and unlike Edward, with his love for me, unlike Conrad Noel, with his unshakeable faith, I had nothing to protect me, nothing but a feeble desire to atone for my silence. Yet, comforting though the souls were in that barren space, they did not seek to detain me. I felt nothing of the innocent lure that Conrad had described, nothing of the emotional frenzy that had so consumed Edward. I felt loved, exonerated, forgiven. The small padlock key with the heart-shaped cut-out I placed on top of the linen fold panelling in the dining room.

There was little more to be done. Late that afternoon, I stood in West Street as autumn breezes hinted of the colder season to come, pulling a soft woollen wrap around my shoulders. I gazed upon the intricate carving on the front of the house and at the Paycocke's ermine tail merchant mark which would forever brand this place on my heart.

I climbed into the motor car and we took the London Road.

Chapter 62
Moving

Martin hadn't moved, was still tucked into the carver in the entrance hall, his arms tight to his chest. He continued to stare into the dying fire. There was plenty of wood stacked up beside the burner and Simon wondered why he hadn't kept the blaze going.

"Hey, Martin?" Simon felt a new lightness, as though worlds had been lifted from his shoulders, or maybe he only felt it because of the depression steaming from Sparrow. Martin didn't reply and then Simon saw the bag beside him, The holdall, unzipped, was overflowing with all his possessions, a stray sweater sleeve dangling from the opening as though it belonged to a body in a trunk. He was leaving?

Simon put his hand on his friend's shoulder. What could he say that would not make Sparrow feel even lower? Martin nodded at the fire, in response to some errant thought. "I'm thirty-five, Simon," he said. "What is there left?"

"It's not all bad, Martin." What could Simon say? "Try and be positive."

"What for? What's the use?" He looked up at Simon, a rawness around his eyes glimmering in the last of the firelight. "What's it all about?"

Simon picked up a couple of logs from the stack and tossed them into the burner.

"Oh, come on, mate. What's happened to the old Martin Sparrow?"

"There is no old Martin Sparrow. This has always been me." He shifted in his seat, moving backwards to where darker shadows lurked. There was a heavy pause, before Martin shrugged and looked over at Simon. "I'll leave you to it, then," he said, scraping the chair on the floorboards.

"What?" Simon replied. He had seen the bag, but Sparrow's words had such an innocuous ring, as though he were popping out to the corner shop for a pint of milk.

"I have to go."

"It's getting dark."

Sparrow picked up his bag, feeling its weight, then put it down again and stuffed the errant sleeve back inside. It caught on the zip.

Simon desperately wanted to help him. "Look, if you want to stick around for a while..."

Sparrow shook his head. "For what? To see my daughter grow up? She's done that, done it all already. Without me. I came back to see the toddler I remembered – don't ask me, I know it's not logical – and she's now a woman, a beautiful young woman."

"I know," Simon said. "Alex, Cassie, too. They'll both be gone soon. I can't... we can't build our lives around them, Martin. Birds fly the nest." He laughed, trying to lift Martin's spirits. "Then again, they're homing pigeons, back to get their washing done and tap us for a handout. Home is a moveable feast."

Martin shrugged. "Yeah, well, you know she left just now, left without even saying goodbye."

"I'm sorry."

Sparrow picked up the holdall again, and this time turned to the door.

Simon made no attempt to stop him. "Where will you go?" he said.

Martin looked up at the carved ceiling, as though he were seeking out the initials. "I don't know. I can sail. It's the only thing I really know how to do. I'll find something. Yeah, I can sail. The rest was all bull. I'm sick of it, Simon, I'm sick of my life."

"Then change it. It's not too late. It depends what you want."

"What *I* want? I'm not even sure what I want myself. A fire. A cat on my knee. Kids. Simple stuff, really. Simple, but bloody hard, you know what I mean?"

Simon nodded. "Stay. Just one more night. Stay over. Don't leave now. Not like this."

"A clean break, Simon, old pal. That's what I need. If I go now, maybe I can do it."

"Yeah, OK. I understand."

"Do you?" Sparrow opened the door. Night had fallen like a steel shutter. The wind hadn't let up and it tore at Sparrow's hair. He slung his coat over a shoulder, oblivious to the dropping temperature. "Cheers, Simon, I owe you everything."

"You owe me nothing. Bloody hell, Martin, put your coat on, it's freezing."

Martin looked at the coat as if not realising that he was carrying it. He slipped it on. "Bye, mate."

The two men stood face to face in the doorway. "Hey, you'll look us up some time, yeah?" Simon said.

Martin smiled, reached forward and rubbed Simon's arm. "Bye, old mate." He turned and walked down West Street towards the bus stop, the street lamps spotlighting him as he went by, until he became no more than a silhouette.

Simon went back indoors.

"Has he gone?" It was Cassie.

Simon nodded. He opened the wood burner and puffed bellows at the remains of the fire. Cassie came up behind him and put her hands on his shoulders. "I don't want to be harsh, Dad, but he did an awful lot of damage."

"Yeah, maybe."

"What do you mean, maybe?"

"Maybe he was the catalyst that brought us all back together again."

He almost believed that. Now it wasn't a case of forgiving Sparrow, more one of accepting what had happened and moving on. What good would it do him to dwell on the past? Sparrow would never forgive *himself* for what he had done - what help would Simon's forgiveness be to him?

Cassie tugged her pashmina into a noose and turned her jacket collar up. She smiled at Simon and pinched him on the cheek. "You're right, Dad. Maybe he was. Bizarrely, hate him as I do."

"Going out?"

"Yeah. Mark... Fitz... is picking me up in a bit."

He stood up and went to give her a hug.

Cassie backed away. "Hey. Hands, Dad."

Simon held up his palms, speckled with soot and ash. "Sorry."

A horn sounded in the street. "That'll be him," Cassie said.

"OK, fine. Will you be back tonight?"

"What do you take me for, Dad?"

"Sorry."

"And stop saying sorry." Cassie leant forward and kissed him on the nose.

Simon smiled. "I will, if you do something about your hair. It's not you."

"It's not my hair you need to worry about, Dad. You wait 'til you see my tattoo."

"What?"

"Only kidding, Pops."

The horn sounded again in the street.

"I really got to go," Cassie said. She opened the door and a gust threw a pile of leaves through the gap. She hesitated and turned to Simon. "Dad?"

"Yes?"

She seemed to look through him, searching for something. "Did you ever have a favourite? Out of me and Alex, I mean? Did you ever have a favourite?"

How could he lie? "Maybe I did," he said. "I always was a sucker for the easy option." He went over and held the door for her, watched her climb into the red Ford Escort.

Fitz leant over and waved.

"Where you off to?" Simon asked. "School Disco?"

"No." Fitz looked perplexed. "Romeo and Juliet," he said.

Simon laughed. They waved goodbye and Cassie tucked her hand inside Fitz's elbow.

The car did a three-point turn and Simon watched it go up the street until all he could see were the starry red pin pricks of its tail lights illuminating the number plate. It seemed familiar. Simon struggled to remember. E90 MPH, ninety miles per hour. Yes, it was the same car he had seen outside Eleanor's house that day, when he'd wanted to scrawl their initials in the grime on the bodywork.

Of course. Yes, of course. That's what happened. No. It couldn't be. Eleanor couldn't have. He rubbed his eyes. *She had. She definitely had. They both had. Eleanor and Fitz.*

Eleanor and Fitz had trussed him up. How they must have laughed at him. It was his own fault, his own stupid fault; damn, he was so gullible. The girls had always been able to pull the wool over his eyes. Who snipped the cat's whiskers? Who spilt the paint on the carpet? Who peeled the edges of the wallpaper away? Not me. Not me. Different times, different girls, but the wool hadn't changed and neither had he, still just as gullible. Robin, Cassie, Alex, now Eleanor. How could he have been so stupid?

Simon put his black woollen coat on and jammed an old beanie on his head. He locked the house and set off into the windy night towards Tilkey Road.

Chapter 63
Beginnings

Imogen looked at her hands, liver spotted and tired. They felt so cold. What a wretched thing it was to be old, the parts of your body which had been so trustworthy letting you down one by one, like an old car unable to satisfy the MOT: clawed fingers; brittle bones; fading memory. She closed her eyes and the past became fresh again, no longer the nineteen eighties, but 1923 once more. How could almost sixty years pass so quickly? What had happened to Edward? Dear, sweet boy, with his jewelled eyes and his earnest love.

Staring out of the window, Imogen watched the grey sea roll up the flat Suffolk shore. What if she had succumbed to him? Where would she be now? The decisions you made rippled like the waves, taking you in unknown, unpredictable directions. She had lived so much of her life in the shadow of her father, Imogen knew that, but it was less of a shadow than a great pool of light. Gussie had been a truly great man; he had illuminated whomsoever he met, moving people by his mere presence. Imogen still met former pupils of his, their memories alive with his inspiration. Too soon. It had all ended too soon. He had never really recovered his career after Paycocke's, she knew that now, and he had died young, so young. Had the sadness of the house touched him? Her breath steamed the window so that the sea receded out of focus. She had never forgotten the plaintive air that pulled at her as she left the house that last time, the desperate melancholy that had stayed with her as the backdrop to her life. At sixteen, the world lies before you to be conquered. Your immortality is not to be questioned. Wistful looks over her shoulder came in her later years, as they did, time after time. The past haunted her.

How could there be regrets? If she had followed Edward on that evening by St. Peter's, when he ran down the hill as though chased by demons, if she had been able to love him, where would she be now?

There was a sound at the front door, the letterbox clacking open and then the sound of mail falling on the coir mat. There were always the everyday things to contend with, things you never realised at sixteen. This was the wallpaper of her late adult life, so much in contrast to the kingfisher existence of her teenage years, darting from one adventure to the next.

She eased herself from the rocker and went out into the hall. Two manilla envelopes lay across each other on the doormat like a crucifix. Dear Conrad, she had not thought of him in years. He died during the war, crippled by illness and almost completely blind, his work done. His grave at Thaxted was fitting, in the shadows of the east wall of the church he had loved. He had never sought the limelight, yet it had sought him and loved him. Forty years on and she missed him still, mischievous and rebellious, yet so honourable, the light in his eyes a sign of his dedication to what was right.

The telephone bill – that could wait. The second envelope was heavier. Imogen slit it with an ivory letter opener and eased out the crisp paper. She sighed. Now it might at last be at an end: it was from Richard Poundlove, her solicitor. She hesitated before she unfolded the letter. And if she had taken this action sixty years ago? What then? How would the world be today? Would there be less sadness, or more? You can only take the decisions as you see fit at the time.

Poundlove had found him. Imogen's fingers trembled as she read his words. Poundlove had found the one man, the one single descendant of a cousin of the usurped Edward, the murdered prince whose remains still lay within Paycocke's House. So there had been a connection after all; there had been an heir. Poundlove advised that such a claim to the throne would never stand, of course, probably never would have.

Imogen felt a peculiar sadness. So it might not have made a difference after all? The thought was acid to her. She had condemned the souls of the princes to their dank prison, and for what? She felt a tear well. Who would not cry for them, she thought, remembering their tomb, who would have such a granite heart that they would not cry?

Imogen had not seen Paycocke's since that lingering look from the back of the motor car in the last embers of that 1923 summer. She could not have borne to visit the house again, she knew, although she had followed its progress over the decades. The National Trust had leased it to a succession of families, none of whom had stayed for very long, and Imogen often wondered if they too had felt the pull of its ghostly residents, and whether they had fallen under the Paycocke's spell just as she and Edward had. She hoped that there had been children, at least. The house deserved children.

Imogen fanned herself with Poundlove's letter. Was it too warm? She felt almost overcome by an unpleasant stifling heat. Perhaps the thermostat was set too high. She returned to the window looking over the sea. It was still misted up, sealing her off from the outside world. She re-read Poundlove's words. Such a gentle man, she thought, and so kind and thoughtful to have done this for her. She must find a way to thank him; yes, she would write to him today.

Opening her writing desk, she took out a pad of blue paper and her fountain pen, scratching her address in the top right corner. She stopped and put her pen down. Her fingers ached more than usual today. How dreadful it was when writing a letter became a chore. She looked at Poundlove's letter once again and knew then what she still had to do. It was too late for her, but the baton must be passed. Standing by the window, she traced the Paycocke's ermine tail in the condensation, and through this she could see the sea rolling towards her once more, inexorable and timeless. As long as there were tides, there was always time.

So there had been a distant heir to the throne.

Dear Mr Fitzwarwick,

You do not know me, but I am writing to you to discharge a burden which has troubled me these many years, and upon which, to my great shame, I have been incapable of acting until now. I have always believed my behaviour to be for the greater good, and that is salve to my conscience. What some may perceive to be the weakness of my silence is at one and the same time its strength, borne out by the peace of our times.

I speak of a matter upon which the dust of centuries has now settled, but whereby your family has been dealt a terrible wrong, denied wealth untold and social standing of great magnitude. It is indeed no exaggeration to say that the entire history of England may have pivoted on the fate of the Fitzwarwick family. Yet this wrong has also been a double-edged sword, one which has spared your lineage murder and deceit across the ages, for who knows how our country might have been had justice been served.

I fear that I cannot redress that injustice, now lost in history, but there remains one bequest you might claim, and with it the eternal peace of your ancestors. There are forces at work about which we know little, Mr Fitzwarwick, this I have witnessed at first hand, and for this reason I implore you not to act with undue haste.

You will find in the camera a film. Although now of some vintage I am assured that it has suffered little in its journey across the decades. There is a very knowledgeable young man in Great Russell Street who will develop it for you. The ensuing photographs will portray the place to which you should go, the merchant's house in which you will discover your heritage. More I need not say, for once in this great house you will be led to the truth.

The house will know you belong there, Mr Fitzwarwick, for you are of it and it is of you. It will draw you in and take you in its heartfelt embrace, change you and all that you know. I know this, for I have felt its charms. It will lead you to what you must do. Accomplish this and the riches of resolution will be yours.

My part in this story is over, Mr Fitzwarwick. I wish you fortune in your quest.

Imogen hesitated. There was no gain to be made from adding her identity to the foot of the letter. Mr Fitzwarwick must determine his own path, without her help, no, without her *interference*. She folded the letter into eight and slipped it into the case of Frannie Noel's camera. She had never again used it. It seemed that her life had been split into two parts, before and after Paycocke's. The house had changed her, moulded her for good or bad, both split her apart and made her whole. She did not even know why she had kept the old camera, still pregnant with its undeveloped photographs. Perhaps it was for this moment. She made a parcel of it and addressed it to Fitzwarwick in Romford. He deserved to know what she had discovered. Maybe he would be braver than she had been.

There was one final thing to do before she could rest. Coggeshall was a good hour's drive away, two perhaps, with the roads as busy as they were these days, but it was a journey she had to make.

When she stood in West Street, it was 1923 all over again. The traffic noise shrank away to a few clamouring engines and the clop of a passing dray. The house had not changed, still regal, still charming and idiosyncratic, the carvings perhaps a little more weathered, the timbers worn smooth in places from the passing touch of the decades. But it was still the Paycocke's House she had fallen in love with when the summer had been young and everything had seemed possible.

The sign was new, of course: 'The National Trust' with its stern list of admission charges and opening times. She looked at her watch. Of course it was open now, how could she have expected otherwise? It had waited for her to come, had known that she must return.

Imogen pushed at the heavy front door. Sticking for a brief instant, it seemed to her to acknowledge who she was and gave way. She paused in the doorway to touch the carpenter's mark and then entered the hall. It was exactly as she remembered. Not, of course, the furniture, which was an eclectic mix of eras, but the room itself, striped with the beautiful studs and the carving on the ceiling beams reaching down to her.

"Let me get the door for you." There was a young man in a linen jacket at her elbow, smiling at her. He wore round spectacles and for a split second she thought it was Gussie. "Are you a member?" he asked.

"Oh… yes. Of course, I'm sorry." She opened her purse.

"The carving is rather splendid," he said, following her line of sight to Thomas and Margaret's initials. "Have you been to Paycocke's before?"

"Oh yes. Oh yes. Many times," she said.

"Well, we do have a short leaflet, if you would like one, or I'll be happy to tell you something of the history of the house…"

Imogen smiled and held up a gloved hand. "Thank you. That is terribly kind, but it won't be necessary. I would like only to see the panelled room."

The custodian gestured her towards the dining room, then retreated behind his table. "Of course," he said. "Please make yourself at home. If you have any questions, don't hesitate to ask."

"Thank you." She stepped over the threshold. It was as it had been, yet there was a shimmer in the air, as there might be over a road on a hot summer's day. Heavens, the panelling was still upside down. Dear Edward. Had he perhaps done it on purpose, so that he might see her one more time to rectify his 'mistake'? She would never know. By its very nature, life left so many loose ends.

She felt the grooves in the linen fold above the fireplace. She was sixteen once more and there was Edward behind her, his green eyes sun-bright and in love. 'Make yourself at home,' the young man had said. She smiled. She *was* home. "I am sorry," she whispered to the panelling. "I am so sorry, so very sorry. I have tried to put things right. Someone will be coming soon. I have written to him. You must help him. He will free you."

Out in the street the sun was brighter, or maybe it was an

optical illusion after having been inside, she didn't know. The mind played so many tricks these days that it was hard to decide where reality ended and fanciful speculation began. At sixteen everything had been so fiercely tangible. She drove back down into the village and saw that it too had hardly changed. It was true that most of the shops were different, and here was a new pillar-box, there a zebra crossing. She stopped for two pedestrians, a woman with a pram and an old man with a stick. He turned to thank her for the courtesy and she saw his eyes, a piercing emerald green, not dulled by life, but shining as though polished by tears. It could not be. It simply could not be. He reached the pavement and turned away. It could not be him. The tricks the mind plays, every day.

*   *   *

So Eleanor had known Fitz. It all seemed too obvious now. And was Fitz the one, the one to whom Eleanor owed the favours? So much deception. She had used him. He didn't understand, tried to dredge up an explanation from his heart but failed. Bile rose and he wanted to stop by the side of the street to be sick. Complete nausea.

And why, after she had got what she wanted, why had she carried on with the pretence, holding him to ransom? Before he could push the doorbell, Simon saw her through the frosted glass, a long blue skirt swishing as she vacuumed the hall. She had taken him for some ride: first the school visit; then the accidental meeting in Sainsbury's; finally the kiss on Clacton pier, the moment he had begun to see her in a new, romantic light. He shook his head, raging at the memory. A new light? Well that light had a dimmer switch and now it was turned down low. He rang the bell.

The noise of the Hoover faded and Eleanor's silhouette approached the door. Simon heard the chain being taken off the latch, and she opened the door wide, smiling and starting to hold out her arms, but stopping short when she saw his face. "Simon?"

No. He knows. Somehow he's found out. Fitz, somehow. No.

Simon shook his head. He looked at her anew, with objectivity, perhaps for the first time seeing how attractive she was. Deadly, he thought, attractive and deadly. His heart grappled with his head and he struggled to hold the tears. "Fitz," he said.

For a moment he thought she would deny it, try to bluster it out, but he knew his face gave away his knowledge. How could it not? The flip side of being gullible was being open and trusting.

Her eyes left his. "I'm sorry," she said.

"Why? I don't understand? Why did you need to hurt me so much? Why did you need to… to pretend?" Simon tried to rein in his emotions. He couldn't let her do this to him. He wouldn't. Whatever she was going to say would be more lies. He had to be ready for them.

"It's not what you think, Simon…"

"Then how is it? No, I don't want to know. Who is he? Who is Fitz? I thought I knew him too and now… Now he's off with my bloody daughter. And it's your fault, Eleanor."

"Simon, please, it's not…" He saw indecision tear at her. What was she hiding?

"Come in. Please come in, Simon. Let's not do this. Not out here."

"No," he screamed. "No. Just when I was getting my life back, just when I thought there was a future…"

A small thin boy with long black hair and torn jeans appeared behind Eleanor. "Mum?"

Simon looked at Jack and pointed at Eleanor. His rage spiralled. "Do you know what your Mum is, Jack? Do you know? Shall I tell him, Eleanor? Shall I tell him?"

Eleanor held her arm across the doorway, as if protecting her son. "It's all right, Jack, go into the kitchen, I'll only be a minute." She glared at Simon. "Leave Jack out of this, Simon. Look…"

"I don't want to look, Eleanor. It's all been a pack of lies, hasn't it?"

She shook her head and showed the first signs of panic.

Simon was calm now; he could afford calm, now that he knew it was over. Over? It had hardly begun and was now almost over. "Tell me, Eleanor. Tell me you didn't lie to me."

Eleanor closed her eyes and for a moment there was a wall of silence between them. As she opened her eyes once more, a tear escaped and rolled down a cheek. More deception, more tricks, Simon thought. "I can't," she said, in a voice so low it was almost lost in the gale.

Her words surprised Simon. At last, it was a line drawn through his life, a line to go with all the other lines. How many new starts could you have? How many lives were you expected to live before you could accept defeat?

"Come in, Simon."

He looked at her. A wave of despair thrashed at his insides.

"Please, Simon, I thought... I never... I thought we... I love you..."

He turned his back on Eleanor, walked up the short path and down the hill. *She thought... She thought...* He shook his head. *So did I.* So many worthless words.

The wind blew dust from the path into his face, specks getting in his eyes and he put his hand up to shield them. His fingertips came away wet. Turning his back on the gusts, he sat down on a wall. Was this how it would always be, then? Would he be destined always to see life through a veil of lies? Did he somehow attract subterfuge? Or was this how all people really behaved? Had he missed something?

Simon lost his train of thought as he sat there and by the time he gathered himself together to get back to Paycocke's he was frozen, his lips hard and cracked from the wind. When he arrived back home, the house was cold, only a few lonely embers glowing in the wood burner. No one was home and Simon sensed no sign of life. It was not just that Sparrow and the girls had gone. Something else was missing.

He walked into the dining room. The light was dim, very dim; they still hadn't fixed the street lamp. He picked up the large rubber torch and played its beam over the linen fold panelling. In the half-light, it was as striking as he had ever seen it. Whatever Paycocke had done, the house would always be his true legacy. Simon inhaled the silence. He pondered that this was probably the last time he would be able to do this. When he reported the discovery in the morning, the place would be invaded by police, historians and the press.

He approached the burial place, dust swimming in the beam of the torch. The skeletons lay impervious, almost regal in their serenity. Who were they? Would he ever know?

This was surely the end of his life at Paycocke's. Maybe, he thought, he ought to just walk away. The house could never be the same for him again. Perhaps that was a good thing. He held the torch still on the smaller of the children. What were their names? Had they once swung between two parents' hands? Had they rushed to their mother's arms with grazed knees, there to be comforted? Had they ever known love? He hoped so. Everyone should know love, even if that love eventually fails. His torchlight wavered and he moved closer, almost poking his head inside the recess.

The reliquary. It had gone. Sparrow. Lousy Sparrow had taken it. Simon laughed at the empty room. He had been duped again. Lies and more lies. He knew he should call the police now, try and stop Martin from getting away. He swept the floor of the cavity with the beam in case he had missed it somehow, but he knew he had been right the first time. It had gone, but there, in its place, was something else. Simon reached in and plucked a small piece of paper from the tomb. It was a receipt, a ticket, the words 'King's Cross Left Luggage' bold across the top. It couldn't be? Surely? Or was it another layer of deceit? And where would this ticket lead him? He thought of tossing it in the wood burner, but couldn't bring himself to do it, for it to be another path not taken. Just in case, just on the slightest off-chance.

So Sparrow had taken the golden case with its priceless cargo. His audacity amazed Simon. What would he gain by it? How far would he get? Would he be able to sell it? Sparrow had deceived him one last time and escaped with the prize, but now he was running away again. It was never *to* something, always away. Had he seen the real Martin this evening, captured a brief glimpse behind the veneer? Who knew? Martin had always found it so easy to lie or hide, and so easy to run.

Simon closed the door to the dining room. Let Sparrow have the golden case if he needed it. No one had to know. Let him run. Let him hide. That was all over for Simon. He knew what was important now. He knew what mattered, what was right.

He opened the massive oak door to the outside and the wind whirled around him. To come so far and yet to fail – that was the one thing he would always regret. It could not be allowed to happen. Huge horse chestnut leaves skittered past him, calling him to follow. There was one more thing. He ran to the kitchen and opened the simmering oven on the Aga. His conker was hot and blackened and he tossed it from palm to palm while it cooled. He wondered if it would be hard enough.

Knotting his scarf, Simon strode into the face of the wind and headed for the Tilkey Road. Whatever happened, there could be no regrets.

THE END